PEOPLE
ANIRUDDHA ROY CHOUDHURY

INDIA · SINGAPORE · MALAYSIA

Notion Press

Old No. 38, New No. 6
McNichols Road, Chetpet
Chennai - 600 031

First Published by Notion Press 2018
Copyright © Aniruddha Roy Choudhury 2018
All Rights Reserved.

ISBN 978-1-68466-158-9

Disclaimer by Author

Contents

Acknowledgements

I am eternally grateful to all those who cared for me, for having constant faith in my writing skills, namely my maternal uncle late Parimal Dasgupta (PhD), Hindustan Times, his wife, late Indrani Dasgupta, my mother Mrs.Kajari Roy Choudhury, President, Purbachal Udayan Sangha (NGO), my father late Gp.Capt.S.K.Roy Choudhury, my maternal uncle late Bhaskar Sen, Avery India Ltd, his wife Maitrayee Sen, retired from All India Radio, Sinjita Gupta my maternal aunt and her amazing husband Commodore Swapan Kumar Gupta (Retd), my vibrant maternal aunt Tuktuk Ray and her dynamic husband Indrajit Ray, my well planned maternal aunt Diyali Lahiri and her gentle, highly learned husband, my uncle Ajoy Lahiri (PhD), my sister Sonali Roy Choudhury (PhD), my brother Aditya Roy Choudhury & his wife Nupur, my daughter Bohnita Roy Choudhury, my nephews Rohan & Ishan Roy Choudhury, my brother Amit Ray & his wife Renee Choudhury, my paternal uncles namely Subhankar Roy Choudhury & my aunt, late Prabhakar Roy Choudhury & family, late Tithankar Roy Choudhury & family, Bhaskar Roy Choudhury & family, my brother Pramit Roy Choudhury, his wife and my little niece Sharanya Roy Choudhury, my paternal aunt Gopa Sengupta & family, late Purnima Choudhury & family, and all the others who had stood by me.

I wish to thank the professional painter plus sketch artist Mrs.Moumita De who has drawn such high quality illustrations, Ms.Sneha Mathew my consultant working with Notion Press, a very patient, wise and knowledgeable professional, and the excellent team at Notion Press including Naveen Valsakumar, Bhargava Adepalley and Jana Pillay, and obviously, all my past and present friends, relatives and acquaintances who have stood by me as the story grew over these past so many years.

Chapter 1

Year 1770: The Beginning

It all began with the seven ships and the Treasures of Zahiruddin Ali.

A secret Journal entry made by a French Officer and later found in the uniform of a British Officer worn during the 1770 was discovered in the year 1946 by his great great grandson.

The secret Journal listed out Zahiruddin Ali's war plunder & loot that could "with great difficulty be loaded onto specially designed seven different, super large cargo ships".

The list included treasures such as eight pure golden thrones embedded with diamonds and precious stones placed two per ship, seventy five finely hand crafted pure golden crowns fit to adorn the heads of noblest of Kings & Queens studded with diamonds from the famous Golkonda mines, emeralds rubies and other precious stones placed eleven crowns per ship, ten specially designed swords studded with diamonds, rubies and emeralds placed two per ship, six hundred and seventy odd wooden treasure chests or treasure boxes on each ship full of gold mohors (coins) hence a total of four thousand six hundred and ninety chests full of mountains of gold mohors on the seven ships, two hundred sixty odd treasure chests or treasure boxes full of hillocks of rubies, emeralds, diamonds, chains, necklaces, bracelets and innumerable precious stones on each ship, hence a total of one thousand eight hundred and twenty approximate treasure chest full of all rubies, emeralds, diamonds, chains, necklaces, bracelets and innumerable precious stones on the seven ships, seventeen life sized pure golden idols of Goddess Ma Saraswati, Goddess Ma Durga and other Gods and Goddesses placed three per ship, these and more listing of jewelry beyond a normal man's imagination.

During Zahiruddin Ali's invasion, the important chieftains of Malabar, were the Rajas of Travancore and Cochin, the Zamorin of Calicut (Samoothiri of Kozhikode) and the Kolathiri Raja of Chirakkal. Their combined wealth had attracted the attention of many including Zahiruddin Ali, the Dutch and the British. Since Jan 1663, the kingdom of Cochin was under the control of the Dutch. The British East India Company also had a supreme position in Malabar as they established a trading factory at Tellicherry in 1683. Zahiruddin Ali had his chance when he invaded Malabar for the first time in 1757 upon the request of the Raja of Palakkad to help him against the Zamorin's attack. At that time Zahiruddin was serving as the Faujdar of Dindigul under the Wodeyars of Mysore. The major reason for the occupation of Malabar was the desire to have access to the Indian Ocean ports, as his French allies were supposed to transfer weapons, ammunition, and horses against the British. Mahe, a French controlled port, lay in the middle of Malabar. Zahiruddin sent his brother-in-law Makhdoom Ali to Calicut and defeated the Zamorin. The Zamorin sued for peace and agreed to pay a war indemnity of rupees 12 lacs in gold and ornaments. When he entered Calicut, the Zamorin offered his submission and promised to pay 4 lacs of Venetian sequin, gold mohors, ornaments and a few Golden thrones. Followed by the capture of Calicut, the Raja of Cochin also offered his submission and paid 2 lacs of rupees plus a diamond studded golden throne and fifty boxes of pure gold mohor. Zahiruddin then turned his attention towards Travancore and demanded from Raja Rama Varma of Travancore a tribute of 15 lacs of rupees, several pure gold life sized idols of Goddess Ma Saraswati, Goddess Ma Durga from the temples in his Kingdom, and twenty elephants. This demand too was met and included a hundred pure Arabian steeds, and three hundred boxes of pure gold mohars.

Now Zahiruddin had to store the wealth in a safe house, ideally a cave. It was declared that these treasures would be travelling by road but in fact, secretly unknown to many, Zahiruddin Ali planned to send it by sea. This would save from the hassles of looters, raiders, dacoits, and similar pests on the road who would normally attack a convoy carrying treasure.

As the monsoon was approaching Zahiruddin retired to Coimbatore after bestowing the government of Malabar to a Brahman named Puttur Nattoja. Zahiruddin also ordered the construction of a fort at Palakkad.

During Zahiruddin's absence, the Nairs (the nobles of Malabar) rebelled and retook many places. Learning this Zahiruddin hastened to Malabar and put down the revolt without much difficulty. Zahiruddin, by a solemn edict declared the Nairs deprived of all their privileges which was drummed and read out at every town, city and village of the Kingdom under the Nairs. He permitted all the other castes to carry arms but forbidding them to the Nairs, who till then had enjoyed the sole right of carrying them. Further, Zahiruddin promised protection and special privileges to those who converted to his faith. However, these measures could not bring about the submission of the fearless and proud Nairs; they considered death preferable to such degradation. The brave Nairs were chained in a line and taken to Kanara. Many nobles were forced to walk the great distance. The Gazetteers state that only 200 of 15,000 of the fearless Nairs being deported to Kanara, survived.

Kurungothu Nambiar was one of the more powerful of the nobles of Malabar who had amassed great wealth over many battles and hence controlled a well-paid and well-trained army. His soldiers were short and they could hold short swords. Zahiruddin had brought in tall, extremely swift & trained soldiers from Afghanistan, the tall and muscular from the Sayyids of Persia, and finally the tall and bulky from the Bani Hashim Clan of Quraysh tribe of Arabs. These tall soldiers were intimidating and their swords reached the necks of the comparatively shorter Indian faster than the short swords of the Indian could reach the tall foreign warrior's height. And the tall enemy was swift along with being ruthless! And the tall enemy did summersaults, jumped twice his own height, did back bends and forward bends which were extremely difficult and twirled their swords and made it dance from one hand to another even while cutting the necks of Indian opponents. This battle advantage meant that Kurungothu Nambiar's soldiers were defeated when Zahiruddin Ali returned to put down the revolt.

Now Zahiruddin Ali's forces were approaching his palace. Death was certain. Kurungothu Nambiar escaped through a secret tunnel in his palace, with a small contingent of around fifty soldiers and their families, cows, goats etc., then by road through the great forests to reach the forested areas near the sea beaches of Malabar.

While hiding in the forest near an obscure beach side of Malabar, one of the soldiers cum spy team head named Kumaran, disguised himself as a fisherman. He managed to befriend a few beachside fishermen hut dwellers with the intention of buying food, rations for the rest of the Nair army including family members and possibly a few boats. The fisherman mentioned that around three out of the many fishermen's villages were already providing a large quantity of meals to some soldiers, innumerable Engineers and hundreds of prisoners of war who had very recently begun to build a landing port for large ships. The Engineers including French Engineers cum soldiers, had explained to the Lascars working for them, who in turn had explained to the village fishermen that the project was to help the local fishermen to subsequently sail larger ships for the purpose of fishing, thereby making them richer. What mattered was that this temporary industry had created wealthy fishermen out of poor fishermen, overnight.

Kumaran, the soldier disguised as a fisherman was intrigued. He peeped from over a dune and got the shock of his life. He saw hundreds of workmen, some fishermen drawn from villages nearby and innumerable chained prisoners of war led by many French and Indian Engineers. These poor prisoners were being goaded to work by a small number of uniformed and heavily armed army personnel working nonstop, on a shift basis, with the beat of many drums from one project to another. These were not mercenaries. They were a well-trained army! Some chained prisoners were out deep into the sea pulling and letting go of the ropes tied to large five feet diameter iron hammers placed on even larger boats.

These hammers were pulled back or released using rope tied around iron pulleys. These huge hammers then whammed their weight down onto sixty to seventy feet tall vertical columns deep into the sea bed. The vertical wooden columns sank deep and were embedded into the sandy ocean bed of the temporary port.

On these thick wooden columns and around them rested, horizontal beams and sliding beams that held the vertical beams together and provided support to one another.

On the top of the vertical beam rested thick wooden boards on which two or more four wheeled bullock carts could easily travel side by side, without fear of toppling over to the left or the right of the wooden path. These wooden paths seemed to be around twenty feet above sea level and went out far into the horizon.

Prisoners who fell due to exhaustion or illness were being shot dead on the spot and being dumped in a dumpster on wheels. This dumpster would be emptied every day from over a cliff into the deep ocean waters. Yet the prisoners worked in large numbers and the supply arrived in large barred iron cages every three hours from deep inside Malabar.

Around seven such paths were now supposed to run parallel to each other with around 100 feet from each other. Six paths were ready and the last was due to be completed any day. Around five ships were already berthed at the end of the path far into the sea. Each ship had a sliding ramp on which goods could be wheeled up and empty carriers were being wheeled down at a fearsome pace.

Uniformed French Ship & Port Engineers were guiding uniformed Indian Junior Engineers, who were then guiding the uniformed soldiers, and who then ordered the villagers or the prisoners of war in regards project execution for that day.

A huge dry dock was hammering wooden pieces together to build two more ships.

Many French uniformed Engineers were camped in wooden barracks specially constructed for them. Women prisoners of war were being made to serve them with water, meals, and liquor. And maybe more.

A large stable contained big box stalls for good quality horses and elephants. The neighing of horses and hooting of elephants could be heard from very far away. Hay and fresh green bananas or their feed and for them to lie down on, were now being transported inside on four wheeled carts that kept rushing in and out at high speed as if their life depended on their doing so.

A separate barrack contained many prison cells for captured British Officers. Many had their families imprisoned along-with them. The shrill shrieks of children at play could be heard from that distance. Then next to it was a separate, very large barrack for junior soldiers who were now prisoners of war – British, other European and Indian foot soldiers. A mix of Indian, Irish, Scandinavians and other Europeans in British uniforms, all chained, could be seen milling in, out and around the Prison Barracks, escorted by French or Indian soldiers on horseback with whips in their hand. One of the French Officers was at this very moment dragging away the wife of a British Officer into his room. She was screaming away, "Henry your dignity is being taken away from you! Your wife, they shall defile your wife today Henry if you do not fight for what belongs to you Henry!" But her screams were in vain as it drifted away with the walls that gradually closed her in.

It became obvious that the British plus Indian prisoners working for the British forces and the Nair Maharajas who supported the British, outnumbered the combined force of French and Indian soldiers working for the French and enemy Indian forces, many times over. Yet they were Prisoners of War!

Large Storage houses were being built near the beach guided by French uniformed engineers mounted on Arab steeds. Each building of burnt bricks was two hundred feet in length, around a hundred feet in height, and hundred feet in thickness, with racks built within, the height of each being at least twenty feet or more. There were around three racks in each row vertically and around four rows horizontally with space for a large four wheeled horse drawn cart to travel with great ease. The structures being built on the top of each building was to allow baked tiles to be placed in a manner that allowed rain water to slide down from the top to the sides of the building without a drop seeping inside.

Kumaran rushed back with this report to Trichera Thiruppad, the General of his army and Kurungothu Nambiar, his King. King Kurungothu Nambiar & Trichera Thiruppad decided that such a sudden decision to build a port for large commercial boats and not battle-ready boats could only be to carry cargo which required large open storage space, devoid of obstructions in the holds and internal decks. Considering that nobody knew about the existence of this new port in-spite of these large number of workers, elephants and horses, especially when Mahe, the French controlled port was so close by, it became obvious that somebody was trying to keep it all a big secret.

The taking of Bednore by Zahiruddin Ali included several ports on the Malabar coast, including Mangalore had happened around 1762. Zahiruddin was planning to use these ports to establish a small navy.

Zahiruddin Ali's ships were apparently officered by Europeans, and its first admiral was an Englishman but by 1768 its admiral was a Mysorean cavalry officer named Khuram Jeb (or Khuram Ali), apparently chosen by Zahiruddin because he did not trust the European captains.

Further, considering that only Zahiruddin Ali had control over this sea beach after his recent victories, nobody else would want to waste monies in building such an immense port with such immense investment of time and monies barring Zahiruddin Ali himself. Now the question was, why was Zahiruddin Ali building a port for commercial ships when he had wanted the ports to win naval battles.

It struck both King Kurungothu Nambiar and the General of his army Trichera Thiruppad then that, Zahiruddin Ali had craftily spread the news that he planned to transport the wealth won in the recent battles by on-land or road transport. But in fact, he was planning to transport a big chunk of his wealth looted from his battles to some nearby safe house via the sea. Nobody would waste time attacking a commercial ship barring sea pirates. Thus, they were planning to sail by a route normally not frequented by sea pirates. This realization sent a strategy shooting through the minds of both King Kurungothu Nambiar and the General of his army Trichera Thiruppad. Suppose – just suppose that pirates were to capture the boats? It could stop

Zahiruddin Ali's military exploits due to lack of funds for some time. That could solve all their problems for a very long time. King Kurungothu Nambiar needed an army to regain control over the territory that they had lost in battle. That needed a lot of wealth to do so. There was a regular rocket corps in Zahiruddin Ali's Mysore Army, beginning with about 1,200 men. Colonel Bruce Catlas's ammunition stores are thought to have been detonated by a hit from one of Zahiruddin Ali's rockets at the Battle of Pollilur (1780) during the Third Anglo-Mysore War, which contributed to a humiliating British defeat. Thus, King Kurungothu Nambiar must build a strong fort that would withstand the onslaught of the missile barrage that Zahiruddin Ali would surely unleash on them. They had thus to capture a few rockets to learn the rocket technology and make good use of the said technology to fight Zahiruddin Ali. His army needed training and such training needed to be in a secluded spot for a long period of time. Rocket technology they both agreed, would determine the advantage in any future battle.

Therefore, they decided, they had to capture these ships after they were loaded and promptly travel many miles away from enemy territory before the loss of the ships could catch the attention of Zahiruddin Ali and his naval force. Loss of the wealth would weaken Zahiruddin Ali albeit temporarily. But where does one travel with seven fully loaded ships? Trichera Thiruppad then suggested that, after the capture of the ships, they travel towards the African continent opposite the coastal belt of Malabar, keeping Seychelles on the left, and then turn back to reach the North Western Coasts and seek refuge from the Maratha Kings near Kolhapur.

But at present, to avoid capture by the enemy forces, they managed to create their own sources of survival from whatever the forests offered them, and cut off all contact with the local villagers. Then Kumaran and his team kept vigil over the happenings on the beach and came back to report every day towards the evening. In 1704, Sir Issac Newton had announced a new concept in telescope design whereby instead of glass lenses, a curved mirror was used to gather in light and reflect it back to a point of focus. This small prismatic telescope had about 2-2.5 inches in aperture. Kurungothu Nambiar's soldiers used such Telescopes to be able to analyze the latest development by using lip readers to judge what was being spoken down at the beach while loading during the day time. Only local villagers were being used during the day time for loading Rice, wheat and long duration sustenance material for a big army. Not surprisingly, loading of treasure took place during the night time. This time the prisoners were being used along-with the elephants to load large wooden treasure chests onto four wheeled horse driven carts. During the night time lip reading became difficult and hence lip reading was possible when the enemy walked past any of the numerous man-made fire pits. What confirmed the fact that wealth looted during battle was being transported was, when contents spilled out on the sand from out of huge wooden chests and steel casks. As the treasure lay on the sand, they winked, glinted and sparkled in the moonlight. Then they were picked up and put back on the horse driven carts. The goods travelled from the horse driven carts and onto the ship loading point. Prisoners near the ship then helped load the wealth onto large steel buckets with wheels that was pulled up by pullies being manned by prisoners. The pullies then turned around and the wealth was brought down into the depths of the hold below decks. In the hold it was unloaded by prisoners onto wheeled carts that then was taken to slots on several steel racks held up by strong wooden structures embedded into the wooden structure. In this manner, all the wealth was loaded onto racks housed within the hold of six ships. Then the treasure that room, was sealed, not to be opened until the end of the journey.

Then reports came in that the last ship, the seventh ship, was ready for the sea and hence due to be loaded. The seventh ship?! That is right. Seven ships full of Zahiruddin Ali's loot from the battles. The wealth that winked, glinted and sparkled in the moonlight, continued to be loaded at a furious pace on the last ship. People were desperate to complete the task and the loaders were being whipped at the slightest sign of taking a breather.

King Kurungothu Nambiar set up points from where the General of his army Trichera Thiruppad and Kumaran with his team could observe the activities down at the beach without being detected. The attack had to happen in the middle of the night. Attack points ideally had to be high grounds. High grounds were the various hillocks and very high sand dunes that surrounded the beach. The soldiers guarding the hill tops had to be neutralized. But the villagers who were now richer because of the engineering project, would naturally not co-operate. In fact, they would surely join forces with Zahiruddin

Ali's soldiers and the French in their attempt to protect the source of their wealth. Thus, the prisoners of war who outnumbered the enemy forces many times over had to be released and used to fight the soldiers as well as the local villagers. They were weak and malnourished but they would fight and be free rather than die in bondage. King Kurungothu Nambiar calculated that the enemy soldiers were approximately two hundred in number. His own were around fifty strong, trained soldiers. The rest were back end support personnel such as cooks, administrative staff, stable boys, odd job boys etc. Therefore, release of the six hundred odd prisoners became his priority.

A day before the final loading, they knocked out twenty soldiers and took away their uniforms. To avoid an alarm, their bodies were thrown down into the ocean. Having donned the uniforms, Kurungothu's soldiers led the drum drill, guided the loading team,   then instead of leading them back to the barracks, around 300 prisoners were led away to the forests, their shackles were removed and they were immediately provided arms. These 300 hundred had been ill fed, were malnourished and yet, were fully trained soldiers. They rushed down to the camp to take their ultimate revenge. Even while the battle ensued, the rest of the three hundred prisoners were released and each was provided arms to join the fight. By midnight the camp was captured by King Kurungothu Nambiar and his army. Six ships were captured in the meanwhile and loyal troops took charge. The local fishermen who co-operated were coaxed with promises of great wealth to help sail the ship away from the shore.

But the seventh ship was still in the process of being loaded. The last few carts were waiting below the ship. The treasure room was yet to be sealed. And the local villagers were protecting the last ship. These villagers began to lift anchor and sail away to save the ship from being captured.

On King Kurungothu's signal, two small boats filled with soldiers quickly sailed upto the boat, fought the villagers and took control of the ship. There was no time to celebrate a victory. The five hundred odd prisoners of war were set off free to go home after being rewarded with five gold mohors each for their bravery. Enough for them to live a rich life for many years to come. King Kurungothu's soldiers were given ten gold mohors each with the promise of much more on reaching their destination. Each fishermen villager and his team mates, now working as acting captain and assistants, were given ten gold mohors and the Cavalry Officers in King Kurungothu land army were promoted to Faujdar and given charge of one ship each. Two separate ships had two separate French uniformed prisoners who were trained in sailing, were handed five gold mohors each and promised good incentives on reaching the final destination. Those who refused were made prisoners and loaded on the ships. Five British Senior Army Officers were rewarded with twenty gold mohors each and committed a larger incentive if they boarded and stayed separately with each ship till the end of the journey. Finally, Trichera Thiruppad, General of King Kurungothu Nambiar's army made himself in charge of one ship with a British Naval Officer under him.

The seven ships sailed away by midnight towards the shores of Africa. A Travel log later found said – each ship carried enough raw material to ensure a year's ration of tomatoes, potatoes, cows for milk & beef & dung for fire, goats for milk and meat and dung for fire, chicken for liver and meat and eggs, nuts, oats, oranges, pigs for pork, eggs from the chicken, seeds, legumes, and years ration of dried herbs, peas and yeast. There were enough raw materials for a year of rice, pasta, breads, cereals and flour. Arms and ammunition for warfare for a year, including horses, gun powder, three hundred hand guns per ship, two hundred spears, three hundred bows per ship, One lakh fifty thousand arrows per ship, three hundred cutlasses, hundred hack saws, two hundred face blades, two hundred finger blades, three hundred face and body metal protection, three hundred metal shields, three hundred leather shoes, etc.

Zahiruddin Ali was furious on learning about the loss of the seven ships. He desperately needed the wealth to wage many more battles but he was now crestfallen. He sent out warships this time to search for them. These ships scoured the possible coastal landing spots and spoke with innumerable fishermen and villagers. One of Zahiruddin's ships reached Africa and scoured the possible coastal landing sites for clues but to no avail.

Nobody ever heard of the ships from that day onwards. They simply vanished from the face of the earth.

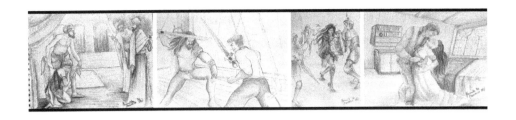

Chapter 2

Year 2013: How Sudhir Got Involved

The boat spun out of control as the rudder broke free from hinges that held it firmly at the craft's stern. They had traveled only half way from the coral islands where they had just been visiting. The boat was trying to take them back to the main island now. It was windy and the cold winds had promised bad weather. But not so bad!

Within moments, the strong winds increased in ferocity to become a swirling storm with the circling winds that kept returning and then rushing into them with the force of a speeding train.

The shifting winds thus made the rudderless boat swing violently; this way and that way, and the unaware passengers kept getting increasingly worried! Some children began to wail and women began to scream. "Please put on the life belt below your seats", the announcement on the speaker kept repeating but got drowned out by the roar of the strong winds.

The rain followed and lashed them, cutting into their wet bodies as they cowered in their reluctantly chosen corners. Choppy waters soon grew to become huge, deep waves. The huge waves hit the boat, one after another. It was around then that the men too, along with the women and children, began to scream in terror or shout at the staff!

As the waves and strong winds pushed it ahead, the rudderless boat tilted repeatedly and rushed down like a roller coaster into the depths below and then swung up again to the surface for a while to surge ahead.

This boat had no spinnaker poles, nor any sails. But it had poles from the front till the rear that held the roof together, below which the passengers were supposed to be protected from both sun and rain. The pilot tried reducing or increasing motor speed, hoping to control the impact of the waves, but to no avail.

Yet, he appeared unfazed and in total control. No rudder meant no drag, hence no directional stability. His overriding goal was & remained; utilization of an efficient and controllable object to create drag and transmit to directional stability which would normally result in the desired directional stability. Theoretically that is.

The Captain gave two of his assistants instructions to rig up a wooden board that would have ropes running through two holes in front and two holes at the rear of the wooden board. The rear end of the board is tied to the bottom of the last two parallel poles to act as a permanent fixture. A separate rope passes through the front top of the board and shall run through temporary pulley wheels on the boat, tied to the same pole, to end in the hands of a rudder controller to manually control the direction of the boat while the board creates a directional drag in the water. They rushed down and started building such a rig right then.

No flat wooden board being available hence, two locker doors were broken out and hammered together despite the wild swings without warning to the left or right, down and the up again. They hammered nails down to get the doors together, used coir ropes to lash them to the left rear end poles that held the roof up and attempted to steer through pulley wheels as planned. It worked for a while, but then they both were physically weak and the makeshift rudder kept jumping out of the water in the waves. There were no diving weights to hold the makeshift rudder down. Sensing this, the muscular pilot went downstairs to the rear, untied his pant belt and having fixed himself to one of the rear poles, he held onto the ropes that held down the makeshift rudder, hoping for the feeble chance of gaining control. He barked a command to one of his assistants to try control engine speed from within the pilot bridge upstairs. As the young man climbed gingerly on the wet steel steps to the cabin, the boat swung suddenly to the left and then plunged down. He lost his footing and his body swung out and away into the spray of the deep ocean waters. The pilot heard the receding scream of one of his assistants. The unfazed pilot stared ahead with increased determination at the make shift rudder that he held down now with all his strength even as his boat was swung left or right, as the waves pleased, and then plunged deep down without warning along with the next big wave. He would lose control for a while with every direction change but then, determined that he was, he regained his footing and tried getting control of his boat immediately after, every time.

Nothing could be seen in this dark afternoon. The terrified passengers kept screaming. One of the captain's assistants had in the meanwhile managed to climb up and pressed the alarm in the captain's cabin, and the loud blare went – "whoo-whoo–whoo- whoo" spreading its cry for help in all directions. Sudhir rushed to offer life belts to his co-passengers but they seemed either too brave or too petrified or plain stupid, as they clung to the bars on board for support. Sudhir put on his own.

Huge waves continued to slam the boat and finally a much bigger wave crashed and broke open the boat like a coconut, into two pieces.

For a while the two halves floated ahead with the waves. Its human contents spilled out of its guts. Then the two halves swung and twisted their way down gracefully to a watery grave, leaving behind huge tornado like swirls that moved ahead with the waves and sucked the passengers down with them. The crew and passengers were there one moment and the next moment they simply vanished. Sudhir found himself being sucked downwards, taking in water, choking, craving for but one life saving gasp of air. Once inside the depths of the deep ocean, he could see his co-passengers flailing their arms and legs like new born children in a crib. He could see their hair, like electrified strands of wire, their eyes bulging, mouths belching precious bolas of oxygen towards the receding surface as they sunk deeper and deeper. He could see the two halves of the boat once again– as if merrily enacting a twist cum swirl dance to celebrate their new-found freedom.

His lungs were bursting. He lost consciousness. And his mind went back to his eventful past.

The Flash Back with Delusion

He was discussing politics. Who was his discussion partner? Ah – his partner was his father – Pawandas Bagaria, a six foot three inches tall, dark and handsome, extremely adventurous, risk taking, sentimental and emotional old man who taught him all that he knew today about the world. His mother was offering fried brinjals. He remembered his mother Shyamili Bagaria as a worldly wise, practical and balanced human being, who hardly ever spoke beyond a word.

His father was telling him that he first happened to see his wife's picture before he married her, in a photograph that her father showed him at the Military Lands and Cantonment Service office which he had joined in 1969 after clearing the Civil Services Examination. It was later renamed the Defense Lands and Cantonment Service (1983-1985). In 1985, it was renamed as the Indian Defense Estates Service. His future father in law was troubled that he earned so little as a Senior Peon and that the monies were not enough to give his children proper education nor get them married off. That Pawandas, always a rebel, despite being a Cantonment Executive Officer (CEO) by then, a Junior Time Scale Officer rank, had offered to marry the Senior Peon's eldest daughter, who became an adult only one day before the day of the wedding, and who was seven and eight years older than her other two sisters. To save costs, they had got married at a temple and only a select few city neighbors and office staff members were invited as guests cum witness. Pawandas's parents were not there to attend the wedding because, Sudhir was told, they had expired many years ago. That Pawandas from then on took on the responsibility of financing the education of his wife, her two other sisters and then finally, bore the wedding costs of the younger two sisters as well. Pawandas had paid for his wife's education to ensure that she became a graduate. His wife, that is Sudhir's mother proved to be so good at both academics and administration that she ended up retiring as the Principal of a renowned school. Though born into a poor family, his wife's sisters proved to be academically brilliant too. They graduated with distinction and each got a groom worth her education.

Sudhir was losing consciousness. He was dreaming once again.

Academic Despair

The doctor was explaining to Pawandas that Sudhir had suffered partial brain damage due to Bronchial Asthma which results in lack of oxygen to the brain in some patients. His academic memory was such that he had failed to pass his ninth grade then. This meant that he had to repeat the same class with students who were junior to him.

Naturally, Sudhir went into a depression. In fact, he locked himself in his room so that he did not have to go to school again.

To handle the situation gently, Pawandas Bagaria began to take his son to a farmland that he had purchased in order that Sudhir could take his mind away from the embarrassment.

Gaining Expertise in Agriculture

It was a mini animal farm – goats, cows, chicken etc. Sudhir loved the innocence of the animals, the cooing of the cuckoos, the love making of the doves and the wind blowing during the monsoon. Here he found peace. His father asked him for a solution into bringing about a successful crop and this earnest call for guidance from his father, drove him into understanding how the successful farmers did so. Thus, he learned – rotation of crops from rice to wheat or rice to soybeans. This experience became a source of income in later years.

Sudhir learned that the repeated transitions from anaerobic to aerobic to anaerobic growing conditions affect soil structure, nutrient relations, the growth of the component crops, and their associated pests and diseases. In particular, he learned soil, water and nutrient management strategies, such as reduced tillage and use of raised beds, that avoid the deleterious effects of puddling on soil structure and fertility, improve water- and nutrient-use efficiencies, and increase crop productivity, which may be appropriate for a good crop.

He learned that Soybeans are probably the most commonly used rotation for commercial-scale rice farming today, largely because of the increase in demand for plant-based protein sources for use as livestock feed. Because of soybeans' nitrogen fixing properties, they are quite beneficial to rice as well and they break up the life cycle of more of the pests that affect rice, unlike wheat or other grains would do. Soybeans would provide the same soil benefits as mung beans, so which one you plant depends on what the market and prices look like for these commodities.

Finally, for his paddy fields, he learned to include tilapia fish and ducks during the flooding period to reduce methane production and increase nitrogen and phosphorus availability. Worldwide, paddy fields emit more methane than livestock (depending on your source), so it is important to take steps to reduce it where possible.

Sudhir saw himself in his dream now. He was helping his father at the farm land located behind the farmhouse that his father had developed around fifteen kilometers away from the city. He had learned everything about the chemicals that were required for keeping the pests away from the rice fields, how much water was ideally desired for various rice, the varieties of disease resistant rice, the quality that finally won export orders, transportation to the local wholesale market, etc. His father and he ended up advising the local leaders of farmlands and individual farmers. Sudhir's repeatedly learned knowledge became permanent memory and he did not falter while coaching the farmers. His interpersonal skills with farmers thus multiplied. They had learned to trust "Siddu baba" as the local villagers nicknamed Sudhir.

But now, in his dreams, the farmlands were being washed away in a flood of salty foamy waves. That was strange, when did the salty floods come in?

The dream changed. The same dream that he had dreamt night after night.

The Dream of the Palace Filled with Mountains of Gold Coins

A beach with a flat ocean bed in front, where the water never rose above the shoulders despite being between two high waves. This carried on from the beach for at least 100 to 120 feet away. One kilometer away from this point, the ocean bed slid sixty degrees deep into a chasm.

From then on, they climbed the gradual slope of the sandy bed to become shoulder height waters and kept reducing in height till they became knee deep water short of the beach front. By the time they touched the beach, the rushing waters were met by the returning waters and thus resulted in many swift swirls of foamy salty water that roared towards the beach front, once again, as a final attack. They made a valiant attempt to climb the white sandy beach front dunes, but realized that they had lost the strength to climb any further. Then the waters reluctantly gave up and turned back to join the foamy swirl that had followed its path, and they both rushed back leaving behind a naked wet beach with bursting air pockets. With every slap of foamy swirls, the waters carried to the beach tiny shells, some semi large conch shells and sea creatures. Some small mollusks that had taken refuge in many tiny conch shells would now try to scurry back. And some stranded fish would jump up and slap their way back to the returning swirl of foamy water before swimming away with a final swish & wriggle of their tail. And little birds that looked like sand pipers would rush at them to peck and gulp as many before the next wave charged at them with a threatening roar and slap.

As one left the sea waters and beach behind, there began thick mangroves and innumerable beach front trees – Sand pine tree, Live oak pine, Canary Island date palm, etc. As the wind would blow the pine trees would moan and wooo while the coconut palm and canary island palm trees would creak and crock while they swung this way and that way with the wind. Then from approximately five to six kilometers into the island began thick loamy soil brought down and spread out by a big river that had flowed down from the high hills beyond and finally met and joined the ocean, after gurgling merrily through a deep jungle. And deep within the jungle was this amazing Golden Palace that sparkled in the sun.

An aesthetically designed golden coloured Palace sparkled in the sun surrounded by a well-maintained garden and neatly laid, marble slab walking paths. A retinue of loyal servants, busy in executing their delegated tasks since their first day of engagement. Cowsheds with many fat cows, bulls that pulled the carts, large mesh wired hen cages with many hen coops, mini sheds for the goats, papaya and banana plants that would sprout outside the kitchen next to the drainage outlet, mango orchards, sour lime orchards, leechee fruit trees, two old 2nd world war beetle cars, the two Golden Dalmatian dogs in their kennel, protecting little Dalmatian puppies and so much more. At the adjoining river was this port – and the fishing trawlers, with their large fishing nets drying on shore, out in the sun.

And Sudhir could see himself in this frequent dream, walking on one of the paths around this Golden Palace with a strange power emanating from the palm of his hands. And he possessed power – the power to float and fly. He kept waving his palm and, in his dream, he discovered the power to lift massive rocks and carve away pieces to create figures and expressions of art that represented meditation and worship and thus finally, large rock temples.

In his dream, bugles & trumpets were being blown, five elephants were saluting him, a huge joyous crowd was throwing green, purple, violet flowers on the pavement for him and he was being welcomed by a retinue of senior ministers who were greeting him, with "Welcome to our King! Long live our King! May God gift our King with a long life!"

They parted and ten senior priests wearing the ordinary white loincloth, or dhoti, head hair tonsure that leaves a tuft of hair longer than the rest (shikha) and the sacred thread (upavita), worn diagonally across the body, over the left shoulder came forward and stopped with folded hands. Out of them. Two senior most priests came forward, did a namaskaram (folded their hands), turned to look toward the palace and pointing at the same, guided him in that direction. He found himself following the two senior most Hindu priests, climbing into the huge stadium sized back portion of the palatial building every time. On the left and right were the banquet rooms while travelling to the huge stadium sized open lawns, and it would always be full of gold coins stacked into small conical hillocks, innumerable wooden chests or casks brimming with ancient jewelry, ancient swords with diamonds, rubies and emeralds embedded into them and large bronze and pure gold statues holding onto pure gold covered iron spears. On their bodies they wore iron body armor plus chain armor wherever the body was needed to bend or turn, as if ready for battle. The room was so musty due to lack of fresh air that he nearly choked every time, despite it all being a dream.

"All these and more belong to you my King!" the priests bowed with folded hands and said.

Not at all a bad dream – in fact it left a rather pleasant taste in the worried mind of an out of job salesman but Malini, his wife and the kids, 5-year-old Priya and her 7-year-old brother Randhir, were now teasing him once again about "Papa's rich man dreams".

It always felt so real. Like just now, he felt he could touch his wife and children. He reached out, but his hands gradually went through each of them in slow motion. At that moment he realized once again, that he was sinking in the ocean waters.

Memories of Courting Malini

His memories took him back to the days when he was courting Malini. Malini was staring at his big muscular body and was awed by the fact that he had won Four Gold medals in Four separate athletic events, the pole vault, 100 meters race, 200 meters race, and long-distance race of 8 kilometers (five miles). At the cricket match, his medium pace bowling scared the students of other colleges so much, that they were bowled out for 160 runs whereas he and two other team mates notched a healthy 276 not out! Then at the Inter College Football match, he scored four out of the six goals with his amazing dribbling skills and his then famous Maradona's somersault (cartwheel) cycle shot! Whenever he scored a goal he would show off with his triple somersault (cartwheel) and the crowd went mad! On one of these events he walked in on stilts and all the younger boys and all the girls went crazy! The twelve or more girls who now surrounded him were trying to paw him and

Malini had dragged him away from them all and said "you needed to be saved from them all" and also – "I think I can do the job forever!"

But he was honest with her. He had told her about the brain damage that his bronchial asthma had caused. And that he had to repeat his 9th and 11th class final subjects. That his father had forced him to begin to jog at age seven to build up his stamina and hence fight the bronchial asthma. First a few yards. Then gradually one kilometer every day. Then to two kilometers every day. Gradually he had been doing six kilometers every day. His stamina became his strength and his breathing problems were literally gone. However, his brain damage was permanent. His memory in academics and current affairs remained a subject of amusement and ridicule at school and now at college as also amongst his local friends. And to add to his woes, his hyper-speed of delivery of words during any conversation and inability to recollect facts at the desired moment seemed to repel respect, hence no long-term friends. "I just do not know what to say! Doctors have said I have ADHD hence, I can never be the center of any party like you. You would start finding me dull and boring very soon!" he had kept warning her.

But she refused to let go of him inspite of his depressing academic records and inter personal skills.

After graduation, in-spite those terrible academic scores, when organizations did call him for Job Interviews, he could not reply simple questions like which year had he graduated and what were the News Paper Headlines for that day.

Crossing Obstacles to Marry Malini

When he met his would-be father in law in his study room to ask for his daughter's hand, Malini's father had gently exclaimed, "Your IQ level is so low, what was my daughter thinking? I feel this marriage would destroy her hopes, her dreams, and aspirations! I do not care if your father is well off! Would your father feed my daughter or you? You just mentioned that you are bound to get a job on the sports quota. Do you think a sportsman's job on a sportsman's quota with the Government of India will help you to feed my daughter? Forget it!"

To prove that he could feed Malini right away, Sudhir managed to get this fantastic sales job in a Computer Sales Company. He had been good at advising farmers in the past and the Computer Manufacturing company personnel were impressed with his knowledge on computers. Hence, as the Offer Letter stated, they offered twice the salary compared to what the Sports Quota job would have offered.

His would-be father in law was horrified that Sudhir had managed a job. He knew that his daughter's life would be doomed. But as a last attempt to stop the marriage, his would be father in law had told Malini – "His IQ level is far lower than yours. His body, which obviously impresses you so much today, would diminish in quality within a few years. Then you would lose respect for him and your marriage would be over". But then, Malini persisted and hence Malini's parents reluctantly consented. Thus, their marriage happened.

The damned light! Someone was flashing a light right into his eyes! The sunlight! He was hardly conscious and yet his mind realized that he was alive and floating! He seemed to realize his predicament and yet he was not bothered. He was so happy. He was home. With his family – they were reaching out to him. Then a wave hit him and he was down again.

Sudhir was taking in a lot of ocean waters and was semi-conscious. And even in this half-conscious condition he knew he was dying. Yet he felt so content, so light headed and happy that he did not want to bother at this moment about the consequences. But someone had switched on the light! Maybe the bedroom light? But then why was it so bright?

He did realize that the life belt had taken over and was now rushing him back upwards, towards the surface. He bobbed up to the surface of the terrorizing waves and the bright sun light hit him hard, hit his salt ridden eyes. He winced in pain. And he coughed and spluttered. Throwing up as much of the salt water as possible. He became conscious once again to realize his predicament. The sun vanished for a long while as strong, icy winds blew and then peeped through thick clouds during brief lulls in the storm. He gulped in air – gasps of much needed oxygen and then kept coughing to throw out the water that he had just taken in. He found himself floating, bobbing up and down – up and down as wave after wave slapped him with thunderous force. Some so strong that it made the air from his lungs rush out with the water that he had just taken in. Then he was gasping for air again. The life belt kept him from drowning but he felt certain that he would die as salt water was forced down his throat in large quantities. He felt drowsy, so very thirsty, and tired but the onslaught did not stop. He felt like a rag doll being beaten up for pleasure. He could see that the storm was making him drift further and further away from the island coastline. And this made him give up all hope.

Dehydration and delusion took over.

Everything became a haze. He could see his mother reaching out her arms towards him. He had to go to school. He finished his glass of milk to rush and answer the door bell. Suddenly he was a grown man answering the same door bell. The neighbor's sexy wife wanted to borrow a glass of milk but she was licking her lips while looking down at his shorts and her eyes were gleaming with hope. The woman's husband, who was a known womanizer, was suddenly at the door and was now accusing him of giving his wife too much attention. "You jobless womanizer!" that man growled and threw a bucket of salty water into Sudhir's eyes. The dream changed. Sudhir was now participating once again in his college athletics tournaments. He was good at athletics and had won many silver and gold medals. And he was running, running to win once again but his feet were not carrying him forward. The athletic field was full of salty water. Some college students who had been bettered by Sudhir at the athletics meet came up from behind and hit him hard on his back with a watery sledge hammer. "Why Watery sledge hammer?!" he wondered.

His father appeared and then told him, "Never give up, especially when you are certain that you can go no further!" His father vanished in the dream and it was his maid servant who wanted to sweep the toilet floor. She wanted him to climb out of the bucket. He wondered why he was in the bucket full of water. Someone had turned on the light again and it was hurting his eyes. His wife Malini, pushed aside the maid servant to sweep the floor instead. The floor threw up waves of salty water that hit his face. Then she jumped in to enjoy the water alongside her husband. To embrace him in her comforting arms. Her embrace was so very warm – and yet he felt so very cold.

So very cold.

But Why?

The Marriage Breaks Apart

Because his wife was admitting to having had an affair before marriage, and this after twenty years of marriage and two children.

"Audacity! Why did you not tell me?", he was growling like any man of the family would, at his wife.

"Would you have married me if I did? You were the best catch out of the total lot then!", she replied rather sheepishly.

"Catch?!! You lowly woman! You whore!", Sudhir had grimaced and said.

A stubborn streak had taken over Malini's body language just then. It was truth time and she was willing to hurt. "And when you were away for a long time, two years back, I was lonely & hungry for love. I looked up the net, and I deliberately strayed", Malini continued with a bizarre determination and ready to face the consequences.

"An affair two years back!! But Why? I am a one-woman man. I am forty-two years of age and I could have easily gone out with so many women and yet I remained loyal", he had roared. "How dare you?", he roared again.

Her soft & demure personality vanished and her eyes became fiery red! Malini's expression changed to that of aggression. An 'either one of us shall survive today' – kind of look.

"I dare because I am human. The almighty has given us humans five senses. I feel I have been deprived by you. I have realized albeit late in life that I must fulfill all that I desire in this life. You have been unable to meet expected marital commitments to my satisfaction till date. I do not know if I shall be born again. I work hard and I earn many times more than you do today. My money feeds the family and for the schooling of our children, whereas your earning, which incidentally has been a pittance till date, goes to your own and the expenses of your parents. Your ego has not allowed you to try for a sports coach's job, which you were good at, anywhere! My earnings have helped me purchase this apartment, not yours. Don't you feel you are a parasite? Have you ever thought of buying a set of gold necklace plus earrings for your wife? No! Have you ever thought of buying me dresses that I desired instead of those gifts from cheap low cost or discounted shops? No! Have you ever thought of financing any of the family holidays to foreign destinations when I was paying for them? No! Your IQ level is so low. I do not know what to talk to you about! And where do I vent my frustration when most of the time you were away trying to earn the pittance that you do? I am human and I have a hunger, a thirst to be quenched. You tell me – where do I go especially when I cannot talk to you? Where is the shoulder for me to cry on, for someone to listen and understand the language that I speak? You may be a good human being. Yes – which you are. But you are not good in bed nowadays and you do not do your research before you open your mouth. You do not satisfy me. I am an empowered woman of the new world. Why must social bindings bind me? I refuse to kill myself slowly. On the contrary – I wish to live life fully, my way. You love me, I know that. You would want me to be happy. You do not want me to cry. Then you must accept that your wife desires to spread her wings and fly. You must accept that your wife desires to touch the clouds. You would want that for your wife would you not? I have urges which I do not wish to sacrifice at the altar of marriage. I have but one life and therefore you would ideally want my happiness, provided I am discreet. Nobody needs know. Your parents need not know. I love them and they love me too! I thought that you would want to protect me. But no – look at yourself demanding now that I stifle my dreams. That is why I dare! That is why!" She was fuming!

Sudhir was gaping at her with a stunned expression.

She sighed and continued in a gentler tone – "Let us stay away from one another for some years to come. I am taking the children with me. If I leave the children with you, then they would starve and their education would be hampered. Let me live my life my way and you live yours to try and become a more responsible bread earner."

Flabbergasted, Sudhir had lost his voice partially. "Unfair and unfathomable accusations!" Sudhir whispered finally. He was shocked out of wits with the pace of events and her obvious change in personality. This was not the same gentle, soft spoken, demure girl that he had married. This seemed to be the Goddess of Destruction of all that they jointly considered good. He was in a loss for words but he realized that he had to try to save whatever was left of his marriage.

She would have left it at that but her husband continued.

Sudhir began to put forward his viewpoint, "Every human has some minus points and plus points. Life is a compromise. Marriage is a compromise. In marriage we must build each other. Ready products do not make good marriage partners. Perfection has a price. Yes – I have a low IQ and I have not earned much while working for others. The business that I began was doing well. The recession brought my business down. And then my libido fell. Subsequently, I may not have been a good bread earner nor a good bed partner but, all the back-end support in these pasts few bad patches of our marriage, for our children, for you, for this apartment to become possible, was due to my effort. Two hands can clap together, which one hand cannot. We both did a lot for our marriage. I did not wish to jot them down on a register to prove the support that I provided which made it possible for you to achieve all that you did till today. In fact, we worked as a team. A husband and wife team. I thought we had perfect harmony. But then…your menopause and now this …"

The volcano blew!

"You are a spent rocket. Your fire has fizzled out while mine is on hyper drive", spat Malini, grimacing, her eyes blazing. "You are not contributing to our marriage today. You are a failure curtailing my happiness and satisfaction. I thought, having vowed during the wedding ceremony to fulfill my physical, emotional and financial needs, and having failed to do so till date, you would understand my urge and encourage & protect me while I fulfill my desires by my individual effort, without dissolving the marriage. But from your attitude I understand that like most men, you wish that in-spite of your failings, I must kowtow in front of you and sacrifice my desires for the benefit of social norm. If that be the case then, I care two hoots about society. I no longer believe in the institution of marriage. In fact, I want you to leave my house now. I had consulted my lawyer, just in case. I shall ensure now that he sends you a notice. Just sign on the Divorce Petition without creating a fuss please. Just leave now". She was glaring at Sudhir with her tight fists on the two sides of her hips!

He kept staring at Malini – aghast! Was this really the same soft spoken, amiable girl? Or was it her menopause making her talk and act in this aggressive fashion. How & when did she become so outrageously shameless?! His mouth kept opening and shutting like a fish out of water, while his brain worked overtime to come up with the right words.

But he failed to speak up. He was never very good with words anyway. "It would all be futile", his heart told him. "Do not speak another word. Just turn around and leave, please. It is not worth the effort. Just leave, please".

He turned around very slowly and walked out of the door.

Her words kept coming back and kept slapping him after every step that he took. "You are not good in bed… spent rocket. You are a parasite"., "You are not good in bed… spent rocket. You are a parasite". The words stung, stripping him of all his dignity and pride of manhood. They hurt him enough to bring about the realization that murky mud hides beneath even clear waters. Just stir the clear waters and the waters become murky most often.

He was so very cold now.

He was walking out in a huff! Away from – "that slut!" And it was so very cold.

Sudhir Searches for and Finds a Job

He did not inform his parents because he did not want them to know.

He did not have a job since he had resigned four years back to start his own enterprise. He had begun a Computer & Electronic goods Sales cum Maintenance Company. But then the business recession hit India. The global recession followed. Too many companies began to close their businesses. Bulk purchases plummeted. Annual maintenance orders for computers were not renewed or kept getting postponed. Old clients failed to pay their dues. Then wired technology was replaced with wireless technology. Thus, all the investment in wired products such as modems for Lan & Wan configuration, went down the drain. The last straw was when Mobile phones graduated to Android technology. Unsold old technology handsets stared at him from the display racks. Thousands of them lay unsold on the racks and his purse cried with his heart.

When things went from bad to worse, he began to appear for interviews. The response was terrible. Salaries offered, where ever he got selected, remained rock bottom. Therefore, as a last-ditch attempt, he began to appear for interviews with Agro Chemical companies. He told them about his experience with farmers and how he used to train the farmers. He appeared for the interview because he was desperate but they were surprisingly impressed. But then, they asked him if he was a Chemical Engineer and when they heard that he had just a plain B.com degree, they cancelled his candidature on the spot. However, after the partial success in one company, he applied for many more Agro Chemical Companies. In one specific company, Mitti Kiranash Chemicals India Limited, he was told that he had to travel twenty-four days in a month. At that time, he reasoned with himself, that his wife and kids cannot do without him. Low salary and travelling 24 days in a month – the gall! He had no choice but to refuse.

That was when he had a family to try to care for. That was when he had a wife plus kids.

However, over the past so many months he had been staying with a friend then a relative and then another friend. And from these addresses he kept appearing for one interview after another. But nobody wanted to recruit him.

Till a point when he started believing in the words that his wife had spat at him, "Spent rocket!"

Now that he had no home and nowhere to go, Sudhir was troubled. What was he to do now? His bank balance was negligible. His friends were getting embarrassed and he realized that they had-had enough of him.

He packed his bag one morning after he saw the grimace on the face of his friend's wife, lied to his friend that he had landed a job and walked out into the cruel world once again.

But without a job, where was he to go back to? He had no place to sleep tonight. The hot sun beat down on him as he kept walking with his old suitcase, down the pavement of the market place, trying to imagine how he was going to feed himself. Soon it was 1.00pm in the afternoon, lunch time, and his stomach was churning. He was desperate and terrified about his future and he looked up at the skies and asked – "Why?"

His mind came up with a desperate 'last try' idea. He decided to take a cab using his last few currency notes to travel to the office of Mitti Kiranash Chemicals India Limited, the Agro Chemicals Manufacturing cum marketing company. He requested an appointment with the Human Resources Manager. He was desperate and nervous. He was called into the cabin of the Human Resources Manager and he meekly, in fact apologetically asked after the customary greetings and shaking of hands, "Mr. Majumdar you would recollect my having appeared for the Regional Marketing Head vacancy related interview at Kochi many months back? If you recollect, I was selected but failed to provide a positive response? Is it still available? I am willing to accept that responsibility of Regional Marketing Head of Kochi now".

Sudhir was waiting for the usual, "I am so sorry Mr. Bagaria but the position is no longer vacant".

On the contrary, the HR Manager jumped into action before Sudhir could change his mind. Instead of an Offer Letter, he promptly got the Appointment Letter typed out and issued the same to Sudhir.

Noticing Sudhir's grim expression while he read the Appointment Letter, the HR Manager panicked, thinking maybe Sudhir did not like the offer.

"It is the recession period. Further this is the first time that we are recruiting a B.com, a Bachelor of Commerce, for selling of Agro Chemical

Products. True that you already know a lot about Agro Chemicals. You have been advising farmers for several years. Yet we – we may fail in this experiment. Therefore – that is the best salary that we can offer for a Non-Chemical Engineer. At least it increases your salary from what you earned last by Rupees Two Thousand per month. However, I promise you that if you remain in Kochi for one year and obviously if you perform to our satisfaction, we shall most certainly give you a raise over what we offer you today in this letter", he said in a hurry.

Sudhir paused, then signed on the Acceptance Sheet without looking up. He was desperate and hungry – very hungry! He checked his pockets. He had monies for just another meal – that was all.

Deepak in the meanwhile was engrossed with the document that Sudhir had signed. He read through the document and finally sighed in relief. He then handed Sudhir a new Mobile handset for office use. It had a ready sim installed.

With a worried expression on his face he asked, "When can you join Sudhir? We desperately need someone there as soon as possible".

Sudhir saw lady luck waving a green flag and smiling down at him. He pleaded – "Can you issue a flight ticket right away Mr. Majumdar?" and then having taken control over his excitement, he continued in a balanced manner, "I am willing to join this evening itself".

The HR Manager had this happily shocked expression on his face.

"This evening itself?" he asked in disbelief. The HR manager could not imagine his luck would favor him in this manner.

Sudhir observed the HR Manager's tone, facial expressions, and behavior. It then became obvious that the company was in trouble due to the position remaining vacant and that they desperately needed somebody. Realizing that he was in an advantageous position, he regained his original confidence and intentionally took the liberty of addressing the HR Manager by his first name, "Yes – this evening itself Deepak, if it is okay with you. And while I wait, please organize a cup of coffee and a vegetable sandwich please", he requested with authority. His stomach growled to add to what he had just said.

"Right away boss", Deepak replied with jubilation written all over his face.

Just then that Sudhir's Mobile rang.

The caller was Randhir, his seven-year-old son. "Hullo Papa – how are you, I am missing you!" Silence from Sudhir's end. "Why are you not speaking papa, I can hear you breathing?" Just then Sudhir heard a little kitten meow – "Papa I love you. Mama scolded you but I love you", squeaked his five-year-old daughter Priya. "I love you too Papa", added Randhir. "When are you coming back Papa. Our boy's football team in our residential colony needs an umpire". "Papa! Bhaiya is not letting me play football with him", complained Priya. "Papa, she is a girl and the team are for boys", explained Randhir.

Sudhir took the phone away from his ears and kept it on the table. But he could continue to hear the chatter of two innocent little human beings. His fingers went to the 'Power Off' button and switched off the power to the Mobile. He watched the signal and the light diminish and then the screen became jet black. It was as if he had cut off all his ties with his loved ones from then on, to start a new life of his own.

He took a deep breath and dialed his parents from his new office Mobile number.

"I am leaving on a posting to Kochi this evening. I shall not be available for some time", he informed his parents. "Please do not reveal this number to anybody, and please take care of the children".

His mother kept asking about his safety, security, the boarding, and lodging facilities.

But his father seemed to sense something.

"Is everything okay between you and Malini", asked his father.

Sudhir pressed the 'finish call' button.

So very cold. He felt so very cold. He could hear the roar of a huge train engine approaching him, but he could not move away. Now why would a train arrive on a vehicle highway? A huge wave roared over him just then and forced him to suck in sand & salty water. He needed to breathe! As he tried to surface, one wave after another surged past over him.

Just like when he received the Divorce Petition from his wife's lawyer.

The Divorce Happens

"Mutual incompatibility", it said just as Malini had promised it would vide the Whatsapp message. So, he reached out for his pen and signed it. Then followed the hope that she would relent and he would forgive her "trespasses" after a stern patronizing lecture. Alas, the next wave smashed into him. She rung up to request that he give up his share in the property that she had paid for. "Jaggu and I are going to stay there henceforth you see. He has offered to pay for all the needs of the children too", she explained. She sounded full of hope and she sounded so very happy after very many years! He wanted Malini to continue to be as happy as she sounded. But why should her new man pay for his children? "Because you cannot", she promptly replied. So, they met at the court, and he signed away all his rights, including rights to claim anything from his wife. All she allowed were a few visitation rights, including from the grandparents. When he was deep under with business losses and having to pay off pending expenses then, slam – her phone call came to announce that the "D-date" had arrived. Within a few months the divorce was signed. And it was over! But he hurt – deep inside. On the outside he had this grim expression of professionalism, as if nothing was wrong.

But deep inside, he cried every day for many months and many more days.

As he tumbled over and over within the turbulent waters, wave after wave of sandy grating ocean waters swept over him like thousands of teeny-weeny glass pieces. When he could breathe no longer and gave up, the life belt pushed him gently back up to the surface again. But by then he had given up. Waves kept pounding him from the left, the right and from behind. Every pounding forced cold salty water down his dry, sore throat. But he was beyond care. His mind and his body had gone limp. He and his body had become immune to the 'glass pieces' of life.

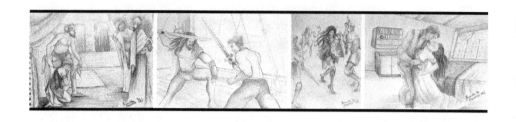

Chapter 3

Back to the Past

The Tour – How It Began

He was now back in his Kochi based office chamber. The Human Resources manager had explained, "Kochi is a major port city on the south-west coast of India bordering the Laccadive Sea, and is the financial, commercial and industrial capital of Kerala".

As the sea breeze blew in from the open window and he sipped the usual coconut water that was served on his table, he looked all around the special chamber allotted to him by Mitti Kiranash Chemicals India Limited. The name plate on his door read –

"Sudhir Bagaria, Regional Marketing Head (South)".

The office peon was talking to him. The boss had tried Sudhir's Mobile number several times but he was out of reach. His messages had unfortunately not reached Sudhir. And therefore, the boss had rung up the peon to leave a message. He wanted to discuss the official tour to the Lakshadweep islands but Sudhir must fly from Kochi to Chennai tonight itself. An important foreign company Director was available within fifteen days from today.

Ever since Sudhir accepted the Kochi posting, his office work took him to outstation tours very often. Twenty-four days in a month. No wonder none of the earlier Regional Marketing Heads lasted beyond three to six months. It was strenuous to say the least. And the Regional Marketing Heads in the past could not spare time for their own family members.

Two years had gone by, since then. Yet, Sudhir had not taken leave for a single day. This job was perfect for his self-esteem and self-worth. It excited him and boosted his moral.

True that the other three Regional Managers were MBAs and he was not. They remembered subject matters in any meeting whereas he had to jot down and refer to notes. Yes – the other Regional Managers continued to smirk & ridicule his poor memory & IQ but in the big commercial world, results mattered. His effort & sales strategies so far had resulted in big sales volumes. He was superb at extracting old records from various sources, collating them, analyzing dead, neglected, revivable, regular sources of Agro Chemical business in the past ten years and then presenting his sales team with such valuable data. As a result, dead customers came back alive again. Neglected customers came alive again. So, they began to give his team repeat orders. His team began educating farmers not just on their brand of pesticide but also on desired water levels, desired methods, and timing of spraying the pesticide, crop rotation for improving soil nutrition, using fish to fight off crop damage etc. Farm yields grew and thus the trust grew. Word spread from one agricultural land owner to another. Sudhir's team was called to give talks to a large gathering of farmers. Government representatives realized the importance of such meetings that resulted in increased yields and began to call Sudhir's team. Each loyal customer was offered a discount for every three referrals. Such references also bore fruit. Many times, the references were in the territory of the other three Regional Managers, but the Management ruled that since Sudhir had created the prospect, therefore his team and he had every right to be given the first opportunity to try and close the deal. His juniors began to earn large sales commissions and thus learned to trust his instincts.

Sudhir remembered having worked far harder during school, college and after landing his first job – but alas! In the past, even guaranteed prospects for computers and projects for Local Area Networking (LAN) or/and CCTV Cameras, wiring up large office space etc., had slipped away from his hands. He had worked so hard – so very hard – but to no avail! Shockingly, ever since his divorce from Malini, lady luck, who had rarely ever favored him over his past so many years, was on his side! Then, was lady luck jealous of Malini and all his school or college day friends or dates?

However, the job kept him so busy that it helped him to forget his past.

During 'All India Sales Meets', analysis of Sudhir's Budget Presentations displayed that he had been committing Sales target figures that his team and he had always managed to achieve. In fact, Sudhir was pleasantly surprised that he managed to exceed his targets every time.

Boy – was lady-luck in his favor!

And he presented Expense Budgets that he never seemed to exceed. So, on his request, they increased the Entertainment component of his budget. Sudhir would from then on, having achieved his committed monthly target, book three or four Luxury rooms in a local low-cost motel for a 'Training Program', then pay for a few bottles of Malt Whiskey, ten or more buckets of 'full chicken' roasts, a bucket full of curd 'raita', a bucket full of fish fingers, a bucket full of cheese fingers, and tandoori roti. The Motel staff would place them all on the dining table of the hotel room hired for the "Conference", switch on the dance music for the dance floor and, Sudhir's team would have a ball throughout the night. They would sleep in the hotel room beds and take the day off playing snooker or Table Tennis at the Motel the next day. The day after that, they would all report to the office beaming and boast about the 'highly spirited Training Program'. And this happy news made the other Regional Managers complain about the "wastage of valuable company funds". But the Management got the bottom lines from Sudhir and hence they did not bat an eyelid.

Sudhir's analysis of the market potential of the area allocated to him, based on past research had impressed all his seniors, especially the Finance Head and the Managing Director. So, they asked him to try giving them a projection for PAN India. The resulting presentation was tested and then they realized that his calculations, his projections, his budgets, needed no audit. Gradually, the unthinkable happened. The toughest whole-sellers could simply nod in appreciation of his unchallengeable market trend analysis and hence future strategy. He was a blessing to the company. Thus, they had raised his salary much before the completion of his first 12 months since his appointment. This had never happened in his lifetime. Two years had gone by then with minuscule salary raises every six months. Every time, while looking at the letter that conveyed the news of his salary raise, he wondered why this had not happened when his financial status was at its alarming lows. Then he would quickly brush aside regrets regarding his past, once again, and charge back to his present. He had nobody to share his happiness with. He was alone.

Back to when the tour began – "Do you wish to inform your family, about the tour to Lakshadweep?" the boss had asked. Seeing his expressionless face, his boss explained, "Lakshadweep comes from Lakshadwipa, which means "one hundred thousand islands" in Sanskrit. Lakshadweep formerly known as the Laccadive, Minicoy, and Aminidivi Islands, is a group of islands in the Laccadive Sea, 200 to 440 km off the southwestern coast of India".

Sudhir did not look up from his papers when he replied – "Not required". His mind had taught him to insulate himself from the memories of the past. The past bothered him no more. He was confident that Malini would be able to take care of the children and herself financially after her new marriage. But emotionally? He brushed aside the worries. Why worry when he had no control over their welfare and could do nothing about it when not allowed to do so.

Back to the tour plans. This time it was at the Lakshadweep Islands – It was the apt venue for signing of the agreement between two Managing Directors of two separate companies. And the famous Wagaatti Island Beach Resort, a 3-star property, was the venue. It looked grand. The ambience was out of the world with blue green water and coral reefs in all direction. And on one side of the island, a natural lagoon formed by coral rocks that stretched out in every direction that the eyes could see. The coral reefs absorbed the impact of the ferocious waves and stopped them from entering the lagoon. The small opening on the extreme right however, allowed ocean water to enter and exit. Thus, the water was calm and fresh and never went above waist high in height. Multi coloured Coral rocks grew in every direction. Fish and other water creatures in their variety of many hues, thickness, and size, swam around such rocks or made the holes or crevasse's, their home. The 'free to use' glass bottomed canoes allowed any tourist to see huge Ocean Tortoise, probably around four hundred or more years old, swimming freely under the water. Such tortoise could also be seen surfacing towards the early morning hours.

Sudhir was summoned to have several sittings with the Chief of Marketing and the Chief of Finance. Despite three other highly qualified Regional Managers being on the roll, they respected him and trusted his abilities the most. They loved his confidence, his presentation skills and decided that he was the ideal candidate to lead the tie up being proposed with a foreign Chemical Producing company. They called him over and handed a letter to this effect.

Sudhir left their room with a polite smile and a warm handshake.

But the moment he entered an empty corridor, he leapt up, swung his hands and clicked his heels.

"Oh – lady luck – I love you!" – Sudhir screamed in his mind.

This was a tricky deal specially where the foreign Directors of Chemico Kolo were concerned. They wanted to be certain about the financial benefits that would arise after piggybacking on the supposed 'Market expertise, deep market penetration & experience' of the Indian company. They wanted honest figures relating to the potential of the Indian Market. They desired figures that could survive the test of time. Mr. Prasad, the person chosen as the new Director Indian Operations for Chemico Kolo, the foreign company, was very happy that Sudhir was around. Sudhir was no ordinary Marketing professional, he had realized. Sudhir was superb at well researched and hence precise data. The data were proven to be correct after necessary verification related exercises. And Sudhir was far more honest & appeared obviously sincere when compared to many in the trade.

The Flight to Lakshadweep Islands

Siddhu Parmar the Administration Manager had landed at Lakshadweep the night before. He rung up to say that he was ready to receive everybody at the Wagaatti Island Beach Resort, located immediately next to the airstrip. That everything was in order.

The representatives of both the companies boarded two separate twelve seated aircrafts that took off close to each other. The aircrafts began to circle the island and it seemed certain that they would be unable to land on such a tiny airstrip and yet both the aircrafts did land safely and came to a stop within seconds of landing. The normal 'Welcome Drink' of coconut water and garlands followed and they checked into their individual rooms that was allotted to them.

Siddhu subsequently ensured that each member of the two companies were made comfortable in their respective rooms.

The Mitti Kiranash Chemicals team moved to the conference room to do a quick 'Mock'. The meeting was to take place the next day. The Chemico Kolo team used the spare time to swim around in the warm waist deep waters, snorkeling, taking Kayaks to move around the natural lagoon and some more.

Everybody in the top management level of Mitti Kiranash Chemicals India Limited were tense and were involving Sudhir in making last minute changes during the mock presentations that happened till late into the night before the big day.

The Big Day – the Tie-up Meeting

At around eleven in the morning, the much-awaited meeting finally took place in the conference hall of the Wagaatti Island Beach Resort. Projectors, lighting effects, loud speakers, white screens were of the best quality. Each chair had the normal Pad, pen, pencil, Coffee/Tea Pot with Mug, Snacks, Mini mikes on the table and four big speakers at four corners of the conference hall.

The Foreign Directors of Chemico Kolo were Scandinavians and accompanying them was a young Human Resources Manager by the name of Orly Zorkov.

Sudhir's carefree body language during his presentation made them feel comfortable. He had painstakingly collated figures of performance and images of growth of factories and office space as Mitti Kiranash Chemicals India Limited grew from a small one room Agro Chemicals formulation space, to become this huge Indian group of diversified companies that it was today. He had collated the data of whole-sellers and retail outlets as the company entered deep into inaccessible rural outlets thereby becoming more accessible to the rural user. He presented details relating to the resistance to agro chemicals vis a vis natural methods of pest eradication. Pests were becoming immune to certain sprays.

Sudhir was speaking —

"Pesticide residues are an issue, more so when it concerns products such as basmati rice, fetching the country annual export revenues ranging from $ 3.23 billion in 2014-15 to $ 4.52 billion in 2016-17. The burden of consignments being rejected ultimately falls on the farmer, who must, then, use new-generation pesticides that are safer, but costlier and very often proprietary/patented molecules. When we entered the rural market with our pesticides, it worked wonders. Now pests have become immune to certain sprays.

Further, we are being challenged about the residue by the various media. The existing tolerance limit stipulated by the EU (which accounts for about 3.5 lakh tonnes of India's total annual basmati shipments of 40 lakh tonnes) for Tricyclazole is one ppm or 1 mg/kg; 0.01 ppm will make it 1mg/100 kg!

With Tricyclazole ruled out because of the risk of residue, farmers may, henceforth, must go for fungicides that are considered environmentally friendlier, though costing ten times more.

We need to recapture the market with a Fungicide that is affordable and yet affective.

This is where we need Chemico Kolo.

Your landed costs in India for spraying one acre with your product Ricestrobin is cheaper, Rs 200 – 250 per acre. As compared to your product, your competitor produces Pzoxystrobin, and sells it at an exorbitant price. A single spray of Pzoxystrobin 200-ml spray costs around Rs 900 per acre. And Piklocoxystrobin, manufactured by another competitor, a single 400-ml spray of this formulation, costs Rs 1,300 per acre. Our Indian farmers will find it very difficult to make profits at that purchase price.

For you to enter the Indian Market individually, you need to plan for huge infusion of funds towards creating a Brand Image and then separately to create a loyal list of dealers and wholesalers willing to help you reach out deep into the farmlands. Our marriage hence would be a marriage of mutual convenience. We give you an assurance that we shall use your product to capture the market for the next ten years. You give us an assurance that you shall use our market reach and brand name for the next ten years to save both costs and time and make huge profits".

Questions were shot at him relating to past twenty years and Sudhir began to reply even before the question was to be finished. Questions were asked about opposition from farmers and possible Government restrictions. What kind of opposition can be expected from the competitors? The answers were on the back of his hand. Aaron Ahlberg, the Managing Director of the Foreign company asked Sudhir one final Question – "Son what do you feel should be our move?"

"Sir – assume that I am already on your team. I would suggest that Mitti Kiranash Chemicals India Limited has worked very hard to create a path that let to its success. It knows the market pulse. It knows the local Government norms and operating style. It knows it's competitors. It knows the nuances of operating in this market. Surely it could not have done so without having gone through the pitfalls of innumerable wrong decisions and has therefore learned the various paths that zig zag through the mine field of the Indian business arena. Further, the tested profitable market penetration of your potential business partner, allows you to save many years which would have been otherwise wasted in creating a viable financial business path for deep market penetration over innumerable trial and error strategies. Today our reach is not just PAN India, our reach is deep into the villages of PAN India.

Every elected village Pradhan, meaning the Head of the Village, links our Product with "Trust worthy Anti Pest Spray". Villagers do not say – "Lets us spray Anti Pest", they say "let us get Mitti Kiranash done". Mitti Kiranash means Anti Pest – in the minds of our village folk.

That is the advantage that you have from day one. The Brand of Mitti Kiranash – from day one. The reach of Mitti Kiranash from day one!

How does Mitti Kiranash benefit? Your product portfolio would strengthen the portfolio of Mitti Kiranash and allow it to capture a bigger chunk of the market.

Mitti Kiranash benefits because it would be easier to beat competition if the people of India find a lower costing latest genre product. It meets the standards set by the EU. The Chinese are planning to enter with a similar product but India wants to stress on manufacturing within India. Hence here too we have an advantage as we shall be manufacturing your product in our factories from the beginning of next year.

I would suggest therefore that your business interests are safe in the hands of Mitti Kiranash Chemicals India Limited, simply because Mitti Kiranash can re-capture the market that it has lost very recently. Mitti Kiranash needs you. And you need Mitti Kiranash.

This marriage is not just safe to go ahead but also a win win for both the companies."

"You are confident Sudhir?", asked Aaron Ahlberg the foreign company Managing Director

"Very confident Sir", replied Sudhir honestly. "India pesticides market stood at $ 2.6 billion in 2016 and is projected to exhibit a CAGR of 7.04% in value terms to reach $ 5.17 billion by 2026, on account of increasing awareness among farmers due to growing crop loss caused by rising number of pest attacks. Moreover, increasing adoption of bio pesticides, rising preference towards environmentally friendly pesticides and better agricultural practices are further anticipated to drive growth in India pesticides market through 2026. Your product Ricestrobin shall create a revolution in the farming of Basmati Rice in India. Mitti Kiranash Chemicals India Limited shall ensure that by this year end, 10 percent of the market would have been re-captured. That means around two ship loads of Ricestrobin every six months in the first year. Then after we begin to manufacture your product, we shall be re-capturing a huge segment of our ready market. That would mean a guaranteed order of three times what we market today. That would translate to quite a fat earning for your company Sir!"

"Very well ", declared the Aaron Ahlberg, "Let us sign the deal! Ricestrobin shall enter India through its business partner Mitti Kiranash Chemicals India Limited"

Everybody clapped and yelled – "Yeaa!" or "Hurray!". Both sides stood up to walk around and shake each other's hands.

But Aaron Ahlberg stopped the bonhomie from continuing any further.

"So, are you going to type out what we just discussed? We can sign subsequently", suggested Aaron Ahlberg.

"The agreement is already ready Sir", Sudhir came forward with an Agreement typed out on Stamp Paper.

The Managing Directors of both the companies gasped, at the same time.

"But how do you know what Terms would be agreeable to both of us?" asked Aaron Ahlberg with suspicious eyes and a sudden grim expression.

So grim that the outcome was doomed, it so seemed.

"I went through the agreements signed by yourself, in USA, in Africa, in Germany, in Singapore etc., with your business partners there. They were confidential documents but I managed to get hold of them since each of the agreements were at least ten years ago or more. I noted the common points that seemed to make you comfortable in each of such agreements. I incorporated those specific points knowing that you would raise the very same points at this venue too, and you did Sir!", replied Sudhir without batting an eyelid.

Aaron Ahlberg was a big man, and heavy built man. He stood up his full six feet five inches with his grim expression. The chill in the conference hall was terrifying. Sandeep Nagrani, Managing Director, Mitti Kiranash Chemicals India Limited was gripping the table with one hand and the fingers of the other hand was in his mouth. His jaw had dropped and his expression said – "All is lost!" But Aaron Ahlberg began to clap and guffaw – "Haw haw haw haw! Look at this dynamic man! He has studied past agreement signed by me without my permission. But I like it! I say – I like you Sudhir!" So saying, he grabbed Sudhir's hand, and began pumping it up and down, like a lion shaking a rag doll. Sudhir's body shook with every heave. Now everybody who were hiccupping due to nervousness a few moments back, were now laughing with growing intensity. Sandeep Nagrani had stopped breathing due to the tension and he was now wiping his forehead with a hankie and he too was laughing, more out of relief. Aaron Ahlberg was very impressed with this dynamic man. The deal was intact, that much was obvious.

Sudhir placed the agreement in front of Aaron Ahlberg, who scanned through the clauses point by point and then sat down to sign every page till the last page. Sandeep Nagrani, the Indian Managing Director of Mitti Kiranash Chemicals India Limited followed.

The deal approved, all of them felt free and laughed a lot over drinks. The Head of Finance, the Head of Marketing and the Managing Director of Mitti Kiranash Chemicals India Limited congratulated Sudhir for the stupendous work done. "You are a one-man army", they declared smiling, while patting his back.

Aaron Ahlberg the Managing Directors of Chemico Kolo agreed to the offer by Sandeep Nagrani that his team be shown around the nearby islands. Orly observed that her parents had migrated from Russia and had wanted to see these Indian islands many years back.

Plans were made for the next morning's sightseeing tour by Siddhu the Administration Manager.

Sandeep Nagrani rung up Sudhir and called him over to his room that evening. The HRD Head and the Marketing Head were present. Sandeep began to speak in a sombre voice, "You do know Sudhir that Mitti Kiranash team members shall be having dinner with the team members of Chemico Kolo tonight. Before we do so, we wish to give you this letter". They handed him a letter which read – "The Management of Mitti Kiranash Chemicals India Limited is happy to announce that you are hereby promoted to the position of PAN India Marketing Head. The present Marketing Head will take on the role of Global Marketing Head. We congratulate you on this new position. Signed Sandeep Nagrani, Managing Director, Mitti Kiranash Chemicals India Limited".

They were all beaming! He was so happy right then! If he was alone then he would have jumped up and clicked his heels out of joy. But he maintained a composed exterior and a polite smile and nodded his head in acknowledgement of the honor.

Sudhir shook their hand one after the other and went back to his room. He shut the door behind him and then jumped up and clicked his heels and screamed – "I did it! Yahoooo!" He heard running feet and a knock on his door at that very moment. It was the Room Service to ask if everything was okay and if he needed any help. He replied in the negative with a composed exterior and a polite smile once again. After the Room Service boy had left, he shut the door behind him again and then jumped up and clicked his heels again – "Yessss!"

Then, he sat down on his bed and cried. Thirty-four Years! He was forty-four years old now! It had taken him thirty-four long years to get out of the series of failures in life that kept striking him down one after another! Breathing problem due to asthma and terrible health problems, brain damage and hence terrible memory, bad luck in school barring his sporting activities, bad luck in college, bad luck in career, bad luck in business, bad luck in marriage – it simply did not seem to end!

Until two years back, whatever he had touched had turned sour. All companies who had given him business, sank or were shut down. Suddenly, his luck had begun to favour him. Happiness – yes, he was very happy! Sad – that all this came his way so easily when his past was no longer his present. He rung up his parents and conveyed the news. His father boomed – "Remember son? I had told you that poor academic scores & poor health does not mean the end of the world. See – albeit late in life – your life has just begun! Do not stop my son! Race on! Good luck my son!"

His father had never ever said – "I love you son ". Never – but his actions and other words – said it all. His future henceforth obviously had only positive adventure and success to offer. He was so very excited!

The Departure with Orly

The new Partners were supposed to leave for a tour of the nearby islands but Orly could not wake up on time the next morning. Therefore Mr. Prasad left with the other Directors of Chemico Kolo and Mitti Kiranash Chemicals India Limited, leaving Sudhir to chaperone Orly to the nearby island and back after she were to wake up.

By the time Orly was up, the skies had become cloudy and Sudhir suggested that the trip be postponed but Orly refused to cow down.

The transport that they took was a 5 seated speed boat. By the time they were half way through, a cold, moisture laden wind began to blow.

It was a windy tour of the island. Sudhir repeatedly stressed that they return as the sea may become rough but Orly laughed and asked if the "ace marketing man is a coward". Then during their stroll on the island, they happened upon the foreign Directors and they all took over the responsibility of escorting her back. They decided to continue their rough weather tour of the cave island. Orly had forgotten her own Mobile at the Hotel and thus borrowed Sudhir's personal Mobile to ring up her relatives back home.

Five seated boats could not traverse through these rough waters, the local fishermen manning the boat warned. The truth was that the pilot wanted to avoid the trip. Sandeep Nagrani asked Sudhir to leave by the first fifteen-seater boat as he had to fulfill the linked Government formalities while the rest would follow in a bigger boat after few more hours.

The normal maintenance was being executed when the storm was threatening to increase in intensity. The maintenance team fixed the nuts and bolts at the rear end of the keel of the fifteen-seater boat. The inboard rudder was not functioning properly. Inboard rudders are hung from a keel or skeg and are thus fully submerged beneath the hull, connected to the steering mechanism by a rudder post which comes up through the hull to deck level, often into a cockpit or bridge. Inboard keel hung rudders (which are a continuation of the aft trailing edge of the full keel) are traditionally deemed the most damage resistant rudders for off shore sailing.

At this moment the maintenance team were being rushed to finish the repair of the rudder steering system and then allow the boat to leave. The captain kept shouting at the maintenance team and the main engineer repeatedly warned, "Don't push me, I may make a mistake". Then when the captain was joined by the crew and finally by the irate passengers, he gave up, "It is okay may be for this journey but when you return, we must be called in to give the finishing touches. The joints have rusted and may crack if you steer extreme left or extreme right too hard", warned the worried engineer.

The Captain brushed aside his warning with a wave of his hand. "Everybody onboard. Everybody onboard!", he announced repeatedly.

Sudhir boarded the boat. He forgot that his personal Mobile had remained with Orly.

The Office Team on That Dark, Stormy Afternoon

Mr. Prasad and the Directors were informed that they would have to put up in the guest house of that island itself until the storm calmed down. Then they heard the plaintive "wooo – wooo" of one of the boats. They were informed that it was the boat that their colleague Sudhir had just left in. It was in trouble. Rescue boats rushed out. And then, soon after, they were informed that it had sunk. The authorities were looking for survivors.

The guests went into a terrified huddle within the secure walls of the guest house. The storm growled and rattled the windows every now and then, as if it wanted to break open the window and drown them all. Orly was now being comforted by the other Directors as she sobbed away in distress, "He warned me about this storm! I should have listened to him. He told me that he has a family. What will become of them now?"

They decided that it would be wise to wait for a while before informing his family. He could just be alive. But silly Orly found Sudhir's family number in his Mobile and rung up his wife's number. As Malini picked up the phone she heard a woman sobbing into the mouthpiece. All she could say was – "Sudhir, sob sob Sudhir…!"

"Hullo, who's this? Hullo? Sudhir? You are not Sudhir. Who are you?", Malini queried.

Orly was sobbing away. All she could manage to blurt out was, "I am sorry. I did not mean any harm, I promise. I am *so* sorry. Please forgive me- *please*. Oh – God! Please forgive me!" Then she started bawling and hung up.

~

After the Storm

Sudhir's Family Immediately After the Storm

Malini and her two children were having dinner with her new husband when the phone rang. Initial jealousy gave way to practical reasoning as the silly Orly sobbed away an apology and begged to be forgiven. Malini was in total control and yet she could sense something terrible had happened to Sudhir. She did not speak a word. She put the Mobile down gently.

Over the past two years, the children visited their grandparents in a chauffeur driven car. Their grandfather would many a time come to pick them up himself. The children answered the calls from the grandparents because Malini refused to take the innumerable calls from Sudhir's parents since the divorce. When the children stayed back with the grandparents then, they were dropped back by their grandfather. He would ring the bell, Malini would open the door and greet him respectfully with folded hands, the children would be handed over and he would leave from the door step itself. For the past two years.

But today, after Orly's telephone call, she dialed the number of her father in law.

The Survivor Who Was Found

The seniors in Sudhir's office had returned to the main island after the storm had died down and were making frantic calls to the authorities for help. It was then that they discovered that the authorities had already been working throughout the night.

Two helicopters had been searching in the choppy waters during the storm but it was dangerous work. The pilots were experts or else the strong winds would have broken apart and blown the helicopters into the dark blue menacing waters below. The copters had been swinging and shaking violently as the pilots maneuvered the craft inspite of the threatening winds even while radioing the result of their search – mile after difficult mile.

They saw floating debris spread over many kilometers. But no signs of life. Nobody.

The search the next morning, after the storm had died down, did not yield anything fruitful. By the evening however, a lot many pieces of debris had floated on to the shore. Luggage, toys, clothes, shoes, wooden pieces of the ill-fated boat. Then they found one who was alive. He was wearing a life belt and clinging onto a wooden plank at the same time. Dehydrated but alive.

And despite his frail condition, he whispered to say, "It was terrible. Nobody – nobody could have survived."

The search was called off after a few days while the various media – News Papers, Radio FM and Television media etc., – continued to investigate the cause, displayed pictures of broken families and urged the reader to do some soul searching. And they got the desired readership attention for maximum financial mileage.

Chapter 4

Sudhir Lands on An Island

Neighbour's Wife Lunges at Sudhir

The birds were chirping all around. It was a usual morning. Sudhir did not want to wake up. The breeze from the open window was so cool. And he felt so tired. He heard shuffling of feet. Malini maybe. But Malini was in the kitchen and would never disturb his sleep after a tiring tour. Kitchen? Malini had divorced him, so why would she be in the kitchen? The neighbor's wife probably, to ask for a cup of milk again. But the shuffling of feet came right upto his bed. Damn the neighbor's wife! She had the audacity to enter his bedroom. He felt so exhausted that opening his eyes was the last thing on his mind. But what is this! She bent over the bed to breathe into his ear and face. She was now kissing him on his cheeks, then his eyes and now his lips. He panicked in his sleep. Her husband would come any moment and break his bones. Today was a Saturday and Malini was home! This could not be, Malini was away with her new husband! He pushed away his neighbor's wife. But the silly woman was now crossing her limits. She was kissing his calf muscle and then his thighs– obviously to excite him! He pushed her away again in his sleep. God! She was dangerously persistent! Didn't she care about social stigma? If only she knew that Malini had left him because of his inabilities. The shameless woman was now tugging at his underwear! But in her excitement, she was neighing & grunting! This must stop, he decided. He had to reprimand her. Having made up his mind he jumped up from his bed, despite his blurred vision, to point a warning finger at her. In his exhausted condition he somehow managed to peep through half-opened, sleepy eyes. The silly woman had grown whiskers and yes – she was grunting in excitement! And she had a tuft of hair on her chin and a face like that of a monkey! He decided that he was hallucinating. She was ugly but not this ugly!

The shock got him back into the real world. It was a monkey! And it was a damn big monkey! A big male monkey that had backed away when he had sat up, but now, with its teeth all bared – it was ready to charge!

Where was he? He looked all around him and he saw miles and miles of sandy beach front with the sea waters behind him that withdrew gurgling & frothing every now and then, to return with a surge to slap his feet with fresh froth & gurgles. And hundreds of tall coconut palm trees ahead. Then followed the jungle of wild growth of mangroves and bushy land in front of him, on his left and on his right. And hundreds of birds chirping, cooing, cawing, screeching away to celebrate the birth of this new day.

And this dangerous male monkey! He looked around for some means of self-defense. He picked up one of the innumerable driftwoods that had floated up to the beach and charged at the monkey. His legs felt wobbly, his body felt heavy and he fell on his knees. The monkey growled with teeth bared in a mock show of strength in front of its gathered brood of female monkeys initially, then it turned around grunting and growling, and fled with its brood in tow.

He looked at his hands and feet. The storm had torn his clothes away barring what was under the life belt. He felt naked but the warm breeze made him feel good, especially now when he was not feeling so strong. In fact, he felt feverish and nauseated.

And he was so exhausted and so very hungry. And thirsty! His parched throat needed immediate attention. His body from head to toe felt like somebody had rubbed him all over with sandpaper.

He staggered up the sandy beach. The sand clung to his feet, thus he almost lost his balance and stumbled. Then he got up once again to stagger ahead but he fell again. Staggering and falling, he braved his way towards the jungle of trees for some sign – any sign of human population. Thick mangroves and innumerable beach front trees – Sand pine tree, Live oak pine, Canary Island date palm, etc., were spread out right in front of him. They all seemed familiar. As the wind would blow, the pine trees would moan and wooo while the coconut palm and canary island palm trees would creak and crock while they swung this way and that way with the wind. He reached the clump of coconut trees and saw no sign of anyone. Sudhir collapsed under the shade of a tree. He tried to shout for help but could manage only to whisper some unfathomable words. He vomited out bile. His mind seemed all muddled up.

He was running a high fever by now and felt very weak. He decided he must find help immediately or else, he would die. So, he had to force himself to walk step by heavy step, many miles, before he came across a deep, dense forest.

With fatigued hands, Sudhir pushed aside creepers, innumerable clusters of low branches and big leaves growing from very old plants. He waded through waste high bushes and puddles of muddy water that were camouflaged by the dry leaves. Falling, clutching onto creepers that hung down from the canopies of the tall tress all around him, he staggered on, his head reeling, pushing forward, then resting his shoulders against a tree, swaying forward inspite of his weakness, then resting again. He did not bother about the screaming monkeys on the tree tops. Nor the many snakes that slithered past as he stepped onto piles of dried leaf that lay on the jungle floor. He had to go on, he decided. He had to try and find somebody – anybody.

Then he heard the sound.

The Wild Animal Attack

The rustling sound of four or more heavy feet pattering on dry leaves – and then – a shrill scream! And then the rapid pattering of feet again – as many feet that would dribble with a football during a football match, followed by a roar and heavy feet and the shrill scream at intervals. This was too much. He was feeling terrible – reeling with high fever, nauseated, exhausted, thirsty, and he so wanted to lie down. But now this danger! He had to have some weapon – any weapon to protect himself. He picked up a thick branch lying down on the forest floor. He tried to hold onto it now – but it felt so heavy, as heavy as would a ton of bricks. Yet, he took a deep breath, spread his legs apart, mustered all his strength and then swung the wooden weapon over his shoulder, ready to bat away the hidden adversary. The sound was fast approaching. It could be upon him any moment. His heart beat rapidly and his eyes gazed with intense concentration towards the direction of the sound.

The pattering sounds, the growls, the grunts, the pattering of feet, kept increasing in volume as it came closer and then closer. He was obviously terrified. It could attack him at any moment now.

And then it did!

It burst out of the jungle with a scream, a grunt and a lunge and he hit it with all his remaining strength.

But what followed the big animal that he hit was even larger — very much larger! As it too lunged forward with a huge roar that reverberated through the jungle till very far in every direction! As it flew towards him in midair, time seemed to slow down, like a slow-motion movie. It had lunged and he was in its path. Then it saw him & the weapon and in a split second, it swerved away from the weapon that had just felled the animal ahead. The second animal jerked in midair, landed to a standstill beside a tree close by and then growled with its teeth laid bare. A black panther! And the animal that he had hit? Sudhir turned his head ever so gently and saw, that the wild boar lay writhing on the jungle floor. A big black wild boar! It was going through the last convulsions of a dying animal. Very cautiously, so as not to threaten the big cat, Sudhir stepped aside from the path of the hunter and the prey. The panther gave him equal respect. It moved aside growling, very cautiously, staring at this strange two-legged man animal. Then the big cat made a gentle detour, keeping a cautious eye on the man. It moved up to the animal that lay on the leafy carpet, picked up the large pig in its mouth, looked at the man, growled, then turning around quickly, lunged back into the deep foliage, and vanished.

And as the foliage parted for the animal, Sudhir thought he saw something familiar below the hill. He could not believe his eyes. He was shivering from fever and his teeth were clattering. Despite this, he threw aside the branch and staggered towards the path of the departing panther. He pushed aside huge money plant leaves, moved aside thick creepers, fell into a puddle, got up and despite the pain, stumbled ahead through a jungle of thick foliage.

Then he saw it again. A huge Golden Palace! It sparkled in the afternoon sun! It looked so familiar. Yes – it was the Golden Palace of his dreams – he had seen it night after night. Repeatedly!

Medicines and Care Offered at the Palace

Huge fishing trawlers anchored far below the hill from which he was looking down, alongside the meandering river that met the sea waters many miles away. He saw some workers weaving ropes out of coconut husk near the river port. He thought he saw many workers – all in uniform, tending to the magnificent garden neatly spread out all around the huge building. Sea birds, so many of them, were calling out to each other as they circled the air and dived down to the ocean to pick on the dead fish that the fishermen were throwing overboard. He stumbled forward.

Sudhir tried to shout for help as he staggered forward, down the hill, but found no voice. He thought he saw people – workers, who were just returning down the hill towards the palace and he called out to them. Some of the workers were pointing up at him from the distance. He could see them getting very excited. He thought he saw people rushing up the hill towards him. Some of them were hailing the workers in the palatial building below. They were all climbing the hill, towards him, in large numbers. Then they reached him. They were dressed in proper uniforms. That meant discipline. Sudhir experienced a surge of relief. He started rambling incomprehensible words. They were making a grab at him as he collapsed in reassured surrender. They were talking in an excited fashion – all at the same time. A cacophony of voices. But he could not make out what they were saying. They were carrying him towards the Palace grounds now. Some people were rushing out from within the palace. They were now staring down at him, trying to talk to him, asking him questions. He tried to answer but could only manage some more unintelligible words. He had no strength left in him to do anything more. His throat was parched and his stomach felt like it had been cut up with so many pieces of glass. His lips were cracked and they hurt. His face was cracked and felt like any Christmas gift wrapping. He whispered the word – "water!"

They rushed away in various directions and rushed back with buckets full of the life saving liquid. He was now being fed with a glass full of water. He vomited the liquid and moaned. They were now feeding him slowly with spoonfuls of the same at measured intervals mixed with sugar and a pinch of salt.

They were now carrying him inside the building on the instructions of an old European looking matriarch.

A tall man attired in pajamas and a night gown, with a pipe in his mouth, seemingly the matriarch's husband, and he gave an approving nod.

They were now carrying him up a flight of stairs with a red carpet. Then they turned right to enter a large bedroom. He was in a half awake, half dream world. He could partially analyse, but it felt like it was all a part of the same dream.

They placed him on a bed next to a window. The same dream obviously. The matriarch pulled the curtains and shut the windows. Some people, possibly the servants – there seemed so many of them, were rushing all around at this very moment and were executing instructions being gently given by her.

An old lady was now helping another wash him and apply some soothing balm all over his face and body. He moaned. His fever was high and so they gave him a head bath. It was as if he was in a coma and yet was waking up with a start every time that they inserted a spoon full of medicine into his mouth. Then he returned to his comatose condition once again. He could sense that they were changing him at intervals, wiping his sweat away with a soothing fresh scented towel, applying the balm at regular intervals, giving him a head bath, inserting spoons full of medicines and then allowing him to rest. A day came when he was being fed a gentle broth though he was in a semi-conscious state. Half of it spilled out from his mouth onto a towel placed below his neck. But he could not muster the energy to wake up to analyze the contents.

Over many days, he realized that his strength was returning. One day he moved his fingers and wriggled his toes and discovered that he had control, that he was indeed alive and was not disabled in any manner.

He called out and realized that his voice had returned. But no one appeared. He called out again and yet nobody appeared. He opened his eyes ever so gently to be met with the glaze of the morning sunlight seeping through a dirty, broken window pane on his left. Broken window pane? A broken window pane in this house of hundred servants? Could not be possible! He turned his head towards the broken window pane again and saw that a lot of cobweb had covered the various corners of the window. And a creeper had grown from outside the window to enter the bedroom through the broken window pane. Some of the leaves within the room were large and the branches were thick and healthy, as if it had been growing within the room for a very long time. For several years!

How was this possible? How could all this obvious neglect not gain the attention of the matriarch? He looked up. The fan that looked so new only yesterday was now rusted and forlorn – hanging in a precarious angle from its hinges. He looked at the walls. The polished, well painted wall paint had peeled away to expose layer over layer of froths of seepage that had dried and caked over one another. He looked at his quilt that had given him warmth and comfort. It was now a torn length of moth-eaten cloth somehow managing to hold on to remnants of what was once a thick, full of silky cotton, velvet quilt. His bed was of solid mahogany but now looked so old and dusty. The paintings on the wall had not been dusted and were hanging at various angles. Some had remnants of faded images. And bats, they were flitting in and out of the room. The stink of decay and neglect!

He pushed himself up on his bed in panic and looked all around him. What is this? Had he become Rip Van Winkle? The man who had woken up to find that the world had changed all around him?

The Shock on Seeing An Empty Palace

Sudhir rushed to look all around the room. He could only but stare. All around him were decaying woodwork, crumbling Victorian furniture, rotting bedsheets, quilts and mattresses. It was obvious. Nobody had been staying in this room for a very long time.

He looked at the large Victorian dressing table. Remnants of the faded mirror showed off a night suit clad, healthy individual, hair neatly combed, neatly shaved with a bedroom slipper to boot! But this was impossible! Who gave him these slippers, who helped him shave and comb his hair, who helped him with medicines and broth and the care that he got? Could all this be a figment of his imagination? Where the hell then did he get these pajamas and night shirt from, he wondered, as he fingered the silky cloth.

He was perplexed. Lost in thought, Sudhir walked up to the cupboard. And tried to open the same. It simply refused to budge. Leaning backwards, he gave it a big tug and it 'whooshed' open. A musty smell of unused material and the layers of dust that had flown into the air, hit his nostrils with a bang. He reeled backwards, repelled by the obnoxious airborne attack. But lo and behold – there they were – hundreds of neatly folded pajamas, night shirts, socks, underwear, shoes, ironed clothes hanging from clothes hangers – all this within the cupboard. But the moment he touched them, the clothes were, he discovered, as brittle as biscuit pieces, because they broke away into tiny pieces of dust in his fingers. These clothes were many years old and unusable.

He remembered the helpers getting luke-warm water from the toilet. He tried opening the toilet door. It creaked open on old hinges to show off a toilet full of cobwebs and dust all around.

The mirror was faded and the toilet cupboards had innumerable dust laden, imported shaving blades, shaving cream, shave lotions and other exclusive toiletries. But the pure brass taps were caked with dust and did not work. The pure brass shower was caked with dust also and obviously did not work. He tried to check on the usability of the shaving blade that was wrapped so neatly in grease paper. Yes, they looked amazingly fresh. And so was the shaving brush made of camel hair, as well as the shaving cream.

This was fantastic. Somebody, or some people were obviously playing a practical joke on him. But it was neither 1st of April, nor was there any reason to joke with him. He decided that he had to find out who or who all were these people who had helped him recover. They must be around but were most certainly hiding somewhere. But why?

He decided to study the building in detail.

Inspection of the Palace Building

The bedroom door creaked opened onto a rectangular shaped, ten feet wide corridor that formed the protective construction around the back portion of the Palace building. And the back portion of the palace building was a very large football stadium sized garden on the ground floor below protected by the corridor at its four corners.

The garden was now inundated with a jungle of shrubs, bushes and innumerable wild trees and creepers. Some of the wild creepers had climbed up the thick pillars that held up the corridor and had carpeted the corridor floor, along with the dried leaves that had blown in from the jungle of trees within the protected garden. Garden Lizards and House Geckos raced around the dried leaves the moment the occasional waft of breeze would blow some leaves around or an adventurous insect would attract their attention. A few tiles from among the tiled canopy that hung away from above the rectangular corridor, held up by solid steel angles, had cracked and broken away at many places thus allowing rain water to trickle in and fall on the corridor floor. Rain water provided sustenance to the new plant life that had taken root on the rotting leaves on the corridor floor.

He treaded carefully over the dry leaves and carpet of creepers lest snakes and dangerous insects were to bite him, while he traversed the total rectangular corridor that surrounded the garden below.

Ten feet high steel framed paintings behind glass fronts, adorned the rectangular corridor walls. Despite the onslaught of various elements over so many years, they still showed off the dignified personalities as if they were there right in front of him. They smiled back at him as if wanting to greet a visitor after so many years.

Each of the rooms on the left-hand side of the corridor were large and banquet room sized, but the rooms were locked.

He peeped through each of the windows one by one. They were decorated with the choicest of linen, expensive furniture, huge beds and tapestry.

One specific room had an enormous study table with a big painting behind the same. It had, like every other room, wall to wall carpeting. He pulled at the lock on the door but it would not budge. So, he went back to the room where he had slept and picked up a hammer that he had found in a handy bag stored in the almirah. He slammed the hammer very hard onto the lock but nothing happened.

He kept repeatedly trying until he got exasperated. He leaned against the pillar, wiped the sweat away from his brows, looked up at one of the smiling personalities in a painting, sighed and jokingly suggested, "Woof! I wish this lock would open". The lock on the door suddenly fell open and dropped on the floor! Sudhir stood gaping at the tough lock that had refused to open or break until now. Then he looked all around the corridor to see if anyone was hiding to control some remote-controlled device. He traversed the total corridor once again. He saw no one. Then he came back and stared at the lady again, on the painting. She seemed familiar! He noticed that it was a painting of the European matriarch who had been issuing instructions when he was being brought in for the first time into this building. The lady on the painting kept smiling. Nothing abnormal. He decided that the lock had opened due to a delayed reaction to his hammering the same. Yet, just to lighten the moment, he decided to humour the painting of the matriarch. He smiled at the matriarch, bowed and said, "Thank you", and then turned to face the door that led to the room.

The Room with the Study Table

The door handle squeaked and squealed as he slid it out of the grooves that had held it in place for so many years. But the door whooshed open to exude the musty smell of a room that had not been opened for several years.

He saw large paintings of foreign, senior, highly decorated British Defense Officers, uniformed dignitaries, and that of Queen Victoria. Strangely, all the windows were shut tight and barricaded with wooden planks, as if someone wanted to shut himself or herself and this mansion away from the outside world.

Sudhir's every step threw up a plume of dust that had settled over so many years on the carpeted floor. He approached the study table. It had a withered British flag along with photograph frames that held faded images of British officers in uniform.

A painting of a battle in progress with British Officers and British sepoys gunning down some "savage" Indian freedom fighters, a painting of British Officers in a successful tiger hunt with a dead tiger at their feet, and that of a young Mohandas Karamchand Gandhi in his prison with some happy British Police Officers posing next to the Prison cell bars.

Some files tied together in an airtight polythene, an old oil lamp, a pen stand, a pen ink container to dip into, a hard leather board (now wrapped in airtight polythene) for the paper to be kept on for quality writing, an imported flask and a glass that was kept upside down.

All around him were mahogany shelves fixed onto the walls that had innumerable books lined up alphabetically on various subjects. All were sealed in airtight polythene. 'Administration of a religiously diverse country, 'The Indian Diaspora', 'Will India remain a British subject', 'Understanding the psychology of an Indian Businessmen', 'Understanding the mind of the Indian terrorist', and so on.

There were two trays with 'In' and 'Out' written on the two of them. The 'In' tray was full of letters that had been undelivered to or not accepted by the addressee and hence returned. All of them were alphabetically numbered. Each Alphabet sometimes had sub – categories. Such as "Son – First Departure". "Son after Selection", "Son after completion of Training", "Son after First Job" and so on and so forth. Each of them was wrapped in airtight polythene.

Curiosity got the better of him and he picked the sealed envelope right at the top wrapped in airtight polythene. He looked all around him, reasoned that nobody could be affected with so many years having gone by, and slit open the first envelope – titled – "Son – First Departure".

Amazingly, it did not crumble in his fingers like the shirt in the almirah did.

"My Dear son Hanuman", it read,
"I am saddened by your sudden departure.

The loss of the boat does not matter to us. The way you risked your life was highly unwarranted. The boat, I was informed after we found it missing, was not sea worthy.

We have come to know after many days of extreme concern for your wellbeing that, you had reached Kochi, had contacted Mr. Peterson for shelter which he gladly provided, especially as he was so very fond of you. This was a matter of relief to all of us over here.

I respect the fact that you want to try to live on your own terms, but I sincerely believe that you would fare better under our parental protection and guidance. Being a Prince, you have been lived a very protected life. Your age, you must understand, does not allow you to realize the problems of sustenance in a cruel world. Every one in this house that you had known as your home, are asking after you, because they all have had a hand in nurturing you. Thus, they love you as much as your parents do. And they are missing you. So are we – your parents.

However, appreciating your desire to be independent, I have sent Karimchand our accountant, along with some monies to your last known address in Kochi. This will help you through until you decide to return.

Yours truly
Your father"

The next envelope was similarly opened and the letter read,
"My Dear son Hanuman,
You must realize that parents yearn to bring forth children in this world for many reasons. Amongst other reasons, one is that they desire to live on through their progeny. Misunderstandings between parent and child are normal. But I would urge you to call a truce and let us be one family again. I wondered how you survived when you refused the financial help via Karimchand. I have got to know through my sources that you were washing dishes in a well-

known restaurant to survive in Kochi. Then you had taken to giving tuitions to certain children.

This is highly embarrassing for a family of our stature. Our Royal family members cannot be seen doing menial labour! We are Royals! We are Maharajas! You are a Prince! Would be Kings have never been seen washing dishes! What would happen of our reputation if people knew? Your Royal cousins are wasting the Royal Purse given to them on luxury cars and a directionless life of luxury. I do not ask you to be like them. I urge you to accept the monies that I send once again through the hands of Karimchand for the minimum comfort that you deserve being from the Royal family. Do also please re-consider the possibility of returning with him.

If you decide not to return, I have asked Mr. Saunders, the Managing Director of Saunders & Company in Kochi to find you suitable employment, obviously to your liking. The company belongs to our royal family. You can, if you so desire grow up the ladder or decide to become the President from the first day. You choose.

We shall be waiting for you my son, the moment that you decide to return, albeit – to visit us for a few days.

Know this my son, that we love you.

Yours truly
Your father"

Sudhir was truly concerned about the poor father of this strange son, Hanuman. The old man was obviously yearning for his son. Why did the son not reply?

He tore open the next undelivered letter. It read,

My Dear son Hanuman,

This may be my last letter to you. I have not been keeping well very recently. This began much before the foreign country officials arrested me for instigating unrest in Nair Dvipa, our own Kingdom.

It has come to our notice that you have renounced the title of Prince of Nair Dvipa and that you have become an Indian Citizen.

I do not wish to disturb your privacy but you have made us all very proud of you my son. We have come to know through sources that you were comfortably employed with the Indian Government and that you cleared the Civil Services Examination of India. I know that you shall get through with flying colors. Academics is in our blood after all.

You are old enough to appreciate that this is the age when I long to be a grandfather. This is the age when I long to hear the pitter – patter of small feet running all around this huge Maharaja's mansion. This is the age when I desire to hear the chirp of little children and the love of their embrace.

I hear that you had got married and that you have a child. Do you suppose you would want to visit us along with your family?

I have been giving a lot of thought to why you would have wanted to leave the comfort of this obvious luxury to strive and survive on your own. And why you would have wanted to resort to risking your life on a rickety boat to get away from what we thought was good for you.

I thought that, maybe it was the discipline that your mother – oh very well – your step mother if you prefer – had brought into the system of this huge establishment. Then I realized that there were many other reasons that collectively drove you out. I recollected the innumerable objections that you had raised about my being pro – British and leasing out our property as an observation base to the Royal Navy. But you must remember that I was a retired Royal Civil Services officer and I guess my loyalties remained. You must know this that I too loved India as much as you and your mother did. I remembered how much you wanted India to be independent from British rule, after all that is what you imbibed from your mother. I remembered your objections about my criticizing the man you admired so much – Mohandas Karamchand Gandhi.

I remembered how much you had loved your first mother. You had willingly allowed her to discipline you. And you were an obedient and faithful child till much after that she suddenly took ill and expired.

You did not mind being disciplined by your second mother either. But you missed your mother by blood so much that you could not accept the disciplined atmosphere without the natural bonding that is present between a natural mother and child. And my work took me away so much that I hardly had the time to give you a warm embrace. And when I did return, instead of my comforting embrace, you were confronted by my reprimanding tone.

I now realize that your rebellion had stemmed from your yearning for that little bit of love that you desired from me but that which was unintentionally denied. We now realize that we were at fault. A lovely child who had lost his mother, should have been handled with increasing moments of love and understanding, rather than the discipline that we thrust upon you. I realize today how much you despised me for having married your second mother.

Why deny this obvious fact that I needed a wife? I feel I have not sinned. At the same time, if I did not commit permanent security to any woman, why then would she want to give her everything to my home front – especially the task of giving you a mother's love?

Trust me my son, circumstances were such that I needed someone to look after my only child – that is you – while re-introducing the discipline that you had accepted so willingly as introduced by your mother, in the home front. I am an administrator after all my son. And I needed to do my job well as a father. I found a woman who was a good administrator too and married her. And I thought she was bloody good at her job, until now! Because I have lost you my son. And I feel I have lost you forever!

Know this my son, if this note were to ever reach you, that, I love you!

God Bless you my son,
Your father".

Tears rolled down Sudhir's eyes. Yet, one letter remained. He could not resist himself.

It read,

"Dearest Hanuman,

It saddens me to convey the news that your father is no more. We have been informed by the Prison Authorities that he died in peace.

We pray for his soul to be content and travel happily to the next life.

You can renounce your Indian citizenship and accept the Crown to become King of Nair Dvipa within thirty-six years of your father's death, as stipulated by our written law. He had tried in vain to have you visit your island kingdom just once especially along with your wife and your child, while he was alive. He so wanted to hold your child in his arms – just once. It was his dying wish that I, his wife and being your mother, should convey the following missive to you.

That he remained loyal to the Queen of England by heart. However, he had asked the British Coastal guard representative to seek an alternative base to continue to ensure British coastal supremacy.

Your father had also framed your newspaper cuttings of Mahatma Gandhi, who you admired so much and has kept them all on his study table, along with the British flag. This, he said, was his sign of showing that he loved you and was willing to compromise with his principles, just so that it can bring you back to this island, some day.

After his death, you had been crowned the Maharaja in absentia. However, we heard that you had renounced the citizenship of Nair Dvipa by becoming a citizen of our fore fathers, which is India. That automatically stops you from becoming our King and automatically makes your son the King in absentia. Yet there is a thirty-six year window within which time, if you return, you can claim the throne and rule this Kingdom. This island, shall remain an independent Kingdom and shall wait for your return. Your father has left all his wealth and estates jointly in your name and mine. Dedicated and loyal Ministers have ensured the appointment of efficient officers to run the country. As I have no other heir but yourself, I have willed that after me, you shall be the rightful owner of all that I own too. If you renounce the throne and your son claims the same, then the wealth, including the Golden Palace becomes his. It does matter to me that you had not accepted me and that you have not learned to love me. Know this that I had always loved you and I shall continue to love you like any natural mother would, till I die and even after. I have instructed the Bank in Zurich to hold my shares and my will, along with yours, in their custody and under their care until you, or your descendants decide to claim your rights. This island and all that you had seen in it my son, yearns for your love and your acceptance.

The King Cherusseri Namboodiri of Nair Dvipa, your father, had been invited by the Queen and had been her guest in London. He had provided temporary access of his island to the British but they had been requested to vacate the land and they have willingly done so. All the countries of the world, India included, have recognized Nair Dvipa, our Kingdom. No country can claim this island barring the King, that maybe you, if you accept the throne. But no Kingdom should remain without a King for very long. There are too many greedy people who would take advantage of the thirty-six year window and claim the throne for themselves. If you decide to abdicate and retire in favor of the next in line for the throne, then all assistance shall be provided to the new Monarch to facilitate such a succession. In any event, if the new Sovereign desires to opt out of his citizenship of the foreign country to which he presently belongs, he must necessarily ensure that this island remains a sovereign independent Kingdom free to align itself with any country as the new Monarch so decides in the interests of the nation.

I shall do my best to trace your whereabouts in order that I may personally deliver this missive into your hands. The Bank Locker and Bank Account Documents, that should ideally have been changed to your name, shall be handed over by myself to you, by hand. The Title Deed to all these lands and the Island itself, with its aborigine inhabitants whose interests you are to safeguard, shall be handed over to you in person too. If I fail then, I guess that I shall be failing in keeping my promise to your father. This would remain my regret. In such an event, this letter shall wait here, till one day that you or your heirs decide to pay this place a visit.

I hope this letter shall find you in the best of health and spirits, my child. Your mother,

Your mother
Queen Gertrude Wallace"

Sudhir sat down on one of the chairs, and wiped the tears away from his eyes. At that very moment a waft of breeze blew the papers away. They flew beyond the desk and settled down on the floor. Sudhir circled the desk and reached down to pick up the precious letters when his eye caught the sight of a letter that lay in the dustbin.

He sat down on the dusty floor to read it too. And the letter read: -
"Attention: His Highness King Cherusseri Namboodiri of Nair Dvipa

Your Highness,
We have as per your instructions done the following,
1) We have followed your son Prince Hanuman from his Hostel till his workplace till today the xxxxx.
2) We have spoken with your employee Mr. Saunders, the Managing Director of Saunders & Company in Kochi and tried to convince Prince Hanuman to go for but one interview, but to no avail.

3) We have successfully convinced the Engineering institute where your son was rejected, to re think. They have, on being suitably remunerated, agreed to admit your son. We have a commitment from their end that they shall maintain utter secrecy regarding this fact

4) We have also visited the offices that were visited by your son for seeking a suitable employment. We have convinced them to suggest to your son to personally visit the names of prospective employers that are considered the top twenty companies in Kochi.

5) We have subsequently primed the Managing Directors of such organizations to appear tough but finally make a suitable job offer to your son. In this manner, he has been made three successful offers. He had, we have learned, accepted and has finally joined the offices of Mc TellyDavid in Kochi.

6) He had been studying for the Indian Civil Services in the meanwhile. We had recruited a man younger than yourself and provided him accommodation near your son's rented apartment. He works as an office boy in a Government establishment but seems to have a pretty good head for the ICS entrance related subjects. This man, on our instructions, had befriended your son and tutored him towards clearing the Civil Services exam. This he did successfully. Your son is now a qualified Government Junior Grade Officer.

7) He later married this man's eldest daughter and they have a son.

8) Your son has taken it upon himself to pay for the education of his sister in laws.

9) We have lost touch with his progress ever since he moved to a new address and have been unable to trace the new address due to the secrecy involved in his new office, till date.

This is always to assure you of our best services.

Our fees for our effort, as agreed is Rupees xxxxxx.

Thanking You,

Your servant forever,

Mathew Johnston McGraw

Private Investigation Professional"

The letter then bore the stamp that read,
"Received total payment of values billed.

Thanking you,
Mathew Johnston McGraw"

Sudhir kept back each letter in their respective envelopes and put them back just as they were in the 'In' Tray. Mathew Jonston Mcgraw's letter also was put in the 'In' tray.

No mention of the name of the son was available anywhere. He found no document or indication anywhere. Sudhir searched for some indication of the family name everywhere. Who were these people? No document was found anywhere! Just this much had become obvious that this old man had paid for his son's career without his son knowing that his life had been protected and literally been financed by his father at the initial stages of his career, until he became untraceable.

His last mother had loved her step son. And that they had expected nothing more than a brief visit from their grandchildren – to touch their progeny, to watch them play and frolic in this huge property. And that the parents had died waiting for this Hanuman and the grandchildren.

He felt only anger for their heartless son Hanuman. Why did the grandchildren not come then? He felt anger for their grandchildren too. What kind of man would refuse to respond to such letters that cried out in pain? What kind of son or grandchild would allow ego to surpass the call of blood?

At the same time, Sudhir felt a pang of respect and admiration for these old people. And he felt sad for them. Albeit the passage of time he felt he wanted to reassure them. To make them feel wanted. They were old enough to be of the age of his mother's or father's parents. But they were not alive any longer for them to hear his soothing words. He decided that he would honor their memory by expressing his love for them by talking to the paintings. That would help drive his loneliness away to some extent. After all, that is all that they had wanted from their son – love. The grand old man's portrait had the portrait of two ladies beside him. One on the left was of the tall European matriarch whose portrait stood next to the entrance to this room. The other portrait on the right of the grand old man's portrait was that of a petite lady clad in a simple sari. Sudhir concluded that these then were the two ladies in the life of the grand old man.

At that moment his stomach churned. He was hungry and thirsty! But no one was around!

He looked all around the big house and found two very old, unused, cob web infested kitchens downstairs. Bats flew in and out of the air vents near the roof. The terrible stink! No fridge, no larder, no storage of tinned food anywhere. Nothing! He was so frustrated and finally, devoid of any solution, he went up again and sat down on the dry leaf covered floor in front of the paintings. They were smiling down at him.

He felt lonely and hungry and he wanted to talk to somebody. At the same time the ludicrousness of the situation made him unwarrantedly witty. He smiled back with tired, frustrated eyes at the painting of the two Matriarchs, and muttered, "Ladies, where do you suppose a visitor may partake of some edibles in the morning, in this mansion?" He laughed at himself for having spoken to the paintings. He got up to turn and walk away. Then good old humour took over. In his loneliness he imagined they were truly there and so he turned back to request, "Ladies, do you suppose I could have some coffee along with my breakfast, please". He turned to walk away again. Then, as if it was an afterthought, he turned back to say, "I just want you to know that your son and your grandchildren may not be here, but you can consider me your grandson until I try and trace your son and his family. That is, if you want me to. And I know your son loved you very much but his pride did not allow him to return and say so". Then he finally turned back to walk towards his bedroom. Saying all this made him feel good. At least he was driving his loneliness away by talking to somebody, albeit a painting.

A sound from within the bedroom along with movement caught his attention. The sound of a door opening! He saw his bedroom door opening suddenly and shutting. Aha – then there was someone and that someone was hiding in his room. He had to catch the person right away. He raced towards his room. Shockingly, as he kept getting closer, the smell of freshly made bacon and eggs hit his nostrils. He pulled open the bedroom door to surprise his benefactor and rushed into his bedroom. And right there on a neatly laid bedside table was freshly prepared breakfast. And the room looked obviously cleaned – probably moments ago. To his amazement, the window had been repaired along with the creepers, the big leaves and the bird poo. The room looked as it had when he was brought in for the first time. Fresh and lived in. He searched everywhere within the room.

But he could not find anybody. He pushed open the toilet door. It was spick and span. And the bathtub had fresh water swishing and swashing even now. Yes – all the taps were functioning!

He rushed to look behind the open toilet door. Nobody!

He looked under the bed and in the freshly cleaned almirah but found nobody hiding anywhere. And the almirah had fresh clothes and undergarments.

This was fantastic! The veranda door had been thrown open to let in fresh air. He rushed to check if anyone was hiding there. Nobody! He looked around the veranda and saw a thick pipe that ran down from the veranda to the garden below. Ah Ha! The person or people who had helped him must have some reason to hide from him. They must have shinnied down this pipe that led down to the garden.

The waft of fresh bacon came to his nostrils once again. His stomach churned. He suddenly realized that he was ravished. He wanted to investigate further but decided to postpone all this for later. He put two fresh apples into his pocket to be consumed later.

He gobbled up everything. Then he burped!

The Area Around the Palace Building

Sudhir rediscovered the stairs that let downstairs and then a path led to the kitchen once again but he found that because all the windows were barricaded and because the house had been thus sealed away, the musty smell had permeated every corner of the huge reception and then the drawing room, and then the dining room and finally the ball room downstairs.

The ball room downstairs along with the toilets too were smelly and dusty, with cobwebs criss – crossing their way all over.

He had just visited the paintings of the old people. Out of normal courtesy and probably to kill his loneliness he greeted the painting of the old man with the pipe as he had the old matriarchs, with a "Very Good Morning to you Sir". "Thank you for the breakfast ladies. Thank you, Sir!". Then he hugged the paintings one by one. He felt good again. He felt he was giving them what their son or their grandchildren should have given them – respect. And lots of love.

At the same time, he felt pampered, especially after the breakfast. He concluded that some loyal servants, who were hiding away from him, were the ones who were serving him. They wanted him to feel that it was all by magic. Ha ha – but he knew better! Old servants who were playing hide and seek were probably listening to him request the painting of the Matriarchs for his meals. Yet that made him feel like – he belonged. That he had a claim to the attention and love that the Matriarchs would have possibly showered on their grandchildren.

He was now standing in the middle of the carpeted steps that led to the drawing room. He looked at the mess around him downstairs. Why did the servants not clean this too? Probably they wanted him to address the Matriarchs before they did so. He looked up at the top of the stairs and shouted, "Ladies. Just suppose that someone would want to clean up this mess and make this place took a bit tidier. Would that not be wonderful? Then let's start with cleaning this huge drawing room. Let me do it with magic! Give me some magical powers – maybe to my fingers?" His stomach was full and he was enjoying talking to his hidden patron. He picked up a stick lying on the staircase, raised it above his head like a sword and declared jokingly, "Ha ha ha! I am Sudhir Bagaria! And I have the power of the Universe!" He kept laughing to himself. He realized the ludicrousness of the situation once again. That he was talking to someone probably hiding in his room while pretending to be talking to the portraits on the floor above. God – this is what loneliness does to you! He was wriggling his fingers pretending to be a magician, while they pointed at the stair steps.

A strange tingling sensation began to build up in his arms right at that very moment. "Ahh!", he exclaimed and began to rub the tinkling spots in his two arms. Then his head began to hum and glow. He began to squirm. His brain was on fire and he held his forehead in his two palms and dropped down on his knees in pain.

"Ahhh!" He grimaced and then winced as his neck with his head bent back due to the searing pain of electrical energy that was surging through his body and his head, and then he grimaced again when it seemed to build up force in his two palms. Some strange power was flowing into him. He felt extremely strong! His palm began to tingle & throb with energy and then his fingers too. Sparks started to burst out of each finger. He was both awed and scared! It seemed he was losing control over his own body and yet it felt so good. Suddenly, his complete body began to glow and hum. It was as if his hands were not his own. His body was not his own.

Magic happened in front of his very eyes just then!

His hands rose all by themselves and swung towards the carpeted floor. A dazzling light buzzed out of his fingers and rushed to strike down on the floor! The dazzling energy seemed to spread within split seconds through the carpeted floor in every direction. The carpet went into waves of convulsions, throwing up the accumulated dust & neglect of so many years. "Wooh!" he exclaimed and fell backwards in shock! Terrified, he climbed a few steps backwards up the stairs from where he had just stood. But what he had started did not stop! The dust from every corner gathered together like a swarm of bees. His arms rose all by themselves again and his fingers crackled with power when they pointed at the curtains. A burst of bright light struck the upholstery, windows and the dust! The old curtains parted, all at the same time. The windows burst open to allow the sunlight to penetrate every nook and corner of the huge ball room sized drawing room. The swarm of dust buzzed out of the window and rushed away towards the far horizon. All this while he kept repeating – "Wow o wooo!", but he could no longer climb backwards as his body flew down to land on his feet in front of the main entrance door. His arms swung towards the mahogany doors at the entrance. And his fingers buzzed out energy – bright waves of energy once again, and it struck the fifteen feet high doors with a – buzz zap!

Maumita De
(MOUMITA DE)

The majestic and huge mahogany main door sprung open suddenly, with a 'swoosh' to allow the river plus ocean fresh cool morning air to blow in, bringing with it the smell of fresh flowers. His body flew up and out of the Palace door to hover over the shrubs below.

His hands went up and his fingers shot out a burst of bright energy –

"ZZZ- ZAPPP!" towards the dry brown wild shrub infested fields all around the palatial building.

Then he saw it. His energy bolt had made the shrubs fold up into itself like a carpet and then vanish into thin air. The wild shrub infested garden became plain light brown mother earth. His fingers hummed out a string of bright sparks and marbled paths began to appear all around the building.

Then a flower garden began to take shape in every direction.

Pots filled with bottle palms began to dot strategic corners of the palatial building. His body flew out of the palace and up into the skies.

The image was exactly as he had seen them when he was brought in. Rows of colorful flowers and well kept, freshly watered gardens. Neatly maintained roads meandered to every possible corner.

His realized that an energy that came from within this building had in part been gifted to him! With profound results – the bursts of energy had brought about a magical change to the garden and the drawing room. But why was tremendous power gifted to him, a marooned outsider?

His body flew back into the drawing room and into an armchair.

Some flower pots with fresh multi-coloured flowers were right at this very moment flying in from the garden, across the room to settle down ever so gently on various window sills in this very huge room

And his fingers were guiding the movement of the pots like a choirmaster would a Philharmonic Orchestra! His fingers buzzed the curtains once again. The curtains and upholstery were climbing down from their perch of so many years and dissolving into dust. Fresh, folded curtains and upholstery were fixing themselves up above each window and door.

The blankets over each chair and table were vanishing. And there in the next room – a fresh table cloth appeared upon the seven seated, 300 dining tables that were spread out in the massive dining room.

And the Ball Room beyond, the dust vanished, old upholstery vanished, dirty walls and chipped away or broken pillars were replaced with fresh paint and repairs – everything became new once again!

Some very powerful forces existed in this house – Ghosts! He decided. This house was haunted! And he scurried to a corner of the immense drawing room and hid behind a huge sofa set. But how could all this happen? He was a firm believer in a scientific base for the existence of everything in this universe. Yet he had just seen the impossible. He was responsible for creating the scientifically impossible! No – he assured himself – you are still out at the sea and you are hallucinating.

Then he slapped himself. Ouch that hurt! Again. Owww – that really hurt! He touched the armchair and sat down once again in the armchair and stayed put to reason with himself.

For obvious reasons he was awed and yet terrified. The supposedly safe boat ride turned out to be a terrible experience. The near drowning experience – how could he forget that! And the endless onslaught of mother nature that had taken him away from his office team – his only family for the past two years – maybe forever. His nearly being mauled by a black leopard. Was his phase of bad luck returning once again to torment him?

Rubbish – he reasoned with himself! Even if science did not work on this island and even if this mansion was full of ghosts – at least they had cared for him while he was recovering. The ghosts protected him till he had regained consciousness.

True – why should he forget the hospitality when he was brought in the first time? Not just the daily nursing. Why forget the sumptuous breakfast? What about their accepting his desire for power to clean the drawing room all by himself? Well – the power to repair the garden and garden path was a bonus!

The doubtful part of him argued – "My cautious nature has kept you alive. What if these powers are not permanent? What guarantee could there be to prove these strange happenings were not intentionally designed to entrap you and subsequently entomb you in this old mansion forever? Caring or no caring ghosts! I am not going to let you take any chances!"

So, he decided to stay put in the sofa for a while. His sofa was resting partly on another sofa. He thought he would push the other chair with a zap of his fingers and he zapped it. But it missed the sofa and hit a sealed bottle fixed at its base to the mantle. He heard a whisper, 'No do not let it open!" He leapt to hold the cap down but it was too late! The bottle began to wizz & fizz immediately, like a bottle of aerated drink and popped open to let out a black robed, slanted eyed man whose, mustache slid down to his lips and below. He began to guffaw – "Hoo hoo hoo hoo! I am free! I am free! Now nobody can stop me!" Sudhir heard a moaning whisper – "Oh Nooo!" Then for a long time nothing happened. Then suddenly, all his "Good Ghosts" explanations went for a spin!

The roof above him collapsed right in front of him. Sudhir jumped back. It fell with a thud where he was a second ago! Then suddenly out of the many spears with shields on the wall, one single spear rose and rushed towards Sudhir! And a deep graveled voice roared – "Aaar dieeee stranger!"

"Oh No!" screamed Sudhir

He told himself – "Fly out of this room! Now!"

Suddenly his body lifted itself and he flew, zipping out of the room and into the drawing room.

"Dieee", the voice chased close behind him into the drawing room and he saw the spear getting closer.

He zipped out of the Mansion, and over the garden. The spear followed him, "Dieee!".

"Fly faster!" Urged the female voice. "Fly away before he kills you! Go now!", urged the female voice.

He saw the deep forests in the near distance from the hills beyond.

He aimed his flight in that direction.

But he fell down to earth and was flat on his back! His powers were gone! He sat up and stared at the approaching spear!

"Oh No!", screamed the female voice.

"Ha ha Stranger! Your powers cannot cross the boundaries of this mansion!"

The spear rushed towards him. A terrible thing happened – Sudhir froze!

But his mind was working at the speed of light. Sudhir remembered his long-distance running days back in school as well as in college. And, the fact that he had won many Gold medals during the hundred-meter sprints. The forests were around six kilometers away. He looked up and saw the spear getting closer every second, which meant certain death if he procrastinated any further! Did he want to die? No! This final decision gave him the impetus he needed today. He turned around, got into a running posture and zipped away at such a pace that even the bad ghost found difficult to keep up.

Chapter 5

Sudhir Meets the Jungle Tribe

Sudhir kept running despite being short of breath. He suddenly realized that he had been running through high bushes and jumping over low-lying branches for quite some time. Soon he was in the periphery of the deep forest. He could hear the crickets and occasional bird song and whooping call of male monkeys high up on the distant canopies. He could hear shrill screeches and chirps of wild animals and birds, a constant sound that were travelling from a far distance to his ears. He looked back and saw the spear far behind him. Very far behind! He slowed down to a walk-through knee-high brush. Step by steady step, he entered the dense forest. The high canopied forest had begun. Thick creepers hung down from the high trees above. He pushed past innumerable creepers. He saw waist high bushes that could easily provide sanctuary to huge snakes or dangerous animals. He waded through them. He saw the huge leaves of the jungle money plants. He brushed past them all. Right at that very moment he felt like he was passing through some waves of endless ocean water. Something was different. Something was changing! The spear blinked a few times behind him and then vanished in the distance! He looked back towards the palace, so far away. He saw it suddenly blink, flash and turn into a ripple of waves a few times before transforming into an old dilapidated building – in front of his very own eyes! He froze. This was all unscientific! Was he scared? He looked at his clothes. No – they had not changed.

It was already late into the evening, and so he climbed up a very high tree, found a resting place protected at the back by a thick branch. No attack could come from behind him. On his left the branch went up and so he was protected from falling off. On his right the branch went up again. And so, he was protected from falling off. He took out the two apples from within his pocket. Leftovers from the morning breakfast, and he munched away at one of them and finished it. Then kept the other back into his pocket for the next day. He kept himself awake for many hours in case wild animals were to attack him, but gradually went off to sleep.

The chirping of the birds early the following morning woke him up. He thought he was waking up in his bed at the mansion and had he not caught hold of nearby branches, he would have fallen thirty feet down from his perch. A cool breeze was blowing, the crickets were busy chirping with the early birds. It was so peaceful. He munched away on the one remaining apple, now his breakfast.

Then he noticed the change. The crickets had stopped chirping. The birds were not calling. There was a pin drop silence. He remained still. A gentle rustle of leaves down below and a "Maaa!" made him look thirty feet down below on his left at a healthy, naked, curly haired, little black boy, no more than five years of age, covering against the fallen branch of a tree. Then there was a rustle and a deep throated "Grrr" around thirty feet below on his right. Sudhir looked down on his right at the source of the new sound below and then froze.

A black panther that now had its eyes on its prey – the little black child with curly hair.

This time, Sudhir decided, he could not let the hunter get this human prey. He scurried down the thick tree making a lot of noise – "Hoi Hoi Hoi! Haiya Haiya Haiya!", he yelled even while climbing down. Then he quickly picked up a big branch from nearby and very cautiously, with his eyes on the panther, moved to stand next to the child. With his eyes on the panther, Sudhir kept massaging the dark boy's curly hair. Despite this, it was obvious that the boy was terrified having seen the panther first and now a total stranger. "I wish to fly!", he told himself, hoping his new powers would not fail him now. But nothing happened – he was not flying. His powers were gone! Sudhir convinced himself that this was a battle that he had to win – powers or no powers! His eyes looked into the panther's blazing eyes. The angry panther bared its teeth and growled to warn Sudhir away from his prey. Sudhir was determined and bared his teeth and growled back. He then spread his legs to brace himself for the panther which was bound to lunge at him. The animal decided to bluff and check Sudhir's reaction. It took two quick menacing steps forward, spat and growled! Sudhir stood his ground and stomped his spread legs like a Sumo wrestler in a crouching position and roared back with the thick branch held high and ready. He had to think quick otherwise the Panther would soon take another two or more steps forward and then surely pounce. Sudhir realized that with his powers gone, he or his stick were no match for this heavy animal. One of its huge paws was enough to finish him off. Yet, he had to save the child.

Sudhir decided to play Rugby in the deep forest! He threw the piece of wood at the panther as one would a spear. In the same stride, he twisted back towards the child, grabbed him, bundled him under one armpit and swerved away from the panther's path to race away over fallen branches, pushing aside huge leaves that rushed towards him to slap him one after the other. He heard the angry growl of a cheated animal and then he could hear the patter patter of four feet, rustle over dry leaves – behind him.

A pea fowl, disturbed by his forward thrust, rushed out of the foliage, and flew up into the skies, into the high forest cover above, with a panicky cackling. "Cuck cuck cuck cuck!"

Pigs, nine or more of them, that were a few moments back snorting into mother earth foraging for tuberous growth, scuttled away in various directions grunting & screaming like little children. Monkeys, hundreds of them, that were a few moments back picking out morsels of insects from each other's bodies, growled imagining an attack, then rushed away from his path to the safety of high branches, whooping and grunting as if to scold Sudhir for the intrusion of their sanctuary.

Sudhir could hear the huffy-growling and steady pattering of four feet following him. He jumped over fallen branches. He had to scare and stall the panther albeit for a moment and so he threw his indigo coloured hanky behind him. The hanky flew at the panther. The animal was frothing from its mouth. It saw the hanky swing its way towards him. Then it swung gently away from the hanky's path and a bit of the froth from his mouth too swung away. The temporary interruption infuriated him further and he roared before he lunged with a "whooaarrre"! Sudhir could hear and sense the lunge.

A few creepers that hung down from the canopies above had dug into mother earth and had become trunks, as thick as a man's arm, some thicker. Some creepers that hung down were thin and young and yet to touch mother earth. Sudhir grabbed one of the thin creepers with his free hand and used his speed to swing away from the animal's path towards a totally different direction. It was then that he saw the stream.

There was a stream that was trickling down the rocks from very high above a nearby hill top that touched the thick clouds and then gurgling happily into the forty feet thick, knee deep water pool below the hill, then pushing itself forward and rushing ahead, cutting its path through the jungle. Lot many creepers hung down from high canopies cradling the banks of this forty feet wide stream.

He had this determined expression despite the sweat streaming away down his face. The moment Sudhir swung away using the hanging creeper, he heard a frustrated "yowl! GGrrrrn!" and some scurrying of four feet trying to balance itself on loose, dry leaf while trying to change direction at high speed. Then another "roar" as the angry animal finally swerved to correct itself and follow the intruder's path.

Sudhir suddenly sensed some fleeting figures through the dense foliage, were running parallel with him, but on the other side of the stream. Ghosts?! He did not have spare moments to analyze anything barring how to get this child out of harm's way.

A huge dead tree trunk had fallen across and become the link from one side of the stream to the other.

Then, for a moment, Sudhir saw them again through the thick foliage. Several naked men with bows and arrows running parallel to him, staring at him, pointing at him, discussing quickly amongst themselves on the other end of the stream. They were around his height, dark complexioned and had curly hair. And they wore a specially designed animal bone protection for their private parts that stuck out like a rhinoceros horn. Animal bone garlands hung from their necks and animal bones pierced their nose. He had to cross over to them but how? It was then that Sudhir noticed the fallen truck and then he saw them pointing at the bridge and asking him to cross over. Sudhir decided that they were the child's family and leapt toward the fallen trunk to cross the stream towards the little wild men. Just then something lunged at him from up above the lower creepers. A very large yellow skinned, polka dotted tree python, as thick as his thighs, maybe more, lunged down at him from a creeper branch that hung right in front of him. Arrows shot out from two of the wild men and pierced the snake's neck from one end to the other and it started writhing on the forest floor behind him. Sudhir did not stop to look back, as he had no spare moments. He rushed ahead on the slippery, moss laden fallen trunk because he could now hear heavy breathing right behind him. Then he was on the other side of the stream and he saw the little men racing alongside. One of them yelled, "Capow Ngigya! Capow Ngigya!" pointing at the child and then making the grabbing sign. Sudhir understood immediately and like in a relay race, he passed on the child to the little man, who grabbed a high creeper and swung away up and high into the foliage above. Sudhir raced ahead with the heavy breathing still behind him. He realized that the little men were running alongside but that one of them had something in their hand, a struggling piglet that even at this moment was squealing away in terror. The panther lunged at Sudhir; the little man threw the piglet in the path of the panther but kept racing ahead. The panther grabbed the screaming piglet in its mouth with a roar and vanished into the deep jungle. Thinking that the danger had passed, Sudhir's pace reduced automatically until he stopped to bend forward, holding his aching stomach with his two hands on his side, and despite heavy breathing, managed to take in precious breaths of air.

Still bent but comparatively comfortable, he looked up and around to realize that he was surrounded by the wild men with menacing expressions, armed with bows and arrows.

With angry faces they were pointing their fingers at him and called him "Agniaw". It meant 'bamboo man' he learnt much later, because he was tall and thin. Then in the direction of the departing panther and they said, "Mrignaw Minsaw Onshoaw". 'Onshoaw' he learnt later, meant 'atheist', or 'non-believer' and 'Mrignaw Minsaw' meant 'live God'.

He understood that the panther was revered by them. Then from threatening words they graduated to threatening gestures with the repeated chanting of "Mrignaw Minsaw Onshoaw". One of them even pointed an arrow at him and muttered, "Agniaw!" and spat on the forest floor. The whole jungle seemed to come alive just then. Little wild men were appearing from everywhere. From out of the bushes, from behind the trees, from out of dug out holes. With spears pointed at him, with every menacing step that they took towards him, they were making cat calls, and jeering at him with that term "Agniaw" being spat out every now and then.

"God!", Sudhir thought turning full circle very cautiously to face his adversaries with his body bent forward, hands spread out and body ready to jump forward, "From the frying pan to the fire! Now I am in real big trouble."

Out of sheer frustration he muttered, "Is there no one who can get me out of this mess?"

Science went for a toss again! He was floating, up, up towards the high canopies.

This was impossible! But it was happening again in-spite of his being far away from the palace! Had his magical powers returned? He floated right up to the branch where the little man and the child now embracing him, were hiding. Sudhir floated down and found his footing on the branch. The little man had an expression of shock and awe on his face and gasped, "Mrignaw Minsaw! Mrignaw Minsaw!" Then, holding on to the child with one hand, he went down on his knees to bow down at Sudhir's feet muttering, "Agniaw Mrignaw Minsaw!

The little men far down below this tree, went down too on their knees and were echoing repeatedly, "Agniaw Mrignaw Minsaw! Agniaw Mrignaw Minsaw! Agniaw Mrignaw Minsaw!"

Just then, the little child lost its balance and fell from the grasp of the wild man on the top branches of the tree towards the forest floor far below and his father screamed in terror. Amazingly, Sudhir found himself flying down towards the falling child in a zip. He analyzed the falling speed and grabbed the child in the safety of his arms. The child was thrilled and screamed happily to the relief of the little men far down below. Sudhir found himself floating down ever so gently and his feet touched the forest floor, equally gently.

Now they were in awe of him. They crawled up to his feet to chant, "Agniaw Mrignaw Minsaw! Agniaw Mrignaw Minsaw! Agniaw Mrignaw Minsaw!"

One of them, an old man with a special headgear, cleared the path for Sudhir with obvious veneration, pointed ahead, up the hill ahead, with his head bowed down. He seemed to be requesting Sudhir to follow him and his people towards a specific direction. "Is he taking me towards security or another bout of trouble?" Sudhir wondered and yet decided to take a chance. Sudhir reasoned that he was now safer than before and decided to walk with them rather than fly. He followed them up a strenuous trial that wound its way up, far above, towards the top of the hill.

It was a long & tough climb which went past many sentry huts. There were sentry huts after every half hour of climbing. Thatched huts on stilts with dried meat hanging from wines strung up between some trees. It was lunch time and he was so very hungry. So, he kept staring at the dried meat at each sentry point.

The old man with the special headgear noticed and signaled at the next sentry point. The sentry had not seen Sudhir's powers and bowed in front of the man with the Head gear but growled with animosity at Sudhir. The man with the head gear barked at him and the sentry rushed forward to cut down one small leg that was hanging amongst many drying pieces and promptly offered the same with fear in his stride as one would approach a stranger. Then on being reprimanded by the man with the head gear, he bowed in front of Sudhir with reluctant reverence and handed over the piece of meat with only two fingers, hands extended from his body as far away from Sudhir and his left leg ready to jump away if the stranger were to bite or attack him. Sudhir stared at the piece. It was obviously uncooked! But he dared not insult the wild curly haired men. His hunger drove him to accept the same and dig his teeth into the tender flesh. Strangely, he relished the dry crust and soft inside of the meat. Instinctively he came out with a," Yyyummmmn!" This expression of approval resulted in a roar of jubilation from the warriors that had followed him from the valley below. They reached their destination finally after a walk of around one hour and forty-five minutes or more. A vast, five times stadium sized plateau on the top of a hill met his eyes.

The top of a hill that had been flattened by the vagaries of nature to become the size of five football fields. On the far-right corner of the plateau was a hillock from which water kept squirting out at regular intervals. There were innumerable thatched huts right at the center of a big man-made clearing on the top of this hill that was pock marked with innumerable trees. In-between these huts, nestled under a huge shady tree was a temple for the Black Panther. Huts continued downhill on all sides of the hill, in small clearings below large leafy trees. The hill climbed down when facing the East, that is right ahead, to a sandy beach far below and then led to a lagoon formed by coral reefs that protected it in all directions from the onslaught of the mighty waves. On the North facing, that is, the left-hand side bottom of the same hill, the river flowed alongside for a very long time and then met the ocean with a roar. The roar could be heard even now along-with the – "twitter twitter" or "cheep chirp" or "kee kee kee" calls of sea birds that flew above them off and on. When one faced the South, that is the right, the undulating green hills swayed their way to a distant horizon to then return and encircle the island from the West, that is behind them. At the center of the island, far into the distant horizon rose the tallest hill, more a mountain, whose peaks got lost amongst the clouds. From this mountain came down the many tributaries and rivers that cut through the hills to finally join the ocean below.

This was one of the villages. The next hill had another village and then the next too! And one large village at the base of the hill after that.

The residents were all very excited and rushing towards them right now. The old man with the special headgear was received with much reverence and made to sit on a huge throne cut into a massive rock now placed inside a thatched hut that was open on all sides. Next to him were four or five other similar thrones cut into rock boulders but much smaller in size. He requested Sudhir to be please seated on his left. He introduced himself as 'Ombasa'. Then, beating his chest he declared himself to be "Powva" and then swept his palm at his village and then the other hill top where Sudhir saw little huts protected under their straw roofs. Sudhir understood that the man with the head gear was the Chief of these two villages. But then Ombasa continued to sweep his palm to the next hill top, then at the little huts down the valley below and then again at himself and then repeated "Powva", beating his chest and nodding his head in the affirmative. Sudhir understood that he meant that he was the Chief of all these villages. Chief Ombasa beckoned at the little man embracing the child and the man rushed forward to fall at his feet. He was introduced as "Nevwat", his mwana (meaning his son). The child followed his father innocently, but walked up to Sudhir, looked up, held his hand and grinned.

The Chief pointed at him and declared, "mjukuu" (meaning the Chief's grandson). Sudhir automatically picked him up in his lap and once again there was a roar of approval with the warriors thumping their spears on the forest floor.

The child's mother came bowing to him. She pointed at the child, introducing him as "Mobi" and herself as "Nankin".

By this time, evening had crept in, and the setting sun painted the horizon into a crimson red canvas. Then, on the signal of the old man, who had introduced himself as the chief, they all went outside the hut to sit down in a circle around a fire lit by the striking of two rocks against each other alongside the pile of dried wood and twigs. And the celebrations began with the beating of big drums that resounded through the deep forests and wild intoxicated dancing by both men and women of the tribe. Sudhir was offered many dried meat pieces, a milky liquid with a pungent smell that soon made his head reel. He saw the dancing figures through hazy eyes. He felt relaxed. When the figures seemed to merge, he refused to accept any further offerings of the heady liquid and watched the drum beats increase in tempo until finally they seemed to be flying like martial art experts of the cinematic kind. It was a beautiful sight. It was a beautiful and relaxed evening after many days of mental turmoil and comparative uncertainty.

Finally, they called it a day and bowed. Sudhir realized that he had to give them a signal and he got up and raised both his hands in the air. This gesture was met with a roar of jubilation once again. However, Sudhir did notice a big group with grim expressions.

The friendly ones led him to a special hut decorated with many garlands made from bones and twigs. He saw that a special bed of straw and bird feather had been prepared for him. Under normal circumstances he would have called 'room service' to change his bed. This time, he crashed and went to sleep.

The Villages of the Tribesmen

Sudhir found that there were four villages of a population of approximately one hundred and fifty village residents each with it's own Chief and village council. They met each other frequently by climbing down their own hill and then climbing up to the next hill top. They all belonged to the same big family of uncles, aunts, grand aunts, grand uncles and married within each other. Each village had its own Chief and village council. The Super Council village named 'Beti Beti', with its own bamboo boundary wall where he stayed belonged to the super council that governed over all the other village Chiefs. The Super Council village named 'Beti Beti' was part of a larger village named 'Zambeke'. But like all the other villages Zambeke village had a Chief below the super council, the Witch Doctor named 'Nksi Nanga' who had the people of all the other villages bowing at his feet. But because Ombasa, the Super Chief of Beti Beti took all the decisions, 'Nksi Nanga' hardly had any power at Zambeke. It became apparent that the super council Chief named Ombasa did not trust Nksi Nanga at all. The next hill top on the South had Omagwena village, and the next hill top after that on the South of Omagwena had the Kavaheke village, and finally the valley settlers were the Kunini Village who thrived in the forests of the valley.

Strange disappearances of Their Tribesmen

Sudhir realized that the tribes' people were normally simple and trusting but had over some years become extremely suspicious of strangers in the forests. The reason became obvious one day when a group of children came back crying, wounded or traumatized after a hunting exercise that they executed to test their ability to hunt like the elders. Girls and women were free to join and they did with their own bows, arrows, spears, knives etc.

They had been attacked by yellow skinned outsiders who wore multi-colour extra skin cover over their bodies and carried boom boom fire sticks. These strangers pointed the sticks at animals high up in the canopies, then boom boom, and the animal would come down hitting one thick branch after another to lie limp and lifeless on the forest floor. Some of their boom boom sticks threw huge cob webs till very far and had been used to capture some village adults and some village children from the hunting party and were taken away forcibly inspite of great resistance from the rest who were beaten up as well as attacked for the purpose of being taken away by force.

The villagers roared on hearing their plaintive cries and rushed out with beating of war drums, bows, arrows, spears etc., but to no avail. The strangers had simply disappeared!

The villages had been losing few people in twos and threes once every year for the past four to five years, not in big numbers but it was enough to mistrust strangers and hence the animosity of the local villagers towards Sudhir.

Nankin and Nevwat Go Permanently Missing

Nankin was Mobi's mother and Nevwat was Mobi's father. Nevwat was the mwana (meaning son) of Ombasa, Chief of the Super council of the Powva tribe.

Hence, he was a very important man.

Hunting was important to feed the family.

Nankin and Nevwat, Mobi's parents, often went out hunting together, hand in hand like two lovers. They were seasoned hunters and were good partners who knew each other's moves. If one shooed the animal to be hunted in one direction then the other waited in the opposite direction for it to be captured.

They would hide in the top foliage of tall trees or bushes that grew everywhere.

One day they crossed the sacred line that protected them from the outside world. They inspected the outside world with caution and then over many months they found their way to the path that led to the sea beaches. They discovered landing tracks that indicated that strangers had landed astride on well chiseled out wooden blocks. Curiosity got the better of them and they followed human tracks to strange wooden huts hidden away by dense foliage. The strangers were obviously in the habit of staying in these wooden huts whenever they landed in these forbidden parts of the forest.

The couple came back and reported these facts to the Chief and were severely reprimanded for having risked their lives to this extant. That evening in front of the villagers of the Powva tribe, the Chief told his people to refrain from venturing beyond the protected zone.

But curiosity got the better of the two lovers cum adventurers and they went off once again but this time to observe the huts from a safe distance, from the top of a hill.

Hidden behind shrubs, from the top of a hill, they looked down the hill at the huts as they heard loud voices and laughter. It was around mid-afternoon. They also heard some animal barking down below! They saw the strangers shedding their multi coloured skin and then putting them on again after a swim in the river that ran along the hut. Some of the animals that looked like a smaller version of a panther kept barking looking up at them up at them. Some of the strangers were looking up at the hill but obviously, could not see them, and asked the animals to stop making that sound.

They kept observing the strange people. A deep growl behind them made them turn their head and they saw one of the four legged animals was snarling at them with teeth bared.

Making a sound would unnecessarily alert the strangers down the hill. They threw a piece of meat at the animal, it sniffed at the dried meat piece but then, looked up at them again, it growled, and then charged at them with an open mouth, fangs bared.

Nankin, Mobi's mother took out her hunting knife and moved aside even in her squatting position, allowing the animal to charge between Nevwat her husband and herself. They pushed their knives into the animal's forelegs and throat but not before it screamed out in pain.

The other four-legged animals down at the bottom of the hill charged up the hill, but this time, followed by their yellow complexioned masters!

Nankin and Nevwat did not wait and rushed out of the protection of the bush to race away towards the protected zone of the big dense forest. But the animals making the barking sound were closing in very fast. And the strangers behind them were following at great speed. Hills had to be climbed down, new hills had to be climbed up, sheer rock surfaces had to be climbed, tall grass shrubs, large leafed money plants, creepers that had climbed high up to the top branches of very tall trees, all and more had to be pushed aside and then travelled. But they did so with ease because they were used to it. But the strangers were making an astounding progress. Then they came to the cliff! On their right, above them was the Kosiya water fall that crashed down from the high hill on their right above and continued with ferocity far below them.

The couple looked back at the yellow skinned strangers, the snarling four legged animals and then they jumped down into the raging river below. When the strangers came up to the cliff, the couple were still falling far below them.

'Nksi Nanga' the Witch Doctor

A dark, six foot two feet tall, mixed breed curly haired man, the deep voiced Witch Doctor was not simply obnoxiously assertive, he was rude, outspoken and disrespectful even with the Supreme Council elders. People respected him because his herbs helped in healing. But they feared him because of his lashing tongue, his aggressive posture if people disagreed, and especially because he claimed to be able to control the bad spirits of this tribe. Though nobody dared accuse him in the open, he was known to be a volatile, physically abusive man who would whip out his poisonous, frog spit laced stone knife, tied to his ankle and his arm, in the dark forest nights, against citizens who dared to question him. The village would find yet another dead villager the next morning with nobody willing to talk. Nobody dared to stand as witness against his atrocities even as he dragged women away into the deep bush against their wishes. The women cried but nobody dared to complain. But he had a huge following of youngsters who were attracted by his audacity and "I care less" swagger. Most of them would copy his mannerisms, especially his sauntering walking style and began to challenge their village elders like their idol.

Private Part Protection

The women wore simple flower garlands and nothing else. Gourds were grown with the sole purpose of being used to create a penis sheath for the men. A gourd is a fruit plant that has a hard shell when dried and was often used as a protection or an ornament or a utensil. Many used it for washing the wooden utensils. Most importantly, it was used as a protection for their private parts. They called it the 'Isembozo' – the Penis Sheath, which began to be used from the moment a little boy became three years of age.

The size served as a functional item initially, rather than a symbol of status. Shape was subject to change. Normally the 'Isembozo' was plain, void of any embellishments, having just a tree bark string to hold it on the body. Shorter Isembozos were more accessible for work especially while running or chasing after a fast prey, while a longer, more decorative one was used for a festival or ceremony.

Scrotum Ball Bags made from dried leather stopped the private part from swinging around wildly especially while chasing a spirited prey in the jungle.

Gradually over the years, when sexual inadequacies were something to be laughed about, and wives were seen to be praying to the lord and the great witch doctor for a solution, even men with inadequacies began to wear long Isembozos to show off huge power. Soon long Isembozos became a sign of virility, a symbol of status and in fact won huge fan following with – "Oohs and aahs" from desperate wives and young girls. The Witch Doctor wore the biggest Isembozo and the largest scrotum bag!

Sudhir refused to wear any under the dried banana leaf. Thus, he had a flat look down there and was rewarded with many sniggers and 'humfs'.

The Village Warriors and Their Ammunition

Though every male and female of these four villages carried arms, were trained in warfare and each contributed his or her bit to the village in some manner or the other, the dedicated soldiers hardly numbered more than forty per village. The grand total of true fighters for all the four villages was hardly one hundred and sixty people at any point of time. And this army believed in loud display rather than brute force at the first stage of battle, shouting and screaming while attacking and scaring one's enemy with scary paint and mask on one's face rather than professional battle techniques. No professional defense or attack techniques were apparent. Lack of education relating to a proper balanced diet, lack of proper hygiene, disease, animals and tsunamis had decimated their numbers to what remained now. Several years back, somebody from outside the village had introduced Herbal medicine to the tribe and though the Witch Doctor reigned supreme in advocating the same, many knew of the right herbs for the right health and vigour related purpose.

The arrow heads and spear heads were from chipped stone, the choppers with sharp edges in front were also of chipped stone. The bow strings were from slices of dried animal skin. Each end of the arrow and the spear had small and large feathers respectively. They used bamboo pipes to shoot out long arrows made from dried river shrub straws. Both arrows as also spear had bird feather at the end to maintain proper flight. Most importantly, they used sling shots where a small rock was placed in a dried animal skin bag and swung several times above one's head before swinging it out to the target at fatal speed.

The jungle people were not fussy about their diet. Survival was priority. Tuna from the ocean waters below, small wild cats, monkeys, squirrels, snakes, wild birds in their variety including pea fowl, bugs within tree trunks, river frogs, river snails, snakes, porcupine – the list was endless. Tiny stone arrow heads dipped in poisonous frog fluid, then shot out from long hollow bamboo poles got best results in targeting animals high up in the leafy canopies above. Then the sling shots with sharpened stones were widely used to target the same target or pigs in a clearing or birds that take sudden flight. Bigger chipped stone spear heads tied with ropes peeled away from trees trunks to snake around long sticks, were used to hunt bigger animals such as wild boar and the huge sized, sharp nailed flightless bird. He discovered later that similar chipped stone ammunition was used to fight inter island tribe warfare several times in their history with tribes of neighbouring islands when the numbers were many times larger than what was there today.

The Village of the 'Powya Tribe'

Powva meant Super Chief and Powva also meant children of God. Each tribal called himself a part of the 'Powya tribe'.

The birds had woken him up. That is what he thought. It was, he discovered when he opened his eyes, the son of Nankin and Nevwat, the little child Mobi, who had crept up to him and had been chattering away despite no response from his end. The child called him "Mahua Mrignaw Minsaw". Sudhir understood very much later that 'Mahua' meant 'good'. And ofcourse the birds were celebrating the dawning of a new day as usual. This tribe resided in the middle of the forest and Sudhir could also hear the call of numerous wild animals.

Mobi had refused to stay with his grandfather because he did not possess the energy to play with him. So, he had moved into Sudhir's hut and Sudhir, knowing that his parents were missing, had adopted him as his own. In fact, everybody began to refer to him as, "the son of the Mahua Mrignaw Minsaw".

It was a beautiful day, with the sun peeping through the strips of cane and bamboo slits, this beautiful child, the sound of wild life and a cool ocean breeze that now blew through the slits.

Sudhir folded his hands behind his head and simply kept listening to the unending chatter of the little child.

As the sun rose further, the tribesmen became busy executing various tasks.

He learned that to ward off mosquitos or pesky flies, it was important to slap one's total body with light brown or reddish river mud. Most villagers were covered in muddy paint for this very reason. It gave everybody a ghoulish appearance but appearances were not as important as survival, immediate relief form pests and immediate comfort.

First Morning Meal in Beti Beti Village

The Super council chief reverently bowed in the morning at his doorstep and looking on his left, beckoned. A woman entered with fresh fruits, a live Tuna (fish) that was still jumping in the basket in which it was being offered to him, and a live wild fowl in a basket prepared with bamboo strips. Obviously, breakfast.

But how could he have the fish or bird raw?! Sudhir gestured that he wanted the fish to be burnt and the fowl to be cooked. The woman fled – giggling.

Sudhir learned later that it was the custom amongst those who were declared to be brave, to eat the tuna and the fowl alive and make a great display of doing so!

The chief came back and with bowed head, listened to and understood what Sudhir was trying to explain. When the chief was explaining what was to be done to a select group of his tribesmen, they tried to cover their laughter but they all finally burst out laughing! They were rolling in mirth on the forest floor holding onto their stomach! The chief stood his ground with a serious look on his face and folded arms. Inspite of their feelings, they set about lighting a fire with two stones being rubbed against each other onto a pile of dry leaves. When the leaves began to smoke, they blew into the pile with a thin bamboo hollow pipe. The first hints of fire appeared. The total lot was immediately transferred to a large mud drum open at the top to place the ceremonial offerings. This mud drum had a hole in its base big enough for three or four adult fists and was now filled with dry twigs and leaves. They then took the fowl away still giggling, killed it, peeled the same, pierced the fowl and the fish with a long stone rod, sharpened like a pencil tip at the front and pushed the stone rod deep into the mud drum. This process drew a lot of attention from the rest of the tribe. And soon others followed suite and laughed at each other's discomfort when they made faces because it tasted bland. Very soon word spread and Sudhir became a laughing stock.

Much later during an evening gathering that day, Sudhir gestured that he had stayed at the Mansion beyond and the whole tribe expressed a strange fear. "Howva!" probably meaning – 'Strange happenings', as understood from their expressions! Sudhir could not agree more.

High Solutions Specialist

Sudhir was practicing his new-found power. He had lost the power to shoot out energy from his fingers. So, he became the 'High solutions' specialist! He would fly out to the highest of branches to pick out the choicest of fruits including coconuts for the tribesmen, aided by Mibo mounted on his back. Mibo and he would pick up birds that had dropped down from their nests high up in the canopies, fly up to the nests and put them back. Mibo and he would race the monkeys to the tree tops. Mibo and he would fly with the sea birds that flew above, within the forested area of course. Having dropped Mibo as an advance party, he would fly with other village children on his back right up to a hill top nearby and sit with them on the peak, staring at and simply admiring the beauty of the ocean beyond. High altitude rides became a popular thrill for the village children. Then the adults too began to generate the courage to fly up into the skies! Nearly everyone in the tribe got the ride, one by one. Sudhir did not mind at all. Mobi and he became a heavy goods transporter and flew back the heavy animals that had been hunted by the tribesmen. Mobi and he loved this new-found power and then Sudhir got a brilliant idea!

He started flying out to the highest branch of the canopies above and would stare out at the far horizon for many hours together, just for any possible sign of an aircraft or any boat. But alas! Then he got another brilliant idea! He waited for a special day when no one was around to watch where he went.

Sudhir came upon such a day suddenly. He decided that if he could fly then he could fly all the way to the next civilized base. So, Mobi mounted his shoulders, Sudhir tried to fly out of the island! He flew high into the air. Wooooooh! The dream of going home was exhilarating. Then he flew hard and fast towards the deep sea. The moment he crossed the sandy beach, he fell like a rock into the sea waters. It was then that he realized that his powers were limited to this island, the palace precincts, this enchanted forest and especially limited to the part where these simple people lived. Was this then his destiny? Mobi and he swam back and walked home to his hut amongst the tribesmen. Mobi had loved the exciting fall from the skies and thinking it was a game, wanted to do it again. But Sudhir was thoroughly disheartened. His head hung low. He realized that he was stuck in this island for a long time to come.

It was on this day that the hunting team returned after a gap of two months. It was announced that Nankin and Nevwat were dead as they had not been found and they had not returned for many days. Hunting parties had gone beyond the protective energy ring but in vain. The Chief of the super council went inside his hut but came back dry eyed. He had to be strong and Ngia Vat his daughter, held him up lest he was to collapse from the feeling of helplessness and inner pain. They could not find Mobi but traced him to the Mohua Minsaw's hut.

That evening the little child named Mobi, the son of Nankin and Nevwat, was declared as the son of the great Mohua Minsaw after Sudhir requested the Chief of the Super Council for this special favour. Mobi was asked who did he choose as his care giver. The little child rushed into Sudhir's warm embrace.

The Chief and the English Language

Ombasa, the Super council chief, was wise and realized the importance of learning the language of a living God. And so, despite the disapproval from the rest of the tribe, Ombasa, his daughter Ngia vat and the Witch Doctor cum village Chief became Sudhir's first pupils. Very soon the Chief and Sudhir could express and understand each other in Pidgin English.

"I Super Council Chief – the Powva. My name Ombasa"

"People outside – my Powva tribe"

"This my daughter Ngia vat".

"This great Witch Doctor Nksi Nanga, and Chief of village Zambeke".

"You are our God. You have returned just as predicted by our elders, to protect us, to take care of us once again. The bigger Gods have sent you to us just as they had once plucked us out from a scary ocean storm and gave us this land many moons ago".

Sudhir did not wish to insult or hurt his belief. He simply nodded.

The Witch Doctor Nksi Nanga expressed his disgust with a "Hrrump!"

Being Accepted By Village Tribals

Mobi, the Chief's grandson had become accepted as Sudhir's son and they spent hours chatting, playing, flying, learning from each other and so much more. But many amongst the tribesmen feared that Sudhir was a dangerous God and they made it obvious that they wished to stay away from him.

Being accepted as God is one thing. Being accepted, liked or loved by the tribesmen was a totally different challenge. The witch doctor realized that this stranger was taking away his importance. So, he began a non-co-operation movement against the one who was God.

Sudhir was and remained an awkward guest, a stranger amongst the tribesmen. He ate differently, spoke a foreign language and hardly mixed with them. Yet their Super council chief got the tribesmen to look after this stranger's every need. Some of them thoroughly disliked this special attention to a stranger, especially the young men. He could very well be one of the kidnappers come to observe who to pick up next! And the ones who had distrusted him from the very beginning added salt to the new feeling of disrespect. The poison of disdain was gradually spreading. The huge witch doctor was a catalyst who willingly continued to stoke the fire.

Sudhir found that they bowed or went down on their knees whenever they saw him and yet the animosity was growing.

He noticed that they would grimace, make faces and smirk behind his back or tried not to smile back when he smiled at them. Many times, when someone bowed and walked past by him, there would be a quick bout of cackling, laughter and sniggering behind Sudhir's back, mainly from by those standing on both sides of the jungle paths.

He knew that he needed temporary security until he found his way back home. Security here translated into meals, a roof above his head and protection from physical harm. He realized that if the majority were to reject him then the chief would be forced to ask him to leave. All he had to do now was to be accepted. He had to do something very fast.

He continued to fly around to help the local tribesmen but many youngsters kept using him. And they continued to snigger behind his back. He thought that if he could discuss with some of them, maybe they could come out with some suggestions on how best to be accepted.

He kept observing them. They were involved in dancing, hunting for sustenance, running through the forests & climbing various hills and then down again for the mere adventure, staying afloat in the beach front sea waters and discussing folklore in the evenings. The women were involved in gathering wild flowers, gathering firewood, mothering little children, creating threads out of crushed tree bark, and then making fine bow strings etc. The moment Sudhir tried to join them, they would either bow and become silent or move away. Barring when the super council chief was around.

One day, Sudhir walked up to a group of young men and women giggling away at one corner of the forest. The moment he walked up, they got up and bowed but started moving away. "Wait!", he pleaded, and they stopped in their tracks. Just then, the huge witch doctor happened to stroll out of nowhere, casually, right up to Sudhir, pointed a finger into Sudhir's face and commented in the local language with a grimace on his face, "Don't you realize you fool that they are all actually afraid of you. They do not like you! They all realize that you are a leech trying to make a fool out of a senile Council Chief. They want you to go back where you came from!" And so saying, he spat on the floor and strode away! With him, the rest of the tribesmen walked away too.

Sudhir stared after them for a very long time. He felt very sad, lonely and very insecure.

He needed a solution to this problem of obvious contempt. He had to become one of them. But how?! How?

He turned around dejected, his head bent down, to walk towards his hut, realizing that once again he was a lonely man trying to win the hearts of strangers in a strange land. He suddenly realized that somebody was blocking his path. He looked up to see 'Ngia vat' meaning 'wild flower', the Super Council Chief's daughter, Mobi's paternal aunt.

She bowed and suggested in all humility, - "The people of this village are all your subjects my lord. But my father's command cannot make them love you!" she bowed again and continued. "You are God and must surely realize that love & respect of your subjects can only be earned through selfless actions and noble deeds. They see you as a stranger. They fear you and have yet to accept you as their own. My father has forced them all to bow in front of you. Thus, they despise you. You are God! But they do not love you. They have no reason to respect you. Give them many reasons to do both, my lord.

Add to our wealth Oh Lord. Make us more successful Oh supreme one. Make us stronger. Make the hearts of those who are afraid of you or those who despise you or are suspicious of you today, so full of happiness that they cannot but talk of anything else but happiness! Then on, you never need to go to them seeking acceptance. From then on you never need to go to them seeking love or respect – oh supreme one. Love & respect of your subjects shall come seeking you!" so saying 'Ngia vat' meaning 'wild flower' smiled, backed away ten paces with her head bowed respectfully, turned and walked gracefully away.

Acceptance Through Games

Much before Sudhir had landed on this huge island, this tribe had graduated over the years to ritual fights or ritual battle between themselves.

Such battles permitted the display of courage, masculinity and the expression of pent up emotion while resulting in relatively few wounds and even fewer deaths. This became a standard form of conflict resolution and a healthy psycho-social exercise.

But the ritualistic exercise was not enough. Nksi Nanga happened to grow up to become who he was. He realized that the young ones had a lot of energy to burn. They needed activity. And they needed lots of excitement to add to their entertainment. What got them all excited was when two tribesmen would argue or fight over the possession of some object, property or person. Then the whole village would get the pleasure of watching men or women wrestling on the forest floor or fighting with stone or wooden weapons, sometimes inflicting grievous wounds. Nksi Nanga instigated the fights to win their following and thus execute his grand plan. He became the face of audacity and macho-ism.

The chief was worried about these outbursts. He was losing control. Unless he found some solution to spend their energies immediately, other than fighting, an all-out war within his tribesmen in the deep forest dwelling tribe was bound to happen.

Sudhir had a suggestion for the chief. He suggested that he be allowed to try and offer various games as a possible avenue for the release of energy. The suggestion was accepted.

Sudhir prepared cricket bats and tried to explain to a few children the rudiments of cricket. However, the children were drawn away by the sniggers & word of mouth propaganda of most youngsters loyal to the witch doctor. The huge witch doctor and his henchmen would always be seen leaning against tree trunks and smirking or sniggering.

Sudhir then tried pole vaulting. He took a long bamboo and vaulted over twenty boys standing in a crowd. Then he vaulted back. Then he somersaulted over many youngsters and then somersaulted back. Soon there were many onlookers as he kept repeating this 'never before' feat. They stared in awe, including the witch doctor and his loyal admirers. Sudhir offered to show some boys how to do the same. Most failed but one managed to race and vault over a small six-foot shrub. Another managed to roll back and roll forward. Instant approval and appreciation for their achievement followed! Then another succeeded and he too won a huge applause. Once again, the third succeeded and everybody was clapping. Very soon innumerable boys were trying out Pole Vaulting, and somersaulting, succeeding and receiving roars of approval and subsequent respect.

Then he created walking stilts out of bamboo poles. He began using stilts to walk around the premises. Onlookers clapped and yippied in appreciation. Now they realized that they can win instant social recognition by succeeding in every game that this God stranger was trying to teach. Very soon many amongst the youngsters were showing off by walking around with stilts, pole vaulting or somersaulting. The witch doctor's groups tried to dissuade them but to no avail, as kids were kids. Then Sudhir declared the great race - a race of stilt walkers, pole vaulters and somersaulters down a village path. Word spread from one village to another and the boys now did not wish to stop practicing for the great event from then on! Pole vaulting, somersaulting, and walking around with stilts became the craze!

When the great day arrived, the venue was a flat ground with specially created hundred meter and two hundred-meter tracks. Huge crowds from all the four villages arrived to participate and view as spectators. Roars of enthused spectators could be heard from very far away into the deep forests beyond. Never had they experienced so much excitement in such harmless games.

Sudhir then started practicing with a ball made from leaves wrapped in wild boar skin leather and stitched together with wild boar skin strings. He started showing off that he could balance the ball on the bat or keep hitting the ball a few feet into the air without letting the ball touch the forest floor. He had a fan following from all the villages now. At first the youngsters sniggered. Some however waited to watch the ball fall. Some sat down when the ball did not touch the forest floor even after fifty odd upward strokes. And when the ball did fall, they let out a unified moan. Sudhir offered the bat to one of the youngsters who tried and failed to keep the ball in the air beyond two such strokes and the other onlookers laughed at his expense. Then one youngster, who belonged to the witch doctor's camp, tried and managed to keep the ball up in the air for ten strokes and that won him a huge lot of applause from the onlookers. Sudhir immediately gave him the stilts to walk on and he succeeded. Everybody clapped and yippied! Especially 'Ngia vat'. She smiled gracefully and clapped her hands in obvious appreciation. Such feminine approval made the young boy try the game again. Others tried too.

The crowd of onlookers swelled. Many more tried and succeeded in increasing their number of successful strokes. And after every successful stroke, they would show off by walking on the stilts, somersaulting or Pole vaulting! It was a permanent revelry time! Very soon most of the youngsters were trying out their hand at these new games. Many of them belonged to the witch doctors' group. It became a new time-consuming attraction – a new fad that earned the winner immediate attention, applause and huge respect.

Everybody clapped and yippied!

Especially 'Ngia vat'. She smiled gracefully and clapped her hands in obvious appreciation.

The witch doctor rushed into the crowd of curious onlookers and growled into the ears of 'Ngia vat', "What are you doing! Encouraging a divide and rule strategy initiated by a total stranger who pretends to be our God?!"

'Ngia vat' did not care to look back. She asked in reply, "A stranger is one who does not recognize the need of the mass. What oh great witch doctor, makes you feel that he is any less a stranger than you are?"

"What do you mean? How dare you compare me, a tribesman of repute, a successful and proven instrument of God's will, to be equal or less than this parasite, this imposter, that has no use to our tribe and feeds on the largesse of your simple father!", growled the huge man.

'Ngia vat' continued speaking with the Witch Doctor standing behind her now, without looking back – "The village rumor speaks of your mother being from a different tribe. If she was given a chance to prove herself then we must all give our God this one chance too Oh Great witch doctor!" Then, she looked back and smiled to ask, "Don't you think so too, oh noble one?"

The reply rubbed salt on an old wound and the witch doctor growled menacingly, "One day I shall breed ten children from that mouth of yours. The first two shall be enough to shut your mouth. The rest would make you learn to respect & fear me and then, I would make you lick my huge boner". And so saying he turned around and stomped away, his head held high. His "twinge" held its head high too!

The witch doctor sent his team and tried his very best to stop these new games repeatedly, but to his dismay, the fire had spread. His grand plan was going haywire ever since this stranger entered his village. He had to kill this stranger if he walked through any lonely stretch of the jungle adjoining the village, ever.

In the meanwhile, after his stint of success, Sudhir did not have much of a problem in moving them towards learning how to play cricket. The participants had to walk on stilts and enter the sports arena. It became an instant hit. Nearly everybody was getting immediate appreciation and applause the moment he would hit a ball for a boundary. Then his team would walk around on stilts or somersault or pole vault to show off a victory! The craze became such that it demanded the chief's personal attention. The chief was forced by common demand to join in as the umpire, as the game took on a serious tone amongst the youngsters. Very soon, the parents could not be kept away from such matches. What followed was an 'all adults team'. This graduated to a mixed team of able youngsters and adults. The best players of a mixed team were then pitted against one another. A huge ground was cleared of all trees and shrubs. Wooden Steps were erected below each of the trees that circled the ground, in order that the tribesmen could view the match perched up on various branches. They could also sit on the steps. Thus, a very large stadium was created.

Many events began to happen within the stadium. And residents of all the villages would gather on preplanned, preannounced days. They would rush in to occupy the best seats.

Sudhir found this the ideal opportunity to teach them to count. The game never started before the crowd roared the numbers from one to one hundred. The huge crowd roared one number to another. One of the cheer leaders was the chief's daughter – 'Ngia vat'. At the count of one hundred, she would stand up to raise her hands.

And then the huge crowd erupted – "Kikat Shuria (Cricket Begin)!"

They soon knew the time and hour of the day. And they remembered, because they practiced and waited for the next game to begin twelve moons away or twelve sunny days away.

Everybody now knew that the father of Pole Vaulting, Somersaulting, Stilt walking, Ball balancing and now 'cricket' – was Sudhir! Acceptance of this great tribe, albeit miniscule acceptance, was achieved.

Since they hardly wore any clothes, Sudhir introduced a uniform that the players meaning the participants, had to wear while participating in the game as a matter of pride and sign of solidarity with any one team. Thus, grass straw tops and long straw underwear for men, grass tops and skirts for women, was introduced initially as a uniform for participants. This soon became a trend as Sudhir requested the painting artists to add colour to the grass skirts from the available red mud of the river banks and the herbs in the forests. The spectators too began to wear the color of their favorite team. The ladies started flaunting skirts along with the little boys and girls who copied their elders. Men wore the skirt more as a sign of solidarity with a team. Now people took sides based on which side hosted their relatives, friends and loved ones. And they ferociously followed the dress code even much after the matches. Soon it became an accepted habit to show off their place in tribal society by wearing a specific colour skirt, top, and straw underwear.

Then one of the villagers who supported Sudhir discovered that mixing specific herbs created a colour blue. He wore a blue skirt and very soon a "Mohua Minshaw" Blue team began to grow fanned by Ngia Vat.

Teaching Them Rugby

Sudhir then moved to teaching them Rugby. Initially the game did not catch on. Sudhir could not understand why. Nksi Nanga the witch doctor felt that this was the best opportunity to ruin Sudhir's reputation. He bowed and with utmost humility sat down with Sudhir to suggest changes. Instead of the Rugby ball, the Witch Doctor suggested that, there should be a live wild boar piglet! Nksi Nanga the Witch Doctor knew that Ngia Vat did not like animals to be unnecessarily hurt. Unless it was needed for food, she would never allow an animal to be used as a tool for a game. This was a good cause because of which Ngia Vat would move away from Sudhir! Many villages would go against such a painful torture of a wild animal. The wild piglet, he slyly suggested, would be released by the umpire into the field and the players at each end had to catch it and touch down on the other side.

And so, it happened just as the Witch Doctor advised. A red rock was handed out as penalty if one were to let the piglet drop from his hands especially if he threw it while trying to pass it on to his team mates. Much to the Witch Doctor's dismay his plan boomeranged! The game became a super-duper success! And all those who believed themselves to be brave and those who did not, fell in love with this war like challenge involved. Shoulders crashed into shoulders with ferocity. And spectators roared when any one player fell subsequent to such an impact. Most importantly, the ferocious players loved the part where they had to chase the wild boar piglet as it squealed and zipped around the field. The excitement of the wild chase was now right here!

Nksi Nanga, the Chief of Zambeke village was coaxed and egged on by his followers into bringing the piglet into the corner of the playground surrounded by a wall of thick bamboo poles that pierced deep into the forest floor, tied together by bamboo strips. The gates would be closed behind him and then the piglet would be released by Nksi Nanga in person.

The wild piglet would squeal and begin running the moment its feet touched the playground. Its survival instinct would make it twist, swerve and turn at amazingly high speed and zip away towards totally different directions, resulting in the chasers losing their balance, stumbling and falling with a thud on the playground. One after the other they fell and yet got up in an instant to get back in the game. The wild people loved the challenge and hence the falls, the roar of the soldiers battling it out on the playground and especially the thrill of a good chase was exhilarating to them. They also loved the pushing and shoving involved while getting hold of the piglet. Shoulders smashing against shoulders to push ahead towards the spirited piglet. Some got bitten, but in-spite of bleeding arms, palms or body parts, they refused to give up. Such was the enthusiasm.

The soldiers of the playground could sense the gaze of the spectators seated behind the high bamboo boundary wall. And they loved the fact that the crowd roared on their every move, especially every touch down!

The players of all the games, whether it be Cricket, Stilt walking, Somersaulting, Pole Vaulting, and Rugby, loved the adulation and the immediate show of support. This support of a roaring crowd pushed their adrenalin to a special high. These games allowed them to show off their technique, stamina and strength – and their style. These games culminated in the show of masculinity! And courage! It created cult figures within a few days! These were wild games! Now obviously these were wildly popular wild games! And the young loafers and vagabonds of yesterday loved it especially because they now had a purpose in tribal society. They had the means to gain the recognition & respect of their fellowmen. Most importantly, their parents were proud of them now.

The Chiefs of three out of the four villages loved it all. This was war! But war without bloodshed! This was fantastic – an answer to their dreams. Nksi Nanga the Chief of this village was seething inside for being such a fool! He had added to the stranger's respect! Nksi Nanga realized that he had dug his own grave for his grand plan!

Obviously "Mahua Mrignaw Minsaw" (good God), that is Sudhir's suggestions were being grudgingly accepted by the youth now. And both the elders as well as the players started bowing in genuine respect. And smiling and waving their hands to get his attention – was but obvious. After all, he had given both the adults as well as given the children, a new life to look forward to in their society. He would not steal their children as would the strangers outside the sacred protected energy circle, the parents decided.

A life of recognition. A life of respect. A life of trust!

Lady luck was by his side once again! Sudhir had proved his worth in tribal society.

A Village Which Was Free to Follow Natural Instincts

Both men and women were good at hunting and coming back with large or small prey. Some failed for many days together, while some excelled every day. Some were good at imitating animal and bird sounds. Some were good at identifying Bee Hives, some at identifying Tree Worms, some at pointing out animal tracks, some knew how to capture snakes. Some artists knew how to paint with earth & leaf colors on the stone walls of the caves, some knew how to dance, some had a lovely voice and could sing, some knew how to make spear tips and arrow tips from granite stones. Some were care givers while some experts at aiding in the birth of a child. Each citizen had a unique talent that was honed over several years.

In the absence of printed notes or coins, each talent allowed barter, wherein the same talent was exchanged for half a pig on one occasion, or a full pea hen on another occasion or a full dead monkey in a special occasion or just a small little tree worm at a bad moment. Such barter was not necessarily fair. If a person, who was highly talented at painting the wall of your hut, was not assertive enough then, he would at best be paid half a pea fowl. Someone who was assertive, would have been paid a full piglet. This little bit of human behavior – assertiveness, and many times aggressiveness, determined success in this wild little world. You got bullied into paying the rightful due or more. In men, a deep voice, tall height, with a fair mix of assertiveness, attracted both success and women. In women, a melodious voice, vibrant and happy nature, a luscious figure and hidden inside that attractive frame -a practical, wise, amiable, easily adjustable nature, made any women the most desired.

But here, each citizen was free to choose his or her mate and life partner. Or change partners at an older age. At such a young age, they seemed to know when their menstrual period would come and when they could 'take the risk'. But for some, during the excitement of an amorous embrace, they happened to cast aside the thought of consequences. Thus, it was but natural to see pregnant young girls going about their daily chores with their family members.

Many failed the test of Khwanga, that is, being able to provide for the family before getting married and in such a case, the new born babies were accepted by the girl's family and brought up as a welcome new member. This supposedly uncultured jungle society did not believe in social stigma.

Some boys succeeded and soon had a hut of their own. He became a Khwanga and only from then onwards they had a say in the tribe's governing body. Many failed to speak up during governing body meetings. Hence those who did, could became natural leaders of the tribe.

Acceptance of the Free Life

All he had wanted was some money to allow him to live a carefree life. He had achieved that albeit late in life, after his divorce. Now all that was gone the moment the boat sank! Why was life being so cruel with him, he wondered. Rare is satisfaction and happiness which were snatched away from his hands and he was thrust by fate into this village!

And now he had to face the free life of these naked people. Initially, Sudhir was shocked out of his wits. If it had been the city, he would simply have walked away from these people. The free life style of this jungle society had shocked him initially.

But men and women were free to mix with one another. No elder forced a couple to remain with one another here. Ability to copulate to satisfy each other's desire was tested. Whether they could adjust and live with the nuances of each other's behavior pattern, was tested. Ability to be assertive and feed the family using one's talent was tested. Each analyzed the worth of the other in their individual life. If living together did not work out then, each was young enough and free to try living with another and then, yet another. The elders did not interfere as happiness and fulfillment was important in this short life of the tribesmen. As is human, many youngsters had high expectations and never found their perfect partner. But they had no regrets about not having tried at all. They tried and then failed. They learned to accept their own faults, thus becoming more responsible citizens, as they understood the failures of those who were like them. Some remained loyal to their old flames, now wives of other men simply because of the fond memories of their past liaison. Peace and adjustability were important to some and hence they accepted women with children from another partner who had moved away, just because the woman brought about a calm and organized atmosphere. It was for them to live together and decide amongst themselves. Many a time if a Khwanga (living together permanently) partner did not return from a hunt or a war with the far away tribes, then, the girl was once again free to choose a temporary or a new Khwanga partner. So it was, with the men. But many a time, they remained single because, nobody could match the memories of the partner who never came back.

Khwanga did not happen overnight. It happened in stages. Stage one was living together. If living together worked out over a self-determined period then they progressed to stage two, that is – Mahua Bkya meaning the boy proves himself to be a trustworthy provider. Finally, they progress to stage three, that is Khwanga, meaning living together permanently. And here, after being permitted by the elders of the tribe, both the girl and the boy chop up bamboo poles, dig holes, pierce the bamboo deep into the holes, collect strong long wooden or bamboo branches for the frame of the circular sliding roof on the top of the hut. And finally, long grass tied down with bamboo strips to the frame, over which three such layers were tied down one after the other thereby ensuring insulation from the vagaries of nature. But if a challenger opposed their Khwanga relationship, he had the option to place his objections in front of his elders. If they failed to provide justice, then the judgment of the super council prevailed.

Because he was stuck here, in his psyche, his subconscious, such free behavior gradually became a part of an accepted norm. He learned to accept such happenings as the behavior of a much-matured society, where today was more important than the next life.

He obviously did not participate, but he had stopped grimacing on seeing it happen literally every day.

Without realizing, his mind delved deep into the repercussions of such a free social fabric, and then, over many days the beauty of this freedom dawned on him.

Chapter 6

The Panther Cub

How Mobi Found the Panther Cub

In the dense jungle of Nair Dvipa, beyond the area of the 'protective energy field' that protected these villages from intruders, there were many ancient Hindu temples that were now inundated with creepers and leafy growth. This meant that these areas were once populated by civilized beings capable of such creative pursuits. As the Black Panther cubs followed their mother, they tried to chase the butterflies and little birds that got flushed out from within the bushes and shrubs.

It was not permitted for both adults as well as children to cross this protective energy field. But several daring villagers, including Mobi's parents ventured beyond the protective energy field, near the temples and vanished for ever. Mobi, the Village Super Council Chief's grandson, now Sudhir's adopted son, loved playing along with his tribesmen and their children near these temples. One day having arrived before they did, he tried climbing the forbidden tall trees. He kept climbing to dizzying heights and the foliage ninety degrees below covered him from being seen by people below. Then, he did not have the courage to climb any further. His village friends sixty degrees below, looked like small ants. Then he saw them. He saw some strange yellow complexioned humans wearing multi coloured body covering and their feet were covered with strange covering too. The Mohua Minshaw had warned him about yellow skinned strangers who had taken his parents away from him. There they were right below in the clearing seventy degrees below. They carried fire sticks that they pointed at the monkeys high up in the trees, then there was a terrible "boom" sound, following which the monkeys screamed and fall from the canopies on which they were perched. These strangers were walking in a single file, chopping away with machetes at the big leaf money plants and creepers and then they arrived at a clearing below his tree, hammered some wooden sticks deep into the earth. They tied strings onto wooden sticks, made a frame for a hut, covered it with a white coloured covering that became many huts into which they vanished. They got some dry wood and set fire to them in the open ground in front of their white huts with a magic instrument. Then they got together some strange containers that made a clanging sound, added water, put the meat hunted a while back into the same and finally added some vegetables. Strangely, they ate the hash with relish! Mobi saw his village tribe members were hidden behind deep bushes and were observing the strangers from not far away.

One of the strangers casually walked into one of the dilapidated temples, there was a "Grrowwl!" and a "Roarr" and the man rushed out screaming with his hands flailing in the air. It was a lactating female Black Panther that raced after him snarling and growling in anger. The stranger's companions picked up their own fire sticks, pointed it at the panther and "boom, boom, boom" the mother Panther lay dead at their feet. They were congratulating themselves, patting each other's shoulders as if they had done a great deed shooting down a lactating mother. Then three of them took their fire sticks and began to search through the temple. Very soon they came out with one panther cub that they held by the nape of its neck even while it kept snarling, "whoaaar" ing and flailing its paws with sharp nails drawn.

They had a good laugh seeing its plight, then they packed up after many hours and went back the way they had come from, carrying the dead black panther plus the little cub. They carried the dead panther exactly as his village folk did with their hunts. They had tied the dead animal's legs to a long pole held up by two people.

The Mohua Minshaw had repeatedly warned him, not to climb down from a tree if he happened to see the yellow skinned strangers and never to make any sound. But, when he saw that their convoy had travelled very far away, Mobi climbed down to investigate their camping site. They had left behind one of their strange utensils in the ashes of the fire. He picked it out and cleaned it with some of the leaf strewn all around. That was when his tribe members rushed in and began to look at the container and touch it with curiosity. It was strong, very strong and did not break inspite of having fallen from the hands of those who were intent on inspecting the same.

That was when he heard the "Meow-Whoar! Meow-Whoar!" followed by silence. His tribe members immediately climbed the nearest tree for safety, because they knew that it was the sound of a panther cub hence the mother, they assumed, would most certainly be nearby. But Mobi had seen the yellow complexioned strangers use their boom boom sticks to kill the poor mother and take one cub away hence, this sound must be, he assumed, from that of another cub and it was obviously scared and hungry.

Mobi entered the temple and saw a portion of the intricately carved rock roof that had collapsed down into what must have been a central prayer hall. Dry tree leaves were strewn all over the floor. He saw a little puffy head peep out from behind a Shiva idol and then vanish behind the same. He approached very cautiously, the damaged roof that had fallen on the floor, with a piece of monkey meat that the visitors had thrown near the fire. He threw it gently near the cub's temporary hideout and saw it come out of a small nook, sniff, pick up the meat piece, chew on it and vanish with it into the same nook where he was earlier. Mobi knew it would not survive without its mother. He grabbed it by the scruff of the neck and brought it out of the temple. His fellow village youngsters panicked and screamed about the mother being nearby. But Mobi was in no mood to listen.

He proceeded with his new friend towards his village. The youngsters followed him to stand outside his home. They wanted to witness a butt whacking! They were certain that the Mohua Minshaw would refuse to accommodate a wild animal, especially a leopard, it being a revered animal, and then he would whack Mobi on his butts. Mobi strode inside and raised his podgy arms towards his father Sudhir. Sudhir sighed in content, picked him and his panther cub up in his strong arms and put them to bed. To Sudhir, this was all he had, his purpose that give him a reason to go on. The kids walked back with dejected faces.

That night the panther cub kept meowing in fear and insecurity and kept Sudhir awake. But Sudhir wanted Mobi to learn to take on the responsibility for a decision that he had made. It happened exactly as planned. Groggy eyed Mobi woke up every now and then to massage the cub back to sleep, every few hours. But every time, Mobi would purr and crawl back into Sudhir's arms, thus waking his father up.

Over the days, 'Mahili', the panther cub learned to trust Mobi and accepted offering of both milk as well as meat pieces every day.

One late evening, when the crickets were chirping away after a heavy rainfall, the moon and the stars shown bright in the skies, 'Mahili' heard a sound, it saw a wild peahen in the jungle. She chewed into the wild pig leather rope tied around her neck and went out by itself to try and catch it. Mobi woke up in the morning to search for the missing cub and followed the paw prints to find that it ended below a very tall tree very far from his village. Mobi looked up and there high up in the tall canopies was the black she-cub, "waaa", "waaa" ing away in terror.

Early in the morning, when Sudhir could not find Mobi, his uncles and aunts rushed out in search of Mobi. Nksi Nanga – the Witch Doctor claimed that he had seen Mobi go with his bow and arrow towards the sea waters. Sudhir flew out to the sea waters. Frantically searching, he made the same mistake in his hurry. He overflew the magic zone from when he had lost his powers every time. He fell into the sea waters, as gleefully witnessed by Nksi Nanga and his eight soldiers hiding in the bushes near the beach.

Mobi in the meanwhile had climbed up the tree and sat on the topmost branch to gently massage the cubs back. "Everything would be okay", he assured the cub and the little darling began to purr in his arms. The strong winds began to blow just then and shook the top of the trees. It was only then that Mobi realized that he had reached the very top of the canopies. As the winds played with his hair, he saw a wonderful scene that he had never seen before. The green jungle of innumerable undulating hills curving away into the distance in every direction. Vast jungles of tree tops till the next hill and then the next, in whichever way he turned his head. Just then from a distant tree top, a big eagle that would normally attack and feed on wild mountain deer and monkeys, had sighted little Mobi. It cocked it's head on the left then right and then focused on Mobi's little head. Then he launched himself into the air.

The sudden howl of innumerable monkeys that were all looking up towards the sky made Mobi look up too, and then he ducked, just in time. The eagle flew by overhead at high speed, it's powerful talons missing him by a whisker but it's talons nicked his little scalp. Mobi lost his balance and fell with the cub in his hand.

Sudhir had lost his flying powers because he had crossed the magic zone where his powers vanish every time. But his mental powers were still intact. He could sense Mobi was in trouble. Mobi was on the verge of falling. So, his mind raced over the jungle to trace the scream of monkeys then, to isolate Mobi's scream. At the spur of the moment his mind reached out and he made two branches reach out, absorb Mobi's fall and cradle the child within their leafy cushion. But his mental strength was waning. He could not hold the two branches together for very long from such a far distance.

Mobi was on the verge of falling from his cushion and he was hanging onto the branches that cradled him and his little cub right now. And those branches were slowly breaking due to his weight. Mobi screamed in terror! His maternal uncle and aunt and many of his village folk had reached the bottom of the tree and were screaming in panic, racing this way and that way, wondering what was to be done. One silly tribesman got ready to shoot a poison dart up into the canopies as was his habit during any hunting spree. "Stupid!", an elder slapped his blow dart down and admonished him. "Aim at the eagle, not at our child!"

The panther cub was terribly scared, hence naturally restless. It was upside down in Mobi's firm arms, "Woaorrr! Woarrr" ing away flailing her four legs in a desperate attempt to free herself and find a firm footing. It began to squirm desperately just as the eagle, high up in the sky, made a U-turn with the intention of targeting his prey again.

"Climb up!" an elder screamed, "Climb up somebody and save the boy!" Mobi's maternal uncle had already begun the strenuous climb towards the high canopies with a wicker basket on his back. But the rest of the village folk became silent spectators fearful of the canopies that reached up into the skies and the delicate, brittle branches at every point till the top that promised certain death especially for a heavy individual.

Sudhir was telepathically communicating with Mobi in the meanwhile.

"I am going to fall and go to the stars where grandmother has gone!" said Mobi with fear in his voice.

"No, you are not!" assured Sudhir. "You wish to do summersaults, go stilt walking and play pig rugby like the elders very soon, do you not!?"

Mobi nodded in the affirmative.

"Then you got to belong to a team Mobi! Which team?"

"The blue team! Your team!" Mobi screamed in terror just as the branch cracked at the joint and bent down a bit more. The terrified crowd below screamed out of concern again.

"Then you got to think very fast like the blue team Mobi! You got to be brave like the blue team Mobi" urged Sudhir even while his mind scoured and identified a branch below, on Mobi's right and he promptly but calmly said, "Look down below on your right Mobi. Do you see a strong branch which will hold your weight?

Mobi very carefully turned his head to the right to look down even while 'Mahili', the panther cub squirmed on seeing the eagle taking a dive in their direction from high up in the skies.

"Now Mobi, hold on to the branch on which you rest now and try to find your footing on that lower branch. It will hold your weight", Sudhir guided gently. Even while he guided Mobi, Sudhir was racing back towards the shore where he was certain he would regain his power to quickly fly to rescue Mobi.

Just then eight of the Witch Doctor's men raced out from behind bushes that bordered the beach front to block his path at that very point from where he would regain his special powers. They were all armed and they roared in unison with painted faces and stomped their feet inside the sea waters! But there were no witnesses to this obvious attempt to block him, barring Nksi Nanga – the Witch Doctor who stood near the trees with a stoic expression.

Sudhir's mind saw the eagle moving fast towards Mobi. "Now Mobi! Grab the branch on which you rest and find your footing below! Now! Do it Now!"

Mobi grabbed the branch with his free hand and found his footing ever so gently, the leaves now above Mobi were blocking the path of the eagle's dive.

The eagle promptly stopped it's charge and landed on a higher branch some distance away but kept cocking his head this way and that way to gauge the next possible strategy to grab Mobi or maybe Mahili, the panther cub.

Sudhir found his path blocked by the Witch Doctor's tribal warriors but he had to regain his power by crossing the magic line, and that meant touching the dry sands of the beach.

He had to think fast as he had to save Mobi! Then he got a bright spark. He used his mind power to send telepathic messages to each warrior as if from each warrior's mother or wife and as if they were calling that warrior home right away due to an emergency. An irritatingly repetitive message that made each warrior shake their heads violently in disbelief initially and, in panic subsequently. Then two of them broke rank and raced away towards the beach to try and rush back to their huts. The enraged Witch Doctor threw two spears at each of them and they collapsed in severe pain.

But that diverted the attention of the others. Confusion about the predicament of their families was obvious on their faces when they received the messages in their mind. But they feared the wrath of the Witch Doctor over these past so many years. While they were staring at their fellow soldiers racing away, they had kept a wary eye on Sudhir. However, the screams of pain of their companions was the diversion that made them look away towards their companions. Sudhir took this opportunity to race past them, he touched the sandy beach, a huge surge of energy rushed through his body and – Vroom! He was flying high up into the skies even as the Witch Doctor looked at his receding figure with disdain!

Just at that very moment, the eagle took off into the air once again having analyzed the position of his prey, it had seen the foliage that protected the prey(s), analyzed the subsequent flapping of wings that would allow a quick exit out of the foliage and finally the power required for full flight over the canopies.

Then he began the nose dive into the fiolage even while Sudhir was zipping above the skies towards where Mobi was.

"Mobi jump!" Sudhir barked. But Mobi was a child and a jump from this height would mean certain death. He would crash through innumerable thick branches and maybe hit his head on his way down. Mobi stalled for a moment and the eagle flew down even closer. The eagle knew that this time his prey(s) could not escape. Mobi's eyes dilated in panic and at that very moment the cub managed to wriggle out of Mobi's grasp, tried to run on the leafy branch. Lost its footing and fell from that great height!

"Nooooo!" screamed Mobi in pain and panic.

"Blue team member Mobi! Jump now!" barked Sudhir once again and Mobi turned away from the eagle and jumped.

The eagle was not going to let go of two of his prey at the same time. It swerved left, swung it's wings back to its tail and zipped down towards Mahili the panther cub. But Mobi's maternal uncle who had nearly reached the top, stretched out the wicker basket, absorbed the cub's fall and having caught the cub in the wicker basket, he brought the basket back behind his shoulders. But just then he saw his nephew zip down in a free fall past him, followed by the determined eagle and Mobi's uncle screamed. So did the crowd, that had swelled to big numbers far below.

The eagle got it talons into position and pushed it forward towards Mobi's soft shoulder tissues. But a high wind whipped up just then and somebody zipped past below the eagle from the left to the right, scooping Mobi into his arms, an inch away from the sharp talons of the huge eagle, and flew up and away towards the skies above. The eagle flew backwards in shock and then began to flap its massive wings "swappap, swappap swappap" to try and comprehend what had just really happened.

Sudhir continued to fly up and high into the sky towards the clouds above the island, with the crowd far below cheering away.

Sudhir flew into the clouds and Mobi looked down at four small villages at one corner and the clouds seemed to play hide and seek with what seemed like big cities of Nair Dvipa on the other corner with many High-rise buildings reaching up towards the skies.

It was then that Sudhir discovered the existence of a civilized society beyond the protected forested lands.

That evening while the villages celebrated Mobi's safe return, Nksi Nanga – the Witch Doctor was absent.

Mahili began to grow fast and very strong. Soon she began to return with small hunts.

Mahili Grows in the Wild

The witch doctor wanted to hurt Sudhir. The only way he could do so was to hurt his adopted son Mobi. And the only way that Mobi could be hurt was to kidnap and sell the Panther cub. Unknown to many, he had begun a contact with the yellow strangers. He got the half-grown panther cub kidnapped and got it sold to a Circus company in Diànlì ji'è de.

A ship full of caged animals, manned by citizens of Diànlì ji'è de, is proceeding at a fast pace away from an island from where some of them were captured. Other animals had been captured from many jungles of other countries. The inmates of this ship were descendants of pirates and were educated but using their education in conducting this illegal trade of selling banned animals and birds. It helped them earn millions.

Amongst the many cages were two Black Panthers, both of whom grew up amongst human beings. One was Mahili, she grew up being pampered with the love and care of Mibo and his fellow villagers. The other was Fùchóu who grew up amongst citizens of Diànlì ji'è de, and remembered being tortured at intervals, struck with hot rods for being a rebel and finally was now being sold off because he refused to be tamed. Neither of the cubs knew about the other being on the Pirate ship that was taking all the animals on board to be sold off to a big circus company by citizens of Diànlì ji'è de.

One of the pirates had a pet monkey that used to once tease Mahili when she was much smaller, while she followed Mibo in his wanderings in the jungle, jumping at butterflies and flushing out fowls from within bushes. The monkey would jump down from the trees to pull the Mahili's tail and leap back to the high branches of trees. Try as she would, Mahili could never get at the monkey.

The monkey remembered the little cub wandering in the jungle just last year. She decided to tease both Mahili and Fuchou at the same time. Mahili was enjoying the teasing but Fuchou was getting terribly irritated.

The monkey pulled back the latch that held the iron door to the cage in which Mahili was held captive. Mahili nudged the door and it swung open. The moment Mahili sauntered out of the cage, the monkey leapt down from the table, pulled the cubs tail very hard and promptly jumped up to the chandelier. Then the monkey leapt down, pulled open the latch to Fochou's door, and leapt back up to the chandelier. But Fochou was extra cautious and he did not react. The monkey had seen his master feeding the cubs with dried meat. She picked up small pieces, and threw them at both Mahili and Fochou. Mahili snapped it up but Fochou was being careful. He knew that the monkey was up to something.

Before the monkey could react, Fochou leapt on the steel gate and it swung open. He then lunged at the main door and was outside within seconds. Mahili followed because the adventure excited her. The monkey followed too, after opening the iron grill gate of every other cage. Parakeets, Peacocks, Hyenas, Geese, Monkeys, rushed out through the open door right up to the deck where sailors were busy at their tasks.

But the panthers found the captain's cabin door ajar. Mahili ambled in on smelling the freshly prepared bacon and eggs!

Hell broke loose on the ship as the Captain standing behind the steering wheel stared as Fochou the wild half-grown panther entered through the entrance to the captain's cabin. He tried to back off but Mobi, used to human beings feeding him by hand, advanced towards him expecting titbits, licking her lips in anticipation. That did it for the captain as his eyes dilated in panic, his voice choked, and he backed off towards the exit door. Just then Fochou the wild panther cub in the company of the Diànlì ji'è de, enters from the door behind the captain and grunts. The captain looks back in panic and jumps and hangs onto the top of the curtain. He looks down to find the first panther cub looking up at him. Mahili the first panther, brushes against the steering wheel and it turns right. Then she brushes again and it continues to turn full circle.

An engine order telegraph or E.O.T., is a communications device used on a ship for the pilot on the bridge to order engineers in the engine room to power the vessel at a certain desired speed. Prior to this system many ships used pull rope bells. Sometimes some ships use both the old pull rope bell system as well as the new EOT system. For urgent orders requiring rapid acceleration, if the EOT fails, then the engine room bell is rung three times.

The man in the engine room nearly got thrown out of his seat by the sharp turn to the right. "Captain you sure you want to return back to shore?" the speaker spoke up.

The captain heard the engine room man and tried to ask him to inform the crew, so that they could save him. But all he could manage was, "Pssst."

"I beg your pardon captain! Did you say something?"

"Psst!" And just then Mahili the cub looked into the captain's eyes and yawned, "Yawrrr!"

The engine room man thought he just heard the captain growl on the microphone. He spoke into his microphone to ask, "You said something captain?"

And just then the cub yawned, "Yawrrr!" and pawed at the pull bell rope, thrice!

"Yeah sure captain! Ha ha ha – Yawrr!" laughed the engine room man and pushed the speed to Flank Speed (full speed).

The thrust threw the captain down on the floor and the freshly cooked bacon and egg salami fell on his face. The egg yolk burst and spread on his face. He froze as Mahili the panther cub sprang up on him and began to lick the egg yolk away from his face.

Fochou in the meanwhile had left the captain's cabin and entered the clothes washing room in search of food. Ten numbers of wicker baskets full of dirty clothes was lined up in one corner. One empty basket was near the washing room floor, far away from the rest. The washing master had been nearly eaten by wild animals in a recent campsite near a jungle. The memory was very fresh. Just then the pup jumped onto the wicker baskets and yawned "Yawwrrr!" The washing master looked at the wild animal seated on the baskets, promptly jumped into the empty basket and pulled the lid above him.

The cook was trying to cut a piece of chicken leg away from the rest of the dressed chicken for the afternoon meal. Having chopped it, he hung his left hand down in which he held the bigger piece. Suddenly, he heard a chomp and felt a tug. He looked down and froze with fear written all over his big eyes. There was Fochou, a big black panther cub looking at him with black eyes with a chicken chunk in his mouth. And it was grinning! He looked right and saw the live chicken room. He lunged towards the door, swung the door handle down to open it, rushed inside, then shut the door behind him, and looked up to find himself staring straight at Mahili, the other cub. She had entered the coop through the door behind, from the laundry room. She had filled her stomach with five chicken and the rest were scurrying all around the coop. She stared at the cook, licked her lips and burped! The cook froze, and could do nothing but stare at her out of fear.

"Do we reduce speed captain?" the engine room man asked. Since he got no reply, the ship flew over the waters at an astounding speed until it hit the sand banks. It lunged forward at great speed over the dry sand, uprooted some coconut trees, and then stopped. Wooden planks piled up on the deck flew over each other and tumbled to finally rest alongside the ship, forming a ramp.

The ship full of animals, now without a captain to steer the same, walked down the ramp and then raced towards the shore. The birds flew screeching into the jungle. The pigs screamed as they rushed into the shrubs. The chicken "cuck cuck cuck" ed in panic, flew into the wild growth and the tree tops and finally rested, secure on various tree tops. The panther cubs sauntered into the wild growth. The cockatoo looked at the captain and said, "You better pull up your socks buddy!" and then flew up into the skies towards the tall trees.

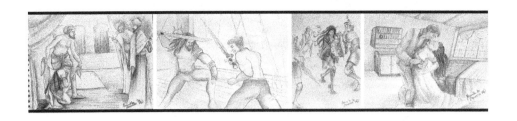

Chapter 7

Sudhir & Ngia Vat Fall in Love

The Accidental Music Instrument

Mobi followed Sudhir everyday to the village school premises, meaning two thatched huts surrounded by wooden planks dug deep into the forest floor. Though Mobi was not yet six years of age, he loved his lessons. Amazingly, he was picking up English Alphabets and numbers much faster than the other kids. Being children, most of the children refused to concentrate. So then, Sudhir made them sing out the alphabets. It worked. He had always carried a bow and few arrows to protect him-self from wild animals. It was by accident that he pulled one string during an English alphabet teaching session.

"Twangggggg!" it went much to his embarrassment. But he noticed that the children seemed to be more attentive.

Then in another class, he subconsciously began to pluck the string as the children sang and he woke up suddenly to the fact that he had a musical instrument. Sudhir discovered that the 'twang' sound had added spice to the excitement of the moment. The little students were thrilled! They were dancing and jumping around while reciting the alphabets!

He experimented further by fixing many strings and fingered them. He found music! Then he experimented with bamboo shoots and made flutes.

The wild man's guitar and flute made a huge splash! The teenaged youngsters absorbed both into their lifestyle as it soon became part of their daily lives, evening dances and special events. Now drums accompanied the new musical addition to their wild lives. And yes – now they had music and dance before and after the games.

The special evening dances became super exciting! The village waited for these special evenings when the musical instruments would arrive. Now boys and girls were practicing with musical instruments at home. And how to woo each other with music. And dancing became even more interesting.

Both young girls or boys as well as the older ladies and older men would bow in front of various girls or boys or women or men to request them to dance.

The women and men would form separate chains facing one another and dance in rhythm. The women would tease with their bottoms swinging left and right with their hands and fingers hiding their behinds while executing rhythmic play of their fingers. The men would swing both their thighs and hips forward and then back, sometimes jumping up with the rhythm. Their strong thigh muscles would gyrate as they stomped the jungle floor and they roared in ecstasy, as if they wanted to eat their partners right then and there. The atmosphere would become hot and mesmerizing.

That Foggy Evening

'Ngia vat' had been coaxing Sudhir to participate for a very long time. But Sudhir kept telling himself that he had failed in marriage and failed as a father. Further he was suffering from a medical problem because of which he could not satisfy his wife. Even if he could, he must not stoop as low as many people in the city would. Civilized society would have asked him to abstain from evil. A part of him continued to feel revulsion towards those in the city who refused to tether their human urges with ancestral social norms and thus proving themselves to be socially irresponsible. He shall not attempt at having another relationship, simply because it would most certainly ruin the life of his new partner, he assured himself.

This evening, he continued to refuse, not just once but several times.

Until the drinks happened. He was tired and they offered him the usual heady drink. He made the mistake of taking one too many. His logical thought process went into a muddle. The young men, the Super Council Chief, his son, the children, were all dancing.

As the evening music and the atmosphere set the evening on fire, he found himself drifting away towards a totally different world. He could see his body down there, one amongst the hundreds of wild people that sat around the fire in the center. He realized that many had accepted him and that fact made him feel good. He had never felt so much at home as today, amongst so many strangers. In the past, those in the city whom he thought he had known the most, had proved to be total strangers, frustrated, sweet talkers masking their pain, with bags full of selfish mystery, and unfulfilled desires. Now looking at these untamed children of God he realized that they were easier to understand and to predict. The city life was just a big stage with city people living double lives. In the city, so many clung onto society monitored monogamy, even while raping so many others with their eyes and mind. All acting out a futile game of togetherness in a rule bound, sacrificial society. He seemed to suddenly understand the beauty of the norms of these hundreds of bodies swaying away with no worries in the world. Their simplicity was genuine. Their smiles were genuine. Their happiness was genuine. Their satisfaction was genuine.

As was usual, the young girls giggled and ran away into the forest and the young men followed suit. Sudhir was pulled away from the dancing crowd into the jungles by somebody. It was Ngia. Her well-formed breasts wobbled up and down behind the top as she danced with the music as if teasing him with her gyrations. Sudhir suddenly saw Malini there right in front of him. So she had decided to come back inspite of his many failings! Ngia saw Sudhir's expression change to that of a man who desired love. He reached out but she stepped back and kept gyrating with the music that now came from beyond the bushes that hid them from the tribesmen. He reached out again and she kept dancing and stepping back again every time.

Very soon the drums accompanied by the music drifted up to the beach and found Sudhir and Ngia dancing face to face, but alone. Ngia held Sudhir by his hand and they danced. Sudhir held her hand and wobbled here and there in drunken ecstasy, wondering how and when Malini came back into his life again. Then his feet got stuck in the wet sand. He was about to fall and that was when Ngia rushed forward to give him support and he fell into her arms. He was sobbing while she comforted him, his head resting on her bosom.

And they kept dancing, he sobbing while being comforted, with their bodies entwined, while the moon gradually played hide and seek behind slight cloud covers and the breeze whispered the happy tidings to the leaves that giggled and fluttered in delight.

Chapter 8

Animosity Between Sudhir and the Witch Doctor

The Witch Doctor Meets the Chief

Much before Sudhir had landed on this island, the witch doctor had barged into the chief's royal hut.

"Who am I?" the witch doctor asked the chief.

"What do you mean?" gently asked a perplexed super council chief in polite reply.

"My mother told me that you knew ", growled the witch doctor.

"Oh!", the chief shrugged his shoulders. "Our tribesmen have always been short in stature. So, it was shocking to see your mother float onto our beach one fine morning. She was nearly dead from drowning. My aunt revived her over many days. Then she saved me while I was hunting in the jungles. I was not super council chief then. I was a youngster somewhere around your age or older. I was not a Chief of one village, like you are today. While I was recouping, I introduced her to the rest of the tribeswomen and our tribal language alongwith its customs. She looked different from our woman. She did not have curly hair like all of us. Her complexion was yellowish whereas we were dark brown or ebony. What was so strange was that she was so much taller than all of us. Nearly two times taller and more. Her shoulders were so much broader. And she was so much stronger. She was obviously from a different tribe. A far away tribe. The senior witch doctor decided that she was a bad omen. They decided that she must die. A few of us lead by my mother and supported by the Super Council Chief, then, pleaded with the senior tribesmen that just because she looked different does not mean that we should kill her. And so, a compromise was reached. It was decided that she be allowed to live but she should never be allowed to live amongst us. She was driven away from our village into the deep forests. Our tribesmen were warned that any further interaction with her would be at the cost of being barred from this tribe forever. No one had the courage to interact with her from then onwards. She built her own hut somewhere in the deep woods and she fended for herself.

Interestingly she hunted so well that she brought many of her hunts as gifts for our tribe's Super chief Baguba, and for our tribesmen as well. She used to leave the kill at our entrance gate and walk away. As she was not allowed inside beyond the boycott line that had been drawn for her, she never dared venture beyond the limit and left her hunt below a tree. The tribesmen grew fond of her over many moons and yet our elders never allowed her into our tribe. We continued to shun her. Then one fine day, she came to the tree and left you behind, with us. You were five years only then. You had curly hair like all of us. Your complexion was brown. Our elders fell in love with you. The elders withdrew the ban on your mother from entering our village and helped her build a hut amongst our own. Your mother and you became part of our tribe from then onwards. And the rest is history. You have been part of our tribe since then".

Both the Chief as well as the witch doctor were silent for a very long time. They were looking at each other.

The Super council chief now asked, "Anything else you want to know?"

"I have curly hair. So, who is my father?" asked the witch doctor

"How should I know? That is for your mother to tell you. Why don't you do back and ask her?" replied the chief.

"Hmmm", growled the huge witch doctor. The Witch Doctor's mother had expired many moons ago.

"Anything else?", queried the chief.

"Can I have your daughter's hand in marriage?"

"Once again, the reply is – No. You may not!"

"Why not!", growled the huge witch doctor, "I can give her a life full of honor and respect. She would be the wife of the witch doctor! Why do you keep refusing me every time I ask for her hand? Why?!"

Ombasa's eyebrows twitched and he had this grim expression on his face, "I have decided and that is final", replied the super council chief.

The angry witch doctor, growled and moved menacingly towards Ombasa with a poisonous stone knife that appeared suddenly in his hand. As if out of nowhere, three armed men appeared from hidden corners of the room and stood with large spears in front of the chief, ready to strike if necessary.

The witch doctor, growled in frustration, stomped his feet hard on the floor and stormed out of the chief's royal hut.

The Faceoff Between the Witch Doctor and the 'Mahua Minshaw'

It was bound to happen. Nksi Nanga the witch doctor felt that if his mother was driven out because she was a stranger then why not this 'Non-Believer of the Black Leopard God'.

He had dared to allow his son Mobi to keep a Leopard cub as a pet! He broke all norms and did everything that the villagers did not! Why could he not live away from this forest and prove his worth at hunting. The fact that Sudhir had already proved his worth in many other ways did not dawn upon the witch doctor's clouded mind.

One day when the person he referred to as 'imposter' was climbing the hill to reach Zambeke village through the dark, late evening jungles, Sudhir heard a rustle of leaves and then dry leaves on the forest floor began to explode and warriors jumped out of the holes! Leaf caps that were flat on the floor a moment ago blew up into the skies to expose many warriors rushing up, who were hidden in the pits below each such leaf cap.

The huge Witch Doctor stood in the path of the 'Mohua Minshaw' with several his followers.

"Ah Witch doctor. What a pleasant surprise! I do hope that you all enjoyed the game", Sudhir asked as if everything was normal.

"I think you are a fraud, an imposter!" growled the big man. "You pretend to be God and yet you live amongst us like a parasite and feed on our charity. What do you say to this accusation?"

Sudhir was smiling when he replied, "You are correct oh great witch doctor. I am not God. I am like any one of you. But while I am here, I will do my best to contribute my bit and prove that I am not as useless as you imagine I am".

"Then why do you not accept that I am God's instrument in this tribe? Why do you not lick my feet and bow like the rest of them do? Why do I not see the obvious veneration on your face that I see in the eyes of the rest", asked a grimacing witch doctor.

A female voice from the jungles spoke up just then, "Because he feels that actions speak louder than simple words or threatening postures that instill fear in the hearts of your tribesmen oh great witch doctor", said 'Ngia Vat' as she emerged from the foliage and brushed off the dust from her body. Alongwith her emerged many of her father's body guards.

The witch doctor did not turn his face. "I see you need female protection to save yourself from the wrath of our tribesmen oh great imposter", growled the huge man.

"Speak for yourself oh great witch doctor", butted in the chief as he too emerged along with many of his warriors and tribesmen from amongst the foliage. "I do strongly believe that the great 'Mahua Minshaw' has earned the respect and love of all our tribesmen. I would advise you to desist from pretending that you represent the minds of all the villagers. You do not! The whole village knows now that you have killed two tribesmen who were instructed by you to stop the Mahua Minshaw from touching the shore and regain his powers. I would advise you to desist from crossing his path again oh great one. Otherwise I would have to take any action deemed necessary in the interests of most of our tribesmen.

So saying, he bowed in front of Sudhir, showed him the path leading up to Zambeke village and followed him along with his soldiers right up to the stairs that led to his hut above, held up by the solid wooden stilts.

A grimacing witch doctor with his armed followers stared after them as they walked away. "You are a coward you imposter! One day you shall have to fight me and then you shall have no option but to die!" he screamed at the departing figure of Sudhir and the people protecting him.

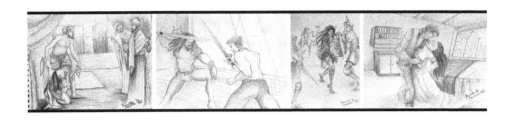

Chapter 9

Ngia Vat and Sudhir Bring Changes to the Village

Herbal Medicines and His Health

The Chief's daughter 'Ngia vat' had moved in with him and began to care for both Mobi, who was her brother's son as well as Sudhir. They were living together under one hut. And both Sudhir as well as Mobi accepted this arrangement because in this strange world, all felt comfortable in each other's company. So Sudhir divulged his private family problems to her. And Mobi told her about his Black Panther cub vanishing into the deep forests, never to return. Both got a warm hug and reassurance. Sudhir narrated the reasons why his wife had moved away from him and the fact that luck had never favored him barring very recently when he had lost everything that he had cared for.

Mobi would insist on sleeping between the two of them and Sudhir would embrace his chubby little friend like one would his own son.

Sudhir was under the supervision of 'Ngia vat' while he consumed the herbs prescribed by her. Ngia vat taught him to identify the herbs and then pluck them gently so as not to damage the leaves. She taught him to identify the herbs that helped him melt body fat inside his arteries. She taught him to identify medicines that boosted his testosterone. As also the medicine to keep his Uric Acid levels at a normal level. How to reduce bone inflammation and hence cure oneself from bone pressing down on nerve junctions. She taught him about herbs that helped in the recovery of damaged nerves, especially those nerves which lead to his private parts. Then she taught him the gentle exercises. She taught him how to twist his body to the extreme right and the left while standing, while bending forward and while touching his toes. She taught him to breathe deep and exhale first with one nasal exit and then another. This was amazing, this was obviously Yoga! How did she, a tribal know this form of exercise?

"A great spirit came to us after the great Tsunami and taught us how to adjust with our pain. To regrow ourselves from within", she replied gently with a warm smile.

He seemed to have recovered his physical abilities over many months and she seemed not just satisfied, she seemed very happy with him. His stamina seemed to shock him now! In the past he never ever lasted beyond five minutes. Now he was at it till much after two hours of rigorous amorous exercise.

Most importantly, he was no longer troubled, nor felt guilty about himself and his past. And yes – his memory had amazingly improved beyond belief.

He wanted to ask her again, "how?". He looked at her soothing expression and he seemed to sense the reply – "The good great spirit…"

Teaching Them Hygiene

Ngia Vat helped him teach hygiene to her people. He designed and supervised the execution of both individual as well as social toilets. He dug up, with the temporary support and help from the sportsmen and a special team of loyal tribesmen, a channel that diverted water from the natural fountain nearby and made it flow all the way to this village. The first to test use this toilet was little Mobi! This canal thus solved the problem of water needed for the toilet, farming of medicinal herbs, as well the needs of the community kitchen that he introduced. In the earlier days, women and children were being dragged away by wild animals and Nksi Nanga's men whenever the ladies went to relieve themselves in the deep forests. Now they lived without fear as, each hut had its own toilet being cleaned every second by the waters in the canal that was made to flow below their bamboo stilt huts. Both security as well as hygiene needs were looked after. This earned Sudhir a huge amount of respect.

But Nksi Nanga the huge witch doctor refused to accept this system of hygiene claiming that the Gods including himself, wanted the tribesmen to visit the forests for their morning chores, alone. Because that is the way it had been since ages. No one, however, listened to him.

The fuming witch doctor planned his next move.

Farming and Permanent Stocks of Food

These people were hunters cum gatherers. There were days when any one family or more would go without any food. Many a time, the man of the family simply failed to come back with a good hunt.

These challenges gave him the chance to introduce a permanent source of food. Sudhir proceeded to teach them farming. And very soon, the crops namely rice and a locally found variety of the potato, were ripe for cutting or extraction.

Poultry

Sudhir had the village people capture pea fowl chicks by the dozen and nurtured them in large wooden slit boxes. They grew up to give both eggs and meat to the village.

How They Learned Latest Fishing Techniques

One group of the tribe has diversified into fishing. Many a time, attempts at fishing yielded no results.

He discovered that they stood in deep waters for long hours just to wait for a big fish to appear within striking distance. Then they would thrust the spear or shoot out an arrow from their bow within split seconds into the big fish and thus capture it for consumption.

It was back breaking work. He taught them to wind the husk of coconuts and long forest root ropes to make strong wicker baskets and forest root ropes to make box traps.

Ponds for Storage of Live Fish

He taught them to burn mud and create mud bricks.

He dug canals for sea water to flow in to a large pond held together with burnt bricks, where the fish would swim into and stay alive. Then he taught them to make nets.

Fishing Nets

The coconut husk was strengthened to make tough ropes and then linked together with strips of bamboo. From these ropes he made fishing nets and the tribesmen learned how to fish in proximity. The yield of fish thus increased.

Rafts & Boats for Sea Fishing

So then, Sudhir helped them design a raft by tying wood pieces together and then taught them how to construct a float.

They were taught how to use the float in the sea, initially in proximity. None of these floats were worthy of long duration sea journeys and yet, provided it was repaired daily then, they were enough for a 'close to land proximity' daily stint of 6 months of fishing. Soon they were enjoying huge yields of tuna.

The tribesmen were jubilant. Now, most of the tribesmen started accepting him as their own. Especially after he suggested that he was as human as all of them. They took this to be his humility.

Sudhir taught them how to preserve this high yield of fish for long periods of time. He taught them how to cut up the fish into manageable pieces and then salting the fish. However, teaching them how to make rafts and such salted fish became the cause of problems in the months to follow. The sad affects shall be detailed in the below detailed narration.

Chapter 10

Personal Challenges

Haircuts and Blades

Gradually but happily, Sudhir started accepting his stay on this island as being permanent.

With no hair cut or shaving possible, Sudhir's beard had grown to unmanageable limits. The hair on his head had grown down to levels which would have put any woman to shame and probably make any man in the city whistle in admiration. With no clothes available, he had taken to wearing the protection for his private parts that the rest of the men in this tribe wore, the 'Isembozo' – the Penis Sheath. Along with that he wore straw shorts and straw tops ofcourse. He looked like a hermit with a rhinoceros horn below to boot! It was when he was contemplating how to solve this problem of unkempt hair that he realized that some of the tribesmen did not seem to be suffering from his problems at all. They had clean shaven cheeks & chins. Strange, that he had not noticed this until now. He decided to investigate. He saw them grinding stones for their weapons. They put a bowl made from baked clay on their head, upside down, while another tribesman would apply a paste extracted from the barks of the Unbuke tree. This paste would create a soapy mixture that softened the skin. Then the blade made from stone was used to shave away unwanted hair. Brilliant! Yet he wanted to keep some of the beard. It made him look different but he did not mind and neither did the tribesmen. He prepared a shaving blade for himself that was sharp enough to cut his beard and the hair on his head to manageable limits off and on. And who would he call to cut them to size? His barber was Ngia Vat, his new room cum soul mate! That is, for some brief period, because very soon, little Mobi insisted that he had first right over Sudhir, and naturally she had to give up her coveted position of chief hair cutter to the little boss!

After every successful hair cut both Sudhir as well as Ngia Vat would blow into Mobi's belly button and he would squirm in uncontrolled laughter!

The Howva Minsaw

The villagers were now putting their children to sleep with the stories of "Yellow skinned strangers would come to take those children away that are awake after pointing at them with boom boom sticks!" The children would promptly shut their eyes and lie still. Then one day a man came running back from his hunt. He was huffing away due to the high-speed marathon. He was very excited and kept pointing at the forest behind him. He had faced or seen some bad Minsaw! The chief was now discussing a possible solution with his tribesmen. Sudhir understood that he was, for some important reason, discussing the tribes 'Mrignaw Minsaw' – 'the live God' – meaning him. Mobi's uncle said something to the child and the little one held Sudhir's hand and led him into the forest with many armed tribesmen, especially the man who had come running back.

They stopped in front of a large cave and the man pointed at the cave and declared, "Howva Minsaw", probably meaning 'God causing strange happenings' or "Bad God". Sudhir understood that whatever strange power was inside was causing awe and fear in the minds of these simple people. He was scared at the Mansion because he had believed that everything had a scientific explanation. After what had happened so far, especially his strange powers, he was a changed man willing to accept that the supernatural was possible. Translated – he was willing to risk entering the cave to investigate the cause of the awe & fear of the little wild men.

He stepped forward but just then, the chief bowed and stopped him in his path. The Chief gestured at one of the armed 'tree climbing' tribesmen, the group that battles from tree tops. The tribesman bowed down in front of the chief and then charged up the hill. He leapt over large rocks, to land with a thump on an uneven rocky path that climbed up the hill, and kept running at great pace to then leap from one rock then over another rock, to proceed towards the cave entrance. Sudhir heard a mechanical roar begin the moment the little man charged and crossed a few rocks up the rocky hilltop cave at the peak. The little tribesmen let out a gasp in unison when the man collided with an invisible barrier forty to fifty feet away from the cave entrance and bounced back flying up into the air, then tumbling down the hill from one rock to another till the base of the hill where the other tribesmen stood. It happened so fast that Sudhir did not have the time to react. The man finally fell with a thud, rolled for a while and remained still, then moaned in pain. He had scars all over his body, the mark of burnt skin at some spots and considering his moans on being touched, innumerable broken bones. The jubilant crowd roared in appreciation of his bravery and the chief nodded in approval. But the man was in no condition to stand or move around for another six months or maybe more. Sudhir's determination wavered.

The chief then stepped aside from Sudhir's path and reverently challenged him to do better than his tribesmen! Nksi Nanga the Witch Doctor and his select few fellow villagers stood clapping and smirking with glee. This was the moment that the Witch doctor was waiting for. Thus, Sudhir realized, this was the moment to prove that he had the desire to protect these simple village folks. He knew, having seen the power of the supernatural forces over these past few months, that whatever or whoever was in the cave, most certainly possessed supernatural powers. He had to prove to these simple people that in-spite of being as normal as any of them, he would die if necessary while trying to protect their interests.

"Hmmm", wondered Sudhir. "An invisible force, acting as a barrier. It meant that the contents within the cave were being protected!" This fact made Sudhir very curious. "What was it within the cave that was being protected? What was it that was so valuable?"

He stepped forward to fly cum jump up the hill with fresh determination.

A mechanical roar begun the moment he crossed a few boulders and the men behind him at the base of the hill, gasped in unison. Sudhir stopped and the roar reduced to a 'wirrrrrr'. Sudhir took another step forward and the 'wirr' came alive again to become a ferociously deep roar. As if warning him away! He stopped. The roar became a 'wirr' again. Sudhir decided to charge come what may, and he leapt up the boulders and flew towards the cave entrance. He could hear the 'wirr' increase in intensity to a roar. His every determined flight movement took him closer to the entrance. The roar by then had increased to a huge, much stronger, last warning roar. He was a few feet from the entrance. He would crash into the magic energy barrier any moment. Then he saw the floating shadow within the cave. The shadow raised its hands and pointed them at him. It obviously had powers to blast him with some strange force. Maybe the blast could kill him. "You!", gasped Sudhir and he braked to a shocked standstill. The shadow stopped to stare at him for some time, smiled at him, gradually brought its hands down, and then it vanished! The roar slowed down to a 'wirrr' then it died down totally and then silence ensued. Strangely, the birds and animals seemed to have fallen silent too! Sudhir flew to the entrance and his feet touched the ground outside the cave. Then he walked in with bated breath, step by cautious step, towards where the shadow was a moment ago. He stopped, peeping left and then right. Then he took his first step into the cave, looked left and then right again and then above. Nothing happened! Having waited for something to happen where he may need to defend himself, he took another step forward and then, he was inside the cave. The tribesmen were holding their breath all this while. Then when he managed to enter the cave without any untoward incident happening, and he could be seen no longer, they all let out a united "OOOhhhhhnnn!" an expression of huge concern.

Mobi had been heard assuring everybody, "There shall come a day when I too shall fly like the Mahua Minshaw!" He escaped the attention of all the villagers at the base camp, somehow managed to approach the stone blocks from a desolate side of the hill and made a determined attempt to "stand by" his adopted father in the hour of his need! Without anyone noticing, he began to climb the hill.

But the rest of the villagers dared not follow Sudhir inside the "Howva Minsaw" cave. Now they waited with bathed breath to see if he would come out at all.

Sudhir moved all around the cave. He saw rooms cut out into the stone walls. And stone beds and stone seats.

Then he saw the wooden cabinet, one study table, one study table chair, one dining table with two chairs. The wooden cabinet had a stack of 10 to 15 files, and that was all! No gold bars, no stacks of silver coins, no large tumblers full of invaluable jewelry, no trunks of hidden treasure – just these files. In 1907, the Belgian-born American Leo Baekeland had already invented Bakelite. These files were wrapped and insulated by a thick airtight plastic cover. "This is ridiculous! This is what that was being protected?!" he wondered.

Nothing seemed to be decayed. He felt they must be fresh. They were in neatly typed out English! All of them were subsequently verified with a signature and stamped in approval followed by another signature to display agreement. He sat down casually to read a few pages from the first file, his eyes popped open, he sat up straight suddenly to read the rest with obvious awe. These minutely descriptive documents were ages old! Then he grabbed the next file. He became excited and he started racing through the pages. He rifled through all the files. Then he went through each of the files again. Deliberately and slowly, at a snail's pace. Then yet again. This carried on for over two hours without a break. He felt tired and his body ached but he carried on. Within two and a half hours he was done. He leaned back to stretch his arms and he let out a yawn. Then he smiled!

Chapter 11

The Treasures of the Lost Seven Ships

The Treasure Files

The first was a file containing News Paper Cuttings of the year 1936 trying to explain how a major battle in history took place during a certain period:

1767–1799 —Mysore Wars: Britain and Mughals versus Mysore, a southern Indian state.

1783 – 9 Apr. Zahiruddin Ali's brother captures the fort named Tablemore from the East India Company.

The second file detailed incidences relating to the year 1782 that added the dots to the first file. In 1782, a huge hoard of Treasure captured by Zahiruddin Ali, was now being supervised & stored by French & Indian soldiers. They were under the command of plunderer cum raider of Kingdoms Zahiruddin Ali, and they were loading these hoards of treasures into seven large ships, when suddenly these seven ships are snatched away from that very secret port by a Nair King of Malabar and his soldiers. Nobody knew where they had gone. No trace of the treasure nor the ships were ever found again.

But the third file had all the details relating to where the ships went.

It read as follows:

FILE NUMBER THREE

The Treasures of Zahiruddin Ali and the seven ships

Captain Kuthiravattathu Nair's Log, Leading Ship Named Shiva Shakti 21st Day of English Month of May 1782

We have captured all the seven treasure ships of Zahiruddin Ali and have sailed towards Africa. We have renamed the ships as Dhruva, Srinjita, Nirbhaya, Shanjukta, Manjula, and finally Payel.

We have captured the journal listing the treasures from a French Officer who was one of the Officers in charge of loading the treasures onto the ships.

Treasure List:

The list included treasures such as

(1) Eight **pure golden thrones** embedded with diamonds and precious stones placed two per ship,

(2) Seventy-five finely **hand crafted pure golden crowns** fit for the noblest of Kings & Queens studded with diamonds, Emeralds rubies and other precious stones placed eleven crowns per ship,

(3) Six hundred and seventy odd wooden treasure chests or treasure boxes on each ship full of **gold mohors (coins)** hence a total of four thousand six hundred and ninety chests full of gold mohors on the seven ships,

(4) Two hundred sixty odd treasure chests or treasure boxes full of **rubies, emeralds, diamonds, chains, necklaces, bracelets and innumerable precious stones** on each ship, hence a total of one thousand eight hundred and twenty approximate treasure chest full of all rubies, emeralds, diamonds, chains, necklaces, bracelets and innumerable precious stones on the seven ships,

(5) Seventeen life sized **pure gold idols of Goddess Saraswati, Goddess Durga alongwith other Gods and Goddesses** placed three per ship, these

(6) and more listing of jewelry & treasures.

Titles of Helping hands:

Titles given to various helping hands on the ship differed from country to country. It was decided to translate for the benefit of the British as follows:

An apprentice in either department shall be known as a topas or topaz. The senior lascar steward shall be known as the butler (either answering to a

European chief steward or in charge of the catering department himself in a small ship). A cook shall be known as a Bhandari.

Senior deck positions shall include seacunny (quartermaster), mistree (carpenter, although a European carpenter shall also be carried), and kussab or cassab (lamp trimmer).

In both deck and rowing room departments, the lascars shall be headed by a serang (equivalent to the boatswain in the deck department), assisted by one or more tindals (equivalent to boatswain's mates in the deck department). We needed cheap labor on board each ship. The foot Indian and French soldiers and the French Officers were strong and able. They were now our prisoners of war and were loaded in large numbers on each ship separately.

All seven ships have made great progress. Our method of one ship remaining in contact with all other ships through messages that went "blink on, blink off, blink on", using a Morse code Lamp. It consumed large dung lit fires stored behind glass domes from within the captain's cabin but operated by the cassabs, and it proved successful. Many a time, one ship conveyed important information – "blink on, blink off, blink on", to another ship which was forwarded to the next ship and so on. It worked wonders as all of us knew the location and happenings within each ship constantly.

Lascars, seamen and all others have been paid as is their due.

The ships, Dhruva, Srinjita, Nirbhaya, Shanjukta, Manjula, Payel have taken the first storm very well.

Captain Kuthiravattathu Nair's Log, Leading Ship, Shiva Shakti 15th Day of English Month of June 1782

The second storm exposed chinks in our armor. Water drops had entered the holds of three new ships, Shanjukta, Manjula, and Payel. Water drops but water alright. A dry atmosphere was very important. A few raw materials displayed signs of fungus. Some were fed to the animals which then displayed signs of illness. The fungus infected raw material was thrown overboard. The second problem was even more serious. We found rats had travelled with the raw material on board our ships.

Captains Log, Shiva Shakti 26th Day of English Month of July 1782

Rationing of food to Lascars has begun on ships named Shanjukta, Manjula, Payel.

Lascars are paid only 5% of their fellow white sailors' wages and are often expected to work longer hours as well as being given food of often inferior quality and in smaller portions. The remuneration for lascar crews remains much lower than European or Negro seamen and the cost of victualing a lascar crew is fifty percent less than that of a British crew, being six pence per head per day as opposed to twelve pence a day. The lascars lived under conditions not unlike slavery, as ship owners could keep their services for up to three years at a time, moving them from one ship to the next on a whim.

Captains Log, Shiva Shakti 14th Day of English Month of August 1782

Doctors on the ships Shanjukta, Manjula, Payel have reported signs of Beri Beri – a disease causing inflammation of the nerves and heart failure, normally due to a poor diet. Oranges and similar sour diet are not available freely on these ships now, hence rationed. Scurvy symptoms have been noticed in some Lascars.

Captains Log, Shiva Shakti 27th Day of English Month of September 1782

The doctors of Shanjukta, Manjula, and Payel are now inundated with patients suffering from following symptoms:
- confusion
- memory loss
- loss of muscle coordination
- visual problems such as rapid eye movement and double vision
- inability to form new memories
- hallucinations
- and bleeding plus swelling from gums

One lascar, on Manjula, a favourite amongst the lascars and much loved due to his amiable nature, was stalking the deck with a cutlass over his head and calling himself the "Maharaja of Varadoda". He was striking everybody who ventured too close. The soldiers overpowered him. The doctor requested that he be handed over for treatment but the soldiers, under the command of the Trichera Thiruppad, General of King Kurungothu Nambiar's army, assisted by the Captain of the ship Butterface Atley the British second in command, ordered that he be thrown overboard.

As a result, there was a lot of whispers to express hurt, which spread like wild fire. Talk of "injustice", talk of "inhuman acts that could not be accepted any longer" became the simmering expression of discontent.

Some lascars subsequently got drunk on Manjula, lost control over their senses, suddenly developed a mad courage to set about looting the ship. Violence broke out between the soldiers and the lascars. The latter have been captured, whipped and asked to walk the plank while all the sailors and lascars watched with fear in their eyes.

Captains Log, Shiva Shakti 14th Day of English Month of October 1782

We have seen an unknown island five days away. Everybody is excited.

Twenty Lascars have died on Payal due to Beri beri and Scurvy. Twelve in Shanjukta. All hell has broken lose on Shanjukta where discipline has been tightened by the acting captain, a Britisher by the name of William Scot, as the Captain, one Sajid Ali has taken ill. Laskars are going hungry as rations have been thrown overboard during the last riot. Hunger has made them desperate. Whipping of unruly lascars have begun, especially after they instigated the French and pro French Indian prisoners. Soldiers have begun checking each Lascar. Anyone found carrying arms and ammunition is whipped with twenty to thirty lashes depending upon the severity of the insubordination.

They have been informed about the unknown island just five days away.

One of the Midshipmen on the Manjula reported the latest, secretly using a light from his cabin window. The Lascars have taken over the ship.

We had lost seventy-six Lascars on Manjula from Beri Beri and Scurvy.

Captain of the ship Butterface Atley the British second in command, was found with his throat slit.

Sravan Ramnath Singh, the acting Captain of Payal was finding it difficult to handle the angry mobs that threatened the soldiers on deck. Forty Lascars have died due to Beri beri or Scurvy on Payal, as reported from a cabin window by a sailor. Discipline had been tightened by Captain Sravan Ramnath Singh. Daily whippings and throwing into the sea of unruly lascars had taken place over the past thirty-five days.

On the evening of 12th October 1782, several amongst the Lascar crew, claiming that they were hungry, drunk on stolen liquor, rushed Sravan Ramnath Singh's cabin and forced their way in after overpowering the marine stationed outside.

They hacked at Sravan Ramnath Singh with knives and cutlasses before throwing him overboard. The mutineers, probably led by a core group of just twenty-two men, went on to murder another eight of Sravan Ramnath Singh's officers: the British first lieutenant, Henry Reed; the British second lieutenant, Henry Foreshaw; the third lieutenant, Archibald McIntosh, Woodrock; the marine commander, Lieutenant Akbar Ali; Boatswain Shivaji Ganesha; Purser Wajid Ali; Surgeon Dr Surya Prakash; and the captain's clerk Nirmal Bera. Two midshipmen were also killed, and all the bodies were thrown overboard. Then they proceeded towards the cabin of Trichera Thiruppad, General of King Kurungothu Nambiar's army and his family consisting of his wife and his daughter. Trichera Thiruppad had given a single shot powder gun to his wife, one to his daughter, one to his daughter's Governess and kept one for himself. The main gunman cum body guard was Kukudia. It was organized that Kukudia the black slave would keep filling the powder in each gun as they finished firing and hand it over to each one of them immediately. Many died from the shots fired by Trichera. But Trichera Thiruppad's daughter and wife had never fired guns before. They had never found the need. They fired in midair and jumped back and away to scream in terror on hearing the explosion so near their ears. But the Governess kept firing before a shot hit her forehead and she slumped down with blood oozing out of her forehead. Shyamala, Trichera' daughter had never seen death so close. She screamed and rushed to embrace her governess and bawled. Her mother coaxed Kukudia to keep firing on her behalf even while teaching her. Kukudia kept firing. Mayuri, Trichera's wife was a soft-hearted philanthropist but she realized the situation demanded that she remained steadfast at the window and play her part at protecting the family. But when she went to the window to fire, she saw a young boy no older than Shyamala, her daughter, staring imploringly into her eyes. She paused but the man behind the boy fired and she slumped to the floor, dead. Trichera stared into the lifeless eyes of his wife's body and his will to fight died at that very moment. His memories raced back to the days when he would return from the innumerable battles and she would rush into his waiting arms. And how baby Shyamala learned to walk, then run, and then boss over her father. He set down his gun on the floor very gently and nodded at Kukudia. Kukudia was trained to follow instructions to the dot. As per Trichera Thiruppad's instructions, he shot his boss in the forehead and knocked his boss's daughter unconscious. Then even while the mutineers kept banging on the entrance door, he opened the secret hatch behind the large painting that looked down into the cruel ocean waters below. It was big enough for two people to exit at the same time. He tied large floats onto Shyamala, Trichera Thiruppad's daughter and pushed her petite frame out of the hatch and let her drop into the ocean below. Then he followed her.

At the beginning of the journey, it was stressed repeatedly on the need for the lower ranks to remain dutiful and obedient to their superior officers. Mutiny was a serious offence.

But the rebellion resulted in the fact that they have now commandeered the ship and are guiding it towards the island where they plan to recoup and refurbish their raw material stocks.

Captains Log, Shiva Shakti 17th Day of English Month of October 1782

On this morning the Captain of Shanjukta reported that a mutiny, hence a great battle was in progress. Hunger, Beri beri, Scurvy had been prevailing for quite some time. The whipping had increased and yet the hungry lascars were desperate enough to attack people serving the senior officers and snatching away their meals. The next report came in after about noon with a lascar messaging secretly that French Officers who were prisoners had led the opposition to the squalor and deprivation down in the decks. The French had known about the war loot stored in the decks below. They spread the word amongst the prisoners and sailors that the hoard belongs to all on board in equal measure. The fact about the treasure was unknown to many lascars.

Greed made them support the French who seized command of the ship and were moving towards the island.

Report is coming in just then that Manjula had hit the coral rocks and was sinking.

When the lifeboats were launched, the idea of equality so seriously instilled among the French seamen, destroyed all subordination. Nearly forty lascars, officers and family jumped into the boats, in defiance of her officers. Then the ship Manjula, began to gurgle and spew out bubbles of air as it began to slide down and then, it was gone!

Captains Log, Shiva Shakti 24th Day of English Month of October 1782

It is said that "when a vessel is lost, the men lose their pay, and the captain his command, all distinction and subordination ceases, and whatever is found on shore or from the wreck belongs to all who find it. The Captain of Shanjukta had sent a message that he alongwith a lot many other officers were at the windows in their cabin that looked down into the sea, ready to jump from the ship. This was because the soldiers had been slaughtered by the mob consisting of sailers, laskars and French Officers. The mutineers were now moving towards the Officer's quarters ready to slaughter officers along with wives and children.

Then news came to Shiva Shakti that Shanjukta's message sender had been shot! He was sending his last message. From then on, contact with Sanjukta was lost.

Finally, it has been realized that there has been no news from the ship, Payel, for a full seven days. That is until today, then we saw a ship in the distant horizon turning towards the island where we were headed. Then it turned towards the corner of the island and that was the last sighting of the ship.

Captains Log, Shiva Shakti 3ʳᵈ Day of English Month of November 1782

We had begun our journey with seven ships. Most hands were soldiers trained and equipped for land based battle. Most had never traveled for such long durations at sea. Most were used to a sunny weather. Most hated remaining wet for long periods of time. And very few were accustomed to sea related illness such as which attacked and put down even the fittest of land based soldiers.

We had to find land! We knelt and we prayed like we had never prayed before.

Then we saw the ship Payel turn the corner of an island.

We headed towards the island. Gone was the desire to touch the shores of Africa or return to the shores of India.

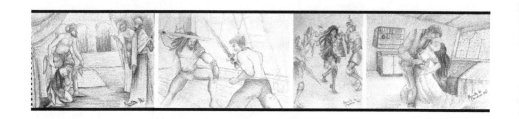

Chapter 12

Establishment of the Nair Kingdom on Nair Dvipa

New Land is Discovered

The Shiva Shakti, Dhruva, Srinjita, and Nirbhaya, dropped anchor under my guidance a few miles from the island. We knew that the coral reefs were sharp and could pierce the hull of our ships. We set out in small boats to the shore and built a base.

Our final tally was that four out of the seven ships had reached the shores of a large island safely.

Shiva Shakti – Dropped anchor

Dhruva – Dropped anchor

Srinjita – Dropped anchor

Nirbhay – Dropped anchor

Shanjukta – Missing

Manjula – Sank

Payel – Missing

We found a large spot in a valley next to a river. Initially makeshift huts were constructed. Subsequently a large boundary wall was constructed with wood from the nearby trees. Black leopards attacked our livestock. For the first few days we lit a fire to ward off wild animals. Then the Bungalows and wooden store houses were constructed.

Then wooden floats were constructed to withstand the pressure of heavy planks to be nailed onto them and then have heavy goods transported from the ships onto a specially constructed dock.

All remaining food stocks were thus gradually transported to wooden store houses created next to many wooden Bungalows, huts and large quarters. We then improved upon the boundary wall. A thirty-foot-high protective wall all around this compound provided further security. We created a second wall alongside the first and then created a walking path high above between the two walls, hence it became an observation post at the top. We increased the size of the compound to allow at least two hundred or more bungalows and family residential quarters for each one of us. Finally, the gold coloured, 'Golden Palace' for the Royal family was completed and the Royal family moved into the same with their retinue of servants.

Even while this was happening, the precious treasure hoard of gold, jewelry, stones, idols, crowns, etc., were transported under vigilant eyes into large storage houses. And we strengthened the path to the ship in such a manner that they became a sturdy, all weather resistant, permanent fixture for future travel overseas. We also began a ship building cum repair yard. This effort was headed by an Indian Engineer named Dhruva Chakravarthy from the land of Bengal. His relatives had died during The Great Bengal Famine of 1770. He could read and write English, Bengali, Urdu and Malayalam very well. Interestingly, he possessed great magnetism that attracted the best Engineers to aid him in his tasks.

Finally, we discovered granite stone hills and we realized that stone can provide stronger protection than wood and hence began a stone quarry. Then we discovered Coal, Iron Ore, and hence begun mining of same. We began to melt sand at high temperature and began to prepare a crude form of glass. Soon we had forty feet high, ten feet thick wall in front of the wooden wall and finally a deep moat filled with water in front of the wall. The thick gate could only be pulled up by pulleys and would not budge otherwise.

There was a severe shortage of manpower and the work involved was huge. Hence, we were willing to accept the rebels from the sunken ships who came floating on rafts, hungry, disheveled and broken.

That is when many disheveled, fatigued and starved survivors of a ship wreck stumbled through the jungles beyond and collapsed in front of our gates. After many days of recovery, they were in a state of health that permitted them to talk. They began to narrate how the ship named Payel sank on the eastern approach to the island. Survivors included French officers, pro French Indian soldiers, sailors, kasabs, cooks, tailors, carpentors, ship building workmen, ship building engineers and many more. The British who had landed with us initially raised a ruckus about accommodating the French officers but to no avail. We needed supervisors and workers. The French officers and their team had gone through a harrowing experience over these past few months. They desired to survive at any cost in a secure and safe environment where daily meals were guaranteed. This was the best sanctuary. So, they were inducted into the nation building team.

English Medium schools that taught French, Sanskrit, Hindi, Malayalam, Telegu, Tamil, Kannada, etc., were constructed. Many teachers were inducted from amongst the various passengers in the ships, soldiers and sailors included.

Then we found Trichera Thiruppad's daughter and Kukudia hiding away in some forest caves, surviving on snakes, squirrels, bats, wild vegetation etc. Kukudia was ready to fiercely protect his boss's daughter at all costs. Then we approached him gently and without causing him much apprehensions, we explained that we were the good guys. Fortunately, Shyamala recognized me as I had met her father several times at his residence.

Kukudia was immediately rewarded with an officer's uniform, all comfort plus ten gold mohors and offered the position of an officer on a ship. He refused and desired to continue his responsibility of protecting Trichera Thiruppad's daughter from then on. Shyamala, was given a bungalow to herself and when she recovered fully, she was introduced to our trained fellow officers. She went on to marry one of them. Kukudia was married off to a local he fell in love with and was given a fully furnished Officer's family quarter behind Shyamala's bungalow. Shyamala joined the Kings Palace as a Junior Accountant and Kukudia was promoted to become her ADC.

By this time, all the survivors, including those who swam to shore from wrecked vessels were aware about the famed loot of war that was being carried within the womb of each ship. Yet each citizen of this new colony assisted in some manner or the other in the transportation of the huge cache of treasure from the four remaining ships onto the shore and into a large specially built and protected treasure house.

This they did in exchange for a fabulous monthly payment in pure gold mohor from the treasure hoard. In addition, they were provided boarding and lodging and protection within the walls of this massive compound stretching miles in every direction.

Yet interestingly, maybe because of the huge number of trained soldiers or the sudden realization of the fact that healthy meals were easily available in this camp compared to the ship or maybe that survival was of prime interest to each and every one, it became obvious that nobody dared to raise the subject of trying to attack or steal the wealth from the King.

The French Designers came up with a brilliant design for a bank building, personnel were interviewed and recruited into various positions within this bank.

A training institute was begun to fill in various vacancies that were expected to arise in the next few years. Subjects such as Accounts & Finance, Administration, Law & Legislation, Arms & Armaments, Medicine, Police, Defense Services, cooking, tailoring, carpenters, ship building for workmen, ship building for engineers etc.

Living facilities that were temporary were now being made permanent. Farming began in earnest. Cow sheds, horse stables, elephant shelters were built in large numbers. It was so planned that common daily consumption goods such as milk, bread, butter, eggs, meat, vegetables etc., were easily available at reasonable cost to all. Transportation from one street corner to another was made possible by horse carts wherein the seating was for ten people or more. Transport on horses, would be provided after every three kilometer radius. Drainage from every house was transported vide a large burnt brick pipe that travelled below the road down to the beach aided by river waters that flowed partially into the drainage pipe at one point.

Bungalows were made more spacious for Officers inside the compound. Large rooms for all others below the officers with family. Inspite of the huge effort to provide common facilities after every three-kilometer radius, many chicken, pigs, goats and horses remained from the four ships including those that had swum ashore. These animals were let free within the compound to feed, breed and multiply. Innumerable little birds in cages were let loose on the island. The Leechee, Mango, Papaya, Guava, Pomegranate, and other fruit seeds were planted under the supervision of a specialized gardener.

The special Pure Gold palace which was being built for the King Kurungothu Nambiar and the living quarters all around the palace for his personal staff, was now complete in all respects.

Naming of the Island

Our Mootha Thampuran, that is the Senior Queen, named the island kingdom 'Nair Dvipa'! We made a new flag. The Flag of Nair Dvipa. From that day on, we all were citizens of our new island Kingdom. We built a printing press and printed our own notes – "Panam Hundred, Panam fifty, Panam ten, Panam five" and the coins, "Nanayam fifty, Nanayam ten, Nanayam five".

Log of Minister of Security & Environment, Nair Dvipa, English Month of November 1783

King Kurungothu Nambiar has got his daughter the Kochu Thampuran, that is the First Princess, Pallavi married off to me. I was thirty years of age when I Captained the King's ship, the **Shiva Shakti** the main ship and since the King had control over all the ships hence, he was the Chief Captain, and I was the **Supervisor on behalf of the Chief Captain** of six other ships plus the Shiva Shakti.

Today, at the age of thirty-one years of age, I am a Prince. As I have displayed excellent man management skills while supervising seven ships out of which four managed to survive with its people, King Kurungothu Nambiar has promoted me to the position of The Minister of Security & Environment of the Island that has been named the Nair Dvipa on this month of November 1783. The foreign country officers and countrymen have been married to locals or have been living with locals and have had children. The trusted members of our army, including the British and the French Officers, have successfully trained others to increase their level of competence. Daily drills are now conducted to ensure their readiness. I have divided the island defense into 'Internal Security' and 'External Security' wherein each division has its own intelligence wing to support efficient functioning. Both divisions are supported by the Naval forces considering that both divisions are affected by incursion by enemy forces using ship or boat into our waters. 'External Security' is further supported by our citizens who trade with foreign nations and assist us in gathering information regards the latest cost of goods that may be produced at a lower cost on our land as also their defense preparedness which includes defense equipment and the technology behind same. I have appointed three separate deputies to look after the administration of separate divisions of this huge island to report to my wife in-spite of my presence. These separate deputies have built roads leading far away into different states on this very island, where land has been allotted at exceedingly reasonable cost to encourage settlement. This allows me to be free to dive into adventures that are delegated by the King to me from time to time. My wife is wise and an able student. She is doing well at the task of **Acting Minister of Security & Environment, Nair Dvipa.**

To allow for instant justice, my wife the Princess, the King, the Queen and I have had various sittings with representatives of sailors, traders, sports professionals, soldiers, craftsmen, artisans, artists etc., and have framed a Legal structure to allow for a fair system of rules, law and order. The three deputies reporting to me were increased to five numbers. The island was divided into five states. Each of these was governed by a Deputy who was now designated as 'Mantri'. Each state was subdivided into separate units known as nads. In turn, the nads, governed by the naduvazhi, were divided into dēsams, the dēsams were themselves divided into 'amsas', the villages. We appointed Nair naduvazhis (governors of nads or city states) and Desavazhis (rulers of Desams). We have built many separate, large buildings in each of the Desams of the island kingdom and each Desavazhis (province comprising several Desams under the control of chieftains, called Desavazhis or 'Administrator') was 'Acting Judge' for all complaints or request for justice if not already heard by the Nair naduvazhis. However, if there was an appeal then it travelled to the palace premises where my wife sat once a week to ensure due justice is granted to the aggrieved party. She was the Supreme Judge to bring about Justice. Because we have citizens of many religious faiths and beliefs, we have made them accept a common law that is applicable in Nair Dvipa in-spite of their religion. We have not permitted minorities to form clusters or cluster communities as that would permit divisions. Instead, all communities have necessarily to live in peace together.

Log of Minister of Security & Environment, Nair Dvipa, English Month of December 1784 to December 1793

I had been instructed by King Kurungothu Nambiar to leave for the Malabar. There had been inter caste clashes notably the captivity of Nairs at Seringapatam, where many were kept captive or killed by forces loyal to Maqbul Alam Khan. Many more became refugees and fled to South Kerala. We were once citizens of the same land. The people there were our brothers. This is the opportunity we needed to make good use of the captured wealth. So we travelled with two ships and joined the forces of the Dharma Raja Karthika Thirunal Rama Varma of Travancore. True that in effect we were supporting the British, who were usurping our lands and yet we had to defeat the greater of the two evils. We were jointly able to defeat the enemy forces in July 1792 at the Third Anglo-Mysore War. We sent up an intelligence gathering unit to support and retain the good and thwart evil forces. We knew that enemy forces are bound to infiltrate our units. Hence each unit became independent and self sufficient. True that one unit will never know about the existence of the other unit and that this may lead to duplication of any effort, but in the end, the goal was achieved inspite of the duplication and deaths due to 'friendly fire'. These independent units then spread out into various countries. The total effort took many years. My forces and I then returned to Nair Dwipa. No one has tried to follow us back to our island. My soldiers and I had been away for nine years.

Log of Minister of Security & Environment, Nair Dvipa, English Month of January 1794

I returned to our island country to find that my son had grown to a full nine years of age. I found something else.

Our son Prince Unni Pushpakan Ambalavasi seems to possess magical powers that has travelled down from his great grand father from his mother's side. I imagined due to lack of any explanation that, these are latent hereditary powers inherent in every human being and that, in some human beings such powers manifest themselves with great intensity and multiply many times over. Such powers respond to the command of a gifted human being.

Such was proved true but the subsequent research produced a good reason which was shocking!

Not satisfied with this self-explanation, I sent out my subjects to the land of our forefathers and they began to study the history of my wife's ancestors. This study included the apparently ridiculous history of our people as narrated from father to son. What became apparent was that such powers had been reported amongst the Brahmins and sometimes in their offspring's inspite of intermarriage with the locals. Our people found that such powers could only be passed down or transferred to a blood descendent. It cannot travel down to any body else. But such powers can be gained by intense mental exercise over several years that would then result in the individual gaining control of his or her physical & mental energies. The powers manifested in our son were because he was a blood relative.

Research Summary of the Source of Phenomenal Out Worldly Powers

Our forefathers had passed down the secret behind the magical powers that certain Daivika Brahmin's possessed. Our forefathers were not Daivika Brahmins in fact! Our history predates the ninth century, as attested by grants of land given to our ancestors by ruling families. Though unbelievable, it was widely believed by our ancestors that their forefathers had travelled from the Daivika planet, far away from planet Prithvi (Earth in later years), where advancement of technology had allowed bases on other nearby planets.

The second Fleet consisting of many Interstellar Crafts, had taken off with fifty thousand disciplined soldiers from the Daivika planet and had vanished around one thousand years ago. This was following a similar disappearance of around fifty interstellar vessels, the first ever interstellar fleet, around two thousand years prior to that, transporting hardened criminals who were in the habit of resorting to guile, snatching, thuggery, thievery, murder, who lacked emotions and refused correction of their mental aberrations. The third fleet of interstellar vessels were technologically many times more superior and advanced in mind control. My wife's ancestors were on the third fleet of ships carrying Scientists, Academicians, and mentally disciplined professionals, who were out on a joint fact finding cum social fabric repair mission. No ship on this venture needed to carry soldiers separately as by this period, the use of mental abilities had reached its zenith. Each citizen had a disciplined, socially responsible, creative mind that allowed for betterment of society alongwith happiness cum satisfaction related rules and regulations. Most importantly each citizen had enough mental energy to be a soldier in his own right. Their job on this assignment was to correct the aberrations to the existing fabric of the planet on which the hardened criminals had landed and to use all their powers to discipline the minds of the said criminals as well as the effected aborigines or citizens.

They had success from the Daivika planet in tracing out a common path taken by both the missions before they had disappeared. As a rule, there were both men and women officers, engineers and workers in all the ships. They were making good progress and were beaming back their regular reports. They were travelling between planets when our ancestors were hit by an interstellar meteorite storm. These ships were moving towards Mars because it was suspected that the earlier crafts had crash landed on that planet and that the citizens of Mars were living an underground existence. Prithvi (Earth in later years) was never their destination. But the storm drove them into the atmosphere of this planet named Prithvi (Earth). It was then that they traced the signals of the Interstellar Crafts that had disappeared. The tracer signal went "beep beep beep" and pinpointed the exact location of the landing or crash site. The first batch with hardened criminals was traced to have crashed in the sea and lands adjoining the North Sea and Malay coast on Prithvi (Earth). The second batch consisting of disciplined soldiers, landed around the Malay coast, Borenta sea, the Kara Sea and East Siberian Sea.

Having thus located the earlier landings, it was imported to spread out and land our ships separately based on where the earlier ships had landed.

For the purpose of immediate security to the body of the present number of Interstellar Crafts and its luminary passengers, each craft was instructed to enter the atmosphere of earth horizontally and at the lowest possible speed to avoid heating up of the body of the crafts. They were instructed to try and land the craft on sea and if not possible then on land. The first craft landed in a place of cold ice where the people were fair as milk like them and as tall as them, had blond hair, possessed great powers like them but were nomads. These nomads claimed that their forefathers had come down from the skies. Another craft that landed near the North Sea found huge damage to the fabric of the original residents. Their forefathers had most certainly come from the second fleet of ships. We understood that they were children of our own planet and went on to repair the damage by providing support to the aggrieved original community. We had to create a settlement for them to survive with dignity and respect. We found, not surprisingly, that our citizens who had landed before us in the first fleet of ships were aggressive, they took with force whatever they desired from the citizens of Prithvi (Earth) and left every attacked settlement in ruin. They lacked ethics, values and refused to believe in commitments. To say ours task of repair of the social fabric was an uphill task was an understatement.

But all the other ships had crashed or landed one by one all over the unknown planet which we now know as Earth. The second fleet of ships had landed in present day Egypt, some in present day Mesopotamia, some in present day Peru, some in present day Germany. We taught the original residents in many worlds including those of the cold countries to dress and speak intelligible words like us instead of jumping around on their hands like wild animals with stone tools.

These primitives, who today ape our every move in the initial days of our visit, would learn to imbibe our mannerisms & great culture and claim it as their own in future. We had hopes that someday into the distant future, they would best be described to be well behaved and well-spoken citizens of that land where fortunate for them, our craft had landed or crashed.

Fifty numbers of our craft crashed near the present-day Malabar Coast near present day India and this crash created a huge mass of land. The locals who saved us discovered our amazing powers. We were white skinned when compared to them. Physically we were large and many times taller than them. Our ancestors saw the locals looking up in awe when they stood up their full height. They said we were, "svarggattil ninn", that is from heaven

How We Got Mistaken to Be Namboodiri Brahmins

By that time Namboodiri Brahmins, who were from Prithvi (Earth) and not from the Daivika planet, were entrenched into the fabric of the Malabar Coast. They were the original residents. The moment we crash landed and we mentioned to the original residents that we were from the Daivika planet, they imagined that we too were Namboodiri Brahmins. This was a very lucky break for us. From that day onwards, we were given the same respect as that was due to Namboodiri Brahmins. This suited us fine as we took on the names of Namboodiri Brahmins and were easily assimilated into the local society.

Some of us travelers from the Daivika planet possessed the skills to read each other's minds, pull, move, push, lift and drop objects using the power of our mind and fingers, burn writing paper merely through our mental power as also to control weather conditions by coaxing natural energies to rain or stop flooding etc. Use of mental energies for such tasks was normal on the Daivika planet as we were taught in our schools to generate the same and then onwards it would automatically pass on to our children. Most importantly, the citizens of Earth could never understand the importance of sound waves and its effect on everything that lived or existed on earth in any form. Usage of sound waves to execute many supposedly impossible tasks for a citizen of Earth, such as carving a statue from out of a big boulder or large piece of rock. Some of us could cure and heal by energies created by high speed vibrations, unseen by the naked eye, using the energy that emanated from our hands and fingers. Some amongst us even had furthered the art of moving at high speeds or using energies to become invisible as also to change our molecular structure and become a different being or object. Some of us used sound waves to bring about rain, heal life threatening wounds and illness, increase yields of crops and such activities. But all amongst us possessed the ability to absorb and retain immense volumes of knowledge. We possessed Engineering and analytical skills, that seemed like magic to the simple people of this planet that was called Earth, especially in the cold countries.

Local kings and chiefs were in awe of our abilities and encouraged us to move to their empires under their control by offering tax-exempt land grants in return for us officiating in Vedic rites that would legitimize the grantors' status as rulers. We brought about rain, brought about fertile lands and healthy crops. We brought about wealth and prosperity by humming out words at a specific speed that energizes the atoms and neutrons of the atmosphere and then takes control over the negative energies that are constantly battling life on earth. We found that the local Kings refused to try and understand the scientific explanation behind sound being able to achieve so much. We thus gained land and improved our influence over the socio-economic life of the region by helping rulers during the wars between the Chola and Chera dynasties when Vedic schools were turned into military academies. Operating from our illam houses, our ownership of agricultural land under the janmi system increased over many centuries and, we established landholding temples. Women travelling with us in the Interstellar crafts from the Daivika planet were many. Yet proximity got many males from amongst us attracted to locals and we married them. That was permitted. However, intimacy with or marriage with anybody immediately related by blood to certified criminals or providing them shelter or support was punishable, hence a strict no no! Our ancestors discovered to their dismay that the brain cells of Non Daivika Planet citizens were not able to break the cell locks that allowed for utilization of greater brain power. Further most were lazy, refused to meditate nor did they try breaking the biological locks that automatically disallowed greater power to and from each brain cell. Which meant that only ten percent of the capability of the brain was being utilized at any one moment. Thus, the elders decided that the younger generation must be dissuaded from marrying the locals otherwise mental abilities would die without our children meditating. By that time, society on Prithvi (Earth) had learned to divide itself as per task or skills learned, for their livelihood. Fathers taught their skills to their children and thus, survival continued. To discourage marriage with the locals which may have resulted in the dilution or the loss of our value systems and genetically empowered mental skills, certain elders took advantage of the existing caste system and taught their children to look down upon, that is disrespect people below their caste. We had to marry within the caste and not below. Hence many remained unmarried. But some carried forward their genes to the next generation without the knowledge of the elders.

About Sanskrit. Whether we picked up the Sanskrit language from the locals or whether the language belonged to us is not known for certain. What is important is that Brahmins have been described to be responsible for the Sanskrit influence on Malayalam.

Supervisory Visits from the Daivika Planet

Once it was confirmed that all our interstellar craft had landed on the planet named Prithvi (Earth), our ancestors decided to ensure supervisory visits at regular intervals.

While approaching the planet Prithvi (Earth), it was very difficult to locate the exact landing spot during any visit. Hence, we executed large deeply etched images on rock surfaces by incising, picking, carving, or abrading them. The size of the etching was spread out over many kilometers and thus could be viewed from high up in the air, especially while entering Prithvi's (Earth's) atmosphere. To ensure that the local aborigines of Prithvi (Earth) did not panic, nor have easy access to such landing spots, we ensured that such landing spots be located on high, inaccessible plateaus or land. We thus had "Monkey point", "Bird Point", "Deer Point", "Long strip landing point" and many more such landing points, mostly on the top of inaccessible plateaus. Wherever the plateaus were absent, flat grounds became a challenge and hence, we chose to erect twenty to thirty feet high, fifteen tonnes or more heavy stone blocks, dug them deep into the ground in a large circle, thus, no aborigine could think of trying to move any of them. In many cases however, aborigines began to chisel out human features on all such heavy stone blocks. We observed such events but we did not interfere as the blocks remained secure.

We discovered that the first fleet of interstellar space craft that carried criminals with undisciplined but powerful minds had found animals but no human beings on the Planet Prithvi (Earth). However, they were in desperate need of labour for their residential quarters and decided to make use of the operational research laboratories on the crashed interstellar crafts to insert their own genes into existing wild apes. The apes gave birth to equally tall and strong but highly resilient and amiable human beings. The first human beings were born! They were always subjugated and made to do all menial labour.

But as each criminal grew in power and wealth, his power to analyze made him desire the wealth of his fellow criminals. To be able to grab what was not his, he created an army of soldiers by once again inserting his genes into available wild apes. These group of warrior armies were tall, strong and powerfully built.

This was a convenient arrangement for the first batch of Intelligent beings albeit criminals, until some from amongst them began to mate with the highly resilient female workers. The offsprings began to think, comprehend and reason like their fathers. Then the numbers of such human beings who began to analyze and reason, began to increase, much to the dislike of the resident criminal minded interstellar travelers. Therefore, at a specific flashpoint, a big group of rebels from amongst the "children of interstellar travelers", were asked to leave. At certain stations of work, some of the rebels attacked their masters and then ran away into the woods.

These new groups of human beings who 'became free', travelled far and wide, multiplied and created new colonies and passed on to their children the knowledge of architecture, mathematics, study of solar systems, medicine, human anatomy and much more, taught to them by their former masters.

Then the second fleet of interstellar travelers, that is, the mentally disciplined soldiers, crash landed on this planet Prithvi, discovered the intelligent human beings created in the research laboratories by their fellow citizens, and found the original criminal citizens of their planet. The criminals were arrested but their vast knowledge of the planet and its resources were constantly required to survive initially and then run the planet. The disciplined fleet members also were in desperate need of labour and thus, continued with the practice of creating further human beings from different parts of planet Prithvi. But these human beings that were created were able to analyze from the moment that they were created. However, they were created with a disciplined, work oriented mind sets and they happened to be honest & responsible human beings.

By the time the third fleet of mentally far advanced citizens crash landed on this planet Prithvi, human beings were spread out all over various parts of planet Prithvi. Many were martial in nature and thus they had formed Kingdoms, did farming, were able to design and manufacture goods and create wealth of their own.

It became obvious that the brain cells of the human beings were not advanced enough to be able to execute the tasks that the interstellar travelers could so easily execute.

However, due to intermarriage with local aborigines over many generations, the ability to use mental power for the manufacture of many interstellar craft became limited to a rare few 'pure citizens. These engineers cum scientists became invaluable, hence became powerful and haughty as they looked down upon their mentally weaker brothers and sisters.

We helped local Kings bring in systems in their operation. We helped him and his subjects realize the importance of 'Mind Control' by creating sound temples that helped amplify the sounds & energies of the mind. We helped build temples with incredibly precise designs that may not be possible for many generations to follow.

For all the above tasks, we needed use of the crafts and hence fuel was required.

But mining of fuel required regular visits to the red planet and we had very few crafts.

For mining of fuel, we increased the production of interstellar craft. The fuel continued to come from the red planet nearby.

To allow for the manufacture & operation of such Intersteller crafts, our ancestors prepared manuscripts detailing how to create the anti-gravity engine for such interstellar craft, how to manufacture a body that would ensure a heat resistant entry into Prithvi's atmosphere, how to ensure pressure inside the craft, what to wear and eat during interstellar travel. How best to manufacture space wear garments? And much more.

Kings, Queens and their ministers freely used such crafts for travel from one region to another.

We flew over the planet Prithvi and created precise maps of each continent. We helped them understand the position of the stars and the moon vis a vis planet Prithvi.

As crops and trade brought about prosperity, the young generation became spoilt and undisciplined. They grew up to become selfish and self-centered. Many desired powers beyond imagination without realizing the negative effects of negatively used power. Power struggles brought about misuse of the crafts loaned by us to the Kingdoms.

The first fleet of interstellar space ships had evil citizens from our planet and they had married with their lab products thus corrupting their minds. When the third fleet of ships landed and the citizens spread out, there were certain degree of dilution of powers after mating with aborigines already possessing corrupt minds, thus this led to the birth of evil-minded individuals possessing our powers. With their power and guile, they took control of large swathes of land, plus ensured a large harem of wives. This success of the negative energy motivated the honest, disciplined minds from amongst us and they too resorted to the very negative activities that we had discouraged. Evil was winning over good. The undisciplined mind was winning over the disciplined mind. But we fought on with our mental powers. The evil forces began to lose until they managed access to and made use of ammunition located in crafts from the first two fleets. Most of such ammunition were environmentally safe, such as the Fire creating weapon, the Flying wheel weapon, the Air Impact weapon etc. But there was one weapon, the Sharva Shrest Astra, that the elders were strongly against using against each other, because it guaranteed total annihilation. But the selfish, evil ones encouraged the use of the same and used it against the good forces. Our engineers cum scientists who made the crafts along with many cities simply evaporated, survivors could not procreate and suffered from innumerable ailments. The effected soil could not be used for farming nor habitation as it had become contaminated. Thus, this powerful weapon became a deterrent in the hands of the evil forces. But use of 'environmentally safe' weapons continued, and brothers fought one another, armies were destroyed, and Kingdoms were won with literally no effort. Evil was gaining control over Prithvi (Earth).

They began to identify and kill all good forces, one by one. This continued until a handful of our engineers cum scientists remained. We were helpless without them, so we all went underground. We vanished into the forests, started living amongst the evil population living in urban and rural population. In order that the evil forces do not gain control over the sacred manuscripts prepared by our elders, we sent out teams to various parts of the world to hide them and keep them in safe custody, ideally in cold, inaccessible mountain tops with the tribes who are resident there. These manuscripts contained detailed step by step secrets about:

(a) how to create the anti-gravity engine for such interstellar craft?

(b) how to manufacture a body that would ensure a heat resistant entry into Prithvi's atmosphere?

How to ensure pressure inside the craft?

(d) what to wear and eat during interstellar travel?

How best to manufacture space wear garments?

(f) how best to get to super warp speed from normal cruise speed?

(g) dos and don'ts when landing on an unknown planet

How to approach Prithvi and recognize the earlier landing spot

And many more subjects.

We had informed our mother planet not to send any further crafts nor engineers as they would be misused. Elders of our mother planet decided that until a suitable soldier is born who would fight back, they shall not appear on Prithvi (Earth).

But we fought back alone, without any help from the elders. We used guerilla warfare, we attacked and vanished, and we caused huge disturbance to transportation of evil weapons and evil acts.

Over these battles for supremacy, inter-family feuds now were aimed at destroying each other's engineers cum scientists dedicated to the task of manufacture of such space crafts & ammunition. The moment most of such specialists died then, any one family group would become weaker in the power struggle. The prosperity & position to negotiate went down for that weaker Kingdom. Kings became desperate to survive but once again their economy was being challenged by the winner in the battle.

There came a time unfortunately when spies working for the evil forces identified the location of, with the help of their evil scientists, the last lot of honest, good energy engineers cum scientists that remained with us. They flew their crafts over our hideouts and they dropped from very high up in the air, the banned weapon, the 'Sharva Shrest Astra' on our people, down below in the hidden valley. There was a huge mushroom cloud that rose up into the skies and then it whipped away in every direction. We watched from the top of a mountain hideout as the high temperature winds blew away thousands of brick houses that we had built. Human beings, animals, birds simply evaporated into thin air by the thousands. The ice on the mountain tops melted due to the heat that remained in the atmosphere for many centuries. The river that flowed down in the valley dried up over many years, the earth became parched dry, the green jungles became devoid of vegetation and any semblance of life evaporated.

And so out of sheer frustration, we did what we should never have done. We took revenge on our enemies. We had hidden away innumerable Sharva Shrest Astra weapons all over the land! We launched all of them at the known habitation of their evil scientists. Once again, we watched as the mushroom clouds rushed high into the skies. Our engineers died because of them and now all their engineers immediately evaporated into thin air. With the death of the last few specialists dedicated to the task of manufacture of such space crafts & ammunition, died the industry of interstellar craft and sophisticated weapons.

A few crafts flew for some more time but due to lack of spare parts, they crossed their life cycle and were grounded. And thus forgotten!

In the meanwhile, Prithvi (Earth) became full of martial races. Empathy, Sympathy, Compassion, Mutual trust, Selflessness, gave way to Suspicion, Guile, Jealousy, Revenge, Greed, Selfishness, Thuggery, Cheating, Lying, and this negative energy spread like wild fire. Good energy managed to survive inspite of all this even while living amongst evil energy.

Our Son Prince Unni Pushpakan Ambalavasi

Back to our son. Because inter marriage had continued in-spite of the ban, and because meditation had refused to catch the attention of the vast majority, many of our planet's children lost their power on Prithvi (Earth). But many a time, it was seen to re-appear in the grandson or granddaughter or great grandchildren. So was the case with our son. Our son's abilities were many at so young an age. For example, to read peoples mind, to change matter, to create huge energies that he releases through his fingers, the ability to lift and pull distant heavy objects to himself, or throw nearby objects, however heavy, far away. Or move oneself through flight or by super human jumps over high obstructions or the ability to stop a blow from an opposite body, all these and more powers seem to be growing day by day. He was awed and scared initially. His mother took him discreetly to an uninhabited area to practice daily, to be able to control his own powers and to be able to release them only when necessary. His mother made him recite a prayer every day, "Oh lord give me the strength to be able to control my power. Give me the strength to ensure that I may fulfill my duties which revolve around my subjects. Give me the strength to ensure that evil thoughts, greed, vengeance, anger, frustration never cloud my mind in the possible event that they were to override my self-discipline. Give me the strength to use this power gifted to me for the good of this planet that you have created and to protect its inhabitants".

Fortunately, he is a kind hearted and a caring person. I returned to find that he did not show off his God given powers unnecessarily. At such a young age, he has used his powers to save two separate wild Tribal groups of around forty to seventy individuals in each group, clinging in mid ocean onto broken palm trees, from drowning. They were affected by a storm that had hit their island and they had been drifting for many days, malnourished and dehydrated. They have dark complexion like many of us after years of intermarriage with the locals, but they are curly haired, stature like ours, use primitive tools and wear no clothing. He has organized a settlement for them in a secluded part of Nair Dvipa at the confluence of the river Satya and the ocean. He took the decision that they shall be protected from the eyes and sight of our modern-day civilization thereby giving them time to mature in their own speed. My son has recommended that we forbid any contact or any attempt to disturb their social norms, and habits, unless so permitted by any of our blood descendants.

Log of Minister of Security & Environment, Nair Dvipa, English Month of August 1805

I had left for the Malabar Coast in 1798 and witnessed from a far distance in 1799 as the British took Srirangapatna from Maqbul Alam Khan. It saddened me that Maqbul Alam Khan was defeated by a foreigner, herein the British, on the land of our ancestors and yet I reasoned that a murderer who like his father had slaughtered so many in his greed for power and wealth, had been punished by the almighty. My men entered Srirangapatna in disguise, even while the smoke of destruction continued to rise high into the skies, and could manage to take away two iron-cased rocket launchers, two serviceable iron-cased rockets and four empty iron-cased rockets.

We returned to Nair Dvipa to do necessary research relating to this rocket technology.

Prince Unni Pushpakan Ambalavasi Becomes King

I have made notes in this log considering that our son, now the King, does not have the time to continue this tradition. Our son Prince Unni Pushpakan Ambalavasi had been crowned the King of Nair Dwipa after my wife abdicated her throne in his favour.

We have in our younger days developed huge jungles of fruit bearing trees, not just because we wanted wild animals to have a sanctuary, but also for a place to reside during our old age.

A hut was built for us old people within our wild life sanctuary. A fair number of assistants accompanied us and hence a small village was born.

Great celebrations marked the occasion of the crowning of our son. He is as pious as his parents and that was a matter of pride for us. He has built seven temples to honor Lord Shiva and Vishnu, all around the island. Interestingly nobody saw work in progress. They suddenly saw a temple on an empty plot of land. Each bolder must have weighed a minimum of a hundred tons or more. The pillars that he cut away from the rocks using only his mind power, were cut down with precision from the top to the bottom. What the local people did not know was that our son had used his mental powers to lift and chip away in great precision at the rocks, to be followed by placing huge pillars and motifs at different locations of the temple using the power of mind alone. The island kingdom has grown to three hundred strong with residents of many faiths and from many countries.

King Unni Pushpakan Ambalavasi has set up an observation camp inside a cave, at a vantage point on a hill top to protect the curly haired tribes he had saved from drowning and then he threw a cloak of invisibility over them to ensure that nobody was to hurt their lifestyle, belief or customs. It also acted as his sanctuary on days when he could not take the hustle and bustle of life anymore.

Trade & Commerce By King Unni Pushpakan Ambalavasi

He has set up trading centers with the British, the French and the Dutch intentionally, in-spite of the fact that they have tried several times, jointly or separately to divide our community and to gain control over the fabled treasures.

True, we wanted them to believe that such stories of unimaginable wealth were fables and nothing more.

Many amongst the foreign traders and many local citizens have tried to search for the sunken ships but in vain. The advantage is that a mist magically appears every time that an unknown ship tries to approach our island kingdom. A force field further stops them from being able to identify any object below the deep waters with sonar or other metal detection or deep ocean imagery related devices.

Log of King Unni Pushpakan Ambalavasi 1805

I do not have the time to make notes as per tradition.

An evil but extremely powerful Royal family member has apparently travelled back in time to cause much harm to Nair Dvipa, its reputation and honour. He calls himself Mogui. Women, meaning house wives, sisters, daughters of fishermen have been enslaved around the Port area and are used as sex slaves.

Resources best used for the development of Nair Dvipa are now being diverted towards the Defense of Nair Dvipa from this Mogui and his evil companions. Word is out that he talks about revenge. It is beyond my comprehension why he would travel back in time to take his revenge and against whom? And why?

There are many large and small islands next to ours. The biggest island immediately next to ours has become his safehouse and he is getting fortifications built that can withstand a big flood. Wonder why he is planning against a super flood. He has travelled back into our time. Does anything happen on this neighbouring island in his time in future that hurts him or his loved ones?

Log of King Marangad Bhavathrāthan Namboothiripad 1840

Our brothers and sisters within the Royal family have begun to make claims on the fabled wealth. My Minister and I consulted each other and assured them a regular monthly Royal Purse but nothing more beyond this. Inspite of this, skirmishes are a regular affair.

Log of King Perikamana Raman Namboothiripad 1880

Our cousins have waged war against each other. The country seems divided. Two of my sons have died in battle trying to protect our Kingdom. My third son is a good for nothing poet cum singer who voyages the world. We have tried giving him minor tasks, for example to deliver certain stocks of rice or spice to distant lands. It would suit us, as well as satisfy his seafaring lust too. The country would be in great peril if he were to ever become the King.

I have identified a young General, from our own community now staying in Kerala who has proven himself in battle and who is also a great leader and strategist. Akavoor Daivikapad seems interested in accepting our daughter's hand in marriage and in taking over the responsibility of keeping this island kingdom together.

A small building close to the river and close to the Ambalavasi village in the Ambalavasi forests was built for us old people within our wild life sanctuary. A fair number of assistants accompanied us and hence a small village was born next to the Ambalavasi village.

Log of Prince Akavoor Namboothiripad, Nair Dvipa, English Month of December 1919

I am Prince Akavoor Namboothiripad, of Nair Dvipa.

There was a large gap in this log due to various challenges that did not permit free time to be easily available.

I am not the descendent of the last King Perikamana Raman Namboothiripad, but I am his son in law. He abdicated the throne in his daughter's favour after getting her married off to me because he felt I was best suited to protect the interests of this island and its residents. The various children of the first King of Nair Dvipa and their cousins, followed by the cousins of their grandchildren, were all enjoying a monthly purse that guaranteed their comfort. They moved around in expensive cars and most did no work for the benefit of the nation. Some got together groups of foreign and local sycophants who egged them on to rebel against the King. I was to quell such rebellions and maintain law, order and peace.

My father in law saw a vision that that there shall be a global war. That by the end of the World war or soon after, the German Empire, Russian Empire, Austro-Hungarian Empire and the Ottoman Empire shall cease to exist. National borders shall be redrawn, with nine independent nations restored or created, and Germany's colonies shall be parceled out among the victors. Britain, France, the United States and Italy shall get maximum mileage out of this war and shall impose their terms in a series of treaties.

He also saw a vision that a third global battle shall take place after two powerful nations began to award sanctions and block trade and commerce against each other in the seas of the Pacific Ocean and the Atlantic Ocean.

Our ancestors have been maintaining a log which was discontinued by them possibly due to one powerful magician named Mogui who had travelled back in time. Every time our last King ventured to search for the unknown time dimension from where he had travelled, there arose other urgent matters that needed to be solved right away. For example, the remaining citizens were dying from plague.

Our focus thus became finding a cure for this medical problem.

But how did all these problems begin?

I hereby restart this log for maintaining a record in perpetuity.

Sailors who were born and brought up on this island, had been travelling to distant lands to gain knowledge, as well as to do trade and commerce.

Such travel also taught us trade. It taught our people that we could give the world something that they needed in exchange for something that we needed.

Our island country had trade with the Great Britain, the USA, the German Empire, Russian Empire, Austro-Hungarian Empire and the Ottoman Empire. We grew large quantities of rice, dal, vegetables, spice and sugar cane. We had enough for ourselves even after we exported a big chunk to the hungry European and USA market. In exchange for the same the British had set up an Embassy cum trading camp on our land. And then a training camp for our army. Whereas the USA provided us loans for the purchase of ammunition and defense equipment manufactured by UK and the USA for our Ocean and land Defense. Why loans? Because we did not wish to disturb the hidden treasure and thus attract attention from the scourge of the world once again.

India remained the only country that had maintained its core values inspite of the torture meted out by the many invaders and now the British rule. Our country, Nair Dvipa, decided to imbibe the fine value systems of the country of our origin.

We had prepared a legal system with its rules and regulations. Gradually, over many years of interaction with various countries around the world, we copy pasted the legal system of India and thus improved our own system, the administrative system, the Government bodies of Nair Dvipa. In fact, we literally copied everything, with the self commitment to modify it subsequently to our country specific requirements.

We desired to create wealth of our own from the land that was gifted to us by the supreme lord. The British wanted to buy land from us but to avoid what had happened in India, we refused sale of land to any foreign individual and to any foreign country. The British wanted to hire land from us to grow Indigo and Opium. We had wisely refused.

Our foreign exchange reserves began to grow. Our banks and financial institutions began to flourish. Our entrepreneurs began to set up operations in many more foreign countries. Our research on Missile & rocket technology saw launches that kept failing.

Some of the researchers of Nair Dvipa were guests of many lands that were being visited to trace potential for trade and commerce. During a few rounds of hard drinks around the Strait of Malacca, or East China Sea, they had unwisely spoken too loud in front of their hosts about the fabled wealth. Some countries were troubled by financial recession and had no other option than to enlist the services of pirates to augment the income for their nation.

This brought in unscrupulous foreigners. They contacted the disgruntled Royal cousins who financed and thus helped the foreigners in instigating riots and political upheavals to try and get at this famed wealth. All such foreign instigators were imprisoned, guillotined or asked to leave our island. But they had also brought in foreign infections for which we had to find a cure.

My Brother in Law Swaminarayanan and Sanya, the Pirate's Daughter (1919)

My brother in law, Swaminarayanan, son of King Perikamana Raman Namboothiripad (1880) seems to have got kidnapped while he was travelling by a merchant vessel from Nair Dvipa towards Formosa to transport spice and opium. The pirates were disgusted by his sloppiness and felt that he could at best be a court musician. He kept reciting poems and singing throughout the day. They decided to initially ask for a small ransom. But the faint-hearted brother in law saw the pirate's daughter from the corner of his eye and unnecessarily had to boast about his royal ancestry. That did it!

And so, the girl, on being tutored by her father, Wúgū, the pirate King of the area around Formosa, intentionally wore flimsy clothing and befriended the "singing Prince of Nair Dvipa". She pretended to reluctantly accept his offer of a drink and then pretended to have got drunk on just a tea spoon full of whiskey. Whereas she was normally adept at polishing off three bottles with no sign of intoxication, this simple, emotional Prince who did not know her history, naturally felt guilty about having got her drunk. Naturally, seeing that she could not walk properly after that tea spoon full of whiskey, he helped her walk back to her room where she had a wardrobe malfunction and he did try to help her into her silk night dress, as requested by her vide her slurred speech.

He did try to help her but then she had a total wardrobe malfunction subsequently! He was so, well, intoxicated by the wealth of this bosomous young lady that he decided to stay back that night in her room, and well, keep trying – "helping her".

But she stopped him from leaving her room for the next three days and then three more days thereafter. He insisted subsequently that his value systems made him commit that he must marry the female outlaw.

They had a son who went away with them on the parents being released from the Nair Dvipa prisons some years later.

It is possible that this son possesses great powers and can travel back in time. How this can be said so confidently is because, the man who visited the period during my great ancestor King Unni Pushpakan Ambalavasi (1805) repeatedly spoke of wanting to take revenge on his, "brothers in the Royal family" and during the time of my great ancestor, a ruffian of his character could never have been related to us.

My Ancestor Gets Attacked By a Person Who Travelled Back in Time

My ancestor the great King Shri Unni Pushpakan Ambalavasi (1805), the one with super powers, has had to face several attacks from strangers & brigands on his island who came to know about the famed treasures. Attacks came from pirates and treasure hunters. They came in various shapes and sizes, for example British, French, Dutch treasure hunters along with pirates who would have gladly slit the throat of our countrymen.

The worst attack came during his reign from Sea Pirates originating from around Formosa who landed at Nair Dvipa during the night, travelled the jungle during the day time and attacked our forces without warning. One such group was led by Móguǐ de érzi who had been boasting about having travelled from the future back into the year 1805, just to "take revenge on my Royal family brothers". Royal family Princes often declared themselves King of independent states and fought against the joint armies. Some imported & used long range rifles with great success. Close-order troop formations disappeared from the Nair Dvipa scene as a result of the success of long-distance rifles, and the cavalry charge was relegated to the past.

Mogui came in with men with arms and ammunition far superior to what was available in the Nair Dvipa army then. During 1805 of Nair Dvipa, the most modern rifle was hand loaded and capable of firing at a range of up to 200 yards (183 meters) for example, the Tauker rifle and the Faper's Kerry Model pistol were being used in bulk. It was only later that we adopted the 11-mm Modell 1871 Lewehr and then the Modell 1871/84 Infanterie-Repetier-Lewehr. Mogui's forces had landed in this time with B.S. Rifle, Caliber. 30 M1, wherein, gas pressure performed automatically the reloading task formerly done by hand. Thus, Rapid gunfire from Mogui's forces routed the King's disciplined, single shot rifle armed forces, one battalion after another.

Mogui was a very cruel pirate who captured one of our important docks and huge tracts of land behind the dock. He remained there for many months torturing, raping and maiming many of our local citizens, forcing them to accept his pagan culture and life style. That Pirate had originated from the lands adjoining the Yellow Sea and the East China Sea.

Móguǐ de érzi was a tall, extremely well built, baritone voiced, selfish, sweet talking, ruthless, heartless, highly sophisticated, antisocial individual who possessed magical powers.

Within a few days of capturing the dock from trained defense personnel and untrained fishermen, he began a harem consisting of the unwilling wives of the soldiers, the helpless fishermen and their unwilling daughters.

Móguĭ de érzi used his great powers to locate one of the sunken ships. Each defense personnel and fisherman were forced to pay a daily tax of two fishes, and at least one gold mohor from the sunken ship that lay far away from the port. Otherwise, his children would be murdered or maimed by Móguĭ de érzi's pirate army. In this manner he had amassed a great number of Gold Mohors and ensured a well-fed army of pirates for a period of approximately two years. He even made the false promise of letting a fisherman's wife go scot free provided the fisherman helped him find the treasure that had landed on shore in the five intact ships.

It is this fisherman who arrived at the Palace of King Shri Unni Pushpakan Ambalavasi, (1805) requesting that we reveal the location of the wealth of our ancestors in order that his wife may be released from the clutches of the powerful Móguĭ de érzi.

He cried his heart out to narrate the plight of too many fishermen who were similarly suffering the humility of their wives & daughters being used as members of Móguĭ de érzi's Harem. And, the fact that Wúgū the Pirate King had evil magical powers that he used to destroy huts and the strongest of hard stone fortifications. That he could enter the minds of the strongest fisherman and use him against his own community.

King Shri Unni Pushpakan Ambalavasi embraced this fisherman and assured him that he shall get his wife back. But how? His every attempt to use his vast army against Mogui's superior arms proved disastrous. Thus, he realized it was important for him to take matters in his own hands. He flew into the skies and landed exactly where the fisherman showed Móguǐ de érzi's camp existed.

He used his invisibility cloak to walk past innumerable tents and brick bungalows but he could not find any trace of Mogui. "Remove invisibility" he said to his mind, as he felt it was not necessary.

"Looking for me?" somebody asked from behind him.

He turned around to see a tall and handsome Prince but, dressed like a Pirate. Interestingly, both were flying at the height of the terrace of a five-floor building.

When King Shri Unni Pushpakan Ambalavasi faced the powerful Móguǐ de érzi they both hovered above the fisherman's village. The King asked Móguǐ de érzi with a grim expression and a deep voice, "What is it that you want? Money? Wealth? I shall give the same to you. Release these innocent people and leave this land that has only strived for peace and prosperity!"

Móguǐ de érzi guffawed while pointing his fingers at the King and then the island below and he said, "I want this island for my country Diànlì jī'è de guójiā, you lousy weakling! Turn around like a good boy and run away so that and I may consider the possibility of letting you live to serve me in perpetuity! I want all these weak people to be the slaves of my country Diànlì jī'è de guójiā! We shall suck Nair Dvipa dry, we shall kill every man, then we shall have every woman of this island to join the harem of every male citizen of Diànlì jī'è de guójiā! Very soon all of you shall speak our language and look like us. We want your wealth and your prosperity and when we leave, you shall be nothing but a dry orange peel to be thrown away into the nearest dustbin!"

Saying this he kept guffawing like a mad man even while his right hand rose lazily up to throw a blast of energy towards King Ambalavasi.

The King realized that he has a lot of anger that cannot be resolved at this moment.

"Mirror his every blast!" the King instructed his mind. The blast bounced back and whammed into Móguĭ de érzi who tumbled in the air to quickly recover and send another blast in the King's direction but this time with his left hand. But that blast too bounced back and hit him with the same force that he had used to send it! He tumbled around in the air and tried to quickly recover. He was grievously hurt by the two blasts. This was when Mogui realized that the King was using the mirror energy and he instructed his mind, "Shatter the mirror!" and the mirror barrier shattered into tiny shards of energy that flew in every direction.

Then within seconds Mogui instructed his mind, "Throw up the heaviest bounders from within the ocean waters below and hit the weakling who dares to call himself the King!" Huge boulders rushed towards the King but became dust even before they reached the King. Mogui threw his 'invade the mind' energy blast down at the village folk and growled, "Nair Dvipa residents rise up into the air and absorb my energies to fight this weak half woman who dares to call himself your King!" The strong, self-confident citizens were not affected by this attempt to control their minds. However, around ten villagers whose minds were weak and easily malleable rose up into the air with their heads bent down as if one were to be asleep. Then all of them raised their heads as one. All had blood shot eyes and all of them roared like wild demons! The King did not wish to hurt his own citizens. He was in a dilemma. They blasted the King from all directions and he got battered and went down on his knees even while in the air! He was seriously wounded!

"Use the Invisibility energy cloak", the King instructed his mind "and make Móguĭ de érzi's pirate colleagues to revolt against their master! Make them blast Mogui from all heights and directions and change their position of attack faster than what Mogui can anticipate!"

Twenty plus some more of Mogui's pirates began to rise with speeds exceeding that which can be seen by the naked eye and even while they rose, they began to fire volley after volley of body penetrating destructive energy. Mogui was shocked to see his own pirate team attacking him. Before he could recover from the shock, the volleys had already penetrated his body and his defenses went down. But the volleys continued and he knew he would die if his body did not repair itself right away. Mogui's mind began to automatically concentrate on self-preservation and self-defense. It lost control over all other energies that ensured him control over any or all people of Nair Dvipa. The citizens of Nair Dvipa came to their senses at that very moment even while in the air and fell into the ocean waters, to swim back safely ashore. But Mogui was losing his supremacy over this battle. His defenses were down as all energies were directed to repair his grievous internal wounds.

It was then that the King sent a 'energy sapper blast'!

Móguǐ de érzi realized that the powers of King Shri Unni Pushpakan Ambalavasi far exceeded his own. He saw the blast of energy racing towards him. He knew that he would become a vegetable with no powers after the blast hit him. He raced away up into the skies to look down upon the vast modern cities and towns of Nair Dvipa for the last time. The blast from the King followed him up like a heat seeking missile! Then before King Shri Unni Pushpakan Ambalavasi could stop him, Mogui threw down a huge force of negative energy that brainwashed within split seconds the minds of many under confident, weak minded citizens to become indifferent to the benefits and facilities already being offered by Nair Dvipa's hard working leaders and elders since the past ages. The unstoppable negative energy kept working even after the 'energy sapper blast' had smashed into Mogui, he grimaced in pain and screamed! The unstoppable negative energy kept working even after Mogui became a surrendered, slumped over body, floating in midair.

But the negative energy continued to execute their task. The negative energy spoke to the minds of the weak and easily malleable minds of Nair Dvipa residents thus, "Diànlì jǐ'è de guójiā my country is the Holy country that feels your pain. Nair Dvipa does not feel your pain! Nair Dvipa leaders and elders fill up their own coffers and neglect the plight of the poor and downtrodden. Our country shall give you the support to fight for your right to get better salaries from the many factories that churn out thousands of dollars for themselves but leave only peanuts for its workers that is you! We shall sell to you all the luxuries that the rich can afford at throw away prices. We shall help you close your own factories that dare to compete with much cheaper products from your favourite country, that is us. We need your help to flood your country with our cheap products. We need your help to become a monopoly! We need your help to destroy our competition in your country and we shall make you rich leaders of your country!" Móguǐ de érzi's negative energy stamped this warped belief into their weak cum malleable minds. His huge force of negative energy continued to erase past faith in oneself, erased past sacrifices made by Nair Dvipa elders, erased past respect for ones parents, erased past respect for Nair Dvipa and erased the immense respect for one's colleagues and friends of Nair Dvipa in the Police, Army, the government, the honest and dedicated work done by citizens to build up a country over so many years, and finally erased the positive feelings for every good deed of every good citizen of Nair Dvipa in the past!

Then the same negative energy filled the empty minds with "Go to Diànlì jì'è de guójiā when I am gone. My countrymen shall provide you free education and a comfortable room, graduation degrees with other fellow students from all over the world and finally reward you with monies to support your fight against any or all mistakes that the hard-working people of Nair Dvipa make! Diànlì jì'è de guójiā shall help you build up the courage to stand up against the positive developments of Nair Dvipa, your country of birth. Have the courage to stand up against those who are making mistakes only because they strive fearlessly to help Nair Dvipa prosper without worrying about the damage to their own reputation or their own families. My country shall support you while you demotivate the very structure that pumps forward the machinery of growth and prosperity of Nair Dvipa. Diànlì jì'è de guójiā shall help your senior students, whose minds have been molded to think in our favour by our countrymen, to go back to Nair Dvipa and gain control over Media, control over the lower courts, High Courts, the various government departments and forces. Then they shall pull you up the ranks to take up positions of control and power. Those even senior to them shall then pull them up even further, into the supposedly holy sanctum of the Supreme Courts of Nair Dvipa! Do not let your Government correct the loopholes in your Election Rules that presently permits funds to be given to political parties with no indication nor explanation of the source of funds. Do not permit registration of the names of citizens. Have the courage to stand against those who desire to protect the fabric of Nair Dvipa and then help us to put you into the seats of power. From then on, we shall help you enrich yourself, provided you run Nair Dvipa exactly in the manner that we suggest you should do!"

Having cast this powerful negative energy into only the weak minded, underconfident and easily malleable citizens of Nair Dvipa, the energy with no form began to laugh like a mad force, as if, it has won the evil battle, inspite of having lost the fight against the good forces. Then it tried to save Mogui!

But King Shri Unni Pushpakan Ambalavasi, like in a smart game of chess used this time to cast a net of protective cover over the fisherman's village and the Palace that even Móguǐ de érzi could not break. The negative energy tried to save Mogui by dividing itself into many small bits of energy. One bit of negative energy pushed the wives of the fishermen in front of themselves even as King Shri Unni Pushpakan Ambalavasi attacked. The King promptly used his mental powers to throw a blanket protective force field over the women and then threw a blast of destructive energy that made the negative energy turn into positive energy dust.

Another bit of negative energy in the meanwhile tried to grab the limp body of Mogui and was about to turn and fly away but the King zipped up at an astounding speed to pin down both the negative energy as well as Mogui in his mental grip then, zapped the negative energy to turn it into positive energy dust. The semi-conscious Móguǐ de érzi squirmed and wriggled his best but could not escape the rope like mental bind.

He was immediately imprisoned in a brown coloured brass metal bottle and the cap was sealed with the condition that it could be only opened by an equally powerful King of Nair Dvipa if he so felt it necessary. All the fishermen were re-united with their wives. Enough Gold Mohors were given to each to reward them for their hard work in extracting them from the deep sea. The balance Gold Mohors, Jewelry and treasures that were extracted from deep sea were then transported to a secret treasury. The fishermen were asked to continue the extraction process under the supervision of a Minister appointed for this purpose.

But various bits of negative energy had spread out to escape the Kings wrath. These energies continued in their negative endeavours to pollute the minds of the weak of Nair Dvipa.

The problems began to surface one by one. Some bit of negative energies began to supervise the departure of citizens of Nair Dvipa to Diànlì jǐ'è de guójiā, the land of the evil Mogui, who wanted to offer Nair Dvipa and most certainly many more countries on a platter to Diànlì jì'è de guójiā, his adopted country. Most certainly the coffers of his adopted country would thus be enriched even while Diànlì jì'è de guójiā wears the shroud of innocence in International forums of justice and denies any connection to the sea pirates, brigands and robbers who waylaid rich traders travelling on the normal trade routes.

As the energy spread out to reach out towards many more malleable minds, students returned from Diànlì jì'è de guójiā with their graduation certificates and hearts filled with disgust, ridicule and with hate for Nair Dvipa. They had been given a purpose and they had the promise of financial support. They began small media companies, they became correspondents, writers, poets, teachers in various institutions of education, lawyers, they even rejoined as students in various Universities in Nair Dvipa to identify pliable students.

Even as the other citizens went about their business not bothering about these negative minded anti nationals in the garb of socially responsible intellectuals, the Diànlì jì'è de guójiā media as well as some new Media companies of Nair Dvipa gave their every negative action the paint of Pro Nair Dvipa superior nationalism! They were branded as the new intelligentsia, the 'Think Tank' of future Nair Dvipa by the Diànlì jì'è de guójiā trained Media!

Only Móguǐ de érzi knew how to stop the growth of this disease. Try as they might, the Kings of Nair Dvipa, starting from King Unni Pushpakan Ambalavasi (1805), then King Marangad Bhavathrāthan Namboothiripad (1840), and then King Perikamana Raman Namboothiripad (1880) could not identify the location of the evil energies that even today continued to supervise the buildup of enemy forces within the country. I tried my best to find ways of travelling into the future to stop the source of the evil energies but to no avail. We realized the crying need to learn the art of travelling through time to correct space and time aberrations. King Unni Pushpakan Ambalavasi (1805) did possess in his days the power to travel forward in time but after being grievously wounded in the last battle with Mogui, he needed to recoup.

But even before he could recoup his vast energies, the attacks from other pirates and foreign residents continued. His own Royal cousins were declaring themselves King in small pockets of Nair Dvipa and had begun to print coins with their faces on the same. Our cousins had become so desperate that they were visiting and interacting with pirates of distant lands. People who called themselves citizens of the land of Diànlì jǐ'è de guójiā were freely interacting with these wayward Royal cousins! These citizens of Diànlì jǐ'è de guójiā, in the garb of tourists, were often seen near the sacred lands of the protected tribes and known to be kidnapping certain tribals who ventured outside the protected zone. The King had a visitor, a good human being, his direct descendant from the future. And following this visit, he made a sudden decision, that all ships shall be put under scrutiny and all pirates shall be tried and if found guilty, shall be put to death! From then on, he dealt with force against all manner of treason and divisions within Nair Dvipa and thus brought the rebels down on their knees. Therefore, he could not muster the energy to fight this strange plague that had the support of Móguǐ de érzi evil super power.

It hit the families of the little dark curly haired people that were saved from the deep ocean from drowning around 1805 by King Unni Pushpakan Ambalavasi. The plague that came from rats brought in by the Pirates, began to decimate their numbers.

Finding a cure took our remaining ancestors to the English occupied India, Great Britain, the USA, the German Empire, Russian Empire, Austro-Hungarian Empire and the Ottoman Empire. They stayed back and reported that they had witnessed a revolution happen. The Industrial revolution that changed the rural economy of certain countries to an industrialized nation. The medical knowledge that our citizens picked up was immense. Our medicinal library is worth boasting about with knowledge brought in from all over the world. But our ancestors also saw the rich become richer and the poor becoming poorer. Money was power and became the identity of a person. Humanity, compassion, mutual respect, respect for nature, – all these values and more got trampled in the race to climb the financial ladder. The ideals of the Planet Daivika were being destroyed slowly. All the representatives of Daivika planet working to stop the negative energies from spreading, were fighting a losing battle.

Not surprisingly, he and his able ministers found the cure to this plague in the Herbs of India, the country of our origin. The knowledge of herbs was passed down over the ages from the sages. The learned ones had landed on planet Earth many ages before the first known landing from planet Daivika. Where did the sages come from? Maybe they came from some other vastly knowledgeable planet that similarly cared for Ethics, Values and Principles. The knowledge of these herbs has now been passed down to the village heads of the many tribes that were being nurtured in the sanctuaries allocated by our ancestors. The herbs were encouraged to grow freely in such sanctuaries in order that the protected residents may benefit from the use of the same. Along-with the herbs, the village council was taught the healing powers of yoga.

Thus, the plague was controlled and King Unni Pushpakan Ambalavasi **(1805)** thought that it was time to recoup his energies. But he did not recoup from the injuries inflicted by the powerful Móguǐ de érzi. He was getting weaker. This was the moment that he abdicated his throne in favour of King Marangad Bhavathrāthan Daivikapad (1840). He made his son promise that the next in generation would continue to try to undo the negative energies that was affecting the minds of Nair Dvipa. But his son failed and so did his grandson King Perikamana Raman Namboothiripad 1880, and now the baton has come into my hands. Now that I am a Prince! Prince Akavoor Nabudiripad in the year 1919!

I had a promise to keep but failed. And it seems that my son Prince Cherusseri Namboodiri did everything within his means to study the possibility of harnessing hundred percent of our brain cells to then stop the growth of negative energies. He kept trying, but to no avail.

I have been suffering from a constant cough and congestion in the chest. The doctors termed it as Consumption, phthisis and the White Plague. I was moved to a separate room away from the rest and administered steam inhalation and was asked to drink hot water. But the racking cough was becoming worse every day.

Our Son Prince Cherusseri Namboodiri 1939

Our son, Prince Cherusseri Namboodiri had returned from his study in London to be able to understand 'Warfare & global Geo Politics' and hence be able to better protect our nation in future. We have placed our secret armies all over the world to discreetly assist friendly nations in their effort to maintain global stability in every sphere. We do not desire credit. But we shall do everything to maintain stability and balance.

Then the First World War, the Great War (1914 to November 1918), or the War to End All Wars, happened! It was a global war originating in Europe. Prince Cherusseri Namboodiri was around 26 years of age then but very mature and worldly-wise. He realized the importance of more than 70 million military personnel, including 60 million Europeans, being mobilized in one of the largest wars in history.

His friends who were commissioned Officers in the United Kingdom, invited him to join them. It was important to take a decision to fight evil forces rather than simply taking a politically correct decision.

My subjects refer to me as "His Highness, First Amongst the Rajas of Nair Dvipa, Lord of Princes, Great Prince over Princes, **King Akavoor Nabudiripad, the lord of Nair Dvipa".**

Prince Cherusseri Namboodiri was trained by British Defense forces both while in Nair Dvipa as well while he was studying in the UK. He was thus invited to join the British forces far above his friends by rank and is referred to as "His Royal Highness". His friends were captains whereas because he was trained by the British forces for many years, he joined as a full Colonel, and having sought our permission, he had given the British landing rights to protect the ocean waters from their enemy forces. A full Colonel by the age of 27 years of age! This was stupendous! By this time, we had improved upon, though not perfected on the steel encased missile technology. Prince Cherusseri Namboodiri placed two very large, long range missile launchers and personally used the same to blast a German ship from the waters using missile technology perfected on our land. We called this model the ND1.

Traders of Nair Dvipa were spread out all over the globe by then, and on the request of the Prince, they provided vital intelligence that strengthened the hands of the British. For his service to the Queens forces he had been awarded the MC in recognition of the performance of further acts of gallantry meriting the award.

Log of King Cherusseri Namboodiri, Nair Dvipa, English Month of December 1922

I am Cherusseri Namboodiri, of Nair Dvipa and became King since 1922. I am now 35 years of age.

My father died due to Consumption, or phthisis or what is also known as the White Plague, within a year of handing over the Kingdom to me. My mother died a few years later. She was treating my father while he was unwell and contracted the infection. I had met an Indian girl, Madhu, in Britain and had married her.

We have a son. Hanuman was born on 16th October 1927 and is a ball of energy when my parents were still alive.

My Royal cousins, inspite of willingly accepting the Royal Purse every month for the past so many ages, have displayed their frustration at not being given a chance to rule Nair Dvipa. I suggested a merit-based rule wherein all willing Royal family members form a core committee to select the next King. But each of them desired to be King without explaining what they desired to do once they sat on the throne. Being a King, they did not understand, desired a lot many sacrifices in life. They were now freely interacting with Pirates and the Diànlì jī'è de guójiā representatives.

Look at me! I could hardly ever give my wife nor my son much time. I was certain that Diànlì jī'è de guójiā would want to capture our lands. Our many power-hungry Royal family cousins had been creating a rift and foreign countries were egging them on even today. The country which had employed pirates to enrich their coffers and subsequently allowed them to retire in peace after having penalized them with a minor fine for their "minor" transgressions, was now power hungry and willing to go to all lengths to expand their geopolitical cum military footprints. I had to have friendly countries supporting me with military might when this was to happen. Geo political necessities thus required that I take sides when the second World War began and thus, I had to move all around the world making friends.

My wife never understood GEO POLITICS, nor the necessity for my effort in this direction. My parents had named me as King and I felt that they could protect my wife and child. But when I was leaving, I could sense the anger cum frustration in the eyes of my young wife. She was a free bird in London hence she hated the constraints of Nair Dvipa. Then when I revealed to her that I was going away without her, she blamed me for making her a mother even before she had the time to enjoy my company while touring the world.

"Take us with you", she had pleaded. "I promise that I shall never come in your way". But I knew if I took my wife and child along then, the fact that they would be under constant observation by the enemy and an easy target for kidnapping and threat, would restrain my movement and strategies. When she realized that her pleas were falling on deaf ears, she turned away to look out of the bedroom window that evening. The window looked out at the deep blue ocean waters and I could sense that her eyes had welled up with tears.

But I had a promise to keep. And so, I turned away towards my responsibilities and left my wife to deal with her emotions and loneliness!

King Unni Pushpakan Ambalavasi (1805) had let his guard down thinking that Móguĭ de érzi was a normal pirate. I cannot trust anybody to that point. I had to identify the den of the negative energies that had corrupted the minds of so many of Nair Dvipa citizens. I began my study of Móguĭ de érzi, dimensions and movement of energies from one time or space dimension to another. I was met with ridicule in scientific circles for having suggested the possibility of movement of energies between dimensions. Why go so far, to even mention that a superior race could have travelled from interstellar space to India, this possibility itself was a subject to be laughed at amongst many famous scientific minds.

My ancestors were from India. To the modern world, India was a Third World country of elephants and snake charmers and not capable of harboring knowledgeable people capable of creating technically superior places of worship. But I know for certain that the temples were created by my people. We created them because the people of earth were unable to use more than 10 percent of their brain cells to energize and bring about their own wellbeing. We had to do it for them. The sound energies that we could create within the temple premises could best be magnified towards Daivika Planet. The energies that we received from the Daivika Planet also came back on the same route.

We could thus create the correct sound waves and ensure rain, good crops and prosperity.

I discovered that there seemed to be a deliberate attempt of our ancestors to hide the fact that they, the extraterrestrial powers were at work in India. It was their modesty that is so missing today. I pointed at the temples strewn all over India, the fine cuts, the groves, nostril holes, eye sockets, machine finish symmetrical idols from the top of a single unbroken pillar till the bottom without any cracks or mismatch in size nor expression. I pointed at marble idols with chiseled polish finish that would require the most expensive of tools in modern technology available today. I pointed at the link of the direction of the deity to the stars above, and most scientists waved it away with "the land of many Gods had cheap labor". When I asked them why Enormous stones have been chiseled and stacked together like a jigsaw puzzle outside the old Inca capital of Cusco, they simply shrugged. How did the NASCA Lines come about and why would anybody labour to attract attention from the skies? Why on a high and dry plateau some 200 miles southeast of Lima, more than 800 long, straight white lines are etched into the Peruvian desert, seemingly at random. Joining them are 300 geometric shapes and 70 figures of animals, including a spider, monkey, and hummingbird. How is it that during a comparatively technologically backward period the Great Pyramid were made of millions of precisely hewn stones weighing at least two tons each. Even with today's cranes and other construction equipment, building a pyramid as big as that of Pharaoh Khufu would be a formidable challenge.

How is it that a huge circle of stones, some weighing as much as 50 tons, sits in the English countryside outside Salisbury? Carved from stone, the nearly 900 human figures of Easter Island are sprinkled along the flanks of the island's extinct volcanoes. The figures average 13 feet tall, weigh 14 tons each and appear to have been chiseled from the soft volcanic tuff found in the Rano Raraku quarry which is far away.

When most qualified and well-read scientists laughed away at all above as acts of whimsical artists, I found it futile to get them to assist me in the great quest to bring back my people from the land of muddled minds. And so, I concentrated in protecting what remained. To do so, I had to learn about the military strategy of "influencing the minds of ordinary residents and the families of military personnel of enemy nations" from the most modern military forces and thus be able to analyze the antidote.

The 2ⁿᵈ World War did not begin until May 1940, as Britain and France were involved in a Phony War between Germany and the Franco-British alliance. The Phony war ended with the Battle of France where Germany invaded Benelux and subsequently France, which forced British troops to escape from Dunkirk. Our secret Nair Dvipa intelligence wing plus army participated in Dunkirk and many died although this fact remains undocumented. My army and I were in the Middle East and North Africa. In 1941, war spread to the Middle East and North Africa as well as the East African Campaign. My countrymen fought alongside the British there too. The United States officially joined the war in December 1941 after the Japanese Attack on Pearl Harbor. We were in Pearl Harbor to assist the Americans though this fact too remains undocumented. My army and I were in El Alamein to secretly assist the British. In 1942, British forces assisted by forces from Nair Dvipa, under Lieutenant General Bernard Montgomery defeated the Axis forces of General Erwin Rommel in the Second Battle of El Alamein, which marked a major turning point in the Western Desert Campaign and the North African Campaign.

Nair Dvipa agents who were resident all over the world had helped in providing relevant information to the Allies for the war effort specially relating to plans & movements by the AXIS. I had to travel globally to co-ordinate the effort. This total effort of intelligence gathering and dissipation of false information to the AXIS, though not acknowledged subsequently by the Allies in Historical battle records, allowed for Battle strategy modifications which proved critical to Allied success in North Africa. Victory for the Allies in this campaign immediately led to the Italian Campaign, which culminated in the downfall of the fascist government in Italy and the elimination of Germany's main European ally.

It was 1937 and I was fifty years of age. I was amid supervising the French support when I received news of my wife's death from Tuberculosis due to depression. Yet it was the very same infection that had affected my parents. I felt guilty and yet I did not have the time to mourn. My son was alone and he was hardly ten years of age. He needed the love of a mother. Further, we had to doubly ensure that the infection that had felled his mother and grandparents did not get at him. No Governess could have taken up such a role. I needed somebody who would settle down permanently at Nair Dvipa. I could only think of the person I trusted the most during my work over all these years and that was Gertrude Wallace, my Executive Assistant cum Secretary. So, I married her at the age of 50 and sent her back to Nair Dvipa.

The war could begin any day due to many countries jointly fighting for what was right. The British Queen had me Knighted. When I was welcomed into the dining room of the Palace after the ceremony, they referred to me as "His Highness, First Amongst the Rajas of Nair Dvipa, Lord of Princes, Great Prince over Princes, Lieutenant-General Sir Cherusseri Namboodiri, Knight Grand Commander of the Order of the Star of Nair Dvipa, Grand Commander of the Order Nair Dvipa, Maharaja of Nair Dvipa". I heard people whispering amongst themselves, "Where is this so-called Nair Dvipa located?" and the reply being whispered, "somewhere near Australia or maybe the Polynesian islands?". Thankfully, nobody knew where we were located. If only they knew that Nair Dvipa was nearly half the size of Australia with fertile land, had no desert land such as Australia possessed, but had undulating hills, lush green jungles. And most importantly, they did not know about the treasure of seven full ships, because if they did, then, treasure hunters would have flocked our shores by undesired numbers.

Gertrude Wallace was known to be efficient and whenever she took on an assignment, she did it well. She believed in systems, rules, efficiency and clockwork operations, like me. But Hanuman, who had accepted the love and discipline of his first mother refused to accept his second mother and subsequently rebelled against her discipline.

I had no powers like that which my grandfather had. Hence, I had urged Gertrude to try and generate her own powers. She has been meditating at the temples of our ancestors and after several years she seemed to be absorbing a strange power that any blood relative could have absorbed in a day. She has committed on using the same for the good of Nair Dvipa and to pass on the throne to our heirs.

She had a glazed expression on her face one day when she predicted many years of gloom for the Royal family in Nair Dvipa.

I was out of Nair Dvipa for many years and not due back for many days. Hence, I could do nothing but trust my Ministers to do their best to try and keep things in order.

By then, education was compulsory for past so many years hence we had eighty percent literacy. Nair Dvipa was a Hindu state but all religions were welcome and there was no discrimination. The same Rules and laws were applicable to all religions. Each High-rise residential building has necessarily to have a playground big enough for all residents. If the residents numbered three hundred couples or more then the park had to be big enough for football, cricket, jogging, swing and slide etc. Each flat had to have a servant quarter for a family of four. Each servant family had to be paid a minimum salary prescribed by the Government, a scooter if not a second-hand car. Education was free for the unemployed and the retired, as also their children and grandchildren provided that, they were below the minimum income bracket. Hence most children of servants received free education and could chose a different profession. Cast or religion had no role in admissions, nor on Job Quota. Quotas were set aside for tuitions to be provided to the financially disadvantaged including free tuitions after school hours or after work hour's time. Educational institutions had to be accredited and were providing education in English, Hindi, Malayalam, Kannada, Tamil, Telegu, Marathi, Bengali, Bhojpuri, and many more languages. English, Hindi, and Malayalam were compulsory languages. Hospitals provided the most modern health care systems with our doctors being invited to give talks on recent discoveries and research related subjects at foreign venues. Alternative medicine was openly practiced provided that the individual or group of individuals had the license to do so from the relevant authorities. The zoos had the finest of healthy animals from all over the world with an environment inside cages that would be as close to their natural habitat as possible.

Health services was free for the unemployed and the retired, provided that, they were below the minimum income bracket. Rations were free for the handicapped, the unemployed and the retired, provided that, they were below the minimum income bracket. Underground Metro Lines and stations crisscrossed to link important cities and towns. There were 150 stations and its total route length was 200 kilometers. The system was mostly underground, with the deepest section 80 meters underground at the Shraddhanjally Metro station, one of the world's deepest during the year 1945. Roads, by-lanes and pedestrians paths were planned far in advance being part of city planning and the population could grow only within these pre-marked pockets. Industrial areas too had preplanned roads, railways, river ports and the airport alongside each such facility to allow ease of doing business. There was a special 'Career Planning Ministry' which looked after all ages and studied the personality, the hobbies, the strong points of each numbered citizen. We noticed that though qualification may be the same, the career path of two different individuals may be different. The candidate would only be happy and satisfied provided the individual chose his career to be based on that subject on which he had spent the maximum hours of the day happily and without being forced. We even encouraged a Private Sector and Defense Services partnership wherein every Defense officer is compulsorily attached to the Private sector for the last four to five years prior to his retirement. This Private-Defense partnership was born when we realized that honest Officers suddenly took to corruption when they realized that their retirement was due and that their children were not yet settled. This partnership allowed the Defense Officer to adjust with the obvious cultural shock and feel secure about his future source of income to look after family expenses especially where the children are yet to be settled and where the Officer continued to bear several responsibilities. We also brought in a blanket Pension scheme for all the Departments that came under the Government of Nair Dvipa. For example, the Police and the Nair Dvipa Bureau of Investigation as well as the Nair Dvipa Research and Analysis wing. Earlier our agents who spied on our behalf were not financially protected if they got caught in enemy lines during any assignment. Now, we showed them off to be employees of any one or other Govt Department and gave their family members the same amount of salary after his being caught, that he would have got were he to be working in Nair Dvipa.

However, a blanket rule for all Government departments that had created a furore but was reluctantly accepted, was where the Pension Department insisted on an "All assignments Completed till date" certificate. If the files allocated to that specific officer while he was on duty was not executed by him within specified time periods then such pensions were halved or cancelled.

The officer could return to his old office and complete the last allocated tasks before being finally released. Further, if there were complaints of corruption, intentional delay in processing of files or actioning per given instructions without justified reason then the Officer or Clerk concerned was asked to appear for an interview and explain his cause for action or inaction. This allowed honest Officers to continue to remain honest today compared to the past when honest officers or clerks got involved in shady deals near the time of their retirement to meet pending financial responsibilities.

My grandfather had already brought in a healthy democracy which encouraged healthy discussions and debates. If any one individual displayed a desire to serve his community and has executed a minimum of two or more projects successfully in or around his area of residence, which has benefitted the local populace, then, he becomes eligible for being sponsored by the Government for standing for elections. His total resume, listing his past achievements, are listed out on line and potential voters get to know his achievements. Achievements were described as bringing about solutions rather than stopping work or stopping progress. Leaders who thwart progress or work were arrested. Hence the democratic process allowed even the farmer to get elected to represent his people. And these farmers sat next to the richest on the land and made growth and development related decisions. Our Royal cousins thus had the right to stand for elections.

Mogui's negative energy had permeated the weak, the underconfident and malleable minds from the bottom to the top rung of Nair Dvipa society. Dirty money began to influence the elections. There were loop holes in our Election Rules & Process. Loop holes that permitted marriage of a Nair Dvipa citizen with any foreign individual, and then granting of citizenship within two years to that foreigner. Further, as per law, any citizen who showed local level development could stand for elections. Hence foreigners began to stand for elections after they became citizens. The strong citizens who desired the good of Nair Dvipa never voted for such unknown foreigners and thus were not affected. But the poor were influenced with money. Naturally because the Election Rules allowed it to do so, anti-Nair Dvipa forces sponsored by the country Diànlì ji'è de guójia swept into the Parliament of Nair Dvipa. Many attempts were made in the name of 'Democracy' to tarnish the image of the

Royalty and they succeeded. The rule of law was cast aside that mandated the requirement of the King's signature on the results, in the absence of which a caretaker Government appointed by the Royal family was to run the country.

Gradually what Mogui had promised, was happening! Normal human to human skirmishes happened all over the world. But many Nair Dvipa Media including the Press deliberately spoke up about one religion attacking another religion. This began to create divisions. The Media showed images of supposed discrimination in favour of one religion against another. This began to create further divisions. Investments from rich nations and industrialists do not come about very easily despite the best effort. The supporters of Diànlì ji'è de guójia took advantage of the global financial crisis and began to blame the "Lethargy on the part of the Royalty leading to lack of economic recovery". Media showed images of vagabonds and beggars to prove their point.

Strangers who had become citizens very recently began to demand quotas in educational institutions and for Government Jobs. They began to pay big money to government officials to change land records on the survey maps to show their name in place of the original owner. They stood in front of large crowds that they had sponsored and blocked normal flow of traffic to enforce their unreasonable demands. The newspapers showed "signs of disenchantment". The ex-students of the country Diànlì ji'è de guójia who had squeezed into Nair Dvipa schools and colleges, now brainwashed the new students to rise against "Dictatorship, the oppression of the poor and the downtrodden of society". The very same ex-students began NGOs to brainwash the minds of the rural mass and then sponsored armed uprisings. Ex-students of Diànlì ji'è de guójia who had joined and risen in the ranks of the media including the Print Media companies, now spoke up against our own Defense Forces and supposed atrocities by the Police Forces. But the moment any news relating to atrocities being committed in Diànlì ji'è de guójiā were reported by the foreign media, the media of Nair Dvipa soft pedaled such news relating to such "internal matters" of a foreign nation. Some Nair Dvipa citizens who desired to sell books recently written by them, shamelessly spoke about the "stress being unfairly put on the helpless Pirates & poor Dacoits cum murderers of Diànlì jî'è de guójiā by the police the Nair Dvipa, the Intelligence wing as well as the Nair Dvipa Defense forces".

The Administrative Services realized too late that the Diànlì ji'è de guójia sponsored movement had taken control over the Media, the Courts and the Intelligentsia.

When the war ended in September 1945, I was awarded the Victoria Cross (VC), a military decoration for the valor "in the face of the enemy". It was normally given to the members of armed forces of some Commonwealth countries. But because I had pledged my country's forces for the cause of Great Britain, an exception was made in our case.

In 1945, I was 58 years of age and my son Hanuman was 18 years of age.

I came back to Nair Dvipa around this time. My son was already a teenager by this time and a guaranteed rebel. I had so many challenges. He was one of them now. Running a country that had gone out of hand was now becoming impossible. To stop further damage, all intended investments by Conglomerates from Diànlì jī'è de guójiā were refused entry because they offered to come in with a "do it or die" condition. The condition being that whatever land was allotted or rented out to such companies from Diànlì ji'è de guójia automatically belonged to Diànlì jī'è de guójiā.

Yet Diànlì ji'è de guójia sponsored candidates in the press, police, and the legal fraternity moved up the ladder, promoted by their corrupt anti national seniors, to control development related decisions. Sabotage of all essential services increased in intensity. Came the time for any election and suddenly banks began to be looted all over Nair Dvipa. It was obvious that terrorists holed up within Nair Dvipa needed operating funds.

It was around the time that railway lines were being stolen and big accidents occurred that my son began to stay away from home for brief periods of time and refused to explain his absence. While he silently had his breakfast, his step mother would gently keep the newspaper that detailed the Nair Dvipa political mess thinking that he would take interest in helping repair the situation. But he too had gone out of our control! Simply to spite his new mother he would pick up the newspaper and throw it into the dust bin without even reading a line. He began to escape his security personnel and mingle with the Nair Dvipa crowd like a commoner. We were very worried especially because too many threats of kidnapping and murder were coming in everyday inspite of our best intelligence officers secretly observing the post offices. We were worried whether he would go out with the wrong girls or if he was being sold drugs by the drug mafia.

Anti-Social Activities to incite religious sentiments and thus embarrass the Pro Nair Dvipa officials in the Government increased by leaps and bounds. And drugs! Opium was being pumped into Nair Dvipa, the schools and colleges at throw away prices! Thus, Raids were conducted, arrests were ensured. Then the Lower Courts and High Courts began to challenge the arrest of genuine criminals, including proven antisocial elements and ensured their bail based on "lack of ample evidence". Soon anti nationals began to be similarly released as their "guilt could not be proven beyond doubt". Interestingly, the media lauded the effort of such judges for having "protected the innocent and righteous" and "decisions in the favour of the nation and justice"!

I was going crazy! My Ministers were going crazy! It was during these difficult times that my son came back one day from his sudden outings with a satchel slung from his shoulders. He looked dreamy eyed and tired out. As if he had not slept for many days. Either that or he was on drugs! One of the maids suggested we check his bag for drugs and my love for my son and fear of losing him to drugs made me rush into his room and thunder an explanation for his sunken eyes. "Are you on drugs?!" I asked. He was tired but my eighteen-year-old son glared back at me and refused to answer.

"Give me your bag!" I thundered.

"Why?", he asked.

I snatched the bag away from his teenaged hands and threw the contents on the bed.

"This is my room and my bag!" he growled.

"I am the King and this Palace is mine! Everything under this roof and on this island belongs to the King. Do you understand?" I growled.

I rummaged through his personal goods and found no drugs.

He was standing with his arms folded on his chest. His breathing was heavy because of the emotions that were welling up and then his tears appeared but he did not speak a word. Like his mother, he turned to face the window that looked out at the deep blue ocean and away from me, forever!

By early the next morning, he had taken a fisherman's boat and was gone! He travelled on a leaky fisherman's motor boat, all alone, to India and never came back! I had lost my son! I had lost my only child!

I sent out our best men to protect him at any cost but without letting him know that we knew his whereabouts.

But that was not the last painful spear in my heart.

Even while I was trying to trace my son, nearly every institution on Nair Dvipa spoke up against the Royal family and its inept management of Nair Dvipa affairs subsequent to the Recession. Diànlì ji'è de guójia had encircled us from every direction by offering high technology ships, submarines, bridges, four to six lane highways, high speed latest technology trains to comparatively poor nations against projects loans that the recipient countries could never repay. This thereby guaranteeing total ownership of that part of land in our neighbouring countries. Diànlì ji'è de guójia now threatened us by blocking our maritime routes and supply routes to our own land if war were to break out with them. They would do the same, if we supported their bigger enemies. Further, unknown to us, they had been grooming media personnel from the child's school days within Nair Dvipa to become their supporters by the time the child became an adult. Similarly, they had been grooming and handholding lawyers right upto our Supreme Courts. The Anti Nair Dvipa Media was so deeply entrenched that our every decision to invest in defense equipment was challenged and our every brave decision to make a Government to Government decision to invest in Defense related equipment was pointed out to be "full of corruption". Skirmishes with our neighbouring island increased and the media blasted the Nair Dvipa Defense for tormenting the helpless, innocent neighbouring island residents. Every time a corrupt man was caught and produced in court, the press, the Television and the Courts would prove him to be the most innocent amongst all in Nair Dvipa.

This torrential rain of praise and good words acted as influencers and hence, anti Nair Dvipa Judges rose faster than the rest to finally enter the sanctum of the Supreme Court. I could do nothing and neither could my closest confidantes.

And it was when two senior lawyers of the Supreme Court suddenly raised the bogie of "the King and his Kingdom's forces putting a spanner in the efficient functioning of the highest court of the country" that it became obvious that Mogui's negative forces had pushed the rot of Anti Nationals right up to the throat of the nation. That the nation was under serious threat from within was an understatement of the day.

I was arrested, the King himself, for instigating unrest and no court allowed my release for five full years. But my trusted Lieutenant kept in touch with me and I kept getting information about Hanuman and his wellbeing.

It was around that time that Hanuman, who was found to be safe and working as a normal citizen with the Indian Government, refused to respond to the title of Grand Commander of the Defense Forces of Nair Dvipa, Prince Hanuman Daivika, of Nair Dvipa. He had however insisted that the emissary paid to befriend my son, refer to him by his mother's family name, Bagaria. He calls himself Pawandas Hanuman Bagaria of India today. He insisted on renouncing his royalty and citizenship of this country of birth because, he hated me and this royalty for all the reasons that his eyes had spoken about when I was checking his bag for drugs that evening. How can I forget the tears that had welled up in his teenaged eyes!

I so wanted to embrace him in my arms then. He was my son. But that part of me which was a King of this land today, facing the challenge of negative forces, gave priority to maintaining a dignified distance and a poised exterior with a normal emotional teenaged child, while all he wanted was a bit of love. I had a duty, that of stopping Mogui's negative energy from growing any further and then cleansing the total system step by step down to the grassroot level. But I had failed my father till date. Now I realize that I had failed my son too.

In the meanwhile, Fifty-five percent of the Parliament voted to end the system of Royalty. I was not keeping well in prison and my lawyers based out of London had advised that I do not sign on the document that permitted the dissolution of the Royal family. The pro foreign country forces decided, with the help of the Nair Dvipa lower courts, that my signature was not necessary. Prior to this, suddenly, a spate of kidnapping of the children or near relatives of loyalists, our Defense and Police Officers began to happen. Honeytraps and bribes to loyalists multiplied. The Nair Dvipa Intelligence wing were reporting about huge monies coming in from Mogui's adopted country every day. Anti-Social elements romped the streets with impunity. The pro Royalty candidates who desired to submit their candidature with the Nair Dvipa Election Commissioner were threatened and manhandled. Children of such potential candidates were warned while coming home from school or college or from work. "Tell your Papa that if he stands for elections then you will get raped and will never be seen again!"

Complaints went to the Chief Election Commissioner. He extended the date for receiving of such nominations. Mogui's lawyers and goons threatened the Commissioner with dire consequences if he dared to continue to extend the dates. The commissioner was due to retire within a few years and settle down in a bungalow in that area. He immediately announced cancellation of the decision to extend the date for receiving applications. The members who wanted to vote for continuation of the old system of Royalty were blackmailed or roughed up and stopped from leaving their homes or entering the parliament. Many were threatened with dire consequences if they dared to speak up in favour of the King and Royalty. The Press branded them as weak-minded opportunists, surviving on the largesse of the supposedly corrupt Royals.

Interestingly the police stood as silent witness and were willing to face the threat of termination rather than face certain death in the hands of this Mafia groomed and financed by Diànlì ji'è de guójia. Media that was friendly to the country of Diànlì ji'è de guójia began to spout venom against the 'Pro Royal' citizens. Loyalists residing all around the country began to feel confused and in fact ashamed about the Royalty that had nurtured Nair Dvipa to this point of all-round development. As the media was their only source of information and the same media spoke only of the atrocities being committed by the King and his henchmen, they were naturally confused. Thus, the media played a big role in changing the opinion of the mass against the King and Royalty. Now the media could not be silenced in a single day. Mobile phone messages were now being designed by a special Defense team of Diànlì ji'è de guójia and these messages began to appear on every Mobile phone in Nair Dvipa. These messages spoke about the only country that could save the citizens of Nair Dvipa and that was - Diànlì ji'è de guójia. To ensure that the takeover of pro Diànlì ji'è de guójia forces was smooth Diànlì ji'è de guójia was sending "consultants & observers" to

Nair Dvipa to provide all assistance during the election process to ensure that "true democracy was restored". A few senior Government Officials from Diànlì ji'è de guójia had been flying in and flying out frequently over the last few months. A compromise was sought between loyalists and the anti-establishment who were obviously guided and sponsored by Diànlì ji'è de guójia. The opposition wanted the Royalty out at any cost. Thus, they were willing to make false commitments of sacrifice. Sacrifices which the Diànlì ji'è de guójia group assured themselves was temporary, were mutually agreed upon. The Loyalists group had managed to negotiate a deal and the Anti-establishment graciously offered to allow the royals to retain the Palace and this part of Nair Dvipa where the tribals reside. Further, the Loyalists had made them agree to hand out a sustenance fee until the end of four more generations. Lastly, we could continue to claim and use our titles but we had no right over the administration and finances of the country any longer. No mention was made of the hidden wealth in any document. The loyalists won the majority votes by getting 49 percent voting in favour of the Royal family. The Anti Royals got 40 percent votes. But the independents happened to be the new citizens of Nair Dvipa who had been citizens of Diànlì ji'è de guójia just a few years earlier to that. The independents won 11% votes and they offered to join hands with the Anti Royals. Thus, they had a total of 51 percent votes. Over all these many years, some bad elements and spoilt children from amongst the disgruntled Royal Family cousins were frequently involved in drunken brawls, forcibly taking away girls from the streets or bars, bullying and showing off their position in Banks, at Restaurants, at Hotels and places of worship. The police were often told to release them after heavy monetary transfers happened every time. The courts too were financially coerced to take a lenient decision in favour of the spoilt Royal cousins. As a result, the Royal family in the Golden Palace suffered a severe blow to their reputation due to such irresponsible cousins and naturally, the popularity with the vote banks went plummeting down. The political conditions were such, that, the arrest of any one such spoilt Royal Cousins would have permitted certain foreign countries to scream about "injustice to democracy". The Anti Royals thus came to power. Fortunately, a lot may citizens of Nair Dvipa may not have liked the Royal family but they loved their country of birth Nair Dvipa and the systems that existed allowing equality, a comfortable, secure and safe existence, especially for the woman.

My son has refused to understand the seriousness of the situation and all our effort seems futile.

The Royalty is over. I remain in prison. The Anti Royals voted to abolish Royalty. They won this resolution by a thin majority. But they did not need my signature, they said.

I end this noting with a sad heart today. I regret not having hugged my son that day. Prince Hanuman Namboothiri, nee Prince Pawandas Hanuman Bagaria of Nair Dvipa refuses to accept any of our letters. The last messenger was told that he had nothing to do with us.

Signed
King Cherusseri Namboodiri,
Nair Dvipa

Sudhir had this shocked expression on his face at this very moment. Could his father Pawandas Bagaria be actually 'Prince Pawandas Hanuman Bagaria'!

Was his father the same King Pawandas Hanuman Bagaria who had refused his throne?! His father!

If this was correct then, that made him a Prince!

A Prince of a non-existent Kingdom but Prince all the same! Prince Sudhir Bagaria! It sounded good!

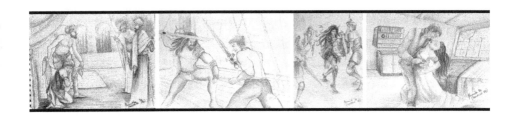

Chapter 13

Sudhir Meets Lost Relatives

Meeting Ancient People

A voice spoke up just then – "There is a slight correction needed in your thought process my child".

Sudhir jumped out of the chair and tried to protect himself!

"Do not worry my child! I shall not hurt you ever", the gentle female voice reassured him. "After your father refused to accept the throne within the mandatory thirty-six-year period, you are automatically, the new King! You are King Sudhir Bagaria nee Daivam Rajam Sudhir Namboodiri, of the Kingdom of Nair Dvipa!"

Sudhir looked all around him and requested – "Would you like to show yourself please?"

A European lady, wearing the attire of a Queen appeared in front of him. The very same lady who was at the cave entrance and the very same lady in the painting in the corridor of the grand palace!

Sudhir rushed to stand up and bowed by instinct, "Ahh Grandmother Gertrude Wallace! It is my honor!"

Queen Gertrude Wallace rushed to embrace Sudhir in a bear hug and cooed, "Your grandmothers and your grandfather wanted to hear the pitter patter of your little feet for so many years. So what, if your steps are belated. It was your first grandmother who suggested that I use my powers to send out my brain waves all over the world, hoping that you would receive it and come to us whenever you may be free. Your dreams were created by us! We kept sending to you many visions of your great palace and its wonderful people. When you did arrive finally in that disheveled state, we thought we were saving a marooned sailor. Then we fell in love with you when you hugged us in the hall way! But we did not know that you were our own blood until later!"

"You could feel my hug?" Sudhir asked with a shocked expression.

"Of course, my darling!" she replied with warmth, "even portraits have a life of its own. It was that hug that told us you were a wonderful human being. But the fact that our powers flowed into you so easily when you asked for the same, now that fact, removed all doubts if any that you were one of us. Because only immediate blood relatives can absorb that tremendous amount of energy within the split second that you did".

Two more figures appeared in front of him just then, in a flash!

"Ahh Grandfather! Daivam King Cherusseri Namboodiri of Nair Dvipa", so saying Sudhir bowed in front of the old King.

"Grandmother Queen Madhu Bagaria of Nair Dvipa", so saying Sudhir bowed in front of the dark-complexioned Indian Queen who stood smiling opposite him.

Instead of bowing in return, they both rushed forward and gave him a bear hug. And then they just did not want to let go of him!

"I am the late King Cherusseri Namboodiri of Nair Dvipa my child. We three survive in spirit form and can be seen by only those who we wish should see us. My second wife made this possible for the three of us aided by the special powers she had absorbed while meditating in the temples.

You are the King now! We are all spirits with special powers. I died in prison waiting for my son, but ohh, you have finally come my grandson! You have finally come", the old King kept repeating in a voice full of emotion while his Indian Queen wept out of happiness. "It would be a pleasure to see a kind man such as yourself sitting on the pure golden throne studded with diamonds, rubies and emeralds, and take control of your Kingdom!"

Sudhir had struggled throughout his life and he had earned every penny through back breaking work. Oh – he knew how much he valued precious money! But a pure golden throne studded with diamonds, rubies and emeralds?!! He did not need a kingdom, he just needed that gold, the diamonds, the rubies, the emeralds and any more treasure that can come into his hands! Wow! Ohh wow!

His grandparents could read his mind and were laughing away because they were already in love with him. Their darling grandson was craving for one single throne whereas the wealth of Nair Dvipa was his own!

Queen Wallace stepped forward and putting her head back to face the skies, she pointed her fingers at Sudhir mumbling "Vajra! Shakti olukaṭṭe! Vajra! Vajra! Vajra!"

A bolt of lightning struck the top of the hill just then, travelled down the body of the hill and this stream of energy flowed through her fingers into Sudhir's body! He immediately fell on his knees grimacing in pain. His head was once again on fire and he grabbed his head with both his hands. Very slowly, the pain reduced. His head had cleared. His eyes were red and glowing! His hair stood up like strands of threads and swaying! He felt powerful!

A roar arose from his chest – "Arouuuuuuhhhhhaaah!"

He looked up to see that Late King Cherusseri Namboodiri, late Queen Madhu Bagaria, and late Queen Gertrude Wallace were looking at him with pride and a new respect. "That energy bolt can light up a city and yet you absorbed it within a second! Your genes allowed you to do so" explained late Queen Madhu Bagaria. "But we are confident that you shall not misuse your power!"

"And what about the famed treasure of the five full ships?" asked Sudhir.

Once again, the grand parents had a good laugh because their darling grandson wanted to discuss about just five full ships!

"None of us know where the treasure has been hidden away by our ancestors", the late Kind replied seriously. "Móguĭ de érzi has offered to release the people of Nair Dvipa in exchange for this famed wealth. Further, he insists that he had won a war against our ancestor and forcibly occupied a corner of Nair Dvipa two centuries back. That is nonsense. One cannot enter anybody's beachfront and claim it as his own. His evil forces demand that we recognize that land to be theirs and hand back part of a strategically located land which we occupy today. That strategically located land is part of an old deep-sea landing dock for large ships that had been used by the British and our combined Naval force during the second world war and now to be also used for submarines. However, it is for you to use your wisdom and experience at man management skills to settle this dispute".

"How do I begin?" asked Sudhir

"Please show us how you can disguise yourself", suggested the late King

"How do I do that?" asked Sudhir

"Instruct your mind to give you the power to change your physical form", suggested the late King

Sudhir's neck bent backwards and his head went back and looked towards the skies, "Give me the power to look like the late King Shri Unni Pushpakan Ambalavasi", Sudhir commanded his mind, without speaking aloud.

Suddenly, Sudhir's whole body morphed into that of the late King Shri Unni Pushpakan Ambalavasi! Sudhir looked at himself in the mirror and saw a distinguished, tall, neatly combed King in Regal dress. When he spoke, his voice sounded dignified and polished. "How do I look my son?", Sudhir asked Late King Cherusseri Namboodiri.

On the spot, Late King Cherusseri Namboodiri, late Queen Madhu Bagaria, and late Queen Gertrude Wallace went down on their knees and bowed in front of him. Sudhir realized the profound effect that his appearance had over them.

"Normal look", he told himself and he morphed back to his true self, his hair came down to his own unkept style. His blood shot eyes became normal.

Late King Cherusseri Namboodiri, late Queen Madhu Bagaria, and late Queen Gertrude Wallace were yet to recover from the speed with which Sudhir was able to transform himself. Their expressions of awe were but obvious!

"Pleasantly shocking!" expressed Queen Madhu Bagaria while exhaling.

"Wow! We never realized that you were so born to be powerful!" expressed Queen Gertrude Wallace with genuine respect.

"I have travelled all over the world. Never before have I seen so much power as I saw with mine own eyes today!" expressed King Cherusseri Namboodiri. He too was holding his breath all this while. "We are so very proud to be your grandparents! However, you need power multiplied a hundred times to better Mogui. You need to plan against the guile and unexpected acts of back stabbing which makes Móguǐ de érzi so dangerous. He enters your mind or the minds of your loved ones. He rarely fires straight. He makes his energy missiles bounce off three different clouds or objects or people before they follow your heat signal and hit you. And he never ever lets out less than three missiles at one time, all from different directions and all of them bouncing off various objects, before they search out your heat signal and hit you. He multiplies his body many times and then you do not know which is the real Móguǐ de érzi. Who do you hit? He throws huge hundred to two hundred-ton boulders at people you love and when you race to stop that boulder, he throws a two-hundred-ton boulder in the opposite direction, at a group of villages that you desire to protect. He feigns to attack at one spot and then actually attacks at a totally unexpected spot. He befriends your enemies and empowers to fight and weaken you. When one dies then another takes over. He attacks when you have tired out. His bag of guile is brimming with the unexpected. Therefore, look at both his hands, his feet and his eyes".

"But I do not have an army nor the ammunition!" argued Sudhir, having brushed his body with his palm.

"You have the tribe that you stay with my son. They are all the army you need", replied late King Cherusseri Namboodiri. "They do not know how to protect themselves from the modern world. Train them. Begin with them".

"Hmmm", thought Sudhir, "I have had to begin from scratch every time over the past so many years!"

Queen Madhu Bagaria looked fondly at her grandson and said, "You need power multiplied a hundred times to battle Mogui. Practice all your available power to the extreme. Know your true self, inside you, that has been unfortunately hidden from the world all these many years. And your wisdom and tenacity shall prevail my son!" assured late King Cherusseri Namboodiri of Nair Dvipa in a doting grandfatherly tone. His two wives nodded in approval with a warm smile on their face.

Sudhir Exits from the Cave of Files

Sudhir finally emerged from within the cave and found to his surprise, little Mobi waiting for him immediately outside the cave with folded legs, all alone. "I missed you!" Mobi moaned with his arms extended towards Sudhir.

His adopted father picked him up in his arms, then to his shoulders, raised Mobi's right hand to yell – "Mahua Minsaw! Mahua Minsaw!", meaning the 'good God'. Little Mobi did not understand what was happening. "Mahua Minsaw! "he peeped in his loudest little voice with both his hands raised. But the tribe's men were not yet willing to accept the concept of a "Good God" within the cave. They roared in approval and obvious admiration for this 'Agniaw Mrignaw Minsaw' who had beaten the 'Howva Minsaw', the "Bad or Evil God".

They had all heard him roar while Sudhir was in the cave and all of them were certain that someone had died there in the cave right then. Naturally if he came out alive then it had to be the 'Howva Minsaw', the "Bad or Evil God" who had died inside.

They surrounded him with "Yippie" and "Aii Yai Yah yah yah" with their spears held high in the air and took turns to inspect his body for injuries if any. Amongst these tribesmen, battle scars were intentionally maintained and displayed to prove bravery. Many were disappointed to see no injuries to prove victory in-spite of supposedly ferocious battle, with a monster inside the cave. But Sudhir could see that the witch doctor had this incredulous expression on his face. He came forward to greet Sudhir with grudging respect and this – "how did you do it?" expression.

Sudhir accepted his extended hand of truce with a warm handshake, but replied his unasked question with a smile that said – "It is a long story brother!"

Mobi's Wild Cub Returns to Attack Yellow Strangers

The cub now named hence known as Mahili, came back with a male panther and began to loiter around the villages. Mahili became everybody's pet and remained a pampered full-grown black female panther that sauntered into one hut then another with no qualms and no fear. But like all wild animals, it would often vanish into the forests with the other panther. And it would return every time with small prey that it would place at the feet of Mobi. Mobi would shake his pet's paw as one would congratulate another hunting partner, then pretend to have a small bite of the prey and finally with much pretentious licking and wiping of lips, return the prey to the bemused panther to be consumed.

One day Mobi accompanied a big group of young hunters and Mahili the female panther followed. Mahili was being a bit too playful and lagged the rest of the group. It would chomp on a tree branch and shake it like a rag doll. It would chase a rabbit to its hole or flush out some birds from a nearby bush. If little Mahili lost sight of Mobi then it would begin to "Youwwrr" in distress. Mobi fell back too to ensure that the cub did not get lost in the wilderness.

The rest of the group had in their enthusiasm to hunt game, gone far ahead. They had crossed the protection line, which was forbidden by the elders, and they did not realize the same. It was during one of these playful moments of the panther scampering upto a high branch of one of the trees and with Mobi following her up to the top, that Mobi heard the "boom boom" sound, the sound of the boom boom sticks being used by the yellow complexioned strangers visiting outside the protected forest. "Run Mobi! Run back home!" his companions screamed in terror from far ahead. Both Mahili and Mobi dived behind a heavy bush of leaves up within the top branches. The male panther vanished. They watched in horror as many strong yellow complexioned strangers dragged away his companions in the distance. The strangers began to fire into every bush to flush out hidden tribals. Two jumped out of a bush, and tried to make a run for it but were promptly captured with nets and dragged away. Mahili growled, rushed down branch to branch and then away inspite of Mobi whispering desperately for it to return. Mahili had vanished into the jungle.

Suddenly a black panther jumped out of some bushes close to where the rest of the tribe had been captured and attacked one of the yellow strangers who was holding onto Jboko a teenaged tribal, and the stranger screamed in terror even while firing his boom boom sticks – "Boom Boom!" but in a totally different direction. But that panther was too quick for them. It pounced at one man's chest to dig her claws deep and then jumped onto another man's shoulders and the claws of her hind legs dug in painfully deep, he nipped onto the calf muscles of yet another yelping stranger. In short – pandemonium ensued. Yellow strangers began to run helter skelter leaving behind their boom sticks and camping material in the backpacks.

"Boom Boom Boom!" they fired in every direction but the male panther and Mahili now went into action. She jumped down from a tree onto the shoulders of a stranger, gave his scalp a swipe, taking off a big chunk of hair from his head. The stranger screamed and Mahili vanished to reappear from a totally different bush to nip the arms of the man holding another boom boom stick. He let go of the stick in terror, screamed and ran towards the shore where his boat was waiting for him and his terrified companions.

Mobi and the rest of the young boys rushed back to the village but after collecting all the boom boom sticks and back packs left behind by the strangers.

The eldest amongst them spoke with their parents and their parents sent word to the Super Council. The Super Council called for a meeting for the next day.

That evening, Mahili was treated to a lot many hugs and back massages and she purred in pleasure. This was her family! The male panther remained outside the village. So, the villagers threw a chunk of meat in its direction. It growled and raced away into the jungle. It returned later to sniff at the chunk of meat, nibble at it for a while, then, he bit the piece and carried it away into the forest cover.

But the attack and victory did amazing things with Mahili's self-confidence.

That evening she went deep into the jungle and got back her first big hunt – a wild boar!

Tribals Learn Boom Boom Stick Use

Sudhir was the guest of the Super Council Chief of all the tribes the next day. He decided that this was not the time nor there was any need to push the fact down their throat that he was the King of the land on which they resided. The Powva tribe were so out of touch with the outside world that comprehension regards a larger world beyond theirs would take time to appreciate and understand.

How then could he train these people who used prehistoric tools to fight their battles? How could they learn to fight the evil army who used modern tools to invade Nair Dvipa and had the support of a powerful sorcerer?!! How could he ensure that his own people, that is the armed forces of Nair Dvipa were to desist infighting between own citizens, the tribesmen?

Further, the Tribals led a peaceful life. Why then would they suddenly begin to train just because he wanted them to train? And why should they want to fight a powerful group and thus endanger their lives for a guest?

But all such apprehensions vanished when the young group, accompanied by Mobi and Mahili appeared for the meeting which had been called by the Super Council. The teenagers had returned panic stricken, but with valuable, modern day arms and a hoard of ammunition to easily last for a full twentyfour months or maybe more.

The elders kept Mobi behind them and took the lead to narrate their adventure with more spice than was necessary. The teenagers went to the point of boasting that they, the terrified teenaged tribals, had beaten up the strangers to a bloody mess. How they bravely snatched away the boom boom sticks from the yellow strangers. Then Sudhir was requested to call Mobi. Sudhir beckoned and while Mobi stood in front of the Super Council he narrated facts exactly as it had happened. Including the ferocity of Mahili, the panther cub and the male panther, inspite of the ferocity of the boom boom sticks.

The tribals of all the villages collected the courage to creep forward with much trepidation and at least peep at the boom boom sticks. Then try to touch the sticks with a lot of anxiety. Sudhir was called and he promptly inserted bullets into the chamber and fired two shots into the air – "Boom boom"! Suddenly everybody had jumped into the nearest bushes!

This gave Sudhir the idea that many more arms and ammunition could be captured from these strangers. He spoke with the Chief and the Chief promptly announced that he and the Super Council would honour any citizen with a huge amount of meat, who can hide away up in the trees near the beach where these strangers land and on seeing any yellow strangers carrying boom boom sticks, they should, without being detected, pass on the message through bird calls to their fellow tribal a few trees away.

It was easy after this meeting to convince the tribals now that they could fight back the yellow skinned strangers simply by carrying and fighting back with equally powerful boom boom sticks. This was, he explained to them, provided they learned how to use the boom boom sticks themselves. The Chief had a second meeting and it was unanimously approved that Sudhir would train the eligible warriors in the use of this powerful boom boom stick.

The prequalification set by the village heads for selection for the training was, that the tribal must not be close to the Witch Doctor. The Chief of the Super Council was in a predicament, and called a large gathering of village chiefs, including the Witch Doctor and explained, "The Witch Doctor has displayed animosity and mistrust towards the Mahua Minshaw. Would the great Witch Doctor ever desire to share his medicine and power related trade secrets with the great Mahua Minshaw? No, he would not. Thus, the Mohua Minshaw is free to pick trusted warriors from amongst us and train them to use the boom boom guns and thus defend our villages from the yellow skinned strangers".

All the village heads knew about the open hostility that Nksi Nanga, the great witch doctor had been displaying ever since the great Mahua Minshaw first stepped on the soil of these villages. Further, Nksi Nanga was known to be aggressive and dangerous. With the knowledge of the use of this boom boom stick, he would become difficult to control. Maybe he would become a menace. They had no difficulty in agreeing with the Chief of the village councils. But Nksi Nanga roared with aggression," These boom boom sticks are now the property of all the villages! Every villager has equal right on using them. We do not care if the fraud who you call Mahua Minsaw does not desire to train a specific few, thereby displaying a desire to create a divide amongst our great tribe. Be as it may, give us our share of the boom boom sticks and we will learn how to use them ourselves!"

It was agreed that two boom boom sticks would be given to each village. The seventh boom boom stick would remain with the Chief of the Super Council. Thus, Nksi Nanga and his loyal group got two boom boom sticks.

The training began within the large Sports Stadium grounds specifically for villagers not loyal to Nksi Nanga. Large round targets were specially prepared as per Sudhir's directions. The Chief posted security guards all around the Stadium to stop peeping toms.

"This Boom boom stick is called a rifle", began Sudhir "and these are bullets". The training programme had managed to easily pull in all the warriors of the villages, plus fresh recruits.

In the meanwhile, Nksi Nanga was trying to fathom the head and tail of this powerful weapon far away from the Sports Stadium. He pointed the gun at a tree, opened his mouth and shouted, "Booom!", but nothing happened. He kept trying until, out of frustration he threw down the rifle on the forest floor, it hit a rock, bounced up and the trigger struck a branch of tree that was sticking out from the forest floor and, "Boom!" the rifle fired. Nksi Nanga and the rest of his loyal team promptly jumped into the nearest shrub.

Mobi was in the stadium and insisted that he wanted to learn too. But Sudhir smiled gently and suggested that the moment he touches the first branch of the Chikka Fruit tree, from then onwards he shall be taught how to use the guns.

Mobi promptly went out of the stadium, made certain villagers allow him to climb onto their shoulders while standing below the tree, he touched the leaf and branches of the Chikka Fruit tree and returned to demand that the great Mahua Minsaw keep his promise.

Sudhir reluctantly gave his adopted son a rifle and was extra careful that Mobi does not get hurt. Everybody sniggered because no child had ever been able to do a man's work.

But Mobi was a quick learner. He sat in the spectator gallery and saw them practice. He observed their every action. Within a few days little Mobi had secretly joined the trainees and he too learned to shoot. Within another few days, his little finger travelled to the trigger and shot eight Bulls Eyes out of every ten shots. Every villager kept looking at each other in awe. Sudhir looked at him with pride and his Mobi beamed!

Thus when the "magic boundary border guards" were appointed, little Mobi stepped forward to request that he be deputed there but once again Sudhir had a smile, a twinkle in his eyes and a gentle suggestion, "Touch that Chikka Fruit tree branch with your fingers but even while your own feet are on the forest floor and you shall be allowed to do anything from then on!"

But Mobi was not to be stopped. When several fully trained warriors were deputed to the beach, which was a part of the unprotected area, Mobi was not to be found for several days. Then he returned from the beach riding on a Punda – a load bearing wild animal that looked like a mix between a donkey and a Zebra, and it carried on its back five boom boom sticks and six sacks of ammunition!

Then the seven-year-old child prodigy looked up at Sudhir as if to ask, "Have I proved my worth?"

Sudhir beaming with pride, picked him up in his arms and hugged him.

Mobi squirmed being embarrassed by this obvious show of affection, but more out of happiness.

Chapter 14

Sudhir Proposes to Ngia Vat

Sudhir Proposes to Ngia Vat

"I need not live a meek person's personality now that I am a King" Sudhir told himself. He was a King of an island. A middle-class individual who had lived a life of struggle to lose everything and then become a King without a Kingdom!

Ngia vat and he loved each other, he reasoned with himself. Law of the Kings of Nair Dvipa permitted the King to marry as many wives as he so pleased. Law of Nair Dvipa protected the King from prosecution in any form or manner from a country to which he had belonged earlier. Ngia vat had cared for him and protected him during the times of stress. She had given him a second life. She had helped him back on the path to becoming a better and healthier human being.

He stood in front of Ngia Vat and asked, "Ngia vat will you be my wife? Can we be Khwanga?"

Ngia Vat's warm embrace was her answer.

He decided to ask the Chief of the Super Council of the tribes for the hand of Ngia vat, his daughter. That both Ngia Vat and he were ready for Khwanga!

Ombasa, the Chief of the Super Council of the tribes was overjoyed! But he reminded Sudhir that as per the rule set by Tribe members, the past was written off, and from that moment onwards, he had to prove himself to be the bravest and the best provider.

The village, barring the Witch Doctor and his cronies, were overjoyed with the prospect of having Sudhir as a son in law, and a separate hut was then made by Sudhir and Ngia vat from the bamboo poles of the forest, the dried leaves to cover the roof, the palm tree leaves to add double protection to the roof against rain. But Sudhir introduced bricks made from baked river mud. And cemented them one above the other with the river mud mixed with the sand from the ocean and the paste from the Bokul Gum Tree. In this fashion, the wall was four layers thick. The villagers were initially amused but when several of the strong villagers failed to break the brick wall, that is when a new respect for Sudhir grew. He dug out a canal from the river, ensured that the mini stream travelled below his toilet and allowed the waste from the toilet to flow away to the paddy fields that he had taught them to grow. This too was of great interest to the villagers. They now thronged in large numbers to personally understand the huge advantage of defecating in a closed room offering privacy, a protected environment when compared to being exposed to attack from wild animals & Nksi Nanga's followers. The women became strong supporters of this arrangement and both brick huts as well as private toilets caught on. Many brick huts with private toilets began to be constructed from then on, and the chief consultant in each case was Sudhir, Ngia vat's would be husband.

"I am a great provider as this will help me feed your daughter" he explained to the Chief of all councils pointing at the solid brick settlement. "I can build ten such strong huts in exchange for two hundred pea fowl, twenty large fish per month and ten sacks of the rice that I have taught you to grow".

"Though you have refused to accept the payment being giving by the tribesmen, these strong structures would certainly stand the test of time", the Chief agreed nodding in the affirmative. And his fellow village heads nodded in agreement.

It was more of less certain that they were Khwanga after the Chief nodded.

The villages came together that evening on hearing the great news. The people of the super council of 'Beti Beti', the Chief and the villagers of 'Zambeke', the Chief and the villagers of 'Omagwena', the Chief and the villagers of 'Kavaheke', and finally the Chief and the villagers of 'Kunini'.

That evening around the fire, while everybody was on their first drink, the Witch Doctor rushed into the gathering with many his armed Tribesmen.

Witch Doctor Challenges Sudhir

"I challenge Ngia Vat's decision to marry a stranger", he boomed "My mother was not allowed inside our village because she was a stranger" he roared looking in every direction with eyes glaring. "Our second law demands that any stranger has to prove that he is the bravest. Yet you have broken this law too. Why? Just because he saves the Chief's grandchild from our Black leopard God? Maybe Gods wanted him to die? Now that you have brought in a stranger then at-least he has to follow one of the laws.

I challenge him to fight with the best four trained warriors and myself. He has the right to live with us if he wins.

Either he wins in a battle against four of our best soldiers and myself or he stays outside our tribe. And if he loses then, he cannot marry one of us!" He looked at the crowd around him and they nodded in approval. They looked at the Chief because they all realized that what he just claimed was in fact a part of their law.

The Chief too knew that he was right. He looked perplexed.

Ngia Vat then spoke up to ask - "Oh great Witch Doctor! If the law demands that he must fight then he shall fight! But what if he wins? What happens if he beats all five of you included yourself, what then? Would you and your henchmen leave the village forever, never to return?" All the seated villagers let out a gasp! Nobody had ever challenged the might of the powerful witch doctor ever before! They waited for his response.

The Witch Doctor, even while looking at Ngia vat, strode right up to her and pleaded, "Why do you do this? I have always loved you and you know that. You never gave me a chance to try and make you happy. You know that I have the respect of everyone in this village. I am the best hunter, the best warrior and can provide for both of us. But you – you have always displayed contempt and disgust for me. You – you want to live permanently with this – this fraud who calls himself God and everyone allows him to feed on the largesse of our innocent Chief! But I love you!" The total village gasped in unison! Never had they seen this great Witch Doctor in such an emotionally weak state.

The Witch Doctor now turned his shaggy head towards Sudhir and growled – "You stranger are a blood sucking leech, a burden on this village!

I shall beat you alone if you have the courage to accept my challenge! But before I fight you, law demands that you fight four others. So, shall it be thus? Or would you rather run away right now to live outside the village you lowly leech?!"

Sudhir did not reply but simply gave a knowing smile.

Another female villager asked, "Oh great Witch Doctor, we urge you to reply Nvia Vat's question. What if you lose the fight and he beat all the other four warriors, then would you and your cronies leave this village forever, never to return?"

A chorus of voices began to ask, "Yes reply! You can also win and the stranger must leave. It is fair that if he wins then you too must have to leave!"

The Witch Doctor suddenly realized how much he was despised by the people of this village. He had reigned supreme through fear but this blood sucking leach of a stranger, he seemed to be gaining in popularity! "Arrrrr!" he roared. "All right I shall leave with my fellow warriors if this puny stranger were to beat five of us! Why five, I shall leave if he beats me alone!"

The village roared in unison and it was decided that the new sports stadium would be the venue for the fight – three nights away. "The great fight shall begin when the sun touches the tips of the top branches of our trees!" the Witch Doctor roared, raising his hands and looking at all the villagers with a sign of victory, and a smug expression on his face. His expression looked like one who imagined that the future had promised him victory!

That night Ngia Vat was very worried and held Sudhir in a close embrace. "Oh, great Lord – Five warriors against one God! You may be God almighty but what if the evil one beats you? I shall then become his slave instead of a free woman as I am with you!"

Sudhir held her chin in his right palm and gently lifted her face to meet his eyes, "Do I look like someone who gets beaten very easily?" he grinned and asked.

She stared into his eyes for a very long time then finally whispered, "I am in love with you!" And she hugged him even tighter, as if she knew she would never ever meet him again.

He flew to the cave and discussed with his grandparents.

"Do not dare to show off your powers against a normal human being", Queen Madhu Bagaria suggested.

"You have the physique and the stamina of a sportsman. You have strategy while they have sheer muscle", Queen Gertrude Wallace suggested

"You believe in justice my son, and you have always been the protector of all that is good! They are your own people. Your goal is to protect them. Your goodness shall win! Your determination shall prevail!" King Cherusseri Namboodiri assured with a soothing tone.

Chapter 15

Village Titans Battle

Sudhir Battles the Huge Nksi Nanga, the Witch Doctor

The event was supposed to begin when the sun rose to the tip of the tallest tree. Meaning mid-afternoon.

Yet people were thronging the boundary wall of the stadium from daylight.

The villagers of 'Zambeke', villagers of 'Omagwena', villagers of 'Kavaheke', villagers of 'Kunini' – all of them! Armed guards were posted on four corners of the stadium and at the gate to avoid any untoward incident.

The entrance gate to the new stadium was yet to be opened but the villagers were banging on the stadium gate much to the chagrin of the security guards posted at that very spot.

Outside the stadium, youngsters were somersaulting, walking around on stilts, doing pole vaulting, practicing balancing a ball on cricket bats. The enterprising lot were selling freshly captured crabs and fish, honey in earthen containers, pots, monkey, birds, porcupine, one flightless bird too.

Then the gates opened with the young wooden gate creaking and groaning at the tough hinges and the villagers swarmed in like flood waters. Each grabbed his or her favorite view point seat, as is human nature. The wise ones grabbed the seats in the front row. The contestants had a box dedicated to themselves. Sudhir had one box whereas the Witch Doctor and his four warriors were in another box. Each box was at the top of the stairs with steps and gate dedicated to each of them and opening into the stadium grounds.

Then the drums boomed out to announce the arrival of the Chiefs. The Deputy Chief of the village of 'Zambeke', The Chief of village of 'Omagwena', The Chief of village of 'Kavaheke', The Chief of village of 'Kunini', came down one by one.

Then came the contestants – Sudhir entered to receive a thunderous applause! He proceeded to his box at the top of the seating arrangement.

The four warriors who were to fight Sudhir entered just then. They too were welcomed with a thunderous roar! They proceeded to their box at the top of the seating arrangement opposite to Sudhir's box.

Finally, the drums boomed once again to announce the arrival of the Super Council.

All within the stadium rose. The Deputy Chief of the village of 'Zambeke'rose to his feet. But the Chief of the village of 'Zambeke' did not rise from his seat within the box.

The Chief of the Super Council rose to speak and raised his hands. Total silence ensued while the wind blew strong and the whispering of tree leaves could be heard.

"Great citizens of our 'Powya tribe'", the Super Council Chief began, "My grandfather told my father and my father told me that many moons ago, a great warrior who flew like a bird and had the power of ten elephants had plucked him and his fellow villagers from the wrath of the ocean Gods and given us sanctuary here. On these very sacred lands! My grandfather and his people were guests of this great powerful God on his lands but he never disturbed our livelihood nor expected anything in return. In fact, when the great sickness came about and our people were dying in large numbers, this God who had plucked him out of the drowning waters came to our assistance once again. He gave us herbs and taught us Yoga. Then again when the great waters swept away our many people when we lived in the lowlands, this great God returned at the time of our great need and created shelters on three separate hill tops and a protected part of the valley below so that we are never ever ravaged by such vagaries of nature again.

For all these he never asked for anything back in return. Never – ever!

All of you had wondered when I invited this great stranger into our midst and gave him special status. Many must surely have felt that this old fool had lost his senses. No, your Chief is not an old fool. My choice has always protected you in the past. I see in this stranger that very God who had saved us from danger every time. I can feel inside me that he is the direct descendant of the very same God. I felt that we the people of all these villages were giving something back in return to that great God by giving to his direct descendant. And whatever we have given to him in return for what he has given us, is very little, a pittance.

But as the rule demands, this great God has been challenged by one of us, 'Nksi Nanga' the great witch doctor, the great Chief of 'Zambeke'!". And then he pointed at the Chief of 'Zambeke'.

'Nksi Nanga' rose up to a standing position and shook his hairy shoulders and head like a mangy dog. He was showing off the longest 'Isembozo' - the Penis Sheath, and Scrotum Ball Bags. And as he shook his powerful shoulders, his Isembozo shook too and the crowd roared in approval with the addition of whistles and cat calls from the young girls.

"Arise Oh great God, arise oh great Chief of 'Zambeke'", continued the Super Council Chief, "this audience of the family of 'Powya' shall witness the unfolding of justice on this great occasion. We urge you to settle your differences and decide who is to remain amongst us. Does this great God who has taught us Pole vaulting, somersaulting, stilt walking, balancing the ball on the bat, cricket, how to make fishing nets and increase our fish yields, how to make boats, how to bake bricks and make brick buildings, has helped us build this great stadium in which we sit today, and music along with counting, how to use boom boom sticks etc., leave us? Or does the great Witch Doctor who has healed so many from amongst us and is presently the Chief of 'Zambeke', a great village – does he leave us?

Today's challenger is the Chief of 'Zambeke' and his four specially trained and seasoned warriors and they all shall fight together against the great God!

Let the mutual settlement begin!" Saying so the Chief of the super council went back to his seat of power amongst the Super Council Chiefs.

The crowd roared as both Sudhir as well as 'Nksi Nanga' the witch doctor and his chosen warriors climbed down from the spectator's box and walked into the sports field which was big enough to be a huge Rugby or football field!

Sudhir stopped at one predetermined and well marked point, and 'Nksi Nanga' the witch doctor and his chosen warriors swaggered up to a mark and stopped on the opposite side facing Sudhir. In the center were the super council of 'Beti Beti', the village of the elders.

The members of the village elders, the supreme council, looked at both the parties and asked, "Are you ready?" Sudhir nodded in the affirmative. But 'Nksi Nanga' the witch doctor and his chosen warriors were raising their hands and looking in every direction as if victory was a foregone conclusion. They too finally answered in the affirmative.

Stone knives, stone tipped spears, bows and arrows, fishing nets were kept on each side. One could choose the weapon that he wanted to use. 'Nksi Nanga's warriors chose daggers, fishing nets, knives and spears. Sudhir chose a net and a wooden stick. Nksi Nanga's warriors looked at each other and sniggered.

The elders moved aside and raised their hands. The moment they would drop their hands, the battle shall begin. There ensued pin drop silence!

Then the elders dropped their hands as one!

Four of Nksi Nanga's warriors began to circle Sudhir in a crouched position. They went around clockwise once and then anti clockwise and then took a jump forward. Sudhir did not look left nor right. He did not flinch! He simply looked straight ahead at the hands and feet of 'Nksi Nanga' the witch doctor. Nksi Nanga kept testing something behind his shoulders.

Suddenly one of the warriors made a lunge at Sudhir with his spear. Sudhir bent backwards and the spear simply rushed and travelled above and away from Sudhir even as he swung back to a vertical position. The warrior followed the spear and Sudhir simply stretched out his legs and lifted it, tripping and flipping his muscular opponent. The warrior went for a toss! The crowd roared! But Sudhir had not flinched from his assigned position.

The four soldiers rushed back to 'Nksi Nanga' the witch doctor for consultation and then rushed back to their original stance of circling Sudhir from four directions.

This time two soldiers, one from the front and one from behind rushed at Sudhir. The ones in front had a spear each and the ones behind had a dagger each. Sudhir shut his eyes and listened but did not flinch. As one got closer from behind, and lunged, Sudhir bent on the right and swung away. In the meanwhile, the one with the spear lunged and pushed his spear deep into the other warrior behind Sudhir while the other pushed his knife into the chest of the person in front of Sudhir. The crowd roared! They fell down gurgling, screaming and writhing on the floor. Nksi Nanga raised an eyebrow in disgust.

The elders beckoned and other warriors rushed in to take the injured warriors away.

The remaining two warriors came rushing back to encircle Sudhir after a quick consultation with 'Nksi Nanga' the witch doctor. Both were extremely cautious. One had picked up a fishing net and was planning to throw his fishing net while the other would pierce Sudhir with the spear and the knife. Sudhir did not flinch. They made various lunges but quickly backed away when Sudhir did not flinch. Then 'Nksi Nanga' barked and one of them threw the fishing net high into the air. Sudhir used his mental powers to make it fly on and hover above 'Nksi Nanga', and then it fell and embraced 'Nksi Nanga' in its tight embrace. While Nksi struggled, the one with the spear lunged at Sudhir and was tossed into the air with Sudhir kicking his legs, and then kick upwards. He rushed up into the skies and then rushed down at a high speed with his spear pointing down but where his colleague unfortunately stood. His colleague died on the spot as the spear pierced his shoulder blade and kept entering right down till its very end. The crowd roared as the warrior screamed!

Thus, now only 'Nksi Nanga' and the terrified spear wielding warrior remained. The other managed to disentangle 'Nksi Nanga' from the fishing net and then discovered that Sudhir had not flinched from his position.

Genuine respect was obvious in the eyes of both 'Nksi Nanga' and the warrior, as they discussed the possible attack strategies. This time both encircled Sudhir but this time Sudhir was extra careful and kept his eyes on 'Nksi Nanga's hands and ankle. Sure enough, Sudhir saw, as his opponent came from behind him, 'Nksi Nanga's hands went behind his back where he had hidden a weapon and he brought out a steel tube rod that sparkled in the afternoon sun. Suddenly a bright bolt of lightning shot out from this steel tube but Sudhir was ready and somersaulted on his right just before it blasted Nksi Nanga's fellow warrior into bits and pieces of meat, blood and bone. The crowd roared but 'Nksi Nanga" kept firing his weapon at Sudhir even as Sudhir somersaulted to dodge the powerful energy bolts every time. This time the bolts of lightning hit the spectators and a woman screamed in terror as her cousin sitting next to her got blasted into simmer-teens! Another got hit in the arm, and now there appeared a gaping hole. Suddenly he was howling in pain. A father was holding onto his little headless child in shock.

The pain and cry of anguish did not perturb 'Nksi Nanga'. That man's cry of anguish hurt Sudhir deep in the heart. He could not understand why but the man's cry made a thousand arrows strike his heart at the same time. The helplessness of innocent spectators made him so very angry! Sudhir kept getting closer and closer to 'Nksi Nanga' with every somersault in-spite of the firing and finally he lunged and grabbed away this deadly weapon from the hands of his opponent. Then he swung 'Nksi Nanga' by his hand and smashed his body onto the stadium floor with his face down, Nksi's hands and feet spread out! The crowd roared and danced around like children! Jubilation was obvious everywhere! They did not notice that Sudhir had twisted 'Nksi Nanga's arms behind his back, thus causing severe pain and was at this very moment asking Nksi, "Where did you get this weapon? Where?!"

"You can go to hell!" 'Nksi Nanga' growled even while grimacing in pain.

Sudhir twisted 'Nksi Nanga's arm harder and the Ex-Chief of 'Zambeke' could hold back no longer, and he screamed. "Where?" Sudhir asked again and then held the tube onto the forehead of the ex-village chief's head! Sudhir saw an amazing transformation in the eyes and expression of 'Zambeke's ex-supremo, that of fear of imminent death, and Nksi Nanga cringed. It became immediately obvious that Nksi had known and probably had, had possession of this weapon for a long time and was successful in keeping this fact secret. But where did he get this high technology weapon? Obviously, an outsider had given it to him. But an outsider could not have entered the protected zone. Then this ex supremo of Zambeke village must have been meeting strangers outside the protected forest zone. That was treason!

"On the count of three I shall fire this tube into your forehead! One, two...!" Sudhir warned

"The submerged ship for God's sake! The submerged ship!" screamed Nksi Nanga.

"What submerged ship? Where is the submerged ship 'Nksi Nanga'?!" Sudhir pushed 'Nksi Nanga's head deeper into the dusty floor, twisting his arm even further, causing excruciating pain.

"On the far end of this island", the ex-Chief screamed, "in the deep seas!"

"Who took you there? How did you get there in the deep seas Nksi?" growled Sudhir.

"A man who can fly, he took me there. I know nothing more! I promise, I speak the truth! Please – please let go of my arm, it hurts!" screamed Nksi.

Sudhir spoke to his own mind. "I need to fly to where he found the tube weapon".

Sudhir held onto 'Nksi Nanga' as he rushed into the skies at supersonic speed, high up into the clouds, then flew down at high speed even while 'Nksi Nanga' screamed in terror looking down at the long fall far below. They were hovering high above the coast but amazingly, his powers remained! It became obvious that he was being given special powers to fulfill a purpose. He was not splashing down powerless into the ocean waters!

"Now tell me where exactly you found this weapon?" Sudhir growled.

Nksi Nanga was terrified and quickly pointed down at a cave entrance, now visible from above, deep into the ocean waters.

And right down there, in the clear waters of the deep ocean, was a huge galleon lying on its side. And strewn all around it were ancient artifacts!

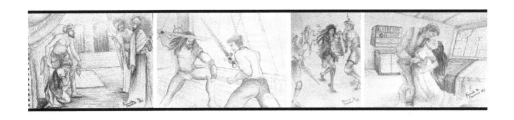

Chapter 16

Sudhir Meets the Aliens Who Created Human Beings

The Ships of Interstellar Space

Sudhir saw the cave from above and told his mind, "I need a strong boat and a chain to hold my prisoner down to the boat.

A flash of light erupted in front of his eyes and the fishing boat for four with a chain on board appeared out of thin air. Then it floated gently down to land on the sea waters exactly above the caves. Sudhir tied 'Nksi Nanga' up to the boat and dived deep into the ocean waters, with the weapon in his hands. There were a lot many fish entering and leaving a cave entrance big enough to allow four 300-seater aircrafts to enter at the same time.

He did not bother about the cave. He began to inspect the artifacts all around the sunken galleon. Old utensils, cutlery, ancient swords, daggers, shields, battering rams, chests full of gold bullion but no weapons. Nothing! He found nothing which could closely resemble a modern-day weapon! His eyes casually glanced at the cave opening. He thought that he saw a sparkle of light falling on glass in water. Nonsense, just fish, he told himself and he looked back at the galleon and the area around. He was losing hope, maybe Nksi Nanga had lied. But he kept shifting the sand and used his mind to x-ray till deep down into the sand, and yet no modern-day weapons.

Then he thought that he saw a sparkle of light once again from within the cave!

He followed the fish swimming lazily into the huge hundred feet high cave mouth and met with a sight that he shall never forget. There docked away on various decks of the cave body were several conical shaped ships, they looked like modern-day submarines, each approximately hundred and fifty feet long and some were many times larger, totaling around twenty ships. Sudhir chose the first. He found that the hatch of one of them opened as he approached. He climbed down the hatch and it closed automatically above him right away. The water drained out automatically and he was able to breathe! This was amazing technology!

"Welcome citizen of Daivika planet! Please mention your name", a female voice asked him

Sudhir continued to be awed but replied, "I am Sudhir Bagaria of Planet Prithvi (Earth). I was an Indian citizen and now I am a citizen of Nair Dvipa, this island. Daivika planet is unknown to me and I am not a citizen of any Daivika planet".

"That is correct Sudhir Bagaria of Earth. However, you share the same genetic code of Daivika planet residents running through your veins. We have sensed that the percentage of Daivika planet blood group within you is around eighty percent, the highest recorded amongst Daivika planet mix with Earth citizens on your planet earth so far".

"So, what is your name and are you a part of a computer programme or are you hiding behind any 'one-way see-through' glass?" asked Sudhir.

"I am an advanced program developed by your great ancestor of Daivika planet. His name was Vakhum Eekhak. You share eighty percent of his Gnome. I operate under a highly complex algorithm designed by your great ancestor" she replied.

"The Daivika planet exists around 70 years away towards the Ekudama Constellation, by the old dry fuel burning ships, and just one month away by these dual negative, positive, magnetic polar energy driven ships.

"Do you have another question Sudhir Bagaria of Earth?" she asked after a pause.

"Where did this weapon come from?" asked Sudhir showing the weapon in his hand.

"That is an accelerated energy drive gun, a primitive weapon by present day standards.

Our ability to tap our brain cells has enabled us to harness energies far beyond your present understanding. Our mental energies can generate blasts many multiple times than this primitive hand-held device in your possession now. One of these was stolen by one of our mix breed citizens with fifty percent blood match named Móguǐ de érzi. These are not toys to be gifted away as one would gift away coloured plastic beads to primitive tribesmen. These are dangerous weapons in the hands of people who wish to cause serious damage to human society", she replied.

"So, when did Móguǐ de érzi visit you, to be able to steal this from you?" Sudhir asked.

"Around two hundred and forty years ago", she replied, "Your blood pressure indicates that you know him and that he scares your mind".

"Scares my mind is precise", Sudhir replied honestly. "Móguǐ de érzi has been able to generate a negative energy that survived for nearly two hundred plus years corrupting the minds of the under confident, weak minded and the malleable minded of my land. His country Diànlì ji'è de guójia is power hungry, greedy and selfish. Even while Morgui remained a prisoner in a bottle that was sealed, these dark forces that he left behind have worked silently and alienated us, the Royal family, from the rest of the citizens. Their minds have been so polluted by the negative forces that, some of Nair Dvipa citizens would fight those who protect me, their King or anybody who is protected by me. Some of my own countrymen, Doctors, Lawyers, Finance people, Sportsmen, Singers, actors, poets, Defense personnel, Real Estate Builders et-all, are all a confused lot, lulled enough to remain silent spectators due to misleading pro-Diànlì ji'è de guójia and anti Nair Dvipa Television, Mobile and Print Media news. Lulled further by the supposed Intelligentsia who had returned fully trained from the land of evil Diànlì ji'è de guójia. Diànlì ji'è de guójia has in its hands corrupt Lawyers and some of the Police personnel who may do everything to harm those that are close to me including the pro King forces. I am not powerful enough to fight Mogui yet. Further, I have yet to get to know from where he gets the energy to keep his negative forces alive; that which does his work in his absence," replied Sudhir in a worried tone.

"Regards your ability to battle Mogui, citizen Sudhir Bagaria, that is no problem!" the lady replied. "We can inject your brain cells with energies that we pumped Mogui's mind with!

There is a history behind this. We saw a human in the ocean water whose genetic coding marked him as a mix breed whose ancestors were citizens of the Daivika planet. He was drowning after his ship got wrecked. We had to rescue him, which is one of our prime directives, that is, to save the lives of the citizens of Daivika planet. Then we gave him a huge amount of power over many months. When he recouped, Móguǐ de érzi's guile amused us as, study of human behavior on this planet is a subject of our study".

Sudhir was shocked. "So, he got his powers from you! It is because of his powers that the minds of our citizens have become corrupt. But I have been tasked by my grandparents to cleanse the minds of my people of all negative forces that corrupt their minds. So can you give me the abilities to cleanse their minds?" Sudhir asked

"That citizen Sudhir Bagaria, can happen only if you defeat Mogui in battle. For this you need a huge surge of permanent power. Such power is no problem for us!" the lady replied. "We shall move you immediately to the Energy ward and pass on the correct dose of energies into your brain cells. Though he shall remain stronger than you, these energies would allow you to be ready to face Móguǐ de érzi, we are confident about this. Subsequently, we shall put you in front of all our database of Inter Dimension movements and Time Travelers that have been happened over the past Five Thousand years. We also have a Database of Time Travelers".

"But how will a database of Inter Dimension Movement help me?" asked Sudhir.

"Very easy citizen Sudhir Bagaria", the lady replied. "We have been cleansing the minds of both negative minded Daivika citizens as well as every other negative minded human being affected by the negative energies of the ships full of crooks, murderers, brigands, thieves, robbers, liars, frauds etc., that had crash-landed or had landed safely on earth. After their minds are cleansed, the negative energies are stored in High Density High Energy Retaining (HDHER) steel casks.

Then we refill their empty minds with an unlimited power bank of energy that keeps telling him, "Can do good hence will do good ", "we shall all have food, clothing and shelter because I shall strive to ensure the same", "we shall achieve with honest deeds, hard work and sincerity", "we all shall have faith in our inner values, our principles and the ethics that we have imbibed from our elders".

This is a lot of hard work considering that Negative energy spreads faster than Positive energy. Negative energy hides whereas Positive Energy shines and shows itself. We can do with a lot many volunteers such as yourself in this noble task.

Now we transport these sealed negative energies stored in HDHER casks to a secret time dimension on this planet and initiate the destruction of such energies through a complex process. Our security systems are extremely tight.

We have had only one case of theft of negative energies and we suspect that the thief was Mogui, because he knows how to travel between time dimensions. Regretfully, we gave him the power to do so!

Negative energies serve either the body to which they belong or they serve a powerful master who releases them but can move them back to the storage space after their job is done. It can thus be recycled endlessly unless stopped by the master. Mogui is obviously the master and is hiding his mirror self in another time & space dimension from where he keeps feeding the negative energies of this time dimension.

You would, on browsing through the database, center on the exact dates that movements have taken place during the time that Mogui threw down the bolt of negative energy on your people. Mogui must have travelled back in time prior to that, followed us and located our storage site. He then must have fooled our security systems and escaped with enough negative energy to pollute your country two times over.

We admit that it is our fault that your countrymen suffer today. A breach in our security system had happened in the past and we have taken corrective action to ensure that it does not get repeated.

We are now willing to help you in identifying the movement in time dimension that matches Mogui's movement. Then the next step would be to identify the co-ordinates and finally we shall assist you in every step to stop the source or dry up the source of endless negative energy that helps Mogui turn your own people against their own country today".

"All right then, let us move to the Energy ward now!" Sudhir requested.

A panel slid open on the side of the ship, a chair flew up to Sudhir and a male voice said, "Good afternoon to you Citizen Sudhir Bagaria of earth. Kindly be seated and please be so kind as to fasten your seat belt. Your safety is our prime concern".

Sudhir saw magnetic levitation rail tracks embedded into the floor of the ship near his feet. These tracks looked more like strips on the floor that came from the panel on the side of the ship. It led down the corridor to the distant end of the ship with junctions that led away into lanes and rooms within lanes.

Sudhir sat on the chair and fastened his seat belt. The chair said – "We shall travel at high speed to the Energy Ward now. Kindly brace yourself.

Your safety is our prime concern. We shall zip away on the count of three. Beginning now - Zero, One, Two, Three, Go!" His neck swung back due to the sudden acceleration but was now being protected by cushioned neck rests at the back and two sides. The chair zipped away at hyper speed where everything became a blur.

Within seconds he was in front of a room that read "Vajra Dvar" meaning the 'Door to Endless Energy'. He now sat opposite a mirror and he saw a metallic helmet that came gently down to rest on his head. Belts appeared automatically around his wrists and ankles to tie him down. "Do not worry Citizen Sudhir Bagaria. This is to restrain you from hurting yourself during the procedure. Kindly brace yourself. Your safety is our prime concern. We shall begin on the count of three", the lady assured. And then a whining sound began. He heard her count, "Three, two, one, zero, go!" Within seconds he experienced a searing, burning pain throughout his brain, many times greater than what he had experienced at the Palace or the Cave, both put together.

A female voice soothingly said, "Your brain cells are opening up now citizen Sudhir Bagaria. Most human brains use a maximum of ten percent of the brain capability and capacity at any one time.

We had MRI technology when we were crib babies of technology. In the olden days, our MRI machines made us believe that we were using 99% of our brain's capacity over many days. That, not all the parts of our brain were always used, we had believed. Every little part of the brain, we believed then, was being used in some manner or the other.

Now we know better. From the moment we began to realize that we had been created by a super being and that each cell had a lock. Our minds were super computers with built in limitations. So, we identified the locks outside each brain cell that brought about the limitations. On a parallel line we studied behavior & feelings. We studied the ways and means to map the speed of electrical energies travelling between two brain cells and their significance to that part of the brain cell as a trigger or effect of any subsequent behavior pattern or feeling. Hence the cause & significance of the energy to each cell was mapped and mock tests done much before the cell locks were finally broken open. Huge amount of energies tumbled out! It was then that we discovered the Power of Sound Energy!

We learned the secrets that allowed building up and concentration of powerful energies, especially the concentration of sound energies. The sages of India had learned and perfected the art of using sounds for good purposes. We discovered the profound affect that sound waves had in bringing about positive feelings, wellbeing, and positive creativity. We realized that interstellar space is made up of huge energies and that any one individual can create interstellar highways on which our spirit form can travel at super high speed. Our brain cells now gave us the ability to see beyond our own time & space dimension. We learned to discipline our minds that otherwise acted like grasshoppers.

We discovered that the sounds, "Shommmm" or "Hommmm" could move objects, and help modify or alter brain waves of a second person. The second person could thus be influenced to do something good. We discovered then the ability to self-heal, the ability to assimilate the energies that float freely around us and then finally, to generate our own energy banks within ourselves.

From that time on, our citizens began to develop mental, analytical and processing skills far beyond our imagination. Mathematics, statistics, computer science, and scientific advances took place by leaps and bounds from then on. Our mind allowed us to travel at supersonic speeds and enjoyed least resistance under water, especially in the turbulent ocean waters. Our mind allowed us to travel beyond dimensions of both time and space on any planet that we desired.

With such superior knowledge and ability, we had developed space crafts like this craft, that could travel to distant planets and stay in specially identified underwater caves. With such knowledge and abilities our ships could get intentionally encased in volcanic liquid which then became volcanic rock, keeping the ship thus encased for millions of years and yet the ship remained active. We began to study and assist the local citizens of neighbouring planets to mature into knowledgeable and responsible beings.

We have by now advanced into generating energies multiplied many times over using our mind. Our body, we realized by then, is simply a biological vessel and that our energies do not die but the body does. In the Planet of Daivika, our minds have graduated to a point where we move around as pure conscious energies. But on earth, we move around with or without bodies. We protect our bodies from harm by switching on or switching off a defense cloak. We heal our bodies with our mental energies. We travel back and forth two dimensions within minutes. That means yes, we travel back and forth the time & space dimensions. We are now a highly advanced race. Yes, we are on earth observing the development of planet earth from close-proximity and constantly trying to repair the damage done by the first fleet of ships that had our anti-social elements".

The buzz went silent and the lady said, "Citizen Sudhir Bagaria, your genetic pattern matches eighty percent of the brain cells of the normal adult Daivika planet citizen. However, we could inject your brain cells with only that much energy that could be absorbed by your cells in one sitting. You have been able to absorb a lot of power and abilities and yet they remain miniscule compared to that which was absorbed by Móguĭ de érzi over a period of six long months. Considering the extreme emergency, we shall follow you and ensure many more sittings, at the rate of one per night. We shall ideally do so when you are asleep during the night. You shall not realize we are doing so. But you shall realize that your powers are increasing with every passing day".

Sudhir nodded to express that he understood and accepted the privilege with dignity.

The virtual image of the lady cocked her head suddenly and said. "We have just received emergency communication from the Daivika planet elders. They consider the conditions of Nair Dvipa to be serious. The elders have pledged total support in your favour".

The lady then said, "We shall now move you to the Database room in order that you may locate Time Travel by individuals and groups. You may also study movement of energies to various dimensions during the time or slightly before Mogui threw down the negative energies on your people".

The Chair moved him at astounding speed over magnetic rails once again and he was soon seated in front of a computer that asked for details, "Which period of Bagaria disappearance should we look for Citizen Sudhir Bagaria?"

"Around two hundred and fifty years back", suggested Sudhir.

But the search drew a blank.

"Maybe not Bagaria! It should be a search for 'residents of Nair Dvipa' don't you suggest that?" Sudhir thought aloud

But "residents of Nair Dvipa" drew a blank.

"Let us search for Pirates employed by the country Diànlì ji'è de guójia", Sudhir suggested.

Sure enough, the search led to a torrential rain of results.

Acts of piracy by the Pirates employed by the country Diànlì ji'è de guójia followed visits to foreign countries by historians and travelers from the land of Diànlì ji'è de guójia over many ages. Innumerable Kings of foreign countries gave such travelers cum historian's food, clothing and shelter considering that it was decent to do so in the past ages. These historians earmarked pockets of wealth that the pirates could then concentrate on. The Pirates did not have to sail the high seas aimlessly waiting for a lucky break, to see and seize the ship laden with wealth. This militarily superior strategy of reconnaissance in every possible direction by supposedly peaceful, learned travelers cum historians bore better results. The act of piracy now became more systematic and result oriented. The ships and the kingdoms of those Kings who offered hospitality were the first to be raided by pirates, brigands and armies. Then they were plundered and destroyed, led and assisted by a powerful magician cum Pirate Chief.

These historians of Diànlì ji'è de guójia over many ages had described a powerful magician cum pirate which matched the description of Mógui de érzi. It matched him in every description over two hundred and fifty years!

In each case, Mogui's Pirate ships were seen sailing nonchalantly into the ports of Diànlì ji'è de guójia and exit the same with no resistance whatsoever. He obviously enriched the coffers of his country Diànlì ji'è de guójia and they were happy about this arrangement.

"This is serious!" exclaimed the female voice, "we thought he had travelled into just one dimension. But from the facts uncovered by you citizen Sudhir Bagaria, we are shocked to realize that we have given him the power to travel back in time repeatedly to cause unforgiveable damage! We wish to consult the Supreme Council immediately!"

There was silence for a full five and more minutes.

Suddenly a deep but gentle male voice spoke up and the sound appeared to resonate from every pore of the space craft, "King Sudhir Bagaria, we the elders of the Supreme Council of Daivika Planet greet you! I am Gyananiyaya Oruvan, one of the senior board members of the Supreme Council of Daivika Planet immediately below honourable Srēṣṭhanāya Oruvan, the Chief of the honourable elders of the Supreme Council of Daivika Planet. We have over the past so many centuries considered ourselves to be superior in our security systems and considered our efficiency to be flawless. It is our honour to be proved wrong by a fellow citizen.

All the honourable elders of the Supreme Council of Daivika Planet are part of this conversation now. Honourable Srēṣṭhanāya Oruvan, the Chief of the honourable elders of the Supreme Council of Daivika Planet, Daivi Ammai Aadarsha Bhattathiripad, Daivi Ammai (Devine mother) Dhanyata Chandrika, Daiva pitava Devvuri Srinivasan, Daivi Ammai Urvashi Nandakumar, and Daiva pitava Dharmarakshak Ayyalasomayajula, are all senior elders of the Supreme Council of Daivika Planet!

You have helped us to identify and understand a major flaw in our procedure to help fellow citizens residing on Planet Earth. We need your assistance to rectify this major tear in the Time & Space Dimension. We need you to travel back in time and stop him as per the time & space dimension co-ordinates of his travel that have just been unearthed by yourself now".

"I shall most certainly assist you honourable Sir, alongwith the honourable elders of the Supreme Council of Daivika Planet!" Sudhir stood up straight and replied. "I am duty bound to brief my grandparents before doing so in order that present day emergencies do not cause them any harm." replied Sudhir with great respect.

"So be it King Sudhir Bagaria of Nair Dvipa", agreed Gyananiyaya Oruvan, one of the senior board members of the Supreme Council of Daivika Planet. "Kindly go ahead and brief your grand parents. Do please convey to him that while you represent us by travelling to the past ages, we shall assist your loved ones here in this age, protecting them and helping them tackle the emergencies that torment them today.

We have found from your brain pattern that you are an honest and responsible individual. We now realize the mistake made by us by allowing Móguǐ de érzi to absorb the great amount of energy that he did. We wish to appoint you, provided you agree, as one of the senior members of the Inter Galactic Justice Core Team. You shall head the Team on Earth and ensure that Justice is served. We wish to put all our ships docked herein alongwith all our

Earth based personnel, under your local command. Each ship has its armory which includes obsolete weapons such as the Accelerated Energy Drive Gun (AEDG). We wish to gift you the AEDG that is in your possession right now.

All of us shall be able to sense your need and be there when you need us. If you feel that any citizen of Daivika planet is causing harm to this planet or its inhabitants, then, we hereby authorize you to pass any judgment or execute any deed as you deem fit for the occasion, on our behalf".

Sudhir bowed in respect as also to acknowledge the request of the elders.

The Chair then rushed him back to the exit chute. He stepped into a chamber that filled with water, then opened into the ocean waters and he rushed up to find both the boat that he had created as well as 'Nksi Nanga' were gone.

Sudhir Briefs His Grand Parents

Sudhir, nee King Sudhir Bagaria of Nair Dvipa was a regular visitor to the cave much to the concern of the tribesmen. They had yet to remove from their minds the association of "Howva Minsaw", meaning 'God causing strange happenings' or "Bad God" with the cave.

Sudhir explained how he beat the five warriors of the Powya tribe including 'Nksi Nanga' the witch doctor and ousted him from the village. That the use of an advanced technology weapon by Nksi Nanga had surprised him. Then he narrated his using Nksi Nanga to locate the source of the weapon and how he accidently discovered the Interstellar crafts hidden in the caves below deep waters of this island. Then he narrated about his being pumped with the cell energies and the opening of his mind from ten percent to forty percent use.

When Sudhir began to discuss about having spoken with an Elder of the Supreme Council of Daivika Planet, this fact made them ask repeatedly as if they had not heard correctly and then they stared in awe at Sudhir. "You mean the Honourable Gyananiyaya Oruvan, one of the senior board members of the Supreme Council of Daivika Planet immediately below honourable Sreṣṭhanāya Oruvan himself, the Chief of the honourable elders of the Supreme Council of Daivika Planet in person, spoke with our grandson?!" the late King asked with eyes of great respect, "this is a great honour my son! This is a great honour indeed!"

"The Honourable Gyananiyaya Oruvan himself, needs your assistance to rectify the major tear in the Time & Space Dimension?! This is indeed a huge challenge especially considering that Mogui remains many times stronger than you inspite of all the power that we have pumped into your brain cells", added late Queen Gertrude.

"The brain cells of the present residents of Daivika Planet, as per what the lady on the interstellar craft told you, has now graduated to a point where they can travel between both time and space dimensions. Further, their minds have become so powerful that they can communicate live with you from the Planet. Now inspite of all this our grandchild has been requested to travel back in time and stop Mogui. Taking into consideration all the facts, it only goes to mean that the Honourable Elders of the Supreme Council of Daivika Planet feel that our grandson is the most suitable soldier amongst all many times more powerful citizens of Daivika citizens presently resident on earth!", analyzed late Queen Madhu.

"True!" analaysed late Queen Gertrude, "Being appointed as the Head of Inter Galactic Justice on Earth and a senior member of the Inter Galactic Justice Core Team is a display of their faith in his potential decisions and of immense respect for our grandchild's abilities! It is possible that the fact that our grandson gives great importance to ethics, values and principles, the core values which the disciplined minds of present-day residents of the Daivika Planet uphold in great esteem, has been a deciding factor".

Then Sudhir moved onto the fact that he planned to visit the Palace after he got married to Ngia Vat. This shook up his grandparents.

"Ahhh! Where is our invitation card?" asked the late King with an expression that he was most certainly not going to miss his grandson's wedding.

"Oh, come along Cheru!" chastised late Queen Gertrude, "they hardly recognize him as their family! And you do not expect the Chiefs of the four villages to come here and give you an invitation card when they do not know whether you exist! This is one wedding that we have to keep ourselves away from".

"Ohh this is my baby's baby!" cried out late Queen Madhu, "can we not find a way out to attend this once in a life time celebration?!"

The crestfallen grandparents from then on listened to what Sudhir had to say with sullen faces.

The fact that he could not find the boat nor Nksi Nanga when he surfaced and his suspicion that Nksi Nanga was linked to Mógui de érzi became obvious when his mind traced him loitering amongst a huge treasure trove in the Palace Ground.

To these much-deprived grandparents, every little discussion with their grandson was fascinating and heartwarming. But every threat to his life was an alarming thought. Hence his question – "Now how do I plan my strategy to combat Mógui de érzi?" was met with "Oh let him have the entire island, the people, the treasures and the Palace, at least we have you! We do not want anything to happen to you!" from the two Queens.

But the King replied, "My son, it has been your destiny to walk the path of pain from your childhood. As is obvious to you, Mógui de érzi will work through many people to hurt and attack you and thus obviously hurt this island. This has always been the strategy of his adopted country through the past so many ages. Diànlì ji'è de guójia is obviously running many countries by proxy and to them this island too is simply a strategically important location to protect their trade and commerce route. The citizens on this island do not matter to them. Mógui is known for his sophisticated glib talk and guile. He is accessing your strength. The fact that your mind could not trace his whereabouts on this island is obviously because he is using an Invisibility Cloak technique that is superior to what is known to any of us. I would recommend that you shift to asking your mind to look for heat signals or areas of air displacement that measures the size of a body. Further, I would suggest that you cloak yourself similarly and your loved ones with an equally high technology of Invisibility cloaking! Further, the spirit world is a different dimension. We are spirits but we can see and touch each other because we have willed it to be so. Henceforth, until further notice, we three can only be seen by the tribe men, Ngia vat your wife and yourself, and no one else".

So, saying he snapped his fingers. Nothing happened! "Sudhir with a foxed expression on his face asked. "But I can see you?!"

"Correct" replied Queen Madhu, "In this room, you and the tribesmen can see us. But nobody else!"

～

Chapter 17

The Wedding

Sudhir's Marriage with Ngia Vat

Sudhir rushed back to a huge welcome party to honour his astounding victory against five adversaries from the 'Powya tribe'. He had become the new star icon of the youngsters. They were now doing away with the swagger in their walk, doing away with the disrespect for one's elders when they spoke, instead they tried to speak in measured dignified tones and they spoke up their minds without hurting their elders. All of them continued to wear the skirts and blouses in support of their favourite teams! A new fervor had taken over the villages.

The next morning, they began to prepare for the Khwanga, the big wedding!

Sudhir was in the newly prepared hut while Ngia Vat was being prepared for the ceremony by the village elders in another hut. Suddenly, Sudhir heard a lot of screaming and commotion happening which did seem out of place. Sudhir went out of the hut to check.

The villagers seemed terribly agitated and were in a frenzy to pick up their spears, bows and arrows as they pointed towards the sky.

"Howva Minsaw, Howva Minsaw", they screamed, meaning 'God causing strange happenings' or "Bad God"!

Sudhir saw Late King Cherusseri Namboodiri, late Queen Madhu Bagaria, and late Queen Gertrude Wallace hovering above the village!

Sudhir was their first and only grandchild! How could they stop themselves from being a part of his celebrations! Yet – arrows were being shot out at them, "Howva Minsaw, Howva Minsaw!", they screamed!

Sudhir quickly flew between his grandparents and the village folk down below and pointing at his grandparents then thumping his chest he declared, "Mahua Minsaw! Mahua Minsaw!", meaning the 'good God'! They stopped shooting out arrows but the doubts and fear did not seem to recede.

Late King Cherusseri Namboodiri, late Queen Madhu Bagaria, and late Queen Gertrude Wallace landed gently within the compound of The Super Council village named 'Beti Beti'. People ran helter skelter and jumped behind bushes and trees to hide or protect themselves.

Sudhir continued to hover and his voice boomed & resonated through the villages as if he was using a loud speaker, "People of the 'Powya tribe'! I am now going to be one of your family members. Like your family members desire to be present when you become Khwanga, here too my family desires to be the guest of the Powya tribe as Ngia Vat and I desire to become Khwanga. How do we treat our guests Oh great people of the Powya tribe? How? By shooting out arrows and spears at them? Or by making them feel comfortable and making them feel welcome? How?"

Ombasa the Chief of the Super Council and the other members of the Super Council were each holding a huge shield and a long spear which pointed menacingly at Late King Cherusseri Namboodiri, late Queen Madhu Bagaria, and late Queen Gertrude Wallace after they had landed gently within the compound of Beti Beti.

But Ombasa was now seen steadily bringing down his shield and then peeping over the same at the three spirits that had just flown into his village.

Sudhir flew gently down and landed next to Ngia vat. Then holding her hand, he led her first to late King Cherusseri Namboodiri and he bowed. Taking the que Ngia Vat too bowed in front of late King Cherusseri Namboodiri! The late King took both his palms to her head and with a voice full of emotion said, "Bless you my child!" and a pure golden crown appeared on her head! Ngia vat touched her head, found the crown and then pleasantly shocked, looked at Sudhir. Sudhir nodded in the affirmative and bowed again in front of the late King with folded hands to thank him for his kindness. Ngia vat too followed suit. The Tribal people began to chatter and whisper in an excited fashion! Then Sudhir walked up to Queen Madhu Bagaria. He touched her feet and the Queen embraced him. Ngia vat too followed suit and the Queen embraced her too. Just then a pure silver laced golden ball necklace appeared around Ngia vat's neck! She gasped and looked at Sudhir for reassurance and Sudhir signaled with his eyes that it was okay! Sudhir bowed again in front of Queen Madhu with folded hands to thank her for her kindness. Ngia vat too followed suit. Then, Sudhir walked up to Queen Gertrude Wallace and she embraced him and Ngia vat and putting both their palms together she handed them a big pure golden Key and declared, "You both are henceforth the protectors of the Island Kingdom of Nair Dvipa, including the famed treasures!" Sudhir bowed to thank her with folded hands and Ngia vat followed suit.

But the Chief of the village Council was feeling uneasy and awkward and therefore Ngia vat bowed, picked up a spear, crashed it on the floor in front of her father Ombasa, and yelled "Turuhusu!" meaning "Permit us". Sudhir followed suit, "Turuhusu!", he roared and the crowd roared in appreciation.

Ombasa then spoke as The Chief of the Tribes – "Ruhusa imetolewa!" meaning "Permission granted". Seeing this the crowd roared and the spear bottoms were thumped down on the forest floor as they sang, "Sasa uwe Raia mzuri! Sasa kwamba umeolewa!" meaning, "Now you be a good Citizen, now that you are married!"

In the meanwhile, Ngia vat went up to her father and whispered into his ear.

Ombasa signaled the rest of the Council members and they all took a step forward and keeping the shield and their spear in front of them bowed to late King Cherusseri Namboodiri, late Queen Madhu Bagaria, and late Queen Gertrude Wallace, reciting, "Mahua Minsaw kowo Karibu! Mahua Minsaw Kowo Karibu!", Mahua Minsaw Kowo meaning the 'group of good Gods', Karibu meaning Welcome!

The rest of the village followed suit. They went down on their knees and bowed in front of Sudhir's elders and began to recite as one, "Ninyi nyote mnakaribishwa!", meaning, you are welcome. "Ninyi nyote mnakaribishwa!", "Ninyi nyote mnakaribishwa!" The sound of this recitation made the birds in the trees, swarm together and fly high up into the skies. Then they flew as one over this august gathering to then broke up into smaller swarms and spread out in all directions like the opening-up of flower petals. It was an amazingly magical sight!

Sudhir had insisted on a Hindu ceremony and explained to the Tribe Leaders how it is done and the meaning or relevance of such a ceremony.

The festivities began. Ngia vat had to be decked up with river mud, flowers and the ceremonial skirt and top for sports events, created by Sudhir for special occasions. All the villagers were thus decked as they would on a sports day. This was a special occasion. Sudhir had to wear the robe made of Wild boar skin.

Sudhir could see his grandparents Late King Cherusseri Namboodiri, late Queen Madhu Bagaria, and late Queen Gertrude Wallace seated under the trees around the village with the village elders. This was one occasion that they obviously did not desire to miss! Their only grandchild getting married! They were so very excited! The late King would walk up to a hut and peep into it and Queen Madhu Bagaria had to pull him out every time and would try to make him behave with a "Shoo!" The two Queens were following the women's group now decking up the 'would be' bride.

The brick hut was ready, Sudhir had insisted on a ceremony and for the first time in the life of this village, Sudhir the groom tied a cane string to his stomach and the other end of the string loped around Ngia vats stomach. Then he led his bride around the fire seven times. This time being his second marriage, Sudhir was very confident while making the commitments to "feed and give all comfort physical or otherwise to my wedded wife". After the wedding, the celebrations of drinking and dancing and eating carried on till very late into the night.

They were Khwanga! Ngia vat and Sudhir were Khwanga! After many years Sudhir was truely happy and confident about his future!

But the happiest were the grandparents and parents.

The old King did not want to go back to the cave. "I really want to know what my grandson is doing inside!" he joked. His two wives had to drag him back with "Leave the young couple alone!"

In the meanwhile, Ombasa was inside his hut and was talking to a piece of panther bone with tears in his eyes, "Oniki see, what your daughter has gone and done! All that you wanted was that she should be Khwanga one day. But that fire brand girl of yours has now gone and selected a God for herself! Oh Oniki – I am so happy for her! Oh Oniki – I wish you were here to see for yourself the happiness in the eyes of our little baby!" And he cried out of happiness holding onto the panther bone.

Chapter 18

Sudhirs First Contact with City People of Nair Dvipa

The Defense Minister & Wánjù Mù'ǒu

Shri Himmat Khan was the Defense Minister of Nair Dvipa and he was a very unhappy man today. Seated immediately behind him were General Cristopher Rodrigues, the Chief of the Army staff (COAS) of Nair Dvipa, Admiral Sudhakar Nattarajan, the Chief of Naval Staff (CNS) of Nair Dvipa and Air Chief Marshal Kuriyedathu Raman Daivika, Chief of the Airstaff (CAS). Seated next to Shri Himmat Khan the Defense Minister around a round table was Shri Sharad Kadju Minister of Home Affairs. Shri Himmat Khan had a sour expression as he was being berated by the present Prime Minister Wánjù Mù'ǒu who had arrived ten years back as a trader from the country Diànlì ji'è de guójia, married a gullible local citizen seven years back, had mysteriously managed to get himself a citizenship card five years back and subsequently got himself elected as the Prime Minister of Nair Dvipa. He had taken full advantage of the loop holes in the Election Rules as were detailed in the Constitution of Nair Dvipa.

"How dare you suggest that you cannot identify the terrorists?!" Wánjù Mù'ǒu was growling at Shyamal Mukherjee, the Director General of Police. Then his voice rose "Go identify them and shoot them down one by one. Tax the rich and powerful amongst the loyalists till they go bust. How dare they stop some innocent tourists of Diànlì ji'è de guójia from taking out a bit of monies from a rich bank?! Eh?! We must encourage tourism. How dare the pro loyals object to an investment by Diànlì ji'è de guójia, a friendly country, in building a ship and submarine manufacture cum repair yard! Diànlì ji'è de guójia is pumping in monies and technology to build this port. Huge monies will be generated when the ships & submarines from our country, oh sorry, I mean from Diànlì ji'è de guójia begin to berth at this new port when complete!" Wánjù Mù'ǒu roured.

"Sir with due respect, Terrorists are those persons who use unlawful violence and intimidation, especially against civilians, in the pursuit of political aims", suggested Shyamal Mukherjee, the Director General of Police, very gently but with a dignified tone. "None of the loyalists are doing so and hence they cannot be labelled as terrorists. And Sir, regarding the bank looting case, we arrested certain miscreants after they were caught them red handed brandishing a gun and looting the bank that you mention, as is clearly obvious from the Video recording. We have the Video recording as proof and we shall present it at the courts." he continued.

"Lastly, as far as the Port is concerned", intervened Shri Himmat Khan, the Defense Minister of Nair Dvipa, "foreign investment of such magnitude is unwelcome if the Parliament has not sanctioned the same. An unlawful act is being unfortunately legalized by allowing Diànlì ji'è de guójia strategic control of such a huge tract of land for a project near our existing defense establishment, without prior sanction from the Nair Dvipa Parliament under the Kings signature as per the existing law which fortunately has not be modified. If Project related personnel from Diànlì ji'è de guójia try to do anything on any part of Nair Dvipa without the Kings signature, as per the existing law, then it will amount to an invasion".

"That is right", intervened Shyamal Mukherjee, the Director General of Police. "This port will open us up for an invasion. Over the years they shall consider that port to be their own property. And when we try to tax them or try to enforce laws relevant to Nair Dvipa, nothing can stop them from aggressively entering our territory controlled by our forces, with the objective of either conquering; liberating or re-establishing control or authority over Nair Dvipa territory; forcing the partition of our country; altering the established government or gaining concessions from said government; or a combination thereof."

Wánjù Mù'ǒu looked unsure and he peeped, "But the Prime Minister of Nair Dvipa can most certainly take a policy decision. We have an elected Government running the country. The King has no say in these matters any longer. We have abolished the Royalty, right?". Then taking on a more aggressive posture, "And my Ministers in the Parliament would certainly vote in favour of my decision!" growled the Prime Minister.

"I am part of that Parliament Sir and in your Ministry!" explained Shri Himmat Khan, the Defense Minister of Nair Dvipa. We chose you as our leader because you promised us a matured Democracy! Do you feel the other Ministers will support a deal with Diànlì ji'è de guójia? Do you feel that any Minister worth his salt, would sell away his country? The Parliament needs a majority to allow a foreign country to keep such a huge tract of land next to a sea port just for themselves and without allowing any audit and checks at regular intervals as it would be ideally desired" answered the Defense Minister. "This would give Diànlì ji'è de guójia a blanket permit to enter our seas as and when they please. This also allows them to invade us with many ships and submarines on the pretext of repair and maintenance. With this open-ended permission, they do not have to enter Nair Dvipa in the cover of the night".

'Wánjù Mù'ǒu glared at Shyamal Mukherjee, the Director General of Police and Himmat Khan the Defense Minister of Nair Dvipa with eyes that displayed loathing for the citizens of Nair Dvipa.

"Do not try to be over smart Mukherjee and Khan!" 'Wánjù Mù'ǒu growled.

Then he bent forward and began to whisper, "Diànlì ji'è de guójia has got people like you imprisoned for spreading anti-development rumours. I cannot remove you because of your stupid laws otherwise I would have kicked both of you out!

Now you report to me and so, just do what you are told! Accept the fact that yours is a stupid country that has allowed another foreign country to take over your Media, your Courts and your intelligentsia over these past so many years! It is too late for your country now to turn back! You belong to us! Learn to accept that! I have won the elections as per the rules of your flawed Electoral

System. Your constitution allowed such loopholes. You may not support my decision but money will make a majority from amongst the Parliamentarians to support just anything! If you refuse my orders then the courts, which are in our hands, will tell you to execute my instructions. Your local laws support my every action and you dare not challenge your local law. Accept the fact that Diànlì ji'è de guójia is today controlling your country by proxy! That is through me! Accept the fact that Nair Dvipa is now effectively an extended territory of Diànlì ji'è de guójia! Hence, you being a senior functionary of Nair Dvipa you must accept the instructions of Diànlì ji'è de guójia because they come through me!

Every loyalist trying to obstruct the project at the port is a terrorist and a potential threat to the friendship with the great country Diànlì ji'è de guójia, who can teach you what is the meaning of a great culture! Over the past so many ages, our citizens have come to this God forsaken land to make you civilized and to teach you how to do trade & commerce. Peaceful traders were branded as Pirates and jailed! Your Law was against them then but Diànlì ji'è de guójia changed that. Now Nair Dvipa law is in the favour of a healthy business dealing with Diànlì ji'è de guójia! These very same traders have sacrificed their life of comfort in Diànlì ji'è de guójia today to give you dimwitted people a helping hand in running this land full of fools, trusting and gullible people. Diànlì ji'è de guójia has ensured that you import low cost goods from them. Diànlì ji'è de guójia goods have become essential for every sphere of manufacturing in Nair Dvipa and if they stop supply to Nair Dvipa then your industry would come to a grinding halt in exactly one day! Diànlì ji'è de guójia does not need Nair Dvipa as much as Nair Dvipa needs Diànlì ji'è de guójia. Your local manufacturing facilities cannot compete with Diànlì ji'è de guójia manufactured goods because of high production costs. See how your greedy factories have begun to close like rats leaving a sinking ship! How would you like it if those greedy manufacturers returned? Eh?" lectured 'Wánjù Mù'ǒu, whispering.

Gopal Patnaik, the Director General of Vigilance and Anti-Corruption Bureau piped in, "at least they would be our brothers and sisters trying to produce within Nair Dvipa and thus bring down imports, thereby helping Nair Dvipa save billions in valuable foreign exchange. The balance of trade is dangerously in favour of Diànlì ji'è de guójia. There may soon come a time when we do not have the monies to pay your friendly country! Sir I would suggest that we become cautious about the Balance of Trade. I disagree with the release of those corrupt importers who do not possess any license to conduct any business in Nair Dvipa".

'Wánjù Mù'ŏu sprang up on his feet and screamed, "Listen you idiots! I am the Prime Minister and I decide what to do and you must do what I order you to do! And this is my last warning to you Khan! Use total force against these street side Romeos who spout poetry and songs in favour of that idiot who you called your King! Or else I get a Diànlì ji'è de guójia junior Sergeant to become your boss", so threatened Wánjù Mù'ŏu and strode out with his Junior Secretary Sashi Padmanabhan who gave a last helpless "Save me from this mess!" expression at those who remained in the conference room and then the door banged shut behind him.

"Sigh! What have we got ourselves into!?" fumed Srikumar Venketasan, the Director General of Coast Guards of Nair Dvipa. "So many people voted against the King but why? It all began with certain enemy nations capturing our media to gradually influence our people over many years. Today they destroy our ethics, values and principles. How? A girl was missing and we found her alive in a bad shape in the ditch outside 'Wánjù Mù'ŏu's house. She described her attackers as a group of men including the Prime Minister! Who dares to arrest him? He picks up our women, school girls, college girls and housewives like we pick up vegetables in the market. The Press and the Courts would come charging at our throats if we dared to arrest him. Who dares to arrest him? Now what are we going to do about Wánjù Mù'ŏu's illegal orders? Arrest the loyalist? On what grounds do we arrest them? Diànlì ji'è de guójia is running our country by proxy and we can do nothing about it!"

"Yes - You can do everything if you want to do something!" spoke a deep voice in a gentle tone.

Everybody stood up assuming that somebody had fixed a hidden microphone to listen to their discussion and was using loud speakers to make them listen to him.

Sudhir appeared in front of them. "I am Sudhir Bagaria, nee Sudhir Nair, son of Prince Pawandas Hanuman Bagaria nee Daivam Prince Pawandas

Hanuman Namboothiri of Nair Dvipa, grandson of Daivam King Cherusseri Namboodiri".

Before he could finish all of them stood at attention and saluted him. "Viśramikkū! Aramse! (Stand at ease!)" Sudhir gave the command and all of them became ramrod straight, chest filled up, and stomach in, legs apart and had moved their hands from their sides to behind their buttocks.

"I have automatically been appointed the King of Nair Dvipa as per the rules & laws put in place by the earliest citizens of this island kingdom. I am using the rights as a King to find out what happened and hence, I am here, amongst you all. Until the Royal family comes back to power please refer to me as Sir and not as 'Your Royal Highness'.

Now, how did Wánjù Mù'ǒu, a citizen of Diànlì ji'è de guójia manage to become a citizen of Nair Dvipa? How did we permit loopholes that allowed his companions, all known criminals, to stand for elections? Within five years of becoming a citizen, what are the loop holes in our Electoral system that he used to become our Prime Minister? It seems huge funds were infused into Nair Dvipa and distributed amongst various leaders or bad elements to guarantee votes at every ward and block level of Nair Dvipa. Why did we not analyze the loans given out by banks to various groups or organizations and the source of finances being used by our candidates, the NGOs, the Foreign Remittances, the siphoning off funds by big corporates, etc.? Why was a mass request to change the Election Process not made by our people till date? How is it possible that inspite of such professionals such as yourself, we failed to realize the threat of past forty years of grooming of Editors and Media personnel by enemy nations harboring negative energies? How is it that our Intelligence department failed to anticipate the takeover of the various Media by Diànlì ji'è de guójia? How is it that we failed to realize the undue attention that the country Diànlì ji'è de guójia gave to our lower and upper courts and finally the Supreme Court? How is it that our laws that allow us to arrest corrupt lawyers and Judges continues to be weak and unimplementable? And finally, how did we not anticipate that these corrupt Judges may someday enter the sanctum of the Supreme Court?

All right Mr. Gopal Patnaik, tell me why is our great nation now in the hands of a foreign nation. Why are we being run by proxy from a foreign land?"

Gopal Patnaik spoke up, "Sir! We all plead guilty! We had become complacent because everything worked systematically as laid out by the last King your Grand Father. By the time we realized that the Foreign nations had taken advantage of our corrupt Media, the corrupt Courts, the corrupt Police it was all too late. The foreign country seeded our minds with doubts about our Royal families. We thought that we had matured as a democracy and no longer needed the Royal family to tell us what to do. A lot many citizens, including I, lobbied against the Royals as it had become a popular movement, instigated by the anti-royal press over many years. Being a democracy, we thought it is okay for them to be free to say what they want. But the press said everything that poisoned the minds of our people. Little did we know that the movement had been instigated by a foreign country and then hijacked by them. We decided that if the fifty-one percent votes have favoured subjugation by foreign forces and misery then it was important for our people to suffer and realize that we all have done wrong before the movers and shakers from amongst us offered them a solution.

Things have gone from bad to worse. The different leaders barging into the office of any company Chairman or residential apartment to demand monies for a cultural event being held in Diànlì ji'è de guójia, the foreign country, this became increasingly unbearable. Companies were on the verge of pulling down their shutters as the seventy percent tax being levied by Wanju Mù'ǒu made doing business unviable. The per month 'protection money' demanded by Wánjù Mù'ǒu subsequently, hammered the nail on the coffin for entrepreneurs. Unemployment has resulted in the fall of any individual's ability to pay for the minimum guaranteed provision of food, clothing and shelter. Purse snatching has now graduated to being followed to the bank and your monies being snatched the moment you withdrew the same. Kidnappings have reached a ludicrous level of audacity. Women were snatched away from husbands or after throwing their children aside, all in full view of the general public and the police. We could now get our relative released from the kidnappers provided we went to the nearest local police station and paid the ransom money with the police acting as the mediators between the kidnappers and the aggrieved individual. Wanju Mù'ǒu has brought in a law that such policemen who acted as mediators cannot be penalized in any manner. And we could do nothing with Wanju supporting the culprits.

Most citizens have finally realized that they can now define lawlessness, corruption, failure of minimum essential services, huge unemployment, enforcing rules and celebrations that are alien to this country, feeling of helplessness and desperation! I feel that they are ready now to go back to your system of Democracy – true Democracy Sir!"

"Mr. Shyamal Mukherjee?" Sudhir asked the Director General of Police.

Shyamal said, "I agree with Mr. Patnaik Sir, that many amongst us who unwittingly voted for the country of Pirates to rule over them, deserved to experience the torture, the humiliation, the corruption, the destruction of business houses, destruction of core values and principles, their wives and daughters being dragged away in front of their eyes, the lawlessness, the helplessness and much more. This subjugation was very necessary because otherwise it would have been impossible for us to explain to the masses what is true subjugation or true suffering. Having gone through hell over these past few years, many have begun to raise their voice but Wanju Mù'ŏu twists our arms and makes us arrest them and ensure false cases are slapped against them with no chance of a bail. Many have expressed their desire to return to the old system but unfortunately there was no King to save them from their misery. Whenever any good citizen would desire to file his nomination papers to stand for elections against Wanju then, he would be threatened with a gun on his head, or his family members would disappear until the end of the elections. The Wanju Mù'ŏu team won the next election and the next and the one after that too, unopposed with every duration being five years. So, your people are resigned to their fate and they continue to suffer. We all have been waiting for a strong and honest leader for Twenty-five years with no hope nor solution until now! However, now that you are here Sir, we say, we are so very happy to see you!"

Sudhir now looked at Himmat Khan the Defense Minister and gestured, asking him for his suggestion.

Himmat Khan said, "We have to be very careful Sir considering that our entire Media including the Editors and their team of reporters is in enemy hands. The honest ones, or the pro country ones have been shot dead or forced to close shop. The migrants from the country of our occupiers use strong arm tactics, kidnappings, murder and mayhem and they have promised 20% of the votes cast by all of Nair Dvipa to Wanju Mù'ŏu in exchange for hard cash. Now that figure is huge and thus you can imagine the number of migrants from their land! Further Shyamal too would agree that corruption has created a rot in not just the Police Force; the courts will always take decisions against the honest government officials and the new King Sir; however shamefully obvious it becomes. The enemy nation is not concerned about our attempts to save our country from their Proxy control, because they know that our Electoral system cannot be changed, because our lawyers are puppets in enemy hands and the Media will always speak in their favour. They are all worried about you Sir! We were visited recently by that evil magician Mogui who tried to take control over our minds but failed miserably. He warned us all about the consequences of supporting you. Meaning they were certain about the possibility of your visit. Even the corrupt police and the lawyers have been warned. Because even the corrupt are finding it difficult to survive under an unreasonable, unpractical foreign government. But what is important that after a long time, we see even the corrupt people smiling happily on hearing about your possible visit. And that got the Prime Minister's brigands very worried. We were happy to see them worried after a long long time Sir!"

"What is certain is that our Electoral system was misused because of loopholes and our existing laws supported such misuse shamelessly", surmised King Sudhir.

"Our Administration is saluting those very criminals who had been imprisoned by them a few years ago. Another loophole.", complained Shyamal Mukherjee, the Director General of Police.

"Therefore, if the existing government has to be removed then we have to do so legally even while we alienate Wanju Mù'ŏu from Diànlì ji'è de guójia", explained Chathura Bandaranayake, Chief of NDI (Nair Dvipa Intelligence), who controlled the intelligence activities & officers globally and within Nair Dvipa. We must thwart any further interference from Diànlì ji'è de guójia the foreign country. I suspect that Diànlì ji'è de guójia may anticipate a 'No Confidence motion' or 'civil disobedience' very soon in the Parliament of Nair Dvipa and send its forces to quell such acts of independence movement".

Then looking at Sudhir he said, "Your Honour, it is important for all of you to know at this juncture that some powerful warships and beach landing craft, all armed to the teeth with latest technology war equipment, have been seen leaving the shores of Diànlì ji'è de guójia. We all must keep each other briefed and remain on the alert for a foreign invasion on Nair Dvipa at any moment! In the event of a victory of the foreign invaders then, my team and I shall have to leave Nair Dvipa for foreign lands to safeguard the detail of our trained assets posted globally."

"Spread the word", instructed Sudhir, "that the King is back! That henceforth policy decisions must not be pushed down to the mass as it is being done under Wánjù Mù'ǒu. All further policy decisions to bring about change must necessarily be brought up by the mass and then the idea can come to Wánjù for his approval".

"Yes Sir!" they all responded at the same time.

Khan the Defense Minster was a very happy man after a long long time.

"Tell everyone that Nair Dvipa shall soon be free!" assured Sudhir and he saw that everybody in the room stood at attention and saluted him.

Sudhir smiled at them and vanished.

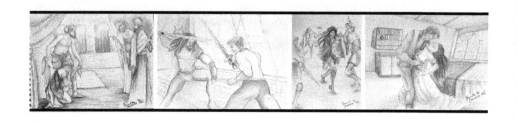

Chapter 19

Sudhir's Time Travel Begins

Sudhir Flies Back in Time to Year 1805

Mógui de érzi was first seen in the year 1805 by King Unni Pushpakan Ambalavasi.

Sudhir realized that he must travel back to that time. He asked his mind for the invisibility cloak and instructed, "Take me to Year 1805". Suddenly his hands stretched upwards and his body rushed towards the skies at supersonic speed. As he moved through the air, it made conical pressure waves in front of and behind him. Within split seconds, he was travelling through a conical tunnel faster than the speed of sound. Just as he broke the sound barrier, there was a sonic boom, then everything seemed to change around him. The speed could not be explained as he zipped past the yesteryears of Prithvi (Earth). He saw Prithvi change many times over as ocean waters backed away from land it had usurped and tectonic plates returned to their original positions. Then there was this mechanical whirr as everything slowed down and finally his body came to a stop. He looked down and saw that Earth looked different.

As he flew back down, the friction began to heat up his body to an unbearable level. "Slow down my descend", he instructed his mind and from then on, his body began to glide down towards Nair Dvipa. He saw hundreds of merchant vessels with sails fluttering against the wind. He flew over the Sea Port and saw sailors from old Asian, Middle East, African, European and some other continents with their wear of the 1800. He realized then that he was in the year 1805.

He flew to the Palace ground and found far below him the uniformed, trained personnel going about their tasks in a methodical fashion. Big Boats entering the river from the ocean, had begun to aim for the port that kissed the river banks near the palace. Pedigreed, pampered dogs were wagging their tales even while scooting all around the huge lawns in front of the palace, immediately after the driveway. Cows were mooing while grazing in the vast green pastures behind the palace after the moat. Horses were neighing while they gamboled, raced and kicked around in these very pastures. Swans and their cygnets were quacking away with each other as they seductively swung their backsides left and then right and then left & right again and ambled away towards the natural lake surrounded by colourlful trees. Children were giggling and skipping in the playground.

The elders however, were a worried lot huddled together, sitting around the dining table, discussing somebody who was hurting the citizens of Nair Dvipa.

King Unni Pushpakan Ambalavasi was walking out of his office towards the people hall where he received his citizens. He had to travel through a carpeted corridor which was not guarded as it was not necessary. Sudhir pointed both his hands towards the head of the King and told his mind, "Give him speed and the battle strategy desired to fight Mogui". The King suddenly went down on his knees and held his head in his two hands.

"You are okay great King! Do not be disturbed by my presence", suggested Sudhir without appearing in front of the King. "It is time for you to fight Mogui the pirate man to man! You have been fed with battle strategy that would allow you to think on your feet and enable you to use your powers wisely and on time".

The King nodded, got up on his feet and having brushed off the dust, strode confidently towards the "people's Darbar"

The Defense Minister, the Finance Minister, the Minister of Internal Intelligence, the Chief of Police, the Chief of Coast Guards were tearing their hair and expressing their woes to their King Unni Pushpakan Ambalavasi. Right in the center of the big group was a trained soldier who had been posted at the port but whose wife had been kidnapped by Mogui and was now a part of his harem. Mogui's pirate companions had advised the sailor to approach the King and ask him about where the treasures from the ships were hidden. If the treasures were found then, his wife would be released and he would be rewarded with ten pure gold mohors.

Sudhir saw King Unni Pushpakan Ambalavasi stand erect in frustration and anger. All his effort to thwart the attacks & torture of his people were in vain. He had the best trained police, coastal guards, Intelligence operatives, and finally the army, but all of them had failed miserably. But the pain in the soldier's voice was too much to bear.

One of the Kings aides whispered into another's ear, "What can our King do when the best armies have failed!"

King Unni Pushpakan Ambalavasi strode up to the soldier, embraced him in his arms and spoke aloud for all to hear, "A soldier's honour is the honour of Nair Dvipa. If the soldier's family is in distress then how can the soldier think about protecting the nation? What is your name soldier?"

"My name is Swarna Kumar your honour!" cried the petrified soldier. He was a broken man and yet the King himself was standing in front of him! Would the King understand his plight? He being a soldier, he could not do anything to protect the honour of his family! What is a soldier without self-respect and honour? "Your honour!", he said in between sobs, "You are our God, the provider of our bread and butter! You are the final protector of the lives of the citizens of Nair Dvipa! I do not care about all those who have failed my Lord. I do not care! I have faith in you my Lord! We have faith in you my lord! We know my lord that only you can do where all have failed!" Having said so, he began to bawl!

Sudhir saw King Unni Pushpakan Ambalavasi place a gentle hand on the soldier's head and then zoom into the skies. The King hovered in the skies to search for Mogui. Then he began to come down with his hands held high in the sky and his feet towards the top steeple of the church near the Prostitution den which had become so popular amongst the foreign traders initially and now amongst the royals from foreign shores who came in hoards, just to sample or buy the wares.

Sudhir watched as King Unni Pushpakan Ambalavasi tried to reason with Mogui and being rudely rebuffed by the youngster who was approximately Sudhir's father's age. Then the battle began where Mogui was gaining an upper hand, unknown to King Unni Pushpakan Ambalavasi, with the help of some black powder he was palming out and throwing from a satchel that he had hung on his back. King Unni Pushpakan Ambalavasi was grievously wounded and it was then that Sudhir, unknown to Mogui, interfered with history. He told his mind, "Seal that satchel permanently that Mogui holds on his back. Let it cut away and fall down below him". Then he told his mind, "Heal King Unni Pushpakan Ambalavasi".

Sudhir saw King Unni Pushpakan Ambalavasi trap Mogui in a vase and make him prisoner. Then King Ambalavasi looked around him and said, "I cannot see you, but I can feel your energy. Why do you not appear in front of me?"

It was then that Sudhir removed the invisible energy from around himself and bowed in front of the King, greeting him with, "I pay my respects oh great ancestor! I bow in respect of you, oh great great Grandfather, King Unni Pushpakan Ambalavasi!"

"So, you have managed to discover the secrets of being able to travel back in time?" King Ambalavasi asked with obvious interest in his eyes.

"Yes, I have, Oh Great great Grandfather King Ambalavasi!" replied Sudhir with great respect.

Then Sudhir told him all about the advances in technology that was to take place over four generations. Mainly in warfare, rifles and guns. How the World War one and then two took place. King Ambalavasi's expression became grim.

Sudhir also explained about the extraction of and then storage of negative or evil energy by an advanced civilization of a distant planet. How evil energies was extracted from the minds of irresponsible antisocial elements who had escaped from the prison ship that had crash-landed on earth and how such negative energies were stored in High Density High Energy Retaining (HDHER) steel casks. How Mogui stole one HDHER steel cask from our alien ancestors, enough to pollute the minds of Nair Dvipa totally. Mogui had been a regular visitor to a specific era to supplement his store. That the Daivika Planet ships located in a deep cave under the ocean had helped him pin point the time periods when many time travel events happened in the past and it was found that it started from or ended around the Formosa region.

Then he asked his great grand father, "Where do you suppose he may have hidden the stolen container of negative energy? Where around the Formosa?" He showed the satchel that Mogui had hidden behind his back and explained, "Mogui surely has a lot of negative energies stored in a safe house where he visits frequently. He has instructed a chunk of such energies to pollute the minds of Nair Dvipa Citizens. And they shall continue to do so and take over Nair Dvipa totally in my time, by the year 2018. The citizens of Nair Dvipa would be devoid of all self-respect, would become filled with disgust and lack of respect for their own nation, for the police, for the defense services, for every department of Nair Dvipa. Their self-worth would fall so low that they would gladly handover Nair Dvipa on a platter to Diànlì ji'è de guójia!"

"He loved his parents", replied King Ambalavasi, referring to Mogui. "Travel to that part of the land to where his parents returned after they left Nair Dvipa".

The suggestion was logical and Sudhir wondered why this common sense had not struck his mind before.

As is Hindu culture, Sudhir touched the feet of his great grandfather to pay his respects.

"Bless you! May you succeed in your search", King Ambalavasi said with his right palm extended over Sudhir's head. A warm energy passed from the palm of King Ambalavasi to Sudhir. Sudhir felt genuine love and care flow through him.

Just then a black ball of energy flew in from the skies, missed the palace by a few inches and bombed the little township nearby.

The township exploded in a plume of black smoke! Amazingly nothing was damaged. No building was damaged, no people died. On the contrary, nobody within the township seemed to notice that they had been bombed with the black energy. They were moving to work and doing their normal chores as if nothing was amiss. Only difference being they kept repeating, "Nair Dvipa has gone to the dogs! Our King is bad, our police is bad, our defense services is evil. We must go to study in Diànlì ji'è de guójia. We must ask Diànlì ji'è de guójia to run our country on our behalf. We must help Diànlì ji'è de guójia to kill our industry and ensure unemployment in Nair Dvipa. We must ask Diànlì ji'è de guójia to help improve our genes by allowing our daughters to be impregnated by the men of Diànlì ji'è de guójia".

They were zombies, and their minds no longer belonged to them. Only a major shock would wake them up!

King Ambalavasi looked at Sudhir with dismay. Sudhir nodded as if to say, "I am on the job Sir!"

He had to find the source of the negative energy that just flew in, right away, before the energy signals died out!

He bowed, turned around and zipped away into the skies.

Sudhir Flies Into the Future to Year 1922

He could immediately read the energy trial signals as they were still fresh.

The black energy had travelled from the future, from the year 1922! This meant that the ball of energy was possibly stored at a safehouse that would exist in the future. He was now in 1805 with his great great grandfather.

Sudhir asked for his invisibility energy cloak and travelled to Diànlì ji'è de guójia in 1922. That is where his parents had taken Mogui the moment that they got released from the prisons of Nair Dvipa.

He found serene beaches and peaceful fishermen the moment he appeared over the Formosa region and began hovering in the skies to observe the conditions of the period.

Then he saw the ships, hundreds of them! Pirate ships being supervised by a senior Diànlì ji'è de guójia official. Most of the ships had heavy cannons. He saw one of the ships sailing away from the rest. Certain smaller boats with sails gave chase and he found this very interesting. As he flew in for a closer look, he saw a much younger version of the picture of Prince Swaminarayanan as was in the wooden frame that he had noticed in the palace drawing room. It was Mogui's father! He was surrounded by pirates who were poking at him with sticks and spear points and laughing like mad men. He suddenly saw a large and tall pirate board the ship from a small sail boat that had been chasing this ship.

Sudhir realized he was Wúgū the pirate king. The big, tall pirate jumped down gently on the deck and then began to approach the prince with menace. He had a wooden leg, an eye patch on the left eye and a knife wound that had cut away a chunk from above his right cheek right down to his teeth that gave him a permanent "skull smirking" look.

"Thok, waph, thok, waph!" his legs made the sound on the wooden decks. Then he looked down on the terrified poet cum prince who had his back against the wooden wall of one of the many cabins on the deck of this ship and then, Wúgū the Pirate King spat on his son in law's face with, "You lousy weakling! An excuse for a King! I made my first mistake in my life by advising my daughter to woo a lousy loser with no sense of how to create wealth! And now he deserts his wife and runs back to his lousy brother who refuses to give him his due share of the kingdom! Eh – what you say – you deserting my daughter, eh? Are you?"

And the pirate king gave the prince a poke in his ribs.

The weak Prince seemed to change in front of Sudhir's eyes. He half stood up inspite of the hand that held him down and said," You father in law, did not ask your daughter to woo me! I wooed her and I proposed! She accepted my proposal and married me! She loves me for who I am and she is proud of the fact that I am a poet, a lyrics writer and a singer. I am not deserting the woman who loves me! I am a struggling trader and not a pirate. My ship is full of the silk cloth that is made here for which I have paid with my own finances. I shall trade it for spice and other goods from Nair Dvipa. I will not resort to snatching, nor piracy nor make monies through dishonest means like you and your pirate friends".

"Hah in love with you! Ho ho ho ho!" Wúgū the pirate king was roaring in laughter while all the pirates were rolling in mirth on the ship deck. Suddenly he became serious and spat, "You disgust my daughter! I have nurtured her in wealth! I have given her everything that she desired whereas you have hurt her with poverty! She did not marry you because you proposed! She was smart enough to accept my plan to trap you into a marriage, you simpleton! You think my daughter, who used to drink like a fish would have got drunk on a single spoon of whiskey! Eh? Ho ho ho ho! You, foolish pip-squeak who pretends to be a royal prince! You have no royalty in you. I feel your mother cheated on your father and had you through a liaison with a vagabond poet cum singer!"

"I do not believe you!" the poet cum singer prince kept trying to stand, blew his chest up and growled, "My wife loves me and she said so even this morning when she heard me recite my poem and encouraged me to remain my honest self. She made me promise that I remain who I am! She," he paused and then continued, "she kissed my lips, and urged me to go to distant lands and earn my monies through respectable trade with Nair Dvipa!"an angry prince Swaminarayanan insisted.

"In fact,", the poet cum singer prince continued, "my son will not learn your nefarious ways! I shall take him back with me to Nair Dvipa and ask my brother to teach him the ways of a Prince while I trade and earn my living for my wife and son and our future!" the now confident and angry prince Swaminarayanan insisted with his eyes staring straight back into the eyes of Wúgū the pirate king.

Just then a little face peeped from the window of a room and peeped," Papa? You okay?"

Wúgū the pirate king saw the little child and roared, "You are taking my grandson away to become a pip-squeak like you?! No, you shall not!" he took out his scabbard threateningly! "He shall grow under my tutelage! He shall learn from me and shall one day rule the seas as one of the most ruthless pirates. And you, pip-squeak, shall die today. Only then can I get my daughter married off to Gunecche my right-hand man with me here!" so saying, he gave an ugly, facially scarred, mean looking pirate a thump on his back.

Prince Swaminarayanan stared with anger at Gunecche the pirate. He must surely have been a very good human being and a handsome man in his time. But he was now an evil, ugly man!

Gunecche gave Prince Swaminarayanan a threatening grin and approached the door that led to the child, little Mogui's room.

Prince Swaminarayanan pushed away the heavy hand of Wúgū the Pirate King with force and the pirate king lost his balance and fell with his scabbard on the deck. The Prince then grabbed Gunecche by his neck from behind and pushed him aside with great strength. The surprised opponent tumbled and fell with a thud. All the pirates were surprised as the poet was known to be a softy.

Wúgū the Pirate king roared in anger. He glared at the pirates who had now surrounded the prince with daggers, cutlasses, swords, single shot guns. Then he nodded, giving them the green signal to attack. They raised their arms and with a horrendous roar that rent the air, and they charged to attack an unarmed man.

Sudhir, had been told never to interfere with history. Though invisible, he decided to change history once again.

He stood alongside Prince Swaminarayanan and the moment the Prince swung his arm to protect himself, Sudhir swung his arm to swat the attacker around ten feet away. Then the moment the Prince faced the wooden wall to save himself from another attack, Sudhir promptly used his back kick to smash into the attacker's face and make him shoot many feet away, tumble and smash into the far away wall. Little Mogui watched his father fight with pride from his window perch. "Yeaa Papa! Go papa! Gooo!" he cheered. Another attacker came charging but this time Prince Swaminarayanan, on hearing the clapping of the hands of his little son, decided to face the killers, come what may!

The attacker came with a dagger and the poet Prince swung his hand meekly and yet the man went flying to the furthest corner of the ship. The

Prince looked at his own fists in amazement. Then the next and the next pirate went flying to various corners of the ship. Prince Swaminarayanan began to enjoy his sudden power and kept swinging left, right and center. And pirates went flying in various directions much to the amazement of the aggressive, no holds barred sea robbers, who were used to a weakling who never reacted to their bullying. Soon the Prince was simply twitching the finger next to his thumb and the pirate would go flying far away!

The attackers went to consult Wúgū the Pirate King and he gave quick instructions. They surrounded him this time in every direction. And they charged as one. This time Sudhir made the prince fly into the skies. As he soured into the clouds, the prince was shocked and then, enjoying himself, he flew down to the huge group at high speed. He saw the panic, the fear, the shock, the awe on their faces. He flew into them, slicing through them even while swinging left and right with his fists and the pirates went flying and hit the wall at various spots all around the ship.

Then Sudhir made Prince Swaminarayanan point at the door which led to his sons' room and the door flung open. His son came out running! Little Mogui squealed in delight.

Sudhir made Prince Swaminarayanan stretch out his arms to receive his son in his embrace so that they could fly away to Nair Dvipa. Little Mogui naturally stretched out his hands to go into his papa's arms. "Weeee Papa weeee! You are so brave papa! You are my brave papa!" Little Mogui obviously adored his gentle papa!

It was then that things got out of hand. Wúgū the Pirate King took his hand back to a satchel behind his back, grabbed a handful of black energy dust and threw it towards Prince Swaminarayanan. Sudhir saw it all happening but it happened within seconds! The poet morphed into a foul-mouthed man who began to spout, "I do not have monies to take care of you, nor your mother! I need my poetry & songs and nothing else. My poetry matters to me and not your mother nor you! You both are a burden and hence I am sailing away from you both. I am running away! Your grandfather wanted me to be a man and hence tried to stop me from running away but I fought them so that I can be free from both of you!"

Sudhir was shocked and lost his concentration! Little Mogui fell but into his grandfather's arms. It was then that Sudhir saw the Pirate King opening his mouth and feeding words into the mouth of the Prince.

Wúgū the Pirate King made little Mogui hate his father, his father's weakness and thus he escaped into his room and locked himself in the same.

Before Sudhir could do anything, the black energy was trying to trace him and Sudhir could feel the search energies touching the air all around him. He had to retreat before their evil could affect his mind.

But what became obvious was that the black energy powder had reached the hands of Wúgū the Pirate king who reigned supreme in the year 1922. What was further obvious, was that the adult Mogui had visited this era and given some or all the evil energy powder to be stored in perpetuity with his grandfather.

Maybe this happened around 1921? Or maybe earlier!

This had to be undone. History had to be changed!

Sudhir Travels Back in Time to the Year 1920 AD

Sudhir realized that Mogui junior had a great chance to have been educated in Nair Dvipa amongst his royal cousins if, he had left with his father.

So, what stopped this from happening? The evil energy powder that little Mogui's grand father already possessed. So, when did Mogui visit him to be able to give the same to him? A year earlier? Two years earlier?

The urgent need was to promptly visit these two periods and check when the transfer took place. Evil dust most certainly affects the user and he tends to become increasingly vile resulting in lack of feelings for fellow beings. So, is it possible that Mogui had been engulfed by the evil dust? He had to investigate right away. Time was of importance here.

He rushed back to the year 1920 in the same region of Formosa.

He saw poverty and desperation in most villages that lined the shores. Every day was a battle to survive. They were desperate enough to dare to fight and snatch away the hard-earned wealth of others to survive and feed their family for that day. Desperation gave them courage to dare or die. Desperation taught them to pick up weapons, sit in small sail boats and charge at larger merchant vessels. Thus, they became pirates.

They attacked Junks that carried valuable goods in an area which was the vital artery of trade via the sea. Then they joined other groups to become bigger. Sudhir saw Pirate fleets exercising hegemony over villages on the coast, collecting revenue by exacting tribute and running extortion rackets.

Sudhir saw that the Pirate galleys were small, nimble, lightly armed, but often heavily manned in order to overwhelm the often-minimal crews of merchant ships. He saw huge cannon armed ships trying to chase these pirate galleys. The galleys would vanish into water lanes, that were meeting points of rivers and the ocean waters that lead deep into the land with villages on either side of the river that provided protection and a quick getaway. Hence in general, these pirate craft were extremely difficult for Government patrolling craft to hunt down and capture.

Sudhir saw how circumstances forced Piracy, which was initially conducted almost entirely with galleys, to gradually move to using highly maneuverable sailing vessels such as xebecs and brigantines which were captured Mediterranean vessels. They were, however, of a smaller type than battle galleys, often referred to as galiots or fustas.

Chapter 20

Wugu the Pirate King & Mogui

Research Material on Wúgū the Pirate King

Sudhir discovered that the Pirate King was a ship loader at the port. Sudhir saw an honest, hardworking man, a loving and caring husband to his wife and an amazing father to his daughter.

He used to complete the tasks given to him and yet many a time, his bosses would refuse to pay him his full dues and many a time, refused to pay at all. His wife, the daughter of a poor Scandinavian priest, found it very hard to meet the expenses of the household and many a day she sacrificed her share of meals so that her husband could go back and work hard.

Then his wife became unwell and his bosses at the port refused him monies for the treatment. He ran from door to door for any small loan to help bring down the fever and the convulsions that his wife was suffering from.

He met many rich men on the street throwing away monies on wasteful expenditures. He begged for a small amount from one of them and that rich man said, "Get your wife for one night and by the next morning she would be hale and hearty! Ha ha ha ha!"

The rich man's guffawing hit a strange nerve in the ship loader's head. That night he sat next to the port praying as he usually did for strength. But tonight, he realized that God helped those who helped themselves! But how was he to help himself? How? Out of sheer frustration he went kicking the sand on the beach until he got tired. His wife had said, with tears in her eyes that, she wanted to live! At this moment he felt so helpless! He stretched out his hands towards the stars and cried out aloud in pain, then picked up a pebble and threw it at the sea. He tore at his hair for some sort of solution and when none appeared in his mind, his frustration surged back and he kicked the sand once again.

"Are you in need of help my son?" a deep voice asked.

He looked up to see a tall stranger.

With tears in his eyes he refused to tell a total stranger about his grave problems at home.

"You have tears in your eyes! I have a small magic that would help you become a better man. It would help you change your life forever! You shall be able to feed your family every day. Your wife would become healthy and happy once again. Take it! I give it to you free of cost. A small gift, a wee bit of magic, from a friend from a distant land".

The Port worker raised his face to look at the small sachet of black powder and said," I do not need magic! I need money to buy medicines for my wife just for today! She needs my help today and I have failed her!"

"No, you have not failed your wife!" reasoned the stranger. "You can still earn and get her back on her feet. From then onwards, you never ever have to be poor again. Try it! Sniff this powder a wee bit! Bring magic into your life!"

The port worker gradually extended his hands towards the sachet of black powder, took the sachet into his hands, took a sniff from the powder and suddenly his whole body was on fire. He became unconscious for a few minutes, but when he woke up, the stranger was not around. He felt very confident and certain that he could change the life of his family. He used to walk with a slump but today, he filled his chest with air and stood his full six feet plus inches, and his muscles bulged out of his torn shirt sleeves.

He began to walk with confident steps towards his boss's bungalow and found a few lights were switched on and a lot of people were making merry. He knocked on the door and a bulky man with a big belly stood at the door with a bottle of liquor in his hand.

"What do you want you beggar!" the rude man asked with liquor fumes reeking out of his mouth.

Wúgū pushed him hard and he fell on his back. Wúgū marched into the drawing room, saw his boss with two women in his arms and each of them had a glass of liquor in their hand.

"I need the monies that you owe me. My wife is unwell" Wúgū said politely

"I told you to send your wife for one evening and you shall be paid much more that what is owed to you, you weakling!" the boss smirked, laughed and said.

Wúgū grabbed his boss by his two feet and gave it a strong tug, pulling him off his cotton filled seating arrangement. Then he kept the momentum and swung his boss against the thick wooden wall. The boss's head hit "thunk" on the thick wall, and he began to bleed. His eyes showed he was terrified.

"The money please", Wúgū looked into the eyes of his boss and growled.

The boss gestured and two powerful bodyguards appeared from behind the curtains. They charged at Wúgū but he smashed his fist first into the neck of one and below the ear of the other. Both collapsed gasping for breath or groaning.

Wúgū picked up his boss by his collar and smashed his fist into his boss's nose. Blood began to spurt like a fountain even while the boss began to scream.

Wúgū put his finger to his lips, "Another noise and I will smash your face again!"

The boss stopped screaming immediately.

"Now the money please", Wúgū calmly requested.

The boss pointed at a big vase, Wúgū found heaps of local currency notes and coins.

"Now, I am going to leave your bungalow", Wúgū explained. "If the local law come to my house then I am going to pay them a bribe, get released and I am going to smash your balls and believe me that it would really hurt! You believe me?" he finished with this threat.

Then he walked out and from that day onwards he always got his payments on time. In fact, he was paid extra to supervise a small group of workers.

Very soon the head worker of the same port came to threaten him to stop helping his team to get their dues. So, he smashed the man's nose, smashed him below his ears, broke the knee cap of five of his gang members and broke the arm of five other of his gang members.

From that day, he controlled a large track of Port Labour force.

His wife became okay, she moved into a bungalow with his daughter and him. They kept a guard dog and five security personal.

"I am so proud of you", she had given him a warm hug, smiled and said.

He was so happy that he decided to go back to the sea shore and he called out for the stranger," Are you there, I need you!"

Amazingly, the man appeared and offered to sell him two casks full of the magic powder. The price? The stranger asked for a shipload of gold coins and gold mohors. Wúgū asked him where would he come across such a ship. So, the stranger pointed at an Indian merchant ship docked at the port.

Out of sheer curiosity he got the cask to stand upright and it stood till his chest. He struck the body and he heard a – "Twangggg!" He got further curious and pried open the top lid and peeped into the cask to see a huge quantity of black powder!

But during that peeping into the vase, he accidently sniffed in a big quantity of the black powder.

That evening, his selected a gang of trusted port hands and he raided the Indian merchant ship. He killed everybody on board and his partners in crime were shocked by his brutality. He did not spare the women and children too. That night the stranger rewarded him with ample number of bags of pure gold coins, which were then distributed amongst his gang members.

Overnight, he became an aggressive thief, a thug, a ruthless murderer who cared for nobody and nothing else but his hunger for money and power. His wife became scared of the new man that her husband had become. Then when he began to display his strength by dragging her out by her hair and beating her in front of his band of thieves and thugs, she began to loathe him. Then, one moonless night, she picked up her meagre belongings and was trying to take her daughter along when she saw him in the distance, returning with his brigands from his murderous exploits. She did not have the time nor the courage to take her daughter along that night. She realized that a child would slow her down and risk getting caught. Therefore, she ran away all by herself, leaving her daughter to her fate.

That night and for many nights Sanya waited for her mother to return. When she realized that she had nobody but her father, she clung to him, and he became her idol.

Sudhir watched the change happening suddenly over a period and specially noticed Wúgū reaching into a leather bag and throwing a powder onto people and their becoming his followers subsequently.

It was the evil powder! But how was this possible? So Mogui had visited his grandfather and thrown the large drum into the sand right in front of him, for him to find.

Sudhir went back into time to identify the period when the cask was dropped.

What he saw shocked him so much that he could not think for some time. He then realized the enormity of the challenge that he now faced!

He used his powers to seal the cask permanently and got it teleported to the intergalactic craft parked under deep water in a cave.

He received a message telepathically, "Thank you! Have received the consignment in order".

He rushed back to the 2000 AD

Trying to Locate Móguǐ De Érzi in 2000 AD

Sudhir was feeling much stronger today. He realized that the Daivika Planet representatives had charged his brain cells further.

The early morning saw Sudhir up in the skies spreading a net of protective energy all around the island, then around important facilities such as the palace and including the village of the 'Powya tribe'.

Móguǐ de érzi was too powerful and did not have to hide. Yet, he was obviously in hiding anywhere on this island. Was he protecting himself or somebody else? Maybe his professional approach was to analyze which King was on the Throne, which person had how much power and how many minds of good people can be taken over to make them leave the good forces and join his evil force.

Sudhir felt that Móguǐ de érzi had something to do with the disappearance of 'Nksi Nanga' the witch doctor. Nksi Nanga could not have untied himself.

Therefore, it was strongly possible that Móguǐ de érzi was observing Sudhir's movements. But Sudhir could not see Móguǐ de érzi. Therefore, Sudhir surmised, Móguǐ de érzi was using his invisibility energy cloak!

Sudhir instructed his mind "Scan the island for Móguǐ de érzi".

But the search brought no results. "Alright, show me Nksi Nanga", he instructed his mind.

Suddenly, a mental video popped up of Nksi Nanga staring around at hundreds of antique wooden Liquor tanks that were held together by strips of pure brass strips. The antique wooden Liquor tanks were full of Diamonds, Jewels and gold mohors which were spilling out from each such wooden tank. A Golden Throne studded with precious stones stood in the corner and Nksi was sitting on the same with his leg swung over one of the arm rests. He was massaging the arm rest and repeating, "He he he! Mine! All mine! He he he!"

"Take me further up to locate the area "Sudhir instructed his mind.

Now he saw the Palace Building and the lush gardens but with workers working under the command of soldiers who were flying around and whipping the workers at intervals!! How were they flying? All the soldiers could not be citizens of the Daivika planet.

He rushed his mind to the ships of the cave. "Where are they getting the soldiers who fly? Are they all citizens of the Mogui's country?" he asked.

"The soldiers who whip your people today are your own soldiers under the mind control of Móguǐ de érzi. They can all execute super human feats under his control. At this juncture Citizen Sudhir Bagaria, you must be extremely careful as his powers far exceed yours even today", the lady on the ship explained.

Sudhir rushed to the cave to consult his elders.

Grandparents Agree to Train Tribals

"I have a question to ask", Sudhir apologetically asked.

"Shoot young man!", boomed the happy old King

"When I first met you all, I saw you all at the Palace. So how come you have been staying in this cave?" Sudhir asked sheepishly.

"He threw us out and he was able to do so because the combined mental power of all three of us could not match that of Mógui de érzi's powers! We escaped when he came charging to destroy our spirit form for eternity!" replied Queen Madhu Bagaria.

"And can he hurt you in this cave or in this village?" asked Sudhir

"My grandfather had made this cave his watch tower, to protect the primitive tribe people", explained the late King. "He had thrown a protective energy umbrella around this area that includes the tribesmen. The protective layer covers a large chunk of the jungle around their villages. That is why Nksi Nanga lost to you in-spite of being so close to Mógui de érzi'. Because Mógui de érzi could see the battle as it progressed but could not interfere because of the protective umbrella.

Now you have thrown another layer. I do not feel that Mógui de érzi can penetrate two layers to hurt the people you care for! But strangely, both the Palace as well as the fisherman's village had been similarly protected by my grandfather and we do not know how Mógui de érzi managed to cut through the protective layer. If he has a new technology superior to ours then you must discover what that is before you plan your attack", finished the late King.

"I have a request", Sudhir peeped

"You proved yourself to be a lion my Son! Your request shall be okayed anyway but shoot!" boomed the late King

Sudhir had been holding his breath and he let out his request like a flash flood, "I want you to begin training the 'Powya tribe' warriors into one of the best Professional fighters. With whatever arms and ammunition are available in their and our armory".

The late King did not bat an eye lid "When do we begin?" all three asked in unison.

"Ahhh – We?" asked a bewildered Sudhir.

"Yes – We!" replied all the three in unison.

"Both men as well as women of our forefathers in my family have been trained for warfare, have proven themselves to be good fighters and hence I can handle the women's division!" added Queen Madhu Bagaria.

"Yes, but your grandmother does not scare me!" the late King pulled his wife's leg.

"Ohh I don't scare you?!" the late Queen Madhu pretended anger and fury and approached the King with an extended fist.

The late King quickly raised both his hands in the air and promptly said with mock fear, "Ohh you do! You most certainly do!" Then he grabbed the late Queen's fist in his hands and kissed the same. Queen Madhu embraced the Late King and purred in his arms.

"And I have always provided good logistics and administrative support", added Queen Gertrude Wallace.

"Ofcourse you always have dear!", said the late King promptly and embraced his second wife too.

So, all four of them flew over the jungles and landed at Beti Beti to be greeted by the Chief of the Supreme Council and Sudhir's wife Ngia Vat.

The council of Chief sat down with the Chiefs of all four Villages, and Ombasa, the Supreme Chief spoke first. "As you all know, the forefathers of these great Mahua Minsaws had brought us to this island and looked after us whenever we were in peril. They now speak of a new peril that threatens to destroy all of us in the next few days. A Howva Minsaw has captured the mind of Nksi Nanga and we know that he can control the minds of us all to fight each other.

These senior Mahua Minsaws have offered to train us to fight like our son in law Mahua Minsaw did the other day while fighting the five brave warrior adversaries. And fight we must, otherwise we may all perish. We need men and women volunteers. How many would volunteer to fight and protect the dignity and existence of the Powya tribe?"

Within a second all the four Chiefs stood up including 'Tai Simba' the new Chief of Zambeke. "I am proud to call you my family! Get your people in each village to join the combined forces for the training to begin at the earliest!" instructed Ombasa

The four Chiefs smashed the end of their spears on the forest floor and roared as one, "Sava!"

And they rushed away towards their villages.

Late King Cherusseri Namboodiri, late Queen Madhu Bagaria, and late Queen Gertrude Wallace were looking tired.

Ombasa signaled his men and then said,

"This training would require dedicated time and energy. It does not make sense for you to return to your spirit abode every day. Kindly be our guest at the special hut which has already been erected for you while we were speaking!" and he guided them reverently towards the hut that stood on twenty stilts. Ngia Vat welcomed them with a Namaste as was taught to her by Sudhir. She was wearing the frilly grass skirt and grass top gifted to her by Sudhir. She bent down and touched the feet of the elders. "Stay blessed my child!" said the King. The two queens gave her a bear hug each and then held her hand to be guided ahead into their quarters.

Ngia Vat turned her head back to look at Sudhir with an expression that asked, "Did I do okay?"

Sudhir smiled, and nodded with a thumps up, then flew and zipped away to the Palace building.

The Training Begins at the Villages of the Tribes

The warriors were mixed in physical structure. Some were short and stocky, some were tall and lanky, some were of normal height of five feet five inches. But all had muscular biceps and triceps and strong muscles thighs and calf muscles.

They came with their long spears, their bows and arrows and shields. Some with their blow pipes with poison darts and some with the pigskin catapults and the small rocks that they would throw at the enemy. They were all very excited and hence thumping their spears on the floor of the huge stadium which had become the venue for the training.

Then silence ensued as the great Mohua Minshaws came flying and began to hover over the stadium.

Then the Ex-King and his two queens landed on a specially built high platform at one end of the stadium, hence the huge gathering now faced them. The Ex- King now spoke with the warriors in their tongue and the voice magically travelled to every corner of the stadium.

"Great warriors of the Powva tribe we greet you!" said the King and the tribe roared as one.

"We greet the elders of Beti Beti, the super council village or the village of the elders. We greet the tribe members of Zambeke. We greet the tribe members of Omagwena. We greet the tribe members of Kavaheke. We greet the tribe members of Kunini!" continued the King. And every mention of a specific village brought about a roar from the warriors of that village.

"We three have been requested by our grandson, who has now become a family member of your great Powva tribe, to train you, so that you may defeat the yellow skin strangers who kidnap your people with boom boom sticks. Many of your Tribe members have captured many boom boom sticks and we shall use these to teach each of you to be able to handle the same to go to battle. We shall teach you to battle not just these bad-bad strangers but also many bad strangers who live in city villages which have baked brick huts, hard as rock, that do not break. And there are many huts built one over another hut and then yet another hut till the structure goes high up into the skies. Some of these city dwellers may wish to harm you with bigger boom boom sticks, many times more powerful than these sticks. At the end of this training you shall be able to defeat many powerful armies!"

The warriors of the Powva tribe roared as one!

The training began the very next day. Camps came up outside the stadium with built in separate toilets and a big reservoir of water. The total lot were broken up into small groups and they were told what was expected of them. Discipline was expected of them. Following orders of their immediate ranking senior with no questions asked, was expected of them. No need for bravado but the need for intelligent warfare tactics and techniques was obvious.

They learned how to dig trenches and how to dig tunnels to travel far and wide without being detected. How to cover the man holes with sticks and leaf and then leap up to attack the enemy. How guerilla warfare and silent attacks are far more successful to ensure maximum fatalities. The boom boom guns were few in numbers. When the enemy is armed with modern tools and you possess primitive tools then how best to stand in a line, shoot the arrow and sit down to reload the arrow, while the line behind you shoots and sits down & reloads the arrow, to allow the third line to shoot. This could be from a flat ground or from the top of a tree or various branches of a tree or a hill top.

Then specially chosen warriors were given powers to fly and attack to scare the enemy. To fly in, pick up the enemy warrior and fly away with shrieks and squeals, thus creating a sense of fear and dread born from superstition. The enemy warrior would be taken high up in the sky for his fellow warriors to see him screaming in terror and then see him drop and keep falling, then being caught just before he is about to strike mother earth and finally being dropped inside the Powva tribe camp to be suitably dealt with by the warriors.

Finally, they were taught how to use the boom boom sticks.

"These boom boom sticks are known to the yellow strangers as guns", began the ex-King.

The First Meeting and Battle with Mógui De Érzi

Sudhir was hovering high above the clouds and looking down at the Palace and the pristine gardens, the chicken pens, the cowsheds, the hills, the river, the boats and the fishermen. Thousands of fishermen!

He did not see the flying soldiers whom he had seen in his vision the other day. But he did see the workers. They were carrying material from within the Palace building onto several large trawlers that were parked alongside the dock. He did not see anybody bullying them nor forcing them. Men, weapon and children were working like disciplined ants in two straight lines, one for entering the building and a separate line for coming out loaded with heavy goods from the building. Some goods were carried by four men, some two and some did it single. But all of them seemed to possess super human strength, enough for them to undertake the task of carrying the heavy valuables without spilling.

He scanned for Mógui de érzi and Nksi Nanga. He traced the latter in a large bedroom with five women who were involving him in various positions of the Kamasutra.

Mógui de érzi could not be traced. He asked his mind to scan for the movement of body heat below him. Mógui de érzi could not be traced. He was not in the Palace. So Sudhir flew down and gently landed at the port and told his mind, "Transform me to a fisherman". And in a flash, he was a bare bodied, thick boned, smelly unwashed person, of medium height, stocky, fat bellied dark sailor with dried red remnants of Betel nut sticking to many of his dirty teeth, with un-kept beard and unkept, dirty, smelly, matted hair on his head. He asked one of the sailors walking in the line ahead of him, "What's up mate? What this line about now say?" The man did not reply nor did he turn around. He continued to walk with his hands down his side. So Sudhir asked the same question of the man behind him. That man too looked straight ahead with his hands down his side.

They were obviously being controlled. Sudhir decided to follow the path and pretended to be one of the hypnotized sailors. He looked straight and like the rest, kept his hands down by his side too.

He walked in through the main entrance door of the palace that he had used to flee the last time. He walked into the same neat and tidy well lit up drawing room but then the line turned right towards a door with stairs that led down. The line 'plick plonked' downstairs then turned left to a huge powerfully lit up cellar, the size of two super-sized ballrooms.

The zombie sailor in front of him stumbled and fell on an obstruction. But he promptly stood up and began to walk straight ahead as if nothing had happened.

Sudhir scanned and saw that the sailor had stumbled on a pile of pure gold mohors!

Right ahead of him was an even bigger pile of thick gold coins!

Then he heard the voices – "No Móguǐ my son, you shall not hurt him", an old man's voice screamed.

"Tā huì sǐ de! He shall die!" a deep and yet hoarse voiced spoke in both his mother tongue as well as in English.

"Dàn wèishéme Móguǐ? But why Móguǐ? the old man's voice asked. He has not hurt you. Why do you wish to hurt him?", continued to ask the old male voice in both his tongue as well as in English.

A bewildered Sudhir looked ahead but saw nobody! He scanned ahead and sensed powerful energy emanating from a wall painting of a Royal in ceremonial dress. Behind him within the painting was the depiction of a Pirate galleon. The painting was talking to a box on the floor that was not moving and was not emanating any heat.

"Ahh so!", realized Sudhir, boxes do not let out much heat energy. "So Móguǐ de érzi has disguised him-self as a box. Interesting battle strategy learned!"

"He wants the treasure. Tā huì sǐ de! He shall die!" growled Móguǐ de érzi.

But the zombie line of sailors seemed not to be bothered by the arguing and therefore he continued to play the hypnotized sailor's role. Each of them was given a small or large item, sometimes boxes of Gold, silver, diamonds, rubies, and they all glistened in the well-lit room.

The first Ballroom sized room, had a small hillock heap of necklaces made from precious stones, bracelets, crowns embedded with precious stones and then he saw the huge gold-plated chest that had fallen on its side thus spilling the contents on the floor.

"Treasure Chests!" Sudhir exclaimed in his mind, "Mountains of gold coins!" he continued to explain to himself in his mind, being in obvious shock. "Gold Chests embedded with precious stones. Hundreds of wooden chests filled with diamonds! Pure golden chairs embedded with precious stones! An armory full of antique arms and body protection armour…" he was now whispering in his mind to himself in shock. These were the very same treasures that he saw night, after night, after night! How could he forget! For the past so many years, his now ex-wife Malini and his children – they had all mocked him about this very dream. But here it was right in front of his very eyes! It was all true! His dream was true! And all those many years his wife had called him a "Non-achiever cum Dreamer!"

He had this expression of awe & bewilderment on his face for a while then quickly controlled himself.

Just then Sudhir heard the voice again!

"Kàn dào. Tā zhīdào wǒ de bǎobèi. These are treasures from only just one ship. The ship that I discovered at the bottom of the ocean, it had all these treasures that are piled up in these two ball rooms. The last King had hidden the treasures from the previous five ships at an unknown destination. Maybe that new Prince who married that tribal woman knows the whereabouts of the rest of the fabled treasure. He knows about my treasure about that I am certain. I can feel it in my bones!", growled Móguǐ de érzi

"This huge treasure hoard spread out in two huge ball rooms is just from one ship alone?!" Sudhir wondered.

The old man's voice reasoned with son, "Your mother and I did not need any treasure barring you. Treasures only bring about pain and sorrow. Your grandfather desired treasures and he died a sad man. But you were our treasure. You were a happy child. We all were so happy! What happened to you? What changed you my son?"

Móguǐ de érzi growled,

"You were always a weak man Papa. Grandfather woke me up to the fact that you too had a right to a share of the Kingdom. We could have lived a rich life like your brothers! But No - you opted to remain silent about your inheritance and both Mama and you remained a middle-class citizen! Then you ran away to this island leaving Ma and me alone back there with grandpa! The cousins got the best of education in foreign countries and enjoyed the best of luxuries whereas they deprived your own son, their blood relative from a fair deal! Why Papa? Because you did not have the courage to demand what was justifiably yours! Now that I am here, do you think that they would be so gracious as to handover my share to me? No, they would not! In this world only the fittest have the right to survive or deserve the riches. Grandpa taught me so! See I have made my mother's countrymen grab this island Kingdom and run it legally by Proxy! All this gold and dimaonds the golden throne, and the chest full of valuables that is here in these two ball rooms is just from a single ship that I discovered Papa, from deep within the ocean waters! Because I worked for all of it Papa!

Enough of hiding! Transform to human!" his command boomed and a devilish, half naked man stood where the box was a few moments ago!

So saying, Mogui sat on the golden throne just to show off his achievements to the Papa whom he had always loved.

"How do I look Papa? Do I look like the King I had deserved to be?

Yet they took it away from me and got me bottled up for so many years! So many years went by because of which I lost the opportunity to see my daughter grow and then my grandson grow up. It is time for me to give my final push. I shall grab today what is due to our family for so many years! I shall ensure that my grandson is not deprived!"

"The old man exclaimed, "You have changed Mogui! You have changed from the sweet, roly-poly ball of loveable cuteness, to this devil who sits on the throne today! You have thrown out my brother's son and his two wives from the palace! That is a horrible thing to do my son! How can you throw somebody out of his own home?

Móguǐ de érzi replied with emotion in his voice, "You call me the devil today Papa? Just because you married the daughter of a pirate, they threw you out of your house too, right Papa? So, I threw out your brother and his two wives! What was wrong in marrying the daughter of a Pirate when you were happy about doing so? You loved Mama and both of you were so happy with each other. Grandpa may have been a Pirate but he had the guts to pamper his daughter and bring her up in luxury. Whereas you gave her a middle-class lifestyle! Did she deserve that? Did I deserve that? Fine they disinherited you because of your supposed misconduct, a view point which I object to! You cannot be punished for robbing that which already belongs to you! Why could you not speak up and ask your sister's husband Prince Akavoor Daivikapad for my rights to a better life style and better education? Why was I, a child who has caused no harm, why was I disinherited?"

The old man did not have a reply and so Móguǐ de érzi growled, "I have always loved you Papa. I have always loved you. Therefore, it hurt more that my Papa was so weak. And therefore, to fight and win what you, my grandson and I deserve, I had to become evil. You displayed your fighting skills several years back when running away using a ship to Nair Dvipa, from your own wife and son. I am so very ashamed of my memories of how they treated you. How they killed you!"

Like all the other zombie sailors, Sudhir was given a box of gold coins and like all the others, he too began to walk back with the line, climbed up the stairs to the drawing room, then turned left towards the exit. As he continued towards the main door, he heard father and son continue their discussion.

Just as he was near the large main door exit, he saw Nksi Nanga emerge naked with two women in his two arms from one of the bedrooms. Each woman had a hypnotic glaze in her eyes. But Nksi was looking at somebody behind Sudhir. "Grandpa Móguǐ! Where are you going in such a hurry?!" he asked lazily.

Sudhir saw from the corner of his left eye that Mogui was standing at the door that led down to the store house! "Aha - so Nksi Nanga's mother was Mogui's daughter!" he realized.

Móguǐ de érzi stood his six feet three inches' tall frame and he began to beam. He looked lovingly at Nksi Nanga, "My darling grandson! I am going out to ensure that your inheritance remains safe in your hands!" So saying, he yelled, "Sea Gull!" and in a flash he was a sea gull! The sea gull flew out of the main door and then out into the blue skies with its shrill, "Kee Kee Kee!"

Sudhir needed to be able to bargain and then thrash out a compromise with Mogui. What could he hold that was valuable to Mogui? Sudhir continued to a large commercial barge and handed his box of gold to another zombie who entered the boat. Then he had a brilliant idea that could lead to a negotiation. He snapped his fingers and all the gold & jewelry from the sealed holds below the decks of all the river barges, got teleported to a preplanned location! Then, like all the rest, Sudhir and all the others went back into the house and back down to the Cellar with its huge hoard of treasure. He could feel the energy of the painting as he walked past the same. On his last visit to the Palace, he had seen this very painting in the drawing room.

"Stop there sailor, I wish to speak with you!" the painting requested. But Sudhir pretended that he had not heard the old man and continued like a zombie with the rest of the zombie sailors. I know that you can hear me young man. I can sense that you are a citizen of the Daivika planet like I. Speak with me sailor!" the old man continued to request.

But Sudhir continued in the line. Suddenly, Sudhir's path was blocked by an old, very well-dressed spirit of a Royal family member. All the other Zombie sailors walked past both Sudhir and the old man. The sailors continued to take possession of boxes and then take the return route.

Sudhir looked up very slowly into the eyes of the old man. It was Prince Swaminarayanan who had married Wúgū the Pirate King's daughter Sanya. Sudhir remembered a much younger man surrounded by pirates on a ship. Sudhir remembered how he had made this prince to fight back the bullying pirates. But today, Sudhir sensed pain in his eyes! A lot of pain!

"You are a Daivika planet citizen, I can feel that, but you certainly do not know that, do you, young sailor? Look at yourself, you are such an unsophisticated mess, just like my son's grandson! You must have been born to a sailor's family by circumstances. I know you heard me speaking with my son. Why do you think all this had to happen young man?" the old man asked.

"Why did my brother disinherit my son? What harm had he caused to them, a child? Look at what has become of him now? Who has pushed him to this path? I have! I accept my failure as a father. But I know that I loved my wife and that I had done nothing wrong by marrying a Pirate's daughter. That new member of the Palace, the one who just married the semi naked tribal woman a few days back, he too has married below the family norm. Will they outcast him now or will they make a different rule for him? Why could they not then allow my son's grandchild, my son's daughter's son, to marry the semi naked tribal woman? It would have been more logical. What do you say to my reasoning my son?"

As Sudhir did not have the details from both the parties, he avoided an answer intentionally. Instead, he asked "So what does your son want now?"

"Now he wants everything! "replied the old man. "He wants to disinherit the Palace Royals in the same manner that my brother disinherited me. Then they bottled my child away for so many years until now! He wants the Palace Royals to be unhappy the same way my family was made to suffer for so many years!"

"And what is your suggestion ", asked Sudhir

"You too like me are a citizen of the Daivika planet. I suggest that you help me stop my son from killing the Palace Royals! That is his way of disinheriting them all! And the only way to stop him is to sit with him and listen to him. Nobody discussed with me. I was not given any chance to explain or reason. I suggest that before he does anything damaging, the new Prince married to that tribal girl of the village must sit with my son and thrash out a compromise".

"You are talking to the wrong man great grandfather!" a voice from behind Sudhir boomed. A massive palm thumped down on Sudhir's shoulder and turned him around and he saw a half-naked Nksi Nanga. "This man is not that young man and he is not anybody who may play any role in our lives. This man is a fat sailor trying to waste your time. Now go back to work fat sailor before I cut your throat" Nksi Nanga growled and pushed Sudhir back to the line. As Sudhir had heard enough, he made his way up to the main exit door alongwith the rest in the line.

Now they had reached the drawing room and were approaching the main door in a straight line that led to the main entrance cum exit door. There were five people in the line ahead of him walking towards the door. He was about to change into a bird and fly away when he heard the faint "Ki Ki Ki" of a sea gull which grew louder every second and suddenly, it flew in "Kee kee kee" and the seagull morphed into Mógui de érzi who rushed from the entrance and began desperately searching through all the faces in the two lines.

Sudhir immediately told his mind, "Do not allow him to sense my heat nor energy! Kill his senses!"

"He is here! He is here!" screamed Mogui. "I felt him from high above in the skies! He has dared to enter my domain! He has dared challenge my might! He has come to once again take everything away from us! Where are you?" he screamed like a madman.

Half naked Nksi Nanga rushed upstairs – "What is wrong grand father?"

"Go away my child! Hide Nksi my darling grandson, he has come to kill you! Hide! Quickly!" he looked with panic-stricken eyes at Nksi and screamed in horror.

Then he grabbed the lead sailor and commanded, "What's happened why can I not sense his presence any longer? You sailor tell me! Are you King Sudhir Bagaria, the one who married Ngia Vat?" But the zombie simply stared ahead with his hands down by his side. When Mogui did not get any reply from the sailor, his face became crimson red with rage compounded by desperation. He swung back with his small knife and cut off the man's throat. The sailor fell dead bleeding from his neck and mouth.

"No grandfather, do not waste your time!" Nksi laughed and said. "None of them are that man who I saw every day for the past so many years! You are an old man now and getting all worked up unnecessarily! Let me go back to that village and pick him out for a fight once again" Nksi Nanga continued to advise his grandfather.

"No Nksi my child, go hide! He is here to kill you!" screamed Mógui de érzi in panic and grabbed the hair of the second sailor and swung his arm to cut the sailor's throat.

"Make me a Panther! "Sudhir spoke to his mind. And flash! The sailor morphed into a Panther, pounced at Mógui de érzi's knife wielding arm, swung him out of the main door and into the garden. As Mógui de érzi kept tumbling over & over due to the momentum of the sudden attack, "Transform to my original Self!", Sudhir told himself and he stood, legs and hands spread out for a fight, where the Panther had crouched a second back.

"It's him grandfather! It is him!" screamed Nksi Nanga from inside the drawing room, now behind Sudhir. Then Nksi Nanga dragged out a spear that hung on the wall and charged, screaming "Aiiii Haiii ya yah!" Sudhir took his left hand behind his back, pointed a finger at the entrance door behind him and whispered, "Door close!" and the main door slammed shut on Nksi Naga's face and smashed his nose!

Mógui de érzi saw the door slam and he winced in pain imagining his grandson's pain but by then he had managed to regain his footing. Then like Sudhir, he too had his hands and legs spread out and was ready for battle.

"Ahh so, my brother's great grandchild! We meet finally!" Mogui smiled and growled.

"I had searched for your father and for you for all these many years", he growled and continued with a grimace. "But I could not find any of you, how sad! Otherwise I would have killed you both by now. When you landed at this palace, I had got the news that a shipwreck by the name of some Bagaria was being treated. I let you run away to the forest because I thought I was letting some shipwreck named Bagaria run away! If I had known, you were the same Late King Cherusseri Namboodiri's grandson then I would have squashed you like a bug and finished you off then and there! Now you chubby faced relative of mine, you stand so vulnerable, so helpless in front of me, just like I did so many years ago when my parents were sent to prison!"

Instead of taking the bait for a fight to the end, Sudhir decided to initiate a discussion. "Mogui I just spoke with your father! There has been a serious misunderstanding and we must talk!" spoke Sudhir.

Mógui de érzi swung his head on the left side and then right side as if assessing Sudhir and replied, "Ofcourse my child! You may want to address me as great grandfather Mogui and not just Mogui, don't you think so? Part of our etiquette but I am sure you have been taught the same by your parents. Yes, we must talk, we must talk my child!" He relaxed as if he was not interested in a fight and, "Come let us sit down on that bench on your left". So saying, he pointed at the bench with the right hand but Sudhir was watching out for his left hand and as expected Mógui de érzi quickly zapped out a very heavy blast from his left hand. Sudhir simply batted it away with his right hand into the skies and zapped Mógui de érzi 's left leg. The blast burned away through Mógui's heavy leather long boots, through the muscles and burned away right till the bone!

Mógui de érzi was not prepared for such power from a comparatively young person, hence he was unprotected. He screamed in pain and fell to grab his burnt ankle. At that very moment Sudhir leapt up into the skies and promptly dived down with the intention of pinning Mógui de érzi down to allow the discussion to happen subsequently. But his opponent was a seasoned player. He swung his body to the left to zap Sudhir with his right hand and the blast hit Sudhir on his left shoulder. Sudhir was not ready for such a fast move. He felt excruciating pain and was thrown back far away. "Repair arm!" he told himself quickly and his arm repaired itself instantly. He stood up to find that Mogui too had repaired his ankle wound and was quickly getting back on his feet.

"Create five of my body reflections to hover above Mogui, and give me the invisibility cloak!", he instructed his mind. And flash! There were five Sudhirs hovering above Mogui!

The five mirror images of Sudhir spoke with Mogui as one, "I do not want us to fight Mogui! I know you feel that there has been injustice! We must not fight! We must sit down for a discussion and come to an understanding!" spoke up all the Sudhirs.

Before Sudhir's mirror images could finish speaking Mogui quickly pointed at all the five Sudhirs and commanded, "Freeze!" And all the Sudhirs froze after finishing the sentence. But the real Sudhir was hidden away by the invisibility cloak.

Mogui floated up in the center of the frozen Sudhirs. "Do you call your own great grandmother by her first name? So how dare you call me Mogui? You want to hide amongst these five and you think I cannot identify who to hit? But I do not intend to find you! So, you wanted to talk eh!? Talk about what? And what else do you want to discuss? How there was a big mistake so many years back? How much you wish that we forget that your great grandfather disinherited a child who had committed no crime? Then you would want to come to a compromise and give us a mere five percent thrown in our direction like one would to a beggar. Right? You are mistaken you dimple cheeked upstart! You all have committed a grave crime many years back. The rules of Intergalactic travel clearly state that no citizen of Daivika planet shall ever cheat or deprive his fellow Daivika planet brother. Your great grand parents have shown my father to have committed a grave crime by marrying the daughter of a Pirate! That is a lie! You married far below your Royal family. You were not disinherited! Marrying the daughter of a Pirate is a decision to marry with any local citizen of earth. It is a case of inter-marriage. It is not a crime. But your family used guile to deprive and disinherit my father and an innocent child! You all need to be punished for misusing an Inter-galactic rule. And I start with you!"

So saying, he blasted at all the five forms of Sudhir, one by one, screaming, "Die! Die! Die! Die! Die! "And when the last of Sudhirs burst into many small pieces and floated away, Mogui came slowly down, landed on the cemented floor, zapped at the entrance door in anger which swung open immediately. He saw his grandson sprawled on his back after getting his face smashed once again just because he was standing in front of the door and watching through the peep hole!

Sudhir saw a grandfather embrace his grandson to help him reduce the pain of the door slam.

Sudhir told his mind, "Fly back to the village!" And he flew back totally invisible, to the village.

Sudhir at the Beti Beti Village in a Dilemma

Sudhir was in a dilemma. He had been taught to do a job well. Now when he took up the sales of computers, he had made it a point to put forward the negatives as well as the positives of buying a PC versus a Laptop. So, his sale for Desk tops were few and his sales figures did not justify doing this business for too long. But when he helped farmers and guided them towards profitability, which resulted in the purchase of the product being sold by Sudhir's company, his sale figures multiplied.

His surmise was that if the end user was benefitted by his guidance, and such guiding steps included earning from the beneficiary then such honest deals were to his liking.

Thus, honesty and sincerity to ensure that both parties benefitted and ensuring that no parties got hurt in the process, must always be the bottom-line.

He was now King of Nair Dvipa, he was also the Head of Inter Galactic Justice on Prithvi (Earth) and a senior member of the Inter Galactic Justice Core Team. Mogui firmly believed that the decision by his ancestors to disinherit him was against intergalactic law, and since Sudhir being the Head of Inter Galactic Justice on Earth was automatically the Arbitrator on behalf of the representatives of the Daivika planet, then, he was duty bound to conduct a neutral investigation and give the aggrieved party due justice. That meant that being the Arbitrator, if his own family was found to be guilty then he would be forced to disinherit his own family and himself from everything.

He explained his dilemma to his grandfather and grandmothers. Ngia Vat was now part of the discussion as she was a family member.

They did not bat an eyelid and gave an all-knowing smile.

The late King was beaming with pride and he said, "My child, we are very proud and honored to be sitting in your company. You have got this sincerity and honesty from your genetic coding. Permit us to present you with the facts relating to Mogui's past and we leave you to make a judgement".

He thus narrated the history of Móguǐ de érzi.

Móguǐ De Érzi's History as Narrated By Daivam King Cherusseri Namboodiri

Móguǐ de érzi's history as narrated by His Highness, First Amongst the Rajas of Nair Dvipa, Lord of Princes, Great Prince over Princes, Lieutenant-General Sir Cherusseri Namboothiri, Knight Grand Commander of the Order of the Star of Nair Dvipa, Grand Commander of the Order Nair Dvipa, Maharaja of Nair Dvipa.

Our ancestors have passed down the history of our home planet from generation to generation. True that over the generations, a lot of ridiculous imagination seeped into the narrative. Yet one can sieve through these narratives to arrive at a plausible history of the Daivika Planet and its residents.

While on their home planet, all citizens of the Daivika planet had to go through a process of self cleansing while they grew up. Normal subjects taught such as, Chemistry, Biology, Physics, Mathematics, foreign languages etc., continued as is done on Prithvi (Earth) today, considering that earth citizens have imbibed our teachings. The first few years went into disciplining the mind to concentrate our mental energies and this included control over our breathing.

Then all citizens are taught that the body is simply a vessel that must be kept healthy and fit in order that we may execute our functions. Thus, came about a body discipline related regime of bending, stretching, coiling, flexing, lifting, pulling and many more exercises that tested the limits of our physical abilities.

While this curriculum was thus being imbibed by the students, the mind of each student was taught to cleanse itself of all negative thoughts. This involved stage by stage, brain cell by brain cell formatting or in other words, deletion of negative feelings such as cheating, guile, misinformation, lying, dis-honor of commitments made, murder, rape, the list goes on. But even while the formatting was being executed, fresh feelings were saved on the partially empty brain cell thus increasing the feeling or sense of responsibility, caring, compassion and understanding.

The final stage was of self control over all such actions by tweaking our genetic coding to ensure that self-control becomes a permanent feature of our mind. Hence a new genetic coding to be passed down generation after generation.

Each student was awarded the graduation certificate of – "Sudh!" meaning "Pure!" because by this stage, every citizen was able to harness the total potential of his brain cells and had realized that the truly disciplined one does not need the body and does not need to be vile or evil. Pure energy did not need a body! One can do everything that one desires to do without the body. And that energy is pure by birth. Hence anyone who absorbs energy must necessarily be pure. But as one gains knowledge, the impurities that travel along with each such knowledge is also absorbed by the student. But self-discipline allows the impurities to be washed away. That self-discipline finally makes one truly "Sudh!" meaning "Pure!"

We had sent several fleets of Intergalactic crafts consisting of ten crafts per fleet with around three hundred personnel in each craft, to venture out to trace uninhabited but livable planets before we had learned the path to become truly "Sudh". The citizens of the Daivika planet needed physical forms way back then because they had yet to learn the art of total mental discipline. By the time we had sent the search fleet with the semi disciplined soldiers, we had progressed vastly in enhancement of our mental abilities. By the time the second 'Search and rectify' fleet had moved out and entered the Prithvi (Earth) atmosphere, we could move around without our bodies and yet we had to use our physical forms on planets such as earth. This was to ensure that we did not scare the citizens of Prithvi.

The first fleet of Intergalactic space fleet containing criminals with powerful minds had found no intelligent beings like themselves, only wild animals including apes all over the planet Prithvi (Earth) when they had crash-landed. They had begun to create secure dwellings for themselves and desired to create secure sources of food and clothing. But they were desperately short of manpower. That is when they made use of the laboratories within each crashed Interstellar craft to insert their own genes into the wild apes. As a result, many children were born from the apes, who were as tall as the criminals but were comparatively docile and amiable. The children lacked the ability to analyze or reason as any other Intergalactic traveler could. These offspring were thus exploited due to their brute strength. This brute strength helped in the construction of strong huts, gathering of heavy wood, hunting of big game, mining for precious metals, manufacturing, grinding, cutting etc., was achieved with great ease.

But the children that they created did not have a very long life. Fresh children had to be created at regular intervals. The bodies of the interstellar travelers had always lasted around three to four hundred years. The laboratory created children could at best last a hundred years but with rapid deterioration happening from the age of fifty years onwards in most cases. The brain cells of these human beings did not have the time to mature into fully operational brain cells until one hundred and sixty years but no creation of theirs lasted that long.

Great empires were built with the help of the armies made up of such human beings. Great mining work was done and as a result, gold, diamonds, rubies, emerald etc., were extracted with great ease.

But many of us married into local human behavior pattern. As a result, a lot of the Daivika planet genetic coding that determined our personalities and our dedication to remain hard working and ruthlessly goal oriented, got diluted especially if negativity was present in the other individual.

The point is that nobody on the planet Prithvi (Earth) had a sticker on his or her forehead that read, "I am good" or "I am bad", and so we took a decision as being part of Intergalactic rule that we may marry any human or any from our own planet, but provided that, his or her family has not been prosecuted for any criminal or anti-social act nor committed any anti-social or anti national activity. The computer program on any hidden Intergalactic Observer craft on Prithvi, can easily remind us about this important rule. The children from such marriages had necessarily to be "cleansed" if signs of negative energies became obvious. Keeping in mind that we wanted to ensure no harm came to Prithvi from our first batch of escaped criminals, this "cleansing" exercise was important to avoid further harm to planet Earth.

The criminals from our planet had landed many years ago exactly in that area where Piracy was born on Prithvi (Earth) subsequently. The criminals of Daivika planet of those periods had never learned that self-discipline in one's work front could help one achieve miracles. One need never go hungry if dedicated hard work continued inspite of the greatest of challenges in one's life. It was important to never give up especially during the most difficult phase of one's life. But the criminals were weak minded and wanted to achieve happiness and satisfaction in the quickest fashion. But the quickest did not assure a guaranteed, honest source of income. Naturally they were hungry and desperate like the Mafia of today. With insecurity forcing the criminals to execute desperate acts to survive or otherwise go hungry, they continued with theft, looting, bullying, threatening, murder, pushing the use of harmful drugs, usurping or forcibly occupying someone's property or land, forcing fellow citizens towards depraving acts such as prostitution, and spreading disinformation which, they used to do on the mother planet. They did anything and everything to earn a living. Cheating, guile, misinformation, lying, dis-honor of commitments made, snatching, murder for profit, rape, lack of compassion, lack of mercy, ruthlessness, drugs, destruction of families, destruction of a whole population, the list goes on.

Marrying into such a family was and remained a strict 'no no'.

But Mogui's father, while travelling in a ship got kidnapped by such pirates. All pirates possess undisciplined minds. True that getting kidnapped by pirates was not his fault. The captain of the Pirates decided that earning a one-time ransom was not good enough. The Nair Dvipa Prince was a potential cash cow! If he could coax his daughter to marry into our Royal family then, he could have a reason to stay near us and milk the Royal family for many years to come.

So, the pirate chief coaxed his only child, his daughter, to woo the Prince of Nair Dvipa!

Now, Self-discipline related exercises are done daily at Nair Dvipa and many parts of the world by citizens of the Daivika planet. Self-discipline allows us to remain insulated from negative thoughts and negative energies that try to woo us. A young scantily dressed girl, who pretends to be drunk and asks for you to take her back to her room, should necessarily ring warning bells in your mind. If this scantily dressed girl executes a wardrobe malfunction the moment you put her on her bed to intentionally show off her young swollen breasts and thick silky thighs, then your alarm bells must tell you to scoot the hell out of that room. But no, the Prince succumbed to exposing himself to – well, her exposed assets and because he stared with big hungry eyes, she pulled him down into her arms that night and quenched his hunger, while the winds moaned in agony to have lost yet another citizen of the mother planet, to well – intoxication!

And so, they fell in "love" and got married. And they kept moaning away behind closed doors for many more nights thereafter, with Wúgū the Pirate King himself keeping vigil outside the bedroom door on his captured ship! Because of this very reason, Pirate ships were permitted for the very first time to enter the sea ports of Nair Dvipa. Not just because of the moaning but because the Prince was married to the Pirate's daughter.

Disqualification was automatic and yet an exception was made in the case of the Prince. Disqualification would have meant that his entry back to the Kingdom of Nair Dvipa would have been permanently barred. But till this point no one had challenged the right of Mogui's parents to their share of the Royal wealth. Hence the accusation that being married to a Pirate's daughter got the Royal family member disqualified from claiming his rights, was not true.

Mogui's grandfather, who was an infamous pirate and his people, were permitted as a special case to enter the Kingdom. But instead of behaving like responsible citizens who earned an honest living; the Pirate and his gang began to loot our long-distance passengers while they travelled on road. And they began to loot our long-distance passengers while they travelled on the sea routes as well. No ship could leave without paying an exit tax in his son in law's name. No ship could enter without paying an entry tax in his son in law's name. But the money did not come to the coffers of the son in law!

The Pirates got emboldened by the embarrassed silence of the Royal family. The Royal family did their best to protect their own but to no avail. The pirates began to rob the transport system that conveyed the taxes collected from far flung areas of Nair Dvipa. The tax collection wagons were attacked by masked brigands and the monies that belonged to the country went into the pockets of the Pirate, Mogui's grandfather. If that was not enough, they murdered or maimed our citizens. So, we arrested the Pirate Chief and locked him away in our cells. His daughter raised hell at home and her husband, that is Mogui's father, helped organize a Jail break wherein the Pirate escaped our Prison system. So, we gave chase but the Pirate was nowhere to be found for many months. We kept advertising in various media that harboring of criminals was an act of Anti Nationalism. But to no avail. And in the meanwhile, the thuggeries and murders re-began in earnest. Suddenly one fine day, a messenger who had gone to deliver an important message to the house of Mogui's father, claimed to have seen the Pirate living in that very house. We conducted a raid; he was identified and arrested once again and was being taken away when Morgui's father ordered that Wúgū the Pirate King be released on his good name. Our forces refused to comply. His wife then shot dead many officers.

Now that is a serious office punishable by the laws of the country and punishable by the laws of the Daivika Planet too. Mogui was then just a child and yet he too was taught how to shoot a few officers on duty. Coaxing and teaching a child to break the law and in fact teaching him to kill a representative of the Police or Army is once again a punishable act. The pirate king escaped our clutches and he sailed away to his hometown which we came to know later was somewhere around what is now known as the Yellow Sea.

Mogui's parents were arrested and we urged that Mogui be allowed to stay back with us. Here again, we made it obvious that no rights to his share of the Royal Family wealth was being denied. But the penalties for breaking the local law had necessarily to be paid. As per the Laws of Nair Dvipa, we were confident about bringing about the discipline in baby Mogui's actions and being responsible for his welfare until he became a responsible adult. But

Mogui's parents insisted that Mogui stay in prison in his mother's company. When children stay with the parents, the child imbibes their teachings. The court was willing to deny access to the parents and the then King was more than willing to bring up the child like his own son and help him imbibe goodness. No right to wealth or education was being denied. But his parents kept sending representations and the court was forced to comply with the request. The King's objection to the ruling was put on record. They were released several years later and were informed that they may please meet the King to collect their share of the Royal Wealth. But the moment they were released, they sailed away. Never to be seen again. Before leaving, they made no effort to collect what was rightfully theirs.

In the meantime, we believe that Mogui's mind got a lot of misinformation from both his grandfather as well as his mother.

Mogui returned several years later as an adult with many years of experience as a Pirate. By that time, we believe, that the poor child's mind was filled with a lot of poison. He did not give us any chance to explain our point of view.

In fact, we did not know that this person was our own Mogui until much later.

He did not return to claim his share. He returned as a seasoned land and sea pirate! He came to cause disruption to our supplies, to attack our money earning sources and seize monies by force, intimidation as also murder of our citizens. He captured and took away ships that belonged to friendly nations approaching our shores, after his people killed the captains and ship mates. Because we did not know that he was our Mogui, we passed a decree offering a reward for his capture dead or alive! He was from then on, a common criminal.

One of the British ship's captain reported that he had seen a Pirate battle ship approaching the waters of Nair Dvipa one day and that as per the demand offered, he was going to fire his cannons. What was alarming, he reported, is that it flew an infamous Pirate ship flag normally seen somewhere around the Yellow Sea and the Formosa region. In that region such ships with such flags were a sure sign of pirates who resorted to looting, murder and mayhem. The flag they flew was known for sparing nobody on the ship that they boarded by force.

The captain of the British ship challenged the Pirate ship and warned him about the consequences if the pirate ship refused to surrender. To this the young Pirate began to laugh! "Tell them that Mogui has returned!" the Pirate roared.

The British did not know who Mogui was. As we had offered a reward, this British Captain fired ten rounds of heavy cannon fire which destroyed the ship totally. When he went to collect the proof, he found only debris. And Mogui was not around.

But the news reached us. The knews of, "Tell them that Mogui has returned!" and then of the debry and nothing else, hurt us terribly.

When Mogui Returned But Back in Time, Now in 1805

Many months went by and he surfaced suddenly once again. Kapoof – and he was there! He had travelled back in the time of **King** Unni Pushpakan Ambalavasi in 1805.

He visited us and destroyed our peace. He seemed to have gained super human magical powers!

We used to have attacks from Pirates. The worst attack came one night from Sea Pirates who landed and hid themselves, travelled the jungle during the day time and attacked our forces without warning. One such group was led by Móguǐ. He simply had to point his finger at five of our people and they would be seen flying away as if hit with a huge force! Very soon he had our huge army protecting the beachfront from invaders, lying dead or unconscious at his feet.

He remained there for nearly two years and some months more kidnapping, torturing, raping, maiming or selling many of our local citizens, forcing them to accept his adopted country's pagan culture and life style. We kept sending our police and then the army personnel based around the port and every time he proved himself many times stronger and hence able to defeat all of them. His lawyers were well paid and no proof could be placed that was strong enough to keep Mogui in prison. Witnesses were not willing to stand as witness against him. We had no well thought out plan to bring about a solution.

We did not know who he was then nor the fact that he was the son of our immediate relative. Then we heard after nearly two years had gone by, the reports of "Tell them that Mogui has returned!" He claimed to be of Royal blood and had been cheated by us.

We came to know that his father, a Royal member of the Palace, had been captured by pirates and had a child from the daughter of the Captain of the Pirate ship who had enticed him on a moonlit night. But our records showed no such incident had ever occurred. Then came the news that he had travelled back in time to "take revenge". Now this bit of important news told us that he was the son of our great grandchild. And he was yet to be born! So, we all had a good laugh at his sense of humour!

Mógui̇ de érzi had obviously grown up to become a selfish, sweet talking, highly sophisticated, tall, extremely well built and baritone voiced, strong individual who possessed magical powers.

Mogui's Harem 1805

What was not funny was that within a few days of capturing the dock from our trained army, he began a harem consisting of the unwilling wives of the helpless soldiers and fishermen and their unwilling daughters.

So we sent soldiers once again with spears and arrows mostly and a few mordern weapons being manufactured in foreign countries in those times. But much to our dismay, his soldiers possessed modern weapons which certainly did not belong to this time. It was as if their weapons belonged to a future time. So was Mogui speaking the truth?!! They had big fire power and to add to that was the fact that Mogui himself possessed magical powers that multiplied the power of each of his soldiers. Each of them could defeat ten of Nair Dvipa soldiers. Thus Nair Dvipa forces were easily defeated by such superior enemy forces.

Mogui's confidence grew and he then graduated to a 'Den for Flesh Trade'. The Port became a favourite for unscrupulous and aggressive foreign traders who followed the law of the fittest, meaning Mogui' law.

The traders travelling from distant lands were lonely and desperate and frequently reached out to the female dancers at the bar. The bars thus had frequent brawls over girls who were much in demand and yet no one got arrested. The demand for bar dancers grew and the bad elements began to get women kidnapped locally and rent them out for the night to these travellers who came by ship.

But soon, the travellers began to make financial offers to be allowed to sail away with some of the women or girls they really liked. Exceptions were made initially as it made business sense, then, it became a profitable norm. Mogui started a division dedicated to selling off the high demand girls from the total lot to these Foreign traders. The business grew to a point where traders began to insist on paying extra for inspecting the goods before purchase, hence began the ritual of, 'disrobe and display for proper inspection'.

Traders who were willing to pay double of that value for "disrobe and display ' were allowed to 'touch' the disrobed goods before purchase. The fullness of the breasts, the attractiveness of the slight swell of the belly, the fullness of the buttocks, the 'lusciousness' of the thick thighs, the list went on. Word spread globally. During special days of the Auction, hundreds of foreign traders would converge from various parts of the world to 'Buy the best".

The port became so popular that women and girls were soon being brought in from foreign countries to be sold at this very port of Nair Dvipa. The Port became a den for carnal activities and related drugs & liquor.

The travellers needed accommodation for the period of their stay. Thus began rent-able accommodation furnished to the taste of those who could afford the same. The accommodation facilities trickled down in reducing proportion to the pocket. Pegion posts used to arrive three months prior to the arrival of a Royal accompanying the trader, to book the desired period of accommodation with the hint of commitment to splurge on the best on offer. A lot many services opened up to cater to the local industry. People made a lot of money and the affluent began to move around in four wheeled horse driven carts. Bugle horns could be heard from very far away to warn pedestrians to stand aside and make way for the speeding VIP carriage that was forgiven for all who came under their wheels. The local economy boomed. Nair Dvipa became famous for all the wrong reasons. Kings, Princes, Royalty, Foreign Dignitaries bagan to visit Nair Dvipa, "Unofficially" like never before.

The demand became so high that soon, women and young girls were being kidnapped from various corners of Nair Dvipa and made to walk behind a caravan to "Break them". Further, until they accepted the trade, they were kept cooped up in a 'sitting position' tight cage.

The ones who fell ill alongwith those who eventually died were kept with the other live women & girls to make them realise the repucussions of non co-operation and staying cooped up in small cages.

Many succumbed under pressure and disrobed in front of their captors but refused to reduce their dignity any further. They refused to disrobe in front of the open public.

To reduce their objections Mogui's thugs had a ruse. The women and girls were often drugged to make them more amiable, liquor was also poured down their throats frequently for the same reason. The co-operative ones were instantly rewarded with good food and a proper bed and obviously no more cage, no more drugs and no more liquor being forced down your throat. She knew she had to co-operate as her future was uncertain. She knew that she had to remain alive as her King had failed to save her people till date.

The Final Day of Auction

Then they were finally disrobed and displayed in front of various prospective buyers based on their "quality". The lowest quality which included the sick, the not so well endowed, were sold off at discounted rates in the open market auctions.

The next best included virgins and otherwise, but necessarily well endowed, extremely attractive and healthy girls and women, who were sold off individually or enmass after being disrobed and displayed in indoor auditoriums where traders who hated travelling alone on the long journey back home by ship, preferred making a last minute buy of one or two companions. And finally the 'High Quality' were virgins but necessarily well endowed, extremely attractive and healthy, and in may cases well read with superb worldly wisdom, who were disrobed and displayed in front of the richest bidder in a private display darbar where he 'felt her over' with every part of his body before he gave the signal with an indulgent wave of his right hand index finger.

Thousands of housewives, daughters, sisters were thus disrobed to display their assets and then sold away to the higest bidder as sex slaves, never to see their families again.

And the King of Nair Dvipa kept getting news that wave after wave of his army personnel and each time attacking with a different strategy, kept failing against Mogui's power.

The Discovery of One of the Sunken Ships

Only five out of the seven ships had reached the shore of Nair Dvipa. The remaining two had sunk near the shore of Nair Dvipa and inspite of several attempts, they could not be located over these several years.

Móguǐ de érzi flew high up into the skies to scan the waters around the island. He scanned for wood, for metal, for heat but to no avail. Inspite of his great powers, he could best locate a strange triangular wood piece jutting out of the sand near a rocky approach. His slave workers dived down to the depths to remove the sand around the triangle and there it was – one of the ships. More workers were engaged and the treasures began to pop up! Each soldier and fisherman were forced to pay a daily tax of two fishes, and at least one gold mohor from the sunken ship that lay far away from the port. Otherwise, his children would be murdered or maimed and his wife would be sold off by Móguǐ de érzi's pirate army. In this manner he had amassed a great number of Gold Mohors and ensured a well-fed army of pirates for a period of approximately two years.

Several representations were made by the parents, husbands, children of kidnapped women and girls to the Palace. King Shri Unni Pushpakan Ambalavasi, who had already failed several times, continued to try and charge Mogui's camp with an even larger army every time. Mogui had proved himself to be far powerful than he thought. Then Mogui made the false promise of letting a fisherman's wife go scot free provided the fisherman helped him find the treasure that had landed on shore in the five intact ships.

It is this fisherman who arrived at the Palace of King Shri Unni Pushpakan Ambalavasi, requesting that we reveal the location of the wealth of our ancestors in order that his wife may be released from the clutches of the powerful Móguǐ de érzi.

He cried his heart out to narrate the plight of innumerable army personnel and fishermen who were similarly suffering the humility of their wives & daughters being used as members of Móguǐ de érzi's for foreign trader's Harem. And, the fact that Wúgū the Pirate King had evil magical powers that he used to destroy huts and the strongest of hard stone fortifications. That he could enter the minds of the strongest fisherman and use him against his own community. That every time he destroyed fortifications with a single blow, he would roar, "Tell them that Mogui has travelled back in time for revenge!"

King Shri Unni Pushpakan Ambalavasi embraced this fisherman and assured him that he shall get his wife back. That is when he made the best decision in his life. "Do not depend on your soldiers who are powerless human beings compared to Mogui", he told himself. He decided that he must fight Mogui himself. Yes, he realized that death was a strong possibility but he and he alone had the power to battle Mogui. He flew into the skies and landed exactly where the fisherman showed Móguǐ de érzi's camp existed.

Mogui was standing on the dome of the Temple near the port built by King Ambalavasi looking at the great expanse of the port city. Since the past ages, the positive energy waves created by the chanting of certain words within the precincts of the temple had so far brought about good rain, good crops and prosperity. King Shri Unni Pushpakan Ambalavasi saw Mogui from high above the clouds and descended very slowly to stand opposite him with twenty feet approximately between them. Mogui got a shock and his body took a defensive stance as nobody could reach the height of the Temples dome and stand on it, barring himself.

"You have spread the word that you belong to our family and that you have travelled back in time! You are therefore my great grandchild. I do not wish to hurt you" began King Ambalavasi. For Mogui, the initial shock on seeing someone standing opposite him was gone. Now Mogui was amused! But the King continued, "Law will take its own course. You can choose between the normal prisons or imprisonment as per our legal norms".

Mogui was seething within, but his face displayed no expression. He had beaten so many mentally powerful human beings in his past and here was this weakling who happened to be his great grandfather, threatening him with imprisonment! Did the fool not realize by now that no prison walls were strong enough to hold him?! He found the situation to be ludicrous and at the same time he was infuriated at his great grandfather's audacity! King Ambalavasi was telling him about the virtues of giving up in front of the court of justice. "How dare he mock my power any further!" and so thinking, he brought dark clouds suddenly to appear above them with bolts of lightning striking the trees around the temple.

"This show of power will do you no good Mogui!" explained the King calmly. "Goodness prevails ultimately because Goodness is persistent and omnipresent".

But Mogui began to guffaw and began drawing power from all around him. Energy particles rushed into him with the roar of rushing ocean water, as if he was a blackhole!

When King Shri Unni Pushpakan Ambalavasi realized that Mogui was in no mood to listen to him he finally asked him out of exasperation, "What is it that you want? Money? Wealth? I shall give the same to you. Release these innocent people and leave this land that has only strived for peace and prosperity!"

Móguǐ de érzi ultimately while pointing his fingers at the King and then the island below and he said, "I want this island for my country Diànlì jī'è de guójiā you lousy weakling great grandfather! Turn around like a good boy and run away so that and I may consider the possibility of letting you live to serve me in perpetuity! I want all these weak people to be the slaves of my country Diànlì jī'è de guójiā! We shall suck Nair Dvipa dry, we shall kill every man, then we shall have every woman of this island to join the harem of every male citizen of Diànlì jī'è de guójiā! Very soon all of you shall speak our language and look like us. Your grandchildren will have our blood in them. We want your wealth and your prosperity and when we leave, you shall be left with no self-confidence, no self-respect. Your self-esteem shall be nothing but a dry orange peel to be thrown away into the nearest dustbin!"

Saying so he kept guffawing like a mad man even while his right hand rose lazily up to throw a blast of energy towards King Ambalavasi. "Mirror his every blast!" the King instructed his mind. The blast bounced back and whammed into Móguǐ de érzi who tumbled in the air to quickly recover and send another blast in the King's direction but this time with his left hand. But that blast too bounced back and hit him with the same force that he had used to send it! He tumbled around in the air. He was grievously hurt by the two blasts. This was when Mogui realized that the King was using the mirror energy and he instructed his mind, "Shatter the mirror!" and the mirror barrier shattered into tiny shards of energy that flew in every direction. Then within seconds Mogui instructed his mind, "Throw up the heaviest bounders from within the ocean waters below and hit the weakling who dares to call himself the King!" Huge boulders rushed towards the King but became dust even before they reached the King. Mogui threw his 'invade the mind' energy blast down at the village folk and growled, "Nair Dvipa residents rise up into the air and absorb my energies to fight this weak half woman who dares to call himself your King!" The strong, self-confident citizens were not affected by this attempt to control their minds. However, around ten villagers whose minds were weak and easily malleable rose up into the air with their heads bent down as if one were to be asleep. Then all of them raised their heads as one. All had blood shot eyes and all of them roared like wild demons! The King did not wish to hurt his own citizens. He was in a dilemma.

They blasted the King from all directions and he got battered and went down on his knees even while in the air! He was seriously wounded!

"Use the Invisibility energy cloak", the King instructed his mind "and make Móguǐ de érzi's pirate colleagues to revolt against their master! Make them blast Mogui from all heights and directions and change their position of attack faster than what Mogui can anticipate!"

Then he flew far away from where he was and the ten villagers kept bombarding his last position.

Even while this was happening, some twenty plus Mogui's pirates began to rise with speeds exceeding that which could be seen with the naked eye and even while they rose, they began to fire volley after volley of body penetrating destructive energy. Mogui was shocked to see his own pirate team attacking him. Before he could recover from the shock, the volleys had already penetrated his body and his defenses went down. But the volleys continued and he knew he would die if his body did not repair itself right away.

Mogui's mind began to automatically concentrate on self-preservation and self-defense. It lost control over all other energies that ensured him control of any or all people of Nair Dvipa. The citizens of Nair Dvipa came to their senses at that very moment even while in the air and fell into the sea waters to swim back safely ashore. But Mogui was losing his supremacy over this battle. His defenses were down as all energies were directed to repair his grievous internal wounds. He was immediately imprisoned in a brown bottle and the cap was sealed with the condition that an equally powerful King of Nair Dvipa could only open it if he so felt it necessary. All the fishermen were re-united with their wives. Enough Gold Mohors were given to each to reward them for their hard work in extracting treasures from the deep sea. The balance Gold Mohors, Jewelry and treasures that were extracted from deep sea were then transported to a secret treasury. The fishermen were asked to continue the extraction process under the supervision of a Minister appointed for this purpose.

All that was very easy, but trying to stop the flesh trade that had international ramifications was a big challenge. Mogui's absence created a vacuum that was filled in by his junior Pirates who had learned the trade by then. When the Royal Police began to raid the hideouts and shut down a junior of Mogui then, innumerable other juniors took up the responsibility of carrying forward the illegal trade. The trade broke up into innumerable heads that catered to the huge International demand. So, we banned ships from transporting female prisoners onboard and we conducted raids on the ships but found nothing. The Royal Police Forces continued to raid ship after ship. We discovered very soon that after the ship had sailed away, mini fishing boats would transport kidnapped women with their hands tied behind their backs and their mouths covered with cloth to the ships anchored deep into the sea.

Thus, we declared the kidnapping of women for the sex trade as punishable with death. That did the trick as all those caught in the subsequent raids were hung up for all to see on road crossings.

We thought that the problem of prostitution was over, but alas! Women who had been kidnapped in the early days, but who were now pariah in their husband's families, requested that they be allowed to survive by attracting foreign customers who travelled on business to Nair Dvipa. They knew no other trade nor source of income, they explained. They declared that either that or the King pay them reparations and damages for having failed to protect their interests in the early days. So, the King began a small protected community of huts, gave them each a small hut and a pension for life hoping that this gesture would stop the act of prostitution. Each such community was tied up with a local school and a hospital. Children of each such community had to admit their children to the nearest school and get themselves treated at the nearest hospital.

But news of some of these women being caught with rich men reached the ears of the palace.

Comparing them with animals, the Ministers around the King however declared prostitution to be an "animal like" activity. That "animals had no control over themselves and thus entertained their base instincts".

To this, the kidnapped women who were now rescued from the trade argued, "But human beings have a normal urge even after they get rescued". And the King, they insisted, had "no right to stop them from fulfilling a God gifted urge".

And so, King Ambalavasi looked away considering that God's creation, a woman, had made a point! But the training camps for self-sustenance in different trades, such are basket weaving, fishing net manufacture, portrait painting, singing, theatre, agriculture produce marketing and distribution etc., continued for those who were interested.

Edicts signed by the King have been distributed all around the cities and towns that one day into the future, one of our grandchildren would be a pirate's son and must be arrested immediately.

Then the King's wounds which refused to heal made him abdicate his throne to his next in line.

The Summary

Late King Cherusseri Namboodiri now looked into Sudhir's eyes and said, "You have heard the details that are relevant to Mogui. He feels he has been wronged. The Planet of Daivika who had set the rules know that he has been intentionally misinformed and brainwashed by his evil grandfather. Mogui is certain that his parents were right and everybody else is wrong. He does not know that we had wanted to adopt him and provide the best of education and care for his wellbeing. He does not know that he too would have had equal say in the wealth of Nair Dvipa provided he had remained in the path of righteousness and goodness instead of following his grandfather's footpath. It is going to be difficult considering his present state of mind to understand laws and the difference between a Pirate girl with an evil mind and a Tribal girl with a simple mind. His energy has gone far beyond repair. It is sad but he must no longer be imprisoned but he must be destroyed.

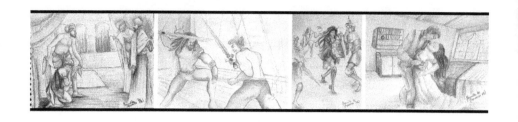

Chapter 21

Sudhir's Ex-wife Vanishes

Sudhir's Ex-wife with His Parents

Malini and her two children stayed in an apartment five minutes away by car from her ex-in-law's place. Her second husband had enough money plus confidence to create much more, unlike her first husband. At the same time, with confidence and money came the huge sexual drive and the fact that he could get a woman anywhere, whenever he wanted. Malini was a senior official in a professional organization and obviously had monies of her own. Initially she waited for him to spend at restaurants and he used to pay. But the sex became routine and gradually, boring. That is when he woke up to decide that, she was not going to make a fool of him by making him spend on her and for her family while she kept her savings intact. Her second husband realized that the attraction was simply because of her menopausal burst of sexual drive. Gradually the drive began to die. But her nature remained intact, the fact that she cared only about her own decisions. He got tired of living with a supposedly empowered, but undisciplined, mistrusting and unreasonable old demanding woman. Initially he had stopped spending on her, then he began to stay away from her home for many days and finally he simply did not return home, ever.

She kept trying searching for him in vain, then out of sheer frustration she once again tried to search for new friends through online websites but to no avail. Her sexual drive was gone! From then on, she had nothing to give. Thus, nobody was willing to adjust with her emotional needs. Nobody was willing to accept the children. Nobody was willing to spend on her – full stop.

Five years had gone by since the boat sinking incident. It seemed like only yesterday. Sudhir's ex-wife was a senior executive. She had to look after both the home front as well as the office. Paying electricity & telephone bills online required time. Lights or fans not working at home needed somebody to visit and follow up with the maintenance staff. Brackish water coming out of the flush required the attention of the maintenance staff of the colony but somebody had to chase after them. Rushing the kids to the bus stop was not always possible especially whenever she had come home late and thus failed to wake up on time. As she kept growing within her organization, she found it hard to keep a balance. Many a time she would find herself reaching home very late into the night. She hardly saw her kids. It was over these many years that she had realized that albeit the lack of income and brains, the huge administrative support her husband had provided to the family, had been taken for granted. Thankfully, Sudhir's father had ensured constant contact with his son's children and did not interfere in his ex-daughter in law's extra marital exploits after her second marriage.

Over time she had realized that all her men friends were temporary. They had no respect for her nor did they desire to take on any responsibility for the children if the relationship was to be allowed to progress further. She had moved away from Sudhir because she had lost respect for him. Her male friends too egged her into getting a divorce for their ulterior motives. Nobody bothered to love the children like a father would. They considered the children to be mere objects to be cooed at, or to be placated with cheap gifts for the ultimate goal, that is, a brief bedroll with their mother. The children were an undesirable baggage. Some eyed the daughter with obvious lust.

The menopause had made her say terrible things. But gradually when the menopause symptoms began to die, she began to feel tired and wanted the company of her closests relatives and friends. But her closest relatives were busy with grown up children. Some just did not wish to suffer her bawling away in self-pity. The females of her school and college met her during the 'friends meet' and they talked about the 'good old days' but they had their individual busy schedules and then they were gone. There was no one who she could confide in as she used to with "brainless" Sudhir. Along with the memories of her sharing her secrets, the memories of the moments that she laughed the most was when she was with Sudhir. That is when the feeling of severe loss hit her, and the realization that her future promised a dreadfully prolonged loneliness.

She would stare at his photographs during spare hours in solitude. She would recollect the moments they had enjoyed together. The children rushing into his arms the moment he came back from his office. Her waiting with her arms on the two sides of her hip, with mock anger for he had neglected her and giving his children too much time. His letting the children go, to open his arms for her and she, rushing into his warm & loving embrace.

Why was she so stupid? Why did she have to send the Divorce petition? And why the hell did he sign it? He should have understood that he had failed to fulfill his marriage vows and she was merely tapping the world to fulfill them. Why did he not understand such a simple thing? Why did God have to make him so stubborn – why! She could see Sudhir in her dream. God was taking Sudhir away right at this very moment in a boat very far – so very far away. She kept calling out to him but he just would not respond!

A deep voice was calling out to her.

Sudhir's father was speaking to her at this very moment. She crashed back to reality. Where was she? She was in the house where her in ex-in-laws stayed. She had taken a flat on rent very close to theirs. At this very moment she was in their drawing room. Her father in-law was sitting besides her applying a wet cloth to her head, while her ex-mother in-law looked after the morning chores and sending the children off to school. Nothing should be disturbed, Sudhir's father had declared. Much before her ex- husband's sinking with the boat, Malini decided that it was wise to stay away from her ex-inlaws in order that she may live her own life in her own manner. But the children needed the protection and the loving security of immediate blood relatives. Especially when her busy schedule meant she was away from her children. Sudhir's father never entered her apartment and she never requested him to enter but he always took the children to school and dropped them back when she returned home. This, she felt was a mature way of handling things.

But today she had rushed into her ex-in-laws house, unannounced, and then had become unconscious.

Somehow this day was special. She had seen Sudhir in her dream.

Today she did what she had never done before. Her dreams were her private matter. But today she could bear the pain of separation no longer. She spoke to her ex-inlaws about Sudhir's strange dreams – the rich dreams – the huge palatial building surrounded by a retinue of loyal servants – and everything else.

Shyamili, Pawan Bagarias's wife's eyes dilated in obvious amazement and terror combined. Her shocked expression mirrored that on her husband Pawan Bagaria's face right now. He suddenly stood up, ramrod straight. "What did you say? Huge palatial building surrounded by a retinue of loyal servants? Did it have Cowsheds with many big & fat cows and the bulls that pulled the carts and the fishing trawlers?"

"Yes", replied a perplexed Malini.

"Did the building have large mesh wired hen cages with many hen coops?", he persisted

"Yes", shocked, Malini paused and then replied.

"And mini sheds for the goats, banana plant orchards, mango orchards, sour lime orchards, well planned and clean paths that led to every corner that any one desired, two old 2nd world war beetle cars?", he seemed to be reminiscing now, as if he was lost in deep thought. He seemed to be talking to himself.

Malini was nodding in the affirmative. She was flabbergasted because Sudhir's parents were never informed about her husband's supposedly silly dreams.

But they seemed to know about his dreams right now. Why then were they so shocked?

Pawandas's eyes were as if lost in a different world. He looked at his ex - daughter-in-law and said in a voice that did not belong to him – "Sudhir is alive!". And so saying, he picked up the phone.

He dialed the number that had belonged to his father so many years ago. After the recent turn of events, he was not surprised when it rang. But it kept ringing and no one picked up the phone.

Then he dialed the number of his colleague in the office where he had worked before.

"Jai Hind! This is DGDE. How may I help you?" a male voice asked.

"This is Pawandas Bagaria, ex Director of DGDE. I wish to talk to Mallik Anand, the Director General please", requested Sudhir's father.

The male assistant exclaimed," Yes Sir! Please be on the line Sir!" and after a wait of a minute Mr. Mallik Anand, the Director General, was on the line.

"Malik here Sir!"

"Malik this is Bagaria. Yes, Good evening! Malik, I did not tell you before, but I am the ex-Prince of Nair Dvipa and my son who automatically becomes the King of Nair Dvipa, is, I feel, in trouble! Yes, do come over so that we can have a detailed private discussion this evening. Yes, thankyou Malik".

Just then he turned to look at his ex-daughter-in-law and he saw a strange illumination all around her, as if one were on fire! And a strange hum seemed to emanate from her, from head to toe! Like a massive electricity generation center!

His wife was staring with her mouth open at this shocking spectacle! Her ex-daughter-in-law was squirming in pain!

Then Malini screamed, there was a buzz like a short circuit, the illumination that emanated from inside her blinked several times and buzzed like sparks during a short circuit, there was a whoomph! And then, pooff - she had vanished! Right in front of their very eyes!

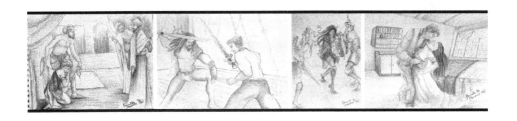

Chapter 22

Outsiders Invade Nair Dvipa

The Primitive Invaders Enter

It is in Human nature to remain curious and so over so many ages human beings made innumerable discoveries.

And so, the 'Powya tribe' learned that they could take their float to other islands close by. Other Powya tribesmen tried the same. Some sank and their families cried in pain. Others came back to report their success stories. Soon they were trying out bold experiments. One or more decided to set up thatched huts on some islands. Some took their families along and settled on them. These settlers reported befriending resident people from other tribes. Tribes who had waged war on the Powya tribe using floats that did not have a long life and repeatedly lost. But that was because the smaller islands were separate tribes and not united. The 'Powya' tribesmen became prosperous as compared to the tribals of other smaller islands. Soon less prosperous tribe leaders met at this island. The technology of the float was bartered away for a hundred monkey skins. Some of them saw the obvious affluence and went away silently without revealing the hatred instigated by jealousy that they now harbored. Jointly these jealous Tribe leaders had a huge number of warriors – wild warriors. Warriors hungry for blood and gore! Warriors used to gain wealth through plunder and loot rather than working hard for the same. And the prospect of a Joint Army got them all very hopeful of victory and that got them very excited. They agreed to share the proceeds of the plunder and loot. Instigating them, uniting them and leading them against the Powya tribe was Nksi Nanga, the Ex Chief of Zambeke village, grandson of Móguĭ de érzi!

The island was protected against an attack. But traders were allowed as their intention was supposedly peaceful.

The raiders disguised as traders came on floats in the middle of the night and landed at the ocean and river confluence, next to the hill protecting entry into the valley. Unknown to Nair Dvipa residents, they killed or captured local village fishermen at the river bank, remained hidden for seven plus months, digging tunnels that travelled under the hill leading to underground natural caverns and boring through rock to emerge into Nair Divpa Land on the other side of the hill. Around five months later, they were ready. Some of them then climbed through the only pass between two hills that allowed them entry into the valley and waited in hiding to charge in the early morning. The warning call of the monkeys high up on the canopies woke up the Powya tribesmen at the base of the hill, within the fort which Sudhir had helped them build.

Some of them woke up to see a huge number of armed tribesmen from other islands all around the fortification. They blew the 'shankha'- the conch shell - that was normally used to signal the beginning of a big hunt or extreme danger. It resonated loud and clear all over the forest and till very far away into the deep blue sea and up to the tribes that resided on the top of three other hills. The sound woke up sleepy Powya tribesmen who grabbed the bows, arrows and spears and roared in unison at the advancing army of the combined opposition, outside the fortification. The combined opposition roared back. The numbers were so huge that they literally carpeted the sandy beach as well as the jungle around the fortification. The chief realized that he was outnumbered!

The rigorous training over the past so many months had taught the Powva tribe warriors the basics of how a trained and synchronized army operates. The importance of discipline, synchronized action under a single command, arrow shooting or spear throwing under a single command, guerilla warfare, passage through hidden tunnels, and much more. They knew that there would be war and hence they did not mind the lack of sleep, the sudden mock battle calls, the guerilla warfare drills, booby traps, the exhaustion, all of this made them realize that this training was desired for past many years.

Then the enemy forces decided to spread dread and fear amongst the Powva tribe with a terrifying roar that, like the Sankha, reached out to the far corners of the forest including the palace.

Mógui de érzi smiled on hearing the roar and relaxed in his armchair in the store room of the Palace. "It has begun father! Justice shall be served," he spoke to the image within the frame.

The Attack at the Old Sea Port

Sudhir heard the 'shankha'- the conch shell blowing - and knew that the villages were in safe hands. Mogui was known for feigning an attack to divert the attention away from the actual attack. The attack on the village with huge number of tribals from neighbouring islands, even though the villages of this island remained protected by double protection energy was obviously to divert his attention away from an actual - many times more powerful attack elsewhere. Where could it be?! He rushed to the port and the fishermen's village that bordered the palace. It looked deceptively calm and peaceful.

It was then that Sudhir used his heat sensors and saw around five modern armoured ships were anchored a few kilometers away from the island of Nair Dvipa and armed personnel on flat bottomed boats carrying mechanized landing crafts were speeding towards the island. But they all had the invisibility cloak around them that only a powerful Daivika planet citizen could generate on their behalf. They all were marked with the country of their origin – "Diànlì jì'è de guójiā"!

He scanned each of the ships for Fire Power and realized that the missiles that they carried were enough to destroy Nair Dvipa.

Nair Dvipa Defense and Administrative forces can protect their seas and inland problems. No foreign army or navy could logically be allowed to interfere in internal matters unless requested by the Prime Minister assisted by majority votes of the Nair Dvipa Parliament. No such permission had been granted. Therefore, this was an invasion!

The foreign invaders had to be destroyed. They were invisible but not protected.

Sudhir sent a telepathy message to Khan, the Defense Minister. "They are here wearing invisible cloaks! Select your best team and prepare for fighting off an invasion. The situation desires a minimum of five percent of Nair Dvipa Sea, Land and Airforce selected by your four Defense Wing Chiefs to the last British Defense Port within fifteen minutes from now. Please keep General Cristopher Rodrigues, Admiral Sudhakar Nattarajan, Air Chief Marshal Kuriyedathu Raman Daivika, and Vice Admiral Srikumar Venketasan, the Director General of Coast Guards informed and ready for five percent of their forces being Teleported. Ensure everybody is onboard as the total of three warships, helicopters, long distance missiles fixed on three tonner trucks, night image detectors etc., would be used from the moment they land at the port."

Khan was one of the retired Army Chiefs himself before he joined the Anti Royals party and became the Defense Minister. But after getting elected, he realized that Nair Dvipa was in danger. He realized after he began getting orders that went against the interests of the country that the complete election process had been managed from a foreign country.

"Yes, Your Highness", replied Khan telepathically. "Doing so right away Sir!"

"I shall continue to be tuned to receive messages by Telepathy from your end." continued Sudhir. Inform India about an attempt by Diànlì jǐ'è de guójiā to forcibly take over our lands. Request India to assist us immediately with beach landing crafts, and mine detectors to fight off Submarines and deep-sea mines, Helicopters armed with missiles, heavy sonic boom cannons, Ships and submarines armed with long distance missiles. Also request them for satellite assistance to detect submarines as well as war ships and approaching missiles.

Sudhir received a Telepathic Message from the Defense Minister, "Forces are ready for action Sir!" Sudhir used his powers to Teleport five percent of Nair Dvipa's Defense capability right to the old ex-English Port. Multiple telepathic broadcasts to Nair Dvipa forces began and Sudhir instructed them to switch on their sonars and Nair Dvipa's own satellite linked Enemy ship cum submarine sensor.

Sudhir teleported the Chiefs of the different wings, along with their immediate juniors into a secret cave on the top of a granite hill that gave them one hundred and eighty-degree view of the sea port and the approaching invading naval force.

Most of the mechanized landing crafts were within touching distance of the shore. Sudhir lost no time and said," Dolphin!" and he was a dolphin in the water. He raced towards the innumerable fast approaching flat boats. But Nair Dvipa could not see them though their sensors were switched on. When a few feet away from them, Sudhir dived deep down and he said, "Whale" and he became a whale. Then he rushed to hit the bottom of the first flat bottomed vessel.

The flat vessel went flying high up into the sky. But the other mechanized landing crafts hit the beach front and spilled out uniformed, professionally trained soldiers who came out shooting from their heavy-duty guns. And they were not invisible! They were sitting ducks in front of Nair Dvipa forces already Teleported to the spot.

"Fire at will!" commanded General Cristopher Rodrigues on his walkie talkie.

The heavy Nair Dvipa shore-based guns boomed – "Boom! Vooom! Phuuui, Fllaaat! Flaath! Boom – Phuuuui, Flaat!"

The beach front became crimson red, close to the colour of the contents of a tomato sauce bottle! Inspite of this Diànlì ji'è de guójia forces kept coming like a thousand cockroaches and kept getting blasted to smithereens!

Frantic calls began to come in from the Prime Minister to the Defense Minister on his Walkie Talkie, "Your forces are shooting at my forces! I mean your forces are attacking the Submarine cum Ship Maintenance team of Diànlì ji'è de guójia! Diànlì ji'è de guójia soldiers are getting massacred! I mean, our forces are firing at peaceful Diànlì ji'è de guójia maintenance Engineers, our most valuable guests of Nair Dvipa! This is in gross violation of an internationally enforceable agreement! Cease fire you fool! There can be severe consequences otherwise!" screamed Wánjù Mù'ou.

Khan twiddled the volume control to "extreme high", the Walkie Talkie made a shrill "Tweee wooo!" sound and the Defense Minister quickly pretended to not have heard Wánjù Mù'ou at all due to the "disturbance". "Hello Honourable Prime Minister! Cannot hear you! Some enemy forces are firing at the civilians of Nair Dvipa! Repeat unknown enemy forces are killing helpless civilians! We are Defending the Port from the attack! Over!" Khan signaled and Admiral Sudhakar Nattarajan immediately instructed the captain of the ship named NS Sindhubal, and it immediately began to fire heavy duty guns at the Latitude and Longitude Telepathically provided by Sudhir. The guns went "Boooom! Vrooom! Pfoooooi – Vvvvpphhaaaatttt! And they exploded with heavy impact on supposedly concealed hidden metal bodies of ships under the command of Diànlì ji'è de guójia. "Sir! The enemy forces are firing heavy guns at us! We must protect Nair Dvipa! Over!"

"No Noo Khan!" screamed Wánjù Mù'ou. "I'll lose my job! They are simply Engineers doing deep sea explosive research with some deep-sea explosives, that's all! Cease Fire! Cease Fire!"

Khan twiddled the volume control to extreme high once again and the Walkie Talkie made a shrill "Tweee wooo!" sound. "Hello! Hello! Cannot hear you Sir! Hullo?! Hullo?!" he pretended to have lost contact. With gestures, he instructed a front-line Havildar to keep twiddling the Walkie Talkie volume control during the duration of this battle. The Defense Minister signaled all guns to commence heavy firing at will. All Aircraft now based at the port flew up into the skies and began firing down into the sea. Based on Latitude & Longitude coordinates provided by Sudhir of a hidden submarine, one of the Nair Dvipa aircraft shot a rocket from a firing range of about one thousand five hundred yards. The rocket had four tail fins for stabilization at the rear and remained lethal even after passing through up to 130 feet of water, giving the pilot a target several times the actual size of the submarine. The rocket hit the sweet spot, that is, 60 feet in front of the rear side of the submarine. Though the submarine could not be seen, the sudden explosion and the expulsion of steel parts and shrapnel out of the water along with a huge mushroom of water that rose into the sky, made the successful impact all too obvious!

Just at that very moment Sudhir felt a tingling sensation in his head and severe pain. Mogui had obviously switched on the mass paralyzing 'brain scream wave'. Mogui's powers were far greater than Sudhir in this respect. The 'brain scream wave' sent out a sound wave at a Very High Frequency like the scratching of the black board with a chalk, "Screeeeee!" It paralyzed brain cells for very long period. Interestingly, Mogui could control the wave to affect only Nair Dvipa forces and not that of his own! This was his display of control over his limitless power!

The pain was so severe that Sudhir went down on his knees. He could not throw his protection energy net very far to protect the Nair Dvipa forces. It fell within a range of twenty feet and then stopped moving out further. The senior Defense Chiefs were with him. He could see Nair Dvipa forces squirming with blood oozing out of their ears, or lying unconscious or struggling with contorted expressions trying desperately to remain in control inspite of the crippling pain in their heads. Sudhir could sense Mógui de érzi, the sheer power of his brain waves was astounding to say the least! That was when the second wave, the third wave and the fourth wave of Diànlì ji'è de guójia mechanized landing crafts rushed onto the Nair Dvipa beach. They began to open to spill out thousands of professionally armed and trained soldiers. These soldiers began to fire missiles from an open tube, recoilless, shoulder launched gun, wherein the reaction gases expelled out of the back of the weapon to compensate the force exerted on the projectile (with a momentum equal to the projectile). The missiles decimated the defense control buildings and the paralyzed forces of

Nair Dvipa. Infrared homing Surface-to-Air missiles targeted the helicopters, and fighter aircrafts. Three Nair Dvipa aircraft and two helicopters went down or exploded before Sudhir gave them the instructions to fly away and out of reach. The large assault ships of Diànlì ji'è de guójia stationed until now in the ocean far away from Nair Dvipa, fired two cruise missiles carrying a warhead of 1,000 pounds of MOABs. It travelled one thousand five hundred miles to strike their target at the forces of Nair Dvipa around the beach. The huge force sucked away oxygen from 1.5 kilometers in every direction, the force mushroomed everything it could carry high up into the skies, an unbearably searing hot air whipped away in every direction pulverizing several buildings, defense equipment and killing life in every form in the vicinity. But by then the Nair Dvipa forces which were based on the beach were defeated. It was like using cannons to kill an unconscious fly!

Nair Dvipa had a small Defense force when compared to the Fire Power of Diànlì ji'è de guójia. Further, Nair Dvipa forces were unable to raise their guns in defense due to the excruciating pain of the 'brain scream wave' switched on by Mogui. And Sudhir obviously was in pain himself and could do nothing!

Sudhir then saw them! Thousands of winged soldiers armed with Laser Guns had flown out of the enemy ships and up into the skies. So numerous in numbers were they that the sun got covered with a dark cloud of winged enemy forces! "What Technolgy is this?" Sudhir wondered in awe.

"We are trying to identify their source", replied the lady from the submerged Interstellar Galactic craft.

"We have analyzed the source to be from Mogui's mind" the lady said after a while. "He has created these creatures from the power that we have given him".

"Shall we intervene King Sudhir?" asked the lady

"If he detects your energy then he would hurt many more of my people". replied Sudhir confidently. "He can sense new energies that may thwart his attack. I cannot risk my citizens being exposed to any further retaliation. Not now and certainly not today. Looks like we have lost this battle for today."

The winged soldiers helped Diànlì ji'è de guójia wingless soldiers and they all clambered onto the Nair Dvipa ships and Defense base building structures and took up positions of control. Soon the flag of Diànlì ji'è de guójia was fluttering on bastions that until today had proudly declared themselves to belong to Nair Dvipa. Sudhir realized that Diànlì ji'è de guójia had won this battle for today by using Mogui's anger over supposed injustice. Any further struggle on the part of Nair Dvipa forces would have meant Hara Kiri! "Do not resist any further!" he instructed Nair Dvipa forces telepathically. "Let them take you as Prisoners of War and live for today. We shall fight back soon when we are ready!"

Khan, the Defense Minister, was crestfallen! He could not look Sudhir in the eye. "Is this why we voted your honour out of power? Is this what we asked for? We voted ourselves into the hands of a representative of a Pirate nation! We got outwitted by them into voting in favour of their Geo political agenda. The Press, the Courts, our Supreme Court, our intelligentsia, all of us, we had worked together to oust the Royalty! We all have made a fool of ourselves! We voted for this invasion! We voted to become a slave country in the hands of a country that will kill our enterprise and leave us poverty stricken?!" He stared down and spoke with a voice full of emotion.

Sudhir embraced him and held him tight while the big man sobbed away.

But any further delay would have resulted in the capture of the Chiefs of the Nair Dvipa forces and Sudhir could not afford that! He grabbed Khan and the senior Defense Chiefs by their mind energies and Teleported them all quickly to their respective offices.

The Near Loss of the Four Villages

The tribes of Komungo, looked different, more Polynesian and had different cultural and religious beliefs from that of the Okimbo, who were from a different White European & Dark African mixed race compared again to the Heroko, Tswanga, and the Mokima tribe who were curly haired, tall, dark chocolate in complexion & well built.

But greed had made them join forces. They were many times taller, healthier and stronger than the Powva tribesmen and it foxed them to find such comparatively weak looking people earning many times more than them. And these weak people were citizens of a village that boasted of a highly advanced system of lifestyle. The enemy forces had never made any effort to earn a good life for themselves and their society. They had survived for that day and for that moment alone as if there was no tomorrow. Hence, they envied the wealth of the next-door neighbor and thus made this plan to loot and plunder just to make them feel small! The easiest method to earn quickly today was to loot the famous hard-earned wealth of the Powva tribe consisting of four villages the Zambeke, Omagwena, Kavaheke, and Kunini villages.

The positive energy protection was provided those who were inside the semi - circle. The positive energy protection stopped those who were outside, from coming in.

But the enemy forces had entered through deep tunnels that had been painstakingly built in total secrecy. And once inside the circle, they were automatically protected.

They were roaring in response to the roar of defiance from the Powva tribesmen who guarded the Kunini village in the valley below. The Kunini blew the sankha and roared! The sankha then the roar woke up the warriors of the Zambeke, Omagwena, Kavaheke villages as well as the elders of the Beti Beti, the super council village or the village of the elders high up on the three hill tops.

The enemy forces obviously planned to defeat each village one by one after having isolated them. They could not climb the hills due to the protective energy barrier placed by the ex-King of Nair Dvipa. Thus, they planned to camp at the base of each hill, including the village at the base of the valley, to stop the food supply route from and to each village and eventually let Powva tribesmen die! If they cannot come out from their protective cocoon, then this blockade by enemy forces would certainly choke each village of all food supplies over some month's time.

In this manner the Kunini village became isolated. Then the Zambeke, followed by the Omagwena and finally the Kavaheke village were barricaded and hence isolated. Subsequently, no village could join the forces of another village and thus each remained cut off and thus could not go out to hunt to feed their family members.

Sudhir flew in just at that very moment having experienced defeat in the hands of Mogui and quickly analyzed the gravity of the situation down below.

Sudhir's late Grandparents were there. Ngia Vat was also present and she kept silent while the rest discussed the repercussions of the fall of the Port and hence the immediate urgency to save the villages from harm.

"We have an emergency situation now", said Daivam late King Cherusseri Namboodiri.

"King Sudhir Bagaria has to look into stopping the breach in the protective layer. We shall sit down now to plan and end the impasse in the rest of Nair Dvipa".

"I have got to seal the tunnels!" Sudhir stood up and said and then he flew away after giving everybody a nod.

"Invisible cloak", he instructed his mand and he promptly became invisible. Sudhir scoured the shrubs and wild growth until the deep jungle began. He saw some enemy Warriors bending to enter the valley out of tunnels and then stand up to their full height. He flew down closer to see the opening to a foxhole tunnel. He mumbled words that created a surge of energy that would travel the length of the tunnel, including its branches and block this route for ever. He quickly sent an energy bolt to that entrance to seal it permanently and several others that he kept identifying based on sudden movement of armed enemy beings. Then he mumbled some more words to create a hard-concrete cement like crust below the protected area. Now nobody could dig his way into the protected area. His conscience said that he could not hurt the enemy forces without cause. They had only raised their voices but they had not hurt anybody within the protected area. He could not hurt or cause harm to the enemy forces until the enemy forces caused harm to the citizens within the protected area. Further, being Head of Inter Galactic Justice on Earth and a senior member of the Inter Galactic Justice Core Team, he was duty bound to bring about a peaceful resolution.

It was at that very moment that the Zambeke, Omagwena, Kavaheke and the Kunini decided to enforce their freedom to move freely on land that belonged to them. Mokkasa Bviki of Kunini village decided to execute a foolhardy act. He walked out of the protective field with a feather from a wild fowl tied on a small twig, a gesture of peace and walked to a flat clearing where he stood holding up the same.

Ariki the chief of the Komungo with muscles bursting out from every part of his body, roared a deep loud roar. He kept roaring with every step forward, his wrists clenched on his two sides.

Mokkasa Bviki raised his right hand in the air, calling for a dialogue. But Aiki kept coming forward roaring menacingly. He reached out behind his back to pull out a large stone hacker blade normally used to cut away a pig's head in one swipe, and then, even while rushing forward, he bent forward to attack.

"We need to talk! This is unnecessary!" shouted Mokkasa Bviki

But Aiki took a long run, roaring all the while, towards Mokkasa Bviki and swung his hacking blade behind his back, ready to be swung forward and then down on Mokkasa Bviki.

Mokkasa had to defend himself from the forward swing of the sharp blade and he swung away from Aiki's path at the last moment, grabbed his opponent's right arm and pushed his feet in front of Aiki's ankle making his opponent trip and fall with a thud on his face.

Aike swung back on his feet and charged at Mokkasa Bviki but the latter stayed on the spot, devoid of any expression, as if expecting nothing. The moment Aiki lunged and swung his blade ninety degrees horizontally from the left to the right, Mokkasa leapt up into the air, with his feet folded under him. He took on a roll and his two feet slammed into the back of Aiki. Aiki' lungs emptied with a "Woooff!" as he rushed forward due to the impact from behind and fell on his face again.

He had lost face twice! Aiki the Chief of the Komungo jumped back on his feet and raised his blade arm high into the air to call for war! "Chargeee!" he screamed.

All the invading tribes from other islands, the Komungo, the Okimbo, the Heroko, the Tswaga, and finally the Mokima charged at a single warrior with a roar that resonated through the deep forests!

To protect Mokkasa Bviki, around fifty warriors rushed out of the protective energy cover of the Kunini village to immediately take positions on his left and right. Seeing the charging warriors Aiki rushed back towards his tribesmen thinking the Kunini warriors were charging at him. The spears and the arrows from the invaders flew towards these fifty warriors before the invaders could reach but the same were deflected using shields, with ease.

Then the first wave of invaders struck with a roar and a "boom, ffllatt, pffatta, Pluttthh, Klak!" of sharp knives, fists and legs against large shields and good training. However, instead of pushing the knives into their opponents, the Kunini village warriors smashed their knife butts, just as trained against the jaws, or the ears, or the solar plexus, or the scrotum, of their opponents. Exasperated after he saw innumerable warriors squirming or writhing in pain on the forest floor, Aiki called for a halt and called one of the Kunini warriors for a quick talk. The warrior looked at Mokkasa Bviki for his approval, and on seeing the latter nod in the affirmative, he moved cautiously towards Aiki. He walked past two of Aiki's warriors. Suddenly, Aiki gave the signal and one of the warriors jumped into the air and pushed his blade deep down into the back of the Kunini warrior.

The blade sliced through bones, cartilage, nerves and lungs! The warrior screamed in excruciating pain and his fellow warriors then had no option but to reply in kind. The invaders had shed the first blood. Hence, blood for blood!

All the villages, the Zambeke, the Omagwena, the Kavaheke, and the Kunini had a good reason to execute the strategies born from intense training as provided by late Lieutenant-General Sir Cherusseri Daivika, the last King of Nair Dvipa. They shot out the fire tipped arrows that flew high into the air from sixty or more very large crossbows per village. Each arrow was ten feet long, had bird feathers at the rear end and the front tip was shaped like a conical pot filled with burning hot oil & sharp stone chips. A wick was lit before the launching of the arrow by a large cross bow and the oil caught fire. This oil on fire exploded a few feet above the warriors along with tiny sharpened star shaped stone chips shooting out in every direction to pierce a minimum of four or more warriors deep into muscles and sinew. The explosion was alien to them. Initially they ran. Then it began to pierce them when they displayed courage and stood their ground. This time, they screamed. But, even before the invaders had time to recoup, the second line of sixty crossbows behind the first, followed by the third line of cross bows behind the second, shot out their arrows. In the meanwhile, the first line and the second line primed their crossbows and were ready to shoot.

The arrows caused a lot of disturbance in the ranks of the various tribes but they changed their strategy by moving under the protection of trees. However, the arrows continued to rain down on those who paid no heed. The invaders dispersed in every direction possible, waiting for another opportunity to regroup and attack.

That was when Sudhir gave his warriors the power to fly and spout fire. Each Powva tribe warrior had intentionally to wear the mask of a demon and paint his body red with black stripes like that of a zebra. They flew out of each village in swarms and looked down on the ocean of invaders and rained fire on them. This sight was 'Black Magic' to these tribe members who had remained isolated from the scientifically advanced cities. They saw demons rising from each village and raining fire. Seasoned tribal warriors were terrified by this sight.

Superstition was further added to the war strategy. The elders entered the minds of the enemy warriors to better understand their worst fears and created holograms of the cause of that fear. The invisibility energy and change form energies were given to specific warriors of the Powva tribe. They flew up to coconut trees, invisible.

A coconut fell from a tree and 'pop' it landed on Ariki. "Ouch!" shouted Ariki and he looked up and around but could not see anybody. Atiu his elder brother felt something warm wrap it's arm around his shoulders from behind. He looked back to see a big leopard staring at him. He froze in fear! "Is your name Atiu?", the leopard growled and asked. Atiu was in shock and kept wondering how is it that a leopard spoke and then how is it that it spoke his tongue. All Atiu could manage was to gulp and nod in the affirmative very slowly with the corner of his eyes watching for any move that the leopard would make. "So, have you come to this island to disturb the peace?" the leopard growled and asked. Terrified Atiu promptly shook his head in the negative. "What about Ariki your brother?" the leopard growled and asked. Then it continued, "Go and ask Ariki. Tell him that I asked. Go on!" and so saying the leopard gave Atiu a push towards his shorter and stockier younger brother. Atiu, with his hands down by his side like a zombie, walked up to Ariki, his younger brother and with a terrified expression on his face asked, "Ariki have you come to this island to disturb peace? No – right? You have not come to this island to disturb peace, right?" Atiu kept giving hints to Ariki, nodding his head in the negative and pointing his eyebrows behind him for Ariki to understand.

"You drunk or something elder brother?" asked Ariki. Then he continued, "We both have come not just to disturb peace, we have come to loot, become rich and cause mayhem! Hah ha ha ha!" Atiu looked crestfallen because he saw that the leopard had appeared from behind Ariki now and had put its arm around him. It whispered, "I love the blood of people who come to disturb peace. Which part of you do I eat first?" Ariki looked back in shock then, terrified, he unwrapped himself away promptly from the leopard's grasp and within seconds zipped away with Atiu in the opposite direction. The warriors that they led stared after them in confusion. Then they saw the Black Leopard which growled and said, "I protect these lands! So, who dares to invade my land? You? Or you? Or you?" Each warrior kept moving one step back in fear even while shaking his head in the negative. Then one by one they ran as fast as they could away from the Leopard.

Fallou of the Okimbo tribe was hiding on the top of a tree camouflaged by huge creeper leaf. He was chewing a beetle leaf waiting for the island residents to climb down the hill so then he would attack and become rich. His mother had run away with a younger man and his father left him with his disciplinarian grandmother. "Get the hell out of bed your lazy bum!" so screaming she would pour cold water on his head. Then she would use a thin reed to spank him on his bottom every time that he came home late and forgot to do the dishes. So, he ran away! That was many years ago, thank God for that! Suddenly he heard a voice, "Fallouuuuuu!". He looked all around him frantically! What the hell! How did she reach this island now? Is she going to make him wash her dishes again? "Fallou? Where are you Fallou?" the voice was coming closer and closer with large leaf being brushed aside. He jumped down from the tree and asked his tribesmen to stop his grandmother. Then he ran as far as his legs would carry him and even further. The warriors that he led stared after him in confusion. This grandmother arrived in a little while searching for Fallou. She had hair standing one foot into the air all around her head wherein, each strand kept waving and squirming as if they were alive. But her face – her face was huge, like that of a pig and she had two knives in her two hands which she kept waving at every warrior while spouting fire! "You hiding Follou?" she shrieked like a banshee. "I shall burn you all alive!" she shrieked. This ghastly sight was too much for the warriors. They had come to fight warriors, not witches like these! It was then that the grand mother sent a blast of fire in their direction and a whole tree branch burnt down to ashes. The warriors jumped in fright and ran away before she could get at them!

Chausiku of the Heroko tribe, and Chege of the Tswaga tribe, were runaway warriors of the Mohinique Kingdom deep in the forests of Katungila. Their group commander of the Mokima tribe was Bakuiri, a tall, heavy built, barrel chested gorilla who killed many soldiers simply by squeezing them to death.

One day their group commander caught both in bed with his wife. The group commander speared his wife dead and then knifed Chausiku in the shoulder and Chege in the leg. Chege pretended to fall, grabbed the spear and ran it through the stomach of the group commander and he collapsed. They had probably killed their group commander which meant a court martial in the jungle as per jungle law and that meant a very long jail term was certain. So, they ran away, came home to lead their army of illiterate fellow villagers to loot and pillage for quick profit. Chege, at this moment was hiding in a deep dugout with a cap of twigs tied together covering the dugout. Chausiku. was looking at the base of the hill from the trees that provided him shade from the strong sun rays. Suddenly, he heard huffing and puffing and a warrior wearing the same grass skirt uniform that he had worn several years ago came rushing in his direction. "Run run! Huf puff! The old man Bakuiri of the Mohinique Kingdom is coming with a sword!" so saying he rushed away into the jungle. Chausiku popped his head out on hearing his supposedly dead boss's name. "old man Bakuiri is here?!" Chausiku had now changed his pan horizon view of the direction from which the warrior had just arrived. Then both Chausiku, and Chege saw old man Bakuiri come chasing in their direction, "Where are the two rascals?" Bakuiri roared in anger, "I shall kill them both!" Chausiku, and Chege ran as far as their legs could carry them with their warriors looking at them running away with a confused look on their face. Then hundreds of flying monsters began to chase the warriors after their leaders began to run away. Screeching, screaming and throwing fire balls down at them. They all ran away terrified!

In this manner the Chief of each invading tribe was made to run away. Once again, the elders entered the minds of the warriors to better understand their worst fears and create a hologram of the cause of that fear. Now wives appeared with broomsticks, mother in laws appeared to pay a visit with a full bag for a month, teachers came with their canes to swipe the terrified warrior on his bottom, the big feet flightless bird came charging, hunger took on a form and charged at the warrior, flying witches appeared screeching and spitting out fire. One by one the invading warriors began to scream in terror and escape into the forests. But the Powva tribe were instructed to tire out the invaders. The instruction was to make them so very tired out that they would then be willing to come to the negotiating table. Thus, the Powva tribe warriors, for the good of the Powva tribe, sent the worst fears of each invader to follow the warriors.

By the evening, the various invading tribes were nowhere to be seen, barring one or two confused or drunk warrior.

Then the leaders came in ones and twos to beg for shelter & protection from the demons! They would do anything if saved from the demons. Anything!

So then on, Sudhir began to execute the "Mind Cleansing process" with each one of them. By the fourth day on the island, their personalities had changed, they were willing to give up their lives for the security of Nair Dvipa and to ensure that their villagers cum Tribe members become 'Good Human Beings".

They were then asked to relocate the fox holes from where they had entered and Sudhir opened each of them to allow them to go home and start life anew.

The Torture and Mayhem in the Cities of Nair Dvipa

The Chiefs of the various Nair Dvipa Defense wings were back in their stations. There was a divide in the Diànlì ji'è de guójia decision making team. One side, did not want to disturb the status of the Nair Dvipa Defense forces. They wanted the facts about takeover of Nair Dvipa to be a bit subtle to avoid condemnation from powerful nations of the world. The other group aggressively wanted to declare victory in an invasion and takeover of a foreign nation. The subtle team seemed to be gaining in strength. The invasion was termed by the Press as "protection of democracy" in response to the call of the Prime Minister of Nair Dvipa to the heads of Diànlì ji'è de guójia. The media kept repeating, "discovery of an attempt to remove elected representatives by force. Investigations are on and the 'save democracy' army sent by Diànlì ji'è de guójia will remain until further notice". Not one media recognized nor praised the sacrifice of the Nair Dvipa forces. All media on the other hand thanked the Diànlì ji'è de guójia for having responded to the "Cry of democracy in distress". The collegium of judges of the Supreme Court had always been held in high esteem over the past so many years. Attempts to bring about punitive action against the Chiefs of the various Defense wings failed in the Parliament. The foreign country sponsored Prime Minister tried his best through his henchmen to file PILs (Public Interest Litigations) to remove the Defense Chiefs but as they had acted in the defense of the country, their "actions were at par with their assigned duties", the Supreme Court decided. But problems arose when a Team of Judges of the Supreme court allocated the file by the Chief Justice relating to the supposed "misconduct" of the Chiefs of Defense of Nair Dvipa, took the above decision in favour of the Chiefs of Defense.

Such a decision irked the two judges immediately below the Chief Justice of the Supreme Court of Nair Dvipa. The media screamed, "Murder of justice – says Diànlì ji'è de guójia". The decision to protect the Defense Chiefs seemed to have hurt the interests of the not so subtle Diànlì ji'è de guójia team. Thus, they instigated these two judges immediately below the Chief Justice to do something unprecedented! They decided to mar the faith of the island nation in this hallowed institution by calling a Press Conference to claim, "Important cases were being allocated to Legal luminaries junior to them hence this amounted to favoritism". They began to claim that "Justice was in danger". That the clean image of the "Repository of Justice" that is the Supreme Court, was being marred by this one individual who in fact had acted as was expected of him. It did not matter to them that the Chief justices of the past in Nair Dvipa too had decided many a time to by-pass the immediate two or more judges below him and allocate important cases to judges of his choice. The fact that the Chief Justice of Nair Dvipa was the

Master of the Roster and had total power to decide who to allocate which file, did not suit these four Judges. The Press kept printing, "Murder of Justice", for many days to come and yet the people of Nair Dvipa were happy with the courage that the Chief Justice has displayed in the face of such Anti Nair Dvipa opposition.

Niar Dvipa forces now saluted with grim expressions on their faces, as forces of Diànlì ji'è de guójia marched by. The Intelligence Chief along with his core team vanished from Nair Dvipa the moment Diànlì ji'è de guójia forces occupied Nair Dvipa. The advantage of the Nair Dvipa Intelligence department was that the foreign based Nair Dvipa intelligence operatives had been encouraged to begin business houses of repute. Thus, they were self-sufficient and self-motivated. The foreign embassies of Nair Dvipa did not have any records of such deep assets, neither did senior cadre Administrative Officials within Diànlì ji'è de guójia itself. A large chunk of Digital files simply vanished along with the main functionaries from the premises. The Media raised a hue and cry along with the Prime Minister but the "traitors" could not be traced. Yet the people of Nair Dvipa were happy with the wisdom that the Chief of Intelligence had displayed, by not allowing confidential papers to fall into the hands of such Anti Nair Dvipa opposition.

Diànlì ji'è de guójia was paranoid about losing control over a new colony and banned gatherings or congregations above two people at any location outside their homes without prior notice to the nearest police stations. Police stations had a huge number of pending files to be cleared every day and this new responsibility added to their work pressure. They began to demand bribes for each file cleared. But marriages, celebrations, cultural events, sports events, competitions etc., needed quick decisions and hence this caused a lot of distress. The most distressed were the public but the happiest were the Ministers who were running Nair Dvipa on behalf of Diànlì ji'è de guójia.

The capital of Nair Dvipa was Suryadham and the metros were Sudukki, a satellite city of Suryadham, the Metro city of Vaynur in the North with its lush green hilly lands, Vasarathod the west based green river valley, Vartayam the Information Systems capital of Nair Dvipa in the South, and finally Maryadatote the land of educated farmers but now infested by proven criminal citizens of Diànlì ji'è de guójia. All of Nair Dvipa cried out in pain as some corrupt and brain washed police, the local MLAs, the local councilors, the local courts, the media, everybody unwittingly or with partial understanding, or with full knowledge, joined hands to support the takeover of Nair Dvipa by Diànlì ji'è de guójia. This takeover happened through proxy representation while the Defense forces, under strict orders from the duly elected Prime Minister, tried its best to adjust to the new command without any obvious display of animosity.

But the local citizens knew no diplomacy and they could not be cowed down as the victorious Diànlì ji'è de guójia army did a Flag March within the capital city of Sudukki. They booed and heckled the Diànlì ji'è de guójia soldiers as they marched in perfect rhythm towards the Army barracks with combat ready Nair Dvipa forces being told to accept the command of Diànlì ji'è de guójia senior military commanders with humility.

Those Defense personnel who were financially well off, and did not need a salary to survive, decided to desert and left for unknown destinations with their family. They were declared as "deserters" and their images appeared in the media to shame them and their family members. Many decided to fight from within and took off their uniform during desired assignments to execute guerilla warfare against the invaders. Many who could not afford not being paid a monthly salary, were sponsored by fellow citizens. Thus, the resistance began.

The port that which had been a den of prostitution, drugs, innumerable deaths and disease, which had been created many ages back by Mogui next to the old British Port, now re-began its operations. Over enthusiastic pirates cum mafia now began to kidnap women locally once again. Lonely Diànlì ji'è de guójia forces were lonely no more as drugged women and girls of Nair Dvipa were thrown into their bedrooms as weekly bonus. Problems for the Anti Royal voters began when their wives, daughters and sisters began to vanish. The modus operandi was cruel and followed under the threat of an armed mafia. The girls or women would be kidnapped, felt and inspected for quality, sent to the dock or shipped away in barred cells never to be seen again.

The media reported, "The Pro Royal forces, desperate to have the King back as a dictator and throttle democracy, have resorted to kidnapping of our wives, daughters and sisters, so says our Prime Minister".

But the Anti Royal voters had their moles within the Pro Royal Forces and by this time they knew that the media report was fake. When their own was in danger then everything else becomes secondary. It was from that point on that the Anti Royal party got divided.

When the police which had many anti royals, refused to help fellow anti royals in identifying the kidnappers and bringing back their families from the prostitution den, the anguished anti royals decided to take matters into their own hands.

When certain anti socials were caught red handed while kidnapping and taking away by force the daughters and wives of Anti Royal voters and the Diànlì ji'è de guójia sponsored court declared that "there was lack of ample evidence to prove the guilt of the kidnappers conclusively", the Anti Royal party got divided even further.

Therefore, the moment the culprits were released from prison due to 'lack of evidence", the anguished Anti Royal caught them, took them away to secluded spots and tried to solicit information regards their missing family members.

The Diànlì ji'è de guójia sponsored Police termed this act as "Anti-Social", and "Creating unrest". and got them arrested. The Diànlì ji'è de guójia sponsored court declared them to be a danger to society, slapped them with the charge of "attempt to murder and sedition" and awarded them with life sentences.

Word of this obvious anarchy, lawlessness, lack of basic security and lack of justice spread like wild fire all over Nair Dvipa.

Thus, was born the Pro-Independence movement!

The Total Breakdown of Law & Order

Diànlì ji'è de guójia sponsored low cost drugs entered the schools and colleges. Dropouts, suicides, murder for drugs began to happen in increasing numbers. Guns, Swords, knives, ammunitions, and arms in their variety which were banned for the public was now being carried in total disregard of earlier laws. Arms manufacturers, all being citizens of Diànlì ji'è de guójia, controlled decisions in Nair Dvipa relating to the right of humankind to live or die. What could one do when law did nothing to protect the weak and the downtrodden? The Diànlì ji'è de guójia sponsored Media now began to advocate Diànlì ji'è de guójia style uniforms for all and sundry. Brown tops and brown pajamas.

Earlier they would mollycoddle the Nair Dvipa Anti Royal Judges, Advocates, Senior Government Officials, Media, Police etc. There was a time when no decision was taken without joint consultation. There was a time when big money exchanged hands to enable every such Bill that enforced and ensured the powers of the Proxy government. The meetings, consultations, and monies kept reducing in frequency and in value. Lack of financial lubrication began to cause friction.

Diànlì ji'è de guójia was expecting the friction and decided to divide and rule by using a foreign religion that was not their own, as a weapon, against the non-conformists of Nair Dvipa. The extremist's version of this foreign religion could now sweep into Nair Dvipa with the pro Diànlì ji'è de guójia media supporting the infiltration under the garb of "human rights", and the anti-Royal media fell into their trap as it helped keep the Royals away. And the innocent citizens of Nair Dvipa who felt good calling themselves "progressive and tolerant" felt that they would be God Blessed supporting the supposed righteous pro Diànlì ji'è de guójia media narrative. In the meanwhile, the enemy nation began to openly favour the extremist version of the foreign religion and made them fight the non-conforming Nair Dvipa citizens.

Interestingly, when a fresh citizen of Extremists religious faith wanted to organize a prayer gathering, or meeting to explain their religion to "Non-Believers" within Nair Dvipa, permission was granted within seconds. "Conversion" was worded as "Being reborn" or "Being purified" and to save themselves from tyranny, or to appease the top bosses, thousands were willingly "reborn" or "purified".

The proxy government of Diànlì ji'è de guójia began to feel super confident about their hold on Nair Dvipa. They felt self-sufficient and hence got arrogant. They felt that they can do without their business partners. And such arrogance began to work wonders for the Pro Royal group.

Diànlì ji'è de guójia brought in the divide and rule policy. Appeasement of an extremist's foreign religion policy to a point where the 'religious tax' was imposed that had necessarily to be paid by everybody in Nair Dvipa amongst other taxes. It made no sense as no development of Nair Dvipa came out of such a tax. The "reborn" or "purified" were asked to wear a light golden necklace which allowed them to get away from payment of this obviously discriminatory "religious tax".

Very soon, those who were not "reborn" or "purified" were stopped at every crossing to pay the "religious tax" for that corner of the city.

That extremist foreign religion did not realize that they were being used. It never occurred to them that when Nair Dvipa would be totally in the hands of Diànlì ji'è de guójia, then, they would be exterminated like pests, or bombed to extinction.

There came about a policy decision to allocate several reserved seats on aircraft, trains, auto rickshaws and underground Metro railways for specific "reborn" or "purified" citizens of Nair Dvipa, normal citizens of Diànlì ji'è de guójia, family members of citizens of Diànlì ji'è de guójia and, "concubines of citizens of Diànlì ji'è de guójia"!

Then the Media personalities began to get affected on being refused seats because certain empty seats were reserved for Diànlì ji'è de guójia citizens as also for the "reborn" or "purified" citizens of Nair Dvipa. So, one of them, the reporter known to many as Nindiya of Vēgattiluḷḷa Vārtta, the TV cum online

Media cum News Print Media giant, wrote, "Do we have to become their concubine to have the right to breathe and move around at our own free will with our own faith and belief within Nair Dvipa?"

Within a few days of such news release, mysterious flying human beings were seen hovering over the apartment of Nindiya. She began to get threat mails, and she was followed wherever she travelled on business. One day, a group of men followed her all the way home and began to taunt her, then surrounded her, then began to touch her inappropriately. When she tried to photograph them, they took away her Mobile phone. There was a police picket and yet they pretended to see nothing and refused to come to her aid. She ran into an apartment which was open and they escorted her into her own apartment. The police came and took her complaint the next morning but no arrests took place. Under instructions of the Chairperson of the media company, a male reporter, a friend of hers, moved in with her to provide her the security that she desired. He would escort her to the office and return with her every day.

Then one day, he was found unconscious on the road. Her colleagues tried searching for Nindiya everywhere but she was not to be found.

But her question "Do we have to become their concubine to have the right to breathe and move around at our free will with our own faith and belief within Nair Dvipa?" began to torture the conscience of the mass. 'Like buttons' spread this message like wild fire thanks to the Social Media. Soon, the otherwise Pro Diànlì ji'è de guójia Senior Reporter named Manjula of a specific media now began to spout venom about "reborn" or "purified" citizens, reservation, and the state of lawlessness. Manjula came out in the open, "We had supported the Diànlì ji'è de guójia running our country rather than the Royals thinking that we would be free from the stifling rules, the supposedly boring discipline that had been introduced ages back by the Royals. We got invited by Diànlì ji'è de guójia to numerous conferences at International Forums wherein we were conferred the honour of being "Intellectuals" and as a result, everybody came to know about us. They rewarded our "modern outlook" wherein we challenged "respect for elders", "respect for some all-powerful energy called Nair Dvipa Gods", "respect for the culture of Nair Dvipa", "respect for the history of Nair Dvipa", "respect for any history that was not in writing", "respect for any history that lacked scientific basis". Hence, we reported in the favour of Diànlì ji'è de guójia in exchange for an increase in our personal wealth and to ensure that the books written by us got free publicity. But now we face an unprecedented emergency that shakes our faith in our past actions. Now we have no option but to reverse the reporting pattern to save Nair Dvipa from the Diànlì ji'è de guójia Government by bringing back the Royals!"

The Diànlì ji'è de guójia leadership were furious! Orders were issued to ensure that the reporter be picked up by the human traffickers and sold off at the port. And because she was "not good to look at", hence the kidnappers disrobed her, felt her over, found her "unsuitable" and she was sold off at a "highly discounted rate" wherein the negotiation, especially the discounted offer, was made in her presence to embarrass, demoralize, and subsequently break her spirit. This bit of news was conveyed by one of the kidnappers who was a plant of the Anti Royal forces. The media went wild but the Diànlì ji'è de guójia leadership running Nair Dvipa did nothing to trace nor save her from the Den of Vice.

Sudhir Re-enters Nair Dvipa

Sudhir came to know about this kidnapping and felt that the political environment permitted his entry into the fray. In the history of Nair Dvipa humankind, the media reports have always determined how the citizens of any country would react to the existing political environment. Every Politician knew that the Media was a slippery fish that could be nobody's friend. How many days can any human survive on a bland diet of non-spicy news?! A majority of Nair Dvipa consumed the maximum quantities of spicy meals and spicy news which, deep in their hypocritical hearts meant, entertainment! Media had to mean drama! Media had to mean sensationalizing mole hills into mountains in the garb of truth. Diànlì ji'è de guójia had not allowed the media of its own country to say anything other than what it desired should be said. Diànlì ji'è de guójia had made the right strategic move by capturing the media of Nair Dvipa over a period of past forty years as a first step to capturing Nair Dvipa for long term commercial exploitation and global strategic control.

And now Diànlì ji'è de guójia made the first two mistakes by antagonizing the media. Sudhir realized that winning a war desired having the media by your side. If he could save the two female reporters and convince them about the importance of the citizens of Nair Dvipa to stick together at this crucial moment then, half the battle was won.

He scanned the port for Manjula's and Nindiya's description and found Manjula in a store room located in the basement of a bungalow near the new port. The foreign resident who had paid to buy her called himself David McDonald and was at this very moment trying to explain to her that he could not afford to pay more otherwise, he would have bought somebody more adjusting and reasonable. Her mouth was covered with duct tape but from her violent body language and facial fury he realized she was obviously unhappy with the humiliation she had suffered and the violation of her body. Her eyes were spouting venom and if expressions could have been a sword then he would have been dead.

The sign board below David's nameplate outside the main entrance gate read, "President of The Kind Nair Dvipa Heart, NGO, Philanthropist, Protector of the weak and downtrodden". Heavily built and armed security guards were patrolling outside the gate and inside the compound of this 'Protector of the weak and downtrodden' individual who ran an NGO financed by dubious foreign entities. His style of philanthropy was interesting. Just yesterday, he had been negotiating with the arms manufacturers of Diànlì ji'è de guójia based out of Nair Dvipa for the purchase of weapons intended to create war and mayhem in an otherwise peaceful country in Africa.

It was around twelve noon and the guards were often trying to avoid the sun rays by walking under the protection of some shaded trees.

Sudhir hovered above the Bungalow and told his mind, "Make me look like David McDonald". Sudhir's form changed to that of a tall European and he landed gently on his feet in the forested area outside the bungalow but within the Bungalow compound. Then, as if returning from an evening stroll, he walked past the dog squad and the armed musclemen all moving around inside the Bungalow compound walls, who nodded to acknowledge him. He nodded back and walked towards the main entrance where a huge seven foot fully uniformed and armed giant with muscles bursting out of his half shirt sleeves was blocking the door. The security guard seemed shocked to see him. The guard instantly looked inside the bungalow because he remembered David having entered around a few hours back, then, he turned his head to stare at Sudhir once again intently and shook his head to wake himself up! As Sudhir approached towards the main entrance the security guard looked confused and took on a defensive stance. He once again looked inside then back at Sudhir and then inside, instinctively flexed his muscles to be ready for action, and then back at Sudhir again. When Sudhir was but a few feet away, the security guard finally relented by saluting him but with suspicion written all over his grim face. He opened the glass door for Sudhir to enter but kept staring into Sudhir's eyes and face for any tell-tale sign of doubt or fear or sweat pouring down his face. Sudhir smiled and saluted back even while striding confidently past the guard and into the Bungalow. The security guard kept staring after him trying to imagine the cause of the change in his snooty, unfriendly boss.

Sudhir walked past five other inhouse servants and attendants to climb down to the basement, after locking the door behind him. Sudhir heard a scuffle and a loud thud. He peeped to find that the real David McDonald had been kicked in the face by Manjula the feisty reporter. He must have tried to touch her inappropriately. David was now sitting on his bottom holding his jaw with his two hands and growling, "You, stupid woman! Why do you not co-operate?! Nobody was willing to pay a penny to buy you! But I had pity on you, see? I was the only one to even consider buying you, see? I paid for buying you and you are my banana to peel, to use and throw away as and when I please. You got to get this simple thing into your skinny head. I own you and I can do with you as I please!"

Saying so he reached out to touch her breasts, she kicked out again but this time he was ready, he moved away and her foot missed him. With that missed kick, she lost her position of defense, he grabbed her little breasts and began to fondle them. Now she was looking really scared!

He was blabbering now even while fondling her breast with one hand, the other was now pointing an accusing finger at her, "If I complain to the Diànlì ji'è de guójia government that you are defective then I shall get a full refund! You know, that don't you? You also know what they would do with you right?

They would do with you what they do with all defective women, they shall give you away to the Diànlì ji'è de guójia front soldiers. The front soldiers cannot afford to buy women and so ten or twenty of them shall mount you every day! For as many days until you are no more! You would love that, would you not? Eh!"

Saying so he smacked her on her buttocks and quickly moved away before she kicked out again. Then he kept spouting his threats while pointing his threatening finger at her. Sudhir could see that she was wincing because of the strong words. And she was terrified having heard him hint the latest threat to her future.

"Make him lose his voice", Sudhir told his mind. David kept trying to threaten Manjula with words that refused to come out of his lips now. Suddenly realizing that he could not speak, he kept clutching his wind pipe and kept shaking his fingers at Manjula. So engrossed was he in threatening the reporter that he did not see Sudhir walk up to stand behind him. David saw Manjula's expression change from shock to bewilderment as she stared with awe at somebody behind him. Very slowly he turned around and David saw two feet and then as he looked up, he saw himself!

"Change David's body for three days to look like Manjula", Sudhir instructed his mind. And David changed into Manjula right in front of the real Manjula's eyes and yet continued to do the task in hand, that of threatening the real Manjula. The latter was now terrified because she had never ever seen a human form morph into another form.

Make the real Manjula look like Nindiya the missing reporter. And Manjula morphed into Nindiya!

Sudhir picked up Manjula's tied up body and having heaved her over his right shoulder, climbed the stairs from the basement to the ground floor, upstairs. David, now looking like Manjula, chased after Sudhir, trying his best to communicate with the household staff and security guards but in vain. Sudhir, looking like David, instructed the household help to lock up Manjula downstairs in the basement. They promptly picked up David and took him down to the basement and then climbed back upstairs after locking the door behind them.

The security guard was the only one to notice that Manjula's body language matched that of his boss and that David was too warm and friendly. But what truly got him suspicious was that he had never seen Nindiya being brought into the building.

Sudhir strode out but this time the security guard saluted straight away and opened the door out for him. Sudhir got into David's car, placed Manjula on the seat beside him and drove out of the Bungalow.

The security guard went to the basement and inspite the objections of the other staff, he requested Manjula to communicate in writing. And Manjula kept writing in unstoppable fury!

After travelling a big distance, both Sudhir & Manjula morphed back to their original bodies while Manjula kept gawking like she had just seen a ghost.

"I am King Sudhir Bagaria of Nair Dvipa and I need your help in gaining independence from Diànlì ji'è de guójia", Sudhir smiled and requested.

Then very gently he snapped his fingers and the sticky tape pasted over Manjula's mouth along with the rope that bound her hands, dropped away like magic! Manjula could finally take a deep breath and having done so she exclaimed, "Phewww! Thankyou your Highness! Thankyou, oh thankyou, thankyou, a million times!" and then "Ohh! Oww wow oww!" as blood surged back into her hands and feet. And so, she flexed her wrists and exercised her stiff body until she felt better.

Tears welled up in her eyes as she whimpered, "That horrible man touched me all over and I could do nothing about it!"

Then rage took over her demeanor and with eyes on fire she growled, "Many other women must have been suffering this humility and pain for all these ages. And they had no one to fight for them! The audacity of the country Diànlì ji'è de guójia! They think that the women of Nair Dvipa can be bought and sold like cattle?" Then, as if realizing the reality, she exclaimed with the same amount of ferocity, "They actually know that nobody can do anything to them inspite of their kidnapping and selling our women of Nair Dvipa!"

Then her tone mellowed to an expression of shame and sorrow. "I spoke on their behalf through my many articles and reports which helped the proxy government win the majority votes in the Nair Dvipa Elections and thus I deserve to be sold off like cattle by them! I sold off my country to a foreign country and I deserved to be punished! I was disrobed and they felt me over like one would a dead, bad quality chicken or fish! I knew I was bad to look at, and I knew that I did not have a good figure like a film star does but they made me feel miserable because of what I was! They began to quote discounted figures that kept going down for selling me off! As if I was waste material to be sold off on discount! I have never been so humiliated, never felt so miserable in my life as within these days of horror! They sold me off for a pittance, because I was not good to look at nor had a fantastic body! A human being, an educated, empowered human being and I was sold off to that European who was pawing me and he was getting ready for doing something dreadful when you stopped him, your Highness! I shall remain eternally grateful Sir! I feel so ashamed of myself Oh great King! I am so ashamed that I happen to be one of the people who gave away Nair Dvipa on a platter to the country Diànlì ji'è de guójia!".

Then she honked into a hanky. As if brushing away the past, she wiped away the tears that were flowing from her eyes with her shirt sleeves as she vents her heart out, and then, she made a determined declaration, "But under your leadership Oh great King, we can once again be the law respecting, free nation that had been created by the Kings of our past. Please forgive me for my foolishness and short sightedness! I shall do everything possible to rally the media people together from now onwards against the bullying and expansionist nation that Diànlì ji'è de guójia has proved itself to be".

Sudhir simply nodded to express that he understood.

Suddenly he put his index finger on his lips and hushed her! A roar passed over them immediately after. They looked up to see around forty to fifty winged humans flying past overhead, looking all around the forested lands below while screeching like banshees. They were searching below them, obviously for them!

Sudhir snapped his fingers. The car vanished and the King became a thick tall tree whereas Manjula became a sapling and they were standing next to each other, but their heads and neck remained intact at the base of the tree. "For our safety", Sudhir explained with a gentle smile.

The winged humans passed over them several times, screeching like banshees searching for a hint of human body heat. Then they gradually drifted away to a distant part of the forests, until they could be seen no more.

Manjula's face was ashen as she was holding her breath and now, she sighed in relief! Then as if realizing where she was, she looked up at her brown branches covered with green leaves that reached up and all around her. She looked down at the bark below her head, then at her roots as it dug deep into mother earth. "Wow! I am a tree!" she exclaimed with a ludicrous look on her face. "I would never have believed that this is ever possible had I not been personally involved your Highness! I am honoured to be under your able protection Sir!"

Sudhir nodded in the affirmative to acknowledge her gratitude with a gentle smile.

"I had a few questions your Highness, if I may ask the same?" she asked with an expression of awe written all over her face.

Sudhir nodded his head in the affirmative with a gentle smile on his face and waited for her query.

Manjula was obviously a well read, self-confident and an empowered citizen. "All this morphing of one body into another body and then my ropes and Sticky plaster falling off by themselves was simply unscientific and logically impossible as per our knowledge of science of today. Yet you did it and continue to do so with ease, like a fish swims in water. What you did could not be magic because magic has a scientific explanation. Therefore, can I safely presume that you possess certain powers that challenge science as we know it on Earth today?"

Sudhir nodded his head in the affirmative with a gentle smile on his face and waited for her next query.

"Are you from Earth?" Manjula the reporter asked.

Sudhir nodded his head in the affirmative with a gentle smile on his face and waited for her next query.

"Sooo, have you been born with these powers or were you gifted these powers?" Manjula asked.

"Both", Sudhir replied gently with a smile on his face and then he waited for her next query.

"Can I safely assume that since your highness has been unable to win the battle that was fought at the beach of Nair Dvipa, then there must be somebody even more powerful than your highness who is supporting and propping up the country Diànlì ji'è de guójia and helping them to rule over us?" Manjula asked.

Sudhir's expression became grim. But he nodded in the affirmative and waited for her next query.

"So why is he doing what he is doing? We all who went against the Royal family had so much hope. That Diànlì ji'è de guójia wanted to execute Engineering projects in Nair Dvipa to develop our economy and genuinely help us build ourselves as a growing nation. They had invested huge amounts of funds from their own sources on developing our infrastructure and we thought that they were our friend. Nair Dvipa has so much potential! Little did we suspect that Diànlì ji'è de guójia had been an expansionist nation since ages past and had been inviting the youth of Nair Dvipa over past forty years to be educated free of cost in their country so that we could be brain washed to believe in their hollow promises. Why does the person who is more powerful than you want to destroy Nair Dvipa in the manner that he is doing so today? Why?" asked Manjula.

And so Sudhir patiently explained how the Daivika Planet citizens landed on Earth, how the old Kings landed on Nair Dvipa, how Mogui got his stupendous powers and how he continued to feel that injustice that had been done to him and his family.

When Sudhir was hovering over the Bungalow it was twelve noon, but by the time he had finished narrating the history of the Daivika planet citizens to Manjula, how Nair Dvipa was born and how Mogui became the devil incarnate, the sun had already set and the crickets had begun to chirp.

"Because we are trees, we shall not feel the cold of these hill slopes as the wind blows. What is important is that we must not travel in the night as Mogui's powers are strongest during night time. He would have known about your escape and would like to fight me now which I can ill afford. Our body heat matches that of all the other trees around us and he shall not be able to trace us though he would try his best to do so. Let us rest for the night here and in the early morning hours we have to be careful to not catch his attention when I travel with you to a safe house".

This was all so unreal for Manjula. Was she human or was she a tree? Did she really see human beings morph into another human form? She had been a rebel from her childhood and thus she had never accepted the norm. She created fresh norms that best suited her future path and then led teams below her to follow her norm. But all that she had seen and experienced till now was beyond the scientifically proven norm. Nobody would believe her if she told them that she was a real tree for one whole night and that she had spent the night with the King! Well, the King and she had not 'spent the night' as in 'slept together' in the real sense of the words but at least they 'stood together' throughout the night! Anyway, nobody would believe her if she told anybody about anything that the King had just told her from this afternoon till this evening. Yet she had seen the impossible happen in front of her very own eyes! She was bound to believe that just anything "unscientific" was possible after this!

The News Two Days Later

This write up made headlines.

"From the Desk of the Editor, 'Satyaṁ', Nair Dvipa, dated 14th May 2017

Diànlì Ji'è De Guójia Invades Nair Dvipa

Diànlì ji'è de guójia has silently taken over our country in collusion with us gullible Press, the gullible Intelligentsia, a few corrupt judges, and many corrupt Government officials and politicians.

Diànlì ji'è de guójia had entered Nair Dvipa with offers of mouth-watering Road projects, Bridge projects, canal projects, and most importantly Seaport & Airport Projects that would have pushed up the economy of Nair Dvipa many folds. They promised to invest astronomical sums which our King had refused to allow. And so, they took the assistance of your Media to influence you all and to brain wash you all to vote against the Royals. Our King had warned us against 'hidden words' within agreements that Diànlì ji'è de guójia wanted us to sign. We discovered the hidden words later, for within the folds of the agreement were those very hidden words that our King had warned us about. Words that said that we 'give away' the land allotted for the project to Diànlì ji'è de guójia in perpetuity! Can one ever knowingly 'give away' one's mother land to a foreign nation? We were fooled into these deals. But International courts too stood by the hidden words initially. At the beginning they too declared that if we were foolish enough into signing such a deal that amounted to selling our country to Diànlì ji'è de then, we deserved to be slaves and no longer independent!

And then began their atrocities as would be expected by a foreigner on a foreign soil. Today they make our own brothers arrest us when we congregate as we always congregated on our own land. Today we need permissions from foreign citizens to breathe on our own soil. Today we cannot protect our own. Our mothers, sisters and daughters are being kidnapped and sold off as if we have been bred by these foreigners for the sex trade.

You my citizens have been silent spectators to atrocities being committed because they have divided us and you cannot fight alone. The total breakdown of law and order has become obvious to you. They force us to accept their religion and make us wear necklaces so that we stand out to be their slaves. They have passed laws that forces us to accept refugees from their country by the ship loads, challenging the King's planned twenty-year permission ban on the entry of illegal migrants. Very soon the citizens of Diànlì ji'è de guójia shall exceed the citizens of Nair Dvipa due to their sheer numbers per fertile male. The colonies that have come up to settle these refugees have no planning, no sanitation, no roads, no schools, no hospitals, no jobs. The funds allocated to bring about such projects are now being siphoned away. The children are left home while the parents strive to eke out a living. The children are thus indulging in increasing number of antisocial activities. They would grow up to become confident criminals if not shown the correct path right away.

And the parents from amongst these refugees of Diànlì ji'è de guójia come to our cities now looking for jobs. Then they see our family members and try to touch them. Drugs have entered every school and college that matters. Guns and dangerous arms and ammunition are being manufactured in Diànlì ji'è de guójia, but stored in Nair Dvipa for quick delivery to neighbouring countries. The manufacturers seek out weaker nations all around the world that are unable to fight back. Such weaker nations are never permitted to sign peace accords. On the contrary they are instigated to go to war with their immediate neighbours and thus skirmishes happen frequently in order that such war equipment may be sold to them! And sold like one would buy toys. Yet our politicians have turned a blind eye till now. So, the illegal migrant use stolen monies to buy these very guns and shoot one another as one would do with toy guns. Corruption has seeped into the edifices of Nair Dvipa. Our police refuse to file our complaints. Our courts refuse to give a ruling in favour of honesty, truth and justice.

Ladies and gentlemen! If there is hell then this is it!

As it is known to all of you in the Press fraternity and many amongst our readers, Manjula, the senior reporter of 'Yathārt'tha Vārtta' the Television cum Social Media company, was kidnapped and sold by certain bad elements the moment she reported against unreasonable and unfair decisions taken by Diànlì ji'è de guójia. Yathārt'tha Vārtta happens to be our family. Yathārt'tha Vārtta happens to a part of our Media fraternity and we shall stand by Manjula and Yathārt'tha Vārtta. You would be happy to know that our King, his Royal Highness King Sudhir Bagaria had single handedly saved Manjula after she was kidnapped and sold. Our King tracked our Press Reporter colleague, saved her from her oppressors and tucked her far away from the vengeance of Diànlì ji'è de guójia, the country that has invaded our lands!

Dear readers, I hereby give you the legal views of two legal luminaries:

Sandeep Vaidya says that there was a window of certain number of years within which the Royal family member, Prince Pawandas (Hanuman) Bagaria nee Prince Daivam Pawandas Hanuman Namboothiri could accept his Kingdom or take the decision to abdicate his thrown. He had abdicated his throne. In such an event Prince Sudhir Bagaria, nee Prince Sudhir Namboodiri, his son, was automatically the King unless he refused in writing, which he has not. During any vote to oust a King, the signature of the King is necessary for the agreement to be legally valid, in the International courts. The King did not sign because he was not present in the Kingdom. Therefore, the King continues to control and be the supreme power of Nair Dvipa. Further, as per our law, any agreement with foreign countries that amounted to selling land or giving away land rights in perpetuity is invalid unless signed and stamped by the King of Nair Dvipa.

Shankar Narain says that as per the Laws of Nair Dvipa, the Elections could not have happened without the signature and seal of the King of Nair

Dvipa. Our King was not present in the city when the first elections took place. Therefore, the very first election and from then on, every other election, and decisions taken, stand null and void, voidable at the option of the King on a case to case basis.

The two legal luminaries have agreed on their legal view that all the elections conducted till date without the signature of the King can, by the law that still exists, be declared null and void. Voidable at the option of the King on a case to case basis. Decisions taken by the present Parliament on a case to case basis, can be declared as going against the interests of Nair Dvipa and hence can stand scrapped with immediate effect as per past laws. This fact has been conveyed on behalf of the King of Nair Dvipa, His Royal Highness Sudhir Bagaria to all the nations globally, as also to important bodies including the United Nations. Most nations have now agreed with the above legal view.

Hence, we the citizens of Nair Dvipa hereby declare the elections that have happened without the seal of the King as invalid as the King had not sanctioned such an election that finally brought about the doom of Nair Dvipa.

King Sudhir Bagaria was and remains the supreme authority of Nair Dvipa till date and any decision regarding the lands of Nair Dvipa by the country Diànlì ji'è de guójia amounts to "acts of an invader" rather than just an innocent act of execution of projects against a twenty-year payment credit.

Our King is our supreme leader, and shall lead us to victory against the invaders.

Long live King Sudhir Bagaria! Long live Nair Dvipa!

Lalithambika Vasudevan,

Editor, 'Satyam', Nair Dvipa

From that day onwards, 'Satyam' was shut down by forces loyal to Diànlì ji'è de guójia. A handful of Media companies that remained loyal to Diànlì ji'è de guójia screamed, "Fugitive Lalithambika Vasudevan is on the run. But she shall be traced, and then hung for instigating anti national sentiments".

But the sentiments of Nair Dvipa were on fire! Nothing could stop the long lines of citizens of Nair Dvipa as they began to form outside the parliament after passing through busy city centers and busy thoroughfares. The Pro Nair Dvipa Press arrived and the images splashed "The Independence struggle begins!" on the first page. Editors got terminated from their jobs but new ones took over to repeat exactly what their predecessors did. Then Diànlì ji'è de guójia sent editors from within their own country and told the publishing team what to say and what to print. The team nodded their heads but printed exactly what the people of Nair Dvipa wanted to read, the true facts. So, they too lost their jobs and thus 'Janaṅṅaḻuṭe Sabdaṁ' (The Voice of the People) a new Online Media sprang up and became popular overnight. Within two nights the readership jumped to Three lakhs and then Five lakhs on the next night and then Ten lakhs by the fifth night! 'CashPurse', the online payment facility allowed readers to donate monies and it flowed into the International bank account of 'Janaṅṅaḻuṭe Sabdaṁ'.

And images of the line of Independence seekers, kept growing. This line kept increasing in numbers as the routine of arresting them kept repeating itself every day and their pictures appeared with shackles on major media which told Nair Dvipa citizens, "Sacrifice your freedom for Nair Dvipa and the King shall give Nair Dvipa freedom!".

The forces loyal to Diànlì ji'è de guójia was finding it difficult to control the unending line of citizens of Nair Dvipa. Their forty-year-old plan of gently brain washing the citizens of Nair Dvipa, especially the pseudo "intellectuals" and then ruling over them by proxy was now being challenged.

That is when Mogui brought in the flying demons once again.

They flew in the sky by the thousands, and began to swoop down on the long lines of citizens of Nair Dvipa moving with placards that declared their true King to be their protector and leader. Terrified citizens began to run helter-skelter. Pandemonium reigned for a while. Then control came about as the birdmen began to drop down from the skies and the citizens of Nair Dvipa roared in jubilation! How did this happen? The King had given strategic instructions and the village warriors had moved in very silently into the midst of Nair Dvipa, dressed in city clothes. They were ready with blowgun pipe darts that they shot out at the necks of such powerful bird men. Mobi had moved in with adult warriors. Curare is a poison that blocks nerve impulses from being sent to the skeletal muscles, effectively paralyzing the muscles of the body. These darts had been coated with Curare and shot out at the birdmen. The birdmen began to drop down like pests being swatted from the skies as the darts shot up towards them in hundreds. Mogui could not be seen but he was enraged and once again he switched on the mass brain paralyzing 'brain scream wave'. But once again, as per strategic instructions of the King, most of Nair Dvipa was ready with ear mufflers and thus very few could hear the shrill ear piercing "screeee" that had damaged so many ear drums when the attack on the beach of Nair Dvipa by Diànlì ji'è de guójia forces had taken place.

Foreign journalists had landed in large numbers and Mogui was advised by his handlers in Diànlì ji'è de guójia to stop himself from causing harm to the general public in plain view of the International Media.

When powerful nations become desperate, they make mistakes.

Diànlì ji'è de guójia's mistake was to allow the news of the arrest of Lalithambika Vasudevan to be printed. Every Nair Dvipa citizen raised a hue and cry! This time Nair Dvipa roared in Defiance! People came out into the streets in large numbers, some shut down their shops for many days, some took leave from their office and they were all very angry. They all were now carrying placards that said, "We are awake and Lalithambika Vasudevan is the reason", "Lalithambika Vasudevan our 'Daiva Mātāv'('Godly mother') shall not be harmed!"

The police came out in large numbers this time but the citizens who came out to voice their protests far outnumbered them. So, the police stood as silent spectators as the citizens roared as one. Gradually, the "Laḷitāmbikaye svatantramāyi nirttū" (Set Lalithambika free from her shackles) morphed into "Niṅṅaḷuṭe sañciyil ninn Nair Dvipa sajjamākkān" (Set Nair Dvipa free from your shackles). Very soon the roars of "Rājāvine nīṇāḷ vāḷaṭṭe" (Long live the King) and "Nam'muṭe rājāv atyunnatanāṇ" (Our King reigns supreme) began to rent the air. Then the army was ordered out and with tears in their eyes, they reluctantly pumped gallons of water through jet hoses on their own brothers and sisters just because an enemy nation now ruled their country and had ordered them to do so.

Locating Nindiya and Arming Oneself

In the meanwhile, Sudhir who had been using his mind to trace heat and voice signals, had managed to trace Nindiya the reporter of Vēgattiluḷḷa Vārtta, the TV cum online Media cum News Print Media giant, imprisoned in a closed cell in the Bungalow of Wánjù Mù'ou the Prime Minister of Nair Dvipa. The Prime Minister lived in a fortress. If Sudhir tried to copy the same strategy as he had used while saving Manjula then this time they would be ready for him. He had to think of something different.

He did not doubt that he had been given immense powers but the doubt remained whether he knew how far he could go in regards to his own abilities. Could he become a mosquito for example? "Why not try becoming a mosquito?" he asked himself. But what if he got fumigated or swatted away or gassed out and then he would be dead! Fear stifled his experimentative spirit. He had to take control over his fear. He began to reassure himself. He had lost the first trial competition and was bound to lose in the actual competition too.

He was sitting worried on the steps of a broken down and dilapidated bungalow hidden away by a deep jungle of trees in the outskirts of the city. Mobi woke up at 12.00 midnight and waddled up to Sudhir, rubbed his eyes with his two palms and grumpily asked, "If it is day time then why is the sun not shining?"

Sudhir did not look up, but kept staring into the distant horizon with its twinkling stars. Mobi came up from behind and hugged Sudhir's neck, put his little head on Sudhir's back and asked, "Why do you not smile nowadays Mohua Minshaw?"

Sudhir gently patted Mobi's little hands and said, "Do you know Mobi that when I was as little as you are today, I had thought that everything is so easy, like in a game in the stadium. You are in the first standard now but I was in the ninth class at that time when I lived in a world of make belief. I remembered the time I had failed in my ninth class and was being taunted on the sports field too. That was when my father had kept his arms around me and had given me a bit of advice.

"When you know your weaknesses and you learn your opponent's strengths then you also have to learn to adapt. When you learn to adapt then you become unstoppable!"

I began to observe how my opponents ran. And I ran like I had never run before! And I won the Gold Medal in the One-hundred-meter sprint, and finally the long-distance race!

This time my opponent is Mogui who had vast experience at using energies of the mind. I must out think Mogui. I must do something that Mogui would never think of doing. I must think of various safeguards that Mogui would create around people important to him. I must bring down such people who are important to him. I must imagine what he would be doing and then outsmart Mogui!

"You can do anything great Mohua Minshaw!" whispered little Mobi staring into his idol's eyes with great admiration. "You can do anything because you have been sent to protect us great Mohua Minshaw and to pamper me. The stars have sent you to protect all that is good in this world, especially me!", he finished with a twinkle in his eyes.

Sudhir stared back with mirth at his son and spanked him on his round bottom, "That's how much I love you!" Sudhir laughed and said. "Oww Mohua Minshaw! That is too much love! It hurts!" So saying, he hugged Sudhir and planted a kiss on his father's cheek.

Sudhir looked into the eyes of innocent mirth and total trust. Then he made his little child stand aside and became a mosquito, a humming bird, a snake, then he became Wánjù Mù'ou the Prime Minister, and finally he became Mogui. His courage and confidence grew with every attempt. So, he decided to change his form as fast as possible. Initially, changing from a mosquito to a humming bird to a snake to Wanju took a full five minutes. He kept practicing and reduced it to one minute!

Little Mobi stared with awe at his hero!

Then Sudhir tried becoming two people at one time, then one person and one object. He became a car and then got down from within that car as Wanju. So, he went ahead and became a car, with Wanju in it and then he became many other motor cyclists on motor cycles escorting Wanju. He realized he could become around ten objects or living beings at any one time. But Mogui could become around two thousand plus birdmen that he had seen flying high in the sky at the sea port. That was truly astounding! He had to equal Mogui's feat if he wanted to help Nair Dvipa become free from Diànlì ji'è de guójia once again. He kept practicing throughout the night. By the early morning he had learned to re-energize himself from the universe and create around sixty-two different objects or living beings. He was far behind the two thousand odd birdmen that Mogui had created. And the amazing fact to note was that each of the birdmen that Mogui had created were able to take their own decision and reacted to different stimuli differently. Further, each of them had skin and bones unlike the empty muscleless forms that he could conjure. He kept practicing because he realized that Mogui was surely planning too and Mogui was desperate to retain Nair Dvipa for himself.

Mogui was powerful at teleportation and Sudhir realized that he had to gain expertise on that front too. He had already teleported the Jewels stored by Mogui on the boats in the river next to the palace to a safe house far away. So, he knew that he could teleport many small and medium objects. Therefore, he kept practicing Teleportation of large number of cars back and forth, large number of trees from an arid region to a monsoon wet region, a flock of birds from one tree to another, a swarm of fish from the ocean to a lake on the top of the mountain, and finally people within a remote village from one part of the village to the other part. Teleportation sapped away a super human level of his mental energies and yet he kept practicing to reduce the time taken to teleport from a full fifteen minutes to five minutes. Then he gradually, and painstakingly over many days brought it down to a second, on the snap of his fingers.

But he realized he was becoming tired immediately after every such exercise of teleportation. And so, he began to practice attracting energy from all around him into his mind to supplement for his loss of energy. He spread out his hands and told his mind, "Draw energy from this universe and re-energize my mind". Bits and pieces of energy came at wavering intervals and gave him brief spurts of energy.

He needed a flow of energy, like Mogui had drawn from the universe when fighting his great grandfather. So, he spread out his hands, closed his eyes and concentrated on trying to see the energy particles around him. He saw through his mind's eye the heat signals of numerous negative and positive energy particles constantly interacting with one another, energizing one another. They were alive and very social and were talking with one another. He began to call on the bits and pieces of energy particles, gently, "Come to me". And some particles came along but that was all. This meant that the energies needed discipline, hence a stronger voice.

He had to create a surge, a constant flow and therefore he gave a command, "All energy particles are to link with each other and flow into my brain cells". In his mind's eye he could see the energy particles talking with one another, linking with one another at a ferocious pace, then forming a stream and when various branches of streams linked up together, they became a roaring river of energy just as it would have sounded when entering Mogui.

Then "vrooooom", the roaring river surged into his brain cells and it felt like rain water flowing over parched land! Wave after energy wave thunder-stormed into his brain! And his thirst was quenched!

He could now finally feel the desired surge of energy that successfully began to revitalize his depleted brain energy cells. Nair Dvipa could finally be freed from the clutches of Diànlì ji'è de guójia with this endless energy.

He suddenly felt courageous, selfless and he was not afraid to die!

He knew then, that though Mogui remained many times stronger, yet, he was ready for the great Mogui!

The Battle for Rescuing Nindiya

Every morning His Excellency, Wánjù Mù'ou, the Prime Minister of Nair Dvipa would travel from the 'Pradhāna Mantri Tāmasikkunnat' (Prime Minister's Residence) to Pradhāna Mantri Jēālisthalatt (The Prime Minter's Work Place) between 10.00am to 11.00am. Prior to this the 'Surakṣā Kramīkaraṇaṁ' (Security Arrangement) required that a phone call is made from the Chief Security Officer to the Chief of Traffic Control. "The Carriage is rolling", he would say on the Walkie Talkie, meaning, that the cavalcade has begun to move out of the Official Residence, and the Chief of Traffic Control would say, "Arrangement is ready and being re-enforced", meaning, that the traffic on the new route for that day had been held back for the cavalcade to travel at high speed, without stopping, to avoid attacks and spoil pre planned assassination attempts. Each time the route taken would be different and never the same. His cavalcade would exit from the Pradhāna Mantri Jēālisthalatt between 7.00pm to 8.00pm and reach the Pradhāna Mantri Tāmasikkunnat by 8.50pm to 9.20pm depending on traffic.

When at home, the Prime Minister would inform Huàirén, his secretary, about his choice of drink and woman for the evening. There were many imprisoned women who were called upon to serve the carnal desires of the Minister, one of them being the recently "acquired" Nindiya, the reporter of Vēgattiluḷḷa Vārtta, the TV cum online Media cum News Print Media. Today he called for her once again.

"Why her sir, every so often?" asked Huàirén, his secretary.

"Because of her luscious body, long hair, doe eyes, thick lips, silky body, big breasts, thick thighs and kiss-able neck corners and armpits!" he laughed and replied with lust written all over his face.

"But", countered Huàirén the secretary, "she is now a broken woman Sir! Her body language says she has given up and you would note that she does not scream in terror any more when you approach her, nor when you invade her body nowadays",

"Yes" replied the Minister, "she gives no resistance any longer! The excitement in invading the body of somebody who resists is many times more exciting than invading a defeated woman. We may have to throw her away soon to the Den of Vice."

Sudhir was seated on the Air Conditioning panel looking down at them and swishing his tail. He had entered as a bumble bee inside the high security bungalow and then seeing the Cheshire cat, he had discarded the body of the bumble bee and entered the body of the house Cheshire cat. It had jumped around and resisted at the initial stage then when the takeover of its mind was complete, it became relaxed.

Everybody had let the cat be around the house after several attempts in the past to chase it away. Considering that it had kept its distance nobody really bothered about its presence until now.

He had to find out the security arrangement before he could execute his plans any further. Surely there would be extra layers of security since the last incident where he had saved the Press woman. Interesting that there was no security in the room inspite of the last incident! This seemed too easy! There was something fishy that did not meet the eye and hence extreme precautions were necessary.

He jumped down, meowed several times, scratched his ears with his hind legs, stretched out his front paws and yawned. Both Wánjù Mù'ou and Huàirén looked casually at the cat and then looked back with a sigh at the list of other girls along with their pictures. Sudhir meowed up to Huàirén and began to brush against his legs. Huàirén kicked out at the cat, but Sudhir sidestepped thus avoided being hurt, then jumped onto the lap of Wánjù Mù'ou and began to purr as if to express happiness.

Wánjù Mù'ou at first screamed in shock and then angrily raised his hands in the air, shouting "Shoo! Security! Shoo! Go away! Security! Shoo! Go away!" with his head bend back as far away from the cat as possible. Sudhir heard running feet. He saw in his mind's eye around seven highly trained security personnel and four plain clothed trained personnel. The plain clothed personnel had been planted as helpers in the kitchen and others for keeping all the rooms or the garden clean. He immediately discarded the cat's body and tried to move into the body of the lead senior security officer rushing towards the room. The security officer tried to resist the takeover and fell, and then Sudhir promptly took over his mind and his body.

Then he got up, rushed inside, and made a grab at the cat. The cat spat and scratched Sudhir's face. "Owwwaa!" he screamed in pretended terror.

That is exactly when the winged birdmen appeared, out of nowhere! They had been obviously wearing invisibility energy cloaks all along, exactly as Sudhir had suspected. He counted two in this room. There were around seven similar sized rooms, one large reception room flanked by small glassed cubicles where visitors were met by the "what do you want of the Prime Minister?" welcome desk, one large Banquet hall and one large conference hall. Therefore, Sudhir presumed that there would be around fourteen to fifteen Bird Men wearing invisibility energy cloaks, spread out in this huge Bungalow with its estate grounds all around it.

The moment the cat scratched Sudhir, supposedly the security officer's face, the first Birdman grabbed the cat by the nape of the cat's neck. While the cat bared its teeth and spat, the second Birdman produced a steel cage out of thin air and opened it allowing the first birdman to push the cat into the cage. Then they walked out of the bungalow bowlegged like cowboys do after a long duration of horse riding. Once outside, they belched fire from their mouths into the cage and burnt the cat alive.

Sudhir ordered the other security guards to take extra precaution for the day. "You and you stay outside the PMs bedroom entrance along with the other two", he instructed two security personnel. "Yes Sir!" they saluted and responded as instructed. He then showed the way forward for Huàirén the secretary. "Let me stay with you Sir! This is just to ensure that nothing goes wrong today".

Much to Sudhir's relief, Huàirén led the way forward making Sudhir's first step of approaching Nindiya easier. What worried Sudhir was the possibility of the security guard remembering that somebody had taken over his body after Sudhir were to jump to another body. Unless he thought up something fast, he would find it difficult to ensure that his effort achieves its desired goal.

Huàirén walked through one corridor to turn right at the dead end, then into another corridor that lead to a door at a dead end. He instructed the man standing next to the door with a key hanging around his neck to open the lock. The door opened into a long corridor with rooms on the left and a glass pane on the right that ran till the end of the corridor. The second grilled door on the left opened to show Nindiya looking like a listless teenager, sitting like a zombie.

Huàirén stretched out his left hand and said, "Come Nindiya! It is your turn once again!"

Nindiya was sitting like a zombie staring straight ahead. She did not look left nor right. She got up very slowly, turned around to face the door and began to move slowly forward. Huàirén hastened her saying, "Come along, we do not have all the time!"

Sudhir hiding in the body of the security guard rushed forward to grab Nindiya by the nape of her neck and began to drag her towards the door. Huàirén was shocked by this action and became immediately concerned about the damage to the 'product' to be used by Wánjù Mù'ou. He slapped the security guard Sudhir, shouting, "The product may get damaged you fool!". Sudhir reacted in pretended anger by grabbing Huàirén by the neck and throwing him to the floor growling, "We security guards are not riff raff to be slapped around! Okay?"

As expected, two Birdmen within the room who were wearing the invisibility energy cloak popped into visibility mode and stood spread legged like cow-boys in front of the security guard with the guns getting ready to shoot. But before they were fully ready Sudhir used his mind energy to kill the surveillance camera, blasted out a surge of super heat energy that burned the birdmen alive on the spot, teleported the ashes of the two burnt birdmen far away from the vicinity, teleported Nindiya to a safe house far away from the vicinity, created a new Nindiya and then entered Huàirén's mind, all in a minute's time.

He was now controlling the minds of Huàirén, the security guard and finally that of the second Nindiya whom he had created.

Sudhir the security guard now escorted Huàirén and Nindiya to Wánjù Mù'ou's room and then he signaled for the two extra personnel he had deputed to that door to open the same. They saluted and opened the door, Sudhir the security guard remained outside, Huàirén walked in with Nindiya and he said, "Sir your sweet dish for dessert!"

"Wow Huàirén!" Wánjù Mù'ou laughed and said, "this is the first time I have heard you use wit and humour! Thank God for a good beginning! Bring her here and leave the room". Huàirén left her near Wánjù Mù'ou's bed, turned around and shut the door behind him.

"Sit on the bed darling!" Wánjù cooed. Then he saw the slits of her thick breasts peeping out from within the cascading folds of silky hair and the pink thighs teasingly exposed from behind the 'see through' nightie he had instructed that she wear. He reached out, touched her thighs with one hand, unzipped himself with the second hand, unbuttoned her top with the same second hand and out popped her breasts as if they longed for his touch! "Oooooooohooo!" he groaned. He reached out and pressed her right breast and, "Pop! Fizzzzzz!", her breast began to deflate like a punctured balloon, "What the?!" exclaimed Wánjù. "Manufacturing defect" said Nindiya very casually. Then she picked up his gun from his bedside, cocked it and before the Birdmen who had crashed into visibility mode could react, she shot Wánjù in the head and shot herself in the head thereafter. Her body lay in a pool of blood as the door broke open and was flooded with security personnel and birdmen.

In the rush for the inhouse ambulance and the inhouse doctor, nobody noticed that Nindiya's supposed dead body was turning to dust and then vanishing into thin air.

Right at that very moment, Sudhir the security officer had rushed to the corridor where the other girls were. He looked in and snapped his fingers. Then the next room and he snapped his fingers again. In this manner he teleported all the twenty-five girls kept as sex slaves of Wánjù Mù'ou. When he returned to the Prime Minister's room, Sudhir found that there was pandemonium and that the late Prime Minister Wanju's people were still in a state of disarray. He left control over the minds of Huàirén and the security guard after wiping their memory clean. Then he teleported himself to where he had sent Nindiya and the other girls.

Sudhir with Nindiya

Sudhir wanted Nindiya the reporter of Vēgattilulla Vārtta, the TV cum online Media cum News Print Media to retain her memories, her pain, her trauma, and her 'never give up' personality. They would help in the imminent battle for independence. But he also wanted her to be fighting fit for the battle that was soon to happen. He had to train her to fight back physically stronger people and be wearing necessary armour to stop lethal attacks which were bound to happen soon.

Nindiya along with all the other girls who were the sex slaves of Wánjù Mù'ou were being treated by specially teleported nurses and doctors who were ensuring Intravenous administration of medicines for post-traumatic stress disorder (PTSD). Subsequently they were ensuring Intravenous vitamin & required body salt infusion. Tests had shown that they all needed bed rest and lots of sleep, So, Sudhir put them all in a Semi Conscious state for seven days with his body repair, mind repair cum energizing rays working along with modern medicine.

When they gained consciousness, Sudhir teleported Lalithambika Vasudevan, Editor, 'Satyam', Nair Dvipa as well as Manjula, the senior reporter of 'Yathārt'tha Vārtta'. Nindiya narrated her horrifying recent past between sobs and wailing while secure in the arms of the colleagues of the media industry.

Her colleagues got increasingly agitated as her narration traversed the path from the gruesome beating of her friend cum bodyguard, her kidnapping, her being forced to partake of liquor and drugs to pacify her, her reaching a destination in a blindfolded state, her meeting His Excellency, Mr. Wánjù Mù'ou the Prime Minister who refused to entertain her pleas to spare her and forced himself on her repeatedly. His boasting that nobody could touch him hence she must accept her fate, and finally to his confident boast over drinks that Diànlì ji'è de guójia shall gradually rule over the whole world with its economic muscle power and the fact that it had taken control over the media of most foreign nations! She had heard the Prime Minister boasting, "There shall come a day when all roads shall lead to Diànlì ji'è de guójia. When all the Kings, Presidents and head of elected governments of any country, shall kowtow in front of the servants of Diànlì ji'è de guójia!"

The Headlines After Nindiya Gets Rescued

The 'Legal Press" reported, "Female Terrorists Storm and murder the PM! Murder of our beloved Prime Minister by a well-planned female team of twenty-five" while the 'Illegal Press' reported, "A womanizer, a tormentor, a rapist killed in self-defense by a female victim!! PM killed by victim!"

Fake videos presented by TV channels that were 'legal' showed Sudhir shooting the PM in the head.

The Illegal TV Channels and online Social Media (Free Press) reported

"Twenty-five women rescued from the residence of His Excellency Wánjù Mù'ou the Prime Minister of Nair Dvipa. One of his victims shoots him dead!"

Another Free Press asked, "How did our great King enter inspite the PM's residence inspite of the tight security? Was the security so bad or was our King so good? And if he can cross such tight security then did he allow his face to be seen on a Video Camera?"

The 'Legal' TV channels invited Anti Royal citizens and made them reply to prepared questions and answers. "Yes, the King is a dictator and will bring back the horrifying days of bondage and slavery", one said. "He will kill many more innocent citizens of Nair Dvipa who do not want him to return, before, we find him and shoot him dead like the dog that he is!" another roared.

Then a social media Video Broadcasting facility brought out a video that went viral. It had two lakh seventy thousand hits within the first five hours!

"I am Lalithambika Vasudevan, Ex-Editor, 'Satyaṁ', Nair Dvipa. Namaskaram!" said the Video image of Lalithambika Vasudevan. "And I am Manjula, the Ex-senior reporter of 'Yathār'tha Vārtta' of Nair Dvipa. Namaskaram!" said the Video image of Manjula.

"Today we reporters speak under one umbrella and with one voice. We speak as 'Janaṅṅaḷuṭe Sabdaṁ' (The Voice of the People) live on 'Truthonline' from Nair Dvipa. Our beloved colleague Nindiya the reporter of Vēgattilul̤a Vārtta, the TV cum online Media cum News Print Media whose boyfriend cum bodyguard was brutally beaten after which she was kidnapped and then ravaged by shockingly someone Nair Dvipa looked upon as next after God, His Excellency Wánjù Mù'ou the late Prime Minister of Nair Dvipa. Yes, that is right, citizens of Nair Dvipa! Our sister Nindiya is alive along with twenty-five other girls who were being used as sex slaves by His Excellency Wánjù Mù'ou the late Prime Minister of Nair Dvipa. And they were all saved by a lone soldier, our King His Royal Highness King Sudhir Bagaria!"

Just then the voice of Nindiya came on line. One could hear her sobbing, "Our King His Royal Highness Sudhir Bagaria saved me from the clutches of Wánjù who under the garb of being our Prime Minister was an evil, ruthless, sex maniac! He kept us as sex slaves! He was a bad man! (Sob) Ohh he was a very bad man! (Sob). He did not spare any of us! We begged him for mercy and yet he forced himself on us repeatedly! We used to dread his coming home from office. And the moment he came home, he called for any one of us!" The camera panned all around the room and counted twenty-five young sobbing girls but their faces were digitally hidden. Then the camera stopped and focused on a weeping Nindiya! "I trusted Diànlì ji'è de guójia! I thought that they wanted the development of the infrastructure of our country! I wrote so many shameful untruths against the Royals just so that they step aside! Now look at us! Look at me! I am ruined because I mistrusted my own King and trusted an outsider! Nobody would believe that I am not a loose woman now! Nobody would respect me any longer! I do not want to live!" she bawled.

Manjula came on line and she sounded distraught and yet angry! "I too was one of the ardent advocates of Diànlì ji'è de guójia investing huge sums in Nair Dvipa and bringing about development at a fast pace compared to the slow-paced development that was being executed by our last King. I too wrote so many shameful untruths against the Royals just so that they step aside! Now look at us! Look at me! They sold me off to a businessperson who visits Nair Dvipa often and displays a Billboard outside his Bungalow gate which says he is a philanthropist! I was going to become a sex slave had our King His Royal Highness Sudhir Bagaria not saved me from the clutches of that vile businessman! The Prime Minister was a very bad man and he was from Diànlì ji'è de guójia! He paid monies to become a Nair Dvipa citizen and got himself elected to rule over us! Diànlì ji'è de guójia is ruling us by Proxy citizens of Nair Dvipa! By proxy! The Prime Minister had kidnapped and imprisoned twenty-five young girls and was using them as sex slaves because Diànlì ji'è de guójia now believes that Nair Dvipa is weak and that we can do nothing! The Vice Den where kidnapped women are used every day by various travelers was started by Diànlì ji'è de guójia. Tomorrow you may be kidnapped and sold to be used by the Vice Den. Will your husband or your parents allow you to be kidnapped and sold? So long as we media personnel are alive, we will not allow you to be kidnapped nor sold! We must throw Diànlì ji'è de guójia out of our land! Will you help your own country to win back her freedom? Then join us with your candles. We will not allow you to be sold! Will you help us to win back our freedom? Then join us! Jai Nair Dvipa! Long live Nair Dvipa! Long Live our King!"

"Did you see that citizens of Nair Dvipa? Did you hear that citizens of Nair Dvipa?" asked the Video of Lalithambika Vasudevan. "I too was one of the ardent advocates of Diànlì ji'è de guójia investing huge sums in Nair Dvipa and bringing about development at a fast pace compared to the slow-paced development that was being executed by our last King. I too wrote so many shameful untruths against the Royals just so that they step aside! Now look at us! Look at me! Now I am to be shot on sight! Today they have declared that I am an anti-national in my own country because Diànlì ji'è de guójia, a foreign country, that runs our country by proxy, has decided likewise. Now Diànlì ji'è de guójia claims that the Nair Dvipa Government has sold the land of our fore-fathers to them. That after such an impossible transaction, the traders from Diànlì ji'è de guójia who came in, bought the rest of Nair Dvipa from willing citizens of Nair Dvipa. This is utter rubbish!

Citizens of Nair Dvipa! We have a law which bars us from selling land to foreigners! We never have and we never will sell our lands to foreigners. Nobody can break an existing law. All such transaction amount to invasion of our lands. They are foreigners who do trickery, occupy our land which amounts to an invasion and today they rule over us! They take away our women and sisters and daughters and sell them away to foreign travelers. Look at the fact that one of our senior reporters Manjula, was sold off to people who come to do business with Nair Dvipa. Who saved her from the den of vice? Our King saved her! His Royal Highness King Sudhir Bagaria saved her! Today it is

Nindiya and before that it was Manjula, tomorrow it would be you! Will your husband or your parents allow you to be kidnapped and sold? So long as we are alive, we will not allow you to be sold! We must join our hands with yours and throw Diànlì ji'è de guójia out of our land! Will you help us to win back our freedom? Then join us with your candles. Jai Nair Dvipa! Long live Nair Dvipa! Long Live our King!"

All three came on line together then, Lalithambika Vasudevan, Manjula, and Nindiya with the rest of the twenty-four rescued girls standing behind them with raised fists and they roared in a single voice, "Join us! We will not allow women of Nair Dvipa to be used and sold like cattle! We shall fight till the end! Long live Nair Dvipa! Long live our King!"

How Diànlì Ji'è De Guójia Fell in the Eyes of Nair Dvipa

Media condemnation was spontaneous and poured in from most nations all over the world.

'CashPurse', the online payment facility allowed readers to donate monies and it flowed into the International bank account of 'Janaṅṇaḷuṭe Sabdaṁ'(the voice of the people).

"The women of the world unite in condemning this horrible crime. We request Nair Dvipa to permit us to inspect the Port for possible violation of the dignity of women and human rights violations on the women of Nair Dvipa. We send our contribution to 'CashPurse' the online payment box and request the citizens of Nair Dvipa to never give up their fight for Independence!"

The Press Communique from the office of Diànlì ji'è de guójia to all nations read, "This is an internal matter of Diànlì ji'è de guójia! Foreign countries are requested to desist from interfering in our internal matters, especially considering our superior fire power and defense ability!"

Reading this threat, most countries began to roar in disgust.

"Shameful! What less can be expected from a country that has always harboured the desire to expand its boundaries after taking control over global media!",

"Shameless Country! Shameless Invaders!",

"Shame shame Diànlì ji'è de guójia! Your man has been shot with his pants down!",

"Diànlì ji'è de guójia does not shake hands! They offer you Pants down Diplomacy!"

The wives of Diànlì ji'è de guójia citizens working at senior positions in Nair Dvipa too felt ashamed! The husbands now found it extremely difficult to operate with their wives asking if they were going to their office to work or to "rape an innocent citizen of Nair Dvipa".

People all around Nair Dvipa were going on long protest marches roaring for, "Independence!" The police were finding it difficult to quell the crowds. The foreign press and television media could not be stopped and kept broadcasting the roars of "frustration and anger at being cheated by a foreign nation". The Anti Royal forces were getting gradually isolated and began to fear for their lives and for their future. Many left with their families for foreign destinations. The foreign press kept covering every possible hint of atrocity or human rights abuse.

One foreign media commented, "Occupation of Nair Dvipa on the pretext of investing in infrastructure and any large project, will now make it impossible for Diànlì ji'è de guójia to sign another contract for infrastructure development!" The situation was getting bad from worse for the Diànlì ji'è de guójia sponsored Government! They had been exposed in the International arena!

Loyal Pro Diànlì ji'è de guójia Judges in The Supreme Court were asked to stall the verdict regards the legitimacy of the election process till this date in Nair Dvipa and hence stall questions regard the Legitimacy of the government in power today without the stamp of the King. But how long could they do so? Any further delay and then it would become obvious that the Supreme Court too was in the hands of Diànlì ji'è de guójia. In fact, the people on the streets were roaring, "Is the Supreme Court a puppet of Diànlì ji'è de guójia?! We demand an answer! We demand an answer now!"

The foreign press asked, "Why is the Supreme Court of Nair Dvipa silent about the legitimacy of the Government in power without the stamp of the King?"

There was a rush to appoint a Diànlì ji'è de guójia friendly Prime Minister in Nair Dvipa but the media blitz by the now famous "three sisters of the media" had shaken the conscience of house wives on a global basis, including in Nair Dvipa. All the Ministers were now shaky. They knew nothing about how to bring about development. They knew how to swindle funds and make money while the sun shines. They did not know which side was going to prove stronger and thus which side to support. Until the ultimate war took place, nobody wanted to occupy the Prime Ministerial hot seat and so a stand by Prime Minister, Nagaraju Pillai an old citizen of Nair Dvipa, was put in place. They thought he was pliable because he hardly ever spoke until then. Because he was pliable, the acting Prime Minister was subsequently confirmed as the Prime Minister.

Everything had happened very quickly and his own supporters had become shaky. Mogui thus lost control over his dignity and poise. Instead of going per protocol through the President of Nair Dvipa, he began to order the Chiefs of Defense directly, in front of the President, the Prime Minister and the senior Secretaries heading departments.

He ordered the birdmen and the soldiers out on the street and at the sea ports. It was then that he was informed about a special reinforcement from Diànlì ji'è de guójia that was rushing towards Nair Dvipa, much larger than the last and equally well armed.

The Police Personnel executed a house to house search very casually. The army, one of the most disciplined forces, searched as ordered in lanes & bye-lanes, in houses, in cars at the road blocks, but the three sisters were not to be found.

The foreign press made them heroes and pro Diànlì ji'è de guójia forces could not do anything to stop them, "The three musketeers of the Media of Nair Dvipa, to whom country and freedom comes before self!" Every nook and corner of Nair Dvipa now had their posters titled, "The Three Freedom Fighters of Nair Dvipa". And, "Selfless Guerilla Warriors of Nair Dvipa!" Right on the top of each poster was the King blessing all of them.

Mogui was desperate, hence the President of Nair Dvipa ordered the army to bomb the four villages that remained under the special protection of the King. A reconnaissance was done of the area and the defense services were shocked. At a certain point there was an invisible energy dome that rose as a wall of energy at ground level and then curved at the top of the villages to the base of the ocean waters and hills on the right, and no human or animal could enter. A small drone bumped into an invisible obstruction at the top where the dome curved down and thus it could not travel into the spherical energy defensive wall.

The heaviest of missiles from high above the skies could not even scratch the dome.

Mogui could not take control over the disciplined minds of the Defense Officers began to clutch at straws when the Defense Chiefs too began to refuse his direct orders.

He sent his employees to use the various media to announce that the man who called himself the King shall fight a duel in the Daivam Surya Sports stadium with Mogui himself. Whoever wins shall decide the fate of Nair Dvipa.

When the media spoke with Sudhir's secretary, he laughed away the offer by Mogui to the King to fight him at the Daivam Surya Sports Stadium, saying, "These are the days of people power and votes in a democracy! Law will take its own course about the Royal family of Nair Dvipa".

Then news came in that Malini, Sudhir's ex-wife, had vanished in front of his parents!

The Great Battle Between the Titans

 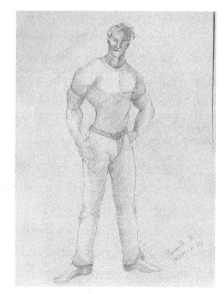

Mogui's powers were far greater than that of Sudhir especially because of the evil energy. To add to that, the dark moon helped Mogui multiply his powers manifold. Mogui could conjure up the dark moon on any evening. He could do so even today!

Sudhir was trapped into coming into Mogui's territory today during night time when he received a mental message fifteen minutes back from Mogui. During the mental message Sudhir heard Malini, his ex-wife's screams in pain and he traced the source to the Daivam Surya Sports stadium. Mogui was holding his ex-wife captive there in a sports stadium!

Sudhir flew through the evening skies to the Daivam Surya Sports stadium to find Mogui standing on a huge temporary performance stage. Mogui held Malini, Sudhir's ex-wife by her scalp hair and kept turning her face for all the spectators who had come to see their King fight Mogui, the evil one. Sudhir looked up and saw the dark moon created by the evil energy gradually engulf the moon that was normally seen every day in the evening sky. He heard a roar of fear and then realized that there was a huge audience behind the lights that were hitting his face and blinding him. Seeing the large numbers of spectators, Sudhir realized that the battle between himself and Mogui that had been repeatedly announced over the past three days all over Nair Dvipa and the International Media, inspite of his denying the same to the media, had been orchestrated by Mogui, who now had him trapped into participating in a combat on a dark moon night.

Sudhir ordered his mind, "Freeze Mogui's hands", but nothing happened. The dark moon had cancelled out his powers. He rushed towards Mogui with clenched fists but Mogui raised his hands and simply sent a shock wave that boxed Sudhir on his solar plexus, between his ribs. Sudhir keeled over, his body rushed backwards due to the ferocious impact and he fell on his knees, in pain.

The crowd moaned as if hurt, "Oooohh!"

Mogui threw a sword at Sudhir and growled, "Pick it up and fight for the life of your ex-wife!" The sword slid from where it fell, and travelled all the way to his feet where it came to rest.

Sudhir did not know how to use a sword! He was educated in an English medium school that did not teach him how to use warfare equipment. He was angry because Malini, his ex-wife, was being hurt and so he picked up the sword with his two hands anyway, tried to balance it with any one hand, finally managed to hold it in his right hand and advanced with angry steps towards Mogui. If he could only get Malini away from Mogui's grasp then he could teleport Malini back to her home in India.

The large screens on both sides of the stage showed a wobbly Sudhir holding onto his sword as if his life mattered to him.

The screens also showed Mogui advancing towards Sudhir with an expressionless face, dragging Malini's petite frame by her hair with one hand. And a sword in his other hand that had suddenly appeared out of nowhere.

Mogui struck Sudhir's sword and kicked Sudhir on his back as he swept past in his charge. The sword went flying out of Sudhir's hands and bounced twice on the stage floor before coming to rest next to a table. Sudhir too, especially due to the kick, rushed into a stack of tables and stools.

Mogui stretched out his hands to the crowd and his expression of ridicule seemed to ask them, "Who do I fight with? This wimp?"

"You are a drunkard who pretends to be a King!" Mogui lied to the crowd while talking to Sudhir. "The King has necessarily to be all powerful. Yet people of Nair Dvipa, your King got beaten by me so easily! This clumsy man does not deserve to be the King of such wonderful people!" roared Mogui for the benefit of the citizens of Nair Dvipa who thronged the stadium grounds in large numbers. His voice travelled all around the stadium especially with the mikes fixed for maximum effect.

The dark energy had created a dark moon high up in the sky and it covered the normal moon that had protected every human being on Prithvi (Earth) over the past so many years.

"Give me the power of vajra, the lightning!" Sudhir instructed his mind but alas, nothing happened.

Sudhir's found his powers weakening until he was devoid of all his powers. He had never learned the art of sword fighting and the dark moon had sapped out so much of his normal human strength that he felt like he had consumed a bottle of the strongest whiskey. He felt drowsy and wobbly. He saw two Mogui's and yet, because he wanted to ensure that Malini was not harmed, he decided he had to fight and protect her. He rushed with wobbly legs towards the sword that lay on the ground. He picked it up and charged towards Mogui.

He wanted to say, "Mogui let go of Malini", but he managed to somehow say, "Mogo lay go o Mai". It was as if inside his mouth, he had swollen cheeks and a swollen tongue.

Mogui batted away the downwards swing of Sudhir's sword and then swiped down hard on Sudhir's right arm.

Sudhir screamed in pain even while moving away on wobbly legs from the return swing of Mogui's sword that now swung past where his neck was a moment ago!

But Mogui had used his mind power and had changed his sword for an axe. Mogui swung exactly where he had hurt Sudhir and once again Sudhir felt a searing pain, he screamed while quickly moving away on wobbly legs.

Mogui sent a "Sap Energy" blast and Sudhir collapsed on his face, on the stadium floor, sapped of all energy to fight back. He stretched out his hands towards the sword but this little effort was so exhausting that he collapsed within seconds.

"Behold!" Roared Mogui. "Behold the man who claims the throne that is committed to ensure the welfare of these noble lands of Nair Dvipa! Look at him! He is a whimpering human being in front of this small knife that I hold against his ex-wife's throat.

He could not pick up that sword that I just threw in front of him. He refuses to fight for his first love, then, how can he protect you, his countrymen?"

Mogui pointed at the sword and roared," Pick up that sword and fight you wimp! Otherwise, on the count of three, I shall slice her throat!"

Sudhir was so exhausted due to the sapping of his normal human energy that he felt like one suffering from a serious bout of Jaundice.

"One!", roared Mogui.

Sudhir dragged himself up to the sword once again. He felt so very weak, and yet he tried and failed again. "Pick up the sword!", he told his mind but nothing happened.

"Two!" roared Mogui.

Sudhir was filled with dread and he looked into the eyes of his ex-wife and he could hear her mind say to him, "I just knew that I was unlucky for you. It made me feel very guilty because you were a good man who was trying so hard to feed his family but you failed repeatedly like you fail now. Being selfish I had clung on to you knowing fully well that I was holding back your success".

Inspite of his severe weakness, Sudhir pushed his body limits to enable himself to squat. Then he held the sword with his two hands and tried to lift the same up with all his might," Unnnnnhhha!" He failed yet again and fell on the floor, exhausted!

As Mogui held the knife against Malini's throat, Sudhir looked up from the sword and saw two tear drops trickle down his ex-wife's eyes, "I knew I had to move away from you, for you to succeed, but you loved me too much and therefore you would have never let me go! I had to be rude with you and say horrible things so that you would not hold me back. But I always loved you and cry today because I still do. I always loved …"

"Three!" roared Mogui and sliced her throat.

"Noooo!" screamed Sudhir and at that very moment there was a powerful lighting that crackled, boomed and burst to strike one of the steel poles that held up the stage. There was a puff and a heavy ball of smoke that mushroomed on a spot on the stage, next to Sudhir.

The smoke disappeared within split seconds, the hologram of honourable Srēṣṭhanāya Oruvan, the Chief of the honourable elders of the Supreme Council of Daivika Planet appeared, he pointed a finger at Sudhir and blasted him with an emergency surge of 'Charge Energy'. Sudhir bounced back on his feet, nodded to thank him, turned towards Mogui, roared in anger and sent a blast at where Mogui had stood a moment ago.

But Mogui had long gone!

And so was the body of his ex-wife, thereby negating the chance of bringing Malini back to life forever!

The Queen Visits the City

The news of the death of Sudhir's first wife had reached far and wide. The International media hit out at, "the cowardice of the evil man who kidnaps, uses and then slaughters in cold blood a helpless woman, simply to fight the King!"

The news had reached Sudhir's parents, his children, his late grandparents, Mobi and finally, Ngia Vat and her village.

Sudhir's grandparents sent his wife Ngia Vat to him to give him comfort during his hour of need in Suryadham, the capital city of Nair Dvipa.

Ngia Vat had since childhood heard the rumours of a "world outside"! But she was never sure that it existed.

The evil Anti Royal papers asked, "Why does the King moan for a woman who had divorced him? Was he planning to double cross the poor tribal girl? Did his first wife come to Nair Dvipa after she realized that her ex-poverty-stricken husband was now actually a King of a big island Kingdom?" They did not know that Mogui had kidnapped the helpless woman.

Many papers and Television media began to repeatedly show videos, that showed or spoke of "Magic and witchcraft was obvious for the first time in the life of Nair Dvipa and probably this planet Earth. Are Mogui and the King human beings or are they from outer space? Mogui the evil wizard covered our moon with a Black moon. Then brought a sword followed by an axe out of thin air. And finally cast a spell on the King that made him weak and helpless. True that Mogui had created unfair battle conditions that suited him the best. But the shocking matter is the fact that everybody saw the hologram of a powerful human being appear to save the King from murder in the hands of evil Mogui and then the fact that the King himself, shot out a powerful blast from his own fingers!" These newspapers sold out all its copies printed in the night and the special two lakhs newspapers distributed as an evening edition, printed that very afternoon! The television media got huge advertisements from global sources which far exceeded that received the whole of last year.

Residents of Suryadham, the capital of Nair Dvipa, had lined up on both sides of the streets when word spread that the Queen, who was a tribal, had planned to venture into the city for the first time after being wed to the new King. Though they had never seen a tribal with their own eyes, the citizens had heard about a secret part of the island where tribals had resided for many ages under the protection of the Royals.

They had recently heard that their King had married one of "them wild jungle women". And the naughty tongues began to wag.

"Do they walk on two legs? Really?!!"

"Do they really sharpen their teeth with rock to bite into wild animals?"

"I heard their men are not as virile as we city dwellers are?!"

"They do not wear any clothes? Really?! None at all?!! Wow!! When are they coming?"

"Does she eat human beings and monkey brains too? Then the King better protect his private parts in the night just in case she gets hungry!"

"How wild is she! I love wild women!"

"Boy I would love to have some women who wants to eat me during the night! Yummmy mummy!"

The Press, both Pro and Anti Royals press, had been giving the expected visit of the queen a lot of time and space.

"Does the queen deserve such disrespect from such obviously jobless, obnoxious, dirty minded vagabonds who unfortunately enjoy the rights of Nair Dvipa being a Nair Dvipa Citizen!?"

"Who gave that half-naked jungle woman the right to call herself Queen and why does she wish to make an entry into Nair Dvipa's capital, Suryadham at this crucial juncture of Nair Dvipa Politics?" asked an Anti-Royal paper with suspicion written into every line." Surely, she has the blessing of that ex-King who had been voted out by all of us. So, has she come to claim the throne? Has the King sent a female to do a man's job now?"

A Pro Royal secret online paper promised, "Her every step will be on a bed of roses because we shall lay it out for her! That is the minimum welcome and comfort that we shall offer the Queen and much more when she honours us with her first visit!"

An Anti-Royal paper showed a cartoon of a King marrying his maid servant with a tribal makeup. While the King was cleaning a bucket, the maid with tribal makeup was climbing out of it, one leg yet remaining to climb out. She had a necklace of skulls in one hand and a pure gold crown in the other! The caption read, "The best that the King could scrape out of his royal marital bucket!"

Another secret Pro Royal online paper reported, "The right to marry a tribal is like any normal right, for example, between two different religions, between two different cultures, between a white and a black or brown, and so many more that a few socially retarded citizens of society find hard to appreciate nor digest. To suggest that such marriage is below our self-esteem, is abhorring! Love does not make exceptions. Our King too did not make any exception! He loved and allowed his heart to decide on his behalf. Commenting on the Queen's background at this juncture exposes the unfortunate lack of mental growth of the individual who utters the negative comments".

And then the big day came, the security was water tight! Balloons and ribbons were torn down by anti-royals but came up again within half an hour.

After becoming the queen, Ngia Vat came to see the outside world that she did not know ever existed. Sudhir's two grand mother spirits had taught her about clothes that city people wear. They told her about the importance of a King and the vastness of his reign. Naturally she was awed beyond what she already was. She so wanted Sudhir to be happy and to be able to meet the expectations of all the people who loved and respected their King, her husband. An airstrip was created in the valley of the tribes. A special team was flown in to deck her up as per city norms. Gold Ear rings, Hair Shampoo, long dress, pearl bead head dress with feathers, the fore head gold plates, gold necklace, silver choker, the tribe's multicoloured side shoulder sash, walking on flat shoes and more.

She was transformed from a plain village girl to a high fashion city beauty!

Initially, Sudhir felt it would be apt to teleport her along with her bodyguards to the city hotel at Suryadham. But he was advised by his grandparents that it would be best if she learns the ways of normal human beings. Initially, she was hesitant about boarding an aircraft and then, after much trepidation, she did.

She arrived at Nair Dvipa's capital, Suryadham, in a specially chartered flight. A see through, aerobridge/airbridge/ air jetty, was unfolded for them to travel through to a special bus.

She was accompanied by thirty of the tribe's best warriors in full sports uniform, as taught to them by Sudhir during his stay with them. Not bothered about their semi nakedness, they seemed bemused by the colour of the skin of the city dwellers.

It was a strange sight for the Airport authorities as well as to the security personnel when semi clad men and women were transferred from the specially chartered aircraft to two specially reserved double decker buses with video monitors linked to the satellite showing different seating arrangement on each bus to each tribal passenger. Each seat had its video monitor. The tribals kept whooping in fear every time they saw a member of their tribe whom they recognized on the screen! They bent away from the screen fearing that it would eat them up too like it had eaten their friend. Then it happened that one of the friends raised his hand from the front seat and kept laughing away on seeing himself on the screen. He laughed at the fact that the screen mimicked his every move. It became a game from that moment onwards, with the tribal being displayed on screen making as many funny faces until the camera moved on to another tribal.

Their lack of contact with the "outside world" found it hard for them to differentiate between skin and clothes. They were innocents in a modern world, and they wore their sports uniforms with pride despite the fact a lot remained to be covered! The cultural shock was obvious but they had been warned and hence they tried very hard not to make it obvious! Accompanying them and providing them with modern security were three bus-loads of modern, fully armed, and trained RED LEVEL security personnel specially provided by Nair Dvipa. RED LEVEL security personnel were combat ready commandos. Even the Anti Royals dared not disrespect the Royals nor dare to disrespect the tribals that were under the protection of the Royals.

The "vroom" of the specially built Air-Conditioned buses could be heard from a distance.

Video cameras of most International Media were mounted on roof tops, street corners, at T- junctions just to catch that little extra glimpse. Latest reports were being flashed every five minutes.

This was a unique occasion for the citizens as they all wished to have a glimpse of the tribal queen, their queen, when the caravan of buses travelled down the streets of the city to an internationally renowned five-star city hotel. The citizens made special flags and waved at the buses as they blared their horns to get a clear path ahead.

The tribals stared with big eyes every time a car would approach them from the opposite lane. They would all get into a crouching position, ready with their bows and arrows or spears. They did not realize that the tinted glasses did not allow the people outside the bus to see them. They would roar as one, grimacing at the approaching vehicle. But every time the car would wizz past causing no harm. The tribals would stare after the vehicle in abject fear and awe. Gradually they got used to the vehicles approaching and whizzing past. They then pointed at the approaching city line of human beings to each other and kept gawking with open mouths. "The human beings on either side of the road, whose skin had strange colours, blue, green, yellow, indigo, multicoloured skin, were waving multi-coloured tree leaves and expressing their desire to wage war!" they explained to each other. And so, they roared back at them too!

Then the bus reached the 5-star hotel specially booked for them. A see through, aerobridge/airbridge/ air jetty, was unfolded for them to travel through. As they walked towards the Hotel, most Nair Dvipa residents were jubilant on seeing the queen for the first time albeit through the aerobridge. To them, semi clad did not matter. To them she was their queen. But to some, she was a sex symbol and they let out wolf whistles.

As they entered the hotel, the existing guests were requested to keep standing but move back against the wall and allow the special guests free passage to pass through. The tribal group consisting of body guards and assistants walked cautiously sideways, one side step at a time, to follow the guide who spoke in their language and now beckoned them to follow him towards the lift. They moved sideways in two separate lines, their backs to one another, pointing their spears or arrows towards the hotel guests. And in the center walked the queen to follow the Tour Guide.

The hotel guests, a large majority being foreign tourists waved at them with various expressions, some of amusement, some of scorn, some of respect, some of lust, some of admiration, some with jealousy and so much more written all over his faces. Some of the men would whistle at the semi clad tribal women, point at them and then take the little finger and thumb to their ears to suggest that the tribal woman rings him back. The protective male warriors raised their Isembozo' - the Penis Sheath and shook it at them. The media happily clicked away the scene for the morning news.

But came the time to get into the lift then, the tribals refused to get in. Nobody could understand why. So, the translator had to come down again and they told him, "This is a man gulping animal! It takes in human beings into its mouth. But when it opens its mouth again then, the human beings have been eaten up!" The ten suites, five on each side, was on the top floor. So, to save time, the translator decided to take the whole lot up by the stairs right up to the top, that is the thirtieth floor. They rushed up with no problems as they were used to similar exercise while climbing up and down the hill at their village. However, by the time the city-based translator, gasping for breath, reached the thirtieth floor, he found them playing football in their individual suits.

During lunch time they came down the stairs again.

The restaurant with French windows on the ground floor, facing the main road, was fully reserved for them where they were served lunch, that is, raw chicken, raw fish, and raw vegetables. The tribals gobbled them up, much to the amusement of the window shoppers who kept recording the "dinner hunting" on their Mobiles. Tribals shooting arrows at chicken that were flying away after escaping from under the serving bowl. A tribal standing on a chair and shooting his spear down at a large fish that had just jumped away from his plate! Another tribal trying to find the lobster that had managed to cling to the hair on the back of his head. Another "phooping" into a bamboo reed to shoot out a coated arrow meant for a small monkey that had escaped his bowl but it hit a waiter's bottom and he collapsed on the spot. Arrows and spears were zipping left and right to strike the wall overhead or the chandelier or the curtain, sometimes missing any waiter or waitress by inches. The bravest waiters and waitresses who were handpicked for this occasion to serve the tribals, were now cowering under the dining table, terrified by the prospect of that accidental spear or arrow striking them on their bottom or some other precious spot! Not to forget that, being speared by a tribal was not insured, considering that they had signed to accept the 'Force Majeure clause'!

Sudhir's instructions were clear," Show them around the city". The VIP group were taken on an "adult supervised" sightseeing tour around the city under high security detail. They saw cars & other vehicles, an airport from outside & airplanes taking off and landing, metro railway, overhead magnetic railway, colorful people singing with musical instruments at street corners, the slums and deprivation vis a vis the wealth and the affluence of the Skyscrapers. When they came back to their room, they were shown how to use the bath tub, the magical shower on rotating a screw, the bath towel, the foam bed, and finally the Television set. They went all around the television sets to try and understand where the people were hiding. They were constantly warned not to throw spears and shoot arrows at the animals being displayed on the Television set. They did not! But all of them cringed on seeing the lion approaching the camera and cheered on seeing the leopard racing after the springbok. They were like children who had discovered a new world! However, Ngia Vat remained silent and aloof throughout the tour and returned with a grim expression. She was worried about her husband, Sudhir.

Finally, the next day was the much publicized visit to the zoo. After the kidnapping of Sudhir's first wife, the international media plus the local "illegal media" lambasted the Government for allowing Mogui to continue to use the stage especially after the police saw him dragging a helpless woman by her hair.

"How could the police remain silent spectators? Have all the law enforcers lost their guts? Is Nair Dvipa now being run by a legal Mafia?! Mafia Dons take decisions and not the Prime Minister?!" roared the international & local Media.

"Zoo trip Royal team to be provided the best security!" commits the Prime Minister, reported all media globally.

Anti Royals joked, "Put them on a lease lest the tribals get hungry!"

The zoo visitors were broken up into ten groups. Ten translators took up the responsibility for each group and showed them around cage by cage. But here Ngia Vat spoke with the animals and they told her about the pain in captivity. She promised them that she would do something about their freedom at the earliest.

Then they boarded the bus to return to the hotel once again. Two jeeps with sirens blaring raced ahead to ensure a clear path, constantly coordinating with security detail on the left and right of the path. After a gap of about fifteen minutes, two motorcycle borne security persons with blaring sirens, followed by one bus full of security personnel ahead of two buses consisting of the Powva tribe. After these two Powva Tribe buses, followed two buses full of security personnel following from behind. And behind these buses were four bike borne commandos chasing after the buses but with a constant eye on the left or the right.

While Sudhir was planning strategy to regain Independence, his wife and her entourage was being followed home by a group of invisible birdmen.

The second bus with Ngia Vat seated in it suddenly began to glow as if ablaze, even while it moved ahead. Suddenly a figure appeared from out of thin air inside the bus, shot out a high energy blast at stupendous speed and the five security guards with latest guns and ammunition, dropped dead. The tribal warriors sitting around Ngia Vat surrounded her to protect her from harm. But the total bus began to hum and glow with greater intensity.

Then suddenly, the glowing bus that seemed on fire from a distance, buzzed like there was a short circuit, blinked several times with innumerable sparks like due to a short circuit, and then, whoomph and pooff – the bus vanished!

Ngia Vat's Kidnapping and the Final Power

The early morning International and pro Royal/pro Nair Dvipa Media went ballistic! Rage was an understatement!

"Is this the 'best security' that Nair Dvipa can provide to the Royal family? Is our King going to lose his second wife too? Is Nair Dvipa going to arrest Mogui now?"

"Queen of Nair Dvipa kidnapped! With thousand being witness, the Special Bullet proof, Air-Conditioned Bus buzzed and then vanished even while the convoy was travelling at high speed on a high security cleared route. The Police force are embarrassed and clueless! The Prime Minister has promised action!" screamed a Pro Royal secret media.

But the pro Diànlì ji'è de guójia press promptly reported, "The Queen hates Nair Dvipa's 'all food cooked' life. Goes missing in Nair Dvipa probably to hunt wild animals! Probably gone back to the jungles. The zoo authorities are requested to be on guard".

Nair Dvipa Pro Royals went wild and then began a riot that shook the world! Many pro Diànlì ji'è de guójia shops, buses, and property was burned beyond recovery.

The International Media had huge material to print finally. They suspected an Alien space ship, some imagined an explosion & evaporation, but all including the Pro Diànlì ji'è de guójia group too were shaken! Now the Pro Diànlì ji'è de guójia wanted to leave Nair Dvipa at the earliest.

Sudhir and his entourage were staying in a huge palatial villa surrounded by green lawns and flower beds and high walls within the city.

Television and Newspaper questioned the Police, the security arrangement, the Hotel and their security and all of them tried but failed to manage an appointment to interview the King. The receptionist refused to entertain the calls, hence the question of the King's Secretary or Executive Assistant sieving the call did not arise.

The same evening, Sudhir received a phone call on his private and highly confidential Mobile number. A deep, yet sugary sweet voice asked, "My dear dear grandson! Have you lost someone valuable by any chance?"

It was Mogui! Sudhir could recognize that voice blindfolded. He sent mind feelers over the Mobile and could now visualize Mogui with wings. With wings? Mogui could fly without wings hence, why the wings?

"This is a call from the lost and found department of Nair Dvipa!" Mogui joked with confidence. "I believe we have found a big number of semi clad tribals including somebody who yearns for her husband's tender touch!! Now I was wondering how much would the International 'Vice Market' quote for each of the "lost tribe" males and females, escorting the woman who keeps asking for you? If you delay in your response then you would surely want to ensure that someone else gives her the tender touch, like I did to your first wife, right? Oh, I was just wondering. How much would someone pay if the maid servant that you married were to be sold off in the International Vice Market, never to be found again?"

Sudhir knew it was useless arguing with or suggesting restraint to such people who have made up their minds. Mogui's huge power multiplied by the negative energy, allowed him to teleport Malini from a country far away from

Nair Dvipa. People like him would simply do what they desire even if you ask them not to do so. They would get especially excited if you threaten them with dire consequences. As stubborn as his last wife was, Mogui was equally unpredictable. Hence, he remained silent and kept listening. He wanted Mogui to keep talking and give away any possible lead in his flow of threats and taunts.

It worked! Mogui continued, "You, my dear dear grandson, need to declare that you are abdicating your throne and that you wish to pass on the crown to my great grandson living in the palace, the one and only Nksi Nanga – the greatest witch doctor!"

Then Mogui's voice became harsh, "You Sudhir whatever your surname is, you will make the declaration within seven days from now, or else, you know the consequences!" And then he switched off the Mobile phone on Sudhir's face!

Sudhir sat down with his head in his hands. His grandparents kept massaging his back gently. Little Mobi embraced his father.

"You have to fight on my son! You cannot lose heart!" advised his grandfather. "You have it in your blood to never give up!"

"That is right son! We can sit down, discuss and a solution would most certainly be brought about" both grandmothers said nearly in one voice.

No one noticed that little Mobi had picked up a machine gun, a ruck sack full of ammunition and had left by the rear door of the villa with a few other villagers who carried their own boom boom guns plus ammunition.

There was thunder and a flash in the cave at that very moment and a luminescent figure floated in the room surrounded by comparatively smaller luminescent figures who kept switching on and off like psychedelic lights. Everybody was shaken and were on guard but the voice of the luminescent figure in the center was gentle and he said,

"Do not be afraid of us King Sudhir Bagaria of Earth, Head of Inter Galactic Justice on Earth and senior member of the Inter Galactic Justice Core Team!

I am Gyananiyaya Oruvan, one of the senior board members of the Supreme Council of Daivika Planet and with us at this every moment is my immediate senior His Honour, Srehanaya Oruvan, the Chief of the honourable elders of the Supreme Council of Nambudiri Planet and these are my fellow board members.

We speak to you from the Daivika Planet using an old technology called 'Body Image & sound Teleporter'. We break the real time Video image including voice, into pulses. These energized pulses are converted to light energy and sent to the highest receiving points on your planet Prithvi (Earth), such as many mountain top landing spots, tips of pyramids and tips of tall temples. Here on Prithvi (Earth), we receive these pulses of Light energy to convert them to pulses of sound and light which then get converted back to real time Video image with the help of onboard satellite converters floating unseen around Earth. This technology allows real time conversation with least signal related disturbances.

Our latest technology allows the image that re-appears on distant planets to touch and manipulate the local energies to make changes or bring about modifications as desired from time to time.

His Honour, Srehanaya Oruvan, the Chief of the honourable elders of the Supreme Council of Daivika Planet would now like to converse with you, if you were to be so kind, Sir!"

Sudhir nodded in the affirmative with a grim expression on his face.

"Ahh King Sudhir Bagaria of Earth! It is an unfortunate moment for all of us on all the planets in this universe! On behalf of the Universe, we have thus appeared to convey our condolences to you and your family", expressed His Honour, Srehanaya Oruvan.

"It is important to understand that the situation is dangerous to say the least. And I wish to quickly dwell over certain points that affect you immediately", the noble one continued.

"You had requested that we do not interfere and we committed not to do so unless you are unable to defend yourself. We truly wanted to stop Mogui from hurting you but we never expected that he would stoop so low as to murder a helpless woman. I had to personally intervene to avoid protocol in regards Interplanetary rules and we are happy that you are alive", expressed His Honour, Srehanaya Oruvan.

"We have noted with great respect & satisfaction that all your past actions, wherein you have used your given powers, were justified, and that you have never misused your powers so far.

You would be doing the right thing if you decide to use your powers now to destroy Mogui and turn him into ash at this very moment, with our assistance", the Chief finished.

Sudhir bowed and said, "I am, we all are honoured oh great Srehanaya Oruvan, Chief of the honourable elders of the Supreme Council of Daivika Planet that, you chose to be by our side at this crucial juncture of space time.

I am thankful that you found my past acts to be justified and that my powers sparingly used. However, oh great leader of the honourable elders of the Supreme Council of Daivika Planet, keeping in view that you respect my past actions, I am certain that you would allow me to make my own assessment of the situation on the ground and subsequently take my own decision", Sudhir bowed and finished with a warm smile.

Srehanaya Oruvan understood that Sudhir was excited and angry with his problems hence he nodded and gave a knowing smile, "We the supreme council respect you and hence expect no less from you! However, considering the seriousness of the situation that you must handle, we have decided that we need to add certain special cells to your existing number of inborn brain cells, as a special case. This is to allow absorption of power never attempted before on Earth! Mogui continues to be far more powerful, many times faster and versatile otherwise! He teleported your ex-wife with astonishing ease, as if it was child's play! There is going to be a great battle now and you would need this extra power to be ready for the battle!"

Sudhir nodded and the Super Council raised their hands as one and pointed them at Sudhir's head. He was standing, suddenly his brain was on fire. He grimaced in obvious pain, became unconscious immediately, his head slumped down, and yet, his body did not fall. His head kept shaking up and down and then sideways violently, like when one accidently touches a live electrical wire. His grandparents tried to rush in to his aid but were met with a protective force that stopped them.

So powerful was the force that Sudhir's body began to float, then glow and hum.

Very slowly the hum reduced to a gradual whirr and then stopped. But the glow became brighter to a point where Sudhir's grand parents had to shade their eyes with their hands. Then Sudhir's body lifted into the air and began to rotate and revolve at a high speed. Soon, his body became a blur of brilliant light! Very gradually the moving body slowed down to became static, settled down on earth with his feet back on the floor and the glow began to reduce to a point where Sudhir regained his normal complexion. But his eyes remained shut and head bowed down like one were to be asleep or in a trance.

After some time, Sudhir woke up with a start, his head went up and he looked all around him trying to fathom what was happening. His eyes met that of his grandparents. His grandparents nodded to confirm that everything was okay.

The supreme elders nodded too and declared, "King Sudhir Bagaria of Earth. You are ready for the greatest battle that Earth has ever seen! This is a very crucial battle. The evil ones who escaped our first fleet of space ships to land on earth have popularized evil to a point on planet earth where it is now good to be evil and evil to be good. Goodness is equated with foolishness. Innocence translates to certain death. The cultures & language of many aborigines have been destroyed. Money is power and can buy anything and anybody. Animals, and sea creatures are being annihilated not for food but for the mere pleasure of killing. Trees are being cut down but fresh saplings are not being planted, forest cover is being depleted just for household luxuries, fossil fuel is being irresponsibly burned. And the leader in this is Diànlì ji'è de guójia, the face of all that is evil, who is now bent on increasing its geographical footprints on Earth.

Diànlì ji'è de guójia looks for a chance to divide and rule. They identify local leaders who are hurt or have been sidelined in a neighbouring country and then this evil country finances them. Mogui was one such disgruntled leader. Diànlì ji'è de guójia is using the Mogui's of this world for its selfish expansion related goals. War equipment that would destroy huge swathes of earth, causing unimaginable damage and destruction is being selfishly produced by Diànlì ji'è de guójia. It plans to spread out it's fangs of evil through guile, misrepresentation, cheating, fraud, and aggression. Everybody has a price, including in Nair Dvipa. Very few honest and sincere people remain who continue to believe in helpfulness and goodness. Prithvi (Earth) today is in grave danger!

You are their only hope King Sudhir Bagaria of Prithvi (Earth)!

Therefore, you have no options but to win!

If you lose this one battle of good over evil then, whatever honesty and goodness remains in this world will be a thing of the past. If you lose then Earth, as we know it today, is doomed! However, there shall be many battle casualties and you may have to bear the burden of losing some of your near and dear ones for ever. To avoid such a possibility, there are a few battle strategies that you may already know but may wish to revise.

For example, there are moments during this great battle when you would feel weak and helpless. You would frequently suffer from the paucity of ideas to protect all that you hold so dear to yourself. But let that weak moment not stop you from making your battle move. During battle you must think on your feet. During these moments, look deep within and quickly recognize your weaknesses. Try to imagine the various attack strategies that your enemy can execute much before he makes his move. When you know your weaknesses and you learn your opponent's strengths then you would also learn to adapt.

When you learn to adapt then you become unstoppable.

From then on it is a mental ping pong ball game of bettering the other's skills.

You may fail to bring him down on his strengths. Bring him down on his weaknesses then! Invade the enemy's mind and know his worst fears. Make his own fears attack him from then onwards. That would make him divert his concentration from fighting just you alone to fighting his own fears too, parallelly.

When you redirect your opponent's energy, you force him to change. When he changes then, he is on untested or uncharted territory. He is bound to make mistakes then. That is when you strike to defeat him! So, in essence, he defeats himself.

Most importantly, Mogui's powers multiply under the protection of the dark moon hence during the night time and in dark places. When you fight him, avoid dark places, caves, dark rooms and dark objects."

Srehanaya Oruvan, Chief of the honourable elders of the Supreme Council of Planet Daivika now looked Sudhir Bagaria straight in the eye and declared, "I personally have complete faith in your command King Sudhir Bagaria! Since this battle is crucial for all of us inter-galactically, we shall remain constantly around you, observing the progress of the battle. We shall intervene only if you ask us to or if we feel that you are down. We cannot allow you to be hurt or killed, hence if we feel that you are in the unfortunate position of not being able to protect yourself nor attacking your enemy to protect your near and dear ones, including the Nair Dvipa Citizens, then, we shall intervene."

Sudhir nodded in the affirmative with a smile and Srehanaya Oruvan, Chief of the honourable elders of the Supreme Council of Daivika Planet and his board of senior members nodded one by one and then, the buzz of a short circuit, the flickering of the lights that surrounded them and then pooff, they vanished!

With his new power Sudhir teleported the total Powva tribe, the Beti Beti, the super council village or the village of the elders, the Zambeke, Omagwena, Kavaheke, Kunini et all and they appeared outside the cave mouth. They were shocked because they were all in their respective huts and the next moment, they were teleported to the cave mouth.

Sudhir did not waste time. He used telepathy and spoke into their minds, "Great people of the Powva tribe. You all had entrusted me with the responsibility of protecting and taking care of Ngia Vat and I have failed you! Ngia Vat has been taken away by force by a very powerful, vile human being called Mogui, who can change human beings into stone, make objects move on their own, kill thousands of the Powva tribe by merely sending a brain generated force towards my family. He takes control over the minds of innocent people and then makes them his unwilling soldiers. All the soldiers who accompanied Ngia Vat have been also kidnapped by this evil man.

His soldiers are controlled by him and share his powers. They can fly with wings, they can blast people with fire from their mouth. Many amongst you have used such power in your land when the outsiders invaded you. But I had never forced you to fight for your land. You joined me in doing so.

Ngia Vat, my wife, had gone to the city outside in the craft that flies and you all had bid her farewell. But this evil man named Mogui and his great grandson, our last witch doctor Nksi Nanga have conspired against all on this island including the Powva tribe. I must fight against the evil people that the powerful Mogui has brought on this island. I must fight Mogui and I must fight Nksi Nanga.

This shall result in a great battle like never before, and I shall put the villages once again in a protective magic cover so that nobody may harm you in any manner, provided you remain within the protected circle.

I want you all to be safe. I need your best wishes. I assure you all that I shall not come back without Ngia Vat. Now I shall send you back to your villages".

"No, you shall not Oh great Mahua Mrignaw Minsaw!" interrupted Ombasa the chief of the Supreme Council. "You shall not send us brave warriors back to be safe while you fight alone to save our daughter!"

The warriors stomped their spears and roared and then the rest of the villagers stomped their feet in protest and roared as one, "We shall go to war with you! Yes, we shall fight! We shall go to war because we are trained to be warriors! You trained us!"

Ombasa the chief of the Supreme Council, along with the Chiefs of Zambeke, Omagwena, Kavaheke, and Kunini villages, strode up to stand in front of Sudhir and said in one voice, "We want to fight to get back our daughter Ngia Vat! We want to fight to protect this island from Mogui, Nksi Nanga and the people that Mogui has brought into this island!" And they stomped their spears and jumped on that spot to roar, "Oyeaha!"

"Very well I agree!", said Sudhir after a brief pause and a sigh. Wars are not won by sentiments, soldiers win it. Soldiers like yourself! I shall have to give you all tremendous powers and then train you regards controlling your powers." declared Sudhir and then he raised his hands in the air and roared, "For Powva! For Nair Dvipa!"

All the villagers, elders, men, women, children, all of them roared as one, "For Powva! For Nair Dvipa!"

Nobody asked where Mobi was. They were confident that he could take care of himself. He had become far too confident hence, independent.

Battle Strategy Revision

Sudhir's grandfather provided Sudhir with a quick verbal material on battle strategy.

"Battles do not begin suddenly. Anyone who desires to win will have over past many years created in the territory of the enemy nation, the foundations for the strategy that he would use on his enemy during a future war. He creates a network of operatives in an enemy country and mock battles happen continuously, thereby honing the skills of the operatives in that country.

Your enemy is trained to identify varying cause of differences and fissures in your country, as is natural in a cross cultural, multi lingual nation such as our nation Nair Dvipa. Your enemy is thus trained to create riots, inter caste wars, influence college students to speak against their nation. The student is trained in the enemy nation in the garb of discounted or free education, to influence the mass in your nation and attain senior positions in your country, to subsequently influence legal judgements against honest hard-working senior Government and Semi Government officials of Nair Dvipa to a point where they are humiliated and feel embarrassed for having done their duty and for being loyal citizens. The student is groomed to influence electoral decisions and speak for the enemy of the nation without even realizing that he is doing so.

Your enemy is trained to enter your country to sacrifice his or her life by marrying senior decision makers of your country and extract valuable secrets. Your enemy is trained to brain wash students good at reporting & writing novels, poetry, sculptures, photography, film making etc., from teen age till adult hood to make them think in favour of your enemy and against Nair Dvipa, and thus get rewarded finally with the brand of being part of the 'intelligentsia'. Your enemy is thus groomed to become a successful editor of media companies that are sponsored by your enemy nation and subsequently spout venom against Nair Dvipa to stop development related activities that would help Nair Dvipa prosper. Most importantly, your enemy is trained to enter the legal profession and become a Judge of the lower courts of Nair Dvipa, with enemy controlled media supporting and tomtomming his every Anti Nair Dvipa act as being "for Nair Dvipa" and "in the best interests of the nation". He uses his position to release every anti national due to "lack of evidence". Finally, your enemy nation pushes a few plants or a few moles working as Judges of the Supreme Court of Nair Dvipa to encourage the elevation of the Anti-National High Court Judge into the hallowed institution of the Supreme Court of Nair Dvipa.

Your enemy nation would also attack the health of your soldiers. Thus, Nair Dvipa had been suffering from Duck Gunia, Vipah Virus, Germ fever and so much more. People were suffering but also getting cured. But what was important is that nobody noticed that the Defense forces too were affected and became "unfit for duty" and hence "not ready for combat" very often. That was mistake number one because Nair Dvipa did not suspect the hand of a foreign country. The fact that Nair Dvipa was made a guinea pig, a testing ground for the efficacy of the products of the labs of Diànlì ji'è de guójia was unknown to Nair Dvipa, and this is unfortunate.

Much before any war happens, the school buses or private vehicles of Defense Officers and senior Government Officials, Pro Nair Dvipa Media Heads, Pro Nair Dvipa Legal luminaries, whose decisions would affect the war effort, are kept under surveillance and the route, normal destination etc., are noted for future use. Long distance cameras take photographs of each sibling of senior decision-making officers. Once identified, Diànlì ji'è de guójia will have done everything to locate the online digital activities and habits of both officers as well as family members. For the officer, and male members of the officer's family, online honey traps are set up and sometimes some gullible officer or son may get attracted to a young girl who blackmails him to a point where Nair Dvipa secrets are given away. Many a time, the officer's wife or daughter is similarly trapped in honeytraps where the man is a trained enemy operative. During any war, these children, if they continue to follow the same route, would become target for kidnapping and thus weakening the concentration and resolve of the officer during a crucial hour of war.

Nair Dvipa had never felt it necessary to spread out a network of operatives in Diànlì ji'è de guójia and to start from scratch in their country now would be a big challenge. That is our area of weakness.

However, we are strong within Nair Dvipa. Nair Dvipa and its people are our strength.

Well, now that you have understood what Diànlì ji'è de guójia has done to Nair Dvipa over these past forty odd years, what is going to be your strategy now?"

Sudhir was so thankful that his late grandfather had a military background and that he was one of the finest in battle strategy! He looked at the spirit of his grandfather with eyes and a smile that said "Thankyou for being my grandfather!".

Then he replied with a gentle smile, "While you were providing me your guidance grandfather, the most important people needed for this battle have already been teleported to the next room. Chathura Bandaranayake, Chief of NDI (Nair Dvipa Intelligence), who controlled the intelligence officers globally and within Nair Dvipa, was in hiding with all the files listing the names of officers under his control globally. This is the time to get him into our battle team. Lalithambika Vasudevan, Editor, 'Satya', Manjula, the senior reporter of 'Yathart'tha Vartta', Nindiya of Vegattilua Vartta, the TV cum online Media cum News Print Media, are in the next room. Nītimān Moonesinghe, head of the Judiciary of Nair Dvipa and the Chief Justice of Nair Dvipa is next door, Shyamal Mukherjee, the Director General of Police of Nair Dvipa, Gopal Patnaik, the Director General of Vigilance and Anti-Corruption Bureau of Nair Dvipa, Vice Admiral Srikumar Venketasan, the Director General of Coast Guards of Nair Dvipa, General Cristopher Rodrigues, the Chief of the Army staff (COAS) of Nair Dvipa, Admiral Sudhakar Nattarajan, the Chief of Naval Staff (CNS) of Nair Dvipa, Air Chief Marshal Kuriyedathu Raman Daivika, Chief of the Airstaff (CAS) and most importantly the present Prime Minister, Nagaraju Pillai, are all in the room next door. Shall we proceed?"

Lieutenant-General Sir Cherusseri Daivika, being a spirit, remained unseen and moved into the huge conference hall created within the cave. Interestingly, the air was fresh and the temperature was mildly cold, hence comfortable.

Delegation of War Strategy

The moment Sudhir entered, everybody in the conference room rose to their feet and stood at attention. Senior Officers trained to salute, did so.

"Good Morning to you gentlemen! Please be seated!", requested Sudhir and all sat down in their seats after Sudhir sat down. Each seat had a mike, a water bottle, a pad and a pencil. Sudhir used telepathy and spoke into their minds,

"You all must be wondering how you all managed to appear under one roof at the same time", began Sudhir. "I teleported you all here. Why? Because all of you have now realized the flaw in your past assumptions that Diànlì ji'è de guójia was a better alternative to the Royals. Now you realize that Diànlì ji'è de guójia has taken over your country and is destroying everything that was good on your land. Diànlì ji'è de guójia is breaking down the value systems that you had held dear. They shall break up your country into little pieces and a lot many foreign countries would shamelessly takeover states that help them profit. They are trying to change your culture, taking away your wife, your sister, your mother and selling them away as commodities to be traded. They are marrying into your families and changing your religion. It may all seem an innocent inter-religion love marriage, but it is important to credit the far-reaching strategy of Diànlì ji'è de guójia. If they could successfully influence Nair Dvipa citizens to a point that they are able to take over Nai Dvipa and Nair Dvipa citizens welcome them then, do please consider the possibility that Diànlì ji'è de guójia may have had influenced the soldiers trained and sent to 'marry and convert' our citizens too.

Legal luminaries have correctly advised that all elections in Nair Dvipa are null and void considering that I had not signed on the very first agreement post the referendum.

Hence, I remain the King, the Defense Services and all the other Government services and facility providers, reports to me with immediate effect."

All the individuals within the room stood up once again and interestingly everybody saluted to show that they accepted his command. Including the representatives of the Press. With one voice they roared, "Yes, Your Royal Highness!"

"As you all know, they have kidnapped the Queen", Sudhir continued I have seven days to abdicate my throne to save her and the other tribals accompanying her. But Diànlì ji'è de guójia has never been known to respect the commitments given by themselves. They will kill the Queen and her entourage any way.

Therefore, each of you will be tasked with specific assignments with immediate affect. We may never meet each other again and hence it is important that you know your specific responsibilities and continue even if anything were to happen to me.

Diànlì ji'è de guójia has sabotaged our electoral system. After you all voted in the referendum and the Royals lost, the Ambassador of Diànlì ji'è de guójia resident in Nair Dvipa went home, after declaring with audacity that he had been tasked to remove the King and that he was going home because his job was over. Ask yourself how he managed to execute his task. He had met certain local anti-social leaders. They were the leaders amongst the 'vote gatherers cum guarantors'. Once the contractual fee was determined they were willing to do everything to help "manage the votes".

Chathura Bandaranayake, Chief of NDI (Nair Dvipa Intelligence), is tasked with identifying the total list plus additions to that list of Vote Ensurers or Middlemen who were used by the Ambassador of Diànlì ji'è de guójia to ensure that the opposition won the election. I want you to use subtle means to make them permanently vanish without anybody becoming any wiser. Nair Dvipa is a big land with many states. If the Ambassador of Diànlì ji'è de guójia could manage to co-ordinate with each of such Vote Ensurers or Middlemen on a PAN Nair Dvipa basis through his state wise operatives then you can imagine what a big operation this was. Chathura Bandaranayake, locate these operatives and neutralize them at the earliest.

Huge sums of monies were involved. Otherwise the vote ensurers would not be interested. Shyamal Mukherjee, the Director General of Police of Nair Dvipa, and Gopal Patnaik, the Director General of Vigilance and Anti-Corruption Bureau of Nair Dvipa, must conduct a joint exercise to identify the source of the huge funds that were given away to the Vote Ensurers or Middlemen on a PAN Nair Dvipa basis through his state wise operative. Subsequently you must stop the opposition from gaining access to such funds.

For the war effort we need funds, huge funds. Diànlì ji'è de guójia too needs funds! We shall offer a War Bond of ND Rs.100 value per bond to the citizens of Nair Dvipa. But Diànlì ji'è de guójia would most certainly conduct a massive exercise of Bank robberies, snatching of valuables, instigating the Government to sign on scam projects, siphoning off monies collected by illegal chit fund schemes, diversion of NGO funds, online hacking into bank accounts or savings accounts of simple or innocent citizens and diverting their funds, hacking into large cash rich organizations plus high net worth individuals and diversion of funds into tax havens etc. Therefore, Shyamal and Gopal, your teams must be tech-savvy and create ample safeguards for all Nair Dvipa citizens.

Further, Shyamal and Gopal, please make a list of all the scams and possible beneficiaries. Locate the Banks or storage points of such ill-gotten wealth. They would have been spread out amongst various junior functionaries. If we cannot punish them legally then put civilians on the job and train them to shoot their way in to raid such storage points and salvage the monies for the use of our war effort. Execute this right away.

Vice Admiral Srikumar Venketasan, the Director General of Coast Guards of Nair Dvipa, General Cristopher Rodrigues, the Chief of the Army staff (COAS) of Nair Dvipa, Admiral Sudhakar Nattarajan, the Chief of Naval Staff (CNS) of Nair Dvipa, Air Chief Marshal Kuriyedathu Raman Daivika, Chief of the Airstaff (CAS) are entrusted with the task of ensuring no more Diànlì ji'è de guójia forces can land on our shores. And the huge force that have entered have to be made to surrender at the earliest on the grounds that their occupation is illegal.

High tech Diànlì ji'è de guójia warships and submarines capable of firing long range MOABs will ideally arrive within normal missile launch distance from the island very soon. It would be impossible to depend on our satellite alone to detect and identify them. Therefore, it is imperative that we drop all around this island our latest long life, under water, self-launch-able unmanned missile bases. Each Nair Dvipa Vessel has been tuned to emit a code that is recognized as being friendly by each underwater missile base. They can detect and differentiate between enemy and friendly submarines and warships. Prime them to launch and destroy all approaching enemy ships and submarines that travel above them, without permission from our Inbound Traffic Controllers. The enemy would surely launch decoys to mislead such missiles. Therefore, modify each of such underwater unmanned long duration base to have rapid fire capability. Put the Nair Dvipa Attack Research Organization (ATO) on the job right away and tell them this is an emergency. Even if one missile is misled by enemy decoys then the balance missiles should find their destination. Issue a warning to every nation around the world that our nation is on high alert considering the immediate threat from Diànlì ji'è de guójia and that no large warship or submarine may traverse our waters without our invitation or permission.

I have messaged Prince Hanuman Daivika, my father, for help from the land of our ancestors, India. I have in the capacity of the King of Nair Dvipa also written to the Prime Minister of India for assistance and have attached the copy of the letter sent to my father, being an ex-Prince of Nair Dvipa. India has always stood by the Downtrodden and disadvantaged of this world. Being a nation of brave hearts, they shall most certainly stand by a country that is being bullied by a larger nation.

In the meanwhile, kindly ask your children and family members to change their online Passwords and User names immediately before resorting to any further Online Social Media activities until further notice. The Nair Dvipa Defense Secrets Act apply even more today. Avoid interacting with strangers and do not upload private images unless you have switched on the 'privacy' option to 'High Alert'. Do not discuss defense related subjects with Non-Defense personnel. Do not permit any vehicle to be parked near any defense establishment without knowing the identity of the owners. Do not permit anybody inside a Defense Establishment without an Identity Card. Considering the emergency, fix Video Cameras at the main gates and ensure the visitor 's claimed identity matches his Nair Dvipa created Bio Metric Recognition details. If it does not match then do not take chances. Put him away in a cell with no legal recourse until the end of this emergency. All defense establishments must ensure that each residential or commercial establishment within two kilometers around the defense bases must possess proof of possessing a Nair Dvipa Digital Identity. Each of such residential or commercial establishments must be checked for possible launch base for shoulder launched mini MOAB missiles.

Recruit and train the best Ethical Hackers to protect all Nair Dvipa facilities from hacking, especially Emergency Services. Essential services will not be allowed to stop for even a minute. Have helicopter landing pads in the premises of each of such essential services establishments.

During the duration of this war, disciplining of erring defense officers becomes the sole responsibility of the Defense services. The Police will have no say on any crime committed by any Defense Personnel during this emergency. The Defense Personnel shall cease to have access to local courts to seek justice for being superseded by a fellow officer or, any other complaint against a fellow officer or, any decision relating to his service with the Defense services during this emergency. Th enemy will try to influence the defense related effort by flexing its muscle in both the Press as well as the Courts and trying to tie the hands of the Defense forces by colouring it's effort as Human Rights violations. The Supreme Court enjoys its individuality and independence. The Defense Services too must be allowed to be independent from the jurisdiction of the courts including the Supreme Court during this emergency.

Mobile phone jammers shall be installed at every defense base to ensure that defense secrets are not clicked and messaged during this war. During the war, proof made available to us relating to use of personal Mobiles by fellow officers will be used to ensure harsh penalties. A crack team of our best IT Personnel will have to design a system that sieves all Mobile messages that arrive on the Mobile phone of any serving or retired defense personnel during this period.

Lalithambika Vasudevan, Editor, 'Satya', Manjula, the senior reporter of 'Yathart'tha Vartta', Nindiya of Vegattilua Vartta, the TV cum online Media cum News Print Media, are entrusted with the task of ensuring that positive pro Nair Dvipa campaigns are initiated. You must ensure that the Neutral Media personnel are identified and protected but that Anti Nair Dvipa Media are identified and the names be conveyed to Chathura Bandaranayake, Chief of NDI (Nair Dvipa Intelligence), for permanent eradication of Anti Nair Dvipa forces within the country.

You would realize that during a war, Diànlì ji'è de guójia is going to throw monies at the Press and ensure Anti King and Anti Nair Dvipa propaganda. They shall try and demotivate the Nair Dvipa Defense services and all the other essential services. The Diànlì ji'è de guójia trained 'intelligentsia' would be paid to instigate the students of all the universities that matter to raise their voice against the King, the Defense services, the Police and the decisions being taken for the defense of the nation during this war. It is important to drown their negative propaganda with our pro Nair Dvipa Campaign. They shall highlight our negatives repeatedly hence you must repeatedly highlight the positive aspects of development that happened during the tenure of the King.

I shall capture the Pro Diànlì ji'è de guójia supposedly legal media channels for some time and make my broadcast wherein I shall declare the fact that the Royalty was and remains in power in Nair Dvipa.

We have in our midst Nagaraju Pillai, the acting Prime Minister who was subsequently confirmed as the Prime Minister, of Nair Dvipa. I request Mr. Nagaraju Pillai to gather people loyal to him. I do believe you have a good majority of the Parliament in your favour. The moment you hear my broadcast, it would be appropriate to declare the Parliament dissolved until the King decides the Ministers.

Finally, Nītimān Moonesinghe, head of the Judiciary of Nair Dvipa and the Chief Justice of Nair Dvipa. You are entrusted with declaring the present Government in power as being illegal without my signature, as declared by me. And that the Defense Services reports to the King with immediate effect. This after you hear my broadcast.

You shall be immediately attacked by Pro Diànlì ji'è de guójia legal luminaries challenging your decision. They would most certainly join hands with the Pro Diànlì ji'è de guójia Media to try and tear your hard-earned reputation apart. They shall do everything to tarnish your image. Consider this sacrifice from your end being for the good of Nair Dvipa. When the Royal family is back in its seat, we shall remove the stain with the help of the media. Then begins the task of protecting & ensuring Justice by listing out corrupt legal luminaries who are throttling justice within Nair Dvipa. They are interfering in the Independence of the Judiciary and the said names must thus be conveyed to Chathura Bandaranayake, Chief of NDI (Nair Dvipa Intelligence), for permanent eradication of Anti Nair Dvipa forces within the country.

Regards ill-gotten wealth of local citizens, stored in foreign locations or, investments in real estate outside India, it is requested that your ruling help us send demands to foreign nations to sell the said properties and repatriate the sums involved, considering that such investments of funds were done without the permission of our country.

The Defense Services needs total independence to operate without fear of legal reprisals during this war. I urge Nītimān Moonesinghe, head of the

Judiciary of Nair Dvipa and the Chief Justice of Nair Dvipa to help us pass a resolution to allow this to happen.

All of you within this room are tasked with putting a stop to funds flowing to pro Diànlì ji'è de guójia forces. This source of generation of funds for the war must be identified far in advance and stopped immediately. Considering that this is an emergency, all such pro Diànlì ji'è de guójia fund Mobilisers need to be eliminated on the spot. No court case will be permitted which allows the culprit to escape the noose. Nītimān, we need your help & guidance to pass a law accordingly.

Most importantly, all of you are tasked with the responsibility of locating the queen of Nair Dvipa. And then conveying the news to me. This news would allow me to take a more coordinated action with all of you, to ensure her safety.

That would be all gentlemen, hope you all do a good job!"

Then, Buzz as if there was a short circuit and, Poof! They had all vanished! They were back in their own place of work as if nothing had happened.

The Media Broadcast

One specific Television channel was shocked to have the acting Prime Minister suddenly walk in to visit them at around ten in the morning.

"Dear citizens of Nair Dvipa, Good afternoon!" the compere opened with a warm tone and a smile. "It is our honour to have a special guest today and we wish to share this good fortune with you. Our Prime Minister, His Excellency Shri Nagaraju Pillai, the Prime Minister of Nair Dvipa has given us a pleasant surprise by visiting us at the Television station today. What a pleasant surprise and what a great honour! Let us all give him a big hand!"

There was a round of loud clapping and applause and the Television camera panned all around the studio and finally pointed at the Prime Minister.

The compere then requested, "We request the Prime Minister, His Excellency Shri Nagaraju Pillai to say a few words. Please Sir!" so saying Padma Vasudevan fixed the collar mike onto His Excellency Shri Nagaraju Pillai.

There was the normal sound of the mike being fixed and then His Excellency Nagaraju Pillai smiled at the camera and began, "Ladies and

Gentlemen, brothers & sisters, granddaughters and grandsons of Nair Dvipa, I greet you all from the bottom of my heart!"

There was a round of loud clapping and applause.

"I have an important announcement to make today. It will change the future for the better and will most certainly repair the past mistakes that many of us have made intentionally and unintentionally in the past.

Citizens of Nair Dvipa. I have been in closed door consultations with eminent lawyers and they all agree that there was a window of certain number of years within which the last Prince could accept his Kingdom or abdicate his thrown. He abdicated his throne and in such an event Prince Sudhir Bagaria, nee Prince Sudhir Namboodiri, his son, was automatically the King unless he refused in writing, which he had not. During any vote to oust a King, the signature of the King is necessary for the agreement to be legally valid. The King did not sign because he was not present in the Kingdom. Therefore, the King continues to control and be the supreme power of Nair Dvipa. Further, as per our law, any agreement with foreign countries that amounted to selling land or giving away land rights in perpetuity is invalid unless signed and stamped by the King of Nair Dvipa.

As per the existing Laws of Nair Dvipa, any number of Elections could not have happened without the signature and seal of the King of Nair Dvipa. Our King was not present in the city when the first elections took place. Therefore, the very first election and from then on, every other election, stands null and void.

I have got the signed resolution of most of the Parliament who have voted to declare that the very first election and from then on, every other election, stands null and void. Hence this Parliament stands dissolved after my declaration on national and international media. We have also resolved that all acquisitions of land without the signature of the King stand null and void, voidable at the option of the King of Nair Dvipa.

His Excellency Shri Nītimān Moonesinghe, head of the Judiciary of Nair Dvipa and the Chief Justice of Nair Dvipa has just declared the present Government in power as being illegal considering that it exists without the signature of the King as declared by His Highness, First Amongst the Rajas of Nair Dvipa, Lord of Princes, Great Prince over Princes, Grand Commander of the Order Nair Dvipa, Maharaja of Nair Dvipa, Shri Sudhir Bagaria. Therefore, the Defense Services reports to His Royal Highness with immediate effect. All forces of Diànlì ji'è de guójia are hereby declared as occupation forces and are warned that they must surrender to the Nair Dvipa forces with immediate affect or face dire consequences.

I hereby declare an emergency which shall remain in force until the King decides otherwise.

Such a broadcast shall most certainly result in unrest. The Police is requested to ensure law and order. Citizens and fellow countrymen, I urge you to ensure restraint and that you remain indoors until the King makes his next announcement and until the conditions are safe.

Ladies and Gentlemen, pan global brothers & sisters, pan global granddaughters and grandsons, I thank you all for having given me the time to convey the decision of our Parliament. From the moment that my broadcast is over, the Parliament stands dissolved and the King is automatically in power. All Government Forces and departments shall henceforth report to the King and nobody else.

I wish you all a good day and a wonderful future! Jay Nair Dvipa! Long live Nair Dvipa! Long live our King!"

And so saying, the Prime Minister went offline and the anchor came online to continue the programe that was temporarily interrupted.

Prior to this broadcast, certain "illegal" online radio and Television channels had been repeatedly broadcasting the King's broadcast, "Dear Citizens our great King, His Highness, First Amongst the Rajas of Nair Dvipa, Lord of Princes, Great Prince over Princes, Grand Commander of the Order Nair Dvipa, Maharaja of Nair Dvipa, Shri Sudhir Bagaria desires to say something very important and of great relevance to you. I hereby pass on the microphone to His Excellency".

"Dear citizens of Nair Dvipa" began Sudhir. "Diànlì ji'è de guójia is a foreign country that has without the signature of the Royal family, occupied our land. They have forced laws upon you that are not acceptable to my countrymen. They seize your wealth by unfair laws. They differentiate between the old citizens and the new illegal migrants from their land and give preference to the latter in any matter. They divide us based on religion and issue badges of honour to those who kowtow before them. They do not dare to fight us directly. Instead they push the people professing a foreign religion into our land thereby making us fight against the new asylum seekers. While we become weaker fighting one another, they will fight with the one who will win but they know that we would be far weaker than what we are today. They seize our women and make monies out of selling of our family members. Being your King I hereby declare that the election process from the very beginning, is Null & Void. The present Parliament is requested to vote against the present government and against tyranny before resigning.

The Supreme Court is requested to pass bills as deemed fit in this regard.

With this broadcast I urge citizens of Nair Dvipa to stand with Nair Dvipa and let us win our freedom. Let us go back to being who we were before. Free citizens of Nair Dvipa!

A long-distance sniper bullet hit the acting PM's head while he was getting into his bullet proof car, with his high security detail firing away at the direction from where it was supposedly fired, but to no avail.

The anchor you allowed the Prime Minister to speak in favour of the King, was also shot dead.

The War Begins

Emergency had been declared in Nair Dvipa by the outgoing Prime Minister and was now being enforced! All roads were empty. Foreign visitors were huddled into hotels waiting for some semblance of peace. Nair Dvipa citizens too remained indoors barring the morning joggers.

Suryadham, the capital city of Nair Dvipa had ensured trees remained shading the side walk that ran parallel to the cyclist's path on the two sides of the two heavy traffic two-way roads that ran parallel to one another. It was as if a colourful painter had splashed the two sides with multicoloured blossoms of Royal Poinciana, or Gulmohar and Bougainvillea trees. The red, purple, pink, violet blossoms had carpeted the side walk creating a royal carpet for the citizens.

Two feet diameter thick plastic pipes ran below the cyclist's path through which the pvc enclosed copper electrical wiring ran from lamp post to lamp post. A central control room per ward kept inspecting the video camera stream per street corner. This helped them know which light was not on even after automatic timers switched on every light all over the city in the evening.

A twenty-foot diameter steel rod structured concrete pipe ran below each main road into which flowed the rain water and other liquid wastes of the road, the pedestrian and the cyclist's path. Drain water outlets were lined one after the other, an outlet every one minute. Man holes every four minutes on the pavement, allowed anybody to climb into the huge drain and out of it in the event of any emergency.

Early in the morning the Koyel birds, the doves, and sparrows would wake up the healthy citizen. The health-conscious citizen would be found jogging or doing a brisk walk even while the world was waking up all around them.

Being on a holiday, Dipak Halder a citizen of India was staying at the Grand Suryastra, a five-star hotel chain, He was in his jogging tracks racing down Ganesh Avenue and he turned right into Aditya Avenue. He saw in the rear-view mini mirror fixed to his long-distance glasses a black six-seater dark glassed vehicle turn the corner of Ganesh Avenue very gently to enter Aditya Avenue and then it slowed down. He did not reduce speed. He noticed that the next crossing allowed him to turn right into Aniruddha Marg and this led to Durga Shrest Marg if he turned right at the next crossing. And then another right turn at the next crossing and he was back at his hotel on Ganesh Avenue.

The car gently increased speed in his rear-view mirror fixed on his glasses. He increased his speed and was very close to the corner to turn right. He saw a huge dust bin before the corner, outside a multi-storied building. He also saw the dark glass window of the car slide down, and a pistol nozzle with a silencer appeared from inside the car! He did not have time to turn the corner but if he ran a bit faster then, he could try and take cover behind the pure steel dustbin. He now began to sprint.

It was then that he heard the "puff" and then "thop" as a bullet missed him and hit the thick bullet proof glass pane of a jewelry store behind him. And "puff" and the next bullet pinged away from the steel lamp post behind him. Now he was sprinting for his life! The third "puff" hit the dust bin with a "bongggngng" just as he raced behind it for protection. Then the sidewalk behind him exploded in a spray of rapid "Puff, puff, puff, puff, puff, puff" and he looked all around him for cover. He knew that if he raced ahead to turn the corner then he would be sprayed with bullets and he would be very dead.

The car screeched to a stop and three armed men from the back seat and one from the front seat sprang out and ran two to the front and two to the back of the dust bin to surround him.

But Dipak Halder was nowhere to be seen! He had vanished!

They rushed back to park below his hotel, "Xié'è de chéngshì, Xié'è de chéngshì, this is Zhū one, over!"

"Xié'è de chéngshì to Zhū one, has the hunting been a success? Over."

"Negative Xié'è de chéngshì! The Indian Shīzi (lion) is as always, smarter than us! He has run into the jungle. Over!"

"You, stupid, ertóng of a Zhu! Either he dies or you die! Now listen to me carefully. Do not come back until you finish the job you, ertóng of a Lǘ! Have I made myself clear?"

"Loud and clear Sir! Over" and the line of the senior sniper went dead.

Dipak Halder was stopped by the security guard at the entrance gate of the hotel. The Hotel senior security personnel arrived to speak with him when he showed his room keys and identity card, "You may be our guest Sir but we cannot allow you to enter the lobby in this, well, uncomfortable attire. Permit us to guide you towards a path that would be most suitable for all of us. Please", the Chief of Security showed the way towards the back entrance from where the raw material for the kitchen entered.

Dipak was escorted to his room, the Chief of Security stood personally by the main door to ask, "Once again sir! You say you fell into an open manhole? In Nair Dvipa? Sir, our municipality does not keep open manholes. But we rang them up and they requested us to apologise to you on their behalf".

Dipak washed away the sewer waste that he had waded through after he had opened the manhole cover, shut it promptly back above him and jumped into the waste to escape the killers. When he popped out of the manhole in front of his hotel, he looked like a black ghost. Most importantly, the smell was so nauseating that people moved far away.

After he had cleaned up, he opened the main door to his room and found a security man who handed him a letter, "We apologise for not having recognised you Sir! We would love to have the pleasure of your company for breakfast in the General Manager's suite. We await an acknowledgement. Daisy Gruper, Client Relations Manager".

Dipak nodded in the affirmative, wrote on the letter, "Invitation accepted!", signed his name and handed over the same to the security personnel.

Within fifteen minutes there was a call on his intercom, "Sir two of our hostesses are outside your door right now to guide you towards the General Manager's suite for breakfast".

Dipak peeped through the 'security eye' and saw two women. He looked left and right but found no one else. He checked the position of the gun tucked into his waist belt and covered it with his grey suit.

Dipak walked along with his two pretty hostesses to the GM's suite. They knocked on the door twice, waited for a second and the door was opened by Ms. Madhu Panduwala, the GM of the property.

"Please come in Mr. Dipak Halder, this way please!" she requested and guided him towards a sofa.

"Would you like tea or would you prefer coffee with your breakfast Mr. Halder?"

"Coffee with milk and five sachets of sugar please", Dipak requested.

A buffet was placed on the long table. Bread slices, Bun slices, bun whole, round buns, sweet buns, jam, jelly, butter, cheese solid, cheese spread, mayonnaise spread, bacon, salami, ham, sausage, fried chicken with chicken broth, roasted mutton pieces with liver sauce, roasted partridge, roasted duck with white sauce, fried potatoes, fried onion leaf, soft boiled onions with salt & pepper, raw beetroot, raw salted sprouts, milk, corn flakes etc

While Dipak munched away on the delicacies, Ms. Madhu Panduwala pecked at a few morsels that she had placed on her plate. "Mr. Haldar we received a call from the Indian High Commission that you were a special guest of Nair Dvipa, that you are an advisor on Human Resources and motivation. We had received a copy of the video from the local municipality wherein you were seen running from a hail of bullets being fired by a group of foreign nationals. We have passed on the same to the Indian High Commission as well as the Nair Dvipa senior police authorities. They shall be here any moment. Ah they are here already!" So saying, she rose to receive two T-shird, plus Bermuda shorts clad individuals.

"Good morning Mr. Halder! My name is Venkataramana Subramanium", said the man who shook his hands first. "We hope you are comfortable? We work with the Nair Dvipa Police. We apologize for the attack on your person and we wondered if you could help us understand why these foreigners would want to attack an advisor on Human Resources and motivation?"

Dipak had his mouth full of fish fillet in his mouth. Even while munching he replied, "Mistaken identity obviously! I am a tourist even though I had an appointment at two local colleges to give a talk on 'How to improve one's career options' last evening and the evening before that", replied Dipak and smiled.

"My name is Naveen Siddharth of the Nair Dvipa Police Intelligence department", spoke up a gentleman who was sitting very quietly in a corner. "We do appreciate Mr. Halder, that the Indian Embassy has conveyed to us that you are a valuable guest. But we are going through a political turmoil and have to handle so many problems.

The foreigners who attacked you were professionals, armed with the latest silencer attached, automatic pistols which we have found are too expensive to import. They are so well planned that they hardly ever make a mistake in identity. I hope what happened this morning would not be adding to our existing problems? We do not wish to be harassed, you would understand."

"This is very disturbing", intervened a dark suited gentleman who had just walked in wearing a grey hanky neatly tucked into his left suit pocket. "My name is Daljit Singh Siddhu, and I am the First Secretary in the High Commission of India in Nair Dvipa. A citizen of India, a friendly country, gets attacked and you begin your sentence suggesting that the added challenge is a harassment?!"

Both the Nair Dvipa Police Officers got up on their feet to salute the First Secretary.

Ms. Madhu Panduwala, the GM of this property, walked up to the First Secretary to shake his hand and introduce herself. Then she offered him to join them for breakfast and he graciously accepted.

But before he was seated, he suggested, "Ms. Panduwala, I take your permission to request Mr. Siddharth and Mr. Subramanium to join us"

"Yes, ofcourse Sir!" Ms. Panduwala smiled and said. Then looking at Mr. Siddharth and Mr. Subramanium she gestured towards the buffet and requested, "Please join us!"

The new group had a quick breakfast and nothing official was discussed barring how the political situation had become super tense.

The moment they had finished and got up to request permission to leave, Daljit Singh Siddhu requested them, "Mr. Siddharth and Mr. Subramanium, kindly ensure that you identify the attempted killers and put them behind bars at the earliest. We want no harm to come to our countrymen".

Just then there was a huge explosion that shook the hotel. Mr. Siddharth and Mr. Subramanium rushed out to investigate and a little while later, screams, wails and moaning of people in pain could be heard. One of the security personnel rushed to inform the GM that people were rushing to help on the 5th floor. Soon hotel security personnel and the local police rushed in and barricaded the floor and the area around the hotel.

Just then gunmen barged into the GMs room and fired indiscriminately in every direction with semi-automatic rifles but there was no one in the room. They searched desperately all around the room, throwing aside sofa sets behind which people may be hiding, they rushed behind tables, and cabinets and book shelves, but found nobody. They rushed out in frustration firing in the air to clear their path to a waiting car on the main road.

They did not know that when the explosion happened, and the security guard rushed in to inform the GM that the 5th floor had been targeted, the GM promptly beckoned her two remaining guests towards a white wall with a painting hanging on it. The moment she pressed down the horn of a deer mounted on the wall, a part of the wall slid aside. She escorted them through a door that was right in front and shut it behind her. The wall with the painting, now behind them, slid back into its original position. Then she escorted them through an airconditioned passage not normally used, to a room with a one-foot thick steel door which opened into an airconditioned five roomed suite with no windows. It was obviously a safehouse fully equipped with a large fridge, an amphitheater with a full wall size television screen, movie hall type slanting floor with slanting chairs, battery backup for five days of power.

The Intercom kept informing the GM about developments while the two VIPs went into a closed cabin for confidential discussions.

It had exploded in room number 505 where Dipak had checked in! A time bomb had caused the explosion and the professionals had left no fingerprints, the security forensic team discovered. It was timed for when Dipak normally entered his room for the past seven days after his jog. Video logs were being checked. Two separate threat calls had come in from untraceable numbers warning them not to accept the commands coming from the office of the King and that the present Government that reported to Diànlì ji'è de guójia continued to be in power inspite of the King's broadcast, Supreme Court' judgement and finally the Prime Minister's declaration.

First Secretary Daljit Singh Siddhu looked at Dipak Halder and explained, "Obviously there are leaks otherwise your visit would have remained a secret".

"We have a job to do" added Dipak. "I find that their operatives are deeply entrenched! The Press in Nair Dvipa is infested by their cadre as in many other countries. My assessment is that, to remove the Pro Diànlì ji'è de guójia forces entrenched into the Media, the Police, the Courts, the Supreme Court of Nair Dvipa is a very long process! However, what we can guide the King to do is to make a louder noise and drown the Pro Diànlì ji'è de guójia media noise to whatever extant possible. The King has sent a message to his father, an Indian citizen asking for military support during this war. He is an ex- Prince of Nair Dvipa and hence is on an Indian Warship to Nair Dvipa that is being escorted by other ships, but they are all on a "NO COMMUNICATIONS" zone. They have to remain silent considering the secrecy".

"I feel India may have to send superior fire power than what has been requested on short notice by the King's father", suggested Daljit. This war will be huge! Our department feels that other countries may pitch in due to their commercial interests involved. Nair Dvipa has discovered Gold Mines, Copper Mines, Coal Cum Diamond Mines, each of the Ports are potential wealth earners. Certain foreign powers may wait for Nair Dvipa to be defeated by Diànlì ji'è de guójia and then they would move in with their ships and fire power, not to protect Nair Dvipa but to occupy such commercially viable states within Nair Dvipa and claim these lands as their extended territories! It is in India's interests to keep Nair Dvipa intact because of the historical links!"

"That is absolutely correct!" intervened Dipak. "We must keep the sharks, wolves and vultures away from Nair Dvipa. I shall submit my assessment. I am booking my return ticket for tonight".

That evening saw the Nair Dvipa forces pushing the Diànlì ji'è de guójia forces in nearly every state into tight corners. Skirmishes grew to become an all-out war between the Nair Dvipa Army and the invasion force of Diànlì ji'è de guójia forces. Diànlì ji'è de guójia forces had been reduced to pockets of resistance. They were using anti-aircraft guns, missiles, grenade launchers, night movement sensor automated guns, night glasses, rapid fire two hundred rounds magazine goozie rifles and more. What was important was that Diànlì ji'è de guójia secret services and trained operatives were everywhere and they were like pin pricks.

Dipak flew back that evening.

Ambassador Kidnaps the Press

The situation was tense for Diànlì ji'è de guójia in Nair Dvipa. They had everything going good for them but then suddenly, they were fighting with their backs against the wall. The Press was a pain.

The local Diànlì ji'è de guójia operatives who had come in on the pretext of being refugees, had spread out and dug deep into Nair Dvipa. They were instructed to locate Lalithambika Vasudevan, ex-Editor, 'Satya', Manjula, the ex-senior reporter of 'Yathart'tha Vartta', and finally Nindiya ex employee of Vēgattiluḷḷa Vārtta, the TV cum online Media cum News Print Media giant. The three were a very important reason for the people of Nair Dvipa to have revolted in this manner.

Nindiya was found shopping for a dress inspite of a strict warning that she must not venture out during the duration of this silent war that Diànlì ji'è de guójia had declared on Nair Dvipa.

Her articles released in various media, after her being saved by the King, repeatedly spoke about sacrificing one's future for a noble cause, that of saving the nation from proxy control. She urged Nair Dvipa towards taking strong decisions during this specific period without fear of commercially hurt Diànlì ji'è de guójia instigating Human Rights related punitive action.

"Diànlì ji'è de guójia being cowards, they would initially resort to a missile warfare and heaps of guile. The days of hand to hand combat are gone!" warned Nindiya. "They would first use the paid media to weaken our police and army by making you fight your own people within Nair Dvipa. They have been sponsoring the instigation of inter religion and inter caste warfare where there were none. When the police or the defense services used force, the paid press screamed "murder of human rights" and both the police as well as the defense forces were demotivated. Therefore, when the war begins, they shall use their control over our media, the Police, the High Courts, and the Supreme Court to tie our hands down and stifle our every move made to protect our own nation", warned Nindiya.

"The only solution therefore is to press the 'restart button' after shutting the window to the world. Let the Nair Dvipa system clean up the mess within the country while the world remains unaware about what is happening after Nair Dvipa has pressed the 'restart button'. When Nair Dvipa's screen comes on again, then the world would see a peaceful country once again, because the deep-rooted evil has been uprooted, chopped into pieces, burnt to ash and washed down the dirty drain! True that the money minded countries that had sponsored and thus invested in inter religion or caste warfare within Nair Dvipa, salivating while thinking about huge volume business gains in future, would want to stop the immediate loss of their mountain sized investments and would thus plan revenge. They would get the Human Rights Sword to dangle above Nair Dvipa from then on, but who cares, the job has been done!" finished Nindiya with relish.

Nindiya's articles had infuriated Diànlì ji'è de guójia because these were exactly their planned strategy and they were being exposed by her articles. Her words scared them because her words were instigating the honest Pro Nair Dvipa press and through the honest press the vast majority of Nair Dvipa, helping the police and Nair Dvipa Government Servants, Nair Dvipa Courts to build up courage and with Diànlì ji'è de guójia's backs already against the wall, this was not to be allowed any further.

Nindiya saw some strangers following her, and recollecting the days of her horror, she quickened her pace and yet they followed. She panicked and began to run through the crowds on the streets, screaming. But having raced through lanes and by lanes, when she realized that nobody had the courage to save her, she hid in crevices between two buildings to take in a few precious breaths. Then realizing that they had seen her again, she ran and they ran after her. She rushed into a clothing shop thinking a dress change would stop them. She pushed aside the owner, grabbed a new dress and ran out through the back door to be now chased by the clothing shop owner too! She dropped currency notes on the street as she ran for the owner to be paid but, street urchins were diving down to make a grab at them thus fighting with the owner for the same notes. She found a bus and boarded the same but they had seen her and began to chase the bus. She paid the bus driver a sum for the full day and he raced the bus without stopping till the Buddha point. She rushed out and ran towards a restaurant at the feet of a forty feet high pure brass Buddha idol. She entered and sat down to have a quick coffee in a dark cabin with a tinted window facing the streets.

A Buddhist monk entered the restaurant just then and without looking left or right headed straight for her chair in the cabin. He carried a tray made from pure wood and on that tray was a prayer bead made of exactly 108 small seed prayer beads.

"Excuse Me Miss?" his asked with a gentle smile.

She smiled back with an expression that asked, "How may I help you?" She then realized that he had this amazing radiance all around his face.

"You have a long and perilous journey my sister", he said very calmly. "Destiny has brought you here today. The Monk superior has sent this prayer bead specially for you! It will keep you safe from the hands of evil. Please wear it from now onwards".

She did not know why but she stood up, bowed and accepted the Buddha Pearls with great reverence and put it on, without looking up. To put it on she had to bend her head down as initially, it seemed heavy. Then when she looked up, he was gone! She looked at the exit door but nobody could have run all the way to the door within a split second! Did she imagine him? But the beads around her neck were genuine! The Buddhist chime bells that hung from the exit door were swinging wildly as if there was great wind. But there was no wind outside!

She looked out of her window. There was danger outside! The stupid bus driver was still standing there with the passengers screaming away at him. Why was he so stupid? Why does he not just drive away? Two black cars screeched to a stop in front of the bus, and the dark suited individuals began to beat up the driver, forcing him to give them the direction that she had taken. When they moved away, his face was a bloody mess but his fingers were still pointing at this restaurant. She did not know what to do.

The black suited gentlemen ran in all directions to surround the restaurant. Then they rushed in with guns drawn but the restaurant was empty barring the waiters wearing saffron coloured uniforms. The suited gentlemen rushed all around the restaurant, from cabin to cubicle, under the tables, behind shelves, in the toilets, they roughed up and threatened the waiters, they opened the back door but their man was still standing there just in case she had tried to exit from behind. They lined up the waiters once again but nobody knew where she had gone. "She had not paid the bill!" they explained.

Angry and frustrated, they left the restaurant, boarded the black vehicles and roared away while reporting on the walkie talkie, "Black Pepper has popped the Pepper Bags. Over!"

After around one hour, when the new lot of guests had come in and gone and when the waiters were discussing in whispers about her sudden disappearance, Nindiya looked down from the hatch in the canopy that covered each cubicle for four. She saw nobody and climbed down gently onto the table and brushed away all the cobwebs that had stuck to her clothes and body. She climbed down to the chair from the table and then to the soft carpeted floor where she sat down on the chair and put on her sports shoes. She walked up to the cashier who was gaping at her with one finger pointing at her, wanting to say something but no sound coming out. She pointed at the menu hanging on the wall, paid for the coffee plus a big tip and walked out. The cashier continued to gape and point at her.

She hailed a taxi and instead of going back to her destination she decided, in case she is followed, it would be best to stay in any hotel for one night.

She checked in at Le Grande Wasabe Hotel, very expensive but the security was tough and had an eye for minor security related detail. She told the reception that she may have been followed and that the security must please be on extra vigil. The GM Mr. Waseem Mallik came over personally to assure her that she was safe.

Within one hour there was a huge commotion on the 1ˢᵗ floor. She had ordered dinner but she was not responding to the door bells. The GM rushed to her door and opened the same with a duplicate key to her room. Her room looked like a tornado had hit it. The window was open and she was missing!

The Legal Press screamed, "Attention seeking, loose character, pseudo media personnel Nindiya vanishes from hotel. Stages her own kidnapping!"

The Pro Royal, pro Nair Dvipa secret online Media roared, "It is high time for all of us to press the 'Restart button' just as Nindiya has been advising us to do for so long. It is high time for us to uproot the brain washed and paid satraps of Diànlì ji'è de guójia in the Media, the Police, the Courts and from within the Government for ever. Press the 'Restart Button' is henceforth our motto! Press the 'Restart Button'!"

Nindiya's disappearance hit emotional Lalithambika Vasudevan very badly. The three of them, including Manjula, had become very close, like three sisters. Her pain flowed like blood in her writeup that followed.

"Mothers of Nair Dvipa will not rest until their daughter is found. Sisters of Nair Dvipa will not rest before the guilty is punished! Brothers of Nair Dvipa are enraged soldiers and they will not rest until Diànlì ji'è de guójia leaves our land!

The little children of Nair Dvipa have learned to mistrust hence detest the face of every Diànlì ji'è de guójia citizen like they have never been detested before. Diànlì ji'è de guójia has declared war on the innocent citizens of Nair Dvipa. They have tried to divide us based on religion and caste. They have tried to force extremists of a foreign religion on our soil under the garb of "human rights". We shall not be divided! We shall not allow extremists on our soil. Let us, citizens of Nair Dvipa teach them the meaning of war! No religion, no caste, but united war! We shall not rest until Nair Dvipa is free of every cloth, every pencil, every breath that was forced upon us by a Diànlì ji'è de guójia citizen. We shall manufacture all that right here, in Nair Dvipa! We shall press the 'Restart Button' from today brothers and sisters! From today!", she roared.

Nair Dvipa read the writeup and roared that day as one! And 'Restart Button' posters appeared at every corner. A few days back, the Nair Dvipa army was thrown back when they attacked three Diànlì ji'è de guójia installations because of their heavy-duty machine-gun fire and because the Nair Dvipa Defense equipment, including aircraft casualties were very high. Missiles fired into the installations never landed because of the anti-missile installations.

But the anger of the citizens drew large crowds who attacked with long battering rams held up by around sixty people and rammed into the steel gate, "whammm!". "Press the 'Restart Button'!" they roared. Then the second group of sixty moved into position, they roared "Press the 'Restart Button'!" then rushed forward as one to whammm the steel gate. And the "whammm!" continued as wave after wave of groups of sixty kept moved into position to roar "Press the 'Restart Button'!"

Then the numbers increased even further and the gates seemed to buckle a little and then gave way. That is when the Diànlì ji'è de guójia forces began to fire on the civilians and the international media began to click. But as one collapsed yet another replaced him and the waves of enraged human ocean roared "Press the 'Restart Button'!" to whamm the gate again! The gate gave way finally and sixty people with a huge battering ram rushed forward inside the premises. But the occupying forces were waiting for them at the other end. The gun fire killed many but the breach was achieved. Then the next wave of battering ram entered the enclosed premises and whammed into the gunners. "Press the 'Restart Button'!" they roared. Then the next lot carrying their battering ram rushed into the premises and turned right to wham into machine gunners hiding inside a fox hole. The machine gunners let out a hail of bullets that laid the first lot of civilians down. But the gunners were soon whammed down to submission by people who immediately replaced the dead and then the army entered to destroy the defense installations including the heavy guns and rapid-fire machine guns with four boxes full of chain bullets.

The Nair Dvipa Defense forces rushed into the barracks and the armory and captured Diànlì ji'è de guójia personnel as well as defense equipment.

The first Diànlì ji'è de guójia defense establishment was down.

Victory was theirs! Nair Dvipa citizens joined hands with the Defense forces to roar as one "Press the 'Restart Button'!"

As word spread, volunteers rushed to various Diànlì ji'è de guójia establishments to assist the Nair Dvipa Defense forces to attack and capture each and every one of Diànlì ji'è de guójia bases.

People rushed in to carry the wounded away to the makeshift medical center in a tent that had been pitched up on short notice by the defense forces. Private doctors joined the Defense Doctors to provide free medical aid and medicines.

Ambulance services rushed in one after the other with their "Pluu Plaa!" sirens and then rushed away to various hospitals all around. Each of the ambulance services had the placard fixed to their body, "Press the 'Restart Button'!"

Many Nair Dvipa citizens had to be hospitalized including senior Pro Nair Dvipa intellectuals and media personnel who had been part of the battering ram team.

The news spread like wild fire much before the media could report the news and the rest of the Diànlì ji'è de guójia army installations put extra personnel on guard duty. Huge crowds of Nair Dvipa civilians joined hands with the Nair Dvipa army and bayed for the blood of Diànlì ji'è de guójia outside the gates of each installation.

The open war had begun!

The Hospital Incident

Lalithambika Vasudevan was visiting a patient in a hospital from yesterday's casualties, and she was told that the patient's room number was 201 whereas it was 203. She opened the door of 201 saw somebody else, apologized and closed the door behind her. She stopped in her tracks while proceeding towards room number 203 because she thought she recognized the bearded old man lying in the Air-Conditioned bed of that special high security room.

The security guard had returned from the toilet and was initially refusing to allow her inside and relented only after she flashed her Media Card. She entered and exclaimed "You! Hiding like the coward that you are!"

"I think you are mistaking me for somebody else my dear lady!" the middle-aged bearded man smiled and remarked gently.

"Don't you dare 'My Dear' me! One cannot forget the face of the representative of the occupying force Ambassador Jiǎohuá hé xié'è! We have heard that you have tried to negotiate with certain powerful cash rich foreign powers requesting them to keep quiet while you defeat us with your defense forces that are on the way, hand in hand with your control over our media, our police, our courts and the vote guarantors staying within our country. You want to cut a deal with these powerful foreign powers regards our Oil extraction wells, Gold Mines, Copper Mines, Coal Cum Diamond Mines, and the fact that each of the Ports are potential wealth earners. You want to cut up Nair Dvipa into so many bits and pieces so that every powerful foreign power grabs a big Nair Dvipa state, and is happy along with you. Your anti Nair Dvipa plans are out in the open you vile Ambassador!

Well, Nair Dvipa will not allow you to win. Nair Dvipa will not allow foreign powers to partner you into cutting us up into bits and pieces.

Our citizens have joined hands with Nair Dvipa Defense forces in routing your army and throwing them out of Nair Dvipa. They were searching for you too! So, you felt hiding away in an air-conditioned hospital is the safest haven for you?! You cowardly Diànlì ji'è de guójia rat!", smirked Lalithambika Vasudevan. "Wearing a beard and moustache does not make any difference to an editor who was once an investigative reporter! I can smell a rat from many miles away!"

The last statement made the huge Ambassador jump out of his bed. He pulled away his beard and moustache and threw them down on the floor. The ambassador was now snarling like a cornered fox and he was seething with anger. The bulky ambassador approached Lalithambika slowly like a huge wolf stalks a sacrificial lamb.

"Ours is a country of lions and we shall soon rule first over Nair Dvipa and then very soon over the world! You had a great chance to be an important part of our global empire! Why are you destroying our effort to rule the world?" Why are you destroying your own chances in the new order? You were doing well, you could have become our valuable lion's tail!"

Instead of replying the Press woman asked "What have you done with Nindiya of 'Vēgattiluḷa Vārtta' you Diànlì ji'è de guójia stooge!?"

Her tone hit him deep inside and he lost his cool, grabbed her by her throat and lifted her up until her feet were dangling below.

"We left her in a room of fifteen men who have not had a woman for many months!" snarled Ambassador Jiǎohuá hé xié'è. "Then, when they are fulfilled and zip up their pants, they shall sell her off at a huge discount in the Vice Den for women! Anything else you wish to ask?"

Lalithambika was finding it difficult to breathe and just when her eyes became all cloudy one of the nurses opened the door and came in with a glass of lemon juice. She gasped, put her hands to her lips in fear and backed away to the wall. The glass in her hands fell to the floor along with the steel serving tray. The clanging sound made the security rush inside. The Ambassador threw Lalithambika to the floor and growled, "I am a servant of Diànlì ji'è de guójia, but not a stooge! And we shall prevail over Nair Dvipa! We are lions and you could have been the lion's tail but you are a fool!"

While he was thus speaking, she had drawn in precious breaths of air and this gave her the opportunity to needle him further. Pointed her finger at Ambassador Jiǎohuá hé xié'è she gasped " We are proud citizens of Nair Dvipa, and we would prefer being a cat's head rather than a lion's tail! Your diplomatic immunity is hereby cancelled Ambassador Jiǎohuá hé xié'è! Run away! Because if the Nair Dvipa citizens get hold of you then they will skin you alive and then hang you up for all the world to see how we treat the Diànlì ji'è de guójia stooges!

And she staggered out due to her difficulty in breathing. After a gap of thirty-five minutes, the mobs rushed into his room. But the bird men had obviously taken him away because he was not in the room. The window curtains fluttered outside the open window.

Sudhir could sense her discomfort from far away but he realized that she was safe and could handle herself. But Mobi had vanished and panic-stricken villagers searched alongwith city police personnel to no avail! And along with Mobi, nineteen other well trained teenaged warriors had also vanished! Sudhir searched for Mobi using his mind energy and saw him surrounded by Mogui's trained soldiers. He could sense severe danger to the life of Mobi and the teenaged warriors!

The lives of both Mobi and Ngia Vat were now in danger.

Little Mobi Attacks Mogui

Little Mobi and his team of teenagers had travelled away from the city towards the palace in the night to avoid being detected and reached the palace ground towards the mid night.

Interestingly, the magical energy that barred city dwellers and strangers from entry, did not bar a single villager from entering the protected area.

Mobi and the teenaged warriors had trained hard under the guidance of the great three spirits. The warriors, Adisa, Chaka, Mogutu, Olatunde, Fatou, Mathembu, Kimaryo, Hodan, Mawuli, Mwamba, Obataiye, Uchechi, Chiamaka, Makalo, Uwimana (female), Obioma (female), Munirah (female), Jabari (female), Dembe (female), a group of nineteen highly motivated teenagers led by a teeny weeny Mobi.

They had climbed the security walls without touching the trip wires and climbed onto the branches of the trees that grew along the boundary wall. Then they climbed down the tree, travelled through the high grass and shrubs until the pure golden palace shown majestically in the moon light in the distance beyond the green lawns and the flower plants. Then before the moon began to set, they raced over the green lawns, lay bamboo poles over the moat filled with brackish water, crossed the same, and shimmied up the rain water pipes that brought rain water down from the path above where the guard paced up and down to ensure security.

They knocked down the three guards unconscious and dragged them to a room behind the door that led to the stairs. The fourth too was dragged to the store room and asked where were the prisoners, especially the queen. After soliciting the information, having knocked him unconscious, this trained but overconfident team got their boom boom sticks ready and attacked the trained security personnel now under the mind control of powerful Mogui. "Rat tat a tat! Rat tat tat a tat a tat!" the total team fired valuable bullets into one or two guards, leaving few more bullets in the chamber.

Security guards appeared from every direction, yet, Mobi and his team kept firing and progressing forward towards the bedroom number twenty-four and twenty-five as revealed by the security guard now locked away in the store room. Then suddenly, when they were but a few yards away, their bodies became stiff as if some super force was wrapping itself around each of them. Their guns began to fly out of their hands and a powerful force pushed them down to the ground.

Bowlegged Birdmen began to appear all around them.

That was when Mogui appeared above them.

Mogui flew out of a window and hovered above them, "Phtew!" he spat on his side. "Now they disrespect my powers by sending children to fight me!"

Sudhir could sense these words and a strange pain hit him in his heart!

Mogui Fights Back

The open central courtyard at the back of the palace after one entered through the back gates, was large enough to hold a big football stadium.

Trained blood hungry Dobermans, German Shepherds, Pit Bulls, and Rottweilers, were growling and barking at little Mobi who was tied down to the wooden plank that had a gilotine blade fixed on the top. "This would be the first execution after a gap of many years", Mogui's evil assistants had boasted.

The nineteen teenagers were standing proudly erect next to nineteen long poles with their hands tied tight behind their back to the same pole.

Mobi's head was to be chopped off and the rest were to be shot dead!

The Palace workers were a big crowd of around three hundred odd pro Royal people and they were made to stand and watch to instill fear into their hearts.

"He shall die because he is the leader of those that have challenged the law of this land. You have attacked the Palace, which is the property of a country being run by an elected Government. You all shall be executed for treason and sedition!" read out one of the Diànlì ji'è de guójia soldiers now protecting the palace.

Muscled Diànlì ji'è de guójia soldiers were having a tough time holding back two hungry black panthers now in two separate cages. One of the cages opened in front of the teenaged village warriors but the chains in the hands of the muscled soldiers held the panther back. It kept roaring and trying to tear away the shackles around its neck, just to pounce at Mobi and have a much-desired meal. It looked left and right and pounced at the guards that held his chains in their hands. But the cage came in between them every time.

A senior Diànlì ji'è de guójia officer appeared on the open veranda that surrounded the central courtyard. He raised a yellow hanky. The moment he would let go, the ferocious black panther would be released. And the nineteen teenaged village warriors would be shot dead by Diànlì ji'è de guójia soldiers.

The crowed of Pro Nair Dvipa, Pro Royal workers moaned and the sound travelled to the forests that surrounded the golden palace. Then Nksi Nanga came down to the courtyard, asked one of the soldiers to step aside and when he delayed, slapped some of the Diànlì ji'è de guójia soldiers. He was a big man and his slap sent the air out of their lungs and they winced in pain. The Palace workers and the other village warriors roared in laughter.

Nksi Nanga looked up at the senior Diànlì ji'è de guójia officer and ordered, "Release the cloth piece!" But the senior Diànlì ji'è de guójia officer was not in a mood to listen to a half-naked tribal. He kept holding onto the hanky. Suddenly, somebody chopped away his hand that held the hanky and both the hand as well as the hanky began to fall towards the courtyard even while the Diànlì ji'è de guójia officer screamed out in pain, looking desperately in every direction to protect himself from his tormentor. But Mogui did not permit him that luxury. For having refused to heed the command of his only grandchild, he picked up his body and threw him down in front of the panther! The panther pounced on the official and even while he kept screaming in pain and panic, the panther tore him apart, roaring and growling!

Mogui appeared in person, floating above the crowd, "My grandson will soon be crowned the King!" he roared while Nksi Nanga beamed in happiness. Everything in this Palace, the treasures of this Palace, the Treasures of Nair Dvipa and the seas around Nair Dvipa will belong to my grandson! All citizens and guests of Nair Dvipa must get into the habit of saluting him and heeding his every command! All who challenge his might shall be punished just as I punished this Diànlì ji'è de guójia ant and I shall now punish these villagers and the punk who leads them." Mogui did not notice that the other senior Diànlì ji'è de guójia officers were glaring at him.

Mogui now looked at his grandson Nksi Nanga with adoring eyes and cooed, "Go and get that village woman you want as your concubine into this courtyard my son. Consume her in this open forum. Let all see how we destroy those who dare to resist us!"

Sudhir received a mind call and heard a scream – Ngia Vat's scream!

Then Mogui spoke into his mind, "You fool! Did you hear that woman of yours scream in pain? My men just branded her with the letter "M" on her buttocks with a searing hot iron. My men have been enjoying the lusciousness of her female security guards one after the other. Your wife is being saved as the special treat – the sweet dish for my grandson. Now he has gone upstairs to bring her down to the open courtyard to consume her in front of all Palace workers and the baby warriors that you sent to fight me!

Ahh! I can feel your anger and frustration! I am loving it but, you deserved this!

That was very very unwise, making such a dreadfully thoughtless declaration of independence from my country when your wife's life is in danger? My grandson was explaining to your wife that you care more about remaining King than you care for her life! And my grandson ran his hands all over her body and told her that he would care for her body more than you do. I keep holding him back but ohh I see him aching to reach out and paw at her body every day! If you do not do as I command then my grandson is free to do with her as he pleases. I cannot stop him from stripping away whatever little that covers her body and seeding her with his future generation, I mean many little, little, little, little, Nksi Nangas".

Sudhir who normally spoke very little, was trying his best to remain within control as he spoke into Mogui's mind now, "How will you feed anybody to your grandson when he is under my protection now Mogui?"

"Ha ha ha ha!" laughed Mogui. "You are a child! That is the oldest bluff and will not work on me! He is with me right here, in the next room with three of your village female security personnel."

"Grandfather please save me!" Nksi Nanga's voice screamed into Mogui's mind.

"What?! How is this possible?! No! It cannot be! Nksi my grandson!" So saying, Mogui flew through the wall into the next room and found the three women lying unconscious, the window open but his grandson was not there! He rushed to look out of the window and saw in the distance a speck of dust going further and further away.

He leapt through the window into the skies at hyper speed. Never had he been so desperate. His grandson was all that remained of his blood line.

When he had returned as a pirate from Diànlì ji'è de guójia to Nair Dvipa he had brought with him pirate citizens from Diànlì ji'è de guójia and had created a small village on an island near Nair Dvipa. He had plans of flooding Nair Dvipa with pirates from his adopted country to take revenge on his uncles and cousins. He wanted to destroy Nair Dvipa and its Royal family for ever. There were around thirty pirate families, three of them of pure Diànlì ji'è de guójia royal blood. When he was imprisoned in the bottle, his daughter was just four years of age and his wife, a pure blood Princess of Diànlì ji'è de guójia, was on that small island near Nair Dvipa waiting for him to return. But he did not return and then when the major flood waters swept over the smaller island some years later, the waters roared into his village and took away his people, including his wife and daughter.

He came to know that his baby was on a raft of reeds that had survived the stormy weather along with his dehydrated wife when the raft drifted and touched the shores of Nair Dvipa. His wife had staggered with their little daughter through deep forests until she saw a cave. In that cave was a witch who rushed forward to scare them away but his wife gave up her life on seeing the first sign of a human being. Seeing that the mother did not breathe any more, the witch adopted the baby girl. But was she really a witch? She was good at collecting herbs from the deep forests as taught to her by Gods who flew in the skies and she became a powerful healer. She learned how to set fire to leaves by rubbing of two stones. She found sea water had salt and salt when dried added taste to the food. When she sprinkled the salt on the fire, it sizzled and crackled in protest. She wrapped the salt in bee wax with a lot of oil in the center from the dried milk of the forest four-legged Two Horned Deer then, it sparkled and burst into flames after the wick made of dry leaves travelled deep down.

So powerful were her medicines and experiments that the Chiefs of the various villages felt threatened by her position in society and hence had her banished from the village. The very same villages that were under the protection of the Kings of Nair Dvipa, these villages had failed to recognize her talent.

His little daughter grew up with and had learned 'witch craft' from her adopted mother. Then her adopted mother died suddenly and his baby was afraid and so lonely. She had just turned nineteen and she was muscular, strong an amazing athlete and adept at hunting. She walked up to the gates of the village but because she was yellow in complexion and because she was so much taller than many of them, they refused to allow her to be a part of them even though she dressed like them, hunted better than them and spoke their language!

Just to be close to them all, she built herself a hut outside, near the gates of the village. Nobody came forward to help his baby and she built her hut all alone. Just to win their hearts, his little baby hunted big animals all by herself and kept it near the gate of the village. Initially there was much resistance but then gradually her gift began to be accepted. This was especially so because the village boys and girls often went off to the forest to hunt and yet, very often, they came back dejected and empty handed.

Soon, she was seen teaching the boys & girls of the village how to hunt better, throw the spear better and how to patiently lie in waiting until the prey was so near that it could not get away. One day, one of them did not return with the group of boys who had gone hunting and the village elders blamed her and her witchcraft. So, his little girl went back into the forests all alone to search for that one boy and she found him high up on a tree wounded, surrounded by black leopards snarling and pawing at him. She beat the drums, blew the horn and made as much noise as possible with the bone anklets tied to her ankles. Finally, she threw the Two Horned Deer oil, encased in salted bee wax. It flew high up into the skies, burst into flames and exploded with a lot of fizz. The leopards leapt down from the high branches in fear and melted away into the deep forests.

His little baby girl had carried that boy into a cave and applied leaves from shrubs all around, to his wounds. She fed him with herbs to bring his fever down and boiled jungle bird in salt water to create a broth which she fed him in spoon fulls every half an hour. She cared for him for several days. When he was strong enough, he had refused to go back to the village, but she dragged him back to the village.

They were thrilled to see him alive and willingly gave her a corner to build a hut inside their village finally, as a reward. His baby girl did not complain while she built another hut all by herself. It was here that the village knew about her giving birth to a child nine months later and Nksi Nanga, who was as dark as all of them, grew up to become one of them. Nobody knew who was the father. His grandson, a royal family member, grew up to become a half-naked tribal villager while his cousins grew up cushioned in luxury, amongst the elite of the cities!

He had lost everybody in his family barring his grandson. And here was somebody flying away with the only living member of his family! He used all his power to zip through the skies at a blazing speed.

In the meanwhile, the Diànlì ji'è de guójia forces were very angry with Mogui for having thrown one of their senior officers in front of a panther.

In their anger they opened the other cage and released the other black panther from its cage. Hunger tearing away at its intestines, the panther charged at Mobi who was right ahead below the guillotine. Mobi was a still a child and he screamed the only name he remembered just then, "Mahiliiiiiiiiiii!"

The panther slammed into a full stop with shock written all over its face!

Then very cautiously, it smelled the air, then ever so gently, she took a cautious foot forward with one foot back just in case. Then she smelled Mobi and seemed to recollect old memories that seemed to be rushing into her mind as displayed by the cocking of her head to the left and to the right as she stared at Mobi. Then she took a final cautious step forward and smelled Mobi again and final confirmation became obvious from her action of jumping all over Mobi, licking his face, whining, crying, running in circles all around Mobi.

It was then that the Diànlì ji'è de guójia forces released the Dobermans, German Shepherds, Pit Bulls, and Rottweilers. They charged at the black panther! The other panther in the open cage door saw his friend was in trouble and tore away from the strong arms that held the steel chains around his strong neck through the bars of the cage, behind him. It dragged the chains tied to its neck and attacked the ferocious, trained dogs with jungle honed ferocity.

Both the male and female panther made short work of the killer dogs.

The Diànlì ji'è de guójia forces raised their guns to fire. A senior officer raised his hanky planning to drop it on the count of three. "Fire on my command! Ready! Aim!"

Just then the man who has raised his hand to give the signal to shoot, went down on his knees holding his head. He seemed to be suffering from a splitting headache. His face grimacing, he looked with tormented eyes at his Deputy, who began to raise his hands to give the command to shoot.

Right then the crowd looked up. There were around a hundred sparrows charging down at the shooters with their claws drawn. They struck first one shooter then the other and then the next. But the next lot of sparrows followed and the charge continued relentlessly.

Many confused Diànlì ji'è de guójia forces forces were standing on jeeps with guns drawn. The jeeps began to move on their own and turned 90 degrees on the right at high speed, thus throwing the soldiers out who were then dragged by local citizens into the unforgiving crowd of Pro Loyal workers.

The other soldiers were on the verge of drawing out their pistols but their own dogs began to behave mysteriously. The dogs, the Dobermans, German Shepherds, Pit Bulls, and Rottweilers that were barking at the crowd a little while back began to take on a glazed expression and charged at their own handlers, biting and sinking their teeth as close to the necks as possible. There was sudden pandemonium.

Other soldiers began to rush out of the fort and it was then that all trained soldiers disguised as the Palace workers shot out their arrows. It flew down like a carpet of needles and finished off the armed soldiers.

Sudhir's forces melted out of the crowd and charged at the disoriented Mogui forces like a flood that roared!

Four of the Diànlì ji'è de guójia forces had Mobi pinned down. Just then a light appeared in the skies and they fell and burst into flames.

The next lot of Diànlì ji'è de guójia soldiers rushed out guns blazing and many Nair Dvipa citizens fell dead.

But just then, the earth opened in front of them and molten lava could be seen and heard gurgling and spitting in anticipation of another offering for hell. The earth caved in below their feet and they vanished screaming and their scream could be heard from very far away even as they kept falling deeper and deeper.

Pro Royal forces rushed forward to help release Mobi and his team from the Guillotine and the poles, respectively.

Mobi thanked them, but instead of leaving through the exit gate, he and his team jumped the wall once again, walked into the dense jungle and then vanished.

But Where Was Mogui's Grandson

Sudhir was already inside the palace unknown to Mogui, and he searched all over, room after room for his wife and her body guards but they were nowhere to be found. But he found Mogui's grandson, in the toilet bath tub with three other hypnotised women. So Sudhir made a biologically twelve-hour life, degradable copy of Mogui's grandson and sent him out to chop off the hands of the foreign invaders. It was then that Mogui contacted Sudhir through mind messaging. Sudhir had no time and so he knocked Nksi Nanga unconscious while he was dipping in the bath tub looking at the girls from under the water. Sudhir then created a hologram of himself and Nksi Nanga and sent them flying away out of the window at high speed towards the distant horizon. He transformed himself into a wooden chair while Nksi Nanga remained invisible under the invisibility cloak. Mogui raced in just then, looked desperately all over the bedroom and the toilet. He looked out of the window, saw the holograms flying away into the horizon and raced out of the window after them.

When Mogui flew out of the palace towards the hologram of two distant individuals flying into the horizon, Nksi Nanga was unconscious and he was wearing an invisibility cloak as put on him by Mobi's adopted father. Sudhir went out and looked down from the veranda into the courtyard and but failed to locate Mobi and his fellow warriors.

He teleported Nksi Nanga, the three village security girls and himself to the old British port where Mogui's most trusted lieutenants was running the 'Fù guǎn' that is, Mogui's vice dens. The vice dens were named Dǐngjí fù zhǔxí, Dì èr gè dòngxué, Dì sān fù dòngxué, and finally the Gōngzhǔ diànxià. At the corner of the street was a hospital started by the last King for the treatment of the girls who were workers in the den and hence had taken ill. Next to the hospital was the Saint Margaret Church where people prayed for the unwell or for those who had died while working in the vice dens. Next to the Church was a large Hindu temple sponsored and built by the last King, followed by a mosque and then a grave yard for the Muslims and separately for the Christians. And next to the grave yard was the Sashan ghat or the cremation ground where Hindu bodies were burnt. Sudhir flew into the Temple, saw many steps to climb up the stairs. One stone had broken and fallen away. Sudhir looked at Nksi Nanga and turned him into a block of stone, inserted him into the position of the missing slab, gave him the ability to understand all languages and flew out to search for his wife. The three girls were placed in the care of the Church. They were given the robe of the nuns and were given due protection. He knew, as a stone in a temple, Nksi would not give off human body heat that can be detected by Mogui. This would make Mogui truly desperate and thus he would make mistakes.

Mogui had by then reached the holograms and found that they turned to dust the moment he touched them, and this fact enraged him further. He rushed back to find the girls gone, the teenaged prisoners to be shot were missing and his grandson was nowhere to be seen. "Aaaaaaarggghhh! Why do I get cheated like this every time? Why?"

Sudhir's hologram appeared in front of Mogui and both remained floating, facing each other, high up in the skies, between the clouds as they drifted by.

Mogui spoke into Sudhir's mind, "If you have the guts then stop attacking my family, let us fight each other, man to man".

"You killed one unarmed woman much weaker than yourself. To fight me, man to man, you used my ex-wife and you used trickery, that is, the black moon, to make me weaker so that you could win. Now you have kidnapped and hold captive my wife and her female & male bodyguards. Before the man to man fight, you may would want to save Nksi Nanga from being branded on his buttock with an 'S' within five minutes!" warned Sudhir

"No! No! Do not hurt my grandson! Please do not hurt my baby's only child. He is the only one left in my blood line!", Mogui pleaded genuinely.

"Does attacking helpless women help your bloodline? Let my wife and the warriors free Mogui!" demanded Sudhir

"What sort of a King are you, my dear dear grandson!" Mogui began to negotiate, "why would you ask for so many people being released in exchange for one person? You must try and be reasonable in your demands"

Sudhir then growled, "You do not feel that your only surviving grandson is worth many more numbers than just those you hold captive?

Listen to my final Offer Mogui. For every wound on my wife, or my people whom you hold captive, your grandson will be inflicted with ten serious wounds. For every torture or lack of comfort, I shall come to know and I shall give the command to my people to respond in ten to one proportion. Now here is what is desired from your end and this is non-negotiable! Deliver the Queen and her guards safe and sound at the temple of the ancient ones. You have two hours. You shall get your grandson after three days from then".

"Three days? Do you think I am a buffoon?!" screamed Mogui.

"You know that I am a man of my word. Three days is to ensure the safety and security of the people of Nair Dvipa. If you do not accept this offer then you may never see your only surviving progeny again! Do you desire that?" bluffed Sudhir in a mild fashion.

Mogui's face became pale. "My grandson is all that I have", he whispered. "I accept your offer", so saying, he vanished.

Mogui's Trickery

Magic on earth is lauded as a slew of a magician's hand. The magician can bring forth rabbit's, pigeons, ribbons, handkerchiefs, and much more from his hat. A magician can bring forward a curtain in front of a woman, lift the curtain and a different woman stands where the last one stood. All scientifically possible tricks.

But the Daivika planet citizens had been able to unlock various cells of their mind and were thus able to tap their minds to be able to do things that cannot be scientifically proved on earth even today.

Mogui landed near the temple at the old port and accompanying him were Ngia Vat and her security guards with their hands tied behind their back. Surrounding him were hundreds of birdmen.

"After I release the prisoners, these birdmen will stay with you for three days! If my grandson is not released on the expiry of three days then, you shall see asteroids crashing in the hundreds on Nair Dvipa", Mogui threatened Sudhir.

Sudhir nodded, staring into Mogui's eyes. There was distrust on both sides and people were ready for an attack.

Mogui's men cut the ropes behind each female warrior and they staggered into the arms of their fellow villagers, exhausted and horrified. Then Mogui cut away the ropes from behind Ngia Vat and Ngia Vat rushed into the arms of Sudhir, "I was so scared!" she whispered into Sudhir's ears.

Mogui looked at Sudhir, smiled benevolently and said, "Very touching! I have kept my part of the bargain. Now we shall wait for the expiry of three days!"

So saying, he turned to go away.

"Wait!" spoke up Sudhir with Ngia Vat clinging to his neck.

Mogui stopped in his tracks and turned around with a frown on his face.

"Your part of the bargain was to bring back my wife and her bodyguards and all the other warriors!" spoke Sudhir very gently. "One hour have now elapsed and sixty minutes remain".

"But how does that matter? You have got what you wanted", argued Mogui.

Sudhir snapped his fingers and Ngia vat and the soldiers began to melt – they were wax figures brought to life by Mogui!

"So what if they are wax images given life for one day?! You too created my grandson's duplicate that did not last for very long. You think I am a fool to handover your family without getting back my grandson"!? roared Mogui.

Instead of replying, Sudhir looked down from the skies towards a factory, "Brand him!"

"Noo no! Stop!" screamed Mogui in panic. Then looking down at the factory below, "He is there is he? In the factory below?"

"Stop! Do not brand him!" Sudhir looked down at the factory and gave his command.

Then looking at Mogui he ordered, "Now release all the people kidnapped by you if you love your one and only remaining blood line and do not want him to be hurt".

Mogui did not reply. Instead he rushed down at stupendous speed to the factory and began to zip search room by room.

Sudhir promptly told his mind, "Create my hologram and make me invisible".

Mogui's search was in vain. Nksi Nanga could not be found anywhere. In fact there was nobody in the obsolete factory. He felt like a fool again and he looked up at Sudhir with blood shot eyes. Before anybody could imagine the move, he let out a series of powerful fire balls towards Sudhir but they missed the target. Instead Mogui's fire balls hit the remaining wax figures of Ngia Vat and her fellow warriors and they exploded into dust. But Sudhir did not respond.

"Mogui think about your grandson before you do anything unwise", said the hologram of Sudhir. "Give back my family, not some people created by your mental power! And take back your real-life grandson, not a temporary biologically degradable copy! Fair deal?" reasoned Sudhir.

Mogui rushed up with a golden shaft in his hand and pointed it at Sudhir's hologram. The hologram promptly had an energy deflector and the bolt from Mogui's shaft hit the deflector and promptly brushed past Mogui after nipping his shoulder muscles hard. "Oof!" he exclaimed.

This enraged Mogui further and he began to hit out at the hologram, one swipe, then second swipe then third and many more. Each time the hologram used a shaft of his own to absorb the impact then, he hit out at Mogui one after the other. Mogui was on guard this time and he deflected each of Sudhir's bolts but he was shocked by Sudhir's speed and dexterity.

Respect made him change battle strategy. He feigned to rush up but sent his hologram up. As Sudhir's invisibility cloak went down and he looked up, Mogui rushed forward, grabbed Sudhir's arm and yelled, "To the 1700 AD!" and after a buzz like a short circuit and a pooff – they had both vanished! They had travelled back in time!

Sudhir and Mogui in the 1700 AD

"Now you shall die in the year 1700 AD. And your family would die with the pain that I have had to suffer on seeing my parents suffer and learning later how my wife, then daughter suffered!" growled Mogui while holding a dagger at Sudhir's throat.

Sudhir and Mogui had appeared on a Pirate ship with swords in the year 1700 AD. Sudhir was shocked because he was now wearing a strange attire. And his hands were in chains whereas Mogui's hands were free! Sudhir had recently travelled back to this time but it was obvious that Mogui was an old hand at time travelling! Mogui saw him gaping at his strange attire and quickly running his hand over it even while looking at his enemy.

"Haaah! Got you!" Mogui roared in evil mirth on seeing the obvious incredulous expression on Sudhir's face. "You have never travelled time! Your hands are in chains. Now I shall never allow you to get back". Then he looked at somebody behind Sudhir and requested, "Mogui my son, can you ensure that this pain in my back side does not follow me back?"

Sudhir immediately created ten Sudhir's in a flash, each dressed exactly as he was right now and each armed with a sword that he had never learned to use. And all of them were without chains! He left behind a hologram in chains in his position and teleported himself to the bow of the ship, then moved to the stern and finally the tower. The different Sudhir's were spread out all over the ship.

He saw Mogui was trying to create a time travel energy circle, by circling his two hands clock wise.

"Block Mogui's ability to link his desire with his mental abilities and hence mental power. Stop both Mogui's from creating any duplicates of themselves. Stop them from flying or travelling time. Stop them from creating any duplicates. Stop them from creating and throwing energy missiles or grenades. Stop them from entering my mind. Stop senior Mogui from becoming invisible or vanishing", Sudhir told his mind very quickly.

The senior Mogui kept desperately trying to create the energy circle but in vain. The energy that he managed to create now dissipated within seconds. Senior Mogui was shocked and had a foxed expression on his face! He had never met with this problem before.

Frustration began to build up to a point that it burst out in his battle charge at one of the true to life holograms of Sudhir. Sudhir's duplicate fought brilliantly with a sword against Mogui, a vastly experienced pirate cum swordsman.

The other Mogui was a younger version of the senior Mogui and seeing him jumping from one part of the ship to another it was obvious he possessed finesse at sword fighting but he knew no magic. An amazing high-speed sword fight ensued between Sudhir's duplicates and the junior Mogui and separately with the senior Mogui. Then various other pirates reporting to the junior Mogui were now spread out all over the ship attacking him.

The sword fight continued to the dining room, destroying cutlery, expensive cut glass, furniture got ripped up, paintings got destroyed, cabinets got sliced up, vases toppled over and broke and much more.

The senior Mogui kept trying desperately to fly back to his time but the desperation was obvious on his face. He got his palms together, began to move them round and round clockwise, formed a ball of energy but the moment he tried to throw it, the energy fizzled out. He was not just puzzled, he was afraid that return to his time was impossible and death was certain.

One of the Sudhir's began to swipe at senior Mogui's sword belt so that he cannot have a sword holder any longer. It worked, and senior Mogui's sword belt fell. But because it held up his trousers, his trousers too began to drop. Mogui senior jumped on to the deck and stretched out his hands to fly but try as much as he could, he could not fly! Now he was really scared. He kept grabbing at his sword belt to hold his trousers up with one hand and the sword with the other! And just then he saw one of the Sudhir duplicates approaching him with a long sword whereas all he had was a short sword.

In the meanwhile, the Sudhir duplicates were defeating each of his pirate mates at sword fighting. Fellow pirates were lying motionless all over the ship. Some intentionally pretending to be dead and opening one eye every two seconds to see if the coast was clear! Casualties were mounting up in a fight brought about by senior Mogui, but that which was taking a wrong turn. Mogui junior was finding it difficult to keep up with the energy and speed of the Sudhir duplicates fighting him.

Then it happened, around sixteen to twenty large battle ships each fixed with powerful cannons surrounded this ship.

"You cannot defeat us", Mogui junior whispered. "All of them will ensure they cut you to pieces" he said, pointing at pirate ships that were lined up one after another all around him. "My grandfather is the King pirate of these seas!"

Sudhir suddenly realized that the King Pirate that Mogui Junior spoke about was in fact Wugu, the Pirate King who had coaxed his daughter Sanya to entice an innocent poet cum singing prince of the Nair Dvipa royal family. And that at this moment, the pirates and privateers reporting to the King of pirates posted at innumerable ships, were waiting for an order to charge at Sudhir! There were at least sixteen to twenty large twenty cannon ships surrounding this ship. Countless number of pirates armed with swords cutlasses, small knives, small pistols and many more weapons, were hanging from the ropes, mast, standing on the parapet of the ship, ready to jump and fight.

What could he do now?

It was time to check if he could match Mogui's ability to create the shockingly large number of bird men that Mogui did. Could he create as many Sudhirs to fight the pirates?

"Create fifty Sudhirs per ship and give each Sudhir a different weapon, a different hairstyle, a different shirt and a different trouser", he instructed his mind. And whoomp! Six hundred and fifty to seven hundred Sudhirs appeared differently dressed, differently armed, with different hairstyles, and they spread out on every ship.

He had done it! He had equaled Mogui's feat!

Senior Mogui, now tied up fighting a Sudhir copy at the crow's nest, stared big eyed at all the Sudhirs. He had his mouth open in shocked realization that Sudhir had managed to match his mental power whereas, as it seemed now, he had lost his own.

Each Sudhir charged into the countless pirates that were so charged to fight him just a moment ago. But now, they were fighting a losing battle against a magician who could multiply himself manifold and was never getting tired of fighting so many pirates.

Strangely the pirates were dying and yet, increasing in number! How was this possible? Were they coming out of some below deck hideout? His mind scan showed no pirates, only guards protecting some women prisoners in barred cells.

The women will have to be rescued later, he made up his mind. But what was important now was, where were these fresh batches of pirates coming from?

Just then he saw an old man shaking his hands in a full circle and pulling out ten to fifteen pro Mogui pirates from some far away destination.

What could he do now? He decided to fight this endless supply of pirates, that old man had to be stopped! But the old man had huge protection! Therefore, Sudhir decided, it was important to have pirates fighting pirates.

Sudhir spoke to his mind, "Bring in Barbary pirates with their ships, pirates and privateers operating from the North African (the "Barbary coast") ports of Tunis, Tripoli, Algiers, Salé and ports in Morocco, who were preying on shipping in the western Mediterranean Sea. Bring in Spanish pirates, bring in British pirates, Gothic pirates, all with their battle-ready ships".

Around twelve large twelve to twenty cannon, battle ready, pirate ships suddenly appeared between the local pirate ships. For a while they stared at each other in astonishment. Then they glared at each other and jumped to the various battle-ready positions on their individual ships. The atmosphere was tense!

Finally, when each of the Sudhirs on each local pirate ship yelled, "Fire!", they fired at each other with vengeance.

Sudhir got just the results that he wanted. The various pirate groups were blowing each other up with their 16 to 18 pounders! Boom! Boom! Boom! Boom! Pow! Pow! Boom!

The ships then began to fire cannons at each other, shattering wood, sea waters rushed into the gaping holes and the damaged ships keeled over on any one direction. Pirates jumped into other ships to carry on the fight.

Their hand arms were lances, machettes (baleng kong), long poles with barbed iron points, bamboo grappling poles, bamboo knives, pikes with bamboo shafts from fourteen to eighteen feet long; these they were throwing at each other from a distance like javelins; they were also attacking each other with a shorter species of pike with shafts of solid wood, the iron part similar to the blade of a dirk, that is a prehistoric dagger for forward trusting and cutting left or right on a forward thrust. They shot out bamboo arrows from bamboo bows tipped with sharp bamboo knives. The dirk was slightly recurved and made sharp on one or both edges. They also used short swords scarcely exceeding eighteen inches in length. The local pirates were short, had no dress sense, smelled like they needed a bath desperately and they looked like they had gone hungry for several days. One or two had hand muskets and pistols, but this and gunpowder was reserved for the leaders of large divisions of desperate, unruly mobs of paid mercenaries, marauders and murderers.

They rushed down from ropes to other ships, they ran down the parapet of the enemy ships, then the swords rushed down on enemy swords, cutlasses, iron rods with "clank, clank, clank, clank, twang, twang, clank". Where opponents were taller or larger, the sea fighting honed desperate pirates began to jump then kick and thump their rock-solid sword handles on the heads of their opponents. They jumped to the liquor casks, then jumped on the captured cloth boxes piled over one another to make mini hillocks and then jumped down on unaware opponents.

But they fought the long sword wielders with a speed and dexterity that amazed the hardy British and Portuguese pirates.

They got down from the larger ships into smaller boats and then rowed upto the British or

Portugese pirate ships.

The decimation continued in equal measure amongst the pirates. When he found any one side losing then Sudhir would teleport a new lot of pirates from a totally different part of the world into the scene.

In the meanwhile, whenever the old man, who was churning out new pirates, was being attacked by opposing pirates, he simply vanished and re-appeared at a new spot on the ship. This shocked Sudhir. One of the Sudhir's had a glimpse of his face and he seemed familiar.

Sudhir promptly scanned for other women on any of the ships and found many prisoners, many female guards, but only one female leader.

Sudhir saw a middle-aged lady standing on the decks of a twelve-cannon pirate ship. He flew down and landed in front of the lady and bowed. The old lady bowed back. "It took you a long time to come back. I was expecting you earlier", she said ever so casually.

"You were expecting me?" Sudhir asked with his eyebrows raised.

"Many years back you had appeared and assured me that you would try and change the past. That I can have my husband back again?", she said confidently.

"I will not allow the past to be changed!" growled a deep voice that emanated from the old man who now glowed like a human on fire.

Sudhir looked behind his back to stare at the old man very intently and then exclaimed in shock, "Honourable Sreehanaya Oruvan, the Chief of the honourable elders of the Supreme Council of Daivika Planet! You have chosen to appear alone! And I see you teleporting pirates thereby making my job difficult. I would then imagine that you appear on your personal capacity and that the Supreme Council of Daivika Planet is not privy to your visit?"

"And the matter will have remained so had you been successful in eliminating Mogui, and his son, but you failed once again!" growled Honourable Sreehanaya Oruvan. "Mogui killed your first wife for God's sake! Any man worth his salt would destroy his wife's killer! Do you not have any respect for the memory of your late wife? Where is the anger? Where is the desire to take revenge? You have so much power, you could have killed them both while you were in Nair Dvipa itself. Kill them now King Sudhir Bagaria of Earth, Head of Inter Galactic Justice on Earth and senior member of the Inter Galactic Justice Core Team!" Sreehanaya Oruvan said in a commanding tone.

"Honourable Sreehanaya Oruvan, I wonder why the Chief of the honourable elders of the Supreme Council of Daivika Planet is so concerned about my respect for my late wife and then, my desired behavior? Is it because of the two High Density High Energy Retaining (HDHER) steel casks, that ensured protective storage of negative energies, but were sold by you to a poor dock worker several years back in exchange for gold coins extracted by him from the deep-sea sunken ships? I feel this is the right opportunity to ask you oh honourable Chief of the honourable elders of the Supreme Council of Daivika Planet, what did you need the gold for?" asked Sudhir in a polite tone, with due respect to the seniority and position of respect that the elder enjoyed.

Sreehanaya Oruvan stared at Sudhir with pain in his eyes. "You know! That is very sad! I liked your spirit! Our Supreme Council could have used your dedication and simple nature to create many colonies on planets yet to be discovered. But now you have to die!" so saying he quickly built up an energy field around Sudhir which immediately bound down Sudhir's arms down by his side. A red glow appeared around Sudhir and a buzz buzz like an electric short circuit began all around Sudhir.

Sudhir realized that his life ended here. His mind went back to the days he failed in his class and hid away from his school to stay far away from the taunts of his fellow students. He had failed a second time but his parents remained calm and did not give up on him.

He failed to feed his family due to many reasons but his wife was patient for several years. He failed to satisfy her and yet she has remained patient for several years.

His true success began slightly before his journey to Nair Dvipa began and spiraled upwards from then on.

Every human is born for a purpose, he told himself right now. He realized that his true purpose was to do good for the people of Nair Dvipa. To bring about justice.

And here was Honourable Sreehanaya Oruvan, the Chief of the honourable elders of the Supreme Council of Daivika Planet attacking him for having realized that the honourable one had been seen selling two High Density High Energy Retaining (HDHER) steel casks several ages ago. But surely the power of the honourable one came from his desire to execute justice. With that logic, the power of Honourable Sreehanaya Oruvan could not be more than the superior power given to him to do good!

So, he told his mind, "Negate the power of Honourable Sreehanaya Oruvan as he misuses his power to execute evil! Let him be docile under my power. Let him speak the truth when questioned by myself".

Honourable Sreehanaya Oruvan immediately stood still, his hands dropped by his two sides. The energy that was whirling around Sudhir began to abate and the red fire glare whirling all around him began to reduce until it vanished totally and Sudhir became free.

"Now Honourable Sreehanaya Oruvan, kindly explain why you sold two High Density High Energy Retaining (HDHER) steel casks several ages ago.

Sreehanaya Oruvan was struggling to escape the grasp of Sudhir's mental powers. He was being forced to speak the truth, "We need gold constantly, even today, to fuel the energies of the dying planets that we had mined for past billions of years. I own a conglomerate that has gold mining interests on several planets. My age is five hundred and seventy-three years. Our spirits do not die. Though we do not need bodies, we appeared inside bodies that was recognized by human beings as being safe. Our bodies survive around four hundred years on earth. Then our spirits take on a different physical form.

We needed a labour force on this planet Prithvi when our first fleet of criminals crash-landed here. That was the opportunity that my grandfather was looking for. He used the criminals to begin a gold mining empire. But other competitors joined in as the returns were very lucrative. So, we used the laboratories within each ship and contributed our genes to create a neutral gender human being, tough and strong but not as smart as we were. However, our scientists could not create perfectly long-lasting physical bodies like ours and hence the human beings began to deteriorate after around the age of fifty years from the day the human being was created. Our laboratory produced human beings were not enough for the labour force that the mines needed. And the human beings were dying by the time they reached the age of seventy-five to eighty years of age. So, we went back to our laboratories and created two different human beings, a man and a woman. We wanted them to procreate and thus generate our much desired labour force. But the human man was uninterested in procreation. And so, we created in the man an urge to get excited on seeing specific or all parts of the female body, and the desire to reach out and touch that which attracted him, to preserve and protect that which he desired. In the woman we created emotions, a desire to be loved, ability to be hurt, and the desire to get excited on being touched by a loved one. That truly helped us multiply our workforce with immediate effect, and we got our desired number of workforces.

The problem began when our home planet citizens began to mate with the women of Prithvi, the ones created in our laboratories. Our laboratory produced man remained simple and extremely hard working, but the women who were born from interacting with our home planet citizens, gave birth to children who were far smarter and business minded than their parents. These women were capable of guile and they began to guide their simple husbands produced from the laboratories. We began to have uprisings under the guidance of the woman at home.

Soon, the men expressed their desire to run the mines under the guidance of their woman at home. We were on the verge of losing control. Prithvi was important to us. It offered greenery and water, that no other planet offered. It produced gold many times multiplied than which is available on other planets in the universe. And I was losing control over the mines as rebellious women led their husbands to take control over the earnings of the mines.

By that time, as per intergalactic norms, we had managed to detect several criminal minded citizens of Daivika Planet especially those who had seeded the laboratory created women. We managed to empty the minds of these criminals of all negative energies and subsequently sealed the energies in High Density High Energy Retaining (HDHER) steel casks.

During the time that the mines got taken away from me one by one, I managed to get myself elected into the Supreme Council of Daivika Planet, and then graduated to the Group of Elders. While visiting one of the storage centers, I had a bright idea and I used my discretion to siphon off two full casks full of negative energy. I decided to seed one group of non-rebellious workers with negative energies and guide them to fight the rebels who had taken over my many mines. But it worked against me as the negative energized workers now began to guide the rebels. They committed many evil deeds that the criminals of my home planet could never imagine. Many more mines went out of my hands.

I did not know what to do with the HDHER casks. They were like huge rocks hanging around my neck. I was flying around Formosa when I saw this poor, hardworking Port Ship Loader who was miserable due to his financial position. I found him crying on the beach one day and I offered him a solution. I gave him a handful of evil energy in a small sachet and asked him to sprinkle some on himself and some on his friends. It worked like magic! He became super confident, assertive, and began to grab what was due to him. He bagan to beat up those who refused his due at the port. Soon the mild-mannered port workers began to look up to him for protection. And he gave them protection. Thus, his followers kept growing until one day, over two years, he found he was a powerful, respected leader!

But that is when he became greedy.

He came to the sea shore once again after around two years later and called for me by name. I appeared in front of him and he asked for some more power, much more power!

This was my opportunity to get rid of the two casks full of negative energy. He had made a lot of monies after he had become assertive. I offered both the casks in exchange for one shipload of gold, which was needed to energize the dying planets being mined by my conglomerate. He asked me to guide him towards any ship that could give me gold in that quantity and I had pointed at the Jalbandhu, a ship from Bharata (India) that belonged to one of the Kings near Malabar. From then on began his days of piracy.

He became my business partner. I pointed out Kingdoms and gold laden ships. In exchange, he would give me sixty percent of the gold. This was an excellent partnership as I did not have to suffer the effort involved in handling the labour force in the gold mines, nor the hassles of mining, then extracting gold. Piracy gave me gold beyond my imagination.

I felt my worries were over, but word spread that two casks were taken out or stolen from one of the storage centers for HDHER casks and that probably, a lot of evil power might have been due to these very casks. I promptly found it easy to blame the King of pirates and thought that my problems were finally solved. I had earned enough in gold by partnering with pirates, to finally retire. But then Mogui had travelled to the past and had seen me sell the casks to his grandfather. I could not allow him to remain alive after that! Therefore, I fed the idea of killing Sanya's husband, that is, the Prince of Nair Dvipa, into the mind of the Pirate King. Maybe then Mogui would fight his grandfather and get killed. I fed into Mogui's mind the idea of kidnapping your grandparents and removing them from power. I fed into his mind the idea of revenge, to destroy all of Nair Dvipa because only then would King Sudhir Bagaria want to stop him. I fed into his mind the desire to kill King Sudhir Bagaria's first wife, because only then would you want to kill him and thus save me from past embarrassment".

Having confessed thus, Sreehanaya Oruvan became silent, but was obviously trying to escape the mental imprisonment on Sudhir's instructions.

Mogui, Sanya that is, Mogui's mother, his grandfather the King of Pirates and the junior Mogui had arrived near the protective energy circle into which Sudhir and Sreehanaya Oruvan were discussing and had the opportunity to listen to the confession.

The King of pirates listened to this and silently disappeared.

All this while the fighting between the many pirate groups continued. The different Sudhir's were inflicting heavy damage to the huge gang of pirates that plied the seas with the King of pirates.

Just then the King pirate appeared on the deck and roared, "stop the fight!", I have your tribal queen! I have your tribal queen!", he kept roaring. But the other opposing pirates did not know what queen and which queen Mogui was roaring about. And so, they kept on slicing down Mogui's men and sinking his ships. But all the Sudhir duplicates looked at him.

"I shall pull the rope now!" he roared and all the Sudhirs turned away from their opponents and flew into the air, ready to protect all that is good and preserve peace.

It was true! Ngia Vat was trying her best to balance on a box with a rope tied around her neck. The other end was being held back by Wúgū the pirate King.

Could this be another duplicate created by Mogui to stall the defeat that they were suffering? Then it struck Sudhir! He had to change strategy right away!

"Ask your father", Sudhir looked at Sanya, the Pirate King's daughter and sent a mental message, "ask your father whether he actually got your husband killed. Ask him whether Honourable Sreehanaya Oruvan is speaking the truth".

Sanya's face had already coloured red when she had heard Sreehanaya Oruvan make such a confession. She rushed to her father and asked gently, "Papa did you kill my husband? Did you kill the man I loved?"

"I do not have the time for all this mushy nonsense!" growled the Pirate King.

"Then the answer is yes!" growled back Sanya. "Just tell me why! Why did you kill such a gentle and kind human being who would never hurt a fly!"

"I got him killed because he was a weak man!", whispered the King of pirates. "Because I wanted to undo the damage to your happiness that I had caused by making you marry him! I wanted your happiness and I thought initially, that marrying a prince would help you get all the riches that you deserved! Then I realized that I had made a terrible mistake. He could at best spout poetry. He did not know how to fight for what was rightfully his own. I thus wanted you to marry the successful pirate assistant who was being groomed by me personally. But you refused!", whispered the Pirate King.

"I refused because I was in love Papa! I refused because I was happy Papa and I trusted the kind & gentle human being that he was. All these many years I felt that he had let me down. That I had trusted him in vain! Now I wish that I had not returned at all to be under your protection and care! At least he would have been alive! You let me down papa! You let me down!", she sobbed.

The Pirate King stepped forward to embrace his daughter but Sanya, his daughter showed her palm upwards to stop him, saying "No Papa! I need to go away from you".

Then she looked up at NgiaVat being held up by her father and said, "If you loved your wife and daughter then you would never have travelled the path of evil. You now hold in your hands the love of the King of another land. What do gain by hurting him again? Has the black energy that you inhale, taken hold of you totally or is there a bit of humanity left? Is there inside you even a small bit of the man whom my mother had loved so much? Is there inside you even a small bit of that man who, while he was poor, would take me in his strong arms to the sea shore, hold his wife's hand even while helping his little baby daughter count the stars in the sky? Is there?"

The eyes of Wugu the Pirate King welled up with tears, "I am the same man, deep inside my mind my darling Sanya! I am the same man who loved your mother and could not bear the sight of her going hungry night after night. I am the same man who could not bear the fact that my wife nearly died several times just because her weak husband did not have the money to buy her medicines! I am the same man who held you close to my chest, and sang lullabies, night after night just because you missed your mother, after she left us! I am the same man who loves you unconditionally, even today!" He pointed at Ngia Vat and said, "This is not the wife of King Sudhir Bagaria! This is just a temporary creation,". He had this, "please try to understand your father", expression on his face. "She is a temporary copy of the Kings wife, created by the Daiva (God), there, under the King's control now!" so saying he pointed at evil Sreehanaya Oruvan and finished.

Just then, Ngia Vat crumbled into dust and the dust blew away into the air! Sudhir did not react though he hurt deep inside.

Evil Sreehanaya Oruvan growled and continued desperately to escape the mental bonds placed by Sudhir on him.

Sanya looked at the junior Mogui and then the senior Mogui. The pure evil that shone from the senior Mogui's face shocked her.

Sanya looked at her son, the senior Mogui, and asked, "Is this what you have become my son? An evil man like your grandfather? Did it never come to your mind that your emotions were being manipulated by an evil outside force? Why did you allow evil to take over your mind? Why? You saw how your grandfather made me do evil deeds. He made me coax my only child to pick up the sword against the family to which he belongs! That is not what a father should ever do! Do you not have even a wee bit of your father's blood in you?"

Senior Mogui replied, "Mama, I saw you die! You died in pain, in vain, waiting for Papa to return! He went away leaving us alone mama! He loved Nair Dvipa more than you and me mama. He admitted so in front of grandpa while on the ship that was leaving! I met his spirit at the island Kingdom, but all he wants to do is to stop me from killing the Royal family. He still loves them more mama. He loves them more than us".

"My son! You heard your grandpa now. He was travelling to Nair Dvipa to earn monies by trading. He wanted to earn the little bit that he could just for you and me, my darling son. But your grandfather stopped him! Your grandfather killed him!" Sanya sobbed.

The King of Pirates stretched out his hands towards his daughter and grandson and said, "All that I had wanted, especially after your mother left us was, to make you happy! I just wanted you to be happy!"and so saying the King of Pirates began to sob. But nobody came forward to hold him in his, or her embrace. He cried alone.

"My father was a weak man", whispered Mogui senior.

"You should be proud of your father", suggested Sudhir. "Your father fought your grandfather on the ship and you cheered him from the window!" added Sudhir and then asked Mogui senior, "Did you not cheer him from the ship window?"

Mogui senior asked in all seriousness, "How do you know that?" Then, an all-knowing expression came over his face and he exclaimed gently, "You helped my father be brave! You helped my brave father fight my grandfather that day! It was you!"

"And had it not been for the black magic that your grandfather began to throw around, your father would have been alive today!" finished Sudhir.

"But I saw my father smiling and singing while fighting! I remember! I so wanted to help my father fight the bad men. I so wanted to stop them from hurting my papa!" Mogui began to reminisce.

Just then, the mentally powerful Sreehanaya Oruvan managed to break Sudhir's mental bonds and leapt into the air roaring, "All you puny human beings and mix breeds shall die today! My problems shall be over at one go!" and so saying he raised his hands intending to crash all his energies into the total lot of them.

Both Sudhir as well as Mogui tried to move but they found their movement as well as their powers were frozen!

It was then that they realised that, nobody would come out of this alive, because, everybody was doomed!

Mobi Fights the Deji Soldiers in the City

It had rained for the past three days. The rivers were in flood. Water hyacinth that had choked the ponds were now being dragged away by the roaring river waters that had entered both ponds as well as low lying farm lands and then flowed away towards the ocean waters.

Mobi was distressed since it was a great dishonor for not being able to save Ngia Vat. He owed it to the Mohua Minshaw, the good God cum father whom he had loved the most, to save his aunt, now the wife of his father!

Ngia Vat had to be traced and saved!

Therefore, it was up to him to find her and save her! But where could her security guards and she be?

Little Mobi sat down with his teenaged warriors and made out a list of possible safehouses where Ngia Vat and her bodyguards could be hidden away by the Mogui and the Diànlì ji'è de guójia troops. Teenaged village warriors now trained in city warfare namely, Adisa, Chaka, Mogutu, Olatunde, Fatou, Mathembu, Kimaryo, Hodan, Mawuli, Mwamba, Obataiye, Uchechi, Chiamaka, Makalo, Uwimana (female), Obioma (female), Munirah (female), Jabari (female), Dembe (female), a group of nineteen highly motivated teenagers led by a teeny weeny Mobi, were now confused because they had tried every possible hideout on this island.

Then one of the pro royal palace guards who spoke the villager's language said that he had seen meals cooked at the palace going by fishing trawlers to a ship anchored in the high seas close to the Palace. He pointed at a ship far away in the horizon. If they could manage a boat ride to that ship and somehow board it then, possibly Ngia vat could be saved. There was a mini township of fishermen, retired police and lower middle-class personnel named 'Dharmashakti gramam', spread out all around the Palace. Many years ago, ever since Mogui had attacked their forefathers, every child was taught to protect himself or herself. Thus, around twenty pro Royal teenagers trained in jungle combat, requested that they be allowed to join and help the villagers. Many of them knew foreign languages and how to launch an attack on an armed merchant ship.

A total battle-ready team of thirty-nine teenaged warriors were yearning to fight the evil forces and rescue the queen.

The township coaxed their elders, managed two fishing trawlers and made the pilot take them as close to the anchored ship as possible. It was late in the evening by the time they reached and darkness had enveloped the skies. Water hyacinth, a free-floating perennial aquatic plant, floated in large numbers into the sea from the many rivers, especially after the recent rains. The clouds covered the moon. Three warriors remained to guard the pilot and boat from harm. The rest slid into the sea waters with little Mobi in the lead. They travelled under the clusters of water hyacinth with straws to help them breathe. The moment the water hyacinth touched the ship they climbed the thick coils of iron that held up the anchor to reach the deck and hid behind fishing nets and large wooden boxes. One of the older villagers grabbed one of the sailors and dragged him to a corner where they began to interrogate him about the whereabouts of Ngia vat, but he spoke in Spanish which they did not understand. One of the palace guards did and he was a polite fifteen years of age. "Where are they hiding the villagers, uncle?" he asked sweetly.

"Grump!" the old man replied with a scowl on his face.

Mobi took out a kitchen knife and brought out a tomato ketchup laced plastic hand that looked like it had been freshly chopped off from a yellow skinned man. "We hate doing this to you but we are left with no options". And so saying, he stabbed at the captured prisoner, the man winched in anticipation of pain, but Mobi simply chopped away some cloth from the man's right sleeve arm. Then he felt the man's right-hand fingers and went up to his elbow.

Then looking at some of his team members, he winked, then whispered to ask, "Shall we chop here around the elbow joint, or there, around his fingers?"

The translator translated into Spanish.

The prisoner's eyes widened in fear and he turned to look at the young boys trying to take a decision regards his hand.

"At his elbow is a better idea, then we can show it to the next man we capture", replied a twelve-year-old.

The prisoner's eyes widened even further, "Why? Why my elbow?", he asked with a voice getting gradually choked due to fear.

"He is right!" intervened another. "Why his elbow? Why not chop away just the skin and muscles to leave him with the bone sticking out?" asked another with a serious expression on his face, but enjoying himself thoroughly.

The man gulped and croaked," Whether you chop my arm, or simply cut away the skin and muscles, in both cases I may bleed to death!"

Mobi looked with concern at the man's arm and declared, "Hmm he is right! He may bleed to death. In fact, death is certain. Unless ofcourse he was to tell us…"

"Sixth door on the deck, right hand side", the frightened man quickly revealed, "four prisoners per cabin from then onwards. One woman has been provided a single cabin. She must be the queen that you are asking about. Four security guards for the total length. Now please do not cut my arm up! You are good boys. Very good boys. Ahh - can I go, please?!"

Marine plants and algae, that is sea weed, floated all around the ship after the recent monsoon, along with the water hyacinth that had come from the inland rivers.

They stuffed his mouth with sea weed, a palm leaf to cover his mouth, tied up the mouth with a coir rope found on the deck near the boxes, tied his hand behind his back, tied a thick cannon hoisting rope to his body and hung him down the side of the ship facing the sea waters.

They hid again when the clouds moved away briefly from the moon, then leapt forward when the moon light disappeared once again due to the dark cloud cover. They were about to turn the corner when they saw a guard marching the other way with his back to them. They shot out a curare laced arrow from a blow pipe and the guard collapsed without a sound. One of the other guards heard the sound and he looked back but by that time the next curare laced arrow had struck his thigh. He had this strange expression of someone intoxicated and then he collapsed on the deck.

The boys crept forward quickly to the first door. They tried to open the latch, it opened easily and it was dark. They entered, found four female warriors, cut the ropes that bound them to the bed and then the new group spread out to open all the doors which were indicated earlier. All the warriors were now armed and began to silently disarm & immobilize the differently posted guards set up by the invading country.

Mobi crept swiftly cabin to cabin until finally, one of the middle rooms, he entered to find a lady armed with a vase and ready to strike. and Mobi entered silently and found the queen, Ngia Vat!

"Binti Ngia Vat, it is me, Mobi!", he whispered.

Ngia Vat saw Mobi and thought initially that he too had been kidnapped. Then on seeing her own bodyguards, she gave him a big hug and indicated with gestures & whispers that it was important now to make a quick retreat.

Most everybody had been offloaded from the ship into the waters under the supervision of Mobi and his team, they had swum the distance to the fishing trawler and had boarded the same, including Ngia Vat. "Boom boom! Rat tat tat tat a tat a tat!" That is when the gunfire started.

One of the guards had seen the silent group of freedom fighters. He had crept back to his barracks and informed the others. They found their innumerable immobilized colleagues and spread out to ensure a synchronized attack. Darkness was a huge problem as the freedom fighters wore black clothing. They saw shadows of the last few of the freedom fighters racing towards the bow of the deck, climbing down the thick coils of iron that held up the anchor and the moment they had a glimpse of the intruders on their ship, the guards began to fire. To protect the rest of the freedom fighters, some of Mobi's team began to climb back and began to return fire, including Mobi.

He switched on and switched off the torch to indicate to the captain of the first fishing trawler carrying most of the rescued body guards as well as the queen, to depart. And "vroom, vroom, swoosh", it began to drift away towards the distant river dock. Ngia Vat was free! He had done his duty! But the guards heard the sound, though they could not make out the source, and so they began to fire into the dark sea waters.

Mobi felt that the queen's life would be in danger and he promptly gave the torch to Munirah his female team mate and requested that he be allowed to use her gun. They had a strategic pact of working together. Munirah pointed the torch at any one of the guards and," Boom", Mobi would fire and make the guard fall. Then the next guard and "boom", he would be down. Then the next was down, but the fourth guard began to run away from the torch light and yet Munirah's torch light followed him all round the limited space from which the ship's guards had began to fire. Mobi's gun followed him and fired again and he was down. This happened even while Mwamba, another of Mobi's team members, was resorting to spurts of rapid fire at the guards who were stopping them from escaping. Mwamba then used a captured grenade launcher and the grenade flew towards a guard's billet through the open window, and the guards within that hideout tried to rush out but were caught in the explosion," Vrhoom!"

There was pandemonium, especially because the deck lights in this part of the ship had been deliberately broken and the guards ran helter-skelter because the darkness made it impossible to spot the enemy!

Mobi indicated that everybody from amongst the remaining few freedom fighters, must dive into the water, and as they went by his command, hence, they did.

Then Mobi jumped, but just then a guard, right from the quarter master's cabin, fired on seeing a silhouette, and "Twack! Twack!" two bullets tore into the boys little frame! To the horror of the boys in the water, Mobi whirled in the air due to the impact, and then smashed into the water from that height of the deck to the waters far below! The boys rushed to him, pushed air into his lungs and dived down into the depts with little Mobi and kept swimming swiftly away underwater to go as far away from the ship as possible before they surfaced to see the guards on the ship firing away into the water where they were a few minutes ago.

They slowly swam back towards the second trawler, even while Mobi kept bleeding into the water.

But the blood attracted two small shore-based sharks and they rushed to attack. They nudged & nipped Olatunde even as he pulled unconscious Mibo with a hold on his chest from below, towards the fishing trawler just a minute away. Olatunde screamed and Kimaryo saw the shark and pulled out both his sword and knife! Just then Obioma, one of the female warriors slightly behind the two male swimmers screamed "shark heading in your direction!".

The smell of fresh blood had got the second shark into a crazy frenzy and both the sharks charged from two different directions towards Mobi, towards Olatunde who was pulling Mobi, and Obioma who was trying to protect the two.

Back to Sudhir's Battle in the Year 1700 Against the Pirates

Sreehanaya Oruvan raised his hands and the negative energies in the air rushed towards him like children rush to their father. His complete body became a beehive of negative energies within split seconds. Both Sudhir as well as Mogui realized that his powers far exceeded their combined powers. If Mogui had become evil, then, Sreehanaya Oruvan, who was the head of Intergalactic Peace, and caretaker of individual peace & harmony, was the father of all that was evil!

Within spilt seconds, thick dark clouds had enveloped the region and darkness spread like thick butter on a fresh toasted bread. Darkness was such that one could not see the other.

A sudden hurricane plus whirlwind brought Ice cold winds with unimaginable speeds and pirates had this incredulous expression combined with extreme fear on their faces as they began to fly away from their ships. Each of them tried to hold onto masts, to anchors, to the window sills, anything to remain alive, but alas! Inspite of Sudhir holding on to other members on the ship, they kept screaming in terror while their bodies flapped around due to the ferocity of the wind.

A strong hum grew in intensity to a point that it sounded like a banshee's shrill threatening call.

Every individual in the vicinity began to glow as if on fire and a "hummm hummmm hummm" deep throated hum now began to emanate from each one of them, including Sudhir and Mogui.

Evil Sreehanaya Oruvan lifted both his palms upwards and every individual in the vicinity began to float up into the air now with the ferocious wind unable to move them and then began the searing heat and severe pain. The heat, was because heartless Sreehanaya Oruvan had began to wave his fingers down and with every finger move, and lightning began to strike Prithvi (Earth) every second with every finger move. "Eeee!", "aaaaaahaa!", "Ooooaaa!", everybody began to scream. Sudhir, the Pirate King and Mogui shut their eyes and bit their lips to stifle the expression of pain.

Then they could take it no more and Pirates and women prisoners below decks began to explode like hot air balloons!

"Aaaaarhh!" Sreehanaya Oruvan roared and growled in satisfaction, "All of you shall die, now! I shall not leave any witness alive!"

Just then "Smash, crackle, boom!" a powerful thunderbolt travelled at an unbelievable speed from far above the clouds and crashed into evil Sreehanaya Oruvan. "Whooomph! Phap!" and he fell down on his face, spread eagled, legs and hands stretched out, and he trembled for a little while and then became unconscious.

All human beings began to gently come down from the sky and their feet touched the earth.

All the honourable elders of the Supreme Council of Daivika Planet had travelled down to earth at hyper speed. Daivi Ammai Aadarsha Bhattathiripad, Daivi Ammai (Devine mother) Dhanyata Chandrika, Daiva

Pitava Devvuri Srinivasan, Daivi Ammai Urvashi Nandakumar, and Daiva Pitava Dharmarakshak Ayyalasomayajula, were present in person!

A lightning bolt came buzz buzz blazing down from far above the dark clouds and stopped to hover above the prone body of Sreehanaya Oruvan.

It was Daiva Pitava (devine father) Gyananiyaya Oruvan, in person!

"You are under arrest Sreehanaya Oruvan!" roared Daiva Pitava (devine father) Gyananiyaya Oruvan, one of the senior board members of the Supreme Council of Daivika Planet, immediately junior to Sreehanaya Oruvan by rank, and he shot out an energy feed blast towards Sudhir. Sudhir revived immediately and was on his feet.

Mogui realised then that he too would be arrested by these senior board members of the Supreme Council of Daivika Planet. Which meant he would not be free any longer. It would have been better to die in the hands of Sreehanaya Oruvan than get arrested. But he saw no escape.

"You are hereby being terminated from the position of the Chief of the honourable elders of the Supreme Council of Daivika Planet", daiva pitava Gyananiyaya Oruvan continued and other board members all around him to look down and glare at the criminal who had misled them for the past several centuries.

Daivi Ammai (Devine mother) Dhanyata Chandrika and Daivi Ammai Aadarsha Bhattathiripad, two of the honourable elders of the Supreme Council of Daivika Planet began to pluck innocent individuals still floating in the sky, from within the raging storm, and Sudhir began to help them out, one by one. They failed to notice that evil Sreehanaya Oruvan had become conscious and was gradually gulping down black powder which was in a sachet in his pocket. Black evil power began to spread through his blood. His muscles began to swell up, his face began to take on the shape of a devil and he began to get ready to attack. Mogui noticed, their eyes met, and Sreehanaya Oruvan nodded.

Sreehanaya Oruvan shot out an energy feed bold towards Mogui, Mogui revived and shot a kill energy bolt towards Sudhir while evil Sreehanaya Oruvan shot out a kill energy blast at Daiva pitava (devine father) Gyananiyaya Oruvan.

Both Sudhir and Gyananiyaya Oruvan used shields and then equal blasts to counter the attack but Mogui had shot out a kill energy blast at both

Daivi Ammai (Devine mother) Dhanyata Chandrika as well as Daivi Ammai Aadarsha Bhattathiripad.

Dhanyata Chandrika swatted away the blast that came to her but Aadarsha Bhattathiripad was carrying a wounded citizen and was late at reacting to protect herself.

The blast hit her and a huge explosion happened! There was a mushroom of energy that travelled in every direction, sending every individual tumbling in various directions.

As people began to recover from the paralysing effect of the blast, both Mogui as well as Sreehanaya Oruvan got up on their wobbly feet and began to circle their hands and palms to create an all-encompassing blast to kill as many as possible. Then when ready, they looked up to find that both Sudhir as well as Gyananiyaya Oruvan had already sent two 'sap power permanently' energy blast and both of such energies hit Mogui as well as Sreehanaya Oruvan "Thwaap!" and "Thwaap!" and they collapsed in helpless heaps.

Sudhir lifted his fingers towards the dark clouds and swept them away as one would erase a sketch from a piece of paper. He then held his palm up towards the hurricane plus whirlwind and it stopped in its tracks as if somebody had applied brakes on a speeding truck. He teleported the kidnapped women within each ship back to their respective homes. He teleported Mogui junior back to the island near Formosa.

He saw honourable Gyananiyaya Oruvan placing both his palms against evil Sreehanaya Oruvan's head to cleanse it of all evil.

It was important that Mogui's mind too should be ready to receive all facts in a positive fashion henceforth. Sudhir therefore placed both his hands on Mogui's head and pressed hard.

An explosion of negative energies flowed up into the skies like a volcano from the heads of both Sreehanaya Oruvan as well as Mogui. A multitude of evil spirits screamed and roared revenge and destruction as they relived their evil memories and then being exposed to the cleansing power of both honourable Gyananiyaya Oruvan and Sudhir, they turned to dust. To be on the safe side, Sudhir took away most of Mogui's powers barring what was necessary to take care of himself.

Then honourable Gyananiyaya Oruvan looked into the eyes of Sreehanaya Oruvan and said, "There was a time when your guidance was all that we needed to make the planets of this universe a better place to live in. We never realized until now who created the first human beings and why. Your confessions now reveal that you needed slaves and created mankind to work in the gold mines. It was you who first mated with the female workforce that you created. The rebellion of intelligent and aware human beings thus happened. It automatically became your duty to protect what you had created but no, you resorted to devious means of controlling and making use of them. You desired to play one against the other. Thus, you had stolen the High-Density High Energy Retaining (HDHER) steel casks that obviously went out of your control and was responsible for evil energy to spread out and create an evil world as we see the world today. Money and possessions are given priority today, whereas values, humanity, concern for welfare of global citizens, all these became secondary. Humankind has no control over its mind and mental discipline is regarded as the enemy of freedom. For all these crimes, we declare that you shall serve your sentence of imprisonment in a solitary cell for the mandatory period of four hundred years, followed by which you shall be put to death!"

Sudhir looked into both Wugu, the Pirate King's and Mogui's eyes and declared, "You both have caused innumerable deaths! You had both willingly consumed the black powder and had allowed it to take over your minds. You have both influenced the poor and hungry human beings of this world towards the wrong path, towards the path of piracy, rape and plunder! You both are responsible for the fact that today, it is good to be bad and bad to be good! For these negative deeds, both of you shall serve your sentences of fifty years each, on the satellite prison that floats around Prithvi, that is 'Chand (moon).'

Sudhir now clicked his two fingers and there was the sound of a roar like an approaching giant ocean wave, the three criminals began to glow as if they were on fire, and then poof, they were gone!

Sudhir now looked at Mogui's mother Sanya, and declared, "you had loved your parents and you tried to protect your father. While learning to love your husband you have learned the true value of goodness that your mother loved so much in your father. You have realized that you had strayed, and now you live a life of painful memories. You have never permitted your father to force you to accept the black powder. You have never consumed the black powder till date because you willed it so.

However, what is to be also considered is the fact that you had committed certain crimes when you were misled by Mugu, the pirate king, your father. For these crimes you shall serve one earth year behind prison cells. Following your release, you shall be provided food, clothing, accommodation, and security, to live your life in prayer and peace.

Sanya looked into Sudhir's eyes and nodded in agreement. "I have but one request before you take me away to the prison", she pleaded.

"Sudhir looked into her eyes as she spoke and nodded, asking her to continue.

"I wish to meet my husband on the ship before he was murdered by my father's men!" Sudhir knew that this was wrong and yet his responsibility was to ensure due justice.

And so, he took her back in time to the ship when her husband was going back to Nair Dvipa laden with silk and other goods to be sold to Nair Dvipa. When they flew in and landed on the deck, Sanya's husband was in the fag end of the fight, wounded, and yet fighting on. Sanya looked with pain in her eyes at Sudhir. Sudhir nodded, pointed at all on the ship and "foom!", he made everybody freeze with a wave of his hand, then gestured to Sanya to go ahead.

Sanya flew down to her husband and hugged him, but he did not move nor respond because he was under the "freeze spell". She went to her little son Mogui, now inside the cabin. "This is my son who would become an evil man and cause harm to our world", she realized. He was looking through the glass window pane at his father, his mouth open in rage, as if screaming for the lord's help to save his Papa, and for grandpa to stop the bad men who were trying to kill his papa! She went forward and hugged her little innocent baby from behind and a tear drop fell from her eyes. Then she went back to her husband and whispered into his ears, "I have always loved you! I have loved your poetry, your ability to write your own lyrics, your ability to sing and most importantly because, you were a good man. Even while you try to fight them today, please sing that song that you sang to me, about the great battle between good and evil. It will give you strength because good may win. And know this my husband, that I have always trusted you, and my love for you will remain alive for ever!"

Then Sudhir made himself and Sanya invisible, floated up into the skies and began to hover, to observe and allow the past to remain as it happened.

The Prince had been fighting a futile battle against seasoned, sea battle honed pirates. But he had this strange, happy smile on his face! And the pirates, to their surprise and amusement, saw that the crazy poet prince, was singing! He was singing aloud with every thrust and swipe of his sword against the evil, heartless pirates!

Three pirates attacked him and he swung his sword to ward off the attack and he sang. Then the next pirate swung his sword and this too was warded off while he sang but, in the meanwhile the third struck his left arm and he went down with a scream and little Mogui screamed, "Papa!" from behind the glass pane.

"This is my son who will regret in later years how he was stopped from fighting alongside his father. He would regret not being able to fight and stop the bad men from hurting his Papa", Sanya realized. Sudhir read her mind.

Sanya struggled in Sudhir's mental grasp but this time Sudhir did not hold her back. Remaining invisible, she flew down to little Mogui and pushed a sword towards him whispering into his ears," Fight with your father my brave little one, fight to protect your father!" And little Mogui fought with all the skills taught to him by his grandfather and his fellow pirates. His father looked at him with a smile and said, "Your mother is with us Mogui!" And then he continued to swoosh and swing his sword.

Little Mogui too was very happy and he said, "I know Papa!" and he touched the wetness on his shirt collar.

And they fought on, father and son and they downed many a pirate! But every good has an end, and hence it was that a sword pierced the heart of little Mogui. This enraged the poet prince and he began to fight like the world would collapse without him! Just then a tall pirate stabbed the prince from behind! The prince had this shocked look on his face and then he smiled and collapsed, dead. Just as he did so, the pirate who pushed the sword into the prince from behind him, could be seen. Sanya saw him and old memories flooded her mind! He was that very pirate named Gunecche. Her father had wanted that she should marry this man. Way back when he was training with her father, she had found him to be a very handsome man. Today she saw the ugliness in him, the evil in him. He did not have the courage to attack her husband from the front. He who attacks from behind is a deceitful man! She tugged at the control of her mind now in the hands of Sudhir and once again Sudhir let her go.

She flew down behind a box, became visible, and came out to stand with a sword in her hand, some distance away from the man she could have married many years ago.

"Ahh Sanya! See! That weak, poet cum singing buffoon is dead, just as your father wanted! He shall never, ever bore you with his version of a song. Now you are mine", and so saying, he made a grab for her right wrist. Sanya swung the sword in her left hand and chopped off his right ear lobe.

"Arrgg you bitch! You spoilt bitch! You need a good lesson before I push between your legs!"and he threw three small knives at her forehead, her chest and her stomach, within spilt seconds of each other!

She batted them away with her sword and then said, "That weak, poet cum singing buffoon was my husband and my son's father. My son and I have always loved that buffoon you killed just now! But you, evil, heartless man you shall never learn to fight like a brave man. You attacked my husband from behind! You killed him from behind because you were afraid that he would kill you if you attacked him from the front! You are a weak coward!"

The Pirate King had left the fight with the prince to his junior. But then he saw an older version of his daughter begin a fight with Gunecche, his junior. He could only stare in shock!

His junior looked at Sanya and attacked screaming, "Aaaayyaaaah!!" and kept throwing small knives with his left hand, then right, and then left, and then right hand again, even while keeping his short sword tucked into his belt, ready to strike. To his shock, Sanya flew up into the sky, each of the knives missed her, and continued to fly by above him. But as he opened his mouth in shock and continued to keep it open while staring at her with big eyes, she flew swiftly behind him and booted him on his back, hard! He raced ahead for some time and then fell flat on his face! The rest of the pirates had a good laugh at his expense.

He then took out the Accelerated Energy Drive Gun (AEDG) - a cylindrical gun that fires a highly strong blast of accellerated energy particles. "It does not need to be reloaded as energy particles are freely available", he smirked and said, pointing it at Sanya. The pirate King came up from behind Gunecche and kicked behind the knee joint, hard! Gunecche collapsed on his knees and the pirate king sliced his throat! Sanya grabbed the gun and kept firing, "Boom!", "Boom", at clusters of pirates who had wounded her husband over the past one hour. And to save themselves, they began to abandon ship!

Sanya walked up to her father and embraced him, "Be good, she requested.

The Pirate King kept staring after the older version of his daughter realizing that he had done a terrible thing. He had failed his wife and now he had ruined his daughter's happiness!

So Sudhir clicked his finger just then and Sudhir & Sanya were gone. Sanya to serve her prison sentence and Sudhir returned to the period where the elders were.

He found all the honourable elders of the Supreme Council of Daivika Planet had gathered in front of him. Daiva Pitava (devine father) Gyananiyaya Oruvan, Daivi Ammai (Devine mother) Dhanyata Chandrika, Daiva Pitava Devvuri Srinivasan, Daivi Ammai Urvashi Nandakumar, and Daiva Pitava Dharmarakshak Ayyalasomayajula were waiting for him with folded palms, out of respect and gratitude.

Sudhir folded his palms to acknowledge their gratitude and just then, all of them received two mental messages. One, that a huge fleet of Diànlì ji'è de guójia ships, aircraft carriers and submarines were approaching Nair Dvipa right now. And two, that Mobi had expired moments ago due to heavy bleeding!

Bidding Farewell to Little Mobi

Mobi lay on the hospital bed! Sudhir looked down at his child. The little baby was looking so helpless and still. His Mobi, who would chirp like a million birds was no more!

The previous evening it had rained cats and dogs. But Nair Dvipa residents came out with their umbrellas to celebrate the courage displayed by this one child. He was just a child and yet he stood against evil forces. In his death, he had given them courage!

They were discussing how the sharks were shot dead and Mobi was pulled up on the second fishing trawler but in vain. He had stopped breathing from much before, even before the sharks had attacked.

The hospital authorities had tried their best.

He now lay so still on the hospital bed as if he was simply sleeping. "Can you check his pulse just once more doctor?" Sudhir urged. The doctors looked at him helplessly.

Mobi's little team came up one by one even as Sudhir sat on the hospital bed and held Mobi close to his chest in silence, without weeping.

Ngia Vat came from behind and touched his shoulders.

The honourable elders of the Supreme Council of Daivika Planet had gathered in front of Sudhir even as he held Mobi close to his chest

Daiva Pitava (devine father) Gyananiyaya Oruvan, Daivi Ammai (Devine mother) Dhanyata Chandrika, Daiva Pitava Devvuri Srinivasan, Daivi Ammai Urvashi Nandakumar, and Daiva Pitava Dharmarakshak Ayyalasomayajula had suffered a serious loss a few hours ago and now this!

Daivi Ammai Urvashi Nandakumar suddenly flew and began to hover above Mobi. Normal human beings around Mobi's hospital bed began to feel uneasy. But not Sudhir because he was looking up and observing her expression and eyes.

"He is alive!", she whispered.

Sudhir rushed up to fly over and above and above Mobi's body. An energy seemed to fly out from Mobi but Daivi Ammai Urvashi Nandakumar was ready. She promptly caught the spirit and threw it back inside the prone body. The little body shook, as if in pain!

Daivi Ammai Urvashi Nandakumar began to recite a strange chant "Tajaka Brahma samastha ulat marge shigrita! Ulat Marge Shigrita! Ulat Marge Shigrita!" and every honourable elder of the Supreme Council of Daivika Planet, alongwith Sudhir began to chant the same, repeatedly.

Suddenly the brilliance that had lit up the cave now appeared next to the hospital bed! A brilliance suddenly appeared and multiplied to a dazzle of light that began to emanate from each honourable elder. The dazzle created a warm charge that travelled from each of them to Mobi's still body. Mobi seemed to change, starting from the feet up to the face, the lips, the eyes, the hair began to burn and a new body seemed to be trying to take shape. After a gap of a few minutes Mobi began to flex his muscles. The dazzle of light extinguished itself and gradually, each of the honourable elders opened their eyes.

"You are back!" Ngia vat screamed out of happiness! She grabbed and hugged Mobi who was unconscious but breathing, Mobi purred out of contentment and the feeling of security, "Wewe ni nyumbani! You are home!" Ngia vat sobbed happily.

"Will you please release me from your embrace? You are hurting me!", whimpered Mobi.

Battle Between 'David' Nair Dvipa and 'Goliath' Diànlì Ji'è De Guójia

Diànlì ji'è de guójia ships, destroyers and submarines thundered towards missile firing range of Nair Dvipa. Standard Displacement of their Battle ship was 39,150 tons, their Full Load was 50,000 tons, they were armed with a battery of nine computer aided missile launchers. They were equipped with Radar & Satellite Evading Technology, cyber security technology. Laser weapon or electromagnetic rail guns were engineered into the design.

The 800-foot, 17,000-ton stealth destroyer cum aircraft carrier, registered on the radar as a small vessel, about the size of a fishing boat. Its computer-guided missile system could hit targets up to 63 miles away, and it was also equipped with a laser weapon or electromagnetic rail gun.

The Nuclear-powered submarines had missile launchers, stealth technology and could strike cities sixty miles away.

Suddenly the Diànlì ji'è de guójia fleet identified a sudden spurt of communications between Indian Battleships, Submarines and Aircraft carriers.

"Enemy hacker neutralized"

"Requesting more energy for Cybersecurity systems"

"Enemy craft within firing range"

"Stealth Systems activated"

"Shields have been increased for protection"

"Launchbases ready and primed"

"Enemy fleet within combat range."

"Maneuvering to engage enemies to port."

Could Diànlì ji'è de guójia attack Nair Dvipa with Indian Forces blocking their path?

They sent out a rude message, "Diànlì ji'è de guójia requests Indian naval exercises be postponed or diverted to any another latitude and longitude! Over!"

Indian response was prompt, "Nair Dvipa has called for our assistance and the International community has been informed accordingly. Battleships of certain other nations are also on the way. We are confident that you do not wish to proceed towards Nair Dvipa, hence you are free to cross and sail by in peace! Over!"

Diànlì ji'è de guójia attack forces now became blunt, "Nair Dvipa is an extended territory of Diànlì ji'è de guójia! The international community has been warned not to interfere as regards matters that do not concern them. We are strong because throughout history we have always despised weakness. We do not have any personal enmity with India. We urge your forces to avoid bravado and clear our path".

"We urge Diànlì ji'è de guójia to respect international sentiments and most importantly international laws. An attack on Nair Dvipa's independence would naturally need our intervention. We represent the international community in safeguarding internationally recognized law. Nair Dvipa has requested our help in avoiding unnecessary bloodshed. Kindly desist from instigating a naval warfare that may mar your international reputation as a strong, respectable & responsible nation".

Diànlì ji'è de guójia fired a missile high into the air as a warning.

Sudhir appeared suddenly in the air to create a protective energy field. The missile hit the field and exploded.

The Diànlì ji'è de guójia ships fired a volley of missiles. All of them exploded on hitting the protective energy field.

The is when they fired their 'magnetic charge buster'. The protective field created by Sudhir was nothing more than a constant chain of static negative-positive magnetic energy field. The thicker the number of chains, better it's elasticity, the more difficult it became to bust it. Diànlì ji'è de guójia threw a charge buster that sucked away the charge of two or more magnets in the chain. That created a riot in the chain and naturally, it collapsed.

Sudhir cast a spell and encased each of the Diànlì ji'è de guójia ships in ice. But the enemy fleet was ready! They created an internal heating system that melted the ice encasing the fleet within thirty minutes.

Sudhir knew that this was the time to ask for the help of the interstellar crafts under his command on Prithvi (Earth). Suddenly twenty Unidentified flying objects surrounded the total naval fleet of Diànlì ji'è de guójia. The lead destroyer cum aircraft carrier rose up in the air and began to rotate around its axis. One by one, all the submarines, and big ships rose in the air and began to rotate around their axis!

They continued to rotate at a very high speed for a full one hour.

Then they flew in the air all the way to Diànlì ji'è de guójia, rotating around their axis. When they touched down at the Diànlì ji'è de guójia airport instead of the sea port, all the officers on the ship got down tottering. They remained in the hospital for many months subsequently.

That day Diànlì ji'è de guójia declared over the media to the International community, "We have always respected international sentiments and have decided to forgive Nair Dvipa for their transgressions on our citizens who were admitted as their guests and then purchased their lands in bits and pieces over many years. This proof of purchase would appear on the Map of Ownership per plot.

Nair Dvipa assured the International community that the value of the land as on the date of purchase shall be reimbursed to Diànlì ji'è de guójia on presentation of proof of a genuinely legal transaction with the original owner confirming in writing that he had sold the said land.

Nair Dvipa declared that their King and Queen would be officially crowned on a specific date and that the Invitation to this ceremony, mentioning the date shall be conveyed to every country vide the normal diplomatic channels.

The battle-ready Indian team went back after a few months after they were certain that Nair Dvipa was safe.

Then the King went missing! When the Nair Dvipa security forces entered his hotel room, they found his suitcase and clothes were laid out on his bed!

In the meanwhile, India felt it was important to ensure that Mrs senior Bagaria and Mr. Pawan Bagaria were successful in their effort to meet their son, the new King and his new family. But how could they when the King and the Queen were missing? The security of the new King was of utmost importance. He had to be traced! The small, secret team had already left for Nair Dvipa from India. It was unsafe to fly by air because there was the possibility that the aircraft would be shot down by Diànlì ji'è de guójia forces, especially because they were sore about the recent insult.

Unknown to the world, a large Indian war ship sped towards Nair Dvipa on a request received "to help trace the King!"

Could it be that enemy forces had kidnapped the King and his Queen?

The Parents Arrive

Normally, no civilians are allowed on any Defense operated combat vessel or aircraft. Serving officers would most certainly be court martialed if they were to break this strict written rule. However, special permission was granted from the very top considering that the family members too played a crucial role in this secret, strategically important Nair Dvipa Rescue Mission being conducted by very senior trained Defense personnel.

The new Bhramastra Ship & Space Ship Builders Ltd, a new Indian Defense venture near Kochi, had begun to build indigenous hi-tech crafts to reduce its dependency on foreign countries.

The large war ship named 'Jalastra Prathama' with 'Vayam Rakshamah' (we protect) painted on its side, was its first indigenously manufactured Amphibious Transport Dock with its indigenous radars and sensors. It featured a well deck, which housed up to four LCM-8 mechanized landing craft that was planned to be launched by flooding the well deck and lowering the hinged gate aft of the ship. Six medium helicopters to be operated simultaneously were ready to use the flight deck during this emergency. The deck was also ready for use for vertical take-off and landing (VTOL) aircraft like the five 'Asman Dhanush'vertical Take off Aircraft, all of them indigenous products of India, which were at this very moment on high alert for this emergency.

'Jalastra Prathama' had at this very moment over 1,000 troops armed with the latest hand held high 'long distance laser' guns, and was fully equipped with extensive medical facilities including four operation theatres, a 12-bed ward, a battle stress treatment ward, a laboratory and a dental center.

The family team following 'Jalastra Prathama' consisted of a Hyper speed 'fly over water' coast guard boat of 30 odd people. No fossil fuel was being used to fly at Hyper speed over the water. It used the latest technology of magnets wherein atmospheric charges were analyzed at the speed of light and the craft produced a charge immediately opposite to the atmospheric charge. If atmospheric charge was negative then the crafts charge became positive and vice versa. This happened at a stupendously high speed thus bringing about a forward or backward or sideways movement.

Sudhir's father, mother, two children, the captain and crew of 5 people and the rest were senior and junior level army and coast guard personnel. But what was sent to do a reconnaissance of the island was the good old Mi8 helicopter that buzzed the island extensively. They flew over Suryadham the capital of Nair Dvipa. The normal city crowd, and the Defense Services of Nair Dvipa welcoming them over radio. Four helicopters of Nair Dvipa flew in and landed to officially welcome the India team. Both the Indian and Nair Dvipa copters flew over the villages. They reported seeing primitive dark people – but no sign of Sudhir or any sign of civilized human beings in the villages.

The copter captain queried, "Victor Tango Five O – Come in. Victor Tango Five O Come In. This is Zulu Yello Bravo Four Nine. Over"

The ships radio officer replied, "Zulu Yello Bravo Four Nine Come In. What is the Status Report? Over"

"The Copter replied, "Hundreds of Primitive People battling each other. War Zone. Repeat - War Zone. No sign of civilized people. Arrows with oil bursting in the skies all around us. I feel we are being shot at. Increasing altitude. Over"

The ships radio officer got up to allow Sudhir's father to instruct, "Report status on Palatial Mansion. Over"

The Mi8 Helicopter turned to buzz over the dilapidated structure, "No sign of life. Repeat – No sign of life. Over"

Sudhir's father queried, "Report on Sea Port – Repeat Sea Port. Over"

The Mi8 copter turned to once again buzz over the old British sea port and reported,

"No sign of life here. Repeat – No sign of Life. Flying to the new Sea Port. Over"

"Sir the new sea port is buzzing with life! People rushing with arms and with ammunition to positions on the roof tops. Port seems to be a fortress. Over!"

Sudhir's father was shocked, "What new sea port!?" Then he sighed and ordered, "Zulu Yello Bravo Four Nine. Do not take chances! Return to Base. Repeat Return to Base. Over"

"Roger that Victor Tango Five O. Over and out", replied the copter pilot and turned around to return.

The Landing of the Rescue Party

The boat tried to dock at the old port but the Captain reported, "Sir the old British port is inaccessible. There seems to be a lot of silt ".

"My family members remain on this boat until we find the island safe for their landing. In the meanwhile, some officers and I will be put on smaller boats and we shall find a suitable landing spot immediately", instructed Sudhir's father.

"Are you sure sir? The tide may not be safe. Would you prefer that some junior officers do a reconnaissance first?" suggested the Captain.

He looked at Pawandas Bagaria's eyes and decided that Sudhir's father was determined. So, he looked at his juniors and barked, "You heard him. Load and lower the boats".

Pawandas Bagaria, some officers and some armed personnel were seated in a smaller boat and they put on their life belts. Then the boat was gradually lowered into the waters with the help of the fixed cranes cum pulleys.

The boat engine came alive and it started purring through the sea waters towards a high beach front. The seamen got down to hold the boat while the members were helped down onto stools placed in the knee-deep water. One by one they were helped to wade onto the shore. Twelve people in all landed on the island. All were armed and ready for action.

Then they saw the majestic, golden coloured, dilapidated palace!

Very cautiously, step by steady step they climbed down to approach the dilapidated mansion. But they seemed to have lost their direction. It was a maze. Pawandas Bagaria looked back at the port, the jungle of growth all around, the cowshed, then he pointed at a direction and said "this way".

Very soon they stood in front of the main gate of the massive palace.

The team members exclaimed "Wow!" all as one. Pawandas Bagaria simply looked all around the mansion and gave instructions. "You four that way. Find any entry into the house. You four this way. Ditto instructions. You and you may please help me open the main door."

The team spread out. Some heavily muscled team members pushed at the main door. Nothing happened. "It is locked sir. We must break it open".

"Try the windows", Pawandas Bagaria instructed.

"Over here sir", called out a team member.

All the windows were shuttered & barricaded from inside. This one was shuttered from outside and barricaded with wooden planks. But the planks had been broken very recently with a rock that lay alongside. A used life belt lay outside this window. The life belt was picked up by one of the coast guard personnel and it read, "Malvindero Enterprises Ltd. Made in India".

The window was shut now and so they pushed it open. It opened inside and some bats that were disturbed by the sudden light, flitted out. The team ducked to get away from their path. They climbed into the palatial drawing room one by one. The room looked musty and unused for a long period of time. White blankets, now greyed or browned by time, covered most of the furniture. The team spread out within the building. "This way sir", shouted an officer. Pawandas went up to where the officer was pointing and saw foot prints on the dusty floor that let from the broken window that they had just entered from, to the kitchens, then back to the drawing room to go up the stairs. They followed the foot prints. The footprints climbed the stairs, reached the landing and turned left towards a half-shut door. One of the officers pushed open the door. It creaked and when pushed further and opened onto a rectangular shaped, ten feet wide corridor that formed the gut of the building, with a very large garden on the ground floor below protected by the corridor at its four corners.

The garden was now inundated with a jungle of shrubs, bushes and innumerable wild trees. Some of the wild creepers had climbed up the thick pillars that held up the corridor and had carpeted the corridor floor, along with the dried leaves that had blown in from the jungle of trees within the protected garden.

The team traversed the total corridor – very cautiously. They peeped through each of the windows one by one. They were decorated with the choicest of linen, expensive furniture, huge beds and tapestry. One specific room had an enormous study table with a big painting behind the same. It had, like every other room, wall to wall carpeting. The door to this room was unlocked. Pawandas signaled not to touch the room.

The footprints first led to a bedroom door and so they decided to inspect the bedroom. A large stone and a broken lock lay alongside.

The bedroom door creaked open. Then they all ducked! Bats and pigeons that had bombarded the room with bird poop were flitting or fluttering out of the room. Thus, the stink of decay and stale bird poop rushed to greet them. They covered their nose. The room had decaying woodwork, crumbling Victorian furniture, rotting bedsheets, quilts and mattresses. It was obvious. Nobody had been cleaning this room for a very long time.

The footsteps led first to the bed of solid mahogany. The bed had been used very recently. The quilt was a torn length of moth-eaten cloth somehow managing to hold on to remnants of what was once a thick, full of silky cotton, velvet quilt.

Footprints traversed to the cupboard, the toilet, the balcony, everywhere!

There was a broken window pane on the left of the bed. A lot of cobweb had covered the various corners of the window as also the room. A creeper had grown outside the window to enter the bedroom through the broken window pane. Some of the leaves within the room were large and the branches were thick and healthy, as if it had been growing within the room for a very long time.

They looked up. A fan, that was now rusted and forlorn – was hanging down on its hinges. They looked at the walls. The polished, well painted wall paint had peeled away to expose layer over layer of froths of seepage that had dried and caked over one another.

The paintings on the wall had not been dusted and were hanging at various angles. Some had remnants of faded images.

The cupboard seemed to have been opened very recently. Hundreds of neatly folded pajamas, night shirts, socks, underwear, shoes, ironed clothes hanging from clothes hangers – all this within the cupboard. But the moment they touched them, the clothes were, they discovered, as brittle as biscuit pieces, because they broke away into tiny pieces of dust in their fingers. These clothes were many years old and unusable.

They moved cautiously towards the toilet. The door creaked open on old hinges to show off a toilet full of cobwebs and dust all around. The mirror was faded and the toilet cupboards had innumerable dust laden, imported shaving blades, shaving cream after shave lotions and other exclusive toiletries. But the pure brass taps were caked with dust and did not work. The pure brass shower was caked with dust also and obviously did not work. He tried to check on the usability of the shaving blade that was wrapped so neatly in grease paper. Yes, they looked amazingly fresh. And so was the shaving brush made of camel hair, as well as the shaving cream.

Pawandas signaled his team to go downstairs, open the main door for the rest of the team and inspect the total building along with the surrounding area. They nodded and walked cautiously downstairs to execute his instructions.

Pawandas moved towards the study.

Garden Lizards and House Geckos raced around the dried leaves the moment the occasional waft of breeze would blow some leaves around or an adventurous insect would attract their attention. A few tiles from among the tiled canopy that hung away from the rectangular corridor, held up by solid steel angles, had cracked and broken away at many places and had allowed rain water to trickle in and fall on the corridor floor. Thereby providing sustenance to the new plant life that had taken root on the rotting leaves on the corridor floor.

He treaded carefully over the dry leaves and carpet of creepers lest snakes and dangerous insects were to bite him.

Ten feet high paintings adorned the corridor walls. Despite the onslaught of various elements over so many years, they still showed off the dignified personalities as if they were there right in front of him. They smiled back at him as if wanting to greet a visitor after so many years.

Each of the rooms on the left-hand side of the corridor were large and banquet room sized, but the rooms were locked.

Then he reached the study. It was unlocked. The broken lock that now lay on the floor, said all.

The door handle squeaked and squealed as he slid it out of the grooves that had held it in place for so many years. But the door whooshed open to exude the musty smell of a room that had not been opened for several years.

He saw large paintings of foreign, senior, highly decorated British Defense Officers, uniformed dignitaries, and that of Queen Victoria. Strangely, all the windows were shut tight and barricaded with wooden planks, as if someone wanted to shut himself or herself and this mansion, away from the outside world.

Then Pawandas saw the footprints. It led from the door to the chairs facing the single master chair on the other end. He followed the footsteps.

Pawandas's every step threw up a plume of dust that had settled over so many years on the carpeted floor. He approached the study table. It had a withered British flag along with photograph frames that held faded images of a young Mohandas Karamchand Gandhi. Pawandas touched the frames ever so gently and sighed. Some files tied together, an old oil lamp, a pen stand, a pen ink container to dip into, a hard leather board for the paper to be kept on for quality writing, an imported flask and a glass that was kept upside down.

All around him were mahogany shelves fixed onto the walls that had innumerable books lined up alphabetically on various subjects. 'Administration of a religiously diverse country', 'The Indian Diaspora', 'Will India remain a British subject', 'Understanding the psychology of an Indian Businessmen', 'Understanding the mind of the Indian terrorist', and so on.

There were two trays with 'In' and 'Out' written on the two of them. The 'In' tray was full of letters that had been undelivered to or not accepted by the addressee and hence returned. But they had been torn open very recently and the contents seemed to have been read very recently.

Pawandas sat down on the dusty chair to read the letter on top, then the other, then the next. Until he had finished reading all of them. Then he read them all over again. He took off his glasses after that, wiped his forehead and sighed.

Then he picked up his Walkie Talkie and spoke into the same, "Victor Tango Five O – Come In. Victor Tango Five O Come In. This is Bravo Bravo Recon. Over"

The ships radio officer replied, "Bravo Bravo Recon Come In. What is the Status Report Sir? Over"

"We have homed in on the landing spot. Repeat – we have homed in on the landing spot. Send repair team along with family members. Repeat – send repair team along with family members. Over and out". Instructed Pawandas.

"Roger that Bravo Bravo Recon. Over and out", replied the ship's Captain.

The Family Lands

They had all the proof that Sudhir was on this island and had stayed in this huge mansion and yet he was nowhere to be found! Sudhir's two children went all around the Palace along with four body guards. They saw the cow shed, the hen cages, the paths that had once led everywhere but were now full of shrubs and wild grass. Everything just as their father had dreamt! They looked at each other as this was shockingly amazing! The children rushed back to explain to their grandmother in an excited fashion – "Dadima! Dadima!" – meaning grandma, "Papa described all this to us. All of this! Papa knew about this place Dadima!"

Just then they heard jungle drums coming from very far away! From deep inside the jungle. They froze! The breeze blew in their direction and they heard the 'Shankha' – the conch shell, "Ooooooooaaaaaahhhnnn".

"Ooooooooaaaaaahhhnnn".

Then they heard the drums again coming from very deep inside the forest, "Do Dum Dum! Do Dum Dum! Do Dum Dum!" and wild men celebrating, "Urrrrrr Hah hhhh!" "Do Dum Dum! Do Dum Dum! Do Dum Dum! Urrrrrr Hah hhhh!" And roars of wild jubilation, "Aiiiiiiiii Ya ya ya ya ya ya ay yahhhh!"

"Mommy", screamed the children and rushed to their grandmother and Mrs. Bagaria grabbed them in her protective embrace. Two coast guard personnel rushed over to them and requested, gasping, "Mam, I think it would be prudent to be inside until further notice!".

Pawandas rushed downstairs and barked orders, "Barricade the Main door! Check all possible breach points. Man, the windows at the four corners of the building. Now! Move! Ask Rudy to fly out to hover over the possible source of the sounds and report. Ask some team members to clean up an area of the land ahead for possible landing and quick evacuation."

"Roger that Sir!"

The personnel rushed to obey orders! Some members of the team got down to swiftly cleaning the area in front of the mansion while others stood guard.

"Bravo Bravo Recon Come In. Bravo Bravo Recon Come in. This is Victor Tango Five O. Repeat – this is Victor Tango Five O. Over", crackled the Walkie Talkie with Pawandas.

"Come in Victor Tango Five O. Report your status. Over", instructed Pawandas.

"Nothing to worry Sir! But there are some small number of wounded uniformed officers of Diànlì ji'è de guójia on many numbers of wooden floats Sir! And they seem to be without paddles. And they are all around us Sir. Would not advice your evacuation by this path. Over"

"Do not do anything "instructed Pawandas "Simply keep an eye on them and report. Over".

"Daddu – I am scared", whispered 10-year-old Priya into her grandfather's ears. Her 12-year-old brother Randhir heard her whisper and asked his grandpa, "Daddu – Those are wild men are they not? Will they eat us!?

Their grandfather simply brought them even closer in reply.

Then they heard the whirr of a faraway helicopter approaching!

Pawandas's Walkie Talkie suddenly came alive, "Bravo Bravo Recon Come In. Bravo Bravo Recon Come In. This is Zulu Yello Bravo Four Nine. Repeat – this is Zulu Yello Bravo Four Nine. Over".

Pawandas replied, "Zulu Yello Bravo Four Nine Come in. Zulu Yello Bravo Four Nine. Come in. Do you know your co-ordinates? Over".

The copter pilot replied, "That is affirmative Sir. Repeat – that is affirmative. Over"

Pawandas then instructed, "Be ready to fire on command Zulu Yello Bravo Four Nine. Over".

The copter pilot then reported, "Bravo Bravo Recon Come In. This is Zulu Yello Bravo Four Nine Reporting Sir! We see hundreds of tribesmen in wooden floats, moving away from the shore in various directions Sir! Feel they have won the battle we had seen a few hours back Sir! Over!"

Pawandas instructed, "Zulu Yello Bravo Four Nine Report on the source of the sound. Over!"

The copter pilot hovered over the victory celebrations, "Hundreds of wild jungle warriors Sir! They seem to be celebrating a victory sir! They seem to waving at us! Yes! They all are waving at us Sir! And they are beating their drums and dancing!"

Then there was a pause and then – "There seems to be a large contingent rushing out of the village fort sir, right now! They seem to be possessing long burning sticks in their hands. They seem to be hundreds of them now. They are moving in your direction Sir! Shall we fire Sir?"

"No! Hold your Fire!" ordered Pawandas, "Just follow them and keep reporting. Over!"

The drums and shrill war cries grew closer and closer. The 'sankha' - conch shell sound resonated through the forest and seemed now like it was very close.

"Bravo Bravo Recon Come In. They are only two hours away from your present location Sir! Would advise immediate evacuation Sir! Until then re-enforcements can be called in now before it is to late Sir! Waiting for your instructions. Over".

Pawandas send down two of his men to help and finish the preparations for a quick airlift. The modern army did not understand what the wild warriors near the ship were trying to do after having slaughtered the uniformed officers of Diànlì ji'è de guójia. The modern army saw the fierce looking warriors and felt that there was no doubt that they had to evacuate by air.

The drums grew closer and closer. The 'Shankha' seemed to be louder - much louder!

Pawandas instructed, "Zulu Yello Bravo Four Nine Report on the location of the approaching warriors. Over!"

"Bravo Bravo Recon Come In. They are 10 minutes away. Repeat – they are ten minutes away from you. Over" the copter warned.

"Zulu Yello Bravo Four Nine - Be ready to fire on command. Over" instructed Pawandas.

"Roger that. Over" replied the copter.

The sound of drums had reached the periphery of the forest. The family had been moved to the dining room downstairs. The kids were whimpering in the laps of their mother and grandmother, who seemed equally worried.

Pawandas was standing at his open window upstairs, in the study, looking at his team working in the shrubs below. The corner most window in the corner most room, two rooms after the study, had been opened too, to gain a vantage point for firing at the enemy that was closing in. He signaled to his team below that they must increase speed and conveyed through gestures that the enemy was just 10 minutes away!

Is my son dead, he wondered? In the hands of these wild men?

Pawandas decided that he had to protect his family at all costs! He had to protect his progeny! Even at the cost of losing his life! Just then – the last letter written by the old man of the house blew away from the heap of letters in the 'In Tray' and floated down to his feet. He picked it up to put it back, and then he noticed a few lines which read –

".............My son....... You are old enough to appreciate that this is the age when I long to be a grandfather. This is the age when I long to hear the pattering of small feet running all around this huge mansion. This is the age when I desire to hear the chirp of little children and the love of their embrace.

I hear that you had got married and that you have a child. Do you suppose you would want to visit us along with your family?......"

He sighed, put the letter back in the 'In tray', marched up to the portrait of the old man and whispered, "I am sorry that I am late father. But I want my son back! I have learned my lesson father – do not hurt my son's family for my mistakes! This is your progeny asking for your forgiveness! The people below are your progeny father. Protect them."

Having said that he walked up to the image of his second and first mother, looked at them for a while, pensively, and then marched back to his point of vigil - at the window.

The roar of a huge army could be heard and then they burst out of the cover of the forests into the open. Hundreds of them. Beating drums "Do Dum Dum! Do Dum Dum! Do dum Dum!" and wild men celebrating, "Urrrrrr Hah hhhh!", "Do Dum Dum! Do Dum Dum! Do dum Dum! Urrrrrr Hah hhhh!" And roars of wild jubilation, "Aiiiiiiiii Ya ya ya ya ya ya ay yahhhh!"

The kids, now in the dining room downstairs, covered their ears both because the sound decibel was so high and because otherwise, it made them afraid.

The helicopter hovered overhead. The "whirrrrr" added to the cacophony of Beating drums "Do Dum Dum! Do Dum Dum! Do dum Dum!" and wild men celebrating, "Urrrrrr Hah hhhh!"

Pawandas kept the Walkie Talkie on the Study table and took the binoculars in his hands. Several naked men with bows, arrows, spears and thick long sticks with a mass tied on the top that were on fire, and they were all staring at this building and pointing at it with excited gestures from the other end of the forest. They were dark featured along with short curly hair and a specially designed animal hide protection for their private parts. Animal bone garlands hung from their necks and animal bones pierced their nose as part of their attire. They had these masks that had the skulls and skins of dead animals on their heads or back. And every time they let out a roar – it sent shivers down his spine.

"Zulu Yello Bravo Four Nine - Be ready to fire on command. Over" instructed Pawandas.

"Roger that. Over" replied the copter pilot as it hovered over the ocean of wild warriors.

Just then the last letter written by the old man flew and slapped onto the face of Pawandas! "What the ...!" exclaimed Pawandas and grabbing the paper in his hands said,

"Zulu Yello Bravo Four Nine - on my command. Over" instructed Pawandas

"Roger that. My finger is on the trigger Sir. Over" replied the copter pilot as it hovered over the ocean of wild warriors.

Pawandas then kept the letter back in the 'In Tray' and returned to the window to put the Binoculars to his eyes. The wind stopped blowing. Even the crickets stopped chirping. Just then the letter written by the old man flew and slapped onto the face of Pawandas – once again! An exasperated Pawandas grabbed the letter in his hands, marched up to his father's portrait and asked in a growl, "Why do you want to disturb me at this juncture father. Do you want to kill your remaining progeny too!" Then Pawandas saw something in his father's eyes – was the expression different from the original portrait?! How was this possible? The portrait was not smiling! Neither were the portraits of his mothers. None of them were smiling! This was truly amazing!

"What is it father?", Pawandas asked. "Is something wrong? Is there something you want to tell me father?"

Just then a gale blew in, the door of the bedroom in which Sudhir had slept, flew open and a small tin can opened and careened his way. In the tin was a small poem. One of the lines read, "Hurried decisions brings about sorrow and in-patient action you shall gain what you may have lost for a while".

Just then the roars of wild jubilation, "Aiiiiiiiii Ya ya ya ya ya ya ay yahhhh!" rent the air.

The Walkie Talkie in the hand of Pawandas crackled, "Bravo Bravo Recon Come In. Bravo Bravo Recon Come In. Give me permission to open Fire. Repeat. Give me permission to Fire Over".

Pawandas read the poem again. Then he rushed with the Binoculars to the open window. He saw a semi naked, bearded wild man approaching. On his shoulders was a little, healthy dark-complexioned child. And he was holding the hand of a decked-up girl – seemed a tribal queen! The wild man could be just five minutes away from this mansion.

"Zulu Yello Bravo Four Nine – Hold your fire. Repeat – Hold your fire. Over" instructed Pawandas. Then he rushed down towards the main door.

"Sir! They are at our door step. Stop Sir! The wild men are outside", shouted a panicked officer. Pawandas opened the main door and rushed out after he looked at them and barked, "Do not fire until I say so".

The Final Moments

"The old man has gone stark mad", gasped the officer, picked up his walkie – talkie and warned the copter, "Zulu Yello Bravo Four Nine – Hold your fire! Repeat – Hold your fire! The boss has gone out on his own to fight them. Over"

"I have my finger on the trigger. Will keep an eye on the boss too. Over", replied the pilot.

Pawandas was running towards the naked bearded man who was walking 2 minutes ahead of the rest of the tribe holding the hands of the queen of the tribe and with the child on his shoulders. The wild warriors seeing the

'Agniaw' charging at their tribesman got agitated and screamed, "Aiiiiiiiii Ya ya ya ya ya ya ay yahhhh!" and charged with a roar.

The pilot did not wait for instructions. He fired a full volley four feet ahead of the first lot of twenty warriors. "Ratt tata – tata – tatat tat," the guns blazed, "Ratat – tatatat – rat tat a tat" the bullets screamed and chewed away the earth from a few feet in front of the warriors. "Phew phwet. Pow Phewt!", was the sound heard by the warriors.

The semi naked, bearded wild man and the queen looked back at their brood and screamed something intelligible in their language and signaled them to stop on their tracks.

Pawandas was at this very moment screaming into the walkie talkie, "Zulu Yello Bravo Four Nine – stop firing. Repeat – stop firing. Over".

Now he was running towards the semi naked, bearded wild man, the child on his shoulders and the tribal queen. Then they were suddenly standing in front of each other. The wind was blowing the semi naked man's hair and beard all around. Then he stepped forward and embraced his father.

Chapter 23

Nair Dvipa Recovers

The Family Reunion

"Papa Shame shame. You are not wearing clothes!" cooed a lankey ten-year-old Priya into her father's ears. She was on his lap. Her brother, twelve-year-old Randhir clung to his father's neck and asked, "Papa why did you go away? I missed you so much!".

Seven-year-old Mobi was standing alone, holding onto the door knob. "That is Mobi, your new brother, from now on!" And then he beckoned Randhir to bring Mobi over to the family group. Both Randhir and Priya walked over to Mobi, Randhir extended his hand and Mobi held his finger to be led to the sofa where Ngia Vat was already seated, being pampered by her mother in law, Sudhir's mother. Senior Mrs. Shyamili Bagaria grabbed her new grandson into her lap and promptly planted six kisses all over his cheeks!

A Nair Dvipa officer came forward, saluted and asked, "Sir the Diànlì ji'è de guójia soldiers who have recently escaped from their barracks need to be lifted from the waters. Shall we do so?"

"Yes Please!" requested Sudhir with a smile.

The Junior Warrant Officers, and Sergeants saluted Sudhir as they marched past him. But when the senior most defense officers began to salute him, Sudhir's children called him aside and asked him, "Our Grand father is the senior defense personnel. Are you saluting our father Mr. Sudhir Bagaria by mistake?"

"Prince Randhir and Princess Priya, I salute him because your father is the King of Nair Dvipa, the Kingdom on which we stand today", so saying he bowed politely and marched away.

"A King?! The King of Nair Dvipa?" Priya asked another senior Defense officer, "Yes Princess Priya! He is all over the latest newspapers. He saved Nair Dvipa from Mogui a powerful wizard from Diànlì ji'è de guójia using his own powerful magical powers! And he has guided us towards throwing out the occupying forces resident in Nair Dvipa!". So saying, he too bowed politely and marched away.

Just then one of the copters had a rotor blade problem and began to totter in midair. Sudhir looked up and shot into the air, held the copter and guided it gently down on the palace ground. Then he flew back to his children.

His children exclaimed, "You can fly too! He was right! You truly possess magical powers!"

Trying to impress his children was not his intention. But because the children had landed at the Palace, he needed a spruced-up Palace. Hence, he clicked his fingers together and the shrubs began to fold up and vanish into thin air. Fresh flowers began to float in from every direction and began to plant itself along with the green carpet grass, tall shady trees, cowsheds, hen coops, water sprinklers, drawing room, dining room, bedrooms, everything changed right in front of everybody's awed eyes! Two golden dalmatians appeared out of nowhere and began to play with Priya and Randhir.

Everyone was smiling and happy. The copter had that was saved had brought in crates of cold drinks, packets of tinned food, fire wood, coal, matchboxes, crates of hard liquor for the officers and for Pawandas etc.

Just then, one of the senior officers came marching up to Sudhir and requested, "Beg your pardon Sir, but the Tribes men are acting a bit strange with the copter. I hope they do not damage it".

Pawandas and Sudhir rushed out to see the Tribesmen pointing arrows at the copter and chanting, "Howva Minsaw", "Howva Minsaw", "Howva Minsaw"

Sudhir rushed to them, massaged their backs, patted the copter and got into the copter. That got them scared again, they were terrified and pointing arrows at the copter they screamed," Aiyeeee, Ya ya ya ya aya a"

Sudhir got out of the copter, raised his hands, patted the copter and declared, 'Mahua Minsaw'. Seeing Sudhir come out safe from the mouth of the flying Monster, the tribesmen bend their heads this way and that way in a crouched position and then some of them were reluctantly made to touch the copter, another was made to enter, then exit the copter and having so honoured him with bravery, they all declared the flying Monster to be 'Mahua Minsaw'.

Another JWO rushed up to suggest they purchase a fresh lot of chicken. "But we had just got a delivery of 300 chickens", asked Mrs.Bagaria senior.

The officer pointed outside. Mrs.Bagaria saw the wild warrior army racing after several chickens in the recently cleared garden. As each of them caught one, they ran away into the bushes to eat it raw!

She looked at the officer and instructed, "Make that 600 chickens then!"

"Yes mam", barked the officer and rushed away to issue instructions.

Another Wild warrior was playing – 'Horsie – Horsie' with Sudhir's children. But every time he would see the beer being served then, he would grab a bottle and polish it off in one gulp. After some time, he was quite a tipsy horsy. And then the horse flopped on the grass – and was snoring! "You are boring "declared Sudhir's daughter and walked up to the next wild man.

The Defense services canteen had sent Pawandas a bill for the material for personal services – Rs. 3 lacs. His wife nearly fainted. But Pawandas happily signed the same. He had his son back after so many years! Out of the bill, Rs.50000 was for only liquor! The Tribesmen had a rollicking time that evening. With bonfires, and unlimited raw chicken that was racing around even at this very moment and salted baked fish!

They were at this moment pointing at Sudhir's mother through heavy eyes and had declared her to be 'Mahua Tinua' – meaning 'the good tiny woman'.

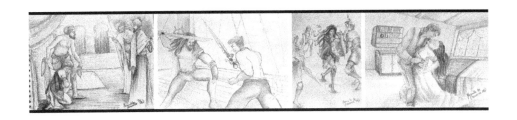

Chapter 24

The Crowning of the King and the Queen

Senior dignitaries from all over the world, including USA, Europe, Asia, including India, were seated within the palace in the grounds behind. Security guards were spread out all over the palace compound.

The tribal army was spread out in the palace ground, now in their traditional sports day attire.

Three cars entered the palace grounds, one with King Sudhir Bagaria and Queen Ngia Vat and the next car with Pawandas Hanuman Bagaria and his wife, Pricess Shyamili Bagaria. In the last were Sudhir's three children, Prince Randhir, Princess Priya and Prince Mobi.

As the three cars entered the palace grounds, bugles & trumpets were being blown, five elephants were saluting him, a huge joyous crowd was throwing green, purple, violet flowers on the pavement for all of them and Sudhir and Ngia vat was being welcomed by a retinue of senior ministers who were greeting them, with "Welcome to our King & Queen! Long live our King & Queen! May God gift our King & Queen with a long life!"

They parted and ten senior priests wearing the ordinary white loincloth, or dhoti, head hair tonsure that leaves a tuft of hair longer than the rest (shikha) and the sacred thread (upavita), worn diagonally across the body, over the left shoulder came forward and stopped with folded hands. Out of them. two senior most priests came forward, did a namaskaram, turned to look toward the palace and pointing at the same, guided them in that direction. They found themselves following the two senior most Hindu priests, climbing into the huge football stadium sized back part of the palatial building. They stopped in front of one of the many treasure rooms. It was full of gold coins stacked into small conical hillocks, innumerable wooden chests or casks brimming with ancient jewelry, ancient swords with diamonds, rubies and emeralds embedded into them and large bronze and pure gold statues holding onto pure gold covered iron spears. On their bodies they wore iron body armor plus chain armor wherever the body was needed to bend or turn, as if ready for battle.

"All these and more belong to you my King & Queen!" the priests bowed with folded hands and said.

The Royal family were guided into a glass chamber that sat parallel to the space where the ceremonial crowing would take place. King Sudhir and Queen Ngia vat were guided towards a pair of pure golden thrones, studded with rubies, diamonds, emeralds, and other precious stones that glistened and winked in the afternoon sun.

The ceremonial guards came riding in on horses that were trained to march with the music. The white peacocks were released just then and flew up into the air "cuck – cuck -cuck" -ing in every direction and from their feet opened and floated down the petals of innumerable flowers, coloured in as many hues as there are in the universe.

The panthers and tigers were marched in just then on a tight pure steel lease. The massive Asian and African elephants followed with the blowing of elephant trumpets.

Nair Dvipa classical dancers joined dangers from the villages of the Powva tribe. Each tribe had its own dancers, from the Zambeke village, Omagwena village, Kavaheke village, and the Kunini village.

The ceremonial guards of the Kings crown came marching in just then followed by horse driven carts that carried two pure golden crowns studded with diamonds from the Wollur Mine, located far away in the southern hills of Nair Dvipa. The head priest in charge of the crowns of the King and the Queen, was escorted down by two tall and strong Powva tribe

Warriors from the Beti Beti village, the super council village or the village of the elders of the Powva tribe.

The head priest walked in the center as the two Powva tribe attendants walked up the steps, one by one with the music right up to the central table on which the crowns were placed accompanied by the thunder of drums.

Unlike normal procedure, both the King and the Queen had to step forward to the centrally fixed marble table on which the crowns were placed. King Sudhir Bagaria was escorted by Prince Mobi while Queen Ngia Vat was escorted by both Prince Randhir, and Princess Priya.

Princess Priya was whispering into the ears of Prince Randhir right now, "Randy bhaiya! I can't believe it, we are a Princess and a Prince! Hee hee!"

"Shhh!!" reprimanded Prince Randhir, without looking at his younger sister.

The head priest stepped forward and requested, "I urge the King of all Kings, the son of the great Prince Pawandas Hanuman Bagaria, to receive his crown in perpetuity!" Sudhir stepped forward and the heavy crown was placed on his head by Ombasa, Chief of the Super council of the Powva tribe.

The head priest now looked at Ngia Vat and requested "I urge the Queen of all Queens, the daughter of Ombasa, Chief of the Super council of the Powva tribe, to receive her crown in perpetuity!" Ngia Vat stepped forward and the heavy crown was placed on her head by Prince Pawandas Hanuman Bagaria.

You are now officially declared the King and Queen of Nair Dvipa.

"You may now declare the celebration, my King", suggested the head priest.

Just at that very moment, Sudhir stepped forward and interrupted the ceremony.

"I wish the attention of my honourable guests from all over the world. I wish to make an important announcement", he said with dignity.

He whispered into the ears of Ngia Vat, his Queen, "Keep this crown meant for a King next to you, and hand it over when I ask for the same", he finished after handing over a box with a pure gold crown studded with diamonds, rubies and emeralds.

The priest stared at the exchange with worried eyes and looked at the senior ministers.

"Ladies and gentlemen! You must certainly have noticed very recently the appearance of certain out of this world people in Nair Dvipa", began King Sudhir Bagaria. "Other than being the King of Nair Dvipa, I also happen to be the Chief of Intergalactic Justice on Prithvi (Earth)!" he finished and waited for any reaction.

The guests and the citizens of Nair Dvipa began to look with shock into each other's eyes! This was obvious admission of interaction with aliens! Cameras began to click and the television cameras began to record.

The senior Ministers of Nair Dvipa began to look at each other with concern written all over their faces. Was this freedom that they had just fought and won going to result in a 'pan to the fire' situation? They had just seen the King handover a crown to his Queen. Was he abdicating his thrown? That would be terrible! Was their King going to take a decision that they may regret?

"Step forward Nksi Nanga!" requested King Sudhir Bagaria.

The guests, the media, the citizens of Nair Dvipa gasped in unison! King Sudhir obviously wanted to execute evil Nksi Nanga in front of the world audience! That was good!

The Media began to click pictures and video record the expected action of belated justice.

Nksi Nanga looked left and then right. He was in chains because of his crimes, and it was impossible that his enemy wanted to call him up to him for a good purpose. The police personnel who had escorted him to his glass cubicle, now pulled him up to a standing position.

"Come forward Nksi Nanga!" requested King Sudhir Bagaria.

The police personnel now helped a reluctant ex-witch doctor forward, but the fear was obvious in the eyes and and his every step. His memory was too fresh! He could still remember Sudhir defeating five of his best warriors in the village stadium. And what terrified him the most was the memory of Sudhir lifting him up and throwing him down on the stadium floor like he would a rag doll. Then, holding his heavy body up by the scruff of his neck and zooming up into the skies as if he were a feather weight mouse!

The crowd now held their breath as Nksi Nanga cringed back against the strong arms of the police personnel who were now thrusting him forward towards King Sudhir.

King Sudhir Bagaria spoke to Nksi Nanga thus, "You Nksi Nanga have served many days and many months in solitary confinement of the prisons of this capital city of Nair Dvipa. The fathers, mothers, wife's and children of the innocent villagers who were slaughtered by the weapon that you had procured from your grandfather Prince Mogui, had met you and wanted that you be punished. The husbands, mothers, sisters, brothers, children of the woman that you raped had wanted justice. They had requested that you be whipped and you were whipped and the affected villagers & other Nair Dvipa citizens were witness. You have cried alone and wept for mercy. From your wealth, that is your share, being a direct descendant of your grandfather, we have compensated each affected tribe member and city dweller with certain sums of gold mohars. Do you have anything to say?"

"I know you want to kill me now, in front of all these people! But please don't kill me! Please! I beg of you! Just give me a second chance!" Tall and bulky Nksi Nanga shoulders shook as he wept. The International and local spectators booed and showed their thumps down. "Die! Die! Die! Die", began the chant.

"Can you hear them Nksi Nanga?" asked King Sudhir Bagaria. "They do not wish that you should live. Give me one good reason why you should live".

"Because I am a child of injustice!" said Nksi with tears flowing from his eyes. "I used to see how the villagers treated my mother and nobody, none of the pro justice chiefs stepped forward to the assistance of a single mother as she fought to feed me and teach me the ways of this world! No one from the village came forward to claim me as his son! As thousands of fathers held their pampered children close to their chest and walked around the village, I stared at them wanting to be held up too, but they glared at me as if I was pariah. They called me a bastard and no one came forward to challenge that insult!"

Sudhir looked at the congregation of villagers and asked," Can anybody please tell me who is Mogui's father from amongst you?"

Ngia Vat glared at her husband as Nksi Nanga was escorted up the stairs in chains by a heavy escort of soldiers. Intergalactic representatives appeared in a flash on his side to try and whisper to him to stop this "foolish decision!"

Nobody stepped forward barring Ngia Vat! Everybody gasped! But she stepped forward and stared at her father Ombasa.

Her father stood up slowly, then stepped forward and stared into the eyes of King Sudhir Bagaria, "I am the father of Nksi Nanga!".

The crowd gasped in shock. Ombasa was a responsible and a respected chief. For him to have neglected the upbringing and protection of his child was unpardonable!

Ombasa walked up to Nksi Nangia and said, "This is why I had refused your request to marry Ngia vat. She was and remains your sister!"

"Ooooohoo!", the crowd gasped in disbelief.

Nksi Nanga stared into the eyes of Ombasa, his father, with tears flowing down his eyes and he said, "When my mother was unwell and could not hunt, nobody came forward to feed me. I went to bed hungry during those days and went hungry for many days during the last few days of my mother!"

Then he looked at King Sudhir Bagaria and continued, "I became who I am because I realized that these were powerful people who decided what was just and what was not just! They were respected because they were strong and when they wronged, nobody cared because nobody dared to question them. I realized that to gain respect in this village and to have a full stomach, I must be stronger than them!" and he gestured towards his father.

"When you arrived, I realized that I may have to see my old days of hunger once again", Nksi continued looking at Sudhir. "I became desperate because memories of my mother dying and my desperation, my helplessness came rushing back to my mind. And that is when I met the man who could fly and who claimed he was my grandfather. And I told him everything! I told him how my grandmother had hung on to a raft in the ocean waters and died on giving my mother away to a medicine woman. How that medicine woman had taught my mother to be strong and self-sufficient. And how I was born due to a wedlock between my mother and this coward who till today did not have the courage to call me his son! That man who flew, he hugged me close to his chest and he wept! He told me that I was a Prince! Even as he wept, he promised me my due. That I was the claimant to my share of wealth that you just spoke about".

Nksi wiped away his tears and continued, "If that is so then I was a Prince too when I took the decision to use the weapon. I was a guardian of justice when I used the weapon. A guardian of justice may take decisions that are for the benefit of the larger sections of society but may result in the deaths of a small section of people. You have punished and whipped a prince like you would punish a common man! Do you not feel that justice has been served? That I have been punished as was due?

Do you not feel that instead of being killed in front of these honourable guests, I should be given a palace of my own?"

The crowd had been stunned into silence. The photographers and cameramen had stopped clicking or recording. There was pin drop silence.

"It becomes my duty to undo an injustice done many ages back! As the Chief of Intergalactic Justice on Prithvi (Earth), I had ordered the arrest very recently of a Prince of this Kingdom. However, as he was being led away, I had made my promise to him which I intend to keep!"

Looking at Nksi Nanga he said, "I never intended to kill you Nksi. I intended to keep my promise made to your grandfather".

Sudhir looked forward at Ombasa and said, "I request honourable Ombasa, the Super Chief of Beti Beti, and the Chief of the Super council of the Powva tribe to step forward. I also request honourable chiefs of the villages of Zambeke, Omagwena, Kavaheke, and Kunini villages to step forward.

The village chiefs were embarrassed but they did step forward.

"What is your decision?" he asked looking at them.

"Ombasa must compensate Nksi Nanga and honourable Ombasa can no longer remain our chief," replied the villagers of villages of Zambeke, Omagwena, Kavaheke, and Kunini villages.

King Sudhir looked at Ombasa and asked, "Are you in agreement with the decision? Do you wish to challenge the verdict?"

"I do not oh great Mohua Minshaw!" replied Ombasa.

Sudhir looked at the guests and citizens of Nair Dvipa.

"When Nksi Nanga's grandfather had become a criminal, he too had spoken about injustice having driven him to commit the unforgivable crimes that he did. The evil energy cannot be held solely responsible. The negative energy found him to be a malleable executive. But what must also be considered is the fact that Mogui could have been kept away from his parents once they were found to be evil and a bad influence on the child. He could have been provided the love and security that would have provided him the atmosphere to become a responsible citizen. The past decisions of Nair Dvipa too are jointly responsible for the crimes that have affected innumerable citizens of Nair Dvipa in the distant past and in the recent past.

Nksi Nanga is correct in demanding justice. And justice has been long overdue for his family.

I hereby declare that Nksi Nanga be crowned the King of the island of Swargbhumi!"

A shocked silence ensued for a while. Then a foreign dignitary began to clap alone. Then another, and then another. Very soon all the dignitaries, the media, the citizens were clapping their hands.

"Bravo! Bravo!", many dignitaries roared with admiration for King Sudhir's brave decision.

"Walk up to me Nksi Nanga!" command King Sudhir Bagaria. "Step forward Ombasa!"

Sudhir beckoned Ngia Vat to hand over the crown and she did.

The shackles that held Nksi Nanga down were unlocked and the chain "clank", clanked down the steps of the stadium as if protesting the decision.

King Sudhir handed Ombasa with a pure golden crown studded with diamonds, rubies and emeralds and requested, "Place the crown on your son's head please!"

Nksi Nanga stepped forward, bent his head and his father placed the crown on his head.

Sudhir then declared, "You are hereby crowned the King of Swargbhumi, the island next to ours! You shall bring about development and the wellbeing of the citizens of the island as you would for your own family!"

Then King Sudhir took a large pure gold key and handed over the key to him saying," This key shall help you unlock the path to happiness, satisfaction and prosperity!"

The crowd roared in acceptance of the King's decision.

King Sudhir Bagaria raised his hands into the air and roared, "I hereby invite my guests from the various countries, senior dignitaries and senior citizens of Nair Dvipa to the banquet hall to join us in our celebrations! For my other fellow citizens, I have a grand party awaiting you at the gardens beyond. Food of your choice and liquor to your liking!" he finished smiling.

The crowd roared in pleasure.

The guests from the various countries and senior dignitaries and senior citizens of Nair Dvipa that King Sudhir Bagaria was talking about, joined him in the massive banquet hall. As they sat down, ten per table, below each bowl was a pure Gold Mohor for each guest, that is, a pure gold coin!

In this huge party, no one realized that Prince Pawandas Hanuman Bagaria was absent.

Down Memory Lane

Pawandas was at this very moment in front of the portrait of his parents. His father and the two mothers in his life.

Pawandas stood in front of a large bedroom and he was staring at the lock. He cussed, "Damn the lock – now how do I open it?" The lock fell open. Pawandas looked all around and found nobody. He entered his mother's room and found that the room was the same as he had last seen it.

He sat down with a bottle and his glass besides him on a dirty sofa. The windows opened suddenly, by themselves. "Mother?" asked Pawandas. A strange glow appeared slowly in front of him. "Mother!" exclaimed Pawandas and embraced the spirit. Pawandas suddenly realized that he was crying, "I missed you. I missed you so much", he whispered. Just then Pawandas sensed another spirit in the room, that of his father.

"I am sorry son. I should have given you more love. I should have been more understanding", his father apologized.

Another spirit arrived, "I loved you my son", his second mother's spirit said. "And I continued to love you even after my demise, my son", she assured him.

Pawandas embraced all of them and said, "Papa. Your progeny is here under your roof. How do you feel?"

"Just as you feel after getting your son back after so many years, my son", his father replied.

"God has various ways of teaching us about what we must do for those we truly love. I learned it just before I died and after I lost you. You have fortunately the rest of your life to relish what you have got back. Cherish what you have got back and teach them about what you have learned my son".

Just then Pawandas noticed an old Gramophone LP Player that would play when the spring was screwed clockwise. "Mama your Record player!" exclaimed Pawandas! Does it work? You both had so many dances together! Why don't you all dance with each other tonight, for me, please".

He put a record on the player and it worked! The soft music spread out its message of happiness to every corner of the room. He saw the old man suddenly appear and ask for the first wife to dance. She graciously accepted his offer and merrily danced away the Rumba, Salsa, Samba, Tango, and finally Waltz. Then it was the turn of the second wife. She too accepted his offer and danced a Foxtrot and the Morris dance. The old man and the two ladies were obviously happy. They had their son amongst them. They were looking into each other's eyes and were so very happy. And they too looked at him with eyes filled with pride. There was this old song, "You are my personal possession, My only love. Du Dud u…" and they looked at him with fondness.

Balloons were being filled up all by themselves and they were bursting all by themselves. Ribbons of confetti were floating all around. The party carried on for very long. He loved the evening. In fact, he loved these lovely people.

The Farewell

The team were all packed to go when the tribesmen raised a hue and cry about his family taking Sudhir and his wife away. So then, Sudhir and his family got down and unpacked. Pawandas looked up at the window of the study room and saw his father smiling!

"Bye Hanuman!", waved Sudhir, grinning at his father

"How did you know about that pet name?" growled Pawandas, with a pretended frown on his face.

"It is all in the files relating to properties and wealth that Nair Dvipa now owns!", teased Sudhir.

"You know something about the wealth that my second mother wrote about Sudhir?", asked Pawandas.

Sudhir pointed at the 6 files on the seat in the copter. "All those details are in the files that I found in the cave. That is when I knew that Pawandas

Bagaria was the son of the grand old man of this huge Mansion Sir. Now Bye Bye!" And so, saying Sudhir shut the door of the copter.

The engine was yet to start.

Pawandas Bagaria, re-opened the door, called Sudhir over, handed back the files to him and said, "Now King of Nair Dvipa, these files are yours!" Then he shut the door of the copter and it flew up into the air.

Sudhir and his family including the children watched as it gradually flew into the deep blue sky. Pawandas looked down at the window below. He waved at the spirits of his parents. And they waved back!

King Nksi Nanga Takes Over Swargbhumi

After Nksi Nanga was crowned King of the small island, the size of Singapore, titled Swargbhumi, next to Nair Dvipa, Sudhir ensured immediate support by posting Heads of departments to further train his juniors. Nksi Nanga promptly declared the small island to be a "free trade island" with "no tax".

Sudhir granted the treasure stored in the palace to Nksi Nanga, Mogui's grand son, which had been extracted from the bottom of the ocean waters. To give him due respect, none of his support team wore clothes, including the women. Neither did the Airport authorities and the life guards at the sea front resorts. Foreigners loved to visit his island.

Sudhir sent a mental message to Mogui in his solitary prison cell, "Justice has been served".

The Dignitaries from a faraway planet were very worried about the decision.

The Rest of the Treasure

Nobody had known where the rest of the treasure was until the Intergalactic Leaders pointed at a floating mountain high up in the clouds. Nobody could see it from below!

Treasure from six out of the seven ships had been stored here by his powerful great grandfather. Treasure from two ships automatically became the share due to Mogui and hence he was handed over treasure from one more ship.

Sudhir found solace with Ngia vat on the top of this floating mountain. It offered solitude and peace!

Sudhir and Ngia Vat had two children.

Chapter 25

Two Years later

The pilot was drinking against regulations. He was singing a lullaby. He was flying a fifteen-seater aircraft which offered drinks free for this holiday package at these coral islands. Everyone was drunk because he had craftily mixed drinks with the fruit juice too. Behind him, a teetotaler was hiccupping while talking to his teetotaler wife. She was hiccupping while replying. The sozzled airhostess somehow balanced her way to the last passenger who kept pressing the bell. The couple's eight month year-old kid. It wanted another helping of "milk". Nah nah ", it cooed, "Du Du", (milk) it demanded and hiccupped! Thrice!

The pilot was explaining to the passengers, "LLay dees and Gen tel men! You zud see on your left the biggest Tuna factory in Nair Dvipa – the 'Agniaw Mrignaw Minsaw - Mary Ann". God knows what the name means but it produces the finesh Tu Tu Tuna which you are going to gorge on at one of the finest ho ho hotels in Nair Dvipa.

And the sce sce scenery is exquisite! You have sea birds flying all around you. One of the passengers looked and there was a man flying on the left of the window. Right there outside his bloody window! He said, "Now that is a lovely bird". Then he kept aside his whiskey bottle!

The pilot looked on his right and saw a boy of around 12 and a girl of 10 years flapping their hands and flying alongside – outside his window! He shook his head and looked again. The children popped their tongue out at him! And he kept staring. He too kept his bottle down.

The flying children waved at him and signaled, "Cheers"!

The Beginning

Story titled - Those Forgotten People

Written by Aniruddha Roy Choudhury

Family Tree

Generation	Year	Family	Family	Family
1st	1762	Daivam King Kurungothu Nambiar		
2nd	1783	Prince Kuthiravattathu Nair son in law (wife Queen Pallavi, the Kochu Thampuran, that is the First Princess)	King Kurungothu Nambiar's	
3rd	1805	Daivam King Unni Pushpakan Ambalavasi	Mógui de érzi, Son of Swaminarayanan & Pirate King, Wugu's daughter Sanya, travels back in time	Curly haired, chocolate complexioned tribes saved from the ocean waters and given permanent shelter in 3 villages in a secluded jungle corner
4th	1840	Daivam King Marangad Bhavathrāthan Namboothiripad 2nd son of Unni Pushpakan Ambalavasi		
5th	1880	Daivam King Perikamana Raman Namboothiripad		
6th	1919	Prince Akavoor Nabudiripad son in law of King Daivam Perikamana Raman Namboothiripad	Son Swaminarayanan Married Pirate King Wugu's daughter Sanya	
7th	1922	Daivam King Cherusseri Namboodiri (Late Marriage)	Mógui de érzi Son of Swaminarayanan & Pirate King, Wugu's daughter, Sanya	
8th	1927	Prince Pawandas Hanuman Bagaria	Mogui's daughter	
9th	1970	Sudhir Bagaria	Nksi Nanga,	

About Nair Dvipa

An island, a democracy under the care of an Ex- Indian Royal Nair family that discovered the island. It is nearly half the size of Australia, located towards Africa as one leaves Kochi, in India. It has no dry land. Hillocks and hills abound in the central region of Nair Dvipa from which the rivers originate and flow down to various parts of Nair Dvipa. Lush green agricultural lands surround each city, feeding it with fresh vegetables, fruits and a variety of non-vegetarian choice of diet.

The capital of Nair Dvipa is Suryadham and the metros are Sudukki, a satellite city of Suryadham, the Metro city of Vaynur in the North with its lush green hilly lands, Vasarathod the west based green river valley, Vartayam the Information Systems capital of Nair Dvipa in the South, and finally Maryadatote the land of educated farmers.

Honourable Elders of the Supreme Council of Daivika Planet

D aivika Planet is several years away from Prithvi (Earth), is inhabited by a very old civilisation that has been able to harness the powers of each brain cell of the brain. They have learned through Yoga to discipline these enormous powers, have travelled planets without the use of intergalactic crafts and do not need a physical form, that is a body. Yet when they visit earth, they create human bodies that are acceptable to the existing citizens and interact as desired.

The honourable elders of the Supreme Council of Daivika Planet are Honourable Srēṣṭhanāya Oruvan, the Chief of the honourable elders of the Supreme Council of Daivika Planet Daiva pitava (devine father) Gyananiyaya Oruvan, Daivi Ammai Aadarsha Bhattathiripad, Daivi Ammai (Devine mother) Dhanyata Chandrika, Daiva pitava Devvuri Srinivasan, Daivi Ammai Urvashi Nandakumar, and Daiva pitava Dharmarakshak Ayyalasomayajula.

About the Author

When the author was a child, he used to daydream, and to that little child, the real world would often merge with the pixies beckoning from behind the clouds, the secret passage in his almirah that led into the netherworld. The Willow and Gulmohar branches ushered him from outside his window to play, the wind actually whispering good tidings into his ears, and so much more.

The author is the son of a highly respected Indian Defense officer, who is no more, and there was once when his parents had a challenging time explaining his 'real world' to his worried school teachers.

Now, after all these many years, it is diplomatic to say, "He has a vivid imagination!"

What profession does a man with, a well, 'a vivid imagination', take up? You are absolutely correct! So, he too, became a salesman, and his 'vivid imagination' was so good that, over thirteen years, he rose up to become a regional manager before he branched off to start his own business, a recruitment consultancy, which has done fairly well over the past twenty-two years.

While travelling back home one day, he began to pen down a recruitment candidate's behaviour traits. At one point he fancied adding an unpredictable twist to that behaviour and just then, a short story was born, then some of them matured to become novels!

CPSIA information can be obtained
at www.ICGtesting.com
Printed in the USA
BVHW031203010219
539256BV00001B/2/P